Bernard Cornwell was born in London and raised in South Essex. Having graduated from London University, he worked for BBC TV for seven years, mostly as a producer on the *Nationwide* programme, before taking charge of the Current Affairs department for the BBC in Northern Ireland. In 1978 he became editor of Thames Television's *Thames at Six*. He is married to an American and now lives in the USA.

D1422065

BY BERNARD CORNWELL

The Sharpe novels
(in chronological order)

The Starbuck Chronicles

BERNARD CORNWELL

REBEL

COPPERHEAD

Grafton

HarperCollins*Publishers*
77–85 Fulham Palace Road
Hammersmith, London W6 8JB

www.harpercollins.co.uk

This omnibus edition published in 2004
by HarperCollins*Publishers*

ISBN 0 00 771207 3

Set in Linotron Ehrhardt

Printed and bound in Great Britain by
Mackays of Chatham plc, Chatham, Kent

REBEL

Rebel is for Alex and Kathy de Jonge,
who introduced me to the Old Dominion

Manassas Battlefield
July 21st, 1861

Sudley Church

Bull Run

Stone Bridge

To Washington, DC

Stone House

Wooden Bridge

Warrenton Turnpike

Henry House

Balls Ford

Beauregard's Headquarters
2 miles

Manassas Gap R.R.

0   1/2 mile

To Manassas Junction

Part One

1

The young man was trapped at the top end of Shockoe Slip where a crowd had gathered in Cary Street. The young man had smelt the trouble in the air and had tried to avoid it by ducking into an alleyway behind Kerr's Tobacco Warehouse, but a chained guard dog had lunged at him and so driven him back to the steep cobbled slip where the crowd had engulfed him.

"You going somewhere, mister?" a man accosted him.

The young man nodded, but said nothing. He was young, tall and lean, with long black hair and a clean-shaven face of flat planes and harsh angles, though at present his handsome looks were soured by sleeplessness. His skin was sallow, accentuating his eyes, which were the same gray as the fog-wrapped sea around Nantucket, where his ancestors had lived. In one hand he was carrying a stack of books tied with hemp rope, while in his other was a carpetbag with a broken handle. His clothes were of good quality, but frayed and dirty like those of a man well down on his luck. He betrayed no apprehension of the crowd, but instead seemed resigned to their hostility as just another cross he had to bear.

"You heard the news, mister?" The crowd's spokesman was a bald man in a filthy apron that stank of a tannery.

Again the young man nodded. He had no need to ask what news, for there was only one event that could have sparked this excitement in Richmond's streets. Fort Sumter had fallen, and the news, hopes, and fears of civil war were whipping across the American states.

"So where are you from?" the bald man demanded, seizing

9

the young man's sleeve as though to force an answer.

"Take your hands off me!" The tall young man had a temper.

"I asked you civil," the bald man said, but nevertheless let go of the younger man's sleeve.

The young man tried to turn away, but the crowd pressed around him too thickly and he was forced back across the street toward the Columbian Hotel where an older man dressed in respectable though disheveled clothes had been tied to the cast-iron palings that protected the hotel's lower windows. The young man was still not the crowd's prisoner, but neither was he free unless he could somehow satisfy their curiosity.

"You got papers?" another man shouted in his ear.

"Lost your voice, son?" The breath of his questioners was fetid with whiskey and tobacco. The young man made another effort to push against his persecutors, but there were too many of them and he was unable to prevent them from trapping him against a hitching post on the hotel's sidewalk. It was mid-morning on a warm spring day. The sky was cloudless, though the dark smoke from the Tredegar Iron Works and the Gallegoe Mills and the Asa Snyder Stove Factory and the tobacco factories and Talbott's Foundry and the City Gas Works all combined to make a rank veil that haloed the sun. A Negro teamster, driving an empty wagon up from the wharves of Samson and Pae's Foundry, watched expressionless from atop his wagon's box. The crowd had stopped the carter from turning his horses out of Shockoe Slip, but the man was too wise to make any protest.

"Where are you from, boy?" The bald tanner thrust his face close to the young man's. "What's your name?"

"None of your business." The tone was defiant.

"So we'll find out!" The bald man seized the bundle of books and tried to pull them away. For a moment there was a fruitless tug of war, then the frayed rope holding the books parted and the volumes spilt across the cobbles. The bald man laughed at the accident and the young man hit him. It was a good hard blow and it caught the bald man off his balance so that he rocked backward and almost fell.

Someone cheered the young man, admiring his spirit. There were about two hundred people in the crowd with some fifty more onlookers who half hung back from the proceedings and half encouraged them. The crowd itself was mischievous rather than ugly, like children given an unexpected vacation from school. Most of them were in working clothes, betraying that they had used the news of Fort Sumter's fall as an excuse to leave their benches and lathes and presses. They wanted some excitement, and errant northerners caught in the city's streets would be this day's best providers of that excitement.

The bald man rubbed his face. He had lost dignity in front of his friends and wanted revenge. "I asked you a question, boy."

"And I said it was not your business." The young man was trying to pick up his books, though two or three had already been snatched away. The prisoner already tied to the hotel's window bars watched in silence.

"So where are you from, boy?" a tall man asked, but in a conciliatory voice, as though he was offering the young man a chance to make a dignified escape.

"Faulconer Court House." The young man heard and accepted the note of conciliation. He guessed that other strangers had been accosted by this mob, then questioned and released, and that if he kept his head then he too might be spared whatever fate awaited the middle-aged man already secured to the railings.

"Faulconer Court House?" the tall man asked.

"Yes."

"Your name?"

"Baskerville." He had just read the name on a fascia board of a shop across the street; "Bacon and Baskerville," the board read, and the young man snatched the name in relief.

11

"Nathaniel Baskerville." He embellished the lie with his real Christian name.

"You don't sound like a Virginian, Baskerville," the tall man said.

"Only by adoption." His vocabulary, like the books he had been carrying, betrayed that the young man was educated.

"So what do you do in Faulconer County, boy?" another man asked.

"I work for Washington Faulconer." Again the young man spoke defiantly, hoping the name would serve as a talisman for his protection.

"Best let him go, Don!" a man called.

"Let him be!" a woman intervened. She did not care that the boy was claiming the protection of one of Virginia's wealthiest landowners; rather she was touched by the misery in his eyes as well as by the unmistakable fact that the crowd's captive was very good-looking. Women had always been quick to notice Nathaniel, though he himself was too inexperienced to realize their interest.

"You're a Yankee, boy, aren't you?" the taller man challenged.

"Not any longer."

"So how long have you been in Faulconer County?" That was the tanner again.

"Long enough." The lie was already losing its cohesion. Nathaniel had never visited Faulconer County, though he had met the county's richest inhabitant, Washington Faulconer, whose son was his closest friend.

"So what town lies halfway between here and Faulconer Court House?" the tanner, still wanting revenge, demanded of him.

"Answer him!" the tall man snapped.

Nathaniel was silent, betraying his ignorance.

"He's a spy!" a woman whooped.

"Bastard!" The tanner moved in fast, trying to kick

12

Nathaniel, but the young man saw the kick coming and stepped to one side. He slapped a fist at the bald man, clipping an ear, then drove his other hand at the man's ribs. It was like hitting a hog carcass for all the good it did. Then a dozen hands were mauling and hitting Nathaniel; a fist smacked into his eye and another bloodied his nose to hurl him back hard against the hotel's wall. His carpetbag was stolen, his books were finally gone, and now a man tore open his coat and ripped his pocket book free. Nathaniel tried to stop that theft, but he was overwhelmed and helpless. His nose was bleeding and his eye swelling. The Negro teamster watched expressionless and did not even betray any reaction when a dozen men commandeered his wagon and insisted he jump down from the box. The men clambered aboard the vehicle and shouted they were going to Franklin Street where a gang was mending the road. The crowd parted to let the wagon turn while the carter, unregarded, edged his way to the crowd's fringe before running free.

Nathaniel had been thrust against the window bars. His hands were jerked down hard across the bar's spiked tops and tied with rope to the iron cage. He watched as one of his books was kicked into the gutter, its spine broken and its pages fluttering free. The crowd tore apart his carpetbag, but found little of value except a razor and two more books.

"Where are you from?" The middle-aged man who was Nathaniel's fellow prisoner must have been a very dignified figure before the jeering crowd had dragged him to the railings. He was a portly man, balding, and wearing an expensive broadcloth coat.

"I come from Boston." Nathaniel tried to ignore a drunken woman who pranced mockingly in front of him, brandishing her bottle. "And you, sir?"

"Philadelphia. I only planned to be here for a few hours. I left my traps at the railroad depot and thought I'd look around the city. I have an interest in church architecture, you see, and

13

wanted to see St. Paul's Episcopal." The man shook his head sorrowfully, then flinched as he looked at Nathaniel again. "Is your nose broken?"

"I don't think so." The blood from his nostrils was salty on Nathaniel's lips.

"You'll have a rare black eye, son. But I enjoyed seeing you fight. Might I ask your profession?"

"I'm a student, sir. At Yale College. Or I was."

"My name is Doctor Morley Burroughs. I'm a dentist."

"Starbuck, Nathaniel Starbuck." Nathaniel Starbuck saw no need to hide his name from his fellow captive.

"Starbuck!" The dentist repeated the name in a tone that implied recognition. "Are you related?"

"Yes."

"Then I pray they don't discover it," the dentist said grimly.

"What are they going to do to us?" Starbuck could not believe he was in real danger. He was in the plumb center of an American town in broad daylight! There were constables nearby, magistrates, churches, schools! This was America, not Mexico or Cathay.

The dentist pulled at his bonds, relaxed, pulled again. "From what they're saying about road menders, son, my guess is tar and feathers, but if they find out you're a Starbuck?" The dentist sounded half-hopeful, as though the crowd's animosity might be entirely diverted onto Starbuck, thus leaving him unscathed.

The drunken woman's bottle smashed on the roadway. Two other women were dividing Starbuck's grimy shirts between them while a small bespectacled man was leafing through the papers in Starbuck's pocket book. There had been little money there, just four dollars, but Starbuck did not fear the loss of his money. Instead he feared the discovery of his name, which was written on a dozen letters in the pocket book. The small man had found one of the letters, which he now opened, read, turned over, then read again. There was nothing private in the

14

letter, it merely confirmed the time of a train on the Penn Central Road, but Starbuck's name was written in block letters on the letter's cover and the small man had spotted it. He looked up at Starbuck, then back to the letter, then up at Starbuck yet again. "Is your name Starbuck?" he asked loudly.

Starbuck said nothing.

The crowd smelled excitement and turned back to the prisoners. A bearded man, red-faced, burly and even taller than Starbuck, took up the interrogation. "Is your name Starbuck?"

Starbuck looked around, but there was no help in sight. The constables were leaving this mob well alone, and though some respectable-looking people were watching from the high windows of the houses on the far side of Cary Street, none was moving to stop the persecution. A few women looked sympathetically at Starbuck, but they were powerless to help. There was a minister in a frock coat and Geneva bands hovering at the crowd's edge, but the street was too fired with whiskey and political passion for a man of God to achieve any good, and so the minister was contenting himself with making small ineffective cries of protest that were easily drowned by the raucous celebrants.

"You're being asked a question, boy!" The red-faced man had taken hold of Starbuck's tie and was twisting it so that the double loop around Starbuck's throat tightened horribly. "Is your name Starbuck?" He shouted the question, spraying Starbuck's face with spittle laced with drink and tobacco.

"Yes." There was no point in denying it. The letter was addressed to him, and a score of other pieces of paper in his luggage bore the name, just as his shirts had the fatal name sewn into their neckbands.

"And are you any relation?" The man's face was broken veined. He had milky eyes and no front teeth. A dribble of tobacco juice ran down his chin and into his brown beard. He tightened the grip on Starbuck's neck. "Any relation, cuffee?"

Again it could not be denied. There was a letter from

15

Starbuck's father in the pocket book and the letter must be found soon, and so Starbuck did not wait for the revelation, but just nodded assent. "I'm his son."

The man let go of Starbuck's tie and yelped like a stage red Indian. "It's Starbuck's son!" He screamed his victory to the mob. "We got ourselves Starbuck's son!"

"Oh, Christ in his holy heaven," the dentist muttered, "but you are in trouble."

And Starbuck was in trouble, for there were few names more calculated to incense a southern mob. Abraham Lincoln's name would have done it well enough, and John Brown's and Harriet Beecher Stowe's would have sufficed to inflame a crowd, but lacking those luminaries the name of the Reverend Elial Joseph Starbuck was next best calculated to ignite a blaze of southern rage.

For the Reverend Elial Starbuck was a famous enemy of southern aspirations. He had devoted his life to the extirpation of slavery, and his sermons, like his editorials, ruthlessly savaged the South's slavocracy: mocking its pretensions, flaying its morals, and scorning its arguments. The Reverend Elial's eloquence in the cause of Negro liberty had made his name famous, not just in America, but wherever Christian men read their journals and prayed to their God, and now, on a day when the news of Fort Sumter's capture had so inspired the South, a mob in Richmond, Virginia, had taken hold of one of the Reverend Elial Starbuck's sons.

In truth Nathaniel Starbuck detested his father. He wanted nothing more to do with his father ever again, but the crowd could not know that, nor would they have believed Starbuck if he had told them. This crowd's mood had turned dark as they demanded revenge on the Reverend Elial Starbuck. They were screaming for that revenge, baying for it. The crowd was also growing as people in the city heard the news about Fort Sumter's fall and came to join the commotion that celebrated southern liberty and triumph.

16

"String him up!" a man called.

"He's a spy!"

"Nigger lover!" A hunk of horse dung sailed toward the prisoners, missing Starbuck, but hitting the dentist on the shoulder.

"Why couldn't you have stayed in Boston?" the dentist complained.

The crowd surged toward the prisoners, then checked, uncertain exactly what they wanted of their captives. A handful of ringleaders had emerged from the crowd's anonymity, and those ringleaders now shouted for the crowd to be patient. The commandeered wagon had gone to fetch the road mender's tar, the crowd was assured, and in the meantime a sack of feathers had been fetched from a mattress factory in nearby Virginia Street. "We're going to teach you gennelmen a lesson!" the big bearded man crowed to the two prisoners. "You Yankees think you're better than us southrons, isn't that what you think?" He took a handful of the feathers and scattered them in the dentist's face. "All high and mighty, are you?"

"I am a mere dentist, sir, who has been practicing my trade in Petersburg." Burroughs tried to plead his case with dignity.

"He's a dentist!" the big man shouted delightedly.

"Pull his teeth out!"

Another cheer announced the return of the borrowed wagon, which now bore on its bed a great black steaming vat of tar. The wagon clattered to a halt close to the two prisoners, and the stench of its tar even overwhelmed the smell of tobacco, which permeated the whole city.

"Starbuck's whelp first!" someone shouted, but it seemed the ceremonies were to be conducted in the order of capture, or else the ringleaders wanted to save the best till last, for Morley Burroughs, the Philadelphia dentist, was the first to be cut free of the bars and dragged toward the wagon. He struggled, but he was no match for the sinewy men who pulled him onto the wagon bed that would now serve as a makeshift stage.

"Your turn next, Yankee." The small bespectacled man who had first discovered Starbuck's identity had come to stand beside the Bostoner. "So what are you doing here?"

The man's tone had almost been friendly, so Starbuck, thinking he might have found an ally, answered him with the truth. "I escorted a lady here."

"A lady now! What kind of lady?" the small man asked. A whore, Starbuck thought bitterly, a cheat, a liar and a bitch, but God, how he had fallen in love with her, and how he had worshiped her, and how he had let her twist him about her little finger and thus ruin his life so that now he was bereft, impoverished and homeless in Richmond. "I asked you a question," the man insisted.

"A lady from Louisiana," Starbuck answered mildly, "who wanted to be escorted from the North."

"You'd better pray she comes and saves you quick!" the bespectacled man laughed, "before Sam Pearce gets his hands on you."

Sam Pearce was evidently the red-faced bearded man who had become the master of ceremonies and who now supervised the stripping away of the dentist's coat, vest, trousers, shoes, shirt and undershirt, leaving Morley Burroughs humiliated in the sunlight and wearing only his socks and a pair of long drawers, which had been left to him in deference to the modesty of the watching ladies. Sam Pearce now dipped a long-handled ladle into the vat and brought it up dripping with hot treacly tar. The crowd cheered. "Give it him, Sam!"

"Give it him good!"

"Teach the Yankee a lesson, Sam!"

Pearce plunged the ladle back in the vat and gave the tar a slow stir before lifting the ladle out with its deep bowl heaped high with the smoking, black, treacly substance. The dentist tried to pull away, but two men dragged him toward the vat and bent him over its steaming mouth so that his plump, white, naked back was exposed to the grinning Pearce, who moved the

18

glistening, hot mass of tar over his victim.

The expectant crowd fell silent. The tar hesitated, then flowed off the ladle to strike the back of the dentist's balding head. The dentist screamed as the hot thick tar scalded him. He jerked away, but was pulled back, and the crowd, its tension released by his scream, cheered.

Starbuck watched, smelling the thick rank stench of the viscous tar that oozed past the dentist's ears onto his fat white shoulders. It steamed in the warm spring air. The dentist was crying, whether at the ignominy or for the pain it was impossible to tell, but the crowd didn't care; all they knew was that a northerner was suffering, and that gave them pleasure.

Pearce scooped another heavy lump of tar from the vat. The crowd screamed for it to be poured on, the dentist's knees buckled and Starbuck shivered.

"You next, boy." The tanner had moved to stand beside Starbuck. "You next." He suddenly swung his fist, burying it in Starbuck's belly to drive the air explosively out of his lungs and making the young man jerk forward against his bonds. The tanner laughed. "You'll suffer, cuffee, you'll suffer."

The dentist screamed again. A second man had leaped onto the wagon to help Pearce apply the tar. The new man used a short-handled spade to heave a mass of thick black tar out of the vat. "Save some for Starbuck!" the tanner shouted.

"There's plenty more here, boys!" The new tormentor slathered his spadeful of tar onto the dentist's back. The dentist twitched and howled, then was dragged up from his knees as yet more tar was poured down his chest so that it dripped off his belly onto his clean white drawers. Trickles of the viscous substance were dribbling down the sides of his head, down his face and down his back and thighs. His mouth was open and distorted, as though he was crying, but no sound came from him now. The crowd was ribald at the sight of him. One woman was doubled over, helpless with mirth.

"Where are the feathers?" another woman called.

19

"Make him a chicken, Sam!"

More tar was poured on till the whole of the dentist's upper body was smothered in the gleaming black substance. His captors had released him, but he was too stricken to try and escape now. Besides, his stockinged feet were stuck in puddles of tar, and all he could do for himself was to try and paw the filthy mess away from his eyes and mouth while his tormentors finished their work. A woman filled her apron with feathers and climbed up to the wagon's bed where, to huge cheers, the feathers were sprinkled over the humiliated dentist. He stood there, black draped, feathered, steaming, mouth agape, pathetic, and around him the mob howled and jeered and hooted. Some Negroes on the far sidewalk were convulsed in laughter, while even the minister who had been so pathetically protesting the scene was finding it hard not to smile at the ridiculous spectacle. Sam Pearce, the chief ringleader, released one last handful of feathers to stick in the congealing, cooling tar then stepped back and flourished a proud hand toward the dentist. The crowd cheered again.

"Make him cluck, Sam! Make him cluck like a hen!"

The dentist was prodded with the short-handled spade until he produced a pathetic imitation of a chicken's cluck.

"Louder! Louder!"

Doctor Burroughs was prodded again, and this time he managed to make the miserable noise loud enough for the crowd's satisfaction. Laughter echoed from the houses and sounded clear down to the river where the barges jostled at the quays.

"Bring on the spy, Sam!"

"Give it him good!"

"Show us Starbuck's bastard!"

Men seized Starbuck, released his bonds and hurried him toward the wagon. The tanner helped them, still striking and kicking at the helpless Starbuck, spitting his hatred and taunting him, anticipating the humiliation of Elial Starbuck's whelp. Pearce had crammed the dentist's top hat onto its owner's grotesque, tar-thick, feathered head. The dentist was shaking, sobbing silently.

Starbuck was pushed hard against the wagon's wheel. Hands reached down from above, grabbed his collar and heaved up. Men pushed at him, his knee cracked hard against the wagon side, then he was sprawling on the wagon bed, where his hand was smeared by a warm patch of spilt tar. Sam Pearce hauled Starbuck upright and displayed his bloody face to the crowd. "Here he is! Starbuck's bastard!"

"Fillet him, Sam!"

"Push him in, Sam!"

Pearce rammed Starbuck's head over the vat, holding his face just inches from the stinking liquid. The vat had been stolen from its coals, but it was big enough and full enough to have retained almost all its heat. Starbuck tried to flinch away as a bubble slowly erupted just beneath his bleeding nose. The tar plopped tiredly back, then Pearce jerked him back upright. "Let's have your clothes off, cuffee."

Hands pulled at Starbuck's coat, tearing off its sleeves and ripping it clean off his back. "Strip him naked, Sam!" a woman screamed excitedly.

"Give his pa something to preach about!" A man was jumping up and down beside the wagon. A child stood by the man, hand at her mouth, eyes bright, staring. The dentist, unremarked now, had sat on the wagon's box, where he pathetically and uselessly tried to scrape the hot tar off his scorched skin.

Sam Pearce gave the vat a stir. The tanner was spitting again and again at Starbuck while a gray-haired man fumbled at Starbuck's waist, loosing the buttons of his pants. "Don't you dare piss on me, boy, or I'll leave you nothing to piss with." He pulled the trousers down to Starbuck's knees, provoking a shrill scream of approval from the crowd.

And a gunshot sounded too.

The gunshot cracked the still air of the street junction to startle a score of flapping birds up from the roofs of the warehouses that edged the Shockoe Slip. The crowd turned. Pearce moved to tear at Starbuck's shirt, but a second gunshot sounded hugely loud, echoing off the far houses and causing the crowd to go very still. "Touch the boy again," a confident, lazy voice spoke, "and you're a dead man."

"He's a spy!" Pearce tried to brazen out the moment.

"He's my guest." The speaker was mounted on a tall black horse and was wearing a slouch hat, a long gray coat and high boots. He was carrying a long-barreled revolver, which he now pushed into a holster on his saddle. It was a marvelously insouciant gesture, suggesting he had nothing to fear from this mob. The man's face was shadowed by the hat's brim, but clearly he had been recognized, and as he spurred the horse forward the crowd silently parted to give him passage. A second horseman followed, leading a riderless horse.

The first horseman reined in beside the wagon. He tilted his hat upward with the tip of a riding crop then stared with incredulity at Starbuck. "It's Nate Starbuck! Yes?"

"Yes, sir." Starbuck was shivering."

"You remember me, Nate? We met in New Haven last year?"

"Of course I remember you, sir." Starbuck was shaking, but with relief rather than fear. His rescuer was Washington Faulconer, father of Starbuck's best friend and the man whose name Starbuck had earlier invoked to save himself from this mob's wrath.

"You seem to be getting a wrong impression of Virginian hospitality," Washington Faulconer said softly. "Shame on you!" These last words were spoken to the crowd. "We're not at war with strangers in our city! What are you? Savages?"

"He's a spy!" The tanner tried to restore the crowd's supremacy.

Washington Faulconer turned scornfully on the man. "And you're a black-assed fool! You're behaving like Yankees, all of you! Northerners might want a mobocracy for a government,

22

but not us! Who is this man?" He pointed with his riding crop at the dentist.

The dentist could not speak, so Starbuck, released from the grip of his enemies and with his trousers safely restored to his waist, answered for his fellow victim. "His name is Burroughs, sir. He's a dentist passing through town."

Washington Faulconer glanced about until he saw two men he recognized. "Bring Mister Burroughs to my house. We shall do our best to make reparations to him." Then, that remonstrance delivered to the shamed crowd, he looked back to Starbuck and introduced his companion, who was a dark-haired man a few years older than Starbuck. "This is Ethan Ridley." Ridley was leading the riderless horse, which he now urged alongside the wagon bed. "Mount up, Nate!" Washington Faulconer urged Starbuck.

"Yes, sir." Starbuck stooped for his coat, realized that it was torn beyond repair, so straightened up empty-handed. He glanced at Sam Pearce, who gave a tiny shrug as though to suggest there were no hard feelings, but there were, and Starbuck, who had never known how to control his temper, stepped fast toward the big man and hit him. Sam Pearce twisted away, but not soon enough, and Starbuck's blow landed on his ear. Pearce stumbled, put a hand out to save himself but only succeeded in plunging the hand deep into the tar vat. He screamed, jerked himself free, but his balance was gone, and he flailed hopelessly as he tripped off the wagon's outer end to fall with skull-cracking force onto the road. Starbuck's hand was hurting, stung by the wild and clumsy blow, but the crowd, with the unpredictability of an impassioned mob, suddenly started laughing and cheering him.

"Come on, Nate!" Washington Faulconer was grinning at Pearce's downfall.

Starbuck stepped off the wagon directly onto the horse's back. He fumbled with his feet for the stirrups, took the reins, and kicked back with his tar-stained shoes. He guessed he had lost his books and clothes, but the loss was hardly important. The books were exegetical texts left over from his studies at the Yale Theological Seminary and at best he might have sold them for a dollar fifty. The clothes were of even less value, and so he abandoned his belongings, instead following his rescuers out of the crowd and up Pearl Street. Starbuck was still shaking, and still hardly daring to believe he had escaped the crowd's torment. "How did you know I was there, sir?" he asked Washington Faulconer.

"I didn't realize it was you, Nate, I just heard that some young fellow claiming to know me was about to be strung up for the crime of being a Yankee, so I thought we should take a look. It was a teamster who told me, a Negro fellow. He heard you say my name and he knew my house, so he came and told my steward. Who told me, of course."

"I owe you an extraordinary debt, sir."

"You certainly owe the Negro fellow a debt. Or rather you don't, because I thanked him for you with a silver dollar." Washington Faulconer turned and looked at his bedraggled companion. "Does that nose hurt?"

"No more than a usual bloody nose, sir."

"Might I ask just what you're doing here, Nate? Virginia doesn't seem the healthiest place for a Massachusetts man to be running loose."

"I was looking for you, sir. I was planning to walk to Faulconer Court House."

"All seventy miles, Nate!" Washington Faulconer laughed. "Didn't Adam tell you we keep a town house? My father was a state senator, so he liked to keep a place in Richmond to hang his hat. But why on earth were you looking for me? Or was it Adam you wanted? He's up north, I'm afraid. He's trying to avert war, but I think it's a little late for that. Lincoln doesn't want peace, so I fear we'll have to oblige him with war." Faulconer offered this mix of questions and answers in a cheerful voice. He was an impressive-looking man of middle years

24

and medium height, with a straight back and wide square shoulders. He had short fair hair, a thick square-cut beard, a face that seemed to radiate frankness and kindness, and blue eyes that were crinkled in an expression of amused benignity. To Starbuck he seemed just like his son, Adam, whom Starbuck had met at Yale and whom Starbuck always thought of as the decentest man he had ever met. "But why are you here, Nate?" Faulconer asked his original question again.

"It's a long story, sir." Starbuck rarely rode a horse and did it badly. He slouched in the saddle and jolted from side to side, making a horrid contrast to his two elegant companions, who rode their horses with careless mastery.

"I like long stories," Washington Faulconer said happily, "but save it for when you're cleaned up. Here we are." He gestured with his riding crop at a lavish four-storied stone-faced house, evidently the place where his father had hung his hat. "No ladies staying here this week, so we can be free and easy. Ethan will get you some clothes. Show him to Adam's room, will you, Ethan?"

Negro servants ran from the house's stable yard to take the horses and suddenly, after weeks of uncertainty and danger and humiliation, Starbuck felt himself being surrounded by security and comfort and safety. He could almost have wept for the relief of it. America was collapsing in chaos, riot was loose on its streets, but Starbuck was safe.

"You're looking a deal more human, Nate!" Washington Faulconer greeted Starbuck in his study, "and those clothes more or less fit. Are you feeling better?"

"Much better. Thank you, sir."

"Bath hot enough?"

"Perfect, sir."

"That eye looks sore. Maybe a poultice before you sleep? We had to call a doctor for your Philadelphia friend. They're trying to unpeel the poor fellow in the stable yard. While my problem

25

is whether to buy one thousand rifles at twelve bucks each."

"Why shouldn't we?" Ethan Ridley, who had settled Starbuck into Adam's room then arranged for his bath and a change of clothes, was now perched on a sofa at the window of Washington Faulconer's study, where he was toying with a long-barreled revolver that he occasionally sighted at pedestrians in the street below.

"Because I don't want to take the first available guns, Ethan," Washington Faulconer said. "Something better may come along in a month or two."

"There's not much better than the Mississippi rifle." Ridley silently picked off the driver of a scarlet barouche. "And the price won't go down, sir. With respect, it won't go down. Prices never do."

"I guess that's true." Faulconer paused, but still seemed reluctant to make a decision.

A clock ticked heavily in a corner of the room. A wagon axle squealed in the street. Ridley lit a long thin cigar and sucked hungrily on its smoke. A brass tray beside him was littered with ash and cigar butts. He drew on the cigar again, making its tip glow fierce, then glanced at Starbuck. "Will the North fight?" he demanded, evidently expecting that a Yankee like Starbuck must have the answer pat.

But Starbuck had no idea what the North intended to do in the aftermath of Fort Sumter's fall. In these last weeks Nathaniel Starbuck had been much too distracted to think about politics, and now, faced with the question that was energizing the whole south country, he did not know what to respond.

"In one sense it doesn't matter if they fight or not," Washington Faulconer spoke before Starbuck could offer any answer. "If we don't seem prepared to fight, Ethan, then the North will certainly invade. But if we stand firm, why, then they may back down."

"Then buy the guns, sir," Ridley urged, reinforcing his

encouragement by pulling the trigger of his empty revolver. He was a lean tall man, elegant in black riding boots, black breeches and a black coat that was smeared with traces of cigar ash. He had long dark hair oiled sleek against his skull and a beard trimmed to a rakish point. In Adam's bedroom, while Starbuck had tidied and cleaned himself, Ridley had paced up and down the room, telling Starbuck how he was planning to marry Washington Faulconer's daughter, Anna, and how the prospect of war had delayed their wedding plans. Ridley had talked of the possible war as an irritation rather than a calamity, and his slow, attractive southern accent had only made the confidence in his voice all the more convincing.

"There goes twelve thousand dollars!" Washington Faulconer now said, evidently putting his signature to a money draft as he spoke. "Buy the guns for me, Ethan, and well done." Starbuck wondered why Washington Faulconer was buying so many rifles, but he did not need to wonder that Faulconer could afford the weapons, for he knew his friend's father to be one of the richest men in Virginia, indeed in all the precariously United States. Faulconer could boast that the most recent survey done of his family's land in Faulconer County had been accomplished by a raw young surveyor named George Washington, and since that day not one acre had been lost to the family and a good many had been added. Among the new acres was the land on which Faulconer's Richmond town house stood—one of the grandest houses on Clay Street that had, at its rear, a wide stable yard with a carriage house and quarters for a dozen grooms and stalls for thirty horses. The house boasted a ballroom, a music room, and what was commonly regarded as Richmond's finest staircase, a magnificent circling stair that swept around and up a gilded well hung with family portraits, the oldest of which had been brought from England in the seventeenth century. The books in Washington Faulconer's study had the family's coat of arms tooled in gold

27

into their leather covers, while the desks, chairs and tables had all been made by Europe's finest craftsmen because, for a man as wealthy as Washington Faulconer, only the very best would do. Flowers stood on every table, not just for decoration, but in an attempt to overwhelm the smell of the city's tobacco factories.

"Now, Nate," Washington Faulconer said heartily when he had decided to buy the twelve-dollar guns, "you promised us a story. There's coffee there, or something stronger? Do you drink? You do? But not with your father's blessing, I'm sure. Your father can hardly approve of ardent spirits, or does he? Is the Reverend Elial a prohibitionist as well as an abolitionist? He is! What a ferocious man he must be, to be sure. Sit down." Washington Faulconer was full of energy and happy to conduct a conversation with himself as he stood up, pulled a chair for Starbuck away from the wall, poured Starbuck coffee, then sat back at his desk. "So come! Tell me! Aren't you supposed to be at the seminary?"

"Yes, sir, I am." Starbuck felt inhibited suddenly, ashamed of his story and of his pathetic condition. "It's a very long tale," he protested to Washington Faulconer.

"The longer the better. So come along, tell!"

So Starbuck had no choice but to tell his pathetic story of obsession, love and crime; a shameful tale of how Mademoiselle Dominique Demarest of New Orleans had persuaded Nathaniel Starbuck of Yale that life had more to offer than lectures in didactic theology, sacred literature or the sermonizing arts.

"A bad woman!" Washington Faulconer said with happy relish when Starbuck first mentioned her. "Every tale should have a bad woman."

Starbuck had first glimpsed Mademoiselle Dominique Demarest in the Lyceum Hall at New Haven where Major Ferdinand Trabell's touring company was presenting the *Only True and Authorized Stage Version of Uncle Tom's Cabin, Complete with Real Bloodhounds.* Trabell's had been the third such

28

traveling *Tom* company to visit New Haven that winter, and each had claimed to be presenting the only true and authorized dramatic version of the great work, but Major Trabell's production had been the first that Starbuck dared attend. There had been impassioned debate in the seminary about the propriety of attending a thespian performance, even one dedicated to moral instruction and the abolition of slavery, but Starbuck had wanted to go because of the bloodhounds mentioned on the playbill. There had been no bloodhounds in Mrs. Beecher Stowe's fine work, but Starbuck suspected the animals might make a dramatic addition to the story, and so he had visited the Lyceum where, awestruck, he had watched as a veritable angel who was playing the part of the fugitive slave Eliza had tripped lightly across the make-believe ice floes pursued by a pair of lethargic and dribbling dogs that might or might not have been bloodhounds.

Not that Starbuck cared about the dogs' pedigree, but only about the angel, who had a long face, sad eyes, shadowed cheeks, a wide mouth, hair black as night, and a gentle voice. He had fallen in love instantly, furiously and, so far as he could tell, eternally. He had gone to the Lyceum the next night, and the next, and the next, which was also New Haven's final performance of the great epic, and on the following day he had offered to help Major Trabell strike and crate the scenery, and the major, who had recently been abandoned by his only son and was therefore in need of a replacement to play the parts of Augustine St. Clair and Simon Legree, and recognizing Starbuck's good looks and commanding presence, had offered him four dollars a week, full board, and Major Trabell's own tutelage in the thespian arts. Not even those enticements could have persuaded Starbuck to abandon his seminary education, except that Mademoiselle Dominique Demarest had added her entreaties to those of her employer, and so, on a whim, and for his adoration of Dominique, Starbuck had become a traveling player.

"You upped stakes and went? Just like that?" Washington

29

Faulconer asked with obvious amusement, even admiration.

"Yes, sir." Though Starbuck had not confessed the full extent of his humiliating surrender to Dominique. He had admitted attending the theater night after night, but he had not described how he had lingered in the streets wanting a glimpse of his angel, or how he had written her name again and again in his notebooks, nor how he had tried to capture in pencil the delicacy of her long, misleadingly ethereal face, nor how he had yearned to repair the spiritual damage done to Dominique by her appalling history.

That history had been published in the New Haven newspaper that had noticed the *Tom* company's performance, which notice revealed that although Mademoiselle Demarest appeared to be as white as any other respectable lady, she was in truth a nineteen-year-old octoroon who had been the slave of a savage New Orleans gentleman whose behavior rivaled that of Simon Legree. Delicacy forbade the newspaper from publishing any details of his behavior, except to say that Dominique's owner had threatened the virtue of his fair property and thus forced Dominique, in an escape that rivaled the drama of Eliza's fictional flight, to flee northward for liberty and the safeguard of her virtue. Starbuck tried to imagine his lovely Dominique running desperately through the Louisiana night pursued by yelping fiends, howling dogs, and a slavering owner.

"Like hell I escaped! I was never a slave, never!" Dominique told Starbuck next day when they were riding the cars for Hartford, where the show would play for six nights in the Touro Hall. "I ain't got nigger blood, not one drop. But the notion sells tickets, so it does, and tickets is money, and that's why Trabell tells the newspapers I'm part nigger."

"You mean it's a lie?" Starbuck was horrified.

"Of course it's a lie!" Dominique was indignant. "I told you, it just sells tickets, and tickets is money." She said the only truths in the fable were that she was nineteen and had been raised in New Orleans, but in a white family that she claimed

30

was of irreproachable French ancestry. Her father possessed money, though she was vague about the exact process whereby the daughter of a wealthy Louisiana merchant came to be performing the part of Eliza in Major Ferdinand Trabell's touring *Tom* company. "Not that Trabell's a real major," Dominique confided to Starbuck, "but he pretends to have fought in Mexico. He says he got his limp there off a bayonet, but I reckon he more likely got stabbed by a whore in Philadelphia." She laughed. She was two years younger than Starbuck but seemed immeasurably older and far more experienced. She also seemed to like Starbuck, who returned her liking with a blind adoration and did not care that she was not an escaped slave. "How much is he paying you?" Dominique asked Starbuck.

"Four dollars a week."

She laughed scornfully. "Robbing you!"

For the next two months Starbuck happily learned the acting trade as he worshiped at the shrine of Miss Demarest's virtue. He enjoyed being on stage, and the fact that he was the son of the Reverend Elial Starbuck, the famous abolitionist, served to swell both Trabell's audiences and receipts. It also brought Nathaniel's new profession to the attention of his father who, in a terrifying fury, sent Starbuck's elder brother, James, to bring the sinner to repentance.

James's mission had failed miserably, and two weeks later Dominique, who had so far not permitted Starbuck any liberty beyond the holding of her hand, at last promised him the reward of his heart's whole desire if he would just help her steal that week's takings from Major Trabell. "He owes me money," Dominique said, and she explained that her father had written to say he was waiting for her in Richmond, Virginia, and she knew Major Trabell would not pay her any of the six months' wages he owed and so she needed Starbuck's help in purloining what was, by rights, already hers. For the reward she was offering, Starbuck would have helped Dominique steal the moon, but he settled for the eight hundred and sixty-four dollars he

31

found in Major Trabell's portmanteau, which he stole while, in the next-door room, the major took a hip bath with a young lady who was hoping for a career upon the stage and had therefore offered herself to the major's professional inspection and judgment.

Starbuck and Dominique fled that same night, reaching Richmond just two days later. Dominique's father was supposed to have been waiting at the Spotswood House Hotel on Main Street, but instead it was a tall young man, scarce a year older than Starbuck himself, who waited in the hotel's parlor and who laughed with joy when Dominique appeared. The young man was Major Trabell's son, Jefferson, who was estranged from his father, and who now dismissed Starbuck with a patronizing ten dollars. "Make yourself scarce, boy," he had said, "before you're strung up for crow bait. Northerners ain't popular in these parts right now." Jefferson Trabell wore buckskin breeches, top boots, a satin vest and a scarlet coat. He had dark knowing eyes and narrow side-whiskers which, like his long black hair, were oiled smooth as jet. His tie was secured with a large pearl pin and his holstered revolver had a polished silver handgrip. It was that revolver rather than the tall young man's dandyish air that persuaded Starbuck there was little point in trying to claim his promised reward from Mademoiselle Dominique Demarest.

"You mean she just dropped you?" Washington Faulconer asked in disbelief.

"Yes, sir." The shameful memory convulsed Starbuck with misery.

"Without even giving you a ride?" Ethan Ridley laid down the empty revolver as he asked the question and, though the query earned him a reproving glance from Washington Faulconer, it was also clear the older man wanted to know the answer. Starbuck offered no reply, but he had no need to. Dominique had made him into a fool, and his foolishness was obvious.

32

"Poor Nate!" Washington Faulconer was amused. "What are you going to do now? Go home? Your father won't be too happy! And what of Major Trabell? He'll be wanting to nail your gizzards to his barn door, won't he? That and get his money back! Is he a southerner?"

"A Pennsylvanian, sir. But his son pretends to be a southerner."

"So where is the son? Still at the Spotswood?"

"No, sir." Starbuck had spent the night in a boarding house in Canal Street and, in the morning, still seething with indignation, he had gone to the Spotswood House Hotel to confront Dominique and her lover, but instead a clerk had told him that Mr. and Mrs. Jefferson Trabell had just left for the Richmond and Danville Railroad Depot. Starbuck had followed them, only to discover that the birds were flown and that their train was already steaming south out of the depot, its locomotive pumping a bitter smoke into the spring air that was so briskly filled with the news of Fort Sumter's capitulation.

"Oh, it's a rare tale, Nate! A rare tale!" Washington Faulconer laughed. "But you shouldn't feel so bad. You ain't the first young fellow to be fooled by a petticoat, and you won't be the last, and I've no doubt Major Trabell's a scoundrel as deep as they come." He lit a cigar, then tossed the spent match into a spittoon. "So what are we going to do with you?" The lightness with which he asked the question seemed to imply that whatever answer Starbuck desired could be easily supplied. "Do you want to go back to Yale?"

"No, sir." Starbuck spoke miserably.

"No?"

Starbuck spread his hands. "I'm not sure I should be at the seminary, sir. I'm not even sure I should have been there in the first place." He stared down at his scarred, grazed knuckles, and bit his lip as he considered his answer. "I can't become a minister now, sir, not now that I'm a thief." And worse than a thief, Starbuck thought. He was remembering the fourth

33

chapter of first Timothy where St. Paul had prophesied how in the latter times some men would depart from the faith, giving heed to seducing spirits and doctrines of devils, and Starbuck knew he had fulfilled that prophecy, and the realization imbued his voice with a terrible anguish. "I'm simply not worthy of the ministry, sir."

"Worthy?" Washington Faulconer exclaimed. "Worthy! My God, Nate, if you could see the plug-uglies who shove themselves into our pulpits you wouldn't say that! My God, we've got a fellow in Rosskill Church who preaches blind drunk most Sunday mornings. Ain't that so, Ethan?"

"Poor old fool toppled into a grave last year," Ridley added with amusement. "He was supposed to be burying someone and damn near buried himself instead."

"So I wouldn't worry about being worthy," Faulconer said scornfully. "But I suppose Yale won't be too happy to have you back, Nate, not if you walked out on them for some chickabiddy trollop? And I suppose you're a wanted man too, eh? A thief no less!" Faulconer evidently found this notion hugely entertaining. "Go back north and they'll clap you in jail, is that it?"

"I fear so, sir."

Washington Faulconer hooted with amusement. "By God, Nate, but you are stuck in the tar patch. Both feet, both hands, ass, crop and privates! And what will your sacred father do if you go home? Give you a whipping before he turns you over to the constables?"

"Like as not, sir, yes."

"So the Reverend Elial's a whipper, is he? Likes to thrash?"

"Yes, sir, he does."

"I can't allow that." Washington Faulconer stood and walked to a window overlooking the street. A magnolia was in bloom in his narrow front garden, filling the window bay with its sweet scent. "I never was a believer in a thrashing. My father didn't beat me and I've never beaten my children. Fact is, Nate, I've never laid a hand on any child or servant, only on my enemies."

34

He spoke sententiously, as though he was accustomed to defending his strange behavior, as in truth he was, for, not ten years before, Washington Faulconer had made himself famous for freeing all his slaves. For a brief time the northern newspapers had hailed Faulconer as a precursor of southern enlightenment, a reputation that had made him bitterly unpopular in his native Virginia, but his neighbors' animosity had died away when Faulconer had refused to encourage other southerners to follow his example. He claimed the decision had been purely personal. Now, the furor long in his past, Faulconer smiled at Starbuck. "Just what are we going to do with you, Nate?"

"You've done enough, sir," Starbuck said, though in reality he was hoping that far more might yet be done. "What I must do, sir, is find work. I have to repay Major Trabell."

Faulconer smiled at Starbuck's earnestness. "The only work around here, Nate, is common soldiering, and I don't think that's a trade to pay off debts in a hurry. No, I think you'd better raise your sights a little higher." Faulconer was taking an obvious enjoyment in solving Starbuck's problem. He smiled, then gestured about the lavishly appointed room. "Maybe you'd consider staying here, Nate? With me? I'm in need of someone who can be my private secretary and do some purchasing as well."

"Sir!" Ethan Ridley sat bolt upright on the sofa, his irate tone betraying that the job being offered to Starbuck was one Ridley considered his own.

"Oh come, Ethan! You detest clerking for me! You can't even spell!" Faulconer chided his future son-in-law gently. "Besides, with the guns purchased, your main job's done. At least for the moment." He sat thinking for a few seconds, then clicked his fingers. "I know, Ethan, go back to Faulconer County and start some proper recruiting. Beat the drum for me. If we don't raise the county, someone else will, and I don't want Faulconer County men fighting for other Virginia regiments. Besides, don't you want to be with Anna?"

"Of course I do, sir." Though Ridley, offered this chance to be close to his betrothed, seemed somewhat less than enthusiastic.

Washington Faulconer turned back to Starbuck. "I'm raising a regiment, Nate, a legion. The Faulconer Legion. I'd hoped it wouldn't be necessary, I'd hoped common sense would prevail, but it seems the North wants a fight and, by God, we'll have to give them one if they insist. Would it offend your loyalties to help me?"

"No, sir." That seemed an entirely inadequate response, so Starbuck imbued his voice with more enthusiasm. "I'd be proud to help you, sir."

"We've made a beginning," Faulconer said modestly. "Ethan has been buying equipment and we've found our guns now, as you heard, but the paperwork is already overwhelming. Do you think you can handle some correspondence for me?"

Could Starbuck handle correspondence? Nathaniel Starbuck would have done all Washington Faulconer's correspondence from that moment until the seas ran dry. Nathaniel Starbuck would do whatever this marvelous, kind, decent and carelessly generous man wanted him to do. "Of course I can help, sir. It would be a privilege."

"But, sir!" Ethan Ridley tried one last patriotic protest. "You can't trust military affairs to a northerner."

"Nonsense, Ethan! Nate's stateless! He's an outlaw! He can't go home, not unless he goes to jail, so he'll just have to stay here. I'm making him an honorary Virginian." Faulconer bestowed a bow on Starbuck in recognition of this elevated status. "So welcome to the southland, Nate."

Ethan Ridley looked astonished at his future father-in-law's quixotic kindness, but Nathaniel Starbuck did not care. He had fallen on his feet, his luck had turned clean round, and he was safe in the land of his father's enemies. Starbuck had come south.

36

2

Starbuck's first days in Richmond were spent accompanying Ethan Ridley to warehouses that held the stores and supplies that would equip the Faulconer Legion. Ridley had arranged for the purchase of the equipment and now, before he left to begin the major recruiting effort in Faulconer County, he made certain Starbuck was able to take over his responsibilities. "Not that you need bother with the finances, Reverend," Ridley told Starbuck, using the half-mocking and half-teasing nickname he had adopted for the northerner, "I'll just let you arrange the transport." Starbuck would then be left to kick his heels in big echoing warehouses or in dusty counting houses while Ridley talked business in the private inner office before emerging to toss another instruction Starbuck's way. "Mister Williams will have six crates ready for collection next week. By Thursday, Johnny?"

"Ready by Thursday, Mister Ridley." The Williams warehouse was selling the Faulconer Legion a thousand pairs of boots, while other merchants were selling the regiment rifles, uniforms, percussion caps, buttons, bayonets, powder, cartridges, revolvers, tents, skillets, haversacks, canteens, tin mugs, hemp line, webbing belts: all the mundane necessities of military paraphernalia, and all of it coming from private warehouses because Washington Faulconer refused to deal with the Virginian government. "You have to understand, Reverend," Ridley told Starbuck, "that Faulconer ain't fond of the new governor, and the new governor ain't fond of Faulconer. Faulconer thinks the governor will let him pay for the Legion, then steal it away from him, so we ain't allowed to have anything to do with the state government. We're not to encourage them, see? So we can't buy goods out of the state armories, which makes life kind of difficult." Though plainly Ethan Ridley had overcome many of the difficulties, for Starbuck's notebook was filling impressively with lists of crates, boxes, barrels and sacks that needed to be collected and delivered to the town of Faulconer Court House. "Money," Ridley told him, "that's the key, Reverend. There's a thousand fellows trying to buy equipment, and there's a shortage of everything, so you need deep pockets. Let's go get a drink."

Ethan Ridley took a perverse delight in introducing Starbuck to the city's taverns, especially the dark, rancid drinking houses that were hidden among the mills and lodging houses on the northern bank of the James River. "This ain't like your father's church, is it, Reverend?" Ridley would ask of some rat-infested, rotting hovel, and Starbuck would agree that the liquor den was indeed a far cry from his ordered, Boston upbringing where cleanliness had been a mark of God's favor and abstinence a surety of his salvation.

Ridley evidently wanted to savor the pleasure of shocking the Reverend Elial Starbuck's son, yet even the filthiest of Richmond's taverns held a romance for Starbuck solely because it was such a long way from his father's Calvinist joylessness. It was not that Boston lacked drinking houses as poverty stricken and hopeless as any in Richmond, but Starbuck had never been inside Boston's drinking dens and thus he took a strange satisfaction out of Ridley's midday excursions into Richmond's malodorous alleyways. The adventures seemed proof that he really had escaped his family's cold, disapproving grasp, but Starbuck's evident enjoyment of the expeditions only made Ridley try yet harder to shock him. "If I abandoned you in this place, Reverend," Ridley threatened Starbuck in one seamen's tavern that stank from the sewage dripping into the river from a rusting pipe not ten feet from the stillroom, "you'd have your throat cut inside five minutes."

"Because I'm a northerner?"

"Because you're wearing shoes."

"I'd be all right," Starbuck boasted. He had no weapons, and the dozen men in the tavern looked capable of slitting a congregation of respectable throats with scarce a twinge of conscience, but Starbuck would not let himself show any fear in front of Ethan Ridley. "Leave me here if you want."

"You wouldn't dare stay here on your own," Ridley said.

"Go on. See if I mind." Starbuck turned to the serving hatch and snapped his fingers. "One more glass here. Just one!" That was pure bravado, for Starbuck hardly drank any alcohol. He would sip at a whiskey, but Ridley always finished the glass. The terror of sin haunted Starbuck, indeed it was that terror which gave the tavern excursions their piquancy, and liquor was one of the greater sins whose temptations Starbuck half-flirted with and half-resisted.

Ridley laughed at Starbuck's defiance. "You've got balls, Starbuck, I'll say that."

"So leave me here."

"Faulconer won't forgive me if I get you killed. You're his new pet puppy, Reverend."

"Pet puppy?" Starbuck bridled at the words.

"Don't take offense, Reverend." Ridley stamped on the butt of a smoked cigar and immediately lit another. He was a man of impatient appetites. "Faulconer's a lonely man, and lonely men like having pet puppies. That's why he's so keen on secession."

"Because he's lonely?" Starbuck did not understand.

Ridley shook his head. He was lounging with his back against the counter, staring through a cracked dirty window to where a two-masted ship creaked against a crumbling river quay. "Faulconer supports the rebellion because he thinks it'll make him popular with his father's old friends. He'll prove himself a more fervent southerner than any of them, because in a way he ain't a southerner at all, you know what I mean?"

"No."

Ridley grimaced, as though unwilling to explain himself, but then tried anyway. "He owns land, Reverend, but he don't use it. He doesn't farm it, he doesn't plant it, he doesn't even graze it. He just owns it and stares at it. He doesn't have niggers, at least not as slaves. His money comes out of railroads and paper, and the paper comes out of New York or London. He's probably more at home in Europe than here in Richmond, but that don't stop wanting him to belong here. He wants to be a southerner, but he ain't." Ridley blew a plume of cigar smoke across the room, then turned his dark, sardonic gaze on Starbuck. "I'll give you a piece of advice."

"Please."

"Keep agreeing with him," Ridley said very seriously. "Family can disagree with Washington, which is why he don't spend too much time with family, but private secretaries like you and me ain't allowed any disagreements. Our job is to admire him. You understand me?"

"He's admirable anyway," Starbuck said loyally.

"I guess we're all admirable," Ridley said with amusement, "so long as we can find a pedestal high enough to stand on. Washington's pedestal is his money, Reverend."

"And yours too?" Starbuck asked belligerently.

"Not mine, Reverend. My father lost all the family money. My pedestal, Reverend, is horses. I'm the best damned horseman you'll find this side of the Atlantic. Or any side for that matter." Ridley grinned at his own lack of modesty, then tossed back his glass of whiskey. "Let's go and see if those bastards at Boyle and Gamble have found the field glasses they promised me last week."

In the evenings Ridley would disappear to his half-brother's rooms in Grace Street, leaving Starbuck to walk back to Washington Faulconer's house through streets that were swarming with strange-looking creatures come from the deeper, farther reaches of the South. There were thin-shanked, gaunt-faced men from Alabama, long-haired leather-skinned horse riders from Texas and bearded homespun volunteers from Mississippi, all of them armed like buccaneers and ready to drink themselves into fits of instant fury. Whores and liquor salesmen made small fortunes, city rents doubled and doubled again, and still the railroads brought fresh volunteers to Richmond. They had come, one and all, to protect the new Confederacy from the Yankees, though at first it looked as if the new Confederacy would be better advised to protect itself from its own defenders, but then, obedient to the insistent commands of the state's newly appointed military commander, all the ragtag volunteers were swept away to the city's Central Fair Grounds where cadets from the Virginia Military Institute were brought to teach them basic drill.

That new commander of the Virginian militia, Major-General Robert Lee, also insisted on paying a courtesy call on Washington Faulconer. Faulconer suspected that the proposed visit was a ploy by Virginia's new governor to take control of the Legion, yet, despite his misgivings, Faulconer could scarcely refuse to receive a man who came from a Virginia family as old and prominent as his own. Ethan Ridley had left Richmond the day before Lee's visit, and so Starbuck was ordered to be present at the meeting. "I want you to make notes of what's said," Faulconer warned him darkly. "Letcher's not the kind of man to let a patriot raise a regiment. You mark my words, Nate, he'll have sent Lee to take the Legion away from me."

Starbuck sat at one side of the study, a notebook open on his knees, though in the event nothing of any great importance was discussed. The middle-aged Lee, who was dressed in civilian clothes and attended by one young captain in the uniform of the state militia, first exchanged civilities with Faulconer, then formally, almost apologetically, explained that Governor Letcher had appointed him to command the state's military forces and his first duty was to recruit, equip and train those forces, in which connection he understood that Mister

41

Faulconer was raising a regiment in Faulconer County?

"A legion," Faulconer corrected him.

"Ah yes, indeed, a legion." Lee seemed quite flummoxed by the word.

"And not one stand of its arms, not one cannon, not one cavalry saddle, not one buttonhook or one canteen, indeed not one item of its equipment, Lee, will be a charge upon the state," Faulconer said proudly. "I am paying for it, down to the last bootlace."

"An expensive undertaking, Faulconer, I'm sure." Lee frowned, as though puzzled by Faulconer's generosity. The general had a great reputation, and folk in Richmond had taken immense comfort from the fact that he had returned to his native state rather than accept the command of Abraham Lincoln's northern armies, but Starbuck, watching the quiet, neat, gray-bearded man, could see little evidence of the general's supposed genius. Lee seemed reticent to the point of timidity and was entirely dwarfed by Washington Faulconer's energy and enthusiasm. "You mention cannon and cavalry," Lee said, speaking very diffidently, "does that mean your regiment, your Legion I should say, will consist of all arms?"

"All arms?" Washington Faulconer was unfamiliar with the phrase.

"The Legion will not consist of infantry alone?" Lee explained courteously.

"Indeed. Indeed. I wish to bring the Confederacy a fully trained, fully equipped, wholly useful unit." Faulconer paused to consider the wisdom of his next words, but then decided a little bombast would not be misplaced. "I fancy the Legion will be akin to Bonaparte's elite troops. An imperial guard for the Confederacy."

"Ah, indeed." It was hard to tell whether Lee was impressed or aghast at the vision. He paused for a few seconds, then calmly remarked that he looked forward to the day when such a

42

Legion would be fully assimilated into the state's forces. That was precisely what Faulconer feared most—a naked grab by Governor John Letcher to take command of his Legion and thus reduce it to yet another mediocre component in the state militia. Faulconer's vision was much grander than the governor's lukewarm ambitions, and, in defense of that vision, he made no response to Lee's words. The general frowned. "You do understand, Mister Faulconer, that we must have order and arrangement?"

"Discipline, you mean?"

"The very word. We must use discipline."

Washington Faulconer ceded the point graciously, then enquired of Lee whether the state would like to assume the cost of outfitting and equipping the Faulconer Legion? He let that dangerous question dangle for a few seconds, then smiled. "As I made clear to you, Lee, my ambition is to provide the Confederacy with a finished article, a trained Legion, but if the state is to intervene"—he meant *interfere*, but was too tactful to use the word—"then I think it only right that the state should take over the necessary funding and, indeed, reimburse me for the monies already expressed. My secretary, Mister Starbuck, can give you a full accounting."

Lee received the threat without changing his placid, somewhat anxious expression. He glanced at Starbuck, seemed curious about the young man's fading black eye, but made no comment. Instead he looked back to Washington Faulconer. "But you do intend to place the Legion under the proper authority?"

"When it is trained, indeed." Faulconer chuckled. "I am hardly proposing to wage a private war on the United States."

Lee did not smile at the small jest, instead he seemed rather downcast, but it seemed triumphantly clear to Starbuck that Washington Faulconer had won his victory over Governor Letcher's representative and that the Faulconer Legion would not be assimilated into the new regiments being hurriedly

43

raised across the state. "Your recruitment goes well?" Lee asked.

"I have one of my best officers supervising the process. We're only levying recruits in the county, not outside." That was not wholly true, but Faulconer felt the state would respect his proprietorial rights inside Faulconer County, whereas if he too openly recruited outside the county the state might complain that he was poaching.

Lee seemed happy enough with the reassurance. "And the training?" he asked. "It will be in competent hands?"

"Extremely competent," Faulconer said enthusiastically, but without adding any of the detail Lee clearly wanted to hear. In Faulconer's absence the Legion's training would be supervised by the Legion's second in command, Major Alexander Pelham, who was a neighbor of Faulconer's and a veteran of the War of 1812. Pelham was now in his seventies, but Faulconer claimed he was as able and vigorous as a man half his age. Pelham was also the only officer connected to the Legion who had ever experienced warfare, though as Ethan Ridley had cattily remarked to Starbuck, that experience had been confined to a single day's action, and that single action had been the defeat at Bladensburg.

Lee's visit ended with an inconsequential exchange of views on how the war should be prosecuted. Faulconer vigorously pressed the necessity of capturing the city of Washington, while Lee talked of the urgent need to secure Virginia's defenses, and afterward, with mutual assurances of goodwill, the two men parted. Washington Faulconer waited until the general had gone down the famous curved staircase, then exploded at Starbuck. "What chance do we have when fools like that are put in command? Dear God, Nate, but we need younger men, energetic men, hard-driving men, not washed-out, cautious buffoons!" He paced the room vigorously, impotent to express the full measure of his frustration. "I knew the governor would try to kidnap the Legion! But he'll need to send someone with

44

sharper claws than that!" He gestured scornfully toward the door through which Lee had left.

"The newspapers say he's the most admired soldier in America." Starbuck could not resist the observation.

"Admired for what? Keeping his pants clean in Mexico? If there's going to be war, Nate, it will not be a romp against an ill-armed pack of Mexicans! You heard him, Nate! 'The paramount importance of keeping the northern forces from attacking Richmond.'" Faulconer gave a rather good imitation of the softspoken Lee, then savaged him with criticism. "Defending Richmond isn't paramount! What's paramount is winning the war. It means hitting them hard and soon. It means attack, attack, attack!" He glanced at a side table where maps of the western part of Virginia lay beside a timetable of the Baltimore and Ohio Railroad. Despite his denial of planning to wage a private war on the North, Washington Faulconer was plotting an attack on the rail line that fed supplies and recruits from the western states to the city of Washington. His ideas for the raid were still forming, but he was imagining a small, fast force of mounted soldiers who would burn down trestles, derail locomotives and tear up track. "I hope the fool didn't see those maps," he said in sudden worry.

"I covered them with maps of Europe before General Lee arrived, sir," Starbuck said.

"You're a brisk one, Nate! Well done! Thank God I've got young men like you, and none of Lee's dullards from West Point. Is that why we're supposed to admire him? Because he was a good superintendent of West Point? And what does that make him? It makes him a schoolmaster!" Faulconer's scorn was palpable. "I know schoolmasters, Nate. My brother-in-law's a schoolmaster and the man isn't fit to be a cookhouse corporal, but he still insists I should make him an officer in the Legion. Never! Pecker is a fool! A cretin! A lunkhead! A heathen! A he-biddy. That's what my brother-in-law is, Nate, a he-biddy!"

Something in Washington Faulconer's energetic tirade triggered Starbuck's memory of the amusing stories Adam liked to tell about his eccentric schoolmaster uncle. "He was Adam's tutor, sir, yes?"

"He tutored both Adam and Anna. Now he runs the county school, and Miriam wants me to make him a major." Miriam was Washington Faulconer's wife, a woman who remained secluded in the country and suffered from a debilitating variety of mysterious maladies. "Make Pecker a major!" Faulconer hooted with derisive laughter at the very idea. "My God, you wouldn't put the pathetic fool in charge of a henhouse, let alone a regiment of fighting men! He's a poor relation, Nate. That's what Pecker is. A poor relation. Ah well, to work!"

There was plenty of work. The house was besieged by callers, some wanting monetary help to develop a secret weapon they swore would bring instant victory to the South, others seeking an officer's appointment with the Legion. A good number of the latter were professional European soldiers on half pay from their own armies, but all such petitioners were told that the Faulconer Legion would elect only local men to be its company officers and that Faulconer's appointed aides would all be Virginians too. "Except for you, Nate," Washington Faulconer told Starbuck, "that's if you'd like to serve me?"

"I'd be honored, sir." And Starbuck felt a warm rush of gratitude for the kindness and trust that Faulconer was showing him.

"You won't find it hard to fight against your own kind, Nate?" Faulconer asked solicitously.

"I feel more at home here, sir."

"And so you should. The South is the real America, Nate, not the North."

Not ten minutes later Starbuck had to refuse an appointment to a scarred Austrian cavalry officer who claimed to have fought in a half-dozen hard battles in northern Italy. The man, hearing that only Virginians would be allowed to command in the

46

Legion, sarcastically enquired how he could reach Washington. "Because if no one will have me here, then by Gott I shall fight for the North!"

The beginning of May brought the news that northern warships had begun a blockade of the Confederate coast. Jefferson Davis, the new president of the Provisional Government of the Confederate States of America, retaliated by signing a declaration of war against the United States, though the State of Virginia seemed in two minds about waging that war. State troops were withdrawn from Alexandria, a town just across the Potomac River from Washington, an act that Washington Faulconer scathingly condemned as typical of Letcher's caviling timidity. "You know what the governor wants?" he asked Nate.

"To take the Legion from you, sir?"

"He wants the North to invade Virginia, because that'll ease him off the political fence without tearing his britches. He's never been fervent for secession. He's a trimmer, Nate, that's his trouble, a trimmer." Yet the very next day brought news that Letcher, far from waiting supine while the North restored the Union, had ordered Virginian troops to occupy the town of Harper's Ferry fifty miles upstream of Washington. The North had abandoned the town without a fight, leaving behind tons of gun-making equipment in the federal arsenal. Richmond celebrated the news, though Washington Faulconer seemed rueful. He had cherished his idea of an attack on the Baltimore and Ohio Railroad whose track crossed the Potomac at Harper's Ferry, but now, with the town and its bridge safe in southern hands, there no longer seemed any need to raid the line farther west. The news of the river town's occupation also promoted a flurry of speculation that the Confederacy was about to make a preemptive attack across the Potomac, and Faulconer, fearing that his rapidly growing Legion might be denied its proper place in such a victorious invasion, decided his place was at Faulconer Court House, where he could hasten the Legion's training. "I'll bring you out to Faulconer County as soon as I

47

can," Faulconer promised Starbuck as he mounted his horse for the seventy-mile ride to his country estate. "Write to Adam for me, will you?"

"I will, sir, of course."

"Tell him to come home." Faulconer raised a gloved hand in farewell, then released his tall black horse to the road. "Tell him to come home!" he shouted as he went.

Starbuck dutifully wrote, addressing his letter to the church in Chicago that forwarded Adam's mail. Adam, just like Starbuck, had abandoned his studies at Yale, but where Starbuck had done it for an obsession with a girl, Adam had gone to Chicago to join the Christian Peace Commission which, by prayer, tracts and witness had been trying to bring the two parts of America back into peaceful amity.

No answer came from Chicago, yet every post brought Starbuck new and urgent demands from Washington Faulconer. "How long will it take Shaffers to make officers' uniforms?" "Do we have a determination of officers' insignia? This is important, Nate! Enquire at Mitchell and Tylers," "Visit Boyle and Gambles and ask about saber patterns," "In my bureau, third drawer down, is a revolver made by Le Mat, send it back with Nelson." Nelson was one of the two Negro servants who carried the letters between Richmond and Faulconer Court House. "The Colonel's mighty anxious to collect his uniforms," Nelson confided to Starbuck. "The Colonel" was Washington Faulconer, who had begun signing his letters "Colonel Faulconer," and Starbuck took good care to address Faulconer with the self-bestowed rank. The Colonel had ordered notepaper printed with the legend "The Faulconer Legion, Campaign Headquarters, Colonel Washington Faulconer, State of Virginia, Commanding," and Starbuck used the proof sheet to write the Colonel the happy news that his new uniforms were expected to be ready by Friday and promising he would have them sent out to Faulconer County immediately.

On that Friday morning Starbuck was sitting down to bring

his account books up-to-date when the door to the music room banged open and a tall stranger glowered angrily from the threshold. He was a tall thin man, all bony elbows, long shanks and protruding knees. He looked to be in early middle age, had a black beard streaked with gray, a sharp nose, slanted cheekbones and tousled black hair, and was wearing a threadbare black suit over scuffed brown work boots; altogether a scarecrow figure whose sudden appearance had made Starbuck jump.

"You must be Starbuck, ah-ha?"

"I am, sir."

"I heard your father preach once." The curious man bustled into the room, looking for somewhere to drop his bag and umbrella and walking stick and coat and hat and book bag, and, finding no place suitable, clung to them. "He was impassioned, yes, but he tortured his logic. Does he always?"

"I'm not sure what you mean. You, sir, are?"

"It was in Cincinatti. At the old Presbyterian Hall, the one on Fourth Avenue, or was it Fifth? It was in '56, anyway, or maybe it was '55? The hall has since burned down, but is no loss to the architecture of what is left of the Republic. Not a fine building in my opinion. Of course none of the fools in the audience noted your father's logic. They just wanted to cheer his every word. Down with the slavocracy! Up with our sable brethren! Hallelujah! Evil in our midst! Slur on a great nation! Bah!"

Starbuck, even though he disliked his father, felt pressed to defend him. "You made your opposition known to my father, sir? Or do you just start quarrels with his son?"

"Quarrels? Opposition? I hold no opposition to your father's views! I agree with them, each and every one. Slavery, Starbuck, is a menace to our society. I simply disagree with your father's contemptible logic! It is not enough to pray for an end to the peculiar institution, we have to propose practical arrangements for its abolition. Are the slaveholders to be recompensed

49

for their pecuniary loss? And if so, by whom? By the federal government? By a sale of bonds? And what of the Negroes themselves? Are we to repatriate them to Africa? Settle them in South America? Or are we to breed the darkness out of them by forcible miscegenation, a process, I might say, which has been well begun by our slave owners. Your father made no mention of these matters, but merely had recourse to indignation and prayer, as if prayer has ever settled anything!"

"You do not believe in prayer, sir?"

"Believe in prayer!" The thin man was scandalized by the very thought of such a belief. "If prayer solved anything there'd be no unhappiness in this world, would there? All the moaning women would be smiling! There would be no more disease, no more hunger, no more appalling children picking their snot-filled nostrils in our schoolrooms, no more sniveling infants brought for my admiration. Why should I admire their mewling, puking, whimpering, filthy-faced offspring? I do not like children! I have been telling Washington Faulconer that simple fact for fourteen years now! Fourteen years! Yet my brother-in-law seems incapable of understanding the simplest sentence of plain-spoken English and insists I run his schoolroom. Yet I do not like children, I have never liked children and I hope that I never shall like children. Is that so very hard to understand?" The man still clung to his awkward burdens, even as he waited for Starbuck's response.

Starbuck suddenly understood who this bad-tempered disorganized man was. This was the he-biddy, the poor relation, Faulconer's brother-in-law. "You're Mister Thaddeus Bird," he said.

"Of course I'm Thaddeus Bird!" Bird seemed angry that his identity needed confirmation. He glared bright-eyed and bristling at Starbuck. "Have you heard a word I said?"

"You were telling me you do not like children."

"Filthy little beasts. In the North, mark you, you raise children differently. There you are not afraid to discipline them.

50

Or beat them, indeed! But here, in the South, we need differentiate our children from our slaves and so we beat the latter and destroy the former with kindness."

"Mister Faulconer beats neither, I believe?"

Bird froze, staring at Starbuck as though the younger man had just uttered an extraordinary profanity. "My brother-in-law, I perceive, has been advertising his good qualities to you. His good qualities, Starbuck, are dollars. He buys affection, adulation and admiration. Without money he would be as empty as a Tuesday night pulpit. Besides he does not need to beat his servants or children because my sister can beat enough for twenty."

Starbuck was offended by this ungrateful attack on his patron. "Mister Faulconer freed his slaves, did he not?"

"He freed twenty house slaves, six garden boys and his stable people. He never had field hands because he never needed them. The Faulconer fortune is not based on cotton or tobacco, but upon inheritance, railroads and investment, so it was a painless gesture, Starbuck, and principally done, I suspect, to spite my sister. It is, perhaps, the one good deed Faulconer ever did, and I refer to the exercise of spitefulness rather than to the act of manumission." Bird, failing to find anywhere to put down his belongings, simply opened his arms and let them all drop untidily onto the music room's parquet floor. "Faulconer wants you to deliver the uniforms."

Starbuck was taken aback, but then realized the subject had abruptly been changed to the Colonel's new finery. "He wants me to take them to Faulconer Court House?"

"Of course he does!" Bird almost screamed at Starbuck. "Must I state the obvious? If I say that Faulconer wishes you to deliver his uniforms, must I first define uniforms? And afterward identify Washington Faulconer? Or the Colonel, as we must all now learn to call him? Good God, Starbuck, and you were at Yale?"

"At the seminary."

"Ah! That explains all. A mind that can credit the bleatings of theology professors can hardly be expected to understand plain English." Thaddeus Bird evidently found this insult amusing, for he began to laugh and, at the same time, to jerk his head backward and forward in a motion so like a woodpecker that it was instantly obvious how his nickname had arisen. Yet if Starbuck himself had been asked to christen this thin, angular and unpleasant man with a nickname it would not have been Pecker, but Spider, for there was something about Thaddeus Bird that irresistibly reminded Starbuck of a long-legged, hairy, unpredictable and malevolent spider. "The Colonel has sent me to run some errands in Richmond, while you are to go to Faulconer Court House," Pecker Bird went on, but in a plump, mocking voice such as he might use to a small and not very clever child. "Stop me if your Yale-educated mind finds any of these instructions difficult to understand. You will go to Faulconer Court House where the Colonel"—Bird paused to make a mocking salute—"wishes for your company, but only if the tailors have finished making his uniforms. You are to be the official conveyor of those uniforms, and of his daughter's manifold petticoats. Your responsibilities are profound."

"Petticoats?" Starbuck asked.

"Women's undergarments," Bird said maliciously, then sat at Washington Faulconer's grand piano where he played a swift and remarkably impressive arpeggio before settling into the tune of "John Brown's Body" to which, without regard to either scansion or tune, he chanted conversationally. "Why does Anna want so many petticoats? Especially as my niece already possesses more petticoats than a reasonable man might have thought necessary for a woman's comfort, but reason and young ladies have never kept close company. But why does she want Ridley? I cannot answer that question either." He stopped playing, frowning. "Though he is a remarkably talented artist."

"Ethan Ridley?" Starbuck, trying to follow the tortuous changes in Bird's conversation, asked in surprise.

52

"Remarkably talented," Bird confirmed rather wistfully, as though he envied Ridley's skill, "but lazy, of course. Natural talent going to waste, Starbuck. Just wasted! He won't work at his talent. He prefers to marry money rather than make it." He accentuated this judgment by playing a gloomy minor chord, then frowned. "He is a slave of nature," he said, looking expectantly at Starbuck.

"And a son of hell?" The second half of the Shakespearean insult slipped gratifyingly into Starbuck's mind.

"So you have read something other than your sacred texts." Bird seemed disappointed, but then recovered his malevolence as he lowered his voice into a confiding hiss, saying, "But I shall tell you, Starbuck, that the slave of nature will marry the Colonel's daughter! Why does that family contract such marriages? God knows, and he is not saying, though at present, mark my words, young Ridley is in bad odor with the Colonel. He has failed to recruit Truslow! Ah-ha!" Bird crashed a demonic and celebratory discord on the piano. "No Truslow! Ridley had better look to his laurels, had he not? The Colonel is not best pleased."

"Who is Truslow?" Starbuck asked somewhat despairingly.

"Truslow!" Bird said portentously, then paused to play a foreboding couplet of bass notes. "Truslow, Starbuck, is our county's murderer! Our outlaw! Our hardscrabble demon from the hills! Our beast, our creature of darkness, our fiend!" Bird cackled at this fine catalog of mischief, then twisted on the piano bench to face Starbuck. "Thomas Truslow is a rogue, and my brother-in-law the Colonel, who lacks common sense, wishes to recruit Truslow into the Legion because, he says, Truslow served as a soldier in Mexico. And so Truslow did, but the real reason, mark my words well, Starbuck, is that my brother-in-law believes that by recruiting him he can harness Truslow's reputation to the greater glory of his ridiculous Legion. In brief, Starbuck, the great Washington Faulconer desires the murderer's approval. The world is a strange place

53

indeed. Shall we now go and buy petticoats?"

"You say Truslow's a murderer?"

"I did indeed. He stole another man's wife, and killed the man thus to obtain her. He then volunteered for the Mexican War to escape the constables, but after the war he took up where he left off. Truslow's not a man to ignore his talents, you understand? He killed a man who insulted his wife, and cut the throat of another who tried to steal his horse, which is a rare jest, believe me, because Truslow must be the biggest horse thief this side of the Mississippi." Bird took a thin and very dark cigar from one of his shabby pockets. He paused to bite the tip off the cigar, then spat the shred of tobacco across the room in the vague direction of a porcelain spittoon. "And he hates Yankees. Detests them! If he meets you in the Legion, Starbuck, he'll probably hone his murdering talents still further!" Bird lit the cigar, puffed smoke and cackled amusement, his head nodding back and forth. "Have I satisfied your curiosity, Starbuck? Have we gossiped sufficiently? Good, then we shall go and see if the Colonel's uniforms are truly ready and then we shall buy Anna her petticoats. To war, Starbuck, to war!"

Thaddeus Bird first strode across town to Boyle and Gambles's huge warehouse where he placed an order for ammunition. "Minié bullets. The nascent Legion is firing them faster than the factories can make them. We need more, and still more. You can provide minié bullets?"

"Indeed we can, Mister Bird."

"I am not Mister Bird!" Bird announced grandly, "but Major Bird of the Faulconer Legion." He clicked his heels together and offered the elderly salesman a bow.

Starbuck gaped at Bird. Major Bird? This ludicrous man whom Washington Faulconer had declared would never be commissioned? A man, Faulconer claimed, not fit to be a cook-house corporal? A man, if Starbuck remembered rightly, who

54

would be commissioned only over Faulconer's dead body? And Bird was to be made a major while professional European soldiers, veterans of real wars, were being turned down for mere lieutenancies?

"And we need still more percussion caps"—Bird was oblivious of Starbuck's astonishment—"thousands of the little devils. Send them to the Faulconer Legion Encampment at Faulconer Court House in Faulconer County." He signed the order with a flourish, Major Thaddeus Caractacus Evillard Bird. "Grandparents," he curtly explained the grandiose names to Starbuck, "two Welsh, two French, all dead, let us go." He led the way out of the warehouse and downhill toward Exchange Alley.

Starbuck matched strides with the long-pacing Bird and broached the difficult subject. "Allow me to congratulate you on your commission, Major Bird?"

"So your ears work, do they? That's good news, Starbuck. A young man should possess all his faculties before age, liquor and stupidity erase them. Yes, indeed. My sister bestirred herself from her sickbed to prevail upon the Colonel to commission me a major in his Legion. I do not know upon what precise authority Colonel Brigadier General Captain Lieutenant Admiral the Lord High Executioner Faulconer makes such an appointment, but perhaps we do not need authority in these rebellious days. We are, after all, Robinson Crusoes marooned upon an authority-less island, and we must therefore fashion what we can out of what we find there, and my brother-in-law has discovered within himself the power to make me a major, so that is what I am."

"You desired such an appointment?" Starbuck asked very politely, because he could not really imagine this extraordinary man wanting to be a soldier.

"Desired?" Pecker Bird came to an abrupt stop on the pavement, thus forcing a lady to make an exaggerated swerve about the obstacle he had so suddenly created. "Desired? That is a pertinent question, Starbuck, such as one might have expected

55

from a Boston youth. Desired?" Bird tangled his beard in his fingers as he thought of his answer. "My sister desired it, that is certain, for she is stupid enough to believe that military rank is an automatic conferrer of respectability, which quality she feels I lack, but did I desire the appointment? Yes I did. I must confess I did, and why, you ask? Because firstly, Starbuck, wars are customarily conducted by fools and it thus behooves me to offer myself as an antidote to that sad reality." The schoolmaster offered this appalling immodesty in all apparent sincerity and in a voice that had attracted the amused attention of several pedestrians. "And secondly it will take me away from the schoolroom. Do you know how I despise children? How I dislike them? How their very voices make me wish to scream in protest! Their mischief is cruel, their presence demeaning and their conversation tedious. Those are my chief reasons." Suddenly, and as abruptly as he had stopped his forward progress, Major Thaddeus Caractacus Evillard Bird began striding downhill again with his long ragged pace.

"There were arguments against accepting the appointment," Bird continued when Starbuck had caught up with him. "First, the necessary close association with my brother-in-law, but upon balance that is preferable to the company of children, and second, the expressed wish of my dear intended, who fears that I might fall upon the field of battle. That would be tragic, Starbuck, tragic!" Bird stressed the enormity of the tragedy by gesturing violently with his right hand, almost sending a passing gentleman's hat flying. "But my darling Priscilla understands that at this time a man must not be seen laggard in his patriotic duty and so she has consented, albeit with sweet reservations, to my going for a soldier."

"You're engaged to be married, sir?"

"You find that circumstance extraordinary, perhaps?" Bird demanded vehemently.

"I find it cause to offer you still further congratulations, sir."

"Your tact exceeds your truthfulness," Bird cackled, then

swerved into the doorway of Shaffer's, the tailors, where Colonel Faulconer's three identical bespoke uniforms were indeed ready as promised, as was the much cheaper outfit that Faulconer had ordered for Starbuck. Pecker Bird insisted on examining the Colonel's uniform, then ordered one exactly like it for himself, except, he allowed, his coat's collar should only have a major's single star and not the three gold stars that decorated the Colonel's collar wings. "Put the uniform upon my brother-in-law's account," Bird said grandly as two tailors measured his awkward, bony frame. He insisted upon every possible accoutrement for the uniform, every tassel and plume and braided decoration imaginable. "I shall go into battle gaudy," Bird said, then turned as the spring-mounted bell on the shop's door rang to announce the entrance of a new customer. "Delaney!" Bird delightedly greeted a short, portly man who, with an owlish face, peered about myopically to discover the source of the enthusiastic greeting.

"Bird? Is that you? They have uncaged you? Bird! It is you!" The two men, one so lanky and unkempt, the other so smooth and round and neat, greeted each other with unfeigned delight. It was immediately clear that though they had not met for many months, they were resuming a conversation full of rich insults aimed at their mutual acquaintances, the best of whom were dismissed as mere nincompoops while the worst were utter fools. Starbuck, forgotten, stood fingering the parcels containing the Colonel's three uniforms until Thaddeus Bird, suddenly remembering him, beckoned him forward.

"You must meet Belvedere Delaney, Starbuck. Mister Delaney is Ethan's half-brother, but you should not allow that unhappy circumstance to prejudice your judgment."

"Starbuck," Delaney said, offering a half bow. He was at least twelve inches shorter than the tall Starbuck and a good deal more elegant. Delaney's black coat, breeches and top hat were of silk, his top boots gleamed, while his puff-bosomed shirt was a dazzling white and his tie pinned with a gold-mounted pearl. He had a round myopic face that was sly and humorous. "You are thinking," he accused Starbuck, "that I do not resemble dear Ethan. You were wondering, were you not, how a swan and a buzzard could be hatched from the same egg?"

"I was wondering no such thing, sir," Starbuck lied.

"Call me Delaney. We must be friends. Ethan tells me you were at Yale?"

Starbuck wondered what else Ethan had divulged. "I was at the seminary, yes."

"I shall not hold that against you, so long as you do not mind that I am a lawyer. Not, I hasten to say, a successful one, because I like to think of the law as my amusement rather than as my profession, by which I mean that I do a little probate work when it is plainly unavoidable." Delaney was being deliberately modest, for his flourishing practice was being nurtured by an acute political sensibility and an almost Jesuitical discretion. Belvedere Delaney did not believe in airing his clients' dirty linen in open court and thus did his subtle work in the quiet back rooms of the Capitol Building, or in the city's dining clubs or in the elegant drawing rooms of the big houses on Grace Street and Clay Street. He was privy to the secrets of half Virginia's lawmakers and was reckoned to be a rising power in the Virginian capital. He told Starbuck that he had met Thaddeus Bird at the University of Virginia and that the two men had been friends ever since. "You shall both come and have dinner with me," Delaney insisted.

"On the contrary," Bird said, "you shall have dinner with me."

"My dear Bird!" Delaney pretended horror. "I cannot afford to eat on a country schoolmaster's salary! The horrors of secession have stirred my appetites, and my delicate constitution requires only the richest of foods and the finest of wines. No, no! You shall eat with me, as will you, Mister Starbuck, for I am determined to hear all your father's secret faults. Does he drink? Does he consort with evil women in the vestry? Reassure me on these matters, I beg you."

"You shall dine with me," Bird insisted, "and you will have the finest wine in the Spotswood's cellars because, my dear Bird, it is not I who shall pay, but Washington Faulconer."

"We are to eat on Faulconer's account?" Delaney asked in delight.

"We are indeed," Bird answered with relish.

"Then my business with Shaffer's will wait for the morrow. Lead me to the trough! Lead on, dear Bird, lead on! Let us make gluttons of ourselves, let us redefine greed, let us consume comestibles as they have never been consumed before, let us wallow in the wines of France, and let us gossip. Above all, let us have gossip."

"I'm supposed to be buying petticoats," Starbuck demurred.

"I suspect you look better in trousers," Delaney said sternly, "and besides, petticoats, like duty, can wait till the morrow. Pleasure summons us, Starbuck, pleasure summons us, let us surrender to its call."

3

Seven Springs, Washington Faulconer's house in Faulconer County, was everything Starbuck dreamed it would be, everything Adam had ever told him it would be, and everything Starbuck thought he might ever want a house to be. It was, he decided from the very first moment he saw it on that Sunday morning in late May, just perfect.

Seven Springs was a sprawling white building just two stories high except where a white clock tower surmounted a stable gate and where a rickety cupola, steepled with a weathervane, graced the main roof. Starbuck had expected something altogether more pretentious, something with high pillars and elegant pilasters, with arching porticoes and frowning pediments, but instead the big house seemed more like a lavish farmhouse that over the years had absent-mindedly spread and multiplied and reproduced itself until it was a tangle of steep roofs, shadowed reentrants and creeper-hung walls. The heart of the house was made of thick fieldstone, the outer wings were timber, while the black-shuttered and iron-balconied windows were shaded by tall trees under which were set white painted benches, long-roped swings, and broad tables. Smaller trees were brilliant with red and white blossom that fell to make drifts of color on the well-scythed lawn. The house and its garden cradled a marvelous promise of warm domesticity and unassuming comforts.

Starbuck, greeted by a Negro servant in the front hall, had first been relieved of the paper-wrapped bundles containing Washington Faulconer's new uniforms, then a second servant took the carpetbag containing Starbuck's own uniform, and afterward a turbanned maid came for the two heavy bundles of petticoats that had hung so awkwardly from Starbuck's saddle bow.

He waited. A longcase clock, its painted face orbiting with moons, stars and comets, ticked heavily in a corner of the tiled hallway. The walls were papered in a floral pattern on which hung gold-framed portraits of George Washington, Thomas Jefferson, James Madison and Washington Faulconer. The portrait of Faulconer depicted him mounted on his magnificent black horse, Saratoga, and gesturing toward what Starbuck took to be the estate surrounding Seven Springs. The hallway grate held the ashes of a fire, suggesting that the nights were still cold in this upland county. Fresh flowers stood in a crystal vase on the table where two newspapers lay folded, their headlines celebrating North Carolina's formal secession to the Confederate cause. The house smelt of starch, lye soap and apples. Starbuck fidgeted as he waited. He did not quite know what was expected of him. Colonel Faulconer had insisted that Starbuck bring the three newly made uniforms directly to Faulconer Court House, but whether he was to be a guest in the house or was expected to find a berth with the encamped Legion, Starbuck still did not know, and the uncertainty made him nervous.

A flurry of feet on the stairs made him turn. A young woman, fair-haired, dressed in white, and excited, came running down the final flight, then checked on the bottom stair with her hand resting on the white-painted newel post. She solemnly inspected Starbuck. "You're Nate Starbuck?" she finally asked.

"Indeed, ma'am." He offered her a small, awkward bow.

"Don't 'ma'am' me, I'm Anna." She stepped down onto the hall floor. She was small, scarce more than five feet tall, with a pale, waiflike face that was so anxiously wan that Starbuck, if he had not known her to be one of Virginia's wealthiest daughters, might have thought her an orphan.

Anna's face was familiar to Starbuck from the portrait that

hung in the Richmond town house, but however accurately the picture had caught her narrow head and diffident smile, the painter had somehow missed the essence of the girl, and that essence, Starbuck decided, was oddly pitiable. Anna, despite her prettiness, looked childishly nervous, almost terrified, as if she expected the world to mock her and cuff her and discard her as worthless. That look of extraordinary timidity was not helped by the hint of a strabismus in her left eye, though the squint, if it existed at all, was very slight. "I'm so glad you've come," she said, "because I was looking for an excuse not to attend church, and now I can talk to you."

"You received the petticoats?" Starbuck asked.

"Petticoats?" Anna paused, frowning, as if the word were unfamiliar to her.

"I brought you the petticoats you wanted," Starbuck explained, feeling as though he was speaking to a rather stupid child.

Anna shook her head. "The petticoats were for father, Mister Starbuck, not me, though why he should want them, I don't know. Maybe he thinks the supply will be constricted by war? Mother says we must stock up on medicines because of the war. She's ordered a hundredweight of camphor, and the Lord knows how much niter paper and hartshorn too. Is the sun very hot?"

"No."

"I cannot go into too fierce a sunlight, you see, in case I burn. But you say it isn't fierce?" She asked the question very earnestly.

"It isn't, no."

"Then shall we go for a walk? Would you like that?" She crossed the hall and slipped a hand under Starbuck's arm and tugged him toward the wide front door. The impetuous gesture was strangely intimate for such a timid girl, yet Starbuck suspected it was a pathetic appeal for companionship. "I've been so wanting to meet you," Anna said. "Weren't you

62

supposed to come here yesterday?"

"The uniforms were a day late," Starbuck lied. In truth his dinner with Thaddeus Bird and the beguiling Belvedere Delaney had stretched from the early afternoon to late suppertime, and so the petticoats had not been bought till late Saturday morning, but it hardly seemed politic to admit to such dalliance.

"Well, you're here now," Anna said as she drew Starbuck into the sunlight, "and I'm so glad. Adam has talked so much about you."

"He often spoke of you," Starbuck said gallantly and untruthfully, for in fact Adam had rarely spoken of his sister, and never with great fondness.

"You surprise me. Adam usually spends so much time examining his own conscience that he scarcely notices the existence of other people." Anna, thus revealing a more astringent mind than Starbuck had expected, nevertheless blushed, as if apologizing for her apparently harsh judgment. "My brother is a Faulconer to the core," she explained. "He is not very practical."

"Your father is practical, surely?"

"He's a dreamer," Anna said, "a romantic. He believes that all fine things will come true if we just have enough hope."

"And surely this house was not built by mere hopes?" Starbuck waved toward the generous facade of Seven Springs.

"You like the house?" Anna sounded surprised. "Mother and I are trying to persuade Father to pull it down and build something altogether grander. Something Italian, perhaps, with columns and a dome? I would like to have a pillared temple on a hill in the garden. Something surrounded by flowers, and very grand."

"I think the house is lovely as it is," Starbuck said.

Anna made a face to show her disapproval of Starbuck's taste. "Our great-great-grandfather Adam built it, or most of it. He was very practical, but then his son married a French lady

63

and the family blood became ethereal. That's what mother says. And she's not strong either, so her blood didn't help."

"Adam doesn't seem ethereal."

"Oh, he is," Anna said, then she smiled up at Starbuck. "I do so like northern voices. They sound so much cleverer than our country accents. Would you permit me to paint you? I'm not so good a painter as Ethan, but I work harder at it. You can sit beside the Faulconer River and look melancholy, like an exile beside the waters of Babylon."

"You'd like me to hang my harp upon the willows?" Starbuck jested clumsily.

Anna withdrew her arm and clapped her hands with delight. "You will be marvelous company. Everyone else is so dull. Adam is being pious in the North, father is besotted with soldiering, and mother spends all day wrapped in ice."

"In ice?"

"Wenham ice, from your home state of Massachusetts. I suppose, if there's war, there'll be no more Wenham ice and we shall have to suffer the local product. But Doctor Danson says the ice might cure mother's neuralgia. The ice cure comes from Europe, so it must be good." Starbuck had never heard of neuralgia, and did not want to enquire into its nature in case it should prove to be one of the vague and indescribable feminine diseases that so often prostrated his mother and elder sister, but Anna volunteered that the affliction was a very modern one and was constituted by what she described as "facial headaches." Starbuck murmured his sympathy. "But father thinks she makes it up to annoy him," Anna continued in her timid and attenuated voice.

"I'm sure that can't be true," Starbuck said.

"I think it might," Anna said in a very sad voice. "I sometimes wonder if men and women always irritate each other?"

"I don't know."

"This isn't a very cheerful conversation, is it?" Anna asked rather despairingly and in a tone that suggested all her

64

conversations became similarly bogged down in melancholy. She seemed to sink further into despair with every second, and Starbuck was remembering Belvedere Delaney's malicious tales of how intensely his half-brother disliked this girl, but how badly Ridley needed her dowry. Starbuck hoped those tales were nothing more than malicious gossip, for it would be a cruel world, he thought, that could victimize a girl as fey and tremulous as Anna Faulconer. "Did Father really say the petti-coats were for me?" she suddenly asked.

"Your uncle said as much."

"Oh, Pecker," Anna said, as if that explained everything.

"It seemed a very strange request," Starbuck said gallantly.

"So much is strange these days," Anna said hopelessly, "and I daren't ask Father for an explanation. He isn't happy, you see."

"No?"

"It's poor Ethan's fault. He couldn't find Truslow, you see, and Father has set his heart on recruiting Truslow. Have you heard about Truslow?"

"Your uncle told me about him, yes. He made Truslow sound rather fearful."

"But he is fearful. He's frightful!" Anna stopped to look up into Starbuck's face. "Shall I confide in you?"

Starbuck wondered what new horror story he was about to hear of the dreaded Truslow. "I should be honored by your confidence, Miss Faulconer," he said very formally.

"Call me Anna, please. I want to be friends. And I tell you, secretly, of course, that I don't believe poor Ethan went any-where near Truslow's lair. I think Ethan is much too fright-ened of Truslow. Everyone's frightened of Truslow, even Father, though he says he isn't." Anna's soft voice was very portentous. "Ethan says he went up there, but I don't know if that's true."

"I'm sure it is."

"I'm not." She put her arm back into Starbuck's elbow and

walked on. "Maybe you should ride up to find Truslow, Mister Starbuck?"

"Me?" Starbuck asked in horror.

A sudden animation came into Anna's voice. "Think of it as a quest. All my father's young knights must ride into the mountains and dare to challenge the monster, and whoever brings him back will prove himself the best, the noblest and the most gallant knight of all. What do you think of that idea, Mister Starbuck? Would you like to ride on a quest?"

"I think it sounds terrifying."

"Father would appreciate it if you went, I'm sure," Anna said, but when Starbuck made no reply she just sighed and pulled him toward the side of the house. "I want to show you my three dogs. You're to say that they're the prettiest pets in all the world, and after that we shall fetch the painting basket and we'll go to the river and you can hang that shabby hat on the willows. Except we don't have willows, at least I don't think we have. I'm not good at trees."

But there was to be no meeting with the three dogs, nor any painting expedition, for the front door of Seven Springs suddenly opened and Colonel Faulconer stepped into the sunlight.

Anna gasped with admiration. Her father was dressed in one of his new uniforms and looked simply grand. He looked, indeed, as though he had been born to wear this uniform and to lead free men across green fields to victory. His gray frock coat was thickly brocaded with gilt and yellow lace that had been folded and woven to make a broad hem to the coat's edges, while the sleeves were richly embroidered with intricately looped braid that climbed from the broad cuffs to above the elbows. A pair of yellow kidskin gloves was tucked into his shiny black belt, beneath which a tasseled red silk sash shimmered. His top boots gleamed, his saber's scabbard was polished to mirror brightness and the yellow plume on his cocked hat stirred in the small warm wind. Washington Faulconer was quite plainly delighted with himself as he moved to watch his reflection in one of the tall windows. "Well, Anna?" he asked.

"It's wonderful, Father!" Anna said with as much animation as Starbuck suspected her capable. Two black servants had come from the house and nodded their agreement.

"I expected the uniforms yesterday, Nate." Faulconer half-asked and half-accused Starbuck with the statement.

"Shaffer's was a day late, sir"—the lie came smoothly—"but they were most apologetic."

"I forgive them, considering the excellency of their tailoring." Washington Faulconer could hardly take his eyes from his reflection in the window glass. The gray uniform was set off with golden spurs, gilded spur chains and golden scabbard links. He had a revolver in a soft leather pouch, the weapon's butt looped to the belt with another golden chain. Braids of white and yellow ribbons decorated the outer seams of his breeches while his jacket's epaulettes were cushioned in yellow and hung with gold links. He drew the ivory-hilted saber, startling the morning with the harsh scrape of the steel on the scabbard's throat. The sun's light slashed back from the curved and brilliantly polished blade. "It's French," he told Starbuck, "a gift from Lafayette to my grandfather. Now it will be carried in a new crusade for liberty."

"It's truly impressive, sir," Starbuck said.

"So long as a man needs to dress in uniform to fight, then these rags are surely as good as any," the Colonel said with mock modesty, then slashed the saber in the empty air. "You're not feeling exhausted after your journey, Nate?"

"No, sir."

"Then unhand my daughter and we'll find you some work."

But Anna would not let Starbuck go. "Work, Father? But it's Sunday."

"And you should have gone to church, my dear."

"It's too hot. Besides, Nate has agreed to be painted and surely you won't deny me that small pleasure?"

"I shall indeed, my dear. Nate is a whole day late in arriving

67

and there's work to be done. Now why don't you go and read to your mother?"

"Because she's sitting in the dark enduring Doctor Danson's ice cure."

"Danson's an idiot."

"But he's the only medically qualified idiot we possess," Anna said, once more showing a glimpse of vivacity that her demeanor otherwise hid. "Are you really taking Nate away, Father?"

"I truly am, my dear."

Anna let go of Starbuck's elbow and gave him a shy smile of farewell. "She's bored," the Colonel said when he and Starbuck were back in the house. "She can chatter all day, mostly about nothing." He shook his head disapprovingly as he led Starbuck down a corridor hung with bridles and reins, snaffles and bits, cruppers and martingales. "No trouble finding a bed last night?"

"No, sir." Starbuck had put up at a tavern in Scottsville where no one had been curious about his northern accent or had demanded to see the pass that Colonel Faulconer had provided him.

"No news of Adam, I suppose?" the Colonel asked wistfully.

"I'm afraid not, sir. I did write, though."

"Ah well. The northern mails must be delayed. It's a miracle they're still coming at all. Come"—he pushed open the door of his study—"I need to find a gun for you."

The study was a wonderfully wide room built at the house's western extremity. It had creeper-framed windows on three of its four walls and a deep fireplace on the fourth. The heavy ceiling beams were hung with ancient flintlocks, bayonets and muskets, the walls with battle prints, and the mantel stacked with brass-hilted pistols and swords with snake-skin handles. A black labrador thumped its tail in welcome as Faulconer entered, but was evidently too old and infirm to climb to its feet. Faulconer stooped and ruffled the dog's ears. "Good boy,

This is Joshua, Nate. Used to be the best gun dog this side of the Atlantic. Ethan's father bred him. Poor old fellow." Starbuck was not sure whether it was the dog or Ethan's father who had earned the comment, but the Colonel's next words suggested it was not Joshua being pitied. "Bad thing, drink," the Colonel said as he pulled open a bureau's wide drawer that proved to be filled with handguns. "Ethan's father drank away the family land. His mother died of the milksick when he was born, and there's a half-brother who scooped up all the mother's money. He's a lawyer in Richmond now."

"I met him," Starbuck said.

Washington Faulconer turned and frowned at Starbuck. "You met Delaney?"

"Mister Bird introduced me to him in Shaffer's." Starbuck had no intention of revealing how the introduction had led to ten hours of the Spotswood House Hotel's finest food and drink, all of it placed on the Faulconer account, or how he had woken on Saturday morning with a searing headache, a dry mouth, a churning belly and a dim memory of swearing eternal friendship with the entertaining and mischievous Belvedere Delaney.

"A bad fellow, Delaney." The Colonel seemed disappointed in Starbuck. "Too clever for his own good."

"It was a very brief meeting, sir."

"Much too clever. I know lawyers who'd like to have a rope, a tall tree and Mister Delaney all attached to each other. He got all the mother's money and poor Ethan didn't get a thin dime out of the estate. Not fair, Nate, not fair at all. If Delaney had an ounce of decency he'd look after Ethan."

"He mentioned that Ethan is a very fine artist?" Starbuck said, hoping the compliment about his future son-in-law might restore the Colonel's good humor.

"So Ethan is, but that won't bring home the bacon, will it? A fellow might as well play the piano prettily, like Pecker does. I'll tell you what Ethan is, Nate. He's one of the finest hunters

69

I've ever seen and probably the best horseman in the county. And he's a damned fine farmer. He's managed what's left of his father's land these last five years, and I doubt anyone else could have done half as well." The Colonel paid Ridley this generous compliment, then drew out a long-barreled revolver and tentatively spun its chambers before deciding it was not the right gun. "Ethan's got solid worth, Nate, and he'll make a good soldier, a fine soldier, though I confess he didn't make the best recruiting officer." Faulconer turned to offer Starbuck a shrewd look. "Did you hear about Truslow?"

"Anna mentioned him, sir. And Mister Bird did, too."

"I want Truslow, Nate. I need him. If Truslow comes he'll bring fifty hard men out of the hills. Good men, natural fighters. Rogues, of course, every last one of them, but if Truslow tells them to knuckle under, they will. And if he doesn't join up? Half the men in the county will fear to leave their livestock unguarded, so you see why I need him."

Starbuck sensed what was coming and felt his confidence plummet. Truslow was the Yankee hater, the murderer, the demon of the hardscrabble hills.

The Colonel spun the cylinder of another revolver. "Ethan says Truslow's away thieving horses and won't be home for days, maybe weeks, but I have a feeling Truslow just avoided Ethan. He saw him coming and knew what he wanted, so ducked out of sight. I need someone Truslow doesn't know. Someone who can talk to the fellow and discover his price. Every man has his price, Nate, especially a blackguard like Truslow." He put the revolver back and picked out another still more lethal-looking gun. "So how would you feel about going, Nate? I'm not pretending it's an easy task because Truslow isn't the easiest of men, and if you tell me you don't want to do it, then I'll say no more. But otherwise?" The Colonel left the invitation dangling.

And Starbuck, presented with the choice, suddenly found that he did want to go. He wanted to prove that he could bring

70

the monster down from his lair. "I'd be happy to go, sir."

"Truly?" The Colonel sounded mildly surprised.

"Yes, truly."

"Good for you, Nate." Faulconer snapped back the cock of the lethal-looking revolver, pulled the trigger, then decided that gun was not right either. "You'll need a gun, of course. Most of the rogues in the mountains don't like Yankees. You've got your pass, of course, but it's a rare creature who can read up there. I'd tell you to wear the uniform, except folk like Truslow associate uniforms with excise men or tax collectors, so you're much safer in ordinary clothes. You'll just have to bluff your way if you're challenged, and if that doesn't work, shoot one of them." He chuckled, and Starbuck shuddered at the errand that now faced him. Not six months before he had been a student at Yale Theological College, immersed in an intricate study of the Pauline doctrine of atonement, and now he was supposed to shoot his way through a countryside of illiterate Yankee haters in search of the district's most feared horse thief and murderer? Faulconer must have sensed his premonition, for he grinned. "Don't worry, he won't kill you, not unless you try and take his daughter or, worse, his horse."

"I'm glad to hear that, sir," Starbuck said drily.

"I'll write you a letter for the brute, though God only knows if he can read. I'll explain you're an honorary southron, and I'll make him an offer. Say fifty dollars as a signing bounty? Don't offer him anything more, and for God's sake don't encourage him into thinking I want him to be an officer. Truslow will make a good sergeant, but you'd hardly want him at your supper table. His wife's dead, so she won't be a problem, but he's got a daughter who might be a nuisance. Tell him I'll find her a position in Richmond if he wants her placed. She's probably a filthy piece of work, but no doubt she can sew or tend store." Faulconer had laid a walnut box on his desk, which he now turned round so that the lid's catch faced Starbuck. "I don't

71

think this is for you, Nate, but take a look at her. She's very pretty."

Starbuck raised the walnut lid to reveal a beautiful ivory-handled revolver that lay in a specially shaped compartment lined with blue velvet. Other velvet-lined compartments held the gun's silver-rimmed powder horn, bullet mold and crimper. The gold-lettered label inside the lid read "R. Adams, Patentee of the Revolver, 79 King William Street, London EC." "I bought her in England two years ago." The Colonel lifted the gun and caressed its barrel. "She's a lovely thing, isn't she?"

"Yes, sir, she is." And the gun did indeed seem beautiful in the soft morning light that filtered past the long white drapes. The shape of the weapon was marvelously matched to function, a marriage of engineering and design so perfectly achieved that for a few seconds Starbuck even forgot exactly what the gun's function was.

"Very beautiful," Washington Faulconer said reverently. "I'll take her to the Baltimore and Ohio in a couple of weeks."

"The Baltimore ..." Starbuck began, then stopped as he realized he had not misheard. So the Colonel still wanted to lead his raid on the railroad? "But I thought our troops at Harper's Ferry had blocked the line, sir."

"So they have, Nate, but I've discovered the cars are still running as far as Cumberland, then they move their supplies on by road and canal." Faulconer put the beautiful Adams revolver away. "And it still seems to me that the Confederacy is being too quiescent, too fearful. We need to attack, Nate, not sit around waiting for the North to strike at us. We need to set the South alight with a victory! We need to show the North that we're men, not craven mudsills. We need a quick, absolute victory that will be written across every newspaper in America! Something to put our name in the history books! A victory to begin the Legion's history." He smiled. "How does that sound?"

"It sounds marvelous, sir."

"And you'll come with us, Nate, I promise. Bring me Truslow, then you and I will ride to the rails and break a few heads. But you need a gun first, so how about this beast?" The Colonel offered Nate a clumsy, long-barreled, ugly revolver with an old-fashioned hook-curved hilt, an awkward swan-necked hammer and two triggers. The Colonel explained that the lower ring trigger revolved the cylinder and cocked the hammer, while the upper lever fired the charge. "She's a brute to fire," Faulconer admitted, "until you learn the knack of releasing the lower trigger before you pull the upper one. But she's a robust thing. She can take a knock or two and still go on killing. She's heavy and that makes her difficult to aim, but you'll get used to her. And she'll scare the wits out of anyone you point her at." The pistol was an American-made Savage, three and a half pounds in weight and over a foot in length. The lovely Adams, with its blue sheened barrel and soft white handle, was smaller and lighter, and fired the same size bullet, yet it was not nearly as frightening as the Savage.

The Colonel put the Adams back into his drawer, then turned and pocketed the key. "Now, let's see, it's midday. I'll find you a fresh horse, give you that letter and some food, then you can be on your way. It isn't a long ride. You should be there by six o'clock, maybe earlier. I'll write you that letter, then send you Truslow hunting. Let's be to work, Nate!"

The Colonel accompanied Starbuck for the first part of his journey, ever encouraging him to sit his horse better. "Heels down, Nate! Heels down! Back straight!" The Colonel took amusement from Starbuck's riding, which was admittedly atrocious, while the Colonel himself was a superb horseman. He was riding his favorite stallion and, in his new uniform and mounted on the glossy horse, he looked marvelously impressive as he led Starbuck through the town of Faulconer Court House, past the water mill and the livery stable, the inn and the courthouse, the Baptist and the Episcopal churches, past

Greeley's Tavern and the smithy, the bank and the town gaol. A girl in a faded bonnet smiled at the Colonel from the schoolhouse porch. The Colonel waved to her, but did not stop to talk. "Priscilla Bowen," he told Nate, who had no idea how he was supposed to remember the flood of names that was being unleashed on him. "She's a pretty enough thing if you like them plump, but only nineteen, and the silly girl intends to marry Pecker. My God, but she could do better than him! I told her so too. I didn't mince my words either, but it hasn't done a blind bit of good. Pecker's double her age, double! I mean it's one thing to bed them, Nate, but you don't have to marry them! Have I offended you?"

"No, sir."

"I keep forgetting your strict beliefs." The Colonel laughed happily. They had passed through the town, which had struck Starbuck as a contented, comfortable community and much larger than he had expected. The Legion itself was encamped to the west of the town, while Faulconer's house was to the north. "Doctor Danson reckoned that the sound of military activity would be bad for Miriam," Faulconer explained. "She's delicate, you understand."

"So Anna was telling me, sir."

"I was thinking of sending her to Germany once Anna's safely married. They say the doctors there are marvelous."

"So I've heard, sir."

"Anna could accompany her. She's delicate too, you know. Danson says she needs iron. God knows what he means. But they can both go if the war's done by fall. Here we are, Nate!" The Colonel gestured toward a meadow where four rows of tents sloped down toward a stream. This was the Legion's encampment, crowned by the three-banded, seven-starred flag of the new Confederacy. Thick woods rose on the stream's far bank, the town lay behind, and the whole encampment somehow had the jaunty appearance of a traveling circus. A baseball diamond had already been worn into the flattest part of the

74

meadow, while the officers had made a steeplechase course along the bank of the stream. Girls from the town were perched along a steep bank that formed the meadow's eastern boundary, while the presence of carriages parked alongside the road showed how the gentry from the nearby countryside were making the encampment into the object of an excursion. There was no great air of purpose about the men who lounged or played or strolled around the campground, which indolence, as Starbuck well knew, resulted from Colonel Faulconer's military philosophy, which declared that too much drill simply dulled a good man's appetite for battle. Now, in sight of his good southerners, the Colonel became markedly more cheerful. "We just need two or three hundred more men, Nate, and the Legion will be unbeatable. Bringing me Truslow will be a good beginning."

"I'll do my best, sir," Starbuck said, and wondered why he had ever agreed to face the demon Truslow. His apprehensions were sharpened because Ethan Ridley, mounted on a spirited chestnut horse, had suddenly appeared at the encampment's main entrance. Starbuck remembered Anna Faulconer's confident assertion that Ridley had not even dared face Truslow, and that only made him all the more nervous. Ridley was in uniform, though his gray woolen tunic looked very drab beside the Colonel's brand-new finery.

"So what do you think of Shaffer's tailoring, Ethan?" the Colonel demanded of his future son-in-law.

"You look superb, sir," Ridley responded dutifully, then nodded a greeting to Starbuck, whose mare edged to the side of the road and lowered her head to crop at the grass while Washington Faulconer and Ridley talked. The Colonel was saying how he had discovered two cannon that might be bought, and was wondering if Ridley would mind going to Richmond to make the purchase and to ferret out some ammunition. The Richmond visit would mean that Ridley could not ride on the raid against the Baltimore and Ohio Railroad, and the Colonel was apologizing for denying his future son-in-law the enjoyment of that expedition, but Ridley seemed not to mind. In fact his dark, neatly bearded face even looked cheerful at the thought of returning to Richmond.

"In the meantime Nate's off to look for Truslow." The Colonel brought Starbuck back into the conversation.

Ridley's expression changed instantly to wariness. "You're wasting your time, Reverend. The man's off stealing horses."

"Maybe he just avoided you, Ethan?" Faulconer suggested.

"Maybe," Ridley sounded grudging, "but I'll still wager that Starbuck's wasting his time. Truslow can't stand Yankees. He blames a Yankee for his wife's death. He'll tear you limb from limb, Starbuck."

Faulconer, evidently affected by Ridley's pessimism, frowned at Starbuck. "It's your choice, Nate."

"Of course I'll go, sir."

Ridley scowled. "You're wasting your time, Reverend," he said again, with just a hint of too much force.

"Twenty bucks says I'm not," Starbuck heard himself saying, and immediately regretted the challenge as a stupid display of bravado. It was worse than stupid, he thought, but a sin too. Starbuck had been taught that all wagering was sinful in the sight of God, yet he did not know how to withdraw the impulsive offer.

Nor was he sure that he wanted to withdraw because Ridley had hesitated, and that hesitation seemed to confirm Anna's suspicion that her fiancé might indeed have evaded looking for the fearful Truslow.

"Sounds a fair offer to me," the Colonel intervened happily.

Ridley stared at Starbuck, and the younger man thought he detected a hint of fear in Ridley's gaze. Was he frightened that Starbuck would reveal his lie? Or just frightened of losing twenty dollars? "He'll kill you, Reverend."

"Twenty dollars says I'll have him here before the month's end," Starbuck said.

76

"By the week's end," Ridley challenged, seeing a way out of the wager.

"Fifty bucks?" Starbuck recklessly raised the wager.

Washington Faulconer laughed. Fifty dollars was nothing to him, but it was a fortune to penniless young men like Ridley and Starbuck. Fifty dollars was a month's wages to a good man, the price of a decent carriage horse, the cost of a fine revolver. Fifty dollars turned Anna's quixotic quest into a harsh ordeal. Ethan Ridley hesitated, then seemed to feel he demeaned himself by that hesitation and so held out a gloved hand. "You've got till Saturday, Reverend, not a moment more."

"Done," Starbuck said, and shook Ridley's hand.

"Fifty bucks!" Faulconer exclaimed with delight when Ridley had ridden away. "I do hope you're feeling lucky, Nate."

"I'll do my best, sir."

"Don't let Truslow bully you. Stand up to him, you hear me?"

"I will, sir."

"Good luck, Nate. And heels down! Heels down!"

Starbuck rode west toward the blue-shadowed mountains. It was a lovely day under an almost cloudless sky. Starbuck's fresh horse, a strong mare named Pocahontas, trotted tirelessly along the grass verge of the dirt road, which climbed steadily away from the small town, past orchards and fenced meadows, going into a hilly country of small farms, lush grass and quick streams. These Virginia foothills were not good for tobacco, less good still for the famous southern staples of indigo, rice and cotton, but they grew good walnuts and fine apples, and sustained fat cattle and plentiful corn. The farms, though small, looked finely kept. There were big barns and plump meadows and fat herds of cows whose bells sounded pleasantly languorous in the midday warmth. As the road climbed higher the farms became smaller until some were little more than corn patches hacked out of the encroaching woods. Farm dogs slept beside the road, waking to snap

77

at the horse's heels as Starbuck rode by.

Starbuck became more apprehensive as he rode higher into the hills. He had the insouciance and cockiness of youth, believing himself capable of any deed he set his mind to achieve, but as the sun declined he began to perceive Thomas Truslow as a great barrier that defined his whole future. Cross the barrier and life would be simple again, fail it and he would never again look in a mirror and feel respect for himself. He tried to steel himself against whatever hard reception Truslow might have for him, if indeed Truslow was in the hills at all, then he tried to imagine the triumph of success if the grim Truslow came meekly down to join the Legion's ranks. He thought of Faulconer's pleasure and of Ridley's chagrin, and then he wondered how he was ever to pay the wager if he lost. Starbuck had no money and, though the Colonel had offered to pay him wages of twenty-six dollars a month, Starbuck had yet to see a cent of it.

By midafternoon the dirt road had narrowed to a rough track that ran alongside a tumbling, white whipped river that foamed at rocks, coursed between boulders and worried at fallen trees. The woods were full of bright red blossom, the hills steep, the views spectacular. Starbuck passed two deserted cabins, and once he was startled by the crash of hooves and turned, fumbling for the loaded revolver, only to see a white-tailed deer galloping away through the trees. He had begun to enjoy the landscape, and that enjoyment made him wonder whether his destiny belonged in the wild new western lands where Americans struggled to claw a new country from the grip of heathen savages. My God, he thought, but he should never have agreed to study for the ministry! At night the guilt of that abandoned career often assailed him, but here, in the daylight, with a gun at his side and an adventure ahead, Starbuck felt ready to meet the devil himself, and suddenly the words *rebel* and *treason* did not seem so bad to him after all. He told himself he wanted to be a rebel. He wanted to taste the forbidden fruits against which his father preached. He wanted to be an intimate of sin, he wanted to saunter through the valley of the shadow of death because that was the way of a young man's dreams.

He reached a ruined sawmill where a track led south. The track was steep, forcing Starbuck off Pocahontas's back. Faulconer had told him there was another, easier road, but this steep path was the more direct and would bring him onto Truslow's land. The day had become hot, and sweat was prickling at Starbuck's skin. Birds screamed from among the new pale leaves.

By late afternoon he reached the ridge line, where he remounted to stare down into the red-blossomed valley where Truslow lived. It was a place, the Colonel said, where fugitives and scoundrels had taken refuge over the years, a lawless place where sinewy men and their tough wives hacked a living from a thin soil, but a soil happily free of government. It was a high, hanging valley famous for horse thieves, where animals stolen from the rich Virginia lowlands were corralled before being taken north and west for resale. This was a nameless place where Starbuck had to confront the demon of the hardscrabble hills whose approval was so important to the lofty Washington Faulconer. He turned and looked behind, seeing the great spread of green country stretching toward the hazed horizon, then he looked back to the west, where a few trickles of smoke showed where homesteads were concealed among the secretive trees.

He urged Pocahontas down the vague path that led between the trees. Starbuck wondered what kind of trees they were. He was a city boy and did not know a redbud from an elm or a live oak from a dogwood. He could not slaughter a pig or hunt a deer or even milk a cow. In this countryside of competent people he felt like a fool, a man of no talent and too much education. He wondered whether a city childhood unfitted a man for warfare, and whether the country people with their familiarity with death and their knowledge of landscape made natural

79

soldiers. Then, as so often, Starbuck swung from his romantic ideals of war to a sudden feeling of horror at the impending conflict. How could there be a war in this good land? These were the United States of America, the culmination of man's striving for a perfect government and a Godly society, and the only enemies ever seen in this happy land had been the British and the Indians, and both of those enemies, thanks to God's providence and American fortitude, had been defeated.

No, he thought, but these threats of war could not be real. They were mere excitements, politics turned sour, a spring fever that would be cooled by fall. Americans might fight against the Godless savages of the untamed wilderness, and were happy to slaughter the hirelings of some treacherous foreign king, but they would surely never turn on one another! Sense would prevail, a compromise would be reached, God would surely reach out his hand to protect his chosen country and its good people. Though maybe, Starbuck guiltily hoped, there would be time for one adventure first—one sunlit raid of bright flags and shining sabers and drumming hoofbeats and broken trains and burning trestles.

"Go one pace more, boy, and I'll blow your goddamned brains to kingdom come," the hidden voice spoke suddenly.

"Oh, Christ!" Starbuck was so astonished that he could not check the blasphemous imprecation, but he did retain just enough sense to haul in the reins, and the mare, well schooled, stopped.

"Or maybe I'll blow your brains out anyhows." The voice was as deep and harsh as a rat-tailed file scraping on rusted iron, and Starbuck, even though he had still not seen the speaker, suspected he has found his murderer. He had discovered Truslow.

4

The Reverend Elial Starbuck leaned forward in his pulpit and gripped his lectern so hard that his knuckles whitened. Some of his congregation, sitting close to the great man, thought the lectern must surely break. The reverend's eyes were closed and his long, bony, white-bearded face contorted with passion as he sought the exact word that would inflame his listeners and fill the church with a vengeful righteousness.

The tall building was silent. Every pew was taken and every bench in the gallery full. The church was foursquare, undecorated, plain, as simple and functional a building as the gospel that was preached from its white-painted pulpit. There was a black-robed choir, a new-fangled harmonium, and high clear-glass windows. Gas lamps provided lighting, and a big black pot-bellied stove offered a grudging warmth in winter, though that small comfort would not be needed for many months now. It was hot inside the church; not so hot as it would be in high summer when the atmosphere would be stifling, but this spring Sunday was warm enough for the worshipers to be fanning their faces, but as the Reverend Elial's dramatic silence stretched so, one by one, the paper fans were stilled until it seemed as if every person inside the church's high bare interior was as motionless as a statue.

They waited, hardly daring to breathe. The Reverend Elial, white haired, white bearded, fierce eyed, gaunt, held his silence as he savored the word in his mind. He had found the right word, he decided, a good word, a word in due season, a word from his text, and so he drew in a long breath and raised a slow hand until it seemed as though every heart in the whole high building had paused in its beating.

"Vomit!" the Reverend Elial screamed, and a child in the gallery cried aloud with fear of the word's explosive power. Some women gasped.

The Reverend Elial Starbuck smashed his right fist onto the pulpit's rail, struck it so hard that the sound echoed through the church like a gunshot. At the end of a sermon the edges of his hands were often dark with bruises, while the power of his preaching broke the spines of at least a half-dozen Bibles each year. "The slavocracy has no more right to call itself Christian than a dog can call itself a horse! Or an ape a man! Or a man an angel! Sin and perdition! Sin and perdition! The slavocracy is diseased with sin, polluted with perdition!" The sermon had reached the point where it no longer needed to make sense, because now the logic of its exposition could give way to a series of emotional reminders that would hammer the message deep into the listeners' hearts and fortify them against one more week of worldly temptations. The Reverend Elial had been preaching for one and a quarter hours, and he would preach for at least another half hour more, but for the next ten minutes he wanted to lash the congregation into a frenzy of indignation.

The slavocracy, he told them, was doomed for the deepest pits of hell, to be cast down into the lake of burning sulfur where they would suffer the torments of indescribable pain for the length of all eternity. The Reverend Elial Starbuck had cut his preaching teeth on descriptions of hell and he offered a five-minute reprise of that place's horrors, so filling his church with revulsion that some of the weaker brethren in the congregation seemed near to fainting. There was a section in the gallery where freed southern slaves sat, all of them sponsored in some way by the church, and the freedmen echoed the reverend's words, counterpointing and embroidering them so that the church seemed charged and filled with the Spirit.

And still the Reverend Elial racked the emotion higher and yet higher. He told his listeners how the slavocracy had been offered the hand of northern friendship, and he flung out his own bruised hand as if to illustrate the sheer goodness of the offer. "It was offered freely! It was offered justly! It was offered righteously! It was offered lovingly!" His hand stretched farther and farther out toward the congregation as he detailed the generosity of the northern states. "And what did they do with our offer? What did they do? What did they do?" The last repetition of the question had come in a high scream that locked the congregation into immobility. The Reverend Elial glared round the church, from the rich pews at the front to the poor benches at the back of the galleries, then down to his own family's pew, where his eldest son, James, sat in his new stiff blue uniform. "What did they do?" The Reverend Elial sawed the air as he answered his question. "They returned to their folly! 'For as a dog returneth to his vomit, so a fool returneth to his folly.'" That had been the Reverend Elial Starbuck's text, taken from the eleventh verse of the twenty-sixth chapter of the Book of Proverbs. He shook his head sadly, drew his hand back, and repeated the awful word in a tone of resignation and puzzlement. "Vomit, vomit, vomit."

The slavocracy, he said, was mired in its own vomit. They wallowed in it. They reveled in it. A Christian, the Reverend Elial Starbuck declared, had only one choice in these sad days. A Christian must armor himself with the shield of faith, weapon himself with the weapons of righteousness, and then march south to scour the land free of the southern dogs that supped of their own vomit. And the members of the slavocracy are dogs, he emphasized to his listeners, and they must be whipped like dogs, scourged like dogs and made to whimper like dogs.

"Hallelujah!" a voice called from the gallery, while in the Starbuck pew, hard beneath the pulpit, James Starbuck felt a pulse of pious satisfaction that he would be going forth to do the Lord's work in his country's army, then he felt a balancing spurt of fear that perhaps the slavocracy would not take its whipping quite as meekly as a frightened dog. James Elial MacPhail Starbuck was twenty-five, yet his thinning black hair and perpetual expression of pained worry made him look ten years older. He was able to console himself for his balding scalp by the bushy thickness of his fine deep beard that well matched his corpulent, tall frame. In looks he took more after his mother's side of the family than his father's, though in his assiduity to business he was every bit Elial's son for, even though he was only four years out of Harvard's Dane Law School, James was already spoken of as a coming man in the Commonwealth of Massachusetts, and that fine reputation, added to his famous father's entreaties, had earned him a place on the staff of General Irvin McDowell. This sermon would thus be the last James would hear from his father for many a week for, in the morning, he would take the cars for Washington to assume those new duties.

"The South must be made to whimper like dogs supping their own vomit!" The Reverend Elial began the summation which, in turn, would lead to the sermon's fiery and emotive conclusion, but one worshiper did not wait for those closing pyrotechnics. Beneath the gallery at the very back of the church a box pew door clicked open and a young man slipped out. He tiptoed the few paces to the rear door, then edged through into the vestibule. The few people who noticed his going assumed he was feeling unwell, though in truth Adam Faulconer was not feeling physically sick, but heartsick. He paused on the street steps of the church and took a deep breath while behind him the voice of the preacher rose and fell, muffled now by the granite walls of the tall church.

Adam looked astonishingly like his father. He had the same broad shoulders, stocky build and resolute face, with the same fair hair, blue eyes, and square-cut beard. It was a dependable, trustworthy face, though at this moment it was also a very troubled face.

Adam had come to Boston after receiving a letter from his

84

father that had described Starbuck's arrival in Richmond. Washington Faulconer had sketched an outline of Nate's troubles, then continued: "For your sake I shall offer him shelter and every kindness, and I assume he will stay here as long as he needs to, and I further assume that need might be for ever, but I surmise it is only the fear of his family that keeps him in Virginia. Perhaps, if you can spare the time from your endeavors," and Adam had smelt the rancor in his father's choice of that word, "you might inform Nate's family that their son is penitent, humiliated and dependent on charity, and so gain for him a token of their forgiveness?"

Adam had wanted to visit Boston. He knew the city was the most influential in the North, a place of learning and piety where he hoped to find men who could offer some hope of peace, but he had also hoped to discover some peace for Nate Starbuck to which end he had gone to the Reverend Elial Starbuck's house, but the reverend, apprised of Adam's business, had refused to receive him. Now Adam had listened to his friend's father preach and he suspected there was as little hope for America as there was for Nate. As the venom had poured from the pulpit Adam had understood that so long as such hatred went unassuaged there could be no compromise. The Christian Peace Commission had become irrelevant, for the churches of America could no more bring peace than a candle flame could melt the Wenham Lake in midwinter. America, Adam's blessed land, must go to war. It made no sense to Adam, for he did not understand how decent men could ever think that war could adjudicate matters better than reason and goodwill, but dimly and reluctantly, Adam was beginning to understand that goodwill and reason were not the mainsprings of mankind, but instead that passion, love and hate were the squalid fuels that drove history blindly onward.

Adam walked the plump ordered streets of residential Boston, beneath the new-leafed trees and beside the tall clean houses that were so gaily decorated with patriotic flags and bunting. Even the carriages waiting to take the worshipers back to their comfortable homes sported American flags. Adam loved that flag, and could be made misty eyed by all it stood for, yet now he recognized in its bright stars and broad stripes a tribal emblem being flaunted in hate, and he knew that everything he had worked for was about to be melted in the crucible. There was going to be war.

Thomas Truslow was a short, dark-haired stump of a man; a flint-faced, bitter-eyed creature whose skin was grimy with dirt and whose clothes were shiny with grease. His black hair was long and tangled like the thick beard that jutted pugnaciously from his dark-tanned face. His boots were thick-soled cowhide brogans, he wore a wide-brimmed hat, filthy Kentucky jeans and a homespun shirt with sleeves torn short enough to show the corded muscles of his upper arms. There was a heart tattooed on his right forearm with the odd word *Emly* written beneath it, and it took Starbuck a few seconds to realize that it was probably a misspelling of *Emily*.

"Lost your way, boy?" This unprepossessing creature now challenged Starbuck. Truslow was carrying an antique flintlock musket that had a depressingly blackened muzzle pointing unwaveringly at Starbuck's head.

"I'm looking for Mister Thomas Truslow," Starbuck said.

"I'm Truslow." The gun muzzle did not waver, nor did the oddly light eyes. When all was said and done, Starbuck decided, it was those eyes that scared him most. You could clean up this brute, trim his beard, scrub his face and dress him in a churchgoing suit, and still those wild eyes would radiate the chilling message that Thomas Truslow had nothing to lose.

"I've brought you a letter from Washington Faulconer."

"Faulconer!" The name was expressed as a joyless burst of laughter. "Wants me for a soldier, is that it?"

"He does, Mister Truslow, yes." Starbuck was making an

86

effort to keep his voice neutral and not betray the fear engendered by those eyes and by the threat of violence that came off Truslow as thick as the smoke from a green bonfire. It seemed that at any second a trembling mechanism could give way in the dark brain behind those pale eyes to unleash a pulverizing bout of destructiveness. It was a menace that seemed horribly close to madness, and very far from the reasoned world of Yale and Boston and Washington Faulconer's gracious house.

"Took his time in sending for me, didn't he?" Truslow asked suspiciously.

"He's been in Richmond. But he did send someone called Ethan Ridley to see you last week."

The mention of Ridley's name made Truslow strike like a starving snake. He reached up with his left hand, grabbed Starbuck's coat, and pulled down so that Starbuck was leaning precariously out of his saddle. He could smell the rank tobacco on Truslow's breath, and see the scraps of food caught in the wiry black bristles of his beard. The mad eyes glared into Starbuck's face. "Ridley was here?"

"I understand he visited you, yes." Starbuck was struggling to be courteous and even dignified, though he was remembering how his father had once tried to preach to some half-drunken immigrant longshoremen working on the quays of Boston Harbor and how even the impressive Reverend Elial had struggled to maintain his composure in the face of their maniacal coarseness. Breeding and education, Starbuck reflected, were poor things with which to confront raw nature. "He says you were not here."

Truslow abruptly let go of Starbuck's coat, at the same time making a growling noise that was half-threat and half-puzzlement. "I wasn't here," he said, but distantly, as if trying to make sense of some new and important information, "but no one told me how he was here either. Come on, boy."

Starbuck pulled his coat straight and surreptitiously loosened the big Savage revolver in its holster. "As I said, Mister

Truslow, I have a letter for you from Colonel Faulconer ..."

"Colonel is he, now?" Truslow laughed. He had stumped ahead of Starbuck, forcing the northerner to follow him into a wide clearing that was evidently the Truslow homestead. Bedraggled vegetables grew in long rows, there was a small orchard, its trees a glory of white blossom, while the house itself was a one-story log cabin surmounted by a stout stone chimney from which a wisp of smoke trickled. The cabin was ramshackle and surrounded by untidy stacks of timber, broken carts, sawhorses and barrels. A brindled dog, seeing Starbuck, lunged furiously at the end of its chain, scattering a flock of terrified chickens that had been scratching in the dirt. "Get off your horse, boy," Truslow snapped at Starbuck.

"I don't want to detain you, Mister Truslow. I have Mister Faulconer's letter here." Starbuck reached inside his coat.

"I said get off that damned horse!" Truslow snapped the command so fiercely that even the dog, which had seemed wilder than its own master, suddenly whimpered itself into silence and skulked back to the shade of the broken porch. "I've got work for you, boy," Truslow added.

"Work?" Starbuck slid out of the saddle, wondering just what kind of hell he had come to.

Truslow snatched the horse's reins and tied them to a post. "I was expecting Roper," he said in impenetrable explanation, "but till he comes, you'll have to do. Over there, boy." He pointed at a deep pit which lay just beyond one of the piles of broken carts. It was a saw pit, maybe eight feet deep and straddled by a tree trunk in which a massive great double-handed ripsaw was embedded.

"Jump down, boy! You'll be bottom man," Truslow snapped.

"Mister Truslow!" Starbuck tried to stem the madness with an appeal to reason.

"Jump, boy!" That tone of voice would have made the devil snap to attention, and Starbuck did take an involuntary step toward the pit's edge, but then his innate stubbornness took command.

"I'm not here to work."

Truslow grinned. "You've got a gun, boy, you'd better be prepared to use it."

"I'm here to give you this letter." Starbuck took the envelope from an inside pocket.

"You could kill a buffalo with that pistol, boy. You want to use it on me? Or you want to work for me?"

"I want you to read this letter ..."

"Work or fight, boy." Truslow stepped closer to Starbuck. "I don't give a sack of shit which one you want, but I ain't waiting all day for you to make up your mind on it either."

There was a time for fighting, Starbuck thought, and a time for deciding he would be bottom man in a saw pit. He jumped, landing in a slurry of mud, sawdust and woodchips.

"Take your coat off, boy, and that hog pistol with it."

"Mister Truslow!" Starbuck made one last effort to retain a shred of control over this encounter. "Would you just read this letter?"

"Listen, boy, your letter's just words, and words never filled a belly yet. Your fancy Colonel is asking me for a favor, and you'll have to work to earn him his answer. You understand me? If Washington Faulconer himself had come I'd have him down that pit, so leave off your whining, get off your coat, take hold of that handle, and give me some work."

So Starbuck left off his whining, took off his coat, took hold of the handle and gave him some work.

It seemed to Starbuck that he was mired in a pit beneath a cackling and vengeful demon. The great pit saw, singing through the trunk, was repeatedly rammed down at him in a shower of sawdust and chips that stung Starbuck's eyes and clogged his mouth and nostrils, yet each time he took a hand off the saw to try and cuff his face, Truslow would bellow a reproof. "What's the matter, boy? Gone soft on me? Work!"

The pit was straddled by a pinewood trunk that, judging by its size, had to be older than the Republic. Truslow had grudgingly informed Starbuck that he was cutting the trunk into planks which he had promised to deliver for a new floor being laid at the general store at Hankey's Ford. "This and two other trunks should manage it," Truslow announced before they were even halfway through the first cut, by which time Starbuck's muscles were already aching like fire and his hands were smarting.

"Pull, boy, pull!" Truslow shouted. "I can't keep the cut straight if you're lollygagging!" The saw blade was nine feet long and supposed to be powered equally by the top and bottom men, though Thomas Truslow, perched on top of the trunk in his nailed boots, was doing by far the greater amount of work. Starbuck tried to keep up. He gathered that his role was to pull down hard, for it was the downstroke that provided most of the cutting force, and if he tried to push up too hard he risked buckling the saw, so it was better to let Truslow yank the great steel blade up from the pit, but though that upward motion gave Starbuck a half second of blessed relief, it immediately led to the crucial, brutal downstroke. Sweat was pouring off Starbuck.

He could have stopped. He could have refused to work one more moment and instead have just let go of the great wooden handle and shouted up at this foul man that Colonel Faulconer was unaccountably offering him a fifty-dollar bonus to sign up as a soldier, but he sensed that Truslow was testing him, and suddenly he resented the southern attitude that assumed he was a feeble New Englander, too educated to be of any real use and too soft to be trusted with real men's work. He had been fooled by Dominique, condemned as pious by Ethan Ridley and now he was being ridiculed by this filthy, tobacco-stained, bearded fiend, and Starbuck's anger made him whip the saw down again and again and again so that the great blade rang through the slashing wood grain like a church bell.

"Now you're getting it!" Truslow grunted.

"And damn you, damn you too," Starbuck said, though under his panting breath. It felt extraordinarily daring to use the swear words, even under his breath for, though the devil above him could not hear the cursing, heaven's recording angel could, and Starbuck knew he had just added another sin to the great list of sins marked to his account. And swearing was among the bad sins, almost as bad as thieving. Starbuck had been brought up to hate blaspheming and to despise the givers of oaths, and even the profane weeks he had spent with Major Trabell's foul-mouthed *Tom* company had not quelled his unhappy conscience about cursing, but somehow he needed to defy God as well as Truslow at this moment, and so he went on spitting the word out to give himself strength.

"Hold it!" Truslow suddenly shouted, and Starbuck had an instant fear that his muttered imprecations had been heard, but instead the halt had merely been called so that the work could be adjusted. The saw had cut to within a few inches of the pit's side, so now the trunk had to be moved. "Catch hold, boy!" Truslow tossed down a stout branch that ended in a crutch. "Ram that under the far end and heave when I tell you."

Starbuck heaved, moving the great trunk inch by painful inch until it was in its new position. Then there was a further respite as Truslow hammered wedges into the sawn cut.

"So what's Faulconer offering me?" Truslow asked.

"Fifty dollars." Starbuck spoke from the pit and wondered how Truslow had guessed that anything was being offered. "You'd like me to read you the letter?"

"You suggesting I can't read, boy?"

"Let me give you the letter."

"Fifty, eh? He thinks he can buy me, does he? Faulconer thinks he can buy whatever he wants, whether it's a horse, a man or a whore. But in the end he tires of whatever he buys, and you and me'll be no different."

91

"He isn't buying me," Starbuck said, and had that lie treated with a silent derision by Truslow. "Colonel Faulconer's a good man," Starbuck insisted.

"You know why he freed his niggers?" Truslow asked.

Pecker Bird had told Starbuck that the manumission had been intended to spite Faulconer's wife, but Starbuck neither believed the story nor would he repeat it. "Because it was the right thing to do," he said defiantly.

"So it might have been," Truslow allowed, "but it was for another woman he did it. Roper will tell you the tale. She was some dollygob church girl from Philadelphia come to tell us southrons how to run our lives, and Faulconer let her stroll all over him. He reckoned he had to free his niggers before she'd ever lie with him, so he did but she didn't anyway." Truslow laughed at this evidence of a fool befuddled. "She made a mock of him in front of all Virginia, and that's why he's making this Legion of his, to get his pride back. He thinks he'll be a warrior hero for Virginia. Now, take hold, boy."

Starbuck felt he had to protect his hero. "He's a good man!"

"He can afford to be good. His wealth's bigger than his wits, now take hold, boy. Or are you afraid of hard work, is that it? I tell you boy, work should be hard. No bread tastes good that comes easy. So take hold. Roper will be here soon enough. He gave his word, and Roper don't break his word. But you'll have to do till he comes." Starbuck took hold, tensed, pulled, and the hellish rhythm began again. He dared not think of the blisters being raised on his hands, nor of the burning muscles of his back, arms and legs. He just concentrated blindly on the downstroke, dragging the pit saw's teeth through the yellow wood and closing his eyes against the constant sifting of sawdust. In Boston, he thought, they had great steam-driven circular saws that could rip a dozen trunks into planks in the same time it took to make just one cut with this ripping saw, so why in God's name were men still using saw pits?

They paused again as Truslow hammered more wedges into

the cut trunk. "So what's this war about, boy?"

"States' rights" was all Starbuck could say.

"What in hell's name does that mean?"

"It means, Mister Truslow, that America disagrees on how America should be governed."

"You could fill a bushel the way you talk, boy, but it don't add up to a pot of turnips. I thought we had a Constitution to tell us how to govern ourselves?"

"The Constitution has evidently failed us, Mister Truslow."

"You mean we ain't fighting to keep our niggers?"

"Oh, dear God," Starbuck sighed gently. He had once solemnly promised his father that he would never allow that word to be spoken in his presence, yet ever since he had met Dominique Demarest he had ignored the promise. Starbuck felt all his goodness, all his honor in the sight of God, slipping away like sand trickling through fingers.

"Well, boy? Are we fighting for our niggers or aren't we?"

Starbuck was leaning weakly on the dirt wall of the pit. He stirred himself to answer. "A faction of the North would dearly like to abolish slavery, yes. Others merely wish to stop it spreading westward, but the majority simply believe that the slave states should not dictate policy to the rest of America."

"What do the Yankees care about niggers? They ain't got none."

"It is a matter of morality, Mister Truslow," Starbuck said, trying to wipe the sweat-matted sawdust out of his eyes with his sawdust-matted sleeve.

"Does the Constitution say anything worth a piece of beaver shit about morality?" Truslow asked in a tone of genuine enquiry.

"No, sir. No, sir, it does not."

"I always reckon when a man speaks about morals he don't know nothing about what he's saying. Unless he's a preacher. So what do you think we should do with the niggers, boy?" Truslow asked.

"I think, sir"—Starbuck wished to hell he was anywhere but in this mud and sawdust pit answering this foulmouth's questions—"I think, sir," he said again as he tried desperately to think of anything that might make sense, "I think that every man, of whatever color, has an equal right before God and before man to an equal measure of dignity and happiness." Starbuck decided he sounded just like his elder brother, James, who could make any proposition sound pompous and lifeless. His father would have trumpeted the rights of the Negroes in a voice fit to rouse echoes from the angels, but Starbuck could not raise the energy for that kind of defiance.

"You like the niggers, is that the size of it?"

"I think they are fellow creatures, Mister Truslow."

"Hogs are fellow creatures, but it don't stop me killing 'em come berry time. Do you approve of slavery, boy?"

"No, Mister Truslow."

"Why not, boy?" The grating, mocking voice sounded from the brilliant sky above.

Starbuck tried to remember his father's arguments, not just the easy one that no man had the right to own another, but the more complex ones, such as how slavery enslaved the owner as much as it enslaved the possessed, and how it demeaned the slaveholder, and how it denied God's dignity to men who were the ebony image of God, and how it stultified the slavocracy's economy by driving white artisans north and west, but somehow none of the complex, persuasive answers would come and he settled for a simple condemnation instead. "Because it's wrong."

"You sound like a woman, boy." Truslow laughed. "So Faulconer thinks I should fight for his slave-holding friends, but no one in these hills can afford to feed and water a nigger, so why should I fight for them that can?"

"I don't know, sir, I really don't know." Starbuck was too tired to argue.

"So I'm supposed to fight for fifty bucks, is that it?"

Truslow's voice was scathing. "Take hold, boy."

"Oh, God." The blisters on Starbuck's hands had broken into raw patches of torn skin that were oozing blood and pus, but he had no choice but to seize the pit saw's handle and drag it down. The pain of the first stroke made him whimper aloud, but the shame of the sound made him grip hard through the agony and to tear the steel teeth angrily through the wood.

"That's it, boy! You're learning!"

Starbuck felt as if he were dying, as if his whole body had become a shank of pain that bent and pulled, bent and pulled, and he shamelessly allowed his weight to sag onto the handles during each upstroke so that Truslow caught and helped his tiredness for a brief instant before he let his weight drag the saw down once again. The saw handle was soggy with blood, the breath was rasping in his throat, his legs could barely hold him upright and still the toothed steel plunged up and down, up and down, up and mercilessly down.

"You ain't gettin' tired now, boy, are you?"

"No."

"Hardly started, we are. You go and look at Pastor Mitchell's church in Nellysford, boy, and you'll see a wide heart-pine floor that me and my pa whipsawed in a single day. Pull on, boy, pull on!"

Starbuck had never known work like it. Sometimes, in the winter, he went to his Uncle Matthew's home in Lowell and they would saw ice from the frozen lake to fill the family ice house, but those excursions had been playful occasions, interspersed with snowball fights or bouts of wild skating along the lake banks beneath the icicle-hung trees. This plank sawing was relentless, cruel, remorseless, yet he dared not give up for he felt that his whole being, his future, his character, indeed his very soul were being weighed in the furious balance of Thomas Truslow's scorn.

"Hold there, boy, time for another wedge."

Starbuck let go of the pit saw's handle, staggered, tripped and half fell against the pit's wall. His hands were too painful to uncurl. His breath hurt. He had been half aware that a second man had come to the saw pit and had been chatting to Truslow these last few painful minutes, but he did not want to look up and see whoever else was witnessing this humiliation.

"You ever see anything to match it, Roper?" Truslow's voice was mocking.

Starbuck still did not look up.

"This is Roper, boy," Truslow said. "Say your greeting."

"Good day, Mister Roper," Starbuck managed to say.

"He calls you mister!" Truslow found that amusing. "He thinks you niggers are his fellow creatures, Roper. Says you've got the same equal rights before God as he has. You reckon that's how God sees it, Roper?"

Roper paused to inspect the exhausted Starbuck. "I reckon God would want me in his bosom long before he ever took that," Roper finally answered, and Starbuck looked unwillingly upward to see that Roper was a tall black man who was clearly amused by Starbuck's predicament. "He don't look good for nothing, does he now?" Roper said.

"He ain't a bad worker," Truslow, astonishingly, came to Starbuck's defense, and Starbuck, hearing it, felt as though he had never in all his life received a compliment half so valuable. Truslow, the compliment delivered, jumped down into the pit. "Now I'll show you how it's done, boy." Truslow took hold of the pit saw's handle, nodded up at Roper, and suddenly the great blade of steel blurred as the two men went into an instant and much practiced rhythm. "This is how you do it!" Truslow shouted over the saw's ringing noise to the dazed Starbuck. "Let the steel do the work! You don't fight it, you let it slice the wood for you. Roper and me could cut half the forests in America without catching breath." Truslow was using one hand only, and standing to one side of the work so that the flood of dust and chips did not stream onto his face. "So what brings you here, boy?"

"I told you, a letter from—"

"I mean what's a Yankee doing in Virginia. You are a Yankee, aren't you?"

Starbuck, remembering Washington Faulconer's assertion of how much this man hated Yankees, decided to brazen it out. "And proud of it, yes."

Truslow jetted a stream of tobacco juice into a corner of the pit. "So what are you doing here?"

Starbuck decided this was not the time to talk of Mademoiselle Demarest, nor of the *Tom* company, so offered an abbreviated and less-anguished version of his story. "I've fallen out with my family and taken shelter with Mister Faulconer."

"Why him?"

"I am a close friend of Adam Faulconer."

"Are you now?" Truslow actually seemed to approve. "Where is Adam?"

"The last we heard he was in Chicago."

"Doing what?"

"He works with the Christian Peace Commission. They hold prayer meetings and distribute tracts."

Truslow laughed. "Tracts and prayers won't help, because America don't want peace, boy. You Yankees want to tell us how to live our lives, just like the British did last century, but we ain't any better listeners now than we were then. Nor is it their business. Who owns the house uses the best broom, boy. I'll tell you what the North wants, boy." Truslow, while talking, was whipping the saw up and down in his slicing, tireless rhythm. "The North wants to give us more government, that's what they want. It's these Prussians, that's what I reckon. They keep telling the Yankees how to make better government, and you Yankees is fool enough to listen, but I tell you it's too late now."

"Too late?"

97

"You can't mend a broken egg, boy. America's in two pieces, and the North will sell herself to the Prussians and we'll mess through as we are."

Starbuck was far too tired to care about the extraordinary theories that Truslow had about Prussia. "And the war?"

"We just have to win it. See the Yankees off. I don't want to tell them how to live, so long as they don't tell me."

"So you'll fight?" Starbuck asked, sensing some hope for the success of his errand.

"Of course I'll fight. But not for fifty dollars." Truslow paused as Roper hammered a wedge into the new cut.

Starbuck, whose breath was slowly coming back, frowned. "I'm not empowered to offer more, Mister Truslow."

"I don't want more. I'll fight because I want to fight, and if I weren't wanting to fight then fifty times fifty dollars wouldn't buy me, though Faulconer would never understood that." Truslow paused to spit a stream of viscous tobacco juice. "His father now, he knew that a fed hound never hunts, but Washington? He's a milksop, and he always pays to get what he wants, but I ain't for sale. I'll fight to keep America the way she is, boy, because the way she is makes her the best goddamned country in the whole goddamned world, and if that means killing a passel of you chicken-shit northerners to keep her that way, then so be it. Are you ready, Roper?"

The saw slashed down again, leaving Starbuck to wonder why Washington Faulconer had been willing to pay so dearly for Truslow's enlistment. Was it just because this man could bring other hard men from the mountains? In which case, Starbuck thought, it would be money well spent, for a regiment of hardscrabble demons like Truslow would surely be invincible.

"So what are you trained to be, boy?" Truslow kept sawing as he asked the question.

Starbuck was tempted to lie, but he had neither the energy nor the will to sustain a fiction. "A preacher," he answered wearily.

The sawing abruptly stopped, causing Roper to protest as his rhythm was broken. Truslow ignored the protest. "You're a preacher?"

"I was training to be a minister." Starbuck offered a more exact definition.

"A man of God?"

"I hope so, yes. Indeed I do." Except he knew he was not worthy and the knowledge of his backsliding was bitter.

Truslow stared incredulously at Starbuck and then, astonishingly, he wiped his hands down his filthy clothes as though trying to smarten himself up for his visitor. "I've got work for you," he announced grimly.

Starbuck glanced at the wicked-toothed saw. "But ..."

"Preacher's work," Truslow said curtly. "Roper! Ladder."

Roper dropped a homemade ladder into the pit and Starbuck, flinching from the pain in his hands, let himself be chivied up its crude rungs.

"Did you bring your book?" Truslow demanded as he followed Starbuck up the ladder.

"Book?"

"All preachers have books. Never mind, there's one in the house. Roper! You want to ride down to the Decker house? Tell Sally and Robert to come here fast. Take the man's horse. What's your name, mister?"

"Starbuck. Nathaniel Starbuck."

The name evidently meant nothing to Truslow. "Take Mister Starbuck's mare," he called to Roper, "and tell Sally I won't take no for an answer!" All these instructions had been hurled over Truslow's shoulders as he hurried to his log house. The dog scurried aside as its master stalked past, then lay staring malevolently at Starbuck, growling deep in its throat.

"You don't mind if I take the horse?" Roper asked. "Not to worry. I know her. I used to work for Mister Faulconer. I know this mare, Pocahontas, isn't she?"

Starbuck waved a feeble hand in assent. "Who is Sally?"

"Truslow's daughter." Roper chuckled as he untied the mare's bridle and adjusted the saddle. "She's a wild one, but you know what they say of women. They're the devil's nets, and young Sally will snare a few souls before she's through. She don't live here now. When her mother was dying she took herself off to Missus Decker, who can't abide Truslow." Roper seemed amused by the human tangle. He swung himself into Pocahontas's saddle. "I'll be off, Mister Truslow!" he called toward the cabin.

"Go on, Roper! Go!" Truslow emerged from the house carrying an enormous Bible that had lost its back cover and had a broken spine. "Hold it, mister." He thrust the dilapidated Bible at Starbuck, then bent over a water butt and scooped handfuls of rainwater over his scalp. He tried to pat the matted filthy hair into some semblance of order, then crammed his greasy hat back into place before beckoning to Starbuck. "Come on, mister."

Starbuck followed Truslow across the clearing. Flies buzzed in the warm evening air. Starbuck, cradling the Bible in his forearms to spare his skinned palms, tried to explain the misunderstanding to Thomas Truslow. "I'm not an ordained minister, Mister Truslow."

"What's ordained mean?" Truslow had stopped at the edge of the clearing and was unbuttoning his filthy jeans. He stared at Starbuck, evidently expecting an answer, then began to urinate. "It keeps the deer off the crop," he explained. "So what's ordained mean?"

"It means that I have not been called by a congregation to be their pastor."

"But you've got the book learning?"

"Yes, most of it."

"And you could be ordained?"

Starbuck was immediately assailed with guilt about Mademoiselle Dominique Demarest. "I'm not sure I want to be, anymore."

"But you could be?" Truslow insisted.

"I suppose so, yes."

"Then you're good enough for me. Come on." He buttoned his trousers and beckoned Starbuck under the trees to where, in a tended patch of grass and beneath a tree that was brilliant with red blossom, a single grave lay. The grave marker was a broad piece of wood, rammed into the earth and marked with the one word *Emly*. The grave did not look old, for its blossom-littered earth ridge was still sparse with grass. "She was my wife," Truslow said in a surprisingly meek and almost shy voice.

"I'm sorry."

"Died Christmas Day." Truslow blinked, and suddenly Starbuck felt a wave of sorrow come from the small, urgent man, a wave every bit as forceful and overwhelming as Truslow's more habitual emanation of violence. Truslow seemed unable to speak, as though there were not words to express what he felt. "Emily was a good wife," he finally said, "and I was a good husband to her. She made me that. A good woman can do that to a man. She can make a man good."

"Was she sick?" Starbuck asked uneasily.

Truslow nodded. He had taken off his greasy hat, which he now held awkwardly in his strong hands. "Congestion of the brain. It weren't an easy death."

"I'm sorry," Starbuck said inadequately.

"There was a man might have saved her. A Yankee." Truslow spoke the last word with a sour hatred that made Starbuck shiver. "He was a fancy doctor from up north. He was visiting relatives in the valley last Thanksgiving." He jerked his head westward, indicating the Shenandoah Valley beyond the intervening mountains. "Doctor Danson told me of him, said he could work miracles, so I rode over and begged him to come up and see my Emily. She couldn't be moved, see. I went on bended knee." Truslow fell silent, remembering the humiliation, then shook his head. "The man refused to move. Said

101

there was nothing he could do, but the truth was he didn't want to stir off his fat ass and mount a horse in that rain. They ran me off the property."

Starbuck had never heard of anyone being cured of congestion of the brain and suspected the Yankee doctor had known all along that anything he tried would be a waste of time, but how was anyone to persuade a man like Thomas Truslow of that truth?

"She died on Christmas Day," Truslow went on softly. "The snow was thick up here then, like a blanket. Just me and her, the girl had run off, damn her skin."

"Sally?"

"Hell, yes." Truslow was standing to attention now with his hands crossed awkwardly over his breast, almost as if he was imitating the death stance of his beloved Emily. "Emily and me weren't married proper," he confessed to Starbuck. "She ran off with me the year before I went to be a soldier. I was just sixteen, she weren't a day older, but she was already married. We were wrong, and we both knew it, but it was like we couldn't help ourselves." There were tears in his eyes, and Starbuck suddenly felt glad to know that this tough man had once behaved as stupidly and foolishly as Starbuck had himself just behaved. "I loved her," Truslow went on, "and that's the truth of it, though Pastor Mitchell wouldn't wed us because he said we were sinners."

"I'm sure he should have made no such judgment," Starbuck said gravely.

"I reckon he should. It was his job to judge us. What else is a preacher for except to teach us conduct? I ain't complaining, but God gave us his punishment, Mister Starbuck. Only one of our children lived, and she broke our hearts, and now Emily's dead and I'm left alone. God is not mocked, Mister Starbuck."

Suddenly, unexpectedly, Starbuck felt an immense surge of sympathy for this awkward, hard, difficult man who stood so clumsily beside the grave he must have dug himself. Or perhaps Roper had helped him, or one of the other fugitive men who lived in this high valley out of sight of the magistrates and the taxmen who infested the plains. At Christmastime, too, and Starbuck imagined them carrying the limp body out into the snow and hacking down into the cold ground.

"We weren't married proper, and she were never buried proper, not with a man of God to see her home, and that's what I want you to do for her. You're to say the right words, Mister Starbuck. Say them for Emily, because if you say the right words then God will take her in."

"I'm sure he will." Starbuck felt entirely inadequate to the moment.

"So say them." There was no violence in Thomas Truslow now, just a terrible vulnerability.

There was silence in the small glade. The evening shadows stretched long. Oh dear God, Starbuck thought, but I am not worthy, not nearly worthy. God will not listen to me, a sinner, yet are we not all sinners? And the truth, surely, was that God had already heard Thomas Truslow's prayer, for Truslow's anguish was more eloquent than any litany that Starbuck's education could provide. Yet Thomas Truslow needed the comfort of ritual, of old words lovingly said, and Starbuck gripped the book tight, closed his eyes and raised his face toward the dusk-shadowed blossoms, but suddenly he felt a fool and an imposter and no words would come. He opened his mouth, but he could not speak.

"That's right," Truslow said, "take your time."

Starbuck tried to think of a passage of scripture that would give him a start. His throat was dry. He opened his eyes and suddenly a verse came to him. "Man that is born of a woman," he began, but his voice was scratchy and uncertain so he began again, "man that is born of a woman is of few days, and full of trouble."

"Amen," Thomas Truslow said, "amen to that."

"He cometh forth like a flower ..."

103

"She was, she was, praise God, she was."

"And is cut down."

"The Lord took her, the Lord took her." Truslow, his eyes closed, rocked back and forth as he tried to summon all his intensity.

"He fleeth also as a shadow, and continueth not."

"God help us sinners," Truslow said, "God help us."

Starbuck was suddenly dumb. He had quoted the first two verses of the fourteenth chapter of Job, and suddenly he was remembering the fourth verse, which asked who can bring a clean thing from an unclean? Then gave its hard answer, no one. And surely Truslow's unsanctified household had been unclean?

"Pray, Mister, pray," Truslow pleaded.

"Oh Lord God"—Starbuck clenched his eyes against the sun's dying light—"remember Emily who was thy servant, thy handmaid, and who was snatched from this world into thy greater glory."

"She was, she was!" Truslow almost wailed the confirmation.

"Remember Emily Truslow—" Starbuck went on lamely.

"Mallory," Truslow interrupted, "that was her proper name, Emily Marjory Mallory. And shouldn't we kneel?" He snatched off his hat and dropped onto the soft loamy soil.

Starbuck also dropped to his knees. "Oh, Lord," he began again, and for a moment he was speechless, but then, from nowhere it seemed, the words began to flow. He felt Truslow's grief fill him, and in turn he tried to lay that grief upon the Lord. Truslow moaned as he listened to the prayer, while Starbuck raised his face to the green leaves as though he could project his words on strong hard wings out beyond the trees, out beyond the darkening sky, out beyond the first pale stars, out to where God reigned in all his terrible brooding majesty. The prayer was good, and Starbuck felt its power and wondered why he could not pray for himself as he prayed for this unknown woman. "Oh God," he finished, and there were tears on his face as his prayer came to an end, "oh dear God, hear our prayer, hear us, hear us."

And then there was silence again, except for the wind in the leaves and the sound of the birds and from somewhere in the valley a lone dog's barking. Starbuck opened his eyes to see that Truslow's dirty face was streaked with tears, yet the small man looked oddly happy. He was leaning forward to hold his stubby, strong fingers into the dirt of the grave as if, by thus holding the earth above his Emily's corpse, he could talk with her.

"I'll be going to war, Emily," he said, without any embarrassment at so addressing his dead woman in Starbuck's presence. "Faulconer's a fool, and I won't be going for his sake, but we've got kin in his ranks, and I'll go for them. Your brother's joined this so-called Legion, and cousin Tom is there, and you'd want me to look after them both, girl, so I will. And Sally's going to be just dandy. She's got her man now and she's going to be looked after, and you can just wait for me, my darling, and I'll be with you in God's time. This is Mister Starbuck who prayed for you. He did it well, didn't he?" Truslow was weeping, but now he pulled his fingers free of the soil and wiped them against his jeans before cuffing at his cheeks. "You pray well," he said to Starbuck.

"I think perhaps your prayer was heard without me," Starbuck said modestly.

"A man can never be sure enough, though, can he? And God will soon be deafened with prayers. War does that, so I'm glad we put our word in before the battles start drowning his ears with words. Emily will have enjoyed hearing you pray. She always did like a good prayer. Now I want you to pray over Sally."

Oh God, Starbuck thought, but this was going too far! "You want me to do what, Mister Truslow?"

"Pray over Sally. She's been a disappointment to us." Truslow climbed to his feet and pulled his wide-brimmed hat over his hair. He stared at the grave as he went on with his tale.

"She's not like her mother, nor like me. I don't know what bad wind brought her to us, but she came and I promised Emily as how I'd look after her, and I will. She's bare fifteen now and going to have a child, you see."

"Oh." Starbuck did not know what else to say. Fifteen! That was the same age as his younger sister, Martha, and Starbuck still thought of Martha as a child. At fifteen, Starbuck thought, he had not even known where babies came from, assuming they were issued by the authorities in some secret, fuss-laden ceremony involving women, the church and doctors.

"She says it's young Decker's babe, and maybe it is. And maybe it isn't. You tell me Ridley was here last week? That worries me. He's been sniffing round my Sally like she was on heat and him a dog. I was down the valley last week on business, so who knows where she was?"

Starbuck's first impulse was to declare that Ridley was engaged to Anna Faulconer, so could not be responsible for Sally Truslow's pregnancy, but some impulse told him that such a naive protest would be met with a bitter scorn and so, not knowing what else to say, he sensibly said nothing.

"She's not like her mother," Truslow spoke on, more to himself than to Starbuck. "There's a wildness in her, see? Maybe it's mine, but it weren't Emily's. But she says it's Robert Decker's babe, so let it be so. And he believes her and says he'll marry her, so let that be so too." Truslow stooped and plucked a weed from the grave. "That's where Sally is now," he explained to Starbuck, "with the Deckers. She said she couldn't abide me, but it was her mother's pain and dying she couldn't abide. Now she's pregnant, so she needs to be married with a home of her own, not living on charity. I promised Emily I'd look after Sally, so that's what I'm doing. I'll give Sally and her boy this homestead, and they can raise the child here. They won't want me. Sally and me have never seen eye to eye, so she and young Decker can take this place

106

and be proper together. And that's what I want you to do, Mister Starbuck. I want you to marry them proper. They're on their way here now."

"But I can't marry them!" Starbuck protested.

"If you can send my Emily's soul to heaven, you can marry my daughter to Robert Decker."

Starbuck wondered how in God's name he was to correct Thomas Truslow's egregious misunderstanding of both theology and the civil powers. "If she is to be married," he insisted, "then she must go before a magistrate and—"

"God bears a bigger clout than a magistrate." Truslow turned and walked away from the grave. "Sally will be married by a man of God, and that's more important than being wed by some buzzard of a lawyer who just wants his fee."

"But I'm not ordained!"

"Don't start that excuse again. You'll do for me. I've heard you, Mister Starbuck, and if God don't listen to your words then he won't listen to any man's. And if my Sally is to be married, then I want her to be properly married by God's law. I don't want her roaming again. She's been wild, but it's time she was settled down. So you pray over her."

Starbuck was not at all sure that prayer could stop a girl roaming, but he did not like to say as much to Thomas Truslow. "Why don't you take her down to the valley? There must be proper ministers there who'll marry them?"

"The ministers in the valley, mister"—Truslow had turned to stab a finger hard into Starbuck's chest to emphasize his words—"were too high and goddamned mighty to bury my Emily, so believe me, mister, they are too high and goddamned mighty to wed my daughter to her boy. And are you now trying to tell me that you're also too good for the likes of us?" His finger rammed one last time into Starbuck's chest, then stayed there.

"I think it would be a privilege to perform the service for your daughter, sir," Starbuck said hurriedly.

107

Sally Truslow and her boy came just after dark. Roper brought them, leading Sally on the horse. She dismounted in front of her father's porch where a lantern-shielded candle burned. She kept her face low, not daring to look up into her father's face. She wore a black bonnet and a blue dress. She was slim waisted, not yet showing her pregnancy.

Beside her was a young man with a round and innocent face. He was clean-shaven, indeed he looked as if he could not grow a beard if he tried. He might have been sixteen, but Starbuck guessed he was younger. Robert Decker had sandy coarse hair, trusting blue eyes, and a quick smile, which he struggled to subdue as he nodded a cautious greeting to his future father-in-law. "Mister Truslow," he said warily.

"Robert Decker," Truslow said, "you're to meet Nathaniel Starbuck. He's a man of God and he's agreed to marry you and Sally."

Robert Decker, fidgeting with his round hat that he held in front of him with both hands, nodded cheerfully at Starbuck. "Right pleased to make your acquaintance, mister."

"Look up, Sally!" Truslow growled.

"I ain't sure I want to be married." She whined the protest.

"You'll do as you're told to do," her father growled.

"I want to be church married!" the girl insisted. "Like Laura Taylor was, by a proper preacherman!" Starbuck hardly heard what she said, or even cared what she said, because instead he was gazing at Sally Truslow and wondering why God ordained these mysteries. Why was some country girl, whelped off an adulteress to a hard-bitten man, born to make the very sun seem dim? For Sally Truslow was beautiful. Her eyes were blue as the sky over the Nantucket sea, her face sweet as honey, her lips as full and inviting as a man's dreams could want. Her hair was a dark brown, streaked with lighter veins and rich in the lantern's light. "A marriage should be proper," she complained, "not like jumping over a broomstick." Leaping a broomstick was the deep country way of wedlock, or the

108

slave's way of signifying a marriage.

"You planning on raising the child on your own, Sally," Truslow demanded, "without marrying?"

"You can't do that, Sally," Robert Decker said with a pathetic anxiety. "You need a man to work for you, to look after you."

"Maybe there won't be any child," she said petulantly.

Truslow's hand moved like lightning, slashing hard and open across his daughter's cheek. The sound of the blow was like a whip cracking. "You kill that baby," he threatened, "and I'll take a leather to your skin that will leave your bones like bed slats. You hear me?"

"I won't do nothing." She was crying, cringing from the vicious blow. Her face had reddened from the slap, but there was still a cunning belligerence in her eyes.

"You know what I do to a cow that won't carry its young?" Truslow shouted at her. "I slaughter 'em. You think anyone would care if I put another aborting bitch under the dirt?"

"I ain't going to do nothing! I told you! I'll be a good girl!"

"She will, Mister Truslow," Robert Decker said. "She won't do anything."

Roper, impassive, stood behind the couple as Truslow stared hard into Robert Decker's eyes. "Why do you want to marry her, Robert?"

"I'm real fond of her, Mister Truslow." He was embarrassed to make the admission, but grinned and looked sideways at Sally. "And it's my baby. I just know it is."

"I'm going to have you married proper," Truslow looked back to his daughter, "by Mister Starbuck, who knows how to talk to God, and if you break your vows, Sally, then God will whip your hide till it bleeds dry. God won't be mocked, girl. You offend him and you'll end up like your mother; dead before your time and food to worms."

"I'll be a good girl," Sally whined, and she looked straight at Starbuck for the first time, and Starbuck's breath checked in

109

his throat as he stared back. Once, when Starbuck had been a small child, his Uncle Matthew had taken him to Faneuil Hall to see a demonstration of the electrical force, and Starbuck had held hands in a ring of onlookers as the lecturer fed a current through their linked bodies. He felt then something of what he experienced now, a tingling thrill that momentarily made the rest of the world seem unimportant. Then, as soon as he recognized the excitement, he felt a kind of desperation. This feeling was sin. It was the devil's work. Surely he must be soul sick? For surely no ordinary, decent man would be so entranced by every girl who had a pretty face? Then, jealously, he wondered whether Thomas Truslow's suspicions were right and that Ethan Ridley had been this girl's sweetheart, and Starbuck felt a stab of corrosive jealousy as sharp as a blade, then a fierce anger that Ridley could deceive Washington and Anna Faulconer. "Are you a proper preacherman?" Sally cuffed her nose and asked Starbuck.

"I wouldn't ask him to wed you otherwise," her father insisted.

"I was asking him myself," she said defiantly, keeping her eyes on Starbuck, and he knew she had seen clean into his soul. She was seeing his lust and his weakness, his sinfulness and his fear. Starbuck's father had often warned him against the powers of women, and Starbuck had thought he had met those powers at their most devilish in Mademoiselle Dominique Demarest, but Dominique had possessed nothing to compare with this girl's intensity. "And if a girl can't ask a preacherman who's marrying her just what kind of a preacherman he is," Sally insisted, "then what can she ask?" Her voice was low, like her father's, but where his generated fear, hers suggested something infinitely more dangerous. "So are you a proper preacherman, mister?" she demanded of Starbuck again.

"Yes." Starbuck told the lie for the sake of Thomas Truslow, and because he dared not let the truth enslave him to this girl.

"I guess we're all ready, then," Sally said defiantly. She did

110

not want to be married, but neither did she want to appear browbeaten. "You got a ring for us, pa?"

The question appeared casual, but Starbuck was immediately aware that it carried a heavy freight of emotion. Truslow stared defiantly at his daughter, the mark of his hand still across her cheek, but she matched his defiance. Robert Decker looked from daughter to father, then back to the daughter, and had the sense to keep his mouth shut.

"The ring's special," Truslow said.

"You holding it for another woman, is that it?" Sally sneered the question, and for a second Starbuck thought Truslow would hit her again, but instead he pushed a hand into a pocket of his coat and brought out a small leather bag. He untied the drawstrings and took out a scrap of blue cloth, which he unwrapped to reveal a ring. It glinted in the darkness, a ring of silver, etched with some design that Starbuck could not decipher.

"This was your mother's ring," Truslow said.

"And Ma always said it should be mine," Sally insisted.

"I should have buried it with her." Truslow gazed down at the ring, which was clearly a relic of great power for him, but then, impulsively, as though he knew he would regret the decision, he shoved the ring toward Starbuck. "Say the words," Truslow snapped.

Roper snatched off his hat while young Decker composed his face into a serious expression. Sally licked her lips and smiled at Starbuck, who looked down at the silver ring laying on the ragged Bible. He saw the ring was engraved with words, but, in the dim light, he could not make them out. My God, he thought, but just what words was he to find for this travesty of a marriage act? This was a worse ordeal than the saw pit.

"Speak up, mister," Truslow growled.

"God has ordained marriage," Starbuck heard himself saying as he desperately tried to remember the marriage services he had attended in Boston, "to be an instrument of his love, and an institution in which we can bring our children into this world to be his servants. The commandments of marriage are simple, that you love one another." He had been looking at Robert Decker as he spoke, and the young man nodded eagerly, as though Starbuck needed the reassurance, and Starbuck felt a terrible sob of pity for this honest fool who was being yoked to a temptress, then he glanced at Sally. "And that you are faithful to each other until death do you part."

She smiled at Starbuck, and whatever words he had been about to say vanished like mist under a midday sun. He opened his mouth to speak, found nothing to say, so closed it.

"You hear the man, Sally Truslow?" her father demanded.

"Hell, yes, I ain't deaf."

"Take the ring, Robert," Starbuck ordered, and was amazed at his temerity. He had been taught in seminary that the sacraments were solemn rituals offered to God by special men, the most Godly of men, yet here he was, a sinner, inventing this tawdry service in the flickering light of a moth-haunted lantern under a nascent Virginia moon. "Put your right hand on the Bible," he told Robert, who lay his work-stained hand on the broken-spined family Bible that Starbuck was still holding. "Say after me," Starbuck said, and somehow he invented a marriage oath that he administered to each in turn, and afterward he told Robert to put the ring on Sally's finger, and then he declared them man and wife, and closed his eyes and raised his shut eyelids to the starry heaven. "May the blessing of Almighty God," Starbuck said, "and his love, and his protection, be with you each, and keep you both from harm from this time on until the world's ending. We ask it in the name of him who loved us so much that he gave his only son for our redemption. Amen."

"Amen to that," Thomas Truslow said, "and amen."

"Praise be, amen." Roper spoke from behind the couple.

"Amen and amen." Robert Decker's face was suffused with happiness.

112

"Is that all there is?" Sally Decker asked.

"The rest of your life is all there is," her father snapped, "and you've made a promise to be faithful, and you keep that promise, girl, or you'll suffer." He snatched at her left hand and, though Sally tried to shrink back, he dragged her hard toward him. He looked down at the silver ring on her finger. "And you look after that ring, girl."

Sally said nothing and Starbuck got the impression that by gaining the ring from her father she had won a victory over him, and the victory was far more important to her than the fact of the wedding.

Truslow let her hand go. "You'll write their names in the Bible?" he asked Starbuck. "To make it proper?"

"Of course," Starbuck said.

"There's a table in the house," Truslow said, "and a pencil in the jar on the mantel. Kick the dog if he troubles you."

Starbuck carried the lantern and the Bible into the house that comprised one simply furnished room. There was a box bed, a table, a chair, two trunks, a fireplace with a pothook, a bench, a spinning wheel, a meal sifter, a rack of guns, a scythe and a framed portrait of Andrew Jackson. Starbuck sat at the table, opened the Bible and found the family register. He wished he had ink to write the entry, but Thomas Truslow's pencil would have to suffice. He looked at the names in the register, which stretched back to when the first Truslows had come to the New World in 1710, and saw that someone had written the fact of Emily Truslow's death on the last filled line of the register, writing her name in ill-formed block capitals and adding Mallory afterward in square brackets in case God did not know who Emily Truslow really was. Above that was the simple record of Sally Emily Truslow's birth in May 1846, and Starbuck realized the girl was just two days over her fifteenth birthday.

"Sunday, May 26, 1861" he wrote with difficulty, hampered by the pain in his blistered hands. "Sally Truslow to Robert Decker, united in holy matrimony." There was a column where

113

the officiating minister was supposed to write his name. Starbuck hesitated, then put his name there: Nathaniel Joseph Starbuck.

"You ain't a real preacherman, are you?" Sally had come into the house and challenged him with her stare.

"God makes us what we are, and what God has made me is not for you to question," Starbuck said as sternly as he could, and felt horribly pompous, but he feared this girl's effect on him and so retreated into pomposity.

She laughed, knowing he had lied. "You got a real nice voice, I will say that." She came to the table and looked down at the open Bible. "I can't read. A man promised to teach me, but he ain't had time yet."

Starbuck feared he knew who the man was, and though one part of him did not want confirmation, another part wanted the suspicion given solidity. "Did Ethan Ridley promise you that?" he asked her.

"You know Ethan?" Sally sounded surprised, then she nodded. "Ethan promised he'd teach me to read," she said, "he promised me a lot, but he hasn't kept a one of the promises. Not yet, anyways, but there's still time, isn't there?"

"Is there?" Starbuck asked. He told himself he was shocked by Ridley's betrayal of the gentle Anna Faulconer, but he also knew that he was horribly jealous of Ethan Ridley.

"I like Ethan." Sally was provoking Starbuck now. "He drew my picture. It was real good."

"He's a good artist," Starbuck said, trying to keep his voice toneless.

Sally was standing over him. "Ethan says he's going to take me away one day. Make me a real lady. He said he'd give me pearls, and a ring for my finger. A gold one. A proper ring, not like this one." She reached out her newly beringed finger and stroked Starbuck's hand, sending a jolt like lightning straight to his heart. She lowered her voice into something scarce above a conspiratorial whisper. "Would you do

114

that for me, preacherman?"

"I'd be happy to teach you to read, Mrs. Decker." Starbuck felt light-headed. He knew he should move his hand from beneath that stroking finger, but he did not want to, he could not. He was captured by her. He stared at the ring. The letters cut into the silver were worn, but just legible. *Je t'aime*, they said. It was a cheap French ring for lovers, of no great value except to the man whose love had worn it.

"You know what the ring says, preacherman?" Sally asked him.

"Yes."

"Tell me."

He looked up into her eyes and immediately had to look down again. The lust was like a pain in him.

"What does it say, mister?"

"It's French."

"But what does it say?" Her finger was still on his hand, pressing lightly.

"It says 'I love you.'" He could not look at her.

She laughed very softly and drew her touch down his hand, tracing the line of his longest finger. "Would you give me pearls? Like Ethan says he will?" She was mocking him.

"I would try." He should not have said it, he was not even sure he had meant to say it, he just heard himself speaking, and there was such a sadness in his voice.

"You know something, preacherman?"

"What?" He looked up at her.

"You've got eyes just like my pa."

"I do?"

Her finger still rested on his hand. "I ain't real married, am I?" She was no longer teasing, but was suddenly wistful. Starbuck said nothing and she looked hurt. "Would you really help me?" she asked, and there was a genuine note of despair in her voice. She had abandoned her flirtation and had spoken like an unhappy child.

"Yes," Starbuck said, even though he knew he should not have promised such help.

"I can't stay up here," Sally said. "I just want to be away from here."

"If I can help you, I will," Starbuck said, and knew he was promising more than he could deliver, and that the promise came from foolishness, yet even so he wanted her to trust him. "I promise you I will help," he said, and he moved his hand to take hold of hers, but then she jerked her fingers away as the cabin door opened.

"As you're here, girl," Truslow said, "then make us some supper. There's a fowl in the pot."

"I ain't your cook any longer," Sally complained, then dodged aside as her father raised his hand. Starbuck closed the Bible and wondered if his betrayal was obvious to Truslow. The girl cooked, and Starbuck gazed into the fire, dreaming.

Next morning Thomas Truslow gave his house and his land and his best leather belt to Robert Decker. He charged the boy only to look after Emily's grave. "Roper will help you with the land. He knows what grows best and how, and he knows the beasts I'm leaving you. He's your tenant now, but he's a good neighbor and he'll help you, boy, but you help him too. Good neighbors make for a good living."

"Yes, sir."

"And Roper will be using the saw pit these next days. Let him."

"Yes, sir."

"And the belt's for Sally. Don't let her be your master. One taste of pain and she'll learn her place."

"Yes, sir," Robert Decker said again, but without conviction.

"I'm going to war, boy," Truslow said, "and the Lord alone knows when I'll be back. Or even if."

"I ought to be fighting, sir. It ain't right that I can't fight."

"You can't." Truslow was brusque. "You've a woman and a child to look after. I've none. I've had my life, so I might as

116

well spend what's left of it teaching the Yankees to keep their thieving hands to themselves." He shifted the tobacco wad in his cheek, spat, then looked back at Decker. "Make sure she looks after that ring, boy. It belonged to my Emily, and I ain't even sure I should have given it to her, except that's what Emily herself wanted."

Sally stayed in the cabin. Starbuck wanted her to come out. He wanted to have a few moments with her. He wanted to speak to her, to say that he understood her unhappiness and that he shared it, but Sally stayed hidden and Truslow did not demand to see her. So far as Starbuck could tell Truslow did not even bid farewell to his daughter. Instead he selected a bowie knife, a long rifle and a pistol, and left the rest of his weapons for his son-in-law. Then he saddled a sullen-looking horse, spent a few private moments at the grave of his Emily, and afterward led Starbuck toward the ridge.

The sun was shining, making the leaves seem luminous. Truslow paused at the ridge's crest, not to gaze back at the home he was leaving, but rather to stare east to where the land lay bright and clean, mile after mile of America, stretching toward the sea and waiting for the butchers to begin its dismembering.

Part Two

5

Dust sifted the air above Richmond's Central Fair Grounds. The dust was being kicked up by the eleven regiments that were marching and countermarching on the massive field that had been abraded free of every last blade of grass, then pounded into a fine powder by the endless exercises of drill that Major General Robert Lee insisted on inflicting upon the recruits who came to defend the Confederacy. The reddish-brown dust had been carried by the wind to settle on every wall, roof and hedge within a half mile of the Fair Grounds so that even the blossoms of the magnolias that edged the site seemed to have been dulled into a curious pale brick color. Ethan Ridley's uniform was powdered with the dust, giving the gray cloth a fleshlike tinge. Ridley had come to the Fair Grounds to find his plump and myopic half-brother, Belvedere Delaney, who was mounted on a sway-backed piebald horse, which he sat with all the elegance of a collapsing sack as he watched the regiments march smartly past. Delaney, though in civilian clothes, saluted the passing troops with all the aplomb of a full general. "I'm practicing for when I join the army, Ethan," he greeted his half-brother, showing no surprise at Ridley's sudden appearance in the city.

"You'll not join the army, Bev, you're too soft."

"On the contrary, Ethan, I am to be a legal officer. I invented the post myself and suggested it to the governor, who was kind enough to have me commissioned. I shall be a captain for the moment, but I shall promote myself if I find that rank too lowly for a man of my tastes and distinction. Well done, men! Well done! Very smart!" Delaney called these encouragements to a bemused company of Alabamian infantry that was marching past the applauding spectators. A visit to these Fair Grounds was a popular excursion for the citizens of Richmond, who now found themselves living in the new capital of the Confederate States of America, a fact that gave especial pleasure to Belvedere Delaney. "The more politicians there are in Richmond then the greater will be the corruption," he explained to Ridley, "and the greater the corruption, the greater the profit. I doubt we shall ever compete with Washington in these matters, but we must do our best in the short time God grants us." Delaney bestowed a beatific smile on his scowling half-brother. "So how long shall you be in Richmond this time? I presume you will be using Grace Street? Did George tell you I was here?" George was Delaney's manservant, a slave, but with the manners and demeanor of an aristocrat. Ridley did not really like the supercilious George, but he had to put up with the slave if he was to use his brother's rooms on Grace Street. "So just what brings you to our fair city?" Delaney enquired.

"Beyond the charms of my company, of course."

"Cannon. Two six pounders that Faulconer discovered in Bowers Foundry. The guns were supposed to be melted down, but Faulconer's bought them."

"No profit for us there, then," Delaney said.

"He needs ammunition"—Ridley paused to light a cigar—"and limbers. And caissons."

"Ah! I hear the soft chink of dollars changing hands," Belvedere Delaney said with delight, then turned to watch a regiment of Virginian militia march past with the fine precision of shuttles on a mechanical loom. "If all the troops were as good as that," he told his half-brother, "then the war would be as good as won, but my Lord, you should see some of the rabble that turns up wanting to fight. Yesterday I saw a company that called itself McGarritty's Mounted Lincoln Killers, McGarritty being their self-proclaimed colonel, you

122

understand, and the fourteen mudsills shared ten horses, two swords, four shotguns and a hanging rope between them. The rope was twenty feet long, with a noose, and more than adequate for Abe, they told me."

Ethan Ridley was not interested in the rarer breeds of southern soldier, but only in the profits he might make with his half-brother's help. "You've got six-pounder ammunition?"

"In lavish quantities, I'm afraid," Delaney confessed. "We're virtually giving the round shot away. But we can certainly make an indecent profit on the canister and shell." He paused to touch his hat to a state senator who had been avid for war before the first guns fired, but who had since discovered a lame leg, a crooked back and a troublesome liver. The invalid politician, propped up with lavish cushions in his carriage, feebly raised his gold-headed cane in response to Delaney's salute. "And I can certainly find some limbers and caissons at a wicked profit," Delaney went on happily.

His happiness was occasioned by the profits that stemmed from Washington Faulconer's insistence that not one boot or button be bought for his Legion from the state, which obstinacy Delaney had seen as his opportunity. Delaney had used his extensive friendships within the state government to buy goods from the state armories himself, which goods he sold on to his half-brother, who acted as Washington Faulconer's purchasing agent. The price of the goods invariably doubled or even quadrupled during the transaction, and the brothers shared the profits equally. It was a happy scheme that had, among other things, brought Washington Faulconer twelve thousand dollars' worth of Mississippi rifles that had cost Belvedere Delaney just six thousand dollars, forty-dollar tents that had cost sixteen dollars, and a thousand pairs of two-dollar boots that the brothers had purchased for eighty cents a pair. "I imagine a gun limber must cost at least four hundred dollars," Delaney now mused aloud. "Say eight hundred to Faulconer?"

"At least." Ridley needed the profits far more than his older

123

brother, which was why he had been so happy to return to Richmond, where he could not only make money, but also be free of Anna's cloying affections. He told himself that marriage would surely make things easier between himself and Faulconer's daughter, and that once he had the security of the family's wealth behind him he would not so resent Anna's petulant demands. In affluence, Ridley believed, lay the solution to all life's griefs.

Belvedere Delaney also liked affluence, but only if it brought power in its wake. He checked his horse to watch a company of Mississippians march by; fine-looking bearded men, thin and tanned, but all armed with old-fashioned flintlocks like the ones their grandfathers had carried against the redcoats. The coming war, Delaney hoped, must be brief, because the North would surely wipe away these enthusiastic amateurs with their homely weapons and gangling gait, and when that happened Delaney intended to realize an even larger profit than the paltry dollars he now made from equipping Washington Faulconer's Legion. For Belvedere Delaney, though a southerner by birth and breeding, was a northerner by calculation, and though he had not yet become a spy he had quietly permitted his friends in the northern states to understand that he intended to serve their cause from within the Virginian capital. And when that northern victory came, as it surely must, then Delaney reckoned that the southern supporters of the legitimate federal government could expect a rich reward. That, Delaney knew, was a long view, but holding the long view while all around him fools gambled their lives and property on the short gave Belvedere Delaney an immense amount of satisfaction. "Tell me about Starbuck," he suddenly asked his brother as they walked their horses about the Fair Grounds perimeter.

"Why?" Ridley was surprised by the abrupt question.

"Because I am interested in Elial Starbuck's son." In truth it had been thoughts of southerners supporting the North and northerners fighting for the South that had made Delaney think of Starbuck. "I met him, did you know?"

"He didn't say anything." Ridley sounded resentful.

"I rather liked him. He has a quick mind. Much too mercurial to be successful, I suspect, but he's not a dull young man."

Ethan Ridley sneered at that generous assessment. "He's a goddamn preacher's son. A pious son of a Boston bitch."

Delaney, who fancied he knew more of the world than his half-brother, suspected that any man who was willing to risk his whole future for some strumpet off the stage was probably much less virtuous and a deal more interesting that Ridley was suggesting, and Delaney, in his long drunken meal with Starbuck, had sensed something complicated and interesting in the younger man. Starbuck, Delaney reflected, had immured himself in a dark maze where creatures like Dominique Demarest fought against the virtues instilled by a Calvinist upbringing, and that battle would be a rare and vicious affair. Delaney instinctively hoped that the Calvinism would be defeated, but he also understood that the virtuous aspect of Starbuck's character had somehow got under his half-brother's skin. "Why do we find virtue so annoying?" Delaney wondered aloud.

"Because it is the highest aspiration of the stupid," Ridley said nastily.

"Or is it because we admire virtue in others, knowing we cannot attain it ourselves?" Delaney was still curious.

"You might want to attain it, I don't."

"Don't be absurd, Ethan. And tell me why you dislike Starbuck so much."

"Because the bastard took fifty bucks off me."

"Ah! Then he did touch you to the quick." Delaney, who knew the extent of his half-brother's greed, laughed. "And how did the preacher's son achieve this appropriation?"

"I wagered him that he couldn't fetch a man called Truslow out of the hills, and goddamn it, he did."

"Pecker told me about Truslow," Delaney said. "But why didn't you recruit him?"

125

"Because if Truslow sees me near his daughter, he'll murder me."

"Ah!" Delaney smiled, and reflected how everyone created their own tangled snares. Starbuck was enmeshed between sin and pleasure, he himself was caught between North and South, and his half-brother was snagged on lust. "Does the murderer have cause to kill you?" Delaney asked, then took a cigarette from a box and borrowed his half-brother's cigar to light it. The cigarette was wrapped in yellow paper and filled with lemon-scented tobacco. "Well?" Delaney prompted Ridley.

"He has cause," Ridley admitted, then could not resist a boastful laugh. "He's going to have a bastard grandchild soon."

"Yours?"

Ridley nodded. "Truslow doesn't know the baby's mine, and the girl's been married off anyway, so all in all I came out smelling like rosewater. Except that I had to pay for the bitch's silence."

"A lot?"

"Enough." Ridley inhaled his cigar's bitter smoke, then shook his head. "She's a greedy bitch, but my God, Bev, you should see the girl."

"The murderer's daughter is beautiful?" Delaney was amused at the thought.

"She's extraordinary," Ridley said with a genuine tone of awe in his voice. "Here, look." He took a leather case from his top uniform pocket and handed it to Delaney.

Delaney opened the case to find a drawing, five inches by four inches, which showed a naked girl sitting in a woodland glade beside a small stream. Delaney was constantly astonished at his half-brother's talent which, though untrained and lazily applied, was still startlingly good. God, he thought, poured his talents into the strangest vessels. "Have you exaggerated her looks?"

"No. Truly no."

"Then she is indeed lovely. A nymph."

126

"But a nymph with a tongue like a nigger driver and a temper to match."

"And you're done with her, yes?" Delaney enquired.

"Finished. Done." Ridley, as he took back the portrait, hoped that was true. He had paid Sally a hundred silver dollars to keep silent, yet he had remained frightened that she would not keep her side of the bargain. Sally was an unpredictable girl with more than a touch of her father's savagery, and Ethan Ridley had been terrified that she might appear in Faulconer Court House and brandish her pregnancy in front of Anna. Not that Washington Faulconer probably minded a man fathering bastards, but whelping them on slaves was one thing and having a girl as wild as Truslow's daughter screaming her outrage up and down the main street of Faulconer Court House was something entirely different.

But now, thank God, Ridley had heard how Sally had been married off to her straw-haired puppy-boy. Ridley had heard no details of the wedding, nothing about the where or the how or the when, only that Truslow had sloughed his daughter off onto Decker and given the couple his patch of stony land, his beasts and his blessing, and by so doing he had left Ridley feeling much safer. "It's all turned out well," he grunted to Delaney, yet not without some regret, for Ethan Ridley suspected that he would never again in his life know a girl as beautiful as Sally Truslow. Yet to lie with her had been to play with fire and he had been lucky to have emerged unscorched.

Belvedere Delaney watched a pack of recruits trying to march in step. A cadet from the Virginia Military Institute who looked about half the age of the men he was drilling screamed at them to straighten their backs, to keep their heads up and to stop looking around like mill girls on an outing. "Does Colonel Faulconer drill his men like this?" Delaney asked.

"He believes drill will only blunt the men's enthusiasm."

"How interesting! Perhaps your Faulconer is cleverer than I thought. These poor devils begin their drill at six in the morning and don't cease till the moon rises." Delaney touched his hat in salute of a judge he frequently met at the brothel on Marshall Street that was always known as Mrs. Richardson's house, though in fact the major shareholder in the house was Belvedere Delaney himself. In times of war, Delaney believed, a man could do a lot worse than invest in weapons and women, and so far Delaney's investments were all showing a fine profit.

"Faulconer believes war should be enjoyed," Ridley said caustically, "which is why he's going on a cavalry raid."

"A cavalry raid?" Delaney said in a surprised tone. "Tell me."

"There's nothing to tell."

"Describe me the nothing, then." Delaney sounded unnaturally petulant.

"Why?"

"For God's sake, Ethan, I am a friend to half the lawmakers in the state, and if Virginia's citizens are waging a private war on the North then the government is supposed to know about it. Or Robert Lee is. In fact Lee's supposed to sanction military movements, even by your incipient father-in-law. So tell me."

"Faulconer's leaving on a raid, or maybe he's already left, I'm not sure. Does it matter?"

"Where? What?"

"He's upset because we let the Yankees occupy Alexandria. He thinks Richmond doesn't care about the war. He says Letcher has always been soft on the North and is probably a secret Union man. He thinks Lee is too cautious, and so is everyone else, and if someone doesn't go and kick the Yankees where it hurts then the Confederacy will collapse."

"You mean the idiot is going to attack Alexandria?" Delaney asked in astonishment. Alexandria was the Virginian town across the Potomac from Washington that, since its abandonment by southern troops, had been heavily fortified.

"He knows he can't attack Alexandria," Ridley said, "so he's

128

planning to cut the Baltimore and Ohio Railroad."

"Where?"

"He didn't tell me," Ridley sounded sour, "but it can't be east of Cumberland, because the trains aren't running between there and Harper's Ferry." Ridley suddenly became alarmed. "For God's sake, Bev, you're not going to stop him, are you? He'll kill me if you do!"

"No," Delaney said soothingly, "no, I'll let him have his fun. So how many men has he taken? The whole Legion?"

"Just thirty men. But you promise me you'll say nothing?" Ridley was terrified that he had been indiscreet.

Delaney could see Robert Lee inspecting recruits on the far side of the Fair Grounds. Delaney had deliberately made himself useful to Lee's office and had found himself being unwillingly impressed by the general's combination of intelligence and honesty. Delaney tried to imagine Lee's fury if he were to discover that Faulconer was free-lancing a raid on the Baltimore and Ohio Railroad, but tempting though it was, Delaney decided he would say nothing to his friends in Virginia's government. Instead he would let the North do the stopping.

For there was still time to write one last letter to a friend in Washington who, Delaney knew, was intimate with the northern government's secretary of war. Delaney reckoned that if the North discovered that he could be a source of useful military information, then their full trust would surely follow.

"Of course I'll say nothing to the governor," he now reassured his terrified younger brother, then sawed on his reins to stop his horse. "Do you mind if we turn back? The dust is irritating my throat."

"I was hoping ..." Ridley began.

"You were hoping to visit Mrs. Richardson's house." That enticement, Delaney knew, was Richmond's main attraction for his half-brother. "And so you shall, my dear Ethan, so you shall." Delaney spurred back toward the city, his good day's work well done.

The raiding party reached the Baltimore and Ohio Railroad two hours before dawn on the sixth day of a journey that Washington Faulconer had confidently predicted would last no more than three. The ride would have taken a full week if Faulconer had not stubbornly insisted on riding throughout the final night. Starbuck, reeling from tiredness and in whimpering agony from his saddle sores, was not at first aware that their journey was almost done. He was slumped in the saddle, half-sleeping, half-scared of falling, when he was suddenly startled by a brilliant glare of light that flared far beneath him in a deep, moon-shadowed valley. For a moment he thought he was dreaming, then he feared he was not dreaming at all but had instead reached the trembling edge of the Valley of Gehenna, the Bible's hell, and that at any moment he would be cast down into the flaming pit where the devils cackled as they tormented the sinners. He even cried out in terror.

Then he came fully awake and realized that Faulconer's bedraggled band of raiders had stopped on the crest of a high ridge and were looking down into a dark valley where a train ran westward. The door of the locomotive's firebox was open, and the furnace's brilliant glow was reflecting on the underside of the boiling smoke plume which looked, Starbuck thought, like the lurid breath of a great dragon. The boiling smoke moved steadily westward, preceded by the feeble glow of the locomotive's oil-fired lantern. No other lights showed, suggesting that the locomotive was hauling freight wagons. The noise of the train changed to a hollow rumble as it crossed trestles spanning a river that lay to Starbuck's left, and he felt a sudden pulse of excitement as he suddenly understood how close they had come to their target.

For the great spume of fiery smoke that ripped through the night marked where the Baltimore and Ohio Railroad ran along the bank of the North Branch of the Potomac River. Until Thomas Jackson had occupied Harper's Ferry, and so cut the rail passage to Washington and Baltimore, this line had been the major link between the western states and the American capital, and even since Jackson's occupation the rails had stayed busy as they fetched supplies, recruits, weapons and food from Missouri, Illinois, Indiana and Ohio, all of them carried to Cumberland where they were reloaded onto canal boats or else onto wagons that were hauled by teams of horses to the Hagerstown depot of the Cumberland Valley Railroad. Colonel Faulconer claimed that if the Baltimore and Ohio could be cut in the Alleghenies west of Cumberland then it might take months before that busy supply line was restored.

That, at least, was the military justification for the raid, though Starbuck knew the Colonel expected to gain much more from this foray. Faulconer believed a successful attack would bolster southern belligerence and hurt northern pride. Better still it would begin the history of the Faulconer Legion with a victory, which was the real reason why the Colonel had led a group of thirty picked horsemen who escorted four packhorses loaded with four barrels of black powder, six axes, four crowbars, two sledgehammers, and two coils of quick-fuse—the materials necessary to destroy the tall trestles of the bridges that carried the Baltimore and Ohio Railroad across the streams and rivers that flowed fast through the Alleghenies.

Three of the Legion's officers accompanied their Colonel on the raid. Captain Paul Hinton was an easygoing man who farmed eight hundred acres in the eastern part of Faulconer County and was a hunting friend of Faulconer's. Then there was Captain Anthony Murphy, who was a tall, black-haired Irishman who had emigrated to America ten years before, planted one spread of cotton in Louisiana, sold the spread before harvest, taken a riverboat north and played twenty-card poker for three days and nights, and stepped off the boat with a pretty Italian girl and enough money to last the rest of his days. He had brought his Italian bride to Virginia, put his money in the Faulconer County Bank and purchased himself four farms to the north of Seven Springs. He kept three slaves on the largest farm, rented out the others, got drunk with his tenants every quarter day and could rarely find anyone rash enough to deal him into a game of bluff. The last officer was Second Lieutenant Starbuck, who had never played poker in his life.

Among the twenty-six men accompanying the four officers was Sergeant Thomas Truslow and a half dozen of the rogues who had followed him down from the hills. Truslow's group rode together, ate together, and treated the three most senior officers with a tolerant disdain, though, to the surprise of all those who knew just how much Truslow hated Yankees, the dour sergeant clearly liked Starbuck, and that acceptance made Starbuck a welcome member of Truslow's group. No one understood the unlikely association, but then no one, not even Colonel Faulconer, had heard about either the prayer Starbuck had offered by Emily's grave or how Starbuck had extemporized a wedding ceremony in the Virginian night.

Not that Faulconer would have been in any mood to have listened to such stories for, as the raiders had moved north and west into the Alleghenies, his dreams of a swift, slashing victory had become mired in rain and fog. The journey had begun well enough. They had crossed the Blue Ridge Mountains into the wide, rich Shenandoah Valley, then climbed into the Alleghenies, and that was when the rains had struck, not gentle rains to swell the growing grain in the valleys, but a succession of sky-lacerating storms that had cracked and ripped the sky as the raiders struggled through the inhospitable mountains. Faulconer had insisted they avoid all settlements, for these regions west of the Shenandoah were hostile to the Confederacy, indeed, there was even talk of this part of Virginia seceding to form a new state altogether, and so Faulconer's men had slunk through the rain-drenched mountains like thieves, not even wearing uniforms. There was no point, the Colonel said, in taking unnecessary risks with the traitorous mudsills of the Alleghenies.

Yet the weather proved far more hostile than the inhabitants. Faulconer became lost in the steep cloud-wrapped mountains, spending one whole day groping west into a blind valley, and it was only Thomas Truslow's canny sense that had brought them back to the right route, and from that moment it had seemed to many of the raiding party that Thomas Truslow had become the real leader of the expedition. He gave no orders, but the horsemen all looked to him rather than the Colonel for a lead. It was Washington Faulconer's resentment of that usurpation of his authority that had made him insist that the raiders keep traveling through the fifth night. It had been an unpopular order, but by enforcing it the Colonel had at least demonstrated who was in command.

Now, perched at last above the railroad, the horsemen waited for the dawn. The clouds of the last few days had torn ragged and a few stars showed around a mist-shrouded moon. Far to the north a tiny spot of light flickered in the far hills that Starbuck realized could be in Pennsylvania. The view from this high crest looked over the misted river, across a strip of Maryland and deep into the hostile north. It seemed incredible to Starbuck that he was poised above a frontier between two warring states; indeed, that America could be at war at all seemed unreal, a denial of all childhood's certainties. Other lesser countries went to war, but men had come to America to avoid war, yet now Starbuck shivered on a mountaintop with the Savage revolver at his side and armed men all around him. No more trains passed. Most of the men slept while a few, like Truslow, squatted at the crest's edge and stared north.

The light seeped slowly from the east to reveal that the horsemen had chanced upon an almost perfect place to cut the railroad. To their left a swift river churned across rocks to join the North Branch of the Potomac, and a high trestle bridge spanned the tributary on a latticework of stilts sixty feet high. There were no guards on the bridge and no blockhouse. Nor were there any farms or settlements within sight; indeed if it had not been for the dull sheen of the steel rails and the spindly lattice of the trellis this could have been unexplored wilderness.

Faulconer gave his final orders as the sky lightened. The raiders would divide into three parties. Captain Murphy would take a dozen men to block the rails leading east, Captain Hinton would take another dozen men west, while the six remaining men, led by the Colonel, would clamber down into the tributary's gorge and there destroy the tall contraption of trestles and rails. "Nothing can go wrong now," Faulconer said, trying to cheer his damp and somewhat dispirited troops. "We've planned it properly." In fact even the most optimistic of the raiders must have realized that the Colonel's planning had been slipshod. Faulconer had not foreseen the possibility of drenching rain and so the powder barrels and quick-fuses had been bereft of tarpaulins. There had been no proper maps provided so that even Truslow, who had crossed these hills a score of times, was not entirely sure what bridge they now threatened. Yet despite all the doubts and difficulties they had succeeded in reaching the railroad, which had proved unguarded, and so, in the first weak light of the new day, they slid and slithered down the steep slope toward the North Branch.

They picketed the horses beside the railroad close to the bridge. Starbuck, shivering in the gray dawn, walked to the gorge's edge to see that the trestles, which had looked so flimsy from the hilltop, were in truth massive timbers that had been stripped of their bark, coated with tar, then sunk into the earth or else braced against the huge boulders that protruded from the chasm's slopes. The trestles were fastened to one another with metal collars, thus linked into a dense trellis structure that rose sixty feet from the stream and spanned two hundred feet across the gorge. The timbers, despite their tar coating, felt clammy, just as the wind that gusted cold from the river felt

134

damp. The clouds were once more building, promising rain.

Captain Hinton's men crossed the bridge, Murphy's went eastward while the Colonel's party, which included Starbuck, struggled down to the bed of the gorge. The slope was slippery and the brush still soaked from the previous day's rain so that by the time the six men reached the bank of the fast-flowing stream their already damp clothes were drenched through. Starbuck helped Sergeant Daniel Medlicott, a morose and uncommunicative man who was a miller by trade, maneuver a barrel of black powder down the steep slope. Washington Faulconer, watching them struggle with the cask, shouted a warning for Nate to beware of a patch of poison ivy, a warning that seemed to disappoint Medlicott. The other three barrels of powder were already at the bottom of the chasm. The Colonel had considered saving two of the gunpowder casks but had decided it was better to make certain that this one substantial bridge was utterly destroyed than to look for a second trestle later in the day. Medlicott stacked the fourth barrel with the others, then knocked its bung out so as to insert a length of quick-fuse. "Powder feels mighty damp to me, Colonel."

"Sir." Faulconer snapped the word. He was trying to persuade his erstwhile neighbors to use the military honorific.

"Still feels damp," Medlicott insisted, obstinately refusing to humor Faulconer.

"We'll try the fuse, and we'll light a fire as well," Faulconer said, "and if the one doesn't work, the other will. So get on with it!" He walked a few paces upstream with Starbuck. "They're good fellows," he said morosely, "but with no idea of military discipline."

"It's a difficult transition, sir," Starbuck said tactfully. He was feeling somewhat sorry for Faulconer, whose hopes for a jaunty and defiant raid had turned into this damp nightmare of delay and difficulty.

"Your fellow Truslow's the worst," the Colonel grumbled. "No respect there at all." He sounded disappointed. He had so

135

wanted Truslow in the Legion, thinking that the man's character would give the regiment a fearsome reputation, yet now he found himself resenting Truslow's truculent and independent manner. Washington Faulconer had corralled himself a tiger and did not know how to handle the beast. "And you're not helping me, Nate," the Colonel suddenly said.

"Me, sir?" Starbuck, who had been feeling sympathy for the Colonel, was taken aback by the accusation.

The Colonel did not respond immediately. He was standing beside the stream and watching Medlicott's men use bowie knives to cut the timber that would be used as firewood around the barrels of gunpowder. "You don't want to be too familiar with these fellows," the Colonel finally said. "One day you'll have to command them in battle and they won't respect you if you don't keep a distance." Washington Faulconer did not look at Starbuck as he spoke, but instead gazed through the trestle at the sliding gray river down which a twisted black tree branch was being carried. Faulconer appeared very miserable. His beard was untrimmed, his clothes damp and dirty, and his normally brisk manner subdued. Bad weather soldiering, Starbuck reflected with surprise, did not seem to suit the Colonel. "Officers should keep company with other officers." The Colonel embroidered his criticism petulantly. "If you're forever with Truslow, how will you command him?"

That was unfair, Starbuck thought, for he had spent far more time on the journey with Washington Faulconer than with Truslow, yet Starbuck dimly understood that the Colonel was jealous that Starbuck, and not he, had so earned Truslow's regard. Truslow was a man whose good opinion other men wanted, and the Colonel clearly thought he deserved it more than some stray student from Massachusetts, so Starbuck said nothing and the Colonel, his complaints against his aide delivered, turned back toward Medlicott. "How much longer, Sergeant?"

Medlicott stepped back from his work. He had stacked the

powder kegs around one of the bridge's tallest legs, then surrounded the gunpowder with a thick stack of brush and logs. "There's a terrible lot of wet in everything," he observed gloomily.

"You've got kindling in there?"

"Plenty of that, Colonel."

"Paper? Cartridges?"

"There's enough to make a fire," Medlicott allowed.

"So when will we be ready?"

"We're as good as ready now, I'd say." Medlicott scratched his head as he considered the answer he had just given, then nodded. "It should do, Colonel."

"You'll go to Hinton." Faulconer turned to Starbuck. "Tell him to pull back over the bridge. Warn Captain Murphy to ready the horses! Tell everyone to look lively now, Nate!"

Starbuck wondered why no signal had been readied to tell everyone to withdraw. A series of gunshots would have served much faster than a damp scramble up the gorge's side to deliver the messages, but he knew this was no time to ask the Colonel a question that would doubtless be construed as critical, and so he simply climbed the gorge's eastern flank, then crossed the trestle bridge to find that Sergeant Truslow had made a huge barricade of felled pine trees to block the line's western approach. Captain Hinton, a short and cheerful man, had been content to let Truslow manage affairs. "I suspect he's stopped trains before," he explained to Starbuck, then proudly showed how, beyond the barricade, the rails had been ripped up and hurled down toward the North Branch. "So the Colonel's ready?"

"Yes, sir."

"Pity. I would rather have liked to have robbed a train. It would have been a new line of work for me, but horribly complicated." Hinton explained that the Truslow method of train robbery demanded that the thieves wait some distance from the barricade, then leap aboard the passing locomotive and its

137

cars. "If you wait for the train to stop before climbing aboard then you're likely to have pesky passengers jumping off with guns and then everything gets rather untidy. You also have to have men on each car to wind the brakes if the train is to stop properly. It seems there's quite an art to these things. Ah well, will you go and fetch the rogue, Nate?" Truslow, with the remainder of Hinton's squad, was a quarter mile down the track, evidently prepared for the complicated business of stopping a train. "Off you go, Nate," Hinton said, encouraging Starbuck.

But Starbuck did not move. Instead he stared down the line to where, beyond the shoulder of the hill, a sudden plume of white smoke was showing. "A train," he said dully, as though he did not really believe his own eyes.

Hinton wheeled round. "Good God, so there is." He cupped his hands. "Truslow! Come back!" But Truslow either did not hear or chose to ignore the summons because he began running west, away from the barricade and toward the train. "The Colonel will just have to wait," Hinton grinned.

Starbuck could hear the train now. It was coming very slowly, its bell clanging and pistons laboring as it climbed the slight gradient toward the curve and the waiting ambush. Behind Starbuck a voice shouted from the gorge, urging him to hurry the withdrawal, but it was all too late for haste to be of any help. Thomas Truslow wanted to rob a train.

Thaddeus Bird and Priscilla Bowen were married at eleven o'clock in the morning in the Episcopal Church opposite the Faulconer County Bank in the main street of Faulconer Court House. It had been threatening rain since dawn, but the weather stayed dry through most of the morning and Priscilla had dared to hope that the rain would hold off altogether, but a half hour before the ceremony the heavens opened. Rain seethed on the church roof, splashed on the graveyard, flooded the main street and drenched the schoolchildren who, in honor

138

of their teachers' wedding, had been given a morning off to attend the service.

Priscilla Bowen, nineteen years old and an orphan, was given away by her uncle who was the postmaster in the neighboring town of Rosskill. Priscilla had a round face, a quick smile and a patient disposition. No one would have called her beautiful, yet after a few moments in her company no one would have dismissed her as plain either. She had light brown hair, which she wore in a tight bun, hazel eyes, which were half hidden by steel-rimmed spectacles, and work-roughened hands. For her wedding she carried a spray of redbud blossoms and wore her best Sunday gown of blue-dyed cambric on which, in celebration of the day, she had pinned a garland of white handkerchiefs. Thaddeus Bird, who was twenty years older than his bride, wore his best black suit, which he had carefully mended himself, and a smile of deep content. His niece, Anna Faulconer, was present, but his sister stayed in her bedroom in Seven Springs. Miriam Faulconer had fully intended to be at the wedding, but the threat of rain and the onslaught of a cold wind had brought on a sudden attack of neuralgia complicated by asthma, and so she had remained in the big house where the servants banked the fires and burned niter papers to relieve her labored breath. Her husband was somewhere beyond the Shenandoah Valley, leading his cavalry raid, and that absence, if the truth were to be told, was why Pecker Bird had chosen this day for his wedding.

The Reverend Ernest Moss conducted the affair, pronouncing Thaddeus and Priscilla man and wife just as a clap of thunder rattled the church shingles and caused some of the children to call out in fright. Afterward the wedding guests all splashed down Main Street to the schoolroom where two tables had been set with corn cake, apple butter, jars of honey, hung beef, apple pie, smoked hams, pickled cucumber, pickled oysters and buckwheat bread. Miriam Faulconer had sent six bottles of wine to her brother's wedding feast and there were also two barrels of lemonade, a jug of beer and a vat of water. Blanche Sparrow, whose husband owned the dry goods store, made a vast pot of coffee on the church stove and ordered two of the Legion's soldiers to carry it to the schoolroom where Major Pelham, dressed in his old United States uniform, made a fine speech. Doctor Danson then gave a humorous speech during which Thaddeus Bird smiled benignly on all the guests and even managed to smile when six of the schoolchildren, coached by Caleb Tennant, who was the Episcopal choirmaster, sang "Flora's Holiday" in thin, rather unconvincing voices.

Afternoon school was necessarily less demanding than usual, yet somehow Thaddeus and Priscilla Bird managed to subdue the excited schoolroom and even persuade themselves that some decent work had been achieved. Priscilla had been appointed as Bird's assistant, which appointment had been intended to release Pecker Bird to his duties in the Faulconer Legion, but in fact Bird still ran the school, for his military duties had proved happily light. Major Thaddeus Bird kept the regiment's books. He compiled the pay lists, noted the punishments, and kept the guard rosters and commissary invoices. The work, he claimed, could have been adequately discharged by a bright six-year-old, but Bird was happy to perform it because, as an integral part of his duties, he was expected to pay himself a major's salary out of his brother-in-law's bank account. Most of the officers were receiving no pay, having private means, while the men were being paid their eleven dollars a month in newly printed Faulconer County Bank dollar bills, which depicted the town's courthouse on the one side and had a portrait of George Washington and an engraved bale of cotton on the other. A legend printed across the bale of cotton read "States' Rights and Southern Liberty. The Faith of the Bank is Pledged to Pay One Dollar on Demand." The bills were not very well printed and Bird suspected they might easily be forged, which was why he took good care to have his own Legion salary of thirty-eight dollars

140

a month paid in good old-fashioned silver coins.

On the evening of his wedding, when the schoolhouse had been swept and the water pumped for the next morning and the firewood stacked beside the newly blacked stove, Bird could at last close his front door, edge past the piled books in the hallway, and offer his new wife a shy smile. On the kitchen table was one bottle of wine left from the wedding feast. "I think we shall have that!" Bird rubbed his hands in anticipatory glee. In truth he was feeling extraordinarily timid, so much so that he had deliberately dallied over his evening chores.

"I thought perhaps we might eat what was left from the wedding?" Priscilla, equally timid, suggested.

"Capital idea! Capital!" Thaddeus Bird was hunting for a corkscrew. He did not often get to drink a bottle of wine in his own house, indeed he could hardly remember the last time he had enjoyed such a luxury, but he was sure there was a corkscrew somewhere.

"And I thought perhaps I might rearrange the shelves." Priscilla watched her husband's frantic attempts to find the corkscrew amidst the jumble of handle-less skillets, holed pans and chipped plates that Bird had inherited from the previous schoolmaster. "If you have no objection," she added.

"You must do whatever you wish! This is your home, my dear one."

Priscilla had already tried to cheer up the dingy kitchen. She had put her wedding spray of redbud blossoms in a vase and pinned strips of cloth to either side of the window to suggest curtains, but somehow the touches did little to alleviate the gloom of the dark, low-beamed, smoke-stained room, which contained a stove, a table, an open hearth with an iron bread oven, two chairs and two old dressers, which were stacked with chipped plates, mugs, bowls, pitchers and the inevitable books and broken musical instruments that Thaddeus Bird accumulated. The illumination in the kitchen, as in the rest of the small house, came from candles, and Priscilla, who was ever

141

mindful of the cost of good wax candles, lit only two as night fell. It was still raining hard.

The corkscrew was at last discovered and the wine opened, but Bird immediately declared himself dissatisfied with the glasses. "Somewhere there are a pair of proper glasses. Ones with stems. The kind they use in Richmond."

Priscilla had never been to Richmond and was about to say that she doubted Richmond glasses could make the wine taste any better, but before she could open her mouth to speak there was a sudden hammering on the front door.

"Oh, no! This is too bad! I expressly said I was not to be disturbed today!" Bird clumsily extricated himself from the cupboard in which he had been searching for wineglasses. "Davies cannot find the muster roll. Or he's lost the pay books! Or he cannot add twenty cents eight times over! I shall ignore it." Davies was a young lieutenant who was supposed to assist Bird with the Legion's paperwork.

"It's raining hard," Priscilla pleaded for the unknown caller.

"I don't care if it's raining fit to drown the planet. I do not care if the animals are lining up two by two to get aboard. If a man cannot be left in peace on his wedding day, when can he hope for rest? Am I so indispensable that I must be dragged from your company whenever Lieutenant Davies discovers that his education is entirely insufficient for the demands of modern life? He was at Centre College in Kentucky. Have you ever heard of such a place? Is it possible that there could be anyone capable of teaching anything worth knowing in Kentucky? Yet Davies boasts of having been educated there! Boasts of it! Why I entrust the regiment's books to him, I don't know. I might as well hand them over to a baboon. Let the fool get wet. Maybe his Kentucky brains will improve after a drenching."

The knocking redoubled in intensity. "I really do think, my dear," Priscilla murmured in the gentlest of all possible reproofs.

"If you insist. You're too kind, Priscilla, altogether too kind.

It's a womanly fault, so I won't dwell on it, but there it is. Too kind altogether." Thaddeus Bird took a candle into the hallway and, still grumbling, made his way to the front door. "Davies!" He snapped as he pulled the door open, then checked, for the caller was not Lieutenant Davies at all.

Instead a young couple stood at Thaddeus Bird's street door. Bird noticed the girl first for, even in the wet windy darkness that threatened to overwhelm his candle's flame, her face was striking. More than striking for she was, Bird realized, truly beautiful. Behind her was a sturdy young man holding the reins of a tired horse. The young man, scarce more than a boy and still with a child's innocence on his face, looked familiar. "You remember me, Mister Bird?" he asked hopefully, then supplied the answer anyway. "I'm Robert Decker."

"So you are, so you are." Bird was shielding the candle flame with his right hand, peering at his callers.

"We'd like a talk with you, Mister Bird," Robert said courteously.

"Ah," Bird said, to give himself time to devise a reason to send them packing, but no reason occurred to him so he stepped grudgingly aside. "You'd better come in."

"The horse, Mister Bird?" Robert Decker asked.

"You can't bring that in! Don't be a fool. Oh, I see! Tie it to the hitching ring. There's a ring somewhere. There, by the step."

Eventually the two young people were ushered into Bird's front parlor. His house had two rooms downstairs, the kitchen and parlor, and a bedroom upstairs, which was reached by a flight of stairs in the next-door schoolroom. The parlor contained a fireplace, a broken armchair, a wooden bench discarded by the church and a table piled high with schoolbooks and sheet music. "It's been a long time since I last saw you," Bird remarked to Robert Decker.

"Six years, Mister Bird."

"That long?" Bird remembered that the Decker family had

fled Faulconer Court House after their father had been involved in an abortive robbery on the Rosskill Road. They had taken refuge in the hills where, judging by Robert Decker's clothes, they had not prospered. "How is your father?" Bird now demanded of Robert.

Decker said his father had been killed by a fall from a bolting horse. "And I'm married now." Decker, who was standing dripping in front of the empty fireplace, gestured at Sally, who was perched warily among the tufts of horsehair that protruded from Bird's sorry armchair. "This is Sally," Decker said proudly, "my wife."

"Indeed, indeed." Bird felt oddly embarrassed, maybe because Sally Decker was a girl of such extraordinary looks. Her clothes were rags and her face and hair were filthy and her shoes were held together with twine, but she was nevertheless as breathtaking a beauty as any of the girls who paraded in their carriages around Richmond's Capitol Square.

"I ain't his real wife," Sally said cattily, trying to hide a ring on her wedding finger.

"Yes, you are," Decker insisted. "We were minister married, Mister Bird."

"Good, good. Whatever." Bird, mindful of his own new minister-married wife in the kitchen, wondered what on earth these two wanted of him. An education? Sometimes a grown pupil came back to Bird and asked the schoolmaster to repair the years of inattention or truancy.

"I came to see you, Mister Bird, because they said you could enlist me in the Legion," Decker explained.

"Ah!" Bird, relieved at the commonplace explanation, glanced from the honest-faced boy to the sullen beauty. They were, he thought, an ill-assorted couple, then he wondered if folks thought the same of Priscilla and himself. "You want to enlist in the Faulconer Legion, is that it?"

"I reckon I do," Decker said, and glanced at Sally, which suggested that she, rather than he, had engendered the wish.

144

"Is it a petticoat?" Bird asked, struck by a sudden and unsavory thought.

Decker looked puzzled. "Petticoat, Mister Bird?"

"You haven't received a petticoat?" Bird asked intensely, clawing his left hand through his ragged beard. "Left on your doorstep?"

"No, Mister Bird." Decker clearly thought his old schoolmaster was at best eccentric, at worst crazy.

"Good, good." Bird did not offer an explanation. In the last two weeks a number of men had discovered petticoats left on their porches or in their wagons. All were men who had failed to volunteer for the Legion. Some were men with ailments, some were the only supporters of large families, others were boys with glowing futures promised at colleges, and only a few, a very few, might have been considered timid, yet the mocking gift of petticoats had lumped them all together in the category of cowardice. The incident had led to bad feeling in the community, dividing those who were enthusiastic for the threatened war against those who believed the war fever must pass. Bird, who knew full well where the petticoats had come from, had kept a politic silence.

"Sally says I ought to join," Decker explained.

"If he wants to be a proper husband," Sally explained, "then he has to prove himself. Every other man's gone to war. Or all the proper men have."

"I wanted to go anyway," Robert Decker went on, "like Sally's father did. Only he'd be real angry if he knew I was here, so I want to be enlisted proper before I go to the camp. Then he can't have me put out, can he? Not if I've been properly signed on. And I want it arranged so that Sally can draw my pay. I'm told they can do that, is that right, Mister Bird?"

"Many wives draw their husbands' pay, yes." Bird glanced at the girl, and was again astonished that such beauty could have been bred in the ragged hills. "Your father's in the Legion?" he asked.

145

"Thomas Truslow." She said the name bitterly.

"Good God." Bird could not hide his surprise that Truslow had whelped this girl. "And your mother," he asked tentatively, "I'm not sure I know your mother, do I?"

"She's dead," Sally said defiantly, intimating that it was none of Bird's business anyway.

Nor was it, Bird allowed, so busied himself by explaining to Decker that he should go to the Legion's encampment and there seek out Lieutenant Davies. He almost added that he doubted anything could be achieved before morning, but he checked himself in case such an observation might suggest he should offer the couple a night's shelter. "Davies, he's your man," he said, then stood up to signify that their business was finished.

Decker hesitated. "But if Sally's father sees me, Mister Bird, before I'm all signed in, he'll kill me!"

"He's not here. He's gone away with the Colonel." Bird gestured his visitors toward the door. "You're quite safe, Decker."

Sally stood up. "Go and look after the horse, Robert."

"But—"

"I said go and look after the horse!" She snapped the order, thus sending the hapless Decker scuttling back into the rain. Once he was safe out of earshot Sally closed the parlor door and turned back to Thaddeus Bird. "Is Ethan Ridley here?" she demanded.

Thaddeus Bird's hand clawed nervously in his tangled beard. "No."

"So where is he?" There was no politeness in her voice, just a bald demand and a hint that she might unleash a violent temper if her demands were frustrated.

Bird felt overwhelmed by the girl. She had a force of character not unlike her father's, but where Truslow's presence suggested a threat of violence coupled with a dour muscular competence, the daughter seemed to possess a more sinuous

146

strength that could bend and twist and manipulate other folk to her wishes. "Ethan is in Richmond," Bird finally answered.

"But where?" she insisted.

Bird was taken aback by the intensity of the question and appalled by its implications. He had no doubts what business this girl had with Ethan and he disapproved of it mightily, yet he felt powerless to resist her demands. "He stays in his brother's rooms. His half-brother, that is, in Grace Street. Shall I write the address down? You can read, yes?"

"No, but others can if I ask them to."

Bird, sensing that he did something wrong, or at least something horribly tactless, wrote his friend Belvedere Delaney's address on a piece of paper and then tried to salve his conscience with a sternly asked question. "Might I ask what your business with Ethan is?"

"You can ask, but you'll get no answer," Sally said, sounding more like her father than she might have cared to know, then she plucked the scrap of paper from Bird's hand and tucked it deep inside her rain-soaked clothes. She was wearing two threadbare homespun dresses dyed in butternut, two frayed aprons, a faded shawl, a moth-eaten black bonnet and an oilcloth sheet as an inadequate cape. She was also carrying a heavy canvas bag, suggesting to Bird that she stood in his parlor with all her worldly goods. Her only adornment was the silver ring on her left hand, a ring that struck Bird as old and rather fine. Sally, returning Bird's appraisal with her scornful blue eyes, had clearly dismissed the schoolmaster as a nonentity. She turned to follow Decker out to the street, but then paused to look back. "Is there a Mister Starbuck here?"

"Nate? Yes. Well, not exactly here. He went with the Colonel. And your father."

"Gone far?"

"Indeed." Bird tried to indulge his curiosity as tactfully as possible. "You've met Mister Starbuck, then?"

"Hell, yes." She laughed briefly, though at what she did not

147

explain. "He's kind of nice," she added in lame explanation, and Thaddeus Bird, even though he was as newly married as a man could be, felt a sudden surge of jealousy against Starbuck. He immediately chided himself for having had such an unworthy envy, then marveled that a daughter of Truslow's could have provoked it. "Is Mister Starbuck a proper preacherman?" Sally frowned at Bird as she asked the odd question.

"A preacherman!" Bird exclaimed. "He's a theologian, certainly. I've not heard him preach, but he isn't ordained, if that's what you mean."

"What's ordained?"

"It is a superstitious ceremony entitling a man to administer the Christian sacraments." Bird paused, wondering if he had confused her with his impiety. "Is it important?"

"To me it is, yes. So he ain't a minister? Is that what you're saying?"

"No, he is not."

Sally smiled, not at Bird, but at some inner amusement, then she ducked into the hall and so out into the wet street. Bird watched the girl climb into the saddle and felt as though he had been scorched by a sudden fierce flame.

"Who was that?" Priscilla called from the kitchen as she heard the front door close.

"Trouble." Thaddeus Bird bolted the door. "Double toil and trouble, but not for us, not for us, not for us." He carried the candle back into the small kitchen where Priscilla was arranging the leftovers from the wedding feast onto a plate. Thaddeus Bird stopped her work, gathered her into his thin arms, and held her close and wondered why he would ever want to leave this small house with this good woman. "I don't know that I should go to war," he said softly.

"You must do what you want," Priscilla said, and felt her heart leap at the prospect that perhaps her man would not march to the guns. She loved and admired this awkward,

148

difficult, clever man, but she could not see him as a soldier. She could imagine the handsome Washington Faulconer as a soldier, or even the unimaginative Major Pelham, or almost any of the sturdy young men who carried a rifle with the same assurance with which they had once wielded a spade or a pitchfork, but she could not envisage her irascible Thaddeus on a battlefield. "I can't think why you should ever have wanted to go for a soldier," she said, but very mildly so that he would not construe her words as criticism.

"Do you know why?" Thaddeus asked, then answered his own question. "Because I have a fancy that I might be good at soldiering."

Priscilla almost laughed, then saw her new husband was serious. "Truly?"

"Soldiering is merely the application of force by intelligence, and I am, for all my faults, intelligent. I also believe that every man needs to discover an activity at which he can excel and it is a constant regret that I have never found mine. I can write a fair prose, it is true, and I am no mean flautist, but those are common enough accomplishments. No, I need to discover an endeavor in which I can demonstrate mastery. Till now I have been too cautious."

"I dearly hope that you will go on being cautious," Priscilla said sternly.

"I have no wish to make you a widow." Bird smiled. He could see his wife was unhappy, so he sat her down and poured her some wine into an inadequate unstemmed glass. "But you should not worry," he told her, "as I daresay it will all prove to be a dreadful fuss about nothing. I can't imagine there'll be any serious fighting. There'll just be a deal of posturing and boasting and much ado about not very much and at summer's end we'll all march home and brag about our bravery, and things won't be a whole lot different than they are now, but, my darling, for those of us who don't join the farce the future will be very bleak."

149

"How so?"

"Because our neighbors will judge us cowards if we refuse to join. We're like men bidden to a dance who cannot abide dancing and who don't even much like music, but who must caper nimbly if we are to sit down to supper afterward."

"You're frightened of Washington sending you a petticoat?" Priscilla asked the pertinent question in a humble voice.

"I'm frightened," Bird said honestly, "of not being good enough for you."

"I don't need a war to show me your goodness."

"But it seems you have one anyway, and your ancient husband shall astonish you with his capabilities. I shall prove to be a Galahad, a Roland, a George Washington! No, why be so modest? I shall be an Alexander!" Bird had made his new wife laugh with his bravado, and then he kissed her and afterward he placed the glass of wine into her hand and made her drink. "I shall be your hero," he said.

"I'm frightened," Priscilla Bird said, and her husband did not know whether she spoke of what this night promised or what the whole summer held in store, so he just held her hand, and kissed it, and promised that all would be well. While in the dark the rain beat on.

6

It began to rain as the train clanked and hissed to a full halt
with the locomotive's great skirtlike cowcatcher just twenty
paces from the gap that Truslow had torn in the rails. The
smoke from the high and bulbous funnel was whipped in the
rainy wind toward the river. Steam hissed momentarily from a
valve, then the locomotive's two engineers were chivied out of
their cab by one of Truslow's men.

Starbuck had already returned to the bridge to shout down
the news of the train to the Colonel who, standing beside the
stream sixty feet below, demanded to know why the appearance
of a train should delay the bridge's destruction. Starbuck had
no good answer. "Tell Hinton to come back across the bridge
now!" Faulconer cupped his hands to shout the order up to
Starbuck. He sounded angry. "You hear me, Nate? I want
everyone back now!"

Starbuck edged past the barricade to see the engineers standing with their backs against the locomotive's huge driving
wheels. Captain Hinton was talking to them, but turned as
Starbuck approached. "Why don't you go and help Truslow,
Nate? He's working his way forward from the caboose."

"The Colonel wants everyone back across the bridge, sir. He
sounds kind of urgent."

"You go and tell Truslow that," Hinton suggested. "And I'll
wait for you here." The hissing locomotive smelt of
woodsmoke, soot and oil. It had a brass-edged nameplate above
the forward driving wheel with the name "Swiftsure" cast into
the metal. Behind the locomotive was a tender stacked high
with cordwood, and beyond the tender four passenger cars, a

151

boxcar and the caboose. Truslow had men inside each car to keep the passengers docile while he went to deal with the guards in the caboose. Those guards had locked themselves in and, as Starbuck started down beside the stalled train, Truslow put his first shots through the caboose's side.

Some women passengers screamed at the sound of the gunshots. "Use your gun if anyone gives you trouble!" Hinton shouted after Starbuck.

Starbuck had almost forgotten the big twin-triggered Savage revolver that he had carried ever since the day he had ridden to fetch Truslow from the hills. Now he tugged the long barrel free. The cars towered above him, their small furnace chimneys wisping dribbles of smoke into the cold wet wind. Some of the car's axle boxes were so hot that the rain falling on their metal cases was boiled into instant steam. Passengers watched Starbuck from behind panes of window glass that were streaked with rain and dirt, and their gaze made Nathaniel Starbuck feel oddly heroic. He was dirty, disheveled, unshaven and with long, uncut hair, but under the passengers' fearful scrutiny he was transformed into a dashing rogue like one of the raiders who galloped the marcher fells in Sir Walter Scott's books. Behind the train's dirty window glass lay the respectable, mundane world which, not six months before, Starbuck had inhabited, while out here was discomfort and danger, risk and devilment and so, with a young man's pride, he strutted before the frightened passengers. A woman put a hand over her mouth, as though shocked to see his face, while a child rubbed a window free of mist just to see Starbuck better. Starbuck waved to the child, who shrank away in fear. "You'll hang for this!" a man with muttonchop whiskers shouted from an open window, and the angry threat made Starbuck realize that the passengers had mistaken Faulconer's raiders for common thieves. He found the idea absurdly flattering and laughed aloud. "You'll hang!" the man shouted, then was told to sit down and shut the hell up by one of the raiders inside the car.

Starbuck reached the caboose just as one of the men inside shouted for Truslow to stop shooting. Truslow, armed with a revolver, had been working his way calmly down the caboose's side, putting a bullet into every third plank and thus driving the inmates to the very back of the wagon, but now, knowing that the next bullet must surely hit one of them, the men inside shouted their surrender. The rear door opened very cautiously and two middle-aged men, one thin and the other fat, appeared on the caboose's platform. "I ain't even supposed to be here," the fat man wailed at Truslow, "I was just taking a ride with Jim here. Don't shoot me, mister. I got a wife and children!"

"Key to the boxcar?" Truslow enquired of the thin man in a very bored voice.

"Here, mister." The thin man, who was uniformed as a guard, held up a heavy ring of keys, then, when Truslow nodded, he tossed it down. The guard, like Truslow, gave the impression of having been through the whole performance before.

"What's in the housecar?" Truslow demanded.

"Nothing much. Mostly hardware. Some white lead." The guard shrugged.

"I'll have a look anyways," Truslow said, "so both you boys come on down." Truslow was very calm. He even thrust his empty revolver into his belt as the two men climbed down to the stones of the railbed. "Hold your hands up. High," Truslow ordered, then nodded at Starbuck. "Search them. You're looking for guns."

"I left mine inside!" the guard said.

"Search 'em, boy," Truslow insisted.

Starbuck found it embarrassing to stand so close that he could smell the fat man's terror. The fat man had a cheap gilt watch chain thick with seals stretched across his belly. "Take the watch, sir," he said when Starbuck's hand brushed against the seals, "go on, sir, take it, sir, please." Starbuck left the

153

watch alone. A pulse in the man's neck fluttered wildly as Starbuck emptied his pockets. There was a flask, a cigar case, two handkerchiefs, a tinder box, a handful of coins and a pocket book.

"No guns," Starbuck said when he was finished with both men.

Truslow nodded. "Any soldiers where you boys come from?"

The two men paused, almost as if they were preparing to lie, then the guard nodded. "There's a whole bunch of 'em 'bout ten mile back. Maybe a hundred horse soldiers from Ohio? They said how they was expecting rebels." He paused, frowning. "Are you rebels?"

"Just plain rail thieves," Truslow said, then paused to jet a stream of tobacco juice onto the ties. "Now you walk back to those soldiers, boys."

"Walk?" the fat man said, aghast.

"Walk," Truslow insisted, "and don't look back or we'll start shooting. Walk between the rails, walk real slow, and just keep going. I'm watching you real good. Start now!"

The two men began walking. Truslow waited till they were out of earshot, then spat again. "Sounds like someone knew we were coming."

"I told no one," Starbuck said defensively.

"I never said you did, never thought you did. Hell, the Colonel's been talking about this raid for days! It's just amazing there ain't half the U.S. Army waiting for us." Truslow climbed up into the caboose and disappeared into its dark interior. "Mind you," he went on, speaking from inside the wagon, "there are men who think you're a spy. Just 'cos you're a Yankee."

"Who says that?"

"Just men. And it ain't anything to worry you. They've got nothing else to talk about and so they wonder what in hell's name a Yankee's doing in a Virginia regiment. You want some coffee off the stove here? It's warm. Ain't hot, just warm."

154

"No." Starbuck was offended that his loyalty had been so impugned.

Truslow reappeared on the back platform with the guard's discarded pistol and a tin mug of coffee. He checked that the gun was loaded then drained the coffee before jumping down to the track. "Right. Now we go and search the passenger cars."

"Shouldn't we leave?" Starbuck suggested.

"Leave?" Truslow frowned. "Why the hell would we want to leave? We just got the son of a bitch train stopped."

"The Colonel wants us to go. He's ready to blow the bridge."

"The Colonel can wait," Truslow said, then gestured Starbuck toward the passenger cars. "We'll start with the last car. If any bastard gives us trouble, shoot him. If any women or kids start screaming, slap them down fast. Passengers are like hens. Once you get 'em flustered they're noisy as hell, but treat 'em tough and they'll stay nice and quiet. And don't take any big stuff, because we've got to ride fast. Money, jewelry and watches, that's what we're after."

Starbuck stood stock still. "You're not robbing the passengers!" He was genuinely shocked at the thought. It was one thing to stride down the train like a freebooter under the gaze of awestruck passengers, but quite another to break the Sixth Commandment. The worst beatings Starbuck had ever taken had been as punishments for theft. When he was four he had helped himself to some almonds from a jar in the kitchen, and two years later he had taken a toy wooden boat from his elder brother's toy chest, and both times the Reverend Elial had drawn blood for a recompense. From that day until Dominique had persuaded him to take Major Trabell's money, Starbuck had been terrified of theft, and the consequences of helping Dominique had only reinforced his childhood lessons that thieving was a terrible crime which God would surely punish. "You can't steal," he told Truslow. "You can't."

"You expect me to buy their belongings off them?" Truslow

asked mockingly. "Now come on, don't lag."

"I'm not helping you steal!" Starbuck stood his ground. He had sinned so much in these last weeks. He had committed the sin of lust, he had drunk ardent spirits, he had made a wager, he had failed to honor his father and mother and he had failed to keep the Sabbath Day holy, but he would not become a thief. He had only helped Dominique steal because she had persuaded him that the money was owed to her, but he would not help Truslow steal from innocent train passengers. So much of sin seemed nebulous and hard to avoid, but theft was an absolute and undeniable sin, and Starbuck would not risk the slippery path to hell by adding that transgression to his woefully long list of wrongdoings.

Truslow suddenly laughed. "I keep forgetting you're a preacherman. Or half a preacherman." He tossed Starbuck the ring of keys. "One of those will open the boxcar. Get inside, search it. You don't have to steal anything"—the sarcasm was heavy—"but you can look for military supplies and if you see anything else worth stealing, you can tell me about it. And take this." Truslow whipped his enormous bowie knife from its scabbard and tossed it to Starbuck.

Starbuck missed the catch, but retrieved the clumsy blade from the railbed. "What's it for?"

"It's for cutting throats, boy, but you can use it for opening boxes. Unless you were planning on using your teeth to get into the crates?"

The heavy brass padlock on the boxcar's sliding door was a good ten feet above the railbed, but a rusted iron stirrup suggested how Starbuck could reach the lock. He pulled himself up and clung precariously to the hasp as he fiddled with the keys. He eventually found the right one, unlocked and slid the heavy door aside, then stepped inside.

The wagon was filled with boxes and sacks. The sacks were more easily opened than the crates and proved to hold seed, though Starbuck had no idea what kind of seed. He trickled the grains through his fingers, then gaped up at the stacked boxes and wondered how he was ever to search them all. The easiest way would have been to hurl the boxes out onto the ground, but the boxes were probably private property and he did not want to risk breaking anything. Most of the crates were marked for collection at either the Baltimore or Washington depot, proof that the occupation of Harper's Ferry had not entirely closed federal traffic through the mountains. One of the crates marked for Washington was a dark-painted box that bore a stenciled and misspelled legend on its side: "1000 Rifle Musket 69IN Cartridgs."

That at least had to be war material, and thus fair plunder. He used the clumsy bowie knife to cut the ropes that had tethered the stacks in place, then began shifting the obstructing crates onto the sacks of seed. It took him the best part of five minutes to reach the dark-painted crate and still more time to lever the well-nailed lid off the heavy box to discover that it was indeed packed with paper cartridges, each one containing a bullet and a measure of powder. Starbuck did his best to hammer the lid back into place, then manhandled the box down to the ground. It was still raining, so he thumped the lid with the heel of his right boot, trying to bang the top down tight and thus keep out the rain.

There was another dark painted box under a second stack and so he climbed back into the boxcar and moved still more crates until he had excavated the second box which, like the first, bore a stenciled legend denoting that its contents were also cartridges. He added that box to the first, then climbed back inside to continue his laborious search.

"What in hell's name are you doing, boy?" Truslow appeared at the boxcar door. He was carrying a heavy leather bag in his right hand and the guard's pistol in his left.

"Those are cartridges"—Starbuck gestured at the two boxes beside Truslow—"and I think there might be more in here."

Truslow kicked the lid off the nearest box, looked down,

then spat tobacco juice over the cartridges. "No more use than tits on a bull."

"What?"

"They're point six nines like I used in Mexico. The rifles the Colonel bought in Richmond are five eights."

"Oh." Starbuck felt himself coloring with embarrassment.

"You could light a fire with these?" Truslow suggested.

"So they're no use?"

"Not to us, boy." Truslow shoved the revolver into his belt then picked up one of the cartridges and bit off its bullet. "Big son of a bitch, ain't she?" He showed Starbuck the bullet. "Anything valuable in there?"

"I've only found the bullets so far."

"Jesus wept, boy." Truslow dropped the heavy leather bag which chinked ominously as it fell, then clambered into the boxcar and seized the bowie knife from Starbuck. "I've got to get our boys out of the cars before the passengers get ideas. I took as many guns as I could, but some of those sons of bitches will have kept them well hid. There's always some bastard who wants to be a hero. I remember a young fellow on the Orange and Alexandria couple of years ago. Thought he would capture me." He spat in derision.

"What happened?"

"He finished his journey in the caboose, boy. Flat on his back and covered with a tarpaulin." As Truslow spoke he wrenched lids off crates, gave the contents a cursory glance, then hurled them out into the rain. A box of china plates decorated with painted lilies smashed itself on the railbed. A clothes mangle followed, then a crate of tin saucepans and a consignment of delicate gas mantles. It had begun to rain more heavily, the drops pattering loud on the boxcar's wooden roof.

"Shouldn't we be leaving?" Starbuck asked nervously.

"Why?"

"I told you. Colonel Faulconer's ready to blow the bridge up."

158

"Who cares about the bridge? How long do you think it will take to rebuild it?"

"The Colonel says months."

"Months!" Truslow was raking through a box of clothes, seeing if anything took his fancy. He decided nothing did and hurled the box out into the weather. "I could rebuild that trestle in a week. Give me ten men and I'll have it up and working in two days. Faulconer don't know goose shit from gold dust, boy." He jettisoned a barrel of soda and another of clearing starch. "There's nothing here," he sniffed, then clambered back to the ground. He glanced west, but the landscape was empty. "Go to the caboose, boy," he ordered Starbuck, "and bring me some hot coals."

"What are you doing?"

"Thinking that if you ask me another goddamned question I'll shoot you. Now go and get me some damned coals." Truslow upended both boxes of .69 cartridges into the boxcar while Starbuck climbed into the caboose where a small pot-bellied stove still burned. There was a zinc bucket of coal beside the stove. He tipped the coal out, used a poker to open the stove's door, then raked a handful of the glowing lumps into the empty bucket.

"Right," Truslow said when Starbuck got back. "Throw the coals onto the cartridges."

"You're going to burn the wagon?" The rain hissed as it fell into the bucket.

"For the Lord's sake!" Truslow grabbed the bucket and chucked the coals onto the spilt cartridges. For a second the coals just glowed among the paper tubes, then the first cartridge exploded with a soft cough and suddenly the whole pile of ammunition was a blazing, exploding, twisting mass of fire.

Truslow picked up his leather bag of loot, then beckoned Starbuck away. "Come on!" Truslow shouted up to the two men he had left in the rear passenger car.

As the guards left each car they warned the passengers that

159

anyone following the raiders would be shot. Most of those raiders were burdened with bags or sacks, and all had the looks of men well satisfied with their work. Some walked backward with drawn pistols to make certain that none of the passengers tried to be heroic. "The trouble's going to come when we're past the barricade," Truslow warned. "Tom? Micky? You hang back with me. Captain Hinton! Get the engineers aboard!"

Hinton chivied the two engineers back into their locomotive's cabin, then followed with his drawn revolver. A second later the great machine gave an enormous hiss of steam, a gigantic clank, and suddenly the whole train jerked forward. A woman in one of the passenger cars screamed. The boxcar was well ablaze now, spewing black smoke into the driving sheets of rain.

"Go on!" Truslow shouted encouragement to Captain Hinton.

The locomotive clanked forward, its funnel giving off small and urgent puffs of gray-white smoke. A black soot smut, hot and sudden, landed on Starbuck's cheek. Hinton was grinning, shouting at the engineer who must have suddenly opened his throttle because the train jerked forward off the rail ends and shoved its cowcatcher deep into the bed. Stones and timber shattered apart. The four drive wheels, each one nearly six foot in diameter, began spinning and shrieking, but they found just enough traction so that, inch by agonizing inch, the monstrous machine shuddered forward as its small front wheels tore up the broken ties. The cowcatcher crumpled in a screech of tearing metal.

Hinton gestured with his revolver and the engineer opened the throttle full and the thirty-ton locomotive lurched forward like a great wounded beast as it toppled a few degrees sideways. Starbuck feared it was about to plunge down the river's bank, dragging its full cars behind, but then, mercifully, the huge machine stuck fast. Steam began to jet from its farther side. One of its small front wheels spun free above the churned dirt while the drive wheels on the farther side of the engine churned a foot-deep trench into the railbed before the engineer disconnected the pistons and more steam slashed out into the rain.

"Set the tender ablaze!" Truslow yelled and Hinton ordered one of the engineers to take a shovel load of red hot timbers from the firebox and thrust it deep into the tender's cordwood. "More!" Truslow urged, "more!" Truslow had found the venting faucet for the tender's water storage tank and turned it on. Water poured out of one end of the tender while the other began to blaze as fiercely as the burning boxcar.

"Go!" Truslow shouted, "go!"

The raiders pushed past the barricade and ran toward the bridge. Truslow stayed with two men to guard against any pursuit as Captain Hinton led the others across the narrow planks laid beside the rails on the trestles. Colonel Faulconer was waiting on the farther bank and shouting at Hinton's men to hurry. "Light the fires! Medlicott!" Faulconer called down into the gorge. "Hurry!" Faulconer shouted at Hinton. "For God's sake! What held you up?"

"Had to make sure the train didn't go back for help," Captain Hinton said.

"No one obeys orders here!" The Colonel had given the order to withdraw at least a quarter hour before and every second of the delay had been an insult to his already fragile authority. "Starbuck!" he shouted. "Didn't I order you to bring the men back?"

"Yes, sir."

"Then why didn't you?"

"My fault! Faulconer," Hinton intervened.

"I gave you an order, Nate!" the Colonel shouted. His other men were already mounted, all but for Medlicott, who had struck a light to the mass of combustibles about the trestle leg. "Now the fuse!" the Colonel shouted.

"Truslow!" Captain Hinton bellowed at the three men left on the far side of the gorge.

161

Truslow, the leather bag in his hand, was the last man away from the barricade. As he crossed the bridge he kicked the planks aside, making pursuit difficult. A gun was fired from the far barricade, the smoke of its powder snatched instantly away by the breeze. The bullet struck a rail on the bridge and whined off across the river. Two dense plumes of smoke from the burning boxcar and tender were drifting low and acrid above the North Branch.

"Fuse is lit!" Medlicott shouted and began clawing his way up the gorge's side. Behind him a dribble of smoke spat and writhed from the lit fuse as it snaked down the slope toward the great heap of timber and brush stacked about the gunpowder.

"Hurry!" the Colonel shouted. A horse whinnied and reared. More men fired from the barricade, but Truslow was across the bridge now and well out of effective revolver range. "Come on, man!" Washington Faulconer shouted. Truslow still had his leather bag, just as all Hinton's men had similar bags. Faulconer must have known from the heavy bags why his order to withdraw had been so long ignored, but he chose to say nothing. Sergeant Medlicott, muddy and damp, scrambled out of the gorge and fumbled for his stirrup just as the smoking fuse darted into the pile of brush. Sergeant Truslow hauled himself into his saddle, and Faulconer turned away. "Let's go!" He led his men off the railroad's embankment. The fire in the gorge had to be quickening, for thick smoke was writhing about the trestle's lattice, though the gunpowder had still not exploded. "Come on!" Faulconer urged, and behind him the horses scrambled and slipped on the muddy slope until, at last, they were concealed from the train by foliage and, though a few random bullets ripped through the leaves and twigs, none of the Legion's men was hit.

Faulconer stopped at the crest and turned to look back at the stricken train. The fires in the boxcar and tender had spread to the cars and the erstwhile passengers, wet and miserable, now clambered up the wet slope to escape the danger.

162

The long passenger cars served like funnels in which the heat roared fierce until the windows cracked open and released billowing gusts of flame that licked into the driving rain.

The train was a blazing wreck, its engine derailed and cars destroyed, but the bridge, which had been the object of the raid, still stood. The fuse had failed to detonate the gunpowder, probably because the powder was damp, while the fire, which had been supposed to dry the powder and then explode it if the fuse failed, now seemed to be succumbing to wet fuel and wind-driven rain. "If you had obeyed my orders," the Colonel charged Starbuck bitterly, "there would have been time to reset the charges."

"Me, sir?" Starbuck was astonished at the unfairness of the accusation.

Captain Hinton was equally surprised by the Colonel's words. "I told you, Faulconer, it was my fault."

"I didn't give you the order, Hinton. I gave it to Starbuck, and the order was disobeyed." Faulconer spoke in a cold, clipped fury, then twisted his horse away and raked back with his spurs. The horse whinnied and started abruptly forward.

"Goddamn Yankee," Sergeant Medlicott said softly, then followed Faulconer.

"Forget them, Nate," Hinton said. "It wasn't your fault. I'll square the Colonel for you."

Starbuck still could not believe that he was being blamed for the failure of the attack. He sat dumbstruck, appalled at the Colonel's unfairness. Down on the rail line, unaware that a handful of the raiders still lingered above them, some of the train's passengers were edging out onto the undamaged trestle while others had begun to pull the barricade clear of the broken tracks. The fire in the gorge seemed to have gone out completely.

"He's used to getting his own way." Truslow pulled his horse alongside Starbuck. "He thinks he can buy what he wants and have it perfect, right from the start."

163

"But I didn't do anything wrong!"

"You didn't have to. He wants someone to blame. And he reckons that if he pisses all over you, then you won't piss back at him. That's why he chose you. He wasn't going to piss on me, was he?" Truslow spurred on.

Starbuck looked back to the gorge. The bridge was undamaged and the cavalry raid, which had been intended as a glorious victory to launch the Legion's triumphant crusade, had turned into a muddled, rain-soaked farce. And Starbuck was being blamed.

"Goddamn it," he swore aloud, defying his God, then turned and followed Truslow south.

"Can this really be it?" Belvedere Delaney had a four-day-old copy of the *Wheeling Intelligencer* that had been brought to Richmond from Harper's Ferry. The *Intelligencer*, though a Virginian paper, was soundly pro-Union.

"What?" Ethan Ridley was distracted and utterly uninterested in whatever the newspaper might have reported.

"Thieves stopped an eastbound passenger train on Wednesday last, one man hurt, locomotive temporarily unrailed." Delaney was condensing the story as he scanned the column. "Four cars badly burned, a boxcar and the passengers looted, rails torn up, replaced very next day." He peered at Ridley through gold-rimmed half-moon reading glasses. "You don't really think this can be the first great triumph of your Faulconer Legion, do you?"

"It doesn't sound like Faulconer. Now listen, Bev."

"No, you listen to me." The half-brothers were in Delaney's rooms in Grace Street. The parlor windows looked through velvet curtains at the graceful spire of St. Paul's and, beyond it, toward the elegant white Capitol Building that was now the seat of the Provisional Confederate government. "You listen, because I am going to read the best part to you," Delaney said with exaggerated relish. "'It might be thought, from their despicable behavior, that the plug-uglies who intercepted the cars on Wednesday were mere vagabond thieves, but thieves do not attempt to destroy railway trestles, and it is that feeble effort of destruction which has convinced authorities that the villains were southern agents and not common criminals, though how it is possible to differentiate, we cannot tell.' Isn't this delicious, Ethan? 'The world is well instructed now in southern manners, for the bravery of the rebels encompassed the robbing of women, the frightening of children, and an abject failure to destroy the Anakansett Bridge which, though lightly toasted, was carrying freight the very next day.' Lightly toasted! Isn't that amusing, Ethan?"

"No, goddamn it, no!"

"I think it's highly amusing. Let's see now, bold pursuit by Ohio cavalry, held up by rains, swollen streams. Rogues got clear away, so clearly the pursuit wasn't near bold enough. Raiders are thought to have retired east toward the Shenandoah Valley. 'Our brethren of eastern Virginia who so like to boast of their greater civilization, seem to have sent these men as emissaries of that vaunted superiority. If this be the best we can hope to see of their belligerent skills then we can rest assured that the nation's crisis will be short-lived and that the glorious Union will be reknit within weeks.' Oh, splendid!" Delaney took off his reading glasses and smiled at Ridley. "Not a very impressive display if it was your future father-in-law. One toasted bridge? He'll have to do better than that!"

"For God's sake, Bev!" Ridley pleaded.

Delaney made a great play of folding the newspaper, then of slipping it into the rosewood rack of other newspapers and journals that stood beside his armchair. His parlor was wonderfully comfortable with leather chairs, a big round polished table, books on every wall, plaster busts of great Virginians and, over the mantel, a massive mirror with a gilded frame of linked cherubs and aspiring angels. Some of Delaney's precious porcelain collection was displayed on the mantel, while other pieces

165

stood among the leather-bound books. Delaney now made his brother wait even longer as he polished the half-moon glasses and carefully folded them into a velvet-lined case. "What on earth," he finally asked, "do you expect me to do about the damned girl?"

"I want you to help me," Ridley said pathetically.

"Why should I? The girl is one of your whores, not one of mine. She sought you out, not me. She's carrying your child, not mine, and her father's revenge threatens your life, certainly not mine, and do I really need to continue?" Delaney stood, crossed to the mantel, and took one of his yellow paper-wrapped cigarettes, which he used to import from France, but which now, he supposed, would become rarer than gold dust. He lit the cigarette with a spill ignited from the coal fire. It was astonishing that he should need a fire this late in the year, but the rains that had come thundering out of the east had brought unseasonably cold winds. "Besides, what can I do?" He went on airily. "You've already tried to buy her off and it didn't work. So clearly you'll just have to pay her more."

"She'll just come back," Ridley said. "And back again."

"So what exactly does she want?" Delaney knew he would have to help his half-brother, at least if he was to go on profiting from the Faulconer Legion purchases, but he wanted to stretch Ethan on the rack a little before he agreed to find a solution to the problem posed by Sally Truslow's unexpected arrival in the city.

"She wants me to find her somewhere to live. She expects me to pay for that, then to give her still more money every month. Naturally I've got to keep her bastard too. Jesus Christ!" Ridley swore viciously as he considered Sally's outrageous demands.

"Not just her bastard, but yours, too," Delaney pointed out unhelpfully. "Indeed, my own nephew! Or niece. I think I'd prefer a niece, Ethan. Would she be a half-niece, do you think? Maybe I could be her half-godfather."

"Don't be so damned unhelpful," Ridley said, then scowled through the window at a city being pounded by rain. Grace Street was almost empty. There was just one carriage clattering toward Capitol Square and two Negroes sheltering in the doorway of the Methodist Church. "Does Mrs. Richardson have anyone who can get rid of babies?" Ridley turned to ask. Mrs. Richardson presided over the brothel in which his half-brother had such a significant investment.

Delaney gave a delicate shrug that might have signified almost anything.

"Mind you," Ridley went on, "Sally wants to keep the bastard, and she says if I won't help her then she'll tell Washington Faulconer about me. And she says she'll tell her father. You know what he'll do to me?"

"I don't suppose he'll choose to have a prayer meeting with you," Delaney chuckled. "Why don't you take the inconvenient bitch down to the Tredegar works and leave her on a spoil heap?" The Tredegar Iron Works by the James River was Richmond's filthiest, darkest and grimmest place, and not many enquiries were made about the tragedies that occurred around its satanic edges. Men died in fights, whores were knifed in its alleys, and dead or dying babies were abandoned in its filthy canals. It was a corner of hell in downtown Richmond.

"I'm not a murderer," Ridley said sullenly, though in truth he had considered some such extraordinary and saving act of violence, but he was much too frightened of Sally Truslow who, he suspected, was hiding a gun somewhere among her property. She had come to him three nights before, arriving at Belvedere Delancy's rooms in the early evening. Delaney had been in Williamsburg, swearing a will, so Ridley had been alone in the apartment when Sally had rung the front bell. He had heard a commotion at the front door and gone downstairs to find George, his brother's house slave, confronting a bedraggled, wet and angry Sally. She had pushed past George who, with his customary and dignified politeness, had been trying to

167

keep her from entering the house. "Tell this nigger to keep his hands off me," she screamed at Ridley.

"It's all right, George. She's my cousin," Ridley had said, then had arranged for Sally's bedraggled horse to be stabled and for Sally herself to be shown upstairs to his brother's parlor. "What the hell are you doing here?" he had asked her in horror.

"I came to you," she announced, "like you said I could." Her ragged clothes dripped water onto Belvedere Delaney's fine Persian rug that lay in front of his red marble fireplace. Wind and rain howled at the casements, but in this warm and comfortable room, insulated by the thick velvet curtains under their deep-tasseled valances, the fire burned softly and the candle flames scarcely flickered. Sally turned about on the rug, admiring the books, the furniture and the leather chairs. She was dazzled by the reflection of candlelight from decanters, from the glint of gilded frames, and from the precious European porcelain on the mantel. "This is nice, Ethan. I never knew you had a brother?"

Ridley had crossed to the credenza where he opened a silver humidor and took out one of the cigars his brother kept for visitors. He needed a cigar to help recover his poise. "I thought you were married?"

"I'll take one of those cigars," Sally said.

He lit the cigar, gave it to her, then took another for himself. "You're wearing a wedding ring," he said, "so you are married. Why don't you go back to your husband?"

She deliberately ignored his question, instead holding her ring finger up to the candlelight. "The ring belonged to my ma and she had it from her ma. My pa wanted to keep it, but I made him give it me. Ma always wanted me to have it."

"Let me see it." Ridley took her finger and felt the thrill he always felt when he touched Sally and he wondered just what accident of bone and skin and lip and eye had made such a terrible beauty out of this foul-mouthed, sour-minded child of the hills. "It's pretty." He turned the ring on her finger, feeling the dry lightness of her touch. "It's quite old, too." He suspected it was very old, and perhaps quite special and so he tried to pull it off her finger, but Sally jerked her hand away.

"My pa wanted to keep it," she looked at the ring, "so I took it away from him." She laughed and drew on the cigar. "Besides, I ain't married proper. No more proper than if I jumped a broomstick."

That was precisely what Ridley feared, but he tried not to show any apprehension. "Your husband will still come looking for you, won't he?"

"Robert?" She laughed. "He won't do anything. A gelded hog's got more balls than Robert. But what about your lady friend? What will your Anna do when she knows I'm here?"

"Will she know?"

"She will, honey, 'cos I'll tell her. Unless you keep your word to me. Which means looking after me proper. I want to live in a place like this." She turned around the room, admiring its comfort, then looked back at Ridley. "Do you know a man called Starbuck?"

"I know a boy called Starbuck," Ridley said.

"A good-looking boy," Sally said coquettishly. A length of ash dropped off her cigar onto a rug. "He was the one that married me off to Robert. My pa made him do it. He made it sound all proper, with a book and all, and he even wrote it down to make it legal, but I know it wasn't proper."

"Starbuck married you?" Ridley was amused.

"He was nice about it. Real nice." Sally cocked her head at Ridley, wanting him to be jealous. "So then I told Robert he should go for a soldier, and I came here. To be with you."

"But I won't be staying here," Ridley said. Sally watched him, her eyes catlike. "I'm going to the Legion," Ridley explained. "I shall just finish my business here, then I shall go back."

"Then I tell you what other business you've got to finish, honey." Sally walked toward him, unconsciously graceful as she crossed the rich rugs and wax-polished boards. "You're going to find me a place to live, Ethan. Somewhere nice, with carpets like this and real chairs and a proper bed. And you can visit me there, like you said you would. Ain't that what you said? That you'd find a place where I could live? Where you'd keep me? And love me?" The last three words were said very softly and so close that Ridley could smell the cigar smoke on her breath.

"I said that, yes." And he knew he could not resist her, but he also knew that as soon as they had made love he would hate Sally for her vulgarity and commonness. She was a child, scarce fifteen, yet she knew her power and Ridley knew it too. He knew she would fight to have her way and she would not care what destruction she caused in the fighting, and so, the very next day, Ridley moved her out of his brother's Grace Street rooms. If Delaney had returned to find any of his precious porcelain broken he would never have agreed to help Ethan, and so Ridley had taken a front room at a boardinghouse on Monroe Street where he registered himself and Sally as a married couple. Now he pleaded for his brother's help. "For God's sake, Bev! She's a witch! She'll destroy everything!"

"A succuba, is she? I'd like to meet her. Is she really as beautiful as your sketch?"

"She is extraordinary. So for God's sake take her from me! You want her? She's yours." Ridley had already tried introducing her to his friends who met to drink in the Spotswood House Saloon, but Sally, even though dressed in newly purchased finery and hugely admired by every officer in the hotel, had refused to leave Ridley's side. She had her claws deep into her man and would not let go for the unknown opportunities of another. "Please, Bev!" Ridley pleaded.

Belvedere Delaney thought how much he hated being called

170

"Bev" as he warmed himself by his small, glowing fire. "You're not willing to kill her?" he asked in a dangerous voice.

Ridley paused, then shook his head. "No."

"And you won't give her what she wants?"

"I can't."

"And you can't give her away?"

"Damn it, no."

"And she won't leave you of her own accord?"

"Never."

Delaney drew on his cigarette, then puffed a reflective smoke ring at his ceiling. "A toasted bridge! I do find that amusing."

"Please, Bev, please!"

"I showed the newspaper to Lee this afternoon," Delaney said, "but he dismissed the account. None of our men, he assured me. He reckons the bridge toasters must have been mere brigands. I think you should find a way of letting Faulconer hear that verdict. Brigands! The word will annoy Faulconer considerably."

"Please, Bev! For God's sake."

"Oh, not for God's sake, Ethan. God wouldn't like what I intend to do with your Sally. He wouldn't like it one little bit. But yes, I can help you."

Ridley gazed at his brother with palpable relief. "What will you do?"

"Bring her to me tomorrow. Bring her to the corner of, say, Cary and Twenty-fourth, that'll be out of the way. At four o'clock. There'll be a carriage there. I may be there or I may not. Find some story that'll get her into the carriage, then forget her. Forget her altogether."

Ridley gaped at his brother. "You're going to kill her?"

Delaney winced at the question. "Please do not imagine I am so crude. I am going to remove her from your life and you are going to be grateful to me forever."

"I will. I promise!" Ridley's gratitude was pathetic.

"Tomorrow then, at four o'clock, at Cary and Twenty-fourth. Now go and be nice to her, Ethan, be very nice, so she suspects nothing."

Colonel Washington Faulconer ignored Starbuck for almost the entire journey home. Faulconer rode with Captain Hinton, sometimes with Murphy, and at other times alone, but always setting a fast pace, as though he wanted to distance himself from the scene of his raid's failure. When he did speak to Starbuck he was curt and unfriendly, though he was hardly any more forthcoming with anyone else. Even so, Starbuck felt hurt, while Truslow was merely amused by the Colonel's sulking. "You have to learn to walk away from stupidity," Truslow said.

"Is that what you do?"

"No, but who ever said I was a good example?" He laughed. "You should have taken my advice and helped yourself to the money." Truslow had made a fair sum from the raid, as had the men who had gone with him into the train.

"I'd rather be a fool than a thief," Starbuck said sententiously.

"No you wouldn't. No sensible man would. Besides, war's coming, and the only way you'll get through a war is by thieving. All soldiers are thieves. You thieve everything you want, not from your friends, but from everyone else. The army won't look after you. The army shouts at you, shits on you and does its best to starve you, so you get by as best you can, and the best getters-by are the ones who thieve best." Truslow rode in silence for a few paces. "I reckon you should be glad you came to say a prayer for my Emily, 'cos it means you've got me to look after you."

Starbuck said nothing. He felt ashamed of that prayer he had uttered beside the grave. He should never have said it, for he was not worthy.

"And I never thanked you for not telling anyone about my Sally, either. How she married, I mean, and why." Truslow cut

172

a slice of tobacco off the plait he kept in a belt pouch and shoved it into a cheek. He and Starbuck were riding alone, separated by a few paces from the men before and those behind. "You always hope your children will do you proud," Truslow went on softly, "but I reckon Sally's a bad one. But she's wed now, and that's the end of it."

Is it? Starbuck wondered, but was not so foolish as to ask the question aloud. Marriage had not been the end for Sally's mother, who had subsequently run off with the small, fierce Truslow. Starbuck tried to picture Sally's face in his mind, but he could not piece it together. He just remembered someone who was very beautiful, and someone he had promised to help if she ever asked. What would he do if she came? Would he run away with her as he had with Dominique? Would he dare defy her father? At night, lying sleepless, Starbuck wove fantasies about Sally Truslow. He knew the dreams were as stupid as they were impractical, but he was a young man and he so wanted to be in love and thus he dreamed the stupid and impractical dreams.

"I'm real grateful you said nothing about Sally." Truslow seemed to want a response, perhaps an affirmation that Starbuck had indeed kept the night wedding a secret instead of making fun of the family's misfortune.

"I never thought to tell anyone," Starbuck said. "It's no one else's business." It was pleasant to sound so virtuous again, though Starbuck suspected his silence about the marriage had been prompted more by an instinctive fear of Truslow's enmity than by any principle of reticence.

"So what did you make of Sally?" Truslow asked in all seriousness.

"She is a very pretty girl." Starbuck gave the response equally seriously, as though he had not imagined riding away with her to the new western lands or sometimes sailing east to Europe where, in his daydreams, he dazzled her with his sophistication in palatial hotels and brilliant ballrooms.

Truslow nodded acceptance of Starbuck's compliment. "She looks like her mother. Young Decker's a lucky boy, I suppose, though maybe he ain't. Prettiness ain't always a gift in a woman, especially if they own a mirror. Emily now, she never thought twice on it, but Sally." He said the name sadly, then rode in silence for a long time, evidently reflecting on his family. Starbuck, because he had shared a moment's intimacy with that family, had unwittingly become a confidant of Truslow who, after his silence, shook his head, spat out his tobacco spittle and declared his verdict. "Some men ain't intended to be family men, but young Decker is. He'd like to join his cousin in the Legion, but he's not the fighting type. Not like you."

"Me?" Starbuck was surprised.

"You're a fighter, boy. I can tell. You won't wet your pants when you see the elephant."

"See the elephant?" Starbuck asked, amused.

Truslow made a face as if to suggest that he was tired of single-handedly correcting Starbuck's education, but then deigned to explain anyway. "If you grow up in the country you're always being told about the circus. All the wonders of it. The freak shows and the animals acts, and the elephant, and all the children keep asking what the elephant is, and you can't explain, so one day you take the children and they see for themselves. That's what a man's first battle is like. Like seeing the elephant. Some men piss their pants, some run like hell, some make the enemy run. You'll be all right, but Faulconer won't." Truslow jerked a scornful head at the Colonel, who was riding alone at the head of the small column. "You mark me well, boy, but I tell you Faulconer won't last one battle."

The thought of battle made Starbuck shiver suddenly. Sometimes the anticipation was exciting, other times it was terrifying, and this time the thought of seeing the elephant was scaring him, perhaps because the raid's failure had shown

174

just how much could go wrong. He did not want to think about the consequences of things going wrong in battle, so changed the subject by blurting out the first question that came to his tongue. "Did you really murder three men?"

Truslow gave him a strange look, as though he did not understand why such a question would ever be asked. "At least," Truslow said scornfully. "Why?"

"So how does it feel to murder someone?" Starbuck asked. He had really wanted to ask why the murders had been committed, and how, and whether anyone had tried to bring Truslow to justice, but instead he asked the stupid question about sensation.

Truslow mocked the query. "How does it feel? Jesus, boy, there are times when you make more noise than a cracked pot. How does it feel? You find out for yourself, boy. You go and murder someone, then you tell me the answer." Truslow spurred ahead, evidently disgusted with Starbuck's prurient question.

They camped that night on a wet ridge above a small settlement where a smelting furnace blazed like the maw of hell and seeped the foul stench of coal smoke up to the ridge where Starbuck could not sleep. Instead he sat with the guards, shivering and wishing the rain would stop. He had eaten his supper of cold dried beef and damp bread with the other three officers, and Faulconer had been livelier than on the previous nights and had even sought some consolation for the raid's failure. "Our powder might have let us down," he said, "but we showed we could be a threat."

"That's true, Colonel," Hinton said loyally.

"They'll have to post guards on every bridge," the Colonel claimed, "and a man guarding a bridge can't be invading the South."

"That's the truth, too," Hinton said cheerfully. "And it could take them days to clear that locomotive off the track. It was dug in brutally deep."

"So it wasn't a failure," the Colonel said.

"Far from it!" Captain Hinton was resolutely optimistic.

"And it was a good piece of training for our cavalry scouts," the Colonel said.

"Indeed it was." Hinton grinned at Starbuck, trying to include him in the friendlier atmosphere, but the Colonel just frowned.

Now, as the night inched by, Starbuck was plunged deep down into a young man's despair. It was not just his alienation from Washington Faulconer that oppressed him, but the knowledge that his life had gone so utterly wrong. There were excuses, good excuses maybe, but at heart he knew he was the one who had gone astray. He had left his family and his church, even his own country, to live among strangers, and the ties of their affection did not run deeply enough or strongly enough to offer him any hope. Washington Faulconer was a man whose bitter disappointment was as sour as the reek of the smelter's furnace. Truslow was an ally, but for how long? And what did Starbuck have in common with Truslow? Truslow and his followers would thieve and kill, but Starbuck could not see himself behaving so, and as for the others, like Medlicott, they hated Starbuck for being an intrusive Yankee, an outsider, a stranger, a favorite of the Colonel's who had become the Colonel's scapegoat.

Starbuck shivered in the rain, his knees drawn up to his chest. He felt utterly alone. So what should he do? The rain dripped monotonously, while behind him a picketed horse stamped the wet ground. The wind was cold, coming up from the settlement with its grim furnace house and rows of dull houses. The furnace illuminated the buildings with a sullen glow against which the tangled trees of the intervening slope were intricately and smokily silhouetted to form an impenetrable tangle of twisted black limbs and splintered trunks. It was a wilderness, Starbuck thought, and at its far side lay nothing but hellfire, and the dark horror of the intervening downward

176

slope seemed a prophecy of all his future life.

So go home, he told himself. It was time to admit that he had been wrong. The adventure was over and he had to go home. He had been made a fool, first by Dominique and now by these Virginians who disliked him because he was a northerner. So he should go home. He might still be a soldier, indeed he should be a soldier, but he would fight for the North. He would fight for Old Glory, for the continuation of a glorious century of American progress and decency. He would give up the specious arguments that pretended slavery was not the issue, and instead join the crusade of righteousness and he suddenly imagined himself as a crusader with a red cross on his white surcoat galloping across the sunny uplands of history to defeat a huge wickedness.

He would go home. He had to go home for his soul's sake, because otherwise he would stay enmeshed in the tangled dark of the wilderness. He was not yet sure just how he would manage to reach home and, for a few wild moments, he toyed with the idea of seizing his horse and just galloping free of this hilltop, except that the horses were all tethered and Colonel Faulconer, fearing a pursuit by northern cavalry, had insisted on setting sentries who would be sure to stop Starbuck. No, he decided, he would wait till he reached Faulconer Court House and there he would seek an honest interview with Washington Faulconer and confess his failure and his disappointment. He would then ask for help to go back home. He had an idea there were truce boats sailing up the James River and Faulconer would surely help him find a berth aboard one of those ships.

He felt the decision settle in his mind, and also the contentment of a choice well made. He even slept a little, waking with a clearer eye and a happier heart. He felt like Christian in *Pilgrim's Progress*, as if he had escaped from both Vanity Fair and the Slough of Despond and were once again heading toward the Celestial City.

177

Next day the raiding party reached and crossed the Shenandoah Valley, and the following morning they rode out of the Blue Ridge Mountains under a clearing sky and a warming wind. Scraps of white cloud blew northward, their shadows flying across the green good land. The disappointment of the raid seemed forgotten as the horses scented home and quickened into a trot. The town of Faulconer Court House was spread before them, the copper-coated cupola of its courthouse bright in the sun and the steeples of its churches rising sharp above the blossom-rich trees. Nearer, beside the quick river, the tents of the Legion lay white in the meadow.

Tomorrow, Starbuck thought, he would seek a long talk with Washington Faulconer. Tomorrow he would confront his mistake and put it right. Tomorrow he would begin to straighten himself with man and God. Tomorrow he would be born again, and that idea cheered him and even made him smile, and then he forgot the thought entirely, indeed he let the whole plan of going back to the North slide free of his mind altogether, for there, coming from the Legion's encampment and mounted on a pale horse, was a young stocky man with a square beard and a welcoming smile, and Starbuck, who had been feeling so lonely and so mistreated, galloped madly ahead to greet his friend.

For Adam had come home.

7

The friends met, reined in, both spoke at once, checked, laughed, spoke again, but were each too full of news and the pleasure of reunion to make much sense of the other. "You look weary." Adam at last managed to edge in an intelligible remark.

"I am."

"I must meet Father. Then we'll talk." Adam spurred on toward Washington Faulconer who, the failure of his raid apparently forgotten, was beaming with happiness at his son's return.

"How did you get back?" Faulconer called as his son galloped toward him.

"They wouldn't let me over the Long Bridge at Washington, so I went upriver and paid a ferryman near Leesburg."

"When did you get home?"

"Just yesterday." Adam reined in to receive his father's greeting. It was plain to everyone that Washington Faulconer's happiness was entirely restored. His son had come home, and the uncertainties of Adam's loyalty were thus resolved. The Colonel's pleasure expanded to include and even to seek forgiveness from Starbuck. "I've been distracted, Nate. You must forgive me," he said quietly to Nate when Adam had gone on to greet Murphy, Hinton and Truslow.

Starbuck, too embarrassed by the older man's apology, said nothing.

"You'll join us for dinner at Seven Springs, Nate?" Faulconer had mistaken Starbuck's silence for pique. "I'd take it hard if you refused."

"Of course, sir." Starbuck paused, then bit an unfair bullet.

179

"And I'm sorry if I let you down, sir."

"You didn't, you didn't, you didn't." Faulconer thus hurriedly brushed away Starbuck's apology. "I've been distracted, Nate. Nothing else. I put too many hopes in that raid, and didn't foresee the weather. That was all it was, Nate, the weather. Adam, come!" Adam had spent much of his morning meeting his old friends in the Legion, but his father now insisted on showing his son around the whole encampment one more time, and Adam good-humoredly expressed his admiration of the tent lines and the horse lines, and of the cook house, the wagon park and the meeting tent.

There were now six hundred and seventy-eight volunteers in the camp, almost all of them from within a half day's ride of Faulconer Court House. They had been divided into ten companies, which had then elected their own officers though, as Faulconer cheerfully admitted, a deal of bribery had been needed to make sure that the best men won. "I think I used four barrels of best mountain whiskey," Faulconer confided in his son, "to make sure that Miller and Patterson weren't elected." Each company had selected a captain and two lieutenants, while some had a second lieutenant as well. Washington Faulconer had appointed his own headquarters staff with the elderly Major Pelham as his second in command and the egregious Major Bird as his over-promoted clerk. "I tried to rid us of Pecker, but your mother absolutely insisted," the Colonel confided in Adam. "Have you seen your mother?"

"This morning, sir, yes."

"And is she well?"

"She says not."

"She usually improves when I go away," the Colonel said in a dryly amused voice. "And these are the headquarter tents." Unlike the bell-shaped tents of the infantry companies the four headquarter tents were large wall-sided ridge tents, each equipped with a groundsheet, camp beds, folding stools, washing bowl, jug and a collapsible camp table which folded into a canvas bag. "That's mine." Faulconer gestured at the cleanest tent. "Major Pelham's is next to me. I'll put Ethan and Pecker over there, and you and Nate can share the fourth tent. I guess that will please you?" Adam and Ridley had both been appointed as captains, while Starbuck was the lowest of the low, a second lieutenant, and together the three young men formed what the Colonel called his corps of aides. Their job, he told Adam, was to be his messengers, as well as to serve as his eyes and ears on the battlefield. He made it all sound very ominous.

The Legion consisted of more than just the headquarters staff and ten companies of infantry. There was a band, a medical unit, a color party, a force of fifty cavalrymen who would be led by a captain and serve as the Legion's scouts, and the battery of two bronze six-pounder cannon, both twenty years old and with smoothbore barrels that Faulconer had purchased from Bowers Foundry in Richmond where the guns had gone to be melted down and so made into newer weapons. He proudly showed the pair of guns to his son. "Aren't they marvelous?"

The guns were certainly smart. Their bronze barrels had been buffed to a sun-reflecting dazzle, the wheel spokes and rims were newly varnished, while the guns' accoutrements, the chains and buckets and rammers and wormscrews, had all been variously polished or painted, yet there was something oddly unsettling about the two weapons. They looked too grim for this summer morning, too full of the menace of death.

"They're not the last word in guns." Faulconer took his son's silence for an unspoken criticism. "They're hardly Parrotts, and not even rifled, but I fancy we can strew a few Yankee corpses across the field with these beauties. Ain't that so, Pelham?"

"If we can find some ammunition for them, Colonel." Major Pelham, who was accompanying the Colonel on this inspection tour, sounded very dubious.

"We'll find ammunition!" Now that his son had returned

from the North, the Colonel's ebullient optimism was wholly restored. "Ethan will find us ammunition."

"He's sent none yet," Pelham answered gloomily. Major Alexander Pelham was a tall, thin, white-haired man whom Starbuck, in the days before the raiding party had ridden north and west, had discovered to be almost perpetually morose. Pelham now waited till the Colonel and his son had ridden out of earshot then cocked a rheumy eye at Starbuck. "The best thing that can happen, Lieutenant Starbuck, is that we never find the ammunition for these cannon. The barrels will probably crack apart if we do. Artillery isn't for amateurs." He sniffed. "So the raid went badly?"

"It was disappointing, sir."

"Aye, so I heard from Murphy." Major Pelham shook his head, as though he had known all along that such adventurousness would be doomed. He was dressed in his old United States uniform that he had last worn in the War of 1812—a faded blue tunic with washed-out braid, buttons bereft of their gilt and crossbelts made of leather as cracked as sun-dried mud. His saber was a huge, black-scabbarded hook of a blade. He winced as the band, which had been practicing in the shade of the Legion's meeting tent, started playing "My Mary-Anne." "They've been playing that all week," he grumbled. "Mary-Anne, Mary-Anne, Mary-Anne. Maybe we can drive the Yankees off with bad music?"

"I like the tune."

"Not when you've heard it fifty times, you won't. They should be playing marching tunes. Good solid marches, that's what we need. But how much drill are we doing now? Four hours a day? It should be twelve, but the Colonel won't permit it. You can rest on it that the Yankees won't be playing baseball like us." Pelham paused to spit tobacco juice. He had an almost mystical belief in the necessity of endless drill and was supported in that creed by all the old soldiers in the Legion, and opposed by the Colonel, who still feared that too much

182

close-order drill would dull his volunteers' enthusiasm. "Wait till you've seen the elephant," Pelham said, "then you'll know why you should be drilling."

Starbuck felt his customary response to the idea of seeing the elephant. First there was a pulse of pure fear, as palpable as a chill of liquid pumped from the heart, then there was a surge of excitement that seemed to come from the head rather than the heart, as though sheer resolution could overcome the terror and thus create a vigorous ecstasy from battle. Then came the unnerving knowledge that nothing could be understood, neither the terror nor the ecstasy, until the mystery of battle had been experienced. Starbuck's impatience to understand that mystery was mixed with a desire to delay the confrontation, and his eagerness with a fervent wish that battle would never happen. It was all very confusing.

Adam, released from his father's company, turned his horse back toward Starbuck. "We'll go down the river and have a swim."

"A swim?" Starbuck feared this activity might be a new enthusiasm in Adam's life.

"Swimming is good for you!" Adam's eagerness confirmed Starbuck's fear. "I've been talking with a doctor who claims that soaking in water prolongs life!"

"Nonsense!"

"I'll race you!" Adam kicked back his heels and galloped away.

Starbuck followed more slowly on his already tired mare as Adam led him around the town on paths he had known since childhood and that led eventually to a stretch of parkland which Starbuck assumed was part of the Seven Springs estate. By the time Starbuck reached the river Adam was already undressing. The water was limpid, tree edged and bright in the spring sunshine. "What doctor?" Starbuck challenged his friend.

"He's called Wesselhoeft. I went to see him in Vermont, on mother's behalf, of course. He recommends a diet of brown bread and milk, and frequent immersions in what he calls a *sitz-bad.*"

"A sitting bath?"

"*Sitz-bad* please, my dear Nate. It works better in German, all cures do. I told Mother about Doctor Wesselhoeft and she promises me she'll try each of his specifics. Are you coming in?" Adam did not wait for an answer, but instead leaped naked into the river. He came up shouting, evidently in reaction to the water's temperature. "It doesn't really warm up until July!" he explained.

"Maybe I'll just watch you."

"Don't be absurd, Nate. I thought you New Englanders were hardy?"

"Not foolhardy," Starbuck quipped, and thought how good it was to be back with Adam. They had been apart for months, yet the very first moment they were back together it seemed as if no time had passed at all.

"Come on in, you coward," Adam called.

"Dear God." Starbuck leaped into the cleansing coldness, and came up shouting just as Adam had done. "It's freezing!"

"But good for you! Wesselhoeft recommends a cold bath every morning."

"Does Vermont not provide asylums for the insane?"

"Probably," Adam laughed, "but Wesselhoeft is very sane and very successful."

"I'd rather die young than be this cold every day." Starbuck scrambled up the bank and lay on the grass under the warm sun.

Adam joined him. "So what happened on the raid?"

Starbuck told him, though leaving out the details of Washington Faulconer's moroseness on the return ride. Instead he made the foray into something comical, a chapter of errors in which no one was hurt and no one offended. He finished by saying he did not think the war would get any more serious than the raid had been. "No one wants a real war, Adam. This is America!"

Adam shrugged. "The North isn't going to release us, Nate. The Union's too important to them." He paused. "And to me."

Starbuck did not reply. Across the river a herd of cows grazed, and in the silence the sound of their teeth tearing at the grass was surprisingly loud. Their cowbells were plangent, matching Adam's suddenly ominous mood. "Lincoln called for seventy-five thousand volunteers," he said.

"I heard."

"And the northern papers say that three times that many will be ready by June."

"You're frightened of numbers?" Starbuck asked unfairly.

"No. I'm frightened of what the numbers mean, Nate. I'm frightened of seeing America struck down into barbarism. I'm frightened of seeing fools ride yelling into battle just for the joy of it. I'm frightened of seeing our classmen become the Gadarene swine of the nineteenth century." Adam squinted across the river to where the distant hills were bright with blossoms and new leaf. "Life is so good!" he said after a while, though with a sad intensity.

"People fight to make it better," Starbuck said.

Adam laughed. "Don't be absurd, Nate."

"Why else do they fight?" Starbuck bridled.

Adam spread his hands, as if to suggest there could be a thousand answers, and none of them significant. "Men fight because they're too proud and too stupid to admit they're wrong," he finally said. "I don't care what it takes, Nate, but we've got to sit down, call a convention, talk the whole thing out! It doesn't matter if it takes a year, two years, five years! Talk must be better than war. And what's Europe going to think of us? For years we've been saying that America is the noblest, best experiment of history, and now we're going to tear it apart! For what? For states' rights? To keep slavery?"

"Your father doesn't see it as you do," Starbuck said.

185

"You know Father," Adam said fondly. "He's always seen life as a game. Mother says he's never really grown up."

"And you grew up before your time?" Starbuck suggested.

Adam shrugged. "I can't take matters lightly. I wish I could, but I can't. And I can't take tragedy easily, at least not this tragedy." He waved toward the cows, evidently intending those innocent and motionless beasts to stand for the spectacle of America rushing headlong into warfare. "But what about you?" He turned to Starbuck. "I hear you've been in trouble."

"Who told you?" Starbuck was instantly embarrassed. He stared up at the clouds, unable to meet his friend's gaze.

"My father wrote to me, of course. He wanted me to go to Boston and plead with your father."

"I'm glad you didn't."

"But I did. Except your father wouldn't receive me. I heard him preach though. He was formidable."

"He usually is," Starbuck said, though inwardly he was wondering why Washington Faulconer could possibly want Adam to plead with the Reverend Elial. Was Faulconer wanting to be rid of him?

Adam plucked a blade of grass and shredded it between his square, capable fingers. "Why did you do it?"

Starbuck, who had been lying on his back, suddenly felt ashamed of his nakedness and so rolled onto his belly and stared down at the clover and grass. "Dominique? Lust, I suppose."

Adam frowned, as if the concept was unknown to him. "Lust?"

"I wish I could describe it. Except that it's overwhelming. One moment everything is normal, like a ship in a calm sea, then suddenly this enormous wind comes from nowhere, this enormous, exciting, howling wind and you can't help it, but just sail madly off with it." He stopped, dissatisfied with his imagery. "It's the sirens' song, Adam. I know it's wrong, but you can't help it." Starbuck suddenly thought of Sally

186

Truslow and the memory of her beauty hurt so much that he flinched.

Adam took the flinch as evidence of remorse. "You have to pay back the man Trabell, don't you?"

"Oh, yes. Of course I do." That necessity weighed heavily on Starbuck's conscience, at least when he allowed himself to remember the theft of Major Trabell's money. Until a few hours ago, when he had still been planning his return north, he had convinced himself that he wanted nothing more than to repay Trabell, but now, with Adam home, Starbuck wanted nothing more than to stay in Virginia. "I wish I knew how," he said vaguely.

"I think you should go home," Adam suggested firmly, "and put things straight with your family."

Starbuck had spent the last two days thinking precisely the same thing, though now he demurred from that sensible plan. "You don't know my father."

"How can a man be scared of his own father, yet contemplate going into battle without fear?"

Starbuck smiled quickly to acknowledge the point, then shook his head. "I don't want to go home."

"Must we always do what we want? There is duty and obligation."

"Maybe things didn't go wrong when I met Dominique," Starbuck said, striking obliquely away from his friend's stern words. "Maybe they went wrong when I first went to Yale. Or when I agreed to be baptized. I've never felt like a Christian, Adam. I should never have let Father baptize me. I should never have let him send me to seminary. I've been living a lie." He thought of his prayers at a dead woman's grave, and blushed. "I don't think I've even been converted. I'm not a true Christian at all."

"Of course you are!" Adam was shocked at his friend's apostasy.

"No," Starbuck insisted. "I wish I was. I've seen other men

187

converted. I've seen the happiness in them, and the power of the Holy Spirit in them, but I've never really experienced the same thing. I've wanted to, I've always wanted to." He paused. He could think of no one else to whom he could speak like this, only Adam. Good honest Adam who was like Faithful to John Bunyan's Christian. "My God, Adam," Starbuck went on, "but I've prayed for conversion! I've begged for it! But I've never known it. I think, maybe, that if I was saved, if I was born again, I'd have the strength to resist lust, but I don't and I don't know how to find that strength." It was an honest, pathetic admission. He had been raised to believe that nothing in his whole life, not even his life itself, was as important as the necessity for conversion. Conversion, Starbuck had been taught, was the moment of being born again into Christ, that miraculous instant in which a man allowed Jesus Christ into his heart as his Lord and Savior, and if a man did allow that marvelous ingress to happen, then nothing would ever be the same again because all of life and all of subsequent eternity would be transmuted into a golden existence. Without salvation life was nothing but sin and hell and disappointment; with it there was joy, love and heaven everlasting.

Except Starbuck had never found that moment of mystical conversion. He had never experienced the joy. He had pretended to, because such a pretense was the only way to satisfy his father's insistence on salvation, yet all his life had been a lie since that moment of pretense. "There's something worse," he confessed to Adam now. "I'm beginning to suspect that real salvation, real happiness, doesn't lie in the experience of conversion at all, but in abandoning the whole concept. Maybe I'll only be happy if I can reject the whole paraphernalia?"

"My God," Adam said, horrified at the very idea of such Godlessness. He thought for a few seconds. "I don't think," he went on slowly, "that conversion depends on an outside influence. You can't expect a magical change, Nate. True conversion comes from an inner determination."

"You mean Christ has nothing to do with it?"

"Of course he does, yes, but he's powerless unless you invite him in. You have to unleash his power."

"I can't!" The protest was almost a wail, the cry of a young man desperate to be released from the travails of religious struggle, a struggle that pitted Christ and his salvation against the temptation of Sally Truslow and Dominique and of all the other forbidden and wonderful delights that seemed to tear Starbuck's soul in two.

"You should begin by going home," Adam said. "It's your duty."

"I'm not going home," Starbuck said, utterly ignoring his recent decision to do just that. "I won't find God at home, Adam. I need to be on my own." That was not true. Starbuck, now that his friend had returned to Faulconer Court House, wanted to stay in Virginia because the summer which had looked so threatening under Washington Faulconer's disapproval was suddenly promising to be golden again. "And why are you here?" Starbuck turned the questioning on his friend. "For duty?"

"I suppose so." Adam was uncomfortable with the question. "I suppose we all look for home when things seem bad. And they are bad, Nate. The North is going to invade."

Starbuck grinned. "So we fight them off, Adam, and that will be the end of it. One battle! One short, sweet battle. One victory, and then peace. You'll get your convention then, you'll get everything you want probably, but you have to fight one battle first."

Adam smiled. It seemed to him that his friend Nate existed only for sensation. Not for thought, which Adam liked to think was his own touchstone. Adam believed that the truth of everything, from slavery to salvation, could be adduced by reason, while Starbuck, he realized, was swayed solely by emotion. In some ways, Adam thought with a surprise, Starbuck resembled his father, the Colonel. "I'm not going to

189

fight," Adam said after a long pause. "I won't fight."

It was Starbuck's turn to be shocked. "Does your father know that?"

Adam shook his head, but said nothing. It seemed that he too was wary of a father's disapproval.

"So why did you come home?" Starbuck asked.

Adam was quiet for a long while. "I think," he said at last, "because I knew that nothing I could say would help any longer. No one was listening to reason, only to passion. The people I thought wanted peace turned out to want victory more. Fort Sumter changed them, you see. It didn't matter that no one had died there, the bombardment proved to them that the slave states would never yield to reason, and then they demanded that I add my voice to their demands, and those demands weren't for moderation anymore, but for the destruction of all this." He gestured at the Faulconer domain, at the sweet fields and heavy trees. "They wanted me to attack Father and his friends, and I refused to do it. So I came home instead."

"But you won't fight?"

"I don't think so."

Starbuck frowned. "You're braver than me, Adam, my God you are."

"Am I? I wouldn't have dared run away with a, with a"—Adam paused, unable to find a word delicate enough to describe the very indelicate Dominique—"I wouldn't have dared risk my whole life for a whim!" He made it sound admirable instead of shameful.

"It was nothing but stupidity," Starbuck confessed.

"And you'd never do it again?" Adam asked with a smile, and Starbuck thought of Sally Truslow, and said nothing. Adam plucked a blade of grass and twisted it about his finger. "So what do you think I should do?"

So Adam's mind was not made up after all? Starbuck smiled. "I'll tell you exactly what to do. Just go along with

190

your father. Play at soldiers, enjoy the encampment, have a marvelous summer. Peace will come, Adam, maybe after one battle, but peace will come, and it will be soon. Why ruin your father's happiness? What do you gain by doing that?"

"Honesty?" Adam suggested. "I have to live with myself, Nate."

Adam found living with himself difficult, as Nate well knew. Adam was a stern and demanding young man, especially of himself. He might forgive weakness in others, but not in his own character. "So why did you come back?" Starbuck went on the attack. "Just to raise your father's hopes before disappointing him? My God, Adam, you talk about my duty to my father, what's yours? To preach to him? To break his heart? Why are you here? Because you expect your tenants and neighbors to fight, but think you can sit the battle out because you've got scruples? My God, Adam, you'd have done better to stay in the North."

Adam paused a long time before responding. "I'm here because I'm weak."

"Weak!" That was the last quality Starbuck would have ascribed to his friend.

"Because you're right; I can't disappoint Father. Because I know what he wants, and it doesn't seem such a great deal to give him." Adam shook his head. "He's such a generous man, and he's so often disappointed in people. I really would like to make him happy."

"Then for God's sake put on the uniform, play soldiers and pray for peace. Besides," Starbuck said, deliberately lightening the mood, "I can't bear the thought of a summer without your company. Can you imagine just me and Ethan as your father's aides?"

"You don't like Ethan?" Adam had detected the distaste in Starbuck's voice and seemed surprised by it.

"He seems not to like me. I took fifty bucks off him in a bet and he hasn't forgiven me for it."

"He's touchy about money," Adam agreed. "In fact I some-times wonder if that's why he wants to marry Anna, but that's a very unworthy suspicion, isn't it?"

"Is it?"

"Of course it is."

Starbuck remembered Belvedere Delaney voicing the same suspicion, but did not mention it. "Why does Anna want to marry Ethan?" he asked instead.

"She just wants to escape," Adam said. "Can you imagine life in Seven Springs? She sees marriage as her ticket to free-dom." Adam suddenly leaped to his feet and scrambled to pull on his trousers, his haste occasioned by the approach of a small dog cart that was being driven by Anna herself. "She's here!" Adam warned Starbuck who, like his friend, hurriedly tugged on his pants and shirt and was just pulling on his stockings as Anna reined in. Her cart was escorted by three yapping spaniels that now leaped excitedly at Adam and Star-buck.

Anna, sheltered from the sun by a wide, lace-fringed para-sol, stared reproachfully at her brother. "You're late for din-ner, Adam."

"My Lord, is that the time?" Adam fumbled for his watch among his rumpled clothes. One of the spaniels leaped up and down at him while the other two lapped noisily from the river.

"It doesn't really matter that you're late," Anna said, "because there's been some trouble at the camp."

"What trouble?" Starbuck asked.

"Truslow discovered his son-in-law had joined the Legion while he was away. So he hit him!" Anna seemed very shocked at the violence.

"He hit Decker?"

"Is that his name?" Anna asked.

"What happened to Decker's wife?" Starbuck asked a little too urgently.

"I'll tell you at dinner," Anna said. "Now why don't you

192

finish dressing, Mister Starbuck, then tie your tired horse to the back of the cart and ride home with me. You can hold the parasol and tell me all about the raid. I want to hear everything."

Ethan Ridley took Sally Truslow to Muggeridge's Drapery and Millinery in Exchange Alley where he bought her a parasol in printed calico to match her pale green linen cambric dress. She was also wearing a fringed paisley shawl, yarn stockings, a wide-brimmed hat trimmed with silk lilies, white ankle-length boots and white lace gloves. She carried a small beaded handbag and, in rude contrast, her old canvas bag.

"Let me hold the bag for you," Ridley said. Sally wanted to try on a linen hat with a stiffened brim and a muslin veil.

"Take care of it." Sally gave him the bag reluctantly.

"Of course." The canvas bag was heavy, and Ridley wondered if she did have a gun in there. Ridley himself had a gun at his hip as part of his uniform. He was in the yellow trimmed gray of the Faulconer Legion, with a saber at his left hip and the revolver on his right side.

Sally turned around in front of the cheval mirror, admiring the hat. "It's real nice," she said.

"You look lovely," Ridley said, though in truth he had found her company ever more grating in these last few days. She had no education, no subtlety and no wit. What she had was the face of an angel, the body of a whore, and his bastard in her belly. She also had a desperation to escape the narrow world of her father's cramped homestead, but Ridley was too concerned for his own future to comprehend Sally's plight. He did not see her as attempting to escape from an unbearable past, but as an extortioner trying to gouge a parasitical future. He did not see the fear in her, only the determination to take what she wanted. He despised her. At night, impassioned, he wanted nothing more than to be with her, but by day, exposed to her crude ideas and lacerating voice, he wanted only to be rid of her. And today he would be rid of her, but first it was necessary to lull her into complacency.

He took her to Lascelles Jewelry store on Eighth Street where he listened to the owner's splenetic complaints about the proposal to lay a railroad line directly outside his shop window. The line, which would run down the center of the steep street, was intended to connect the Richmond, Fredericksburg and Potomac rails with the Richmond and Petersburg line so that military supplies could be carried across the city without the need to unload one set of rail wagons into horse-drawn carts. "But have they considered the effect upon trade, Captain Ridley? Have they? No! And who will buy fine jewelry with locomotives smoking outside? It's preposterous!"

Ridley bought Sally a filigree necklace that was flashy enough to please her and cheap enough not to offend his parsimony. He also bought a narrow gold ring, scarce more than a curtain band, which he pushed into his uniform pocket. The purchases, with the parasol and linen hat, cost him fourteen dollars, and the brisket of beef that he bought as dinner in the Spotswood House cost another dollar thirty. He was lulling Sally's apprehensions, and the price was worth it if she went quietly to whatever fate awaited her. He gave her wine to drink with the meal, and brandy afterward. She wanted a cigar and was quite unworried that no other lady in the dining room chose to smoke. "I've always liked a cigar. My ma used a pipe, but I like a cigar." She smoked contentedly, oblivious of the amused stare of the other diners. "This is real nice." She had taken to luxury like a starved cat to a creamery.

"You should get used to this sort of place," Ridley said. He lolled in his chair, an elegantly booted leg propped on the cold radiator that stood beneath the window and looked onto the hotel's courtyard. His scabbarded saber hung from its slings on the radiator's purge valve. "I am going to make you a lady," he lied to her. "I am going to teach you how a lady speaks, how a lady behaves, how a lady eats, how a lady dances, how a lady

194

reads, how a lady dresses. I am going to make you into a great lady."

She smiled. To be a great lady was Sally's dream. She imagined herself in silks and lace, ruling a parlor like the one in Belvedere Delaney's house, no, an even bigger parlor, a vast parlor, a parlor with cliffs for walls and a vaulted heaven for a ceiling and golden furniture and hot water all day long. "Are we really looking for a house this afternoon?" she asked wistfully. "I'm real tired of Mrs. Cobbold." Mrs. Cobbold owned the boardinghouse in Monroe Street and was suspicious of Ridley's relationship with Sally.

"We're not looking for a house," Ridley corrected her, "but a set of rooms. My brother knows some that are for rent."

"Rooms." She was suspicious.

"Large rooms. Tall ceilings, carpets." Ridley waved his hands to suggest opulence. "A place you can keep your own niggers."

"I can have a nigger?" she asked excitedly.

"Two." Ridley embroidered his promise. "You can have a maid and a cook. Then, of course, when the baby comes, you can have a nurse."

"I want a carriage, too. A carriage like that." She gestured through the window at a four-wheeled carriage that had an elegant shell body slung on leather springs and a black canvas hood folded back to reveal an interior of scarlet buttoned leather. The carriage was drawn by four matching bays. A Negro coachman sat on the box while another black, either slave or servant, handed a woman up into the open coach.

"That's a barouche," Ridley told her.

"Barouche." Sally tried the word and liked it.

A tall, rather cadaverous man followed the woman into the barouche. "And that," Ridley told Sally, "is our president."

"The skinny one!" She leaned forward to stare at Jefferson Davis who, his top hat in his hand, was standing in the carriage to finish a conversation with two men who stood on the hotel

195

steps. His business finished, President Davis sat opposite his wife and crammed the glossy hat on his head. "Is that really Jeff Davis?" Sally asked.

"It is. He's staying in the hotel while they find him a house."

"I never thought I'd see a president," Sally said, and watched wide-eyed as the barouche turned in the courtyard before clattering under the arch into Main Street. Sally smiled at Ridley. "You're trying real hard to be nice, aren't you?" she said, as though Ridley had personally arranged for the president of the Provisional Government of the Confederate States of America to parade for Sally's benefit.

"I'm trying real hard," he said, and reached across the table to take hold of her left hand. He drew it toward him and kissed her fingers. "I'm going to go on trying real hard," he said, "so that you'll always be happy."

"And the baby." Sally was beginning to feel motherly.

"And our baby," Ridley said, though the words very nearly stuck in his craw, but he managed to smile, then took the new gold ring out of his pocket, shook it free of its small wash-leather bag and placed it on her ring finger. "You should have a wedding ring," he explained. Sally had started to wear the antique silver ring on her right hand, and her left was consequently bare.

Sally examined the effect of the small gold ring on her finger, then laughed. "Does this mean we're married?"

"It means you should look respectable for a landlord," he said, then took her right hand in his and tugged the silver ring over her knuckle.

"Careful!" Sally tried to pull her hand away, but Ridley kept firm hold.

"I'm going to have it cleaned," he said. He placed the silver ring in the wash-leather bag. "I'll take good care of it," he promised, though in truth he had decided that the antique ring would make a good keepsake to remember Sally by. "Now come!" He glanced at the big clock above the carving table.

196

"We have to meet my brother."

They walked through the spring sunshine and folks thought what a fine couple they made; a handsome southern officer and his beautiful, graceful girl who, flushed with wine, laughed beside her man. Sally even danced a few steps as she imagined what happiness these next months would bring. She would be a respectable lady, with her own slaves and living in luxury. When Sally had been small her mother would sometimes talk about the fine houses of the wealthy and how they had candles in every room and feather mattresses on every bed and ate off golden plates and never knew what the cold was. Their water did not come from a stream that froze in winter, their beds had no lice and their hands were never chipped and sore like Sally's. Now Sally would live just like that. "Robert said I'd be happy if I just stopped dreaming," she confided in her lover, "and if he could see me now!"

"Did you tell him you were coming here?" Ridley asked.

"Of course not! I'm not wanting to see him ever again. Not till I'm a great lady and then I'll let him open my carriage door and he won't even know who I am." She laughed at that fine revenge on her previous poverty. "Is that your brother's coach?"

They had come to the corner of Cary Street and Twenty-fourth. It was a grim quarter of town, close to the York River Railroad that lay between the cobbled street and the rocky riverbank. Ridley had explained to Sally that his brother did business in this part of town, which is why they needed to walk through its streets. Now, on the point of ridding himself of the girl, he felt a pang of remorse. Her company this afternoon had been light and easy, her laughter unforced, and the glances of other men in the streets had been flatteringly jealous. Then Ridley thought of her ambition that was so unrealistic and of the threat she represented, and so he hardened his heart to the inevitable. "That's the carriage," he said, guessing that the big, ugly, close-curtained coach was indeed Delaney's vehicle,

197

though there was no sign of Delaney himself. Instead there was a massive Negro on the box and two gaunt sway-backed horses in the delapidated harness.

The Negro looked down at Ridley. "You Mister Ridley, Massa?"

"Yes." Ridley felt Sally's hands clutch fearfully at his arm.

The Negro knocked twice on the coach roof and the curtained door opened to reveal a thin, middle-aged white man with a gap-toothed grin, dirty hair and a walleye. "Mister Ridley. And you must be Miss Truslow?"

"Yes." Sally was nervous.

"Welcome, ma'am. Welcome." The ugly creature leaped down from the carriage to offer Sally a deep bow. "My name is Tillotson, ma'am, Joseph Tillotson, and I am your servant, ma'am, your most obedient servant." He looked up at her from his bowed position, blinked in astonishment at her beauty and seemed to leer in anticipation as he swept his hand in an elaborate gesture inviting her into the coach's interior. "Be so pleased, dear lady, as to step inside the coach and I shall wave my wand and turn it into a golden carriage fit for a princess as lovely as you." He snuffled with laughter at his own wit.

"This ain't your brother, Ethan." Sally was suspicious and apprehensive.

"We're going to meet him, ma'am, indeed we are," Tillotson said and offered her his grotesque welcoming bow again.

"You're coming, Ethan?" Sally still clung to her lover's arm.

"Of course I am," Ridley reassured Sally, then persuaded her to walk toward the coach as Tillotson folded down a set of steps covered in threadbare carpet.

"Give me your parasol, ma'am, and allow me." Tillotson took Sally's parasol, then handed her up into the dark, musty interior. The coach's windows were covered by leather-blinds that had been unrolled from their spindles and nailed to the bottom sill. Ridley stepped toward the coach, uncertain what to do next, but Tillotson pushed him unceremoniously away,

198

folded up the carriage steps then leapt nimbly into the coach's dark interior. "Got her, Tommy!" he shouted to the driver. "Go on!" He tossed the brand-new parasol into the gutter and slammed the door.

"Ethan!" Sally's voice called in pathetic protest as the big coach lurched forward. Then she called again, but louder. "Ethan!"

There was the sound of a slap, a scream, then silence. The Negro coachman cracked his whip, the carriage's iron-rimmed wheels screeched on the cobbles as the heavy vehicle slewed around the corner, and thus Ridley was rid of his succuba. He felt remorse, for her voice had been so pathetic in that last desperate cry, but he knew there had been no other alternative. Indeed, he told himself, the whole wretched business had been Sally's own fault, for she had made herself into a nuisance, good for one thing only, but now she was gone and he told himself he was well shot of her.

He still held Sally's heavy bag. He pulled it open to find there was no gun inside, just the one hundred silver dollars he had originally paid to bribe her into silence. Each coin had been separately wrapped in a torn sheet of blue sugar paper, as if each was peculiarly special, and for a moment Ridley's heart was touched by that childish tribute, but then he realized that Sally had probably wrapped the coins to stop them chinking and thus attracting predatory attention. Whatever, the coins were now his again, which only seemed right. He tucked the bag under his arm, pulled on his gloves, tipped his uniform hat over his eyes, tugged his saber to a jaunty angle, and sauntered slowly home.

"It seems"—Anna reached across the table for a bread roll that she broke into two, then dipped one half in gravy as a titbit for her noisy spaniels—"that Truslow has a daughter, and the daughter got herself pregnant, so he married her off to some poor boy and now the daughter's run away and the boy's in the Legion, and Truslow is angry."

"Damned angry," her father said in high amusement. "Hit the boy."

"Poor Truslow," Adam said.

"Poor boy." Anna dropped another morsel of bread among her yapping, scrapping dogs. "Truslow broke his cheekbone, isn't that right, Papa?"

"Broke it badly," Faulconer confirmed. The Colonel had managed to repair the ravages imposed on him by the abortive cavalry raid. He had bathed, trimmed his beard and donned uniform so that he once again looked like a dashing soldier. "The boy's called Robert Decker," the Colonel went on, "the son of Tom Decker, you remember him, Adam? Wretched man. He's dead now, it seems, and good riddance."

"I remember Sally Truslow," Adam said idly. "A sullen thing, but real pretty."

"Did you see the girl when you were up at Truslow's place, Nate?" Faulconer asked. The Colonel was trying very hard to be pleasant toward Starbuck to show that the morose disregard of the last few days was over and forgotten.

"I don't remember noticing her, sir."

"You would have noticed her," Adam said. "She's kind of noticeable."

"Well, she's bolted," Faulconer said, "and Decker doesn't know where she's run to, and Truslow's mad at him. Seems he gave the happy couple his patch of land and they've just left it in Roper's care. You remember Roper, Adam? He's living up there now. Man's a rogue, but he knew how to manage horses."

"I don't suppose they were ever properly married." Anna found the plight of the unhappy couple far more interesting than the fate of a freed slave.

"I doubt it very much," her father agreed. "It would have been one quick jump over the broomstick, if they were even that formal."

Starbuck stared down at his plate. Dinner had been a dish of

200

boiled bacon, dried corn pie and fried potatoes. Washington Faulconer, his two children and Starbuck had been the only diners, and Truslow's attack on Robert Decker the only topic of conversation. "Where can the poor girl have gone?" Adam asked.

"Richmond," his father said instantly. "All the bad girls go to Richmond. She'll find herself work," he said, glancing at Anna and making a rueful face, "of a kind."

Anna blushed, while Starbuck was thinking that Ethan Ridley was also in Richmond. "What happens to Truslow?" he asked instead.

"Nothing. He's already full of remorse. I put him in the guard tent and threatened him with ten kinds of hell." In fact Major Pelham had arrested Truslow and done all the threatening, but Faulconer did not think the distinction important. The Colonel lit a cigar. "Now Truslow's insisting that Decker join his company and I suppose I'd better let him. It seems the boy's got relatives in the company. Can't you keep those dogs quiet, Anna?"

"No, Father." She dropped another scrap of gravy-soaked bread into the noisy free-for-all. "And speaking of jumping over broomsticks," she said, "you all missed Pecker's wedding."

"That was a very proper wedding, surely?" her brother said sternly.

"Of course it was. Moss officiated very damply and Priscilla looked almost pretty." Anna smiled. "Uncle Pecker glowered at us all, it poured with rain and Mother sent six bottles of wine as a present."

"Our best wine," Washington Faulconer said stonily.

"How would Mother have known?" Anna asked innocently.

"She knew," Faulconer said.

"And the schoolchildren sang a very feeble song," Anna went on. "When I get married, Father, I do not want the Tompkinson twins singing for me. Is that very ungrateful?"

"You'll get married in St. Paul's, Richmond," her father

said, "with the Reverend Peterkin officiating."

"In September," Anna insisted. "I've talked with Mama, and she agrees. But only if we have your blessing, Papa, of course."

"September?" Washington Faulconer shrugged, as though he did not much mind when the wedding took place. "Why not?"

"Why September?" Adam asked.

"Because the war will be over by then," Anna declared, "and if we leave it later then there'll be bad weather for the Atlantic crossing, and Mother says we need to be in Paris by October at the latest. We'll have a winter in Paris, then go to the German spas in the spring. Mama says you might like to come, Adam?"

"Me?" Adam seemed surprised at the invitation.

"To keep Ethan company while Mama and I take the waters. And to be Mama's escort, of course."

"You can go in uniform, Adam." Washington Faulconer clearly did not resent being left out of the family expedition. "Your mother would like that. Full-dress uniform with saber, sash and medals, eh? Show the Europeans how a southern soldier looks?"

"Me?" Adam asked again, this time of his father.

"Yes, you, Adam." Faulconer tossed his napkin onto the table. "And talking of uniforms, you'll find one in your room. Put it on, then come to the study and we'll fit you out with a saber. You too, Nate. Every officer should carry a blade."

Adam paused and for a second or two Starbuck feared that this was the moment when his friend would make his pacifist stand. Starbuck tensed for the confrontation, but then, with a decisive nod that suggested he had made his choice only after a great effort of will, Adam pushed back his chair. "To work," he said quietly, almost to himself, "to work."

The work proved to be a glorious early summer of drumbeats and drill, of exercises across pastureland and of comradeship in tented encampments. They were hot days of laughter, weariness, sore muscles, tanned skin, high hopes and powder-stained faces. The Legion practiced musketry until the men's shoulders were bruised from the impact of the guns and their faces smeared black by the explosion of the percussion caps and their lips powder stained from biting open the paper-wrapped cartridges. They learned to fix bayonets, to form a firing line and to make a square to fend off cavalry. They began to feel like soldiers.

They learned to sleep through discomfort and discovered the long loping march rhythm that would see a man through endless, sun-racked days on heat-baked roads. On Sundays they formed a hollow square for a service of prayer and hymns. Their favorite was "Fight the Good Fight," while in the evenings, when men were feeling maudlin for their families, they loved to sing "Amazing Grace" very slowly so that the sweet tune lingered in the hot evening air. On other nights of the week groups of men formed Bible classes or prayer meetings, while some played cards or drank the liquor that was sold illegally by peddlers come from Charlottesville or Richmond. Once, when Major Pelham caught such a peddler, he broke the man's entire stock of stone-bottled mountain whiskey, though the Colonel was less inclined to take the hard line. "Let them have their good time," Faulconer liked to say.

Adam feared that his father was trying too hard to be popular, yet in fairness the lenience was all a part of Washington Faulconer's theory of soldiering. "These men aren't European peasants," the Colonel explained, "and they certainly ain't northern factory drudges. These are good Americans! Good southerners! They've got fire in their bellies and liberty in their hearts and if we force them into hours of drill and yet more drill and still more drill we'll simply dull them into witless fools. I want them eager! I want them to go into battle like horses fresh off a spring pasture, not like nags coming off winter hay. I want them full of spirit, élan, the French call it, and it's going to win us this war!"

"Not without drill, it won't," Major Pelham would answer

gloomily. He was allowed to give four hours of drill a day and not a minute more. "I'll warrant Robert Lee is drilling his men in Richmond," Pelham would insist, "and McDowell his in Washington!"

"I warrant they are too, and so they should, just to keep the rogues out of mischief. But our rogues are better quality. They're going to make the best soldiers in America! In the world!" And when the Colonel was in this sublime mood neither Pelham, nor all the military experts in Christendom could have changed his mind.

So Sergeant Truslow simply ignored the Colonel and made his company do the extra drill anyway. At first, when Truslow had come down from his high home in the hills, the Colonel had imagined employing him as one of the fifty cavalrymen who would be the Legion's outriders and scouts, but somehow, after the raid, the Colonel felt less willing to have Truslow so close to headquarters, and so he had let Truslow become company sergeant to Company K, one of the two skirmishing companies, but even from there, on the outer flank of the Legion, Truslow's influence was baleful. Soldiering, he said, was about winning battles, not about holding prayer meetings or hymn singing, and he immediately insisted that Company K triple the amount of time it spent in drill. He had the company out of bed two hours before dawn and, by the time the other companies were just beginning to light their breakfast fires, Company K was already tired. Captain Roswell Jennings, K Company's commanding officer who had secured his election with lavish quantities of homemade whiskey, was happy so long as Truslow did not demand his presence at the extra sessions.

The other companies, seeing the extra snap and pride in Company K, had begun to lengthen their own time on the parade ground. Major Pelham was delighted, the Colonel held his peace, while Sergeant Major Proctor, who had been Washington Faulconer's bailiff, deviled through his drill books to find new and more complicated maneuvers for the rapidly improving Legion to practice. Soon even old Benjamin Ridley, Ethan's father, who had been a militia officer in his younger days, but who was now so fat and ill that he could scarcely walk, grudgingly admitted that the Legion was at last beginning to look like real soldiers.

Ethan Ridley had returned from Richmond with caissons, limbers and ammunition for the two artillery pieces. The Legion was now fully equipped. Each man had a double-breasted gray jacket with two rows of brass buttons, a pair of ankle-high boots, gray trousers and a round cap with a crown and visor stiffened with pasteboard. He carried a knapsack for his spare clothes and personal belongings, a haversack for his food, a canteen for water, a tin cup, a cap box on his belt to hold the percussion caps that fired his rifle, and a cartridge box for the ammunition. His weapons were one walnut-stocked 1841 Model Rifle, a sword-handled bayonet and whatever personal weapons he chose to carry. Nearly all the men carried bowie knives, which they were certain would prove lethal in the hand-to-hand combat they confidently expected. Some men had revolvers, and indeed, as the June days lengthened and the rumors of impending battle intensified, more and more parents provided their soldier sons with revolvers in the belief that the weapon would be a lifesaver in battle.

"What you need," Truslow told his men, "is one rifle, one mug, one haversack, and damn all else." He carried a bowie knife, but only for scavenging and cutting brush. Everything else, he told them, was just weight.

The men ignored Truslow, trusting instead in the Colonel's largesse. Each man was issued an oilcloth groundsheet in which he rolled two gray blankets. Washington Faulconer's only economy was a refusal to buy the Legion any greatcoats. The war, he declared, could not possibly last into the cold weather, and he was not spending his money to provide the men of Faulconer County with churchgoing coats, but only to make a

205

great name for themselves in the history of southern independence. He did provide each man with a sewing kit, towels and a clothes brush, while Doctor Billy Danson insisted that every Legionnaire also carry a roll of cotton strips for bandages.

Major Thaddeus Bird, who had always been fond of long walks and was the only one of Faulconer's officers who resolutely refused to ride a horse, contended that Truslow was right and that the men had been provided with altogether too much equipment. "A man can't march cumbered like a mule," he contended. The schoolmaster was ever ready to express such military opinions, which were just as readily ignored by the Colonel, though as the summer passed a group of younger men found themselves drawn more and more to Bird's company. They would meet in his yard of an evening, sitting on the broken church bench or on stools fetched from the schoolhouse. Starbuck and Adam went frequently, as did Bird's deputy, Lieutenant Davies, and a half dozen other officers and sergeants.

The men would bring their own food and drink. Priscilla would sometimes have prepared a salad or a plate of biscuits, but the real business of the evenings was either to make music or else to raid Bird's jumbled pile of books for passages to read aloud. Then they would argue into the darkness, setting the world to rights as Adam and Starbuck used to do when they were at Yale, though these new evenings of discussion were laced with news and rumors of the war. In western Virginia, where the Colonel's raid had been so damply disappointing, the Confederacy suffered new defeats. The worst was at Philippi where northern forces won a humiliatingly easy victory that the northern newspapers dubbed the "Philippi Races." Thomas Jackson, fearing to be cut off in Harper's Ferry, abandoned the river town, and that event made it seem to the young officers in Faulconer Court House that the North was invincible, but then, a week later, came reports of a skirmish on the seaboard of Virginia where northern troops had sallied inland from a coastal fortress only to be bloodily repulsed in the fields around Bethel Church.

Not all the news was true. There were rumors of victories that never happened and peace talks that never occurred. One day it was announced that the European powers had recognized the Confederacy and that the North was consequently suing for peace, but that turned out to be false even though the Reverend Moss had sworn on a stack of Bibles that it was the gospel truth. Bird was amused by the summer's alarms. "It's just a game," he said, "just a game."

"War is hardly a game, Uncle," Adam chided.

"Of course it's a game, and the Legion is your father's toy and a very expensive one too. Which is why I hope we never get used in battle because then the toy will be broken and your father will be inconsolable."

"Do you really hope that, Thaddeus?" his wife asked. She liked to sit in the garden till dark, but then, because she had taken over sole responsibility for the school, she would go to bed and leave the men to argue by candlelight.

"Of course I hope that," Bird said. "No one in his right mind wants a battle."

"Nate does," Adam said teasingly.

"I said 'in his right mind,'" Bird pounced. "I am careful to be precise with my words, perhaps because I never went to Yale. Do you really want to see battle, Starbuck?"

Starbuck half-smiled. "I want to see the elephant."

"Unnecessarily large, gray, curiously wrinkled and with burdensome droppings," Bird remarked.

"Thaddeus!" Priscilla laughed.

"I hope there's peace," Starbuck amended his wish, "but I am half-curious to see a battle."

"Here!" Bird tossed a book across to Starbuck. "There's an account of Waterloo in there, I think it begins on page sixty-eight. Read that, Starbuck, and you'll be cured of your desire to see elephants."

"You're not curious, Thaddeus?" his wife charged him. She was sewing a flag together, one of the many banners that would be used to decorate the town on the Fourth of July, which was now just two days away and was to be marked by a great gala at Seven Springs. There would be a feast, a parade, fireworks and dancing, and everyone in town was expected to contribute something to the celebration.

"I'm a little curious, of course." Bird paused to light one of the thin, malodorous cigars that he favored. "I have a curiosity about all the extremes of human existence because I am tempted to believe that truth is best manifested in such extremes, whether it be in the excesses of religion, violence, affection or greed. Battle is merely a symptom of one of those excesses."

"I would much rather that you applied yourself to the study of excessive affection," Priscilla said mildly, and the young men laughed. They were all fond of Priscilla and touched by the evident tenderness that she and Bird felt for each other.

The talk drifted on. The yard, which was supposed to supply the schoolmaster with vegetables, had become overgrown with black-eyed Susans and daisies, though Priscilla had made space for some herbs that were pungent in the evening warmth. The back of the yard was bounded by two apple trees and a broken fence beyond which was a meadow and a long view across the wooded foothills of the Blue Ridge Mountains. It was a lovely peaceful place.

"Are you taking a servant, Starbuck?" Lieutenant Davies asked. "Because if so I have to put his name in the servants' book."

Starbuck had been daydreaming. "A servant?"

"The Colonel, in his wisdom," Bird explained, "has decreed that officers may provide themselves with a servant, but only, mark this, if the man is black. No white servants allowed!"

"I can't afford a servant," Starbuck said. "White or black."

"I was rather hoping to make Joe Sparrow my servant," Bird said wistfully, "though unless he blacks his face now, I can't."

"Why Sparrow?" Adam asked. "So you could whistle at each other?"

"Very amusing," Bird was entirely unamused. "I promised Blanche I would keep him safe, that is why, but the Lord only knows how I'm supposed to do that."

"Poor Runt," Adam said. Joe Sparrow, a thin and scholarly sixteen-year-old, was universally known as Runt. He had won a scholarship to the University of Virginia where he was supposed to begin his studies in the fall, but he had broken his mother's heart by joining the Legion. He had been one of the recruits shamed into volunteering by receiving a petticoat. His mother, Blanche, had pleaded with Washington Faulconer to excuse her boy, but Faulconer had been adamant that every young man had a duty to serve. Joe, like many of the men, was a three-month volunteer, and the Colonel had assured Blanche Sparrow that her son would have served his stint by the time his first semester began.

"The Colonel really should have excused him," Bird said. "This war shouldn't be fought by bookish boys, but by men like Truslow."

"Because he's expendable?" one of the sergeants asked.

"Because he understands violence," Bird said, "which we all have to learn to understand if we are to be good soldiers."

Priscilla peered at her stitches in the fading light. "I wonder what happened to Truslow's daughter?"

"Did she ever talk with you, Starbuck?" Bird asked.

"With me?" Starbuck sounded surprised.

"It was just that she asked for you," Bird explained. "On the night that she came here."

"I thought you didn't know her?" Adam said idly.

"I don't. I met her at Truslow's cabin, but not to notice."

209

Starbuck was glad that the dusk hid his blush. "No, she didn't speak to me."

"She asked for you and for Ridley, but of course neither of you was here." Bird checked suddenly, as though aware that he had been indiscreet. "Not that it matters. Did you bring your flute, Sergeant Howes? I was thinking we might attempt the Mozart?"

Starbuck listened to the music, but he could find no joy in it. In these last weeks he felt he had come to an understanding of himself, or at least he had found an equilibrium as his moods had ceased to oscillate between black despair and dizzy hope. Instead he had taken pleasure in the long days of work and exercise, yet now the reminder of Sally Truslow had utterly destroyed his peace. And she had asked for him! And that revelation, so casually made, added new and bone-dry fuel to Starbuck's dreams. She wanted his help, and he had not been here, so had she gone to Ridley? To that goddamned son of a supercilious bitch Ridley?

Next morning Starbuck confronted Ridley. They had hardly spoken in the last few weeks, not out of distaste, but simply because they kept separate friends. Ridley was leader of a small group of hard-riding, hard-drinking young officers who thought of themselves as rakes and daredevils and who despised the men who gathered in Pecker Bird's garden to talk away the long evenings. Ridley, when Starbuck found him, was stretched full-length in his tent, recovering, he said, from a night in Greeley's Tavern. One of his cronies, a lieutenant called Moxey, was sitting on the other bed with his head in his hands, groaning. Ridley similarly groaned when he saw Starbuck. "It's the Reverend! Have you come to convert me? I'm beyond conversion."

"I'd like a word with you."

"Go ahead." Under the sunlit canvas Ridley's face looked a sickly yellow.

"A word alone."

Ridley turned to look at Moxey. "Go away, Mox."

"Don't mind me, Starbuck, I am oblivious," Moxey said.

"He said to go away," Starbuck insisted.

Moxey looked up at Starbuck, saw something hostile in the tall northerner's face, so shrugged. "I am gone. I am vanishing. Goodbye. Oh, my God!" This last was in greeting to the brightness of the morning sun.

Ridley sat up and swung round so that his stockinged feet were on the groundsheet. "Oh, God." He groaned, then groped inside one of his boots where he evidently kept his cigars and matches at night. "You're looking awful grim, Reverend. Does goddamn Pelham want us to march to Rosskill and back? Tell him I'm sick." He lit the cigar, inhaled deeply, then looked up at Starbuck with bloodshot eyes. "Lay your word on me, Starbuck. Do your worst."

"Where's Sally?" Starbuck blurted out the question. He had meant to be altogether more circumspect, but when the moment of confrontation came he could find no words other than the simple, bald question.

"Sally?" Ridley asked, then feigned disbelief. "Sally! Who in the name of God is Sally?"

"Sally Truslow." Starbuck was already feeling foolish, wondering just what obscure yet undeniable passion was driving him to this humiliating enquiry.

Ridley shook his head tiredly, then sucked on the cigar. "Now why in the name of God, Reverend, would you think that I would know the first goddamned thing about Sally Truslow?"

"Because she ran away to Richmond. To you. I know that." Starbuck knew no such thing, but Pecker Bird, pressed hard, had admitted giving Sally the address of Ridley's brother in Richmond.

"She never found me, Reverend," Ridley said. "But what if she had? Would it have mattered?"

Starbuck had no answer to that question. Instead he stood

foolish and uncertain between the folded back flaps of Ridley's tent.

Ridley hawked a gob of spittle that he shot past Starbuck's boots. "I'm interested, Reverend, so tell me. Just what is Sally to you?"

"Nothing."

"So why the hell are you bothering me this early in the goddamned morning?"

"Because I want to know."

"Or is it that her daddy wants to know?" Ridley asked, betraying his first uncertainty of the conversation. Starbuck shook his head and Ridley laughed. "Are you on heat for her, Reverend?"

"No!"

"But you are, Reverend, you are. I can tell, and I'll even tell you what to do about it. Go to Greeley's Tavern in Main Street and pay the tall woman in the taproom ten bucks. She's an ugly cow, but she'll cure your ailments. You got ten bucks left of that fifty you took off me?" Starbuck said nothing and Ridley shook his head, as if despairing of the northerner's common sense. "I ain't seen Sally for weeks. Not for weeks. She's married, I hear, and that was the end of her for me. Not that I ever knew her well, you understand me?" He stressed the question by jabbing the lit end of the cigar at Starbuck.

Starbuck wondered just what he had expected to achieve by this confrontation. A confession from Ridley? An address where Sally might be found? He had made a fool of himself, betraying his own vulnerability to Ridley's mockery. Now, as awkwardly as he had begun the confrontation, he tried to back out of it. "I hope you're not lying to me, Ridley."

"Oh, Reverend, there's so little you understand. Like good manners for a start. You want to accuse me of lying? Then you do it with a sword in your hand, or with a pistol. I don't mind facing you in a duel, Reverend, but I'll be damned if I have to sit here and listen to your goddamn whining and bitching without so much as a mug of coffee inside me. You mind asking my son of a bitch servant to get me some coffee on your way out? Hey, Moxey! You can come back in now. The Reverend and I have finished our morning prayers." Ridley looked up at Starbuck and jerked his head in curt dismissal. "Now go away, boy."

Starbuck went away. As he walked back down the tent lines he heard a mocking burst of laughter from Ridley and Moxey and the sound made him flinch. Oh God, he thought, but he had just made such a fool of himself. Such a goddamned fool. And for what? For a murderer's daughter who just happened to be pretty. He walked away, defeated and disconsolate.

8

Independence Day dawned clear. It promised to be hot, but there was a blessed breeze coming off the hills and the only clouds were wispy, high, and soon gone.

In the morning the Legion cleaned their uniforms. They used wire brushes, button sticks, blacking and soap until their woolen coats and trousers, leather boots and webbing belts were as spotless as honest effort could achieve. They blacked their ammunition pouches, scrubbed their canteens and haversacks, and tried to unwrinkle the pasteboard tops and visors of their forage caps. They polished their belt buckles and hat badges, then oiled the walnut stocks of their rifles until the wood shone. At eleven o'clock, anticipating the girls who would even then be gathering in the grounds of Seven Springs, the companies formed in full uniform and kit. The fifty cavalrymen made an eleventh company that formed ahead of the others, while the two cannon, which had been pulled from the ruts their wheels had made in the long grass and then attached to their limbers, paraded with the regimental band at the rear of the Legion.

The Colonel was waiting at Seven Springs, leaving Major Pelham in temporary command. At five minutes past eleven Pelham ordered the Legion to stand to attention, to order arms, to fix bayonets and then to shoulder arms. Eight hundred and seventy-two men were on parade. They were not the Legion's full strength, but those recruits who were too new to have learned their drill had been sent ahead to Seven Springs where they were employed in nailing strips of red baize to the church benches, which were being used for the communal dinner. Two massive tents had been raised on the south lawn to offer shade

214

to the visitors, and a cook house established close to the stables where a pair of beefs and six hogs were being roasted whole by sweating cooks who had also been seconded from the Legion. The ladies of the town had donated vats of beans, bowls of salad, trays of corn cakes and barrels of dried peaches. There were pones of cornbread, and stands of sweet cured hams, smoked turkey and venison. There was hung beef with apple sauce, pickled cucumbers and, for the children, trays of doughnuts sprinkled with sugar. The teetotalers were provided with lemonade and sweet water from Seven Springs' best well, while the rest had casks of ale and barrels of hard cider brought from the cellar of Greeley's Tavern. There was wine available in the house, though past experience suggested that only a handful of gentry would bother with such a refined beverage. The provisions were generous and the decorations lavish as they always were at Seven Springs on Independence Day, but this year, in an attempt to demonstrate that the Confederacy was the true inheritor of America's revolutionary spirit, Washington Faulconer had been especially munificent.

At eight minutes past eleven Sergeant Major Proctor ordered the Legion to advance and the band, led by the Bandmaster August Little, played "Dixie" as the fifty cavalrymen led the Legion out of the field. The cavalrymen rode with drawn sabers and the companies marched with fixed bayonets. The town was deserted, because the townsfolk had all gone to Seven Springs, but the troops made a fine show as they marched past the flag-hung courthouse, and under the banners strung across the streets, and past the Sparrow's dry goods store that had a fancy window of eight large sheets of plate glass, which had been brought out from Richmond just one year before and were large enough to serve as a giant mirror in which the passing companies could admire their only slightly distorted selves. The march was noisy, not because anyone was speaking, but because the men were still not used to carrying their full kit. Their canteens banged against their bayonets, and their tin cups, hanging

215

off the knapsacks, clanged against their cartridge boxes.

The first spectators were waiting just inside the white gates of the Seven Springs estate. They were mostly children who, equipped with paper flags of the Confederacy, ran alongside the troops as they marched beneath the avenue of live oaks that led from the Rosskill Road to Seven Springs' front door. The Legion did not march all the way to the house but instead struck off the driveway where a gap had been made in the snake fence beyond the trees and so circled the house to approach the flag-decked south lawns through two ever-thickening lines of onlookers who applauded the fine-looking troops. The cavalry, curbing in their excited horses to make them step high, made a particularly noble display as they rode past the reviewing stand on which Washington Faulconer presided with a politician who, until secession, had sat in the United States Congress. Faulconer and the erstwhile congressman were flanked by the Reverend Moss, Judge Bulstrode and Colonel Roland Peny-crake, who was ninety-seven years old and had been a lieu-tenant in George Washington's army at Yorktown. "I don't mind him remembering Yorktown," Washington Faulconer told Captain Ethan Ridley, who was the aide accompanying the Colonel on Independence Day, "but I do wish he didn't keep reminding us at such length." But on this day, of all days, it was churlish to deny the old man his moment of glory.

Adam, dressed in his fine uniform, led the cavalrymen. Major Pelham rode a plump docile mare at the head of the ten companies, while Major Pecker Bird, whose gorgeous uniform had arrived from Richmond to the general amusement of the Legion and chagrin of his brother-in-law, marched on foot at the head of the band. Second Lieutenant Starbuck, who had no real duties this day, rode the mare Pocahontas just behind Major Bird, who made no effort to keep in step with the drum-beat but strolled long-legged and easy just as if he were taking one of his day-long country walks.

Once on the south lawns the cavalry, whose function was

purely decorative this day, galloped once around the makeshift parade ground, then disappeared to place their horses in a paddock. The two guns were unharnessed from their limbers and parked on either side of the reviewing stand in front of which, and before the delighted gaze of nearly three thousand spectators, the Legion went through its maneuvers.

They marched in column of companies, each company four ranks deep, then deployed into a two-ranked line of battle. There was not quite enough space at the flanks of the parade ground for the whole line of battle, but Sergeant Truslow, K Company's sergeant, had the sense to hold his men back, which somewhat spoiled the next display, Pelham's pride, which demonstrated how the Legion would form a square to repel cavalry, though in the end the square was decently enough formed and only a true expert could have detected that one corner of the formation was slightly battered. The officers, all of them except Major Bird on horseback, were corralled in the center of the square where the band played a gloomy version of "Massa in the Cold Cold Ground." The Legion then came out of square to form two columns of companies, the band quickened into "Hail, Columbia," the crowd cheered, the Colonel beamed, and then Captain Murphy, who had appointed himself chief artillerist to the Legion, spurred forward with his gunners.

The two cannon were charged with bags of gunpowder, but without any shot or shell. The Legion possessed none of the new-fangled friction primers with which to ignite the powder, so instead Murphy used two homemade primers constructed from straw tubes filled with grade-one rifle powder. The straws were placed in the touchholes and thence down through holes pierced in the powder bags, then, on a nod from the Colonel, and just as Bandmaster Little finished playing "Hail, Columbia," the gunners applied lit matches to the primers.

There were two glorious bangs, two spears of flame, two boiling clouds of gray-white smoke and a host of startled birds

217

sprang up from the shade trees behind the reviewing stand. The spectators gave a satisfying gasp.

The cannon shots presaged the speeches. Colonel Peny-crake's speech was thankfully brief, for the old man was short of breath, then the erstwhile congressman gave a seemingly interminable peroration after which Washington Faulconer gave a fine, spirited address that first regretted the necessity of war, but then described the nest of northern vipers which, with hissing mouths, flickering tongues and noxious breath, were spreading their reeking poison across the land. "Yet we southerners know how to treat snakes!" The crowd cheered. Even the assembled black slaves, brought by their owners to the annual feast and confined to a small roped enclosure to one side of the assembly, cheered the Colonel's sentiments. The Colonel, whose voice was strong enough to reach across the whole assembly, spoke of the two races that had arisen in America, which races, though sprung from common parentage, had been separated by climate, morals and religion, and had thus grown apart until now, he declared, their ideas of honor, truth and manliness were so different that the two could no longer abide under the same government.

"The northern race must go its own way," the Colonel declared, "while we southerners, who have always been in the forefront of America's fight for Liberty, Truth, Decency and Honor, will keep alive the shining dream of the Founding Fathers. Their sword has passed to us!" And he drew the bright blade presented to his grandfather by Lafayette and the crowd cheered for the idea that they, and not the degenerate, factory-sweated, education-spoilt, Roman-Catholic infested northerners were the real heirs of those great Virginian revolutionaries, George Washington and Thomas Jefferson and James Madison.

The Colonel concluded his remarks by saying he did not think the struggle would be long. The North had blockaded southern ports and the South had responded by forbidding the export of cotton, which meant the great mills of England would inevitably fall silent, and England, he reminded the crowd, would die without the cotton to feed its mills. If the blockade was not lifted then, within weeks, the world's greatest navy would be off the coast of the Confederacy and the Yankees would flee back to their harbors like snakes to their nests. Yet the South must not look to Europe, Faulconer hurried on, nor need it look to Europe, for southern fighting men would see the Yankees off southern soil without European help. Soon, the Colonel said, the Yankees will regret their temerity, for they will be sent packing and running and screaming and hollering. The crowd liked that.

The war would be over within weeks, the Colonel promised, and every man who helped achieve victory would be honored in the new Confederacy whose flag would fly forever among the banners of the nations. That was the cue for the Legion's flags to be brought forward and presented. And, astonishingly, the Colonel's wife had stirred herself out of her sickroom to be the donor of the two colors.

Miriam Faulconer proved to be a thin, black-haired woman with a very pale face in which her eyes seemed unnaturally large. She was dressed in a purple silk so dark that it appeared almost black, and had a dark, semitransparent veil falling from her hat. She walked very slowly, so that some of the spectators thought she must surely falter before she reached the reviewing stand. She was accompanied by her daughter and by the six ladies of the town who had been chiefly responsible for sewing the two heavy banners of gorgeously fringed silk that would now be the battle flags of the Faulconer Legion.

The first flag was the new Confederate flag. It had three broad horizontal stripes, the upper and lower ones red and the center stripe white, while the upper quadrant by the staff displayed a blue field on which were sewn seven white stars to represent the first seven states to secede. The second color was an adaptation of the Faulconer coat of arms and displayed

219

three red crescents on a white field, with the family's motto, "Forever Ardent," embroidered in letters of funereal black silk along its bottom edge.

The band, having no formal national anthem to play, kept silent, all except the drummers, who tapped a solemn beat as the colors were brought forward. Adam, appointed head of the color party, stepped forward to receive the flags accompanied by the two men chosen to be the standard bearers. One was Robert Decker, whose mended face was marvelously earnest as he advanced beside Adam, while the other was Joe "Runt" Sparrow, who took the Faulconer flag after it had first been handed by Anna to her brother. Adam shook the folds out of the silk, then gave the flag to Joe Sparrow, who seemed almost overwhelmed by the weight of the heavy banner. Then Miriam Faulconer, assisted by the ladies, handed forward the yellow-fringed Confederate flag. For a moment Adam looked reluctant to take it from his mother, then he stepped back and passed the flag to Robert Decker who proudly raised the new color high.

The spectators gave a cheer that died rather raggedly as the crowd realized that the Reverend Moss, who had been waiting patiently all day, now offered his prayer of blessing. The prayer was so long that some of the spectators thought that Joe Sparrow would surely keel over before the invocation was done. Worse, the smell of the roasting meat was ever more tantalizing, yet still Moss insisted on calling the Almighty's attention to the Legion, to its two flags, to its officers, and to the foe whom Moss prayed would be smitten mightily by the Legion. He might have gone on for even longer had he not paused for a deep breath, which gave old Colonel Penycrake a chance to intervene with a surprisingly loud amen, which was so soundly echoed by the crowd that Moss was forced to let the rest of his prayer go unspoken. The Colonel, unable to let the moment pass without a final word, shouted that the Legion would bring the colors home just as soon as the

220

Yankees were roundly whipped. "And that won't be long! By Jiminy it won't be long!" And the crowd cheered and even the Colonel's Negro servants cheered while the band struck up Dixie.

The Colonel then paraded the colors in front of the Legion, letting each man see the two flags close up, and afterward, it already being near to two o'clock and one of the beefs already smelling more like a burnt offering than a dinner, Judge Bulstrode administered the Oath of Confederate Loyalty, which the men pronounced in loud, confident voices, and then, thus sworn to their brand-new country, they gave three cheers for the Colonel and his wife and, the hurrah given, the Legionnaires were ordered to open ranks, stack arms, unsling knapsacks and were so dismissed to their food.

Adam led Starbuck toward the open-sided tent where the guests of honor were seated. "You have to meet Mother."

"Do I really?" The pale, dark-robed Miriam Faulconer looked rather formidable.

"Of course you do." Adam stopped to greet Major Pelham's elderly sister, a tall dignified spinster whose faded clothes spoke of the hardship she endured to keep up appearances, then he and Starbuck touched their hats to the erstwhile congressman's wife, who complained how much she regretted leaving Washington's sophisticated society for the more homely surroundings of Richmond, and then at last Adam was able to draw Starbuck forward to the tent where his mother held court amidst her attendant ladies. Miriam Faulconer was enthroned in a high-backed upholstered chair brought from the house while the pale and timid-looking Anna sat at her side in a much smaller chair and cooled her mother's face with a fan made from filigreed ivory. "Mother," Adam said proudly, "this is my friend Nate Starbuck."

The big eyes, so oddly luminous under the deep shade of the dark purple hat, looked up at Starbuck. He guessed

Adam's mother had to be at least forty years old, yet, to Starbuck's astonishment, she appeared hardly a day over twenty. Her skin was as smooth, white and clear as a child's, her mouth was wide and full, her eyes strangely sad, and her gloved touch, in Starbuck's nervous hand, as light as a songbird's bones. "Mister Starbuck," she said in a very soft and breathy voice. "You are welcome."

"Thank you, ma'am. This is an honor."

"To meet me? I think not. I am a most insignificant person. Am I not insignificant, Anna?"

"Of course not, Mama. You are the most significant person here."

"I can't hear you, Anna, speak up."

"I said you are significant, Mother."

"Don't shout!" Miriam Faulconer flinched from her daughter's scarcely audible voice, then looked up at Starbuck again. "I am afflicted with ill health, Mister Starbuck."

"I am sorry to hear that, ma'am."

"Not so close, Anna." Mrs. Faulconer gestured the fan away from her cheek, then pushed the veil fully back from the brim of her hat. She looked, Starbuck thought guiltily, very beautiful and very vulnerable. No wonder that a young Washington Faulconer had fallen in love with this village girl, daughter of Rosskill's postmaster, and married her despite his parents' opposition. She was a rare thing, fragile and lovely, and rarer still when Starbuck tried to imagine her as Miriam Bird, sister to the prickly Thaddeus. "Do you like it in Virginia, Mister Starbuck?" Miriam Faulconer asked in her sibilant, quiet voice.

"Yes, ma'am, very much. Your husband has been very kind to me."

"I'd forgotten how Washington can be kind," Miriam Faulconer said softly, so softly that Starbuck was forced to lean down to hear her small voice. The still air under the tent's awning smelt of newly cut grass, eau de cologne and

222

camphor, the last, Starbuck supposed, rising from the stiff folds of Miriam Faulconer's purple dress, which must have been drenched in the liquid as a repellent for moths. Starbuck, uncomfortably close to Mrs. Faulconer, marveled that anyone's skin could be so white and smooth. Like a corpse, he thought. "Adam tells me you are a very good friend to him." The corpse spoke softly.

"I am most proud of that opinion, ma'am."

"Is friendship more important than filial duty?" There was a cat's claw of nastiness in the question.

"I am not competent to judge," Starbuck said in defensive politeness.

"Closer, Anna, closer. You wish me to die of the heat?" Miriam Faulconer licked her pale lips, her big eyes still on Starbuck. "Have you ever considered a mother's distress, Mister Starbuck?"

"My mother likes to remind me of it constantly, ma'am." Starbuck gave a swipe of his own claw back. Miriam Faulconer just gazed unblinking, weighing Starbuck and not seeming to like her judgment.

"Not so close, Anna, you will scratch me." Miriam Faulconer pushed her daughter's fan a half inch farther away. She wore a black-stoned ring on one slender finger, intriguingly worn outside the black lace glove. She had a necklace of black pearls and a brooch of carved jet was pinned to the heavy folds of dark purple silk. "I think," Miriam Faulconer said to Starbuck with an undeniable note of dislike in her voice, "that you are an adventurer."

"Is that such a bad thing to be, ma'am?"

"It is usually a selfish thing."

"Mother ..." Adam intervened.

"Be quiet, Adam, I have not asked for your opinion. Closer, Anna, bring the fan closer. Adventurers cannot be relied upon, Mister Starbuck."

"I am sure, ma'am, that there have been many great and

223

reliable men who did not shirk from adventure. Our own Founding Fathers, indeed?"

Miriam Faulconer ignored Starbuck's words. "I shall hold you responsible for my son's safety, Mister Starbuck."

"Mother, please ..." Adam again tried to intervene.

"If I require your contribution, Adam, be assured I shall ask you for it, and until then be so good as to stay quiet." The claws were out now, bright and sharp. "I do not want you, Mister Starbuck, leading my son into adventures. I would have been happy had he pursued his pacific ventures in the north, but it seems that the belligerent party has won his soul. That party, I think, includes you, and I do not thank you for it. So be assured, Mister Starbuck, that I shall hold you and my husband jointly responsible for my son's safety."

"I am honored by your trust, ma'am." At first Starbuck had thought this woman a vulnerable, pitiful beauty, now he thought her a bitter witch.

"I am pleased to have seen you," Mrs. Faulconer said in much the same tone she might have used to express some mild satisfaction at having seen a strange beast in a traveling menagerie, then she looked away and a radiant smile came to her face as she reached both hands toward Ethan Ridley. "My dear Ethan! I just knew Washington would keep you from me, but you're here at last! I have been talking with Mister Starbuck and am consequently in need of some diversion. Come and sit here, take Anna's chair."

Adam drew Starbuck away. "Dear Lord, I am so sorry," he said. "I know she can be difficult, but I don't know why she chose today of all days."

"I'm used to it," Starbuck said. "I have a mother too." Though Starbuck's mother was nothing like the soft-spoken and thin Miriam Faulconer. Jane Abigail MacPhail Starbuck was a tall, fleshy, loud-spoken woman who was large in everything except the generosity of her spirit.

"Mother's often in pain." Adam still wanted to make

224

excuses for his mother. "She suffers from something called neuralgia."

"So Anna told me."

Adam walked in silence, looking down at the ground, and at last shook his head. "Why do women have to be so difficult?" He asked it so wanly that Starbuck could not help bursting into laughter.

Adam's gloom did not last long for he was being reunited with old friends from all across the county, and he was soon leading a troop of young people in the various amusements that had been laid out in Washington Faulconer's park. There were archery butts with straw men targets dressed in striped clothes and top hats, supposedly representing Yankees, and any man who signed up as a recruit could fire a Model 1841 rifle at one of the Yankee dummies. If such a recruit put a bullet clean through one of the targets pinned to a straw man's chest he received a silver dollar. There were water-filled horse troughs where the children could duck for apples, a steeple-chase for officers and challengers, tugs-of-war between the ten infantry companies and a ganderpull.

"Ganderpull?" Starbuck asked.

"You don't have ganderpulls in Boston?" Adam asked.

"No, we have civilization instead. We have things called libraries and churches, schools and colleges ..."

Adam hit his friend, then skipped out of retaliatory range. "You'll enjoy a ganderpull. You hang up a goose, grease its neck with butter, and the first person who manages to pull the bird's head off gets to take the body home for supper."

"A live goose?" Starbuck was horrified.

"It would be too easy if it were dead!" Adam said. "Of course it's alive!"

But before any of these diversions could be tasted the two friends had to go to the summerhouse where a pair of photographers had set up their chairs, tripods, frames and processing wagons. The two men, specially brought out from

Richmond at Washington Faulconer's expense, were charged with taking a picture of any man in the Legion who wanted his portrait made. The pictures, printed within ornate borders, would make keepsakes for the families left behind and mementoes for the men themselves in the long years ahead. The officers could have their portraits printed as *cartes de visite*, a fashionable conceit that appealed hugely to Washington Faulconer, who was first into the photographer's chair. Adam was next.

The process was long and complicated. Adam was seated in a high-backed chair that held at its rear a metal frame into which his head was pushed. The frame, hidden by his hair and cap, would keep his head perfectly still. His saber was drawn and put into his right hand and a pistol into his left. "Do I really have to look so pugnacious?" he asked his father.

"It's the fashion, Adam. Besides, one day you'll be proud of this picture."

The Legion's twin colors were arrayed behind Adam who then, stiff and awkward, stared into the photographer's machine as the sweating assistant dashed out of the wagon and into the summerhouse with the wet glass plate. The plate was put into the camera, Adam was told to take a deep breath and hold it, then the cover was whipped off.

Everyone in the room held their breath. A fly buzzed round Adam's face, but a second assistant waved a towel to drive it away.

"If you must," the photographer told Adam, "you can breathe out, but very slowly. Take care not to move your right hand."

It seemed an age, but at last Adam could relax as the glass plate was reshrouded in its wooden box and rushed off to the wagon for development. Starbuck was then positioned in the frame, his skull painfully inserted in the metal jaws and he too was caparisoned with saber and pistol, and instructed to hold his breath as the wet glass plate was exposed inside the big wooden camera.

Adam immediately began to make faces over the photographer's shoulder. He grimaced, squinted, blew out his cheeks and waggled his fingers in his ears until, to his delight, Starbuck began laughing.

"No, no, no!" The photographer was distraught and slammed a cover over the plate. "It may not have been exposed long enough," he complained, "you will look like a ghost," but Starbuck rather liked that spectral thought and had no need of a *carte de visite*, let alone a keepsake, and so he wandered off through the crowd, eating on a hunk of bread and pork while Adam went to ready his horse for the steeplechase. Ethan Ridley was expected to win the race, which carried a generous fifty-dollar purse.

Sergeant Thomas Truslow had been playing bluff with a group of his cronies, but now stirred himself to watch as the horses thumped past on their first circuit of the steeplechase course. "I've got money on the boy," he confided in Starbuck. "Billy Arkwright, on the black." He pointed toward a skinny boy riding a small black horse. The boy, who looked scarce a day over twelve, was trailing a field of officers and farmers whose horses seemed to sail over the big fences before they turned out to the country for the second time around. Ridley was comfortably in front, his chestnut jumping surely and scarcely winded after the first circuit, while Billy Arkwright's horse seemed too delicate to keep up, let alone survive the long second time around.

"You look as if you've lost your money," Starbuck said happily.

"What you know about horses, boy, I could write in the dust with one bladderful of weak piss." Truslow was amused. "So who would you put your money on?"

"Ridley?"

"He's a good horsemen, but Billy'll beat him." Truslow

watched as the horsemen disappeared into the country, then shot Starbuck a suspicious look. "I hear you were asking Ridley about Sally."

"Who told you that?"

"The whole goddamn Legion knows, because Ridley's been telling them. You think he knows where she is?"

"He says not."

"Then I'd be obliged if you let sleeping bitches lie," Truslow said grimly. "The girl's gone, and that's all there is to it. I'm shot of her. I gave her a chance. I gave her land, a roof, beasts, a man, but nothing of mine was ever good enough for Sally. She'll be in Richmond now, making her living, and I daresay it'll be a good living until she crawls back here scabbed with the pox."

"I'm sorry," Starbuck said, because he could think of nothing else to say. He was just glad that Truslow had not asked why he had confronted Ridley.

"There's no harm done," Truslow said, "except that the damned girl took my Emily's ring. I should have kept it. If I don't die with that ring in my pocket, Starbuck, then I won't find my Emily again."

"I'm sure that's not true."

"I'm sure of it." Truslow stubbornly stuck to his superstition, then nodded to the left. "There, what did I tell you?" Billy Arkwright was three lengths ahead of Ethan Ridley, whose mare was now lathered with sweat. Ridley was slashing with his whip at the mare's laboring flanks, but Arkwright's small-boned black was comfortably ahead and stretching its lead. Truslow laughed. "Ridley can kick the belly out of that horse, but she won't go no faster. There ain't another step in her. Go on, Billy-boy! Go on, boy!" Truslow, his money won, turned away even before the race finished.

Arkwright won by five lengths, going away, and after him a weary stream of muddied men and horses galloped

228

home. Billy Arkwright received his purse of fifty dollars, though what he really wanted was to be allowed to join the Legion. "I can ride and shoot. What more do you want, Colonel?"

"You'll have to wait for another war, Billy, I'm sorry."

After the steeplechase there were four ganderpulls. The birds were hung on a high beam, their necks were greased, and one by one the young people ran and leaped. Some missed entirely, others caught hold of a neck but were defeated by the butter, which made the geese necks slippery, while some were struck by a gander's sharp beak and went off sucking blood, but eventually the birds died and their heads were ripped free. The crowd cheered as the blood-drenched winners walked away with their plump prizes.

The dancing began at nightfall. Two hours later, when it was fully dark, the fireworks crackled and blazed above the Seven Springs estate. Starbuck had drunk a lot of wine and felt mildly tipsy. After the fireworks the dancing began again with an officers' cotillion. Starbuck did not dance, but instead found himself a quiet shadow under a tall tree and watched the dancers circle beneath the moth-haunted paper lanterns. The women wore white dresses garlanded with red and blue ribbons in honor of the day's festival while the men were in gray uniform and their sword scabbards swung as they turned to the music's lilt.

"You're not dancing," a quiet voice said.

Starbuck turned to see Anna Faulconer. "No," he said.

"Can I lead you into the dance?" She held out a hand. Behind her the windows of Seven Springs were lit with celebratory candles. The house looked very beautiful, almost magical. "I had to escort Mother to bed," Anna explained, "so I missed the entrance."

"No, thank you." Starbuck ignored her outstretched hand, which invited him into the cotillion.

"How very ungallant of you!" Anna said in hurt reproof.

"It is not a lack of gallantry," Starbuck explained, "but an inability to dance."

"You can't dance? People don't dance in Boston?"

"People do, yes, but not my family."

Anna nodded her comprehension. "I can't imagine your father leading a dance. Adam says he's very fierce."

"He is, yes."

"Poor Nate," Anna said. She watched Ethan Ridley put his hand into the fingers of a tall lithe beauty, and a look of puzzled sadness showed briefly on her face. "Mother was unkind to you," she said to Starbuck, though she still watched Ridley.

"I am sure she did not mean to be."

"Are you?" Anna asked pointedly, then shrugged. "She thinks you are luring Adam away," Anna explained.

"To war?"

"Yes." Anna at last looked away from Ridley and stared up into Starbuck's face. "She wants him to stay here. But he can't, can he? He can't stay safe at home while other young men go to face the North."

"No, he can't."

"But Mother doesn't see that. She just thinks that if he stays at home he can't possibly die. But I can see how a man couldn't live with that." She looked up at Starbuck, her eyes glossed by the lantern light, which oddly accentuated her small squint. "So you have never danced?" she asked. "Truly?"

"I've never danced," Starbuck admitted, "not one step."

"Perhaps I could teach you to dance?"

"That would be kind."

"We could start now?" Anna offered.

"I think not, thank you."

The cotillion ended, the officers bowed, the ladies curtseyed and then the couples scattered across the lawn. Captain Ethan Ridley offered his hand to the tall girl, then walked

230

her to the tables where he courteously bowed her to her seat. Then, after a brief word with a man who looked like the girl's father, he turned and searched the lantern-lit lawns until he saw Anna. He crossed the lawn, ignored Starbuck, and offered his fiancée an arm. "I thought we might go for supper?" Ridley suggested. He was far from drunk, but neither was he entirely sober.

But Anna was not ready to go. "Do you know, Ethan, that Starbuck can't dance?" She asked not out of any mischief, but simply for something to say.

Ridley glanced at Starbuck. "That doesn't surprise me. Yankees aren't much good for anything. Except preaching, maybe." Ridley laughed. "And marrying. I hear he's good at marrying people."

"Marrying people?" Anna asked, and as she spoke Ridley seemed to understand that his tongue had run away with him. Not that he had any chance to retract or amend the statement, for Starbuck had lunged past Anna to seize hold of Ridley's crossbelt. Anna screamed as Starbuck yanked Ridley hard toward him.

A score of men turned toward the scream, but Starbuck was oblivious of their interest. "What did you say, you son of a bitch?" he demanded of Ridley.

Ridley's face had gone pale. "Let go of me, you ape."

"What did you say?"

"I said let go of me!" Ridley's voice was loud. He fumbled at his belt where a revolver was holstered.

Adam ran toward the two men. "Nate!" He took Starbuck's hand and gently pried it free. "Go, Ethan," Adam said and slapped Ridley's hand away from the revolver. Ridley lingered, evidently wanting to prolong the confrontation, but Adam snapped his command more sharply. The altercation had been swift, but dramatic enough to send a frisson of interest through the big crowd around the dancing lawn.

Ridley stepped back. "You want to fight that duel, Reverend?"

"Go!" Adam showed a surprising authority. "Too much drink altogether," he added in a voice loud enough to satisfy the curiosity of the spectators. "Now go!" he said again to Ridley, and watched as the tall man strode away with Anna on his arm. "Now what was that about?" Adam demanded of Starbuck.

"Nothing," Starbuck said. Washington Faulconer was frowning from the far side of the lawn, but Starbuck did not care. He had found himself an enemy and was astonished by the pure hardness of the hate he felt. "Nothing at all," he nevertheless insisted to Adam.

Adam refused to accept the denial. "Tell me!"

"Nothing. I tell you, nothing." Except that Ridley evidently knew that Starbuck had performed a travesty of a marriage service for Decker and Sally. That service had stayed a secret. No one in the Legion knew. Truslow had never talked of what had happened that night, nor had either Decker or Starbuck, yet Ridley knew of it, and only one person could have told him, and that person was Sally. Which meant that Ridley had lied when he swore he had not seen Sally since her marriage. Starbuck turned on Adam. "Will you do something for me?"

"You know I will."

"Persuade your father to send me to Richmond. I don't care how, but just find a job for me there and make him send me."

"I'll try. But tell me why, please."

Starbuck walked a few paces in silence. He remembered feeling something like this during the painful nights when he had waited outside the Lyceum Hall in New Haven, desperate for Dominique to appear. "Suppose," he finally said to Adam, "that someone had asked for your help and you had promised to give it, and then you found reason to believe that person was in trouble. What would you do?"

"I'd help, of course," Adam said.

"So find me a way of reaching Richmond." It was madness, of course, and Starbuck knew it. The girl meant nothing to him, he meant nothing to her, yet once again, just as he had in New Haven, he was ready to throw his whole life on a chance. He knew it was a sin to pursue Sally as he did, but knowing he toyed with sin made it no easier to resist. Nor did he want to resist. He would pursue Sally whatever the danger, because, so long as there was a sliver of a chance, even a chance no bigger than a firefly's glow in the eternal night, he would take the risk. He would take it even if it meant destroying himself in the pursuit of it. That much, at least, he knew about himself, and he rationalized the stupidity by thinking that if America was set on destruction then why should Starbuck not indulge in the same joyous act? Starbuck looked at his friend. "You're not going to understand this," he said.

"Try me, please?" Adam asked earnestly.

"It is the pure joy of self-destruction."

Adam frowned, then shook his head. "You're right. I don't understand. Explain, please."

But Starbuck just laughed.

In the event a trip to Richmond was easily arranged, though Starbuck was forced to wait for ten long days until Washington Faulconer found his reason to make a journey to the state capital.

The reason was glory, or rather the threat that the Legion would be denied its proper part in the glorious victory that would seal Confederate independence. Rumors, which seemed confirmed by newspaper reports, spoke of imminent battle. A Confederate army was gathering in the northern part of Virginia to face the federal army assembled in Washington. Whether the southern concentration of forces was meant as a preparation for an attack on Washington or whether it was gathering to defend against an expected Yankee invasion, no one knew, but one thing was certain: the Faulconer Legion had not been summoned to the gathering of the host.

"They want all the glory for themselves," Washington Faulconer complained, and declared that the infernal jackanapes in Richmond were doing everything possible to thwart the Legion's ambitions. Pecker Bird remarked privately that Faulconer had been so successful in keeping his regiment free of the state's intervention that he could hardly now complain if the state kept their fighting free of Washington Faulconer's interference, yet even Bird wondered whether the Legion was to be deliberately kept out of the war for, by the middle of July, there was still no summons from the army and Faulconer, knowing that the time had come to humble himself before the hated state authorities, declared he would go to Richmond himself and there offer the Legion to the Confederacy's service. He would take his son with him.

"You don't mind if Nate comes, do you?" Adam asked.

"Nate?" Faulconer had frowned. "Wouldn't Ethan be more useful to us?"

"I would be grateful if you took Nate, Father."

"Whatever." Faulconer found it hard to resist any of Adam's requests. "Of course."

Richmond seemed strangely empty to Starbuck. There were still plenty of uniformed men in the city, but they were mostly staff officers or commissary troops, for most of the fighting men had been sent northward to the rail junction at Manassas where Pierre Beauregard, a professional soldier from Louisiana and the hero of Fort Sumter's bloodless fall, was gathering the Army of Northern Virginia. Another smaller Confederate force, the Army of the Shenandoah, was assembling under General Joseph Johnston, who had taken over the command of the rebel forces in the Shenandoah Valley, but Faulconer was eager that the Legion should join Beauregard, for Beauregard's Army of Northern Virginia was closer to Washington and thus, in Faulconer's opinion, more likely to see action.

"Is that indeed what he believes?" Belvedere Delaney asked. The attorney had been delighted when a nervous Starbuck, presuming upon his one brief meeting with the attorney, called at Delaney's Grace Street rooms on the evening of his arrival in Richmond. Delaney insisted he stay for supper. "Write a note to Faulconer. Say you've met an old friend from Boston. Say he's enticed you to a Bible class at the First Baptist Church. That's an entirely believable excuse and one that no one will ever want to explore. My man will deliver the note. Come inside, come inside." Delaney was in the uniform of a Confederate captain. "Take no notice of it. I am supposed to be a legal officer in the War Department, but truly I wear it only to stop the bloodthirsty ladies enquiring when I intend to lay down my life for Dixie. Now come inside, please."

Starbuck allowed himself to be persuaded upstairs into the comfortable parlor where Delaney apologized for the supper. "It will only be mutton, I fear, but my man does it with a delicate vinegar sauce that you will enjoy. I must confess that my greatest disappointment in New England was the cooking. Is it because you have no slaves and thus must depend on wives for your victuals? I doubt I ate one decent meal all the time I was in the North. And in Boston! Dear Lord above, but a diet of cabbage, beans and potatoes is scarcely a diet at all. You are distracted, Starbuck."

"I am, sir, yes."

"Don't 'sir' me, for God's sake. I thought we were friends. Is it the prospect of battle that distracts you? I watched some troops throw away their dice and packs of playing cards last week! They said they wanted to meet their Maker in a state of grace. An Englishman once said that the prospect of being hanged next morning concentrates a man's mind wonderfully, but I'm not sure it would make me throw away my playing

235

cards." He brought Starbuck paper, ink and a pen. "Write your note. Will you drink some wine as we wait for supper? I hope so. Claim to be immersed in Bible study." Starbuck eschewed the wilder part of Delaney's fancy, merely explaining to Washington Faulconer that he had met an old friend and would therefore not be at Clay Street for supper.

The note was sent and Starbuck stayed to share Delaney's supper, though he proved a poor companion for the plump, sly attorney. The night was hot and very little breeze came past the gauze sheets that were stretched across the open windows to keep the insects at bay, and even Delaney seemed too listless to eat, though he did keep up a lively if one-sided conversation. He asked for news of Thaddeus Bird and was delighted to hear that the schoolmaster was a constant irritation to Washington Faulconer. "I should have dearly liked to have been at Thaddeus's wedding, but alas, duty called. Is he happy?"

"He seems very happy." Starbuck was almost too nervous to make conversation, but he tried hard. "They both seem happy."

"Pecker is an uxorious man, which makes her a lucky girl. And of course Washington Faulconer opposed the marriage, which suggests it might be a good match for Pecker. So tell me what you think of Washington Faulconer? I want to hear your most salacious opinions, Starbuck. I want you to sing for your supper with some intriguing gossip."

Starbuck eschewed the gossip, instead offering a conventional and admiring opinion of Faulconer, which left Delaney entirely unconvinced. "I don't know the man well, of course, but he always strikes me as empty. Quite hollow. And he so desperately wants to be admired. Which is why he freed his slaves."

"Which is admirable, surely?"

"Oh to be sure"—Delaney was deprecating—"except that the proximate cause of the manumission was some interfering woman from the North who was far too pious to reward Faulconer with her charms, and the poor fellow has spent the ten years since trying to persuade his fellow Virginian landowners that he isn't some dangerous radical. In truth he's just a little rich boy not quite grown up, and I'm not at all sure there's anything under that glossy exterior except a superfluity of money."

"He's been good to me."

"And he'll go on being good to you so long as you admire him. But after that?" Delaney picked up a silver fruit knife, and mimicked the action of slitting his throat. "Dear sweet God, but this night is hot," he leaned back in his chair and stretched his arms wide. "I did some business in Charleston last summer and took supper at a house where every place at table was provided with a slave whose job was to fan our brows. That sort of behavior is a bit overripe for Richmond, more's the pity." He chattered on, talking of his travels in South Carolina and Georgia while Starbuck picked at the mutton, drank too much wine, tried a little of the apple pie, and finally pushed his plate away.

"A cigarette?" Delaney suggested. "Or a cigar? Or do you still refuse to smoke? You're quite wrong in that refusal. Tobacco is a great emollient. Our Heavenly Father, I think, must have intended everything on earth to be of specific use to mankind and so he gave us wine to excite us, brandy to inflame us and tobacco to calm us. Here." Delaney had crossed to his silver humidor, cut the stem of a cigar and handed it to Starbuck. "Light it, then tell me what ails thee." Delaney knew that something extraordinary must have driven Starbuck to this desperate visit. The boy looked almost feverish.

Starbuck allowed himself to be persuaded to take the cigar, as much as anything else by the promise that tobacco was a soothing agent. His eyes stung from the smoke, he half-choked on the bitter taste, but he persisted. To have done less

237

would have been to show himself less than a grown man and, on this night when he knew he was behaving like a half-grown youth, he needed the trappings of adulthood. "Do you think," he asked as an elliptic introduction to the delicate matter that had brought him to Delaney's door, "that the devil also put some things on earth? To snare us?"

Delaney lit a cigarette, then smiled knowingly. "So who is she?"

Starbuck said nothing. He felt such a fool, but some irresistible compulsion had driven him to this foolishness, just as it had compelled him to destroy a career for the sake of Dominique Demarest. Washington Faulconer had told him that such destructive obsessions were a disease of young men, but if so it was a disease that Starbuck could neither cure nor alleviate, and now it was driving him to make a fool of himself before this clever lawyer, who waited so patiently for his answer. Starbuck still paused, but at last, knowing that procrastination would serve no longer, he admitted his quest. "Her name is Sally Truslow."

Delaney offered the faintest, most private of smiles. "Do go on."

Starbuck was actually trembling. The rest of America was poised at the edge of battle, waiting for that terrible moment when a schism would be ripped into a gulf of blood, but all he could do was quiver for a girl he had met but for one lame evening. "I thought she might have come here. To these rooms," he said lamely.

Delaney blew a long plume of smoke that rippled the candles on the polished dining table. "I smell something of my brother here. Tell me all."

Starbuck told all, and the telling seemed pathetic to him, as pathetic as that far off day when he had confessed his foolishness to Washington Faulconer. Now he limpingly talked of a promise made in a dusky night, of an obsession he could not properly describe and could not justify and could not really

238

account for, except to say that life would be nothing unless he could find Sally.

"And you thought she might be here?" Delaney asked with friendly mockery.

"I know she was given this address," Starbuck said pointedly.

"And so you came to me," Delaney said, "which was wise. So what do you want of me?"

Starbuck looked across the table. To his surprise he had smoked the cigar down to an inch-long stub, which he now abandoned with the mangled remains of his pie. "I want to know if you can tell me how to find her," he said, and he thought how futile this quest was, and how demeaning. Somehow, before he arrived in this elegant room, Starbuck had believed that his search for Sally was a practical dream, but now, faced with confessing his obsession to this man who was a virtual stranger, Starbuck felt utterly foolish. He also sensed the hopelessness of searching for one lost girl in a town of forty thousand people. "I'm sorry," he said, "but I should never have come here."

"I seem to remember telling you to seek my help," Delaney reminded him, "though admittedly we were both quite drunk at the time. I'm glad you came."

Starbuck stared at his benefactor. "You can help me?"

"Of course I can help you," Belvedere Delaney said very calmly. "In fact I know exactly where your Sally is."

Starbuck felt the elation of success and the terror of confronting that success to discover it was a sham. He felt as if he were at the very edge of a chasm and he did not know whether it was to heaven or to hell that he would leap. "So she's alive?" he asked.

"Come to me tomorrow evening," Delaney said in oblique answer, then held up a hand to check any further questions. "Come here at five. But—" He said the last word warningly.

"Yes?"

Delaney pointed his cigarette across the table. "You will owe me a debt for this, Starbuck."

Starbuck shivered despite the warmth. A soul was sold, he suspected, but for what coin? But nor did he really care because tomorrow night he would find Sally. Perhaps it was the wine, or the heady tobacco fumes, or else the thought of all his dreams coming to a resolution, but he did not care. "I understand," he said carefully, understanding nothing.

Delaney smiled and broke the spell. "Some brandy? And another cigar, I think." It would be amusing, Delaney thought, to corrupt the Reverend Elial Starbuck's son. Besides, if Delaney was honest, he rather liked Nathaniel Starbuck. The boy was naive, but there was steel inside him and he had quick wits even if those wits were presently obliterated by desire. Starbuck, in short, might be useful one day, and if that usefulness was ever needed Delaney would be able to call in the debt that he was forging this night out of a young man's obsession and desperation.

For Delaney was now an agent of the North. A man had come to his chambers, posing as a client, and there produced a copy of Delaney's letter offering to spy for the North. The copy had been burned, and the sight of the burning paper had sent a shiver of nerves through Delaney's soul. From now on he knew himself to be a marked man, liable to the death penalty, yet still the rewards of that loyalty to the North were worth the risk.

And the risk, he knew, could be very short-lived. Delaney did not believe the rebellion could last even to the end of July. The North's new army would roll majestically across the pathetic rebel forces gathered in northern Virginia, secession would collapse and the southern politicians would then whimper that they had never meant to preach rebellion anyway. And what would become of the little people betrayed by those politicians? Starbuck, Delaney supposed, would be sent back to his ghastly hellhound of a father and that would be the end

240

of the boy's one adventure. So let him have a last, exotic moment to remember his whole dull life through and if, perchance, the rebellion did last a few months more, why, Starbuck would be an ally whether he wanted to be or not. "Tomorrow night, then," Delaney said mischievously, then raised his brandy glass, "at five."

Starbuck spent the next day in a torment of apprehension. He dared not tell Washington Faulconer what irked him, he dared not even tell Adam, but instead he kept a feverish silence as he accompanied father and son to the Mechanics Hall in Franklin Street where Robert Lee had his offices. Lee had now been promoted from head of Virginia's forces to be the Confederate president's chief military adviser, yet he still retained much of his state work and was, Faulconer was told, gone from the capital to inspect some fortifications that guarded the mouth of the James River. A harassed clerk, sweating in the outer office, said that the general was expected back that afternoon, or maybe next day, and no, it was not possible to make any appointment. All petitioners must wait. At least a score of men were already waiting on the landing or on the wide stairs. Washington Faulconer bristled at being lumped as a petitioner, but somehow kept his patience as the clock ticked and the clouds gathered dark over Richmond.

At a quarter to five Starbuck asked if he might leave. Faulconer turned angrily on his aide, as though about to refuse permission, but Starbuck blurted out an excuse of not feeling well. "My stomach, sir."

"Go," Faulconer said irritably, "go." He waited until Starbuck had gone down the stairs, then turned on Adam. "What the hell is the matter with him? It isn't his stomach, that's for sure."

"I don't know, sir."

"A woman? That's what it looks like. He's met an old friend? Who? And why doesn't he introduce us? It's a whore, I tell you, a whore."

"Nate doesn't have the money," Adam said stiffly.

"I wouldn't be so certain." Washington Faulconer walked to the window at the end of the landing and stared gloomily into the street where a tobacco wagon had lost a wheel and a crowd of Negroes had gathered round to offer the teamster advice.

"Why wouldn't you be certain, Father?" Adam asked.

Faulconer brooded for a moment, then turned on his son. "You remember the raid? You know why Nate disobeyed my orders? So that Truslow could steal from the passengers in the cars. Good Lord, Adam, that's not warfare! That's brigandry, pure and simple, and your friend condoned it. He risked the success of all we had achieved to become a thief."

"Nate isn't a thief!" Adam protested vigorously.

"And I trusted him with matters here in Richmond," Washington Faulconer said, "and how am I to know if his accounting was fair?"

"Father!" Adam said angrily. "Nate is not a thief."

"And what did he do to that *Tom* company fellow?"

"That was ..." Adam began, but then did not know how to continue, for it was certain that his friend had indeed stolen Major Trabell's money. "No, Father." Adam persisted in his stubborn denial, though a lot more weakly.

"I just wish I could share your certainty." Faulconer looked gloomily down at the landing floor that was stained with dried tobacco juice that had missed the spittoons. "I'm not even sure any longer that Nate belongs here in the South," Faulconer said heavily, then looked up as a clatter of boots and a murmur of voices sounded in the downstairs hall.

Robert Lee had arrived at last, and Starbuck's character could be momentarily forgotten so that the Legion could be offered for battle.

George, Belvedere Delaney's house slave, had conducted Starbuck as far as the front door of the house in Marshall Street

242

where he had been greeted by a middle-aged woman of stern looks and apparent respectability. "My name is Richardson," she had told Starbuck, "and Mister Delaney has given me his full instructions. This way, sir, if you would."

It was a whorehouse. That much an astonished Starbuck realized as he was escorted through the hallway and past an open parlor door beyond which a group of girls sat dressed in laced bodices and white underskirts. Some smiled at him, others did not even look up from their hands of cards, but Starbuck faltered as he understood what trade was carried on in this comfortable, even luxurious house with its dark rugs, papered walls and gilt-framed landscapes. This was one of the dens of iniquity against which his father preached the awful threat of everlasting torture, a place of hellish horrors and unbridled sins, where a varnished hall stand with brass hooks, an umbrella tray and a beveled mirror held three officers' hats, a silk top hat and a cane. "You may stay as long as you like, young man," Mrs. Richardson said, pausing beside the hall stand to pass on Delaney's instructions, "and there will be no charge. Please be careful of the loose stair rod."

Mrs. Richardson led Starbuck up a stairway that was papered in flock and lit by a fringed oil lamp that hung on a long brass chain suspended from the stairwell's high ceiling. Starbuck was in uniform and his scabbarded saber clattered awkwardly against the banisters. A curtained arch waited at the top of the stairs and beyond it the light was even dimmer, though not so dim that Starbuck could not see the framed prints on the wall. The pictures showed naked couples and at first he did not believe what he saw, then he looked again and blushed for what he did indeed see. A stern part of his conscience instructed him to turn back now. For all of his life Starbuck had struggled between sin and righteousness and he knew, better than any man, that the wages of sin were death, yet if all the choirs of heaven and all the preachers of earth had bellowed that message into his ears Starbuck could not have turned back at that moment.

He followed the black-dressed Mrs. Richardson down the long passage. A Negro maid carrying a cloth-covered bowl on a tray came the other way and stood aside to let Mrs. Richardson pass, then grinned cheekily at Starbuck. Some voices laughed in a nearby room, while from another a man's voice gasped excitedly. Starbuck felt light-headed, almost as if he was going to faint as he followed Mrs. Richardson around a corner and down a short flight of steps. They turned yet another corner, climbed a second short stair and then at last Mrs. Richardson brought out her ring of keys, selected one and pushed it into the door's lock. She paused, then turned the key to push open the door. "Go in, Mister Starbuck."

Starbuck went nervously into the room. The door closed behind him, the key turned in the lock, and there was Sally. Alive. Sitting in a chair with a book in her lap and looking even more beautiful than he had remembered her. For weeks he had tried to conjure that face in his dreams, but now, faced with the reality of her beauty again, he realized how inadequate those conjurations had been. He was overwhelmed by her.

They stared at each other. Starbuck did not know what to say. His saber scabbard scraped dully against the door. Sally was wearing a dark blue robe and her hair was gathered in heavy loops on top of her head and tied with pale blue ribbons. There was a fresh scar on her cheek, which did not make her any less beautiful, but oddly made her more fascinating. The scar was a white streak that slashed off her left cheekbone toward her ear. She stared at him, seemingly as surprised as he was nervous, then she closed the small book and put it on the table beside her. "It's the preacherman!" She sounded pleased to see him.

"Sally?" Starbuck's voice was uncertain. He was as nervous as a child.

"I'm Victoria now. Like the queen?" Sally laughed. "They

244

gave me a new name, see? So I'm Victoria." She paused. "But you can call me Sally."

"They lock you in?"

"That's just to keep the customers out. Sometimes the men run wild, at least, the soldiers do. But I ain't a prisoner. I got a key, see?" She pulled a key out of her robe pocket. "And I mustn't say *ain't*. Mrs. Richardson doesn't like it. She says I mustn't say *ain't* and I mustn't say *nigger* neither. It ain't nice, see? And she's teaching me to read as well." She showed her book to Starbuck. It was a McGuffey's *Reading Primer*, the very first in the series and a book that Starbuck had disposed of when he was three years old. "I'm getting real good," Sally said enthusiastically.

Starbuck wanted to weep for her. He did not really know why. She looked well, she even sounded happy, yet there was something pathetic about this place that made him hate the whole world. "I was worried about you," he said lamely.

"That's nice." She gave him a half smile, then shrugged. "But I'm doing fine, real fine. Except I'll bet that piece of shit Ethan Ridley didn't worry about me?"

"I don't think he does, no."

"I'll see him in hell." Sally sounded bitter. A rumble of thunder sounded above the city, followed a moment later by the heavy sound of rain falling. The new drops twitched the tight-stretched gauze insect curtains that were pinned across the two open windows. It was dusk and summer lightning flickered pale across the western sky. "We've got wine," Sally said, reverting to cheerfulness, "and some cold chicken, see? And bread. And these are sugar fruits, see? And nuts. Mrs. Richardson said I was getting a special visitor and the girls brought all this up here. They can look after us real well, see?" She stood and crossed to one of the open windows, staring past the gauze at the ashen sheets of lightning that flickered in the gathering darkness. The summer air was heavy and sultry, suffused with Richmond's tobacco smell that filled

245

Sally's large room which, to Starbuck's innocent eye, looked distressingly ordinary, rather like a well-furnished hotel bedroom. It had a small coal grate in a black metal fireplace, a brass fender, flowered wallpaper and framed mountain landscapes on its walls. There were two chairs, two tables and a scatter of rugs and the ubiquitous spittoons on the polished wood floor. There was also a wide bed with a carved hardwood headpiece and a heap of white pillows. Starbuck tried hard not to look at the bed while Sally still gazed through the gauze at the western horizon where the lightning stuttered. "I sometimes look over there and I think of home."

"Do you miss it?"

She laughed. "I like it here, preacherman."

"Nate, call me Nate."

She turned from the window. "I always wanted to be a fine lady, see? I wanted everything nice. My Ma used to tell me about a real nice house she once went to. She said it had candles and pictures and soft rugs and I always wanted that. I hated living up there. Up at four in the morning and hauling water and always so cold in winter. And your hands were always sore. Bleeding even." She paused and held up her hands, which now were white and soft, then she took a cigar from a jar on the table where the food had been placed. "You want a smoke, Nate?"

Starbuck crossed the room, cut the cigar, lit it, then took one for himself. "How did you find me?" Sally asked.

"I went to Ethan Ridley's brother."

"That Delaney? He's a strange one," Sally said. "I like him, I think I like him, but he's not like Ethan. I tell you, if I see Ethan again, I swear I'll kill the son of a bitch. I don't care if they hang me, Nate, I'll kill him. Mrs. Richardson swears that he won't be allowed to see me if he comes here, but I hope he does. I hope that son of a bitch comes in here and I'll stick him like a hog on a slab, so I will." She sucked on the cigar, making its tip glow a brilliant red.

"What happened?" Starbuck asked.

She shrugged, sat in a chair by the window and told how she had come to Richmond to find Ethan Ridley. For three or four days he had seemed friendly, even kind to her, but then he had told her they were going in a carriage to look at some rooms he planned to rent for her. Except there were no rooms, only two men who had carried her off to a cellar in the eastern end of the city and there they had beaten her, raped her and beaten her again until she had learned to be obedient. "I lost the baby," she said bleakly, "but they wanted that, I reckon. I mean I wasn't any good to them pregnant, not here." She waved around the room, hinting at her new trade. "And of course, he arranged it."

"Ridley?"

Sally nodded. "He had it all arranged. He wanted rid of me, see? So he had two men take me. One was a nigger, I mean a black, and the other used to be a slave trader, see, so they knew how to break people like my pa used to break horses." She shrugged and turned toward the window. "I guess I needed breaking, too."

"You can't say that!" Starbuck was appalled.

"Oh, honey!" Sally smiled at him. "How the hell am I to get what I want in this world? You give me that answer? I ain't born to money, I ain't educated for money, all I got is what men want." She drew on the cigar, then took a glass of wine from Starbuck. "A lot of the girls here started that way. I mean they have to be broken in. It ain't nice, and I don't care if I never see those two men again, but I'm here now, and I'm mended."

"They scarred you?"

"Hell, yes." She touched her left cheek. "Ain't too bad, though, is it? They did other things. Like if I wouldn't open my mouth? They had this machine they use on slaves who won't speak. It goes round your head and has a piece of iron here." She demonstrated by jabbing the cigar toward her lips,

247

then shrugged. "That could hurt. But all I had to do was learn to be good and they stopped using it."

Starbuck was filled with inchoate indignation. "Who were the two men?"

"Just men, Nate. It don't matter." Sally made a dismissive gesture, as though she did not really blame them for what had happened. "Then after a month Mister Delaney came to the house and he said he was real shocked at what was happening to me, and he said it was all Ethan's fault, and Mrs. Richardson came as well, and they took me away and made a real fuss of me and brought me here, and Mrs. Richardson said I didn't really have much of a choice any longer. I could stay here and make money or they'd put me back on the street. So here I am."

"You could go home, surely?" Starbuck suggested.

"No!" Sally was vehement. "I don't want to be at home, Nate! Father always wanted me to be a boy. He reckons everyone should be happy with a log house, two hunting dogs, an axe and a long rifle, but that ain't my dream."

"Do you want to go away?" Starbuck asked her. "With me?"

She smiled pityingly at him. "How are we going to do that, honey?"

"I don't know. Just leave here. Walk north." He gestured toward the darkening sky that was filled with a new hard rain, and even as he made the suggestion he knew it was hopeless.

Sally laughed at the very thought of walking away from Mrs. Richardson's house. "I've got what I want here!"

"But ..."

"I've got what I want," she insisted. "Listen, people ain't no different to horses. Some are special, some are workers. Mrs. Richardson says I can be special. She don't waste me on every customer, only the special ones. And she says I can leave here if a man wants me and can pay for me proper. I mean I can leave anyway, but where am I going to go? Look at me!

I've got dresses and wine and cigars and money. And I won't do this forever. You see the carriages go by with the rich folks? Half those women started like me, Nate!" She spoke very earnestly, then laughed when she saw his unhappiness. "Now listen. Take off that sword, sit down proper, and tell me about the Legion. Make me real happy and tell me Ethan has shot himself. You know that son of a bitch took my Ma's ring? The silver ring?"

"I'll get it back for you."

"No!" She shook her head. "Ma wouldn't want that ring in this place, but you can get it for Pa." She thought for a second, then smiled wanly. "He loved my Ma, you know, he really did."

"I know. I saw him at her grave."

"Course you did." She took a crystalized cherry and bit it in half, then tucked her legs up onto the chair. "So why did you call yourself a preacherman? I often wondered about that."

So Starbuck told her about Boston and the Reverend Elial Starbuck and the big dark brooding house on Walnut Street that always seemed filled with the dangerous silences of parental anger and the smell of wax and wood oil and Bibles and coal smoke. Darkness fell over Richmond, but neither Starbuck nor Sally moved to light a candle, instead they talked of childhood and of broken dreams and how love always seemed to trickle through the fingers when you thought you had a grasp of it.

"It was when Ma died that everything went wrong for me," Sally said, then she gave a long sigh and turned in the darkness to look at Starbuck. "So you reckon you'll stay here? In the South?"

"I don't know. I think so."

"Why?"

"To be near you?" He said it easily, like a friend, and she laughed to hear it. Starbuck leaned forward, his elbows propped on his long legs and wondered about the real truth of his answer. "I don't know what I shall do," he said softly. "I know I'm not going to be a preacher now, and I don't really know what else I can be. I could be a schoolteacher, I guess, but I'm not really sure I want to do that. I'm no good at business, at least I don't think I am, and I don't have the money to become a lawyer." He paused, drawing on his third cigar of the evening. Delaney had been right, it was soothing.

"So what are you going to sell, honey?" Sally asked ironically. "I've been taught real good what I have to sell, so what about you? No one looks after us for nothing, Nate. I learned that. My Ma might have done that for me, but she's dead, and my Pa." She shook her head. "All he wanted was for me to be a cook and a hog slaughterer and a fowl keeper and a farmer's woman. But that ain't me. And if you ain't a lawyer or a preacherman or a teacher, then what in hell's name are you going to be?"

"That." He gestured at the discarded saber that was propped in its cheap scabbard against the windowsill. "I'm going to be a soldier. I'm going to be a very good soldier." It was strange, he thought, but he had never said this before, not even to himself, but suddenly it all made such sense. "I'm going to be famous, Sally. I'm going to ride through this war like a, like a ..." He paused, seeking the right word, then suddenly a bout of thunder cracked overhead, shaking the very house, and at the same instant a bolt of lightning sizzled through the Richmond sky like white fire blazing. "Like that!" Starbuck said. "Just like that."

Sally smiled. Her teeth looked very white in the darkness, and her hair, when the sheet lightning blanched the night, reflected like dark gold. "You won't get rich being a soldier, Nate."

"No, I guess I won't at that."

"And I'm expensive, honey." She was only half teasing him.

250

"I'll find the money somehow."

She stirred in the dark, stubbing out her cigar and stretching her slender arms. "They've given you tonight. I don't know why, but I guess Mister Delaney likes you, right?"

"I think he does, yes." Starbuck's heart was thumping in his chest. He thought how very naive he had been about Delaney, then how much he owed Delaney, and then how little he knew about Delaney. How blind he had been, he thought, how trusting. "Does Delaney own this place?" he asked.

"He has a bit of it, I don't know how much. But he's given you tonight, honey, all night, right till breakfast, and after that?"

"I said I'll find the money." Starbuck's voice was choked and he was trembling.

"I can tell you how to earn it forever. For as long as you and I still want it." Sally spoke soft in the darkness and the rain drummed on the street and on the roof.

"How?" It was a miracle Starbuck could speak at all, and even so the word came out like a croak. "How?" He said it again.

"Kill Ethan for me."

"Kill Ethan," Starbuck said as though he had not heard her correctly, and as though he had not spent these last days persuading himself that Ethan was his enemy and fantasizing a young man's dreams of how he would destroy his enemy. "Kill him?" he asked in dread.

"Kill that son of a bitch for me. Just kill him for me." Sally paused. "It ain't that I mind being here, Nate, in fact it's probably the best place for me, but I hate that son of a bitch for telling me lies, and I hate that he thinks he got away with telling me lies, and I want that son of a bitch dead and I want the last thing he hears on this earth to be my name so he don't ever forget why he's gone to hell. Will you do that for me?"

Dear God, Starbuck thought, but how many sins were here brought into one foul bundle? How many entries would the

251

Recording Angel be making in the Lamb's Book of Life? What hope of redemption was there for a man who would contemplate murder, let alone commit it? How wide the gates of hell gaped, how searing the flames would be, how agonizing the lake of fire, and how long would all eternity stretch if he did not stand now, fetch his sword, and walk out from this den of iniquity into the cleansing rain. Dear God, he prayed, but this is a terrible thing, and if you will just save me now then I will never sin again, not ever.

He looked into Sally's eyes, her lovely eyes. "Of course I'll kill him for you," he heard himself saying.

"You want to eat first, honey? Or later?"

Like a slash of lightning, white across the sky, he would be marvelous.

Part Three

9

Orders came from Richmond that directed the Legion to the rail junction at Manassas where the rails of the Orange and Alexandria met the Manassas Gap line. The orders did not arrive till three days after Washington Faulconer had returned from Richmond, and even then the permission seemed grudging. The order was addressed to the commanding officer of the Faulconer County Regiment, as though the Richmond authorities did not want to dignify Washington Faulconer's achievement in raising the Legion, but at least they were allowing the Legion to join General Beauregard's Army of Northern Virginia as Faulconer had requested. General Lee had enclosed a curt note regretting that it was not in his power to attach the "Faulconer County Regiment" to any one particular corps in Beauregard's army, indeed he took care to note that, because the regiment's availability had been made known to the authorities at such short notice and because the regiment had undertaken no brigade training of any kind, he doubted whether it could be used for anything other than detached duties. Washington Faulconer rather liked the sound of such duties until Major Pelham dryly noted that detached duties usually meant serving as baggage guards, railroad sentries or prisoner of war escorts.

If Lee's note was calculated to pique Washington Faulconer, it succeeded, though the Colonel declared it was no more than he expected from the mudsills in Richmond. General Beauregard, Faulconer was certain, would prove more welcoming. Faulconer's greatest concern was to reach Manassas before the war ended. Northern troops had crossed the Potomac in force

255

and were said to be slowly advancing toward the Con-federate Army, and rumor in Richmond claimed that Beauregard planned to unleash a massive encircling move that would crush the northern invaders. The rumors added that if such a defeat did not persuade the United States to sue for peace, then Beauregard would cross the Potomac and capture Washington. Colonel Faulconer dreamed of riding his black charger, Saratoga, up the steps of the unfinished Capitol Building and in the fulfillment of that dream he was willing to swallow the worst of Richmond's insults, and thus the day after the arrival of the churlish order the Legion was woken two hours before dawn with orders to strike the tent lines and load the baggage wagons. The Colonel anticipated a swift march to the rail depot at Rosskill, yet somehow everything took much longer than anyone expected. No one seemed entirely certain how to disassemble the eleven giant cast-iron camp stoves that Faulconer had bought, nor had anyone thought to order the Legion's ammunition to be fetched out of its dry storage at Seven Springs.

News of the move also provoked the mothers, sweethearts and wives of the soldiers to bring one last gift to the encampment. Men who were already laden down with haversacks, weapons, knapsacks, blankets and cartridge boxes were given woolen scarves, coats, capes, revolvers, bowie knives, jars of preserves, sacks of coffee, biscuits and buffalo robes, and all the time the hot sun rose still higher and the camp stoves were still not disassembled, and one of the wagon horses cast a shoe, and Washington Faulconer fumed, Pecker Bird cackled at the confusion and Major Pelham had a heart attack.

"Oh, good Christ!" It was Little, the bandmaster, who had been complaining to Pelham that there was not enough wagon space for his instruments when suddenly the elderly officer made an odd clicking noise in his throat, gasped one huge, despairing breath inward, then toppled from his saddle. Men dropped whatever they were doing to gather round the thin motionless body. Washington Faulconer spurred toward the gawking spectators and waved them back with his riding crop. "Back to your duties! Back! Where the hell's Doctor Danson? Danson!"

Danson arrived and stooped over the still form of Pelham, then declared him dead. "Out like a candle!" Danson struggled to his feet, putting his trumpet-stethoscope back into a pocket. "Damned good way to go, Faulconer."

"Not today, it isn't. Damn you! Back to work!" He pointed his riding crop at a staring soldier. "Go on, away with you! Who the hell's going to tell Pelham's sister?"

"Not me," Danson said.

"Goddamn it! Why couldn't he have died in battle?" Faulconer turned the horse. "Adam! Duty for you!"

"I'm supposed to be going to the Rosskill depot, sir."

"Ethan can go."

"He's fetching the ammunition."

"Damn Rosskill! I want you to go to Miss Pelham. My best regards to her, you know what to say. Take her some flowers. Better still, fetch Moss on your way. If a preacher isn't any good with the bereaved, then what the hell use is he?"

"You want me to go to Rosskill afterward?"

"Send Starbuck. You tell him what to do." Starbuck had not been in the Colonel's best books since the night in Richmond when he had stayed out till well past breakfast and had then refused to say where he had been. "Not that you need to be told what he's been doing," the Colonel had grumbled to his son that morning, "because it stands out a mile, but he might have the decency to tell us who she is."

Now Nate was ordered to ride to the Rosskill depot of the Orange and Alexandria Railroad and tell the depot manager to prepare for the Legion's arrival. Faulconer, who was a director of the railroad, had already sent a letter that, in anticipation of the orders from Richmond, had required two trains to be prepared for the Legion's journey, but someone now had to ride to

257

the depot and order the engineers to fire up their boxes and so raise steam. One train would consist of the railroad director's car, which was reserved for Faulconer and his aides, and sufficient second-class passenger cars to carry the Legion's nine hundred and thirty-two men, while the second train would consist of boxcars for supplies and horses, and open wagons for the Legion's wagons, cannon, limbers and caissons. Adam handed Starbuck a copy of his father's letter and a copy of the written orders that had been dispatched to the depot manager at dawn. "Roswell Jenkin's company is supposed to be there by eleven, though God knows if they'll be ready by then. They're going to make ramps."

"Ramps?"

"To get the horses into the wagons," Adam explained. "Wish me luck. Miss Pelham is not the easiest of women. Dear God."

Starbuck wished his friend good luck, then saddled Pocahontas and trotted her out of the chaotic encampment, through the town and down the Rosskill road. The town, which held the nearest railroad depot to Faulconer County, was twice the size of Faulconer Court House and had been built where the foothills finally gave way to the wide plain that stretched to the distant sea. It was an easy downhill ride. The day was hot and the cows in the meadows were either standing under shade trees or else up to their bellies in the deep cool streams. The roadside was bright with flowers, the trees heavy with leaf, and Starbuck was happy.

He had a letter to Sally in his saddlebag. She had wanted him to send her letters and he had promised to write as often as he could. This first letter told of the last days of training and of how the Colonel had given him the mare, Pocahontas. He had kept the letter simple, the words short and the letters big and round. He had told Sally how he loved her, and he guessed that was true, but it was a strange kind of love, more like a friendship than the destructive passion he had felt for Dominique.

Starbuck was still jealous of the men Sally would lie with, as any man surely should be jealous, but Sally would have none of his jealousy. She needed his friendship as he needed hers, for they had come together in the thunder-riven night like two lonely children needing comfort, and afterward, lying happily in the bed where they had smoked cigars and listened to the dawn rain, they had agreed to write, or rather Starbuck had agreed to write and Sally had promised she would try to read his letters and one day she would even try to write back so long as Starbuck promised on his honor not to laugh at her efforts.

He stopped at the Rosskill post office and sent the letter, then rode on to the depot, where the manager was a plump, sweating man named Reynolds. "There are no trains," Reynolds greeted Starbuck in his small office next to the telegraph room.

"But Mister Faulconer, Colonel Faulconer, specifically requested two sets of cars, both with locomotives—"

"I don't care if God Almighty ordered the cars!" Reynolds was a plump man, sweating in his woolen railroad uniform, who was clearly tired of the exigencies that wartime had imposed upon his careful timetable. "The whole railroad's only got sixteen locomotives and ten of those have gone north to move troops. We're supposed to do things railroad fashion, but how can I keep order if everyone wants locomotives? I can't help you! I don't care if Mister Faulconer is a director, I don't care if all the directors were here begging for cars, I can't do anything!"

"You have to help," Starbuck said.

"I can't make cars, laddie! I can't make locomotives!" Reynolds leaned across his table, sweat dripping down his face into his ginger beard and mustaches. "I am not a miracle worker!"

"But I am," Starbuck said, and he took out the big Savage revolver from the holster at his waist, pointed it just to one side of Reynolds and pulled the trigger. Smoke and noise filled the room as the heavy bullet smashed through the timber wall to leave a ragged, splintered hole. Starbuck holstered the smoking gun. "I am not a laddie, Mister Reynolds," he calmly told the gaping, astonished manager, "but an officer in the army of the Confederate States of America and if you insult me once again I shall put you against that wall and shoot you."

For a second Starbuck thought that Reynolds was going to follow Major Pelham into an early grave. "You're mad!" the railroad man finally said.

"I think that's probably true," Starbuck agreed placidly, "but I shoot better when I am mad than when I am sane, so let us now decide how you and I are going to move the Faulconer Legion north to Manassas Junction, shall we?" He smiled. It was Sally, he decided, who had released this confidence in him. He was actually enjoying himself. Goddamn it, he thought, but he was going to be a good soldier.

Yet Reynolds suspected there were no available passenger cars within fifty miles. All he had in the depot were seventeen old house cars. "What are house cars?" Starbuck asked politely, and the frightened manager pointed through his window at a boxcar.

"We call them house cars," he said in the same nervous voice that he had used to reassure the telegraph operator and two assistants who had run to his office to enquire about the shooting.

"How many men can we fit into a house car?" Starbuck asked.

"Fifty? Sixty maybe?"

"Then we have just enough." The Legion had not reached Faulconer's target of one thousand men, but over nine hundred had volunteered, making it into a formidable regiment. "What other cars do you have?" Starbuck asked.

There were just two gondola cars, which were simple open wagons, and that was all. One of the gondola cars and eight of the boxcars were in desperate need of repair, though Reynolds thought they could be used, but only at the slowest possible speed. There were, he said, no locomotives available, though when Starbuck put a hand toward the big Savage revolver, Reynolds hastily remembered that a locomotive was expected to pass through the depot on its way to Lynchburg, where it was going to collect a train of platform cars loaded with cut timber that was being carried to the coast to build artillery revetments.

"Good!" Starbuck said. "You'll stop the locomotive and turn it round."

"We don't have a roundhouse here."

"The engine can travel backward?"

Reynolds nodded. "Yes, sir."

"And how far is it to Manassas?"

"A hundred miles, sir."

"Then we shall go to war backward," Starbuck said happily.

Washington Faulconer, when he led the Legion's cavalry unit into the depot at midday, was furious. He had expected two trains to be waiting, one of them with the director's private car attached, but instead there was just a mutinous engineer with a single backward-facing locomotive and tender that was attached to seventeen boxcars and two gondola cars, while the telegraph operator was attempting to explain to Lynchburg why the locomotive would not be arriving, and Reynolds was trying to clear the track northward past Charlottesville. "For God's sake, Nate," the Colonel exploded, "why is everything such a mess?"

"Wartime, sir?"

"Damn it! I gave you simple enough orders! Can't you do the simplest thing?" He spurred off to abuse the grumbling engineer.

Adam looked at Starbuck and shrugged. "Sorry. Father's not happy."

"How was Miss Pelham?"

"Awful. Just awful." Adam shook his head. "And soon, Nate, there'll be scores of women getting that same news.

Hundreds." Adam turned to look down Rosskill's Depot Street where the first of the Legion's infantrymen had come into sight. The marching column was flanked by twin ragged processions of wives, mothers and children, some of whom were carrying knapsacks to relieve their men of their equipment's weight. "Dear God, this is chaos," Adam said. "We were supposed to have left three hours ago!"

"I'm told that in war nothing ever goes to plan," Starbuck said happily, "and that if it does, you're probably being whipped. We have to get used to chaos, and learn to make the best of it."

"Father's not good at that," Adam confessed.

"Then it's a good job he's got me." Starbuck smiled benignly at Ethan Ridley, who had ridden in with the approaching Legion. Starbuck had decided he would be very pleasant to Ridley from now until the end of Ridley's life. Ridley ignored him.

The Colonel had originally supposed that the Legion would be entrained in comfort by ten that morning, yet it was not till five in the evening that the single train limped slowly north. There was enough room for the infantrymen, three days' supply of food and all the Legion's ammunition, but precious little else. The officers' horses and servants were put into the two gondola cars. The Colonel would travel in the caboose, which had arrived with the locomotive, while the men were given the boxcars. The Colonel, mindful of his duties as a director of the line, gave strict orders that the cars were to arrive at Manassas Junction undamaged, but no sooner had he spoken than Sergeant Truslow found an axe and smashed a hole in the side of a boxcar. "A man needs light and air," he growled at the Colonel, then swung the axe again. The Colonel turned away and pretended not to notice the orgy of destruction as the Legion began its enthusiastic ventilation of the wooden boxes.

There was no room on the train for the Legion's cavalry, which had to be left behind, along with the two six-pounder guns, their caissons and limbers, the cast-iron camp stoves and all the wagons. The Legion's tents were slung into the boxcars at the last moment and Bandmaster Little took his instruments, claiming they were medical supplies. The Legion's colors were almost left behind in the confusion, but Adam saw the twin leather flag cases abandoned on a gun caisson and stowed them in the caboose. The depot was chaotic as women and children sought to say goodbye to their men, and as the men, exhausting the water in their canteens, tried to fill the small round bottles from the outflow of the depot's stilt-legged water tank. Faulconer was shouting last-minute instructions for the cavalry, artillery and wagon train, which would now travel north by road. He reckoned they should take three days to make the journey while the train, even with its damaged axle boxes, should make it in one. "We'll see you in Manassas," the Colonel told Lieutenant Davies, who was to be in charge of the convoy, "or maybe in Washington!"

Anna Faulconer, driving her small cart, had arrived from Faulconer Court House and insisted on handing out small Confederate flags that she and the servants at Seven Springs had embroidered. Her father, impatient at the delay, ordered the engineer to sound the whistle to summon the men back to the boxcars, but the sound of the shrieking steam frightened some of the horses in the gondola cars and one Negro servant had his leg broken when Captain Hinton's mare kicked back. The servant was carried off the train and, in the delay, two men from E Company decided they did not want to fight and deserted, but three other men insisted on being allowed to join the Legion there and then and so climbed aboard.

Finally, at five o'clock, the train began its journey. It could go no faster than ten miles an hour because of the broken axle boxes and so it limped north, its wheels clanking across the rail joints and its bell clanging a mournful sound over the water meadows and green fields. The Colonel was still furious at the day's delays, but the men were in high spirits and sang cheerfully as their slow train chugged away from the hills, its smoke drifting among trees. They left the convoy of wagons, guns and cavalry behind and steamed slowly into the night.

The train journey took almost two days. The crowded cars spent twelve hours waiting at the Gordonsville Junction, another three at Warrenton, and endless other minutes waiting while the tender was fueled with cordwood or its water tank charged, but at last, on a hot Saturday afternoon, they reached Manassas Junction where the Army of Northern Virginia had its headquarters. No one in Manassas knew the Legion was coming or what to do with them, but finally a staff officer led the Legion north and east from the small town along a country road that wound through small steep hills. There were other troops camped in meadows, and artillery pieces parked in farm gates, and the sight of those other troops gave the Legion an apprehensive feeling that they had joined some massive undertaking that none of them truly understood. Till now they had been the Faulconer Legion, safe in Faulconer Court House and led by Colonel Faulconer, but the train had abruptly brought them to a strange place where they were lost in an incomprehensible and uncontrollable process.

It was almost dark when the staff Captain pointed to a farmhouse that lay to the right of the road on a wide, bare plateau. "The farm's still occupied," he told Faulconer, "but those pastures look empty, so make yourselves at home."

"I need to see Beauregard." Faulconer sounded irritable, made so by the evening's uncertainty. He wanted to know where exactly he was, and the staff officer did not know, and he wanted to know precisely what was expected of his Legion, but the staff officer could not tell him that either. There were no maps, no orders, no sense of direction at all. "I should see Beauregard tonight," Faulconer insisted.

"I guess the general will be real pleased to see you, Colonel," the staff officer said tactfully, "but I reckon you'd best still wait for morning now. Say at six o'clock?"

"Are we expecting action?" Faulconer asked pompously.

"Sometime tomorrow, I guess." The staff officer's cigar glowed briefly. "The Yankees are up that a way," he gestured vaguely eastward with his lit cigar, "and I guess we'll be crossing the river to give them a howdy, but the general won't be giving his orders till morning. I'll tell you how to find him, and you be there at six, Colonel. That'll give you boys time to have yourselves a prayer service first."

"A prayer service?" Faulconer's tone suggested the staff officer was touched in the head.

"Tomorrow's the Lord's Day, Colonel," the captain said reproachfully, and so it would be, for the next day would be Sunday, July 21, 1861.

And America would be broken by battle.

By two o'clock on Sunday morning the air was already stiflingly hot and breathlessly calm. The sun would not rise for another two and a half hours yet, and the sky was still star bright, cloudless and brilliant. Most of the men, even though they had lugged their tents the long five miles from the rail junction to the farm, slept in the open air. Starbuck woke to see the heavens like a brilliant scatter of cold white light, more beautiful than anything found on earth.

"Time to get up," Adam said beside him.

Men were waking all around the hilltop. They were coughing and cursing, their voices made loud by nervousness. Somewhere in the dark valley a set of harness chains jangled and a horse whinnied, and a trumpet called reveille from a far encampment, its sound echoing back from a distant dark slope. A cockerel crowed from the farmhouse on the hill where dim lights showed behind curtained windows. Dogs barked and the cooks banged skillets and kettles.

"'The armorers'"—Starbuck still lay on his back, staring up at the sharp-edged stars—"'accomplishing the knights,

265

with busy hammers closing rivets up, give dreadful note of preparation.'"

Adam would normally have taken pleasure in capping the quotation, but he was in a silent, subdued mood and so said nothing. All along the Legion's lines the smoky fires were being coddled into life to throw a garish light on shirt-sleeved men, stands of rifles and the white conical tents. The thickening smoke shimmered the stars.

Starbuck still gazed upward. "'The cripple tardy-gaited night,'" he quoted again, "'who like a foul witch doth limp so tediously away.'" He was delivering the quotations to disguise his nervousness. Today, he was thinking, I shall see the elephant.

Adam said nothing. He felt that he had come to the brink of a terrible chaos, like the abyss across which Satan had flown in *Paradise Lost*, and that was exactly what this war meant for America, Adam thought sadly—the loss of innocence, the loss of sweet perfection. He had joined the Legion to please his father, now he might have to pay the price of that compromise.

"Coffee, Massa?" Nelson, Faulconer's servant, brought two tin mugs of coffee from the fire he had tended all night behind the Colonel's tent.

"You're a great and good man, Nelson." Starbuck sat up and reached for the coffee.

Sergeant Truslow was shouting at Company K, where someone had complained that there was no bucket with which to fetch water and Truslow was bellowing at the man to stop complaining and go steal a damned bucket.

"You don't seem nervous." Adam sipped the coffee, then grimaced at its harsh taste.

"Of course I'm nervous," Starbuck said. In fact the apprehension was writhing in his belly like snakes boiling in a pit. "But I have an idea that I might be a good soldier." Was that true, he wondered, or was he just saying it because he wanted it to be true? Or because he had boasted of it to Sally? And was

266

that all it had been? A boast to impress a girl?

"I shouldn't even be here," Adam said.

"Nonsense," Starbuck said briskly. "Survive one day, Adam, just one day, then help make peace."

A few minutes past three o'clock two horsemen appeared in the regiment's lines. One man was carrying a lantern with which he had lit his way across the hilltop. "Who are you?" the second man shouted.

"The Faulconer Legion!" Adam called back the answer.

"The Faulconer Legion? Jesus wept! We've got a Legion on our goddamned side now? The damned Yankees might as well give up." The speaker was a short balding man with intense, button-black eyes that scowled from an unwashed face above a dirty black mustache and a ragged spade beard. He slid out of his saddle and paced into the firelight to reveal skeletally thin legs bowed like razor clam shells that looked entirely inadequate to support the weight of his big belly and broad, muscled torso. "So who's in command here?" the strange man demanded.

"My father," Adam said, "Colonel Faulconer." He gestured at his father's tent.

"Faulconer!" The stranger turned toward the tent. He was wearing a shabby Confederate uniform and was clutching a brown felt hat so battered and filthy that it might have been spurned by a sharecropper.

"Here!" The Colonel's tent was lit within by lanterns that cast grotesque shadows every time he moved in front of their flames. "Who is it?"

"Evans. Colonel Nathan Evans." Evans did not wait for an invitation but pushed through Faulconer's tent flap. "I heard troops arrived here last night and I thought I'd say howdy. I've got half a brigade up by the stone bridge and if the bastard Yankees decide to use the Warrenton Pike then you and I are all that stands between Abe Lincoln and the whores in New Orleans. Is that coffee, Faulconer, or whiskey?"

"Coffee." Faulconer's voice was distant, suggesting he did

not like Evans's brusque familiarity.

"I've my own whiskey, but I'll have a coffee first and thank you kindly, Colonel." Starbuck watched as Evans's shadow drank the Colonel's coffee. "What I want you to do, Faulconer," Evans demanded when the coffee was drained, "is move your boys down to the road, then on up to a wooden bridge here." He had evidently opened a map that he spread on Faulconer's bed. "There's a deal of timber around the bridge and I guess if you keep your boys hidden then the sons of bitch Yankees won't know you're there. Of course we may all end up being about as much use as a pair of balls on a shad-bellied priest, but on the other hand we may not."

Evans's staff officer lit a cigar and gave Adam and Starbuck a desultory glance. Thaddeus Bird, Ethan Ridley and at least a score of other men were openly listening to the conversation inside the tent.

"I don't understand," Faulconer said.

"It ain't difficult." Evans paused and there was a scratching sound as he struck a match to light a cigar. "Yankees are over the stream. They want to keep advancing on Manassas Junction. Capture that and they've cut us from the valley army. Beauregard's facing them, but he ain't the kind to wait to get hit, so he plans to attack on their left, our right." Evans was demonstrating the moves on his map. "So Beauregard's got most of our army out on the right. Way over eastward, two miles away at least, and if he can get his pants buttoned before noon he'll probably attack later today. He'll hook round the back of the bastards and kill as many as he can. Which is dandy, Faulconer, but suppose the sons of bitches decide to attack us first? And suppose they ain't as dumb as northerners usually are and instead of marching straight into our faces suppose they try to hook around our left? We're the only troops to stop them. In fact there's nothing between us and Mexico, Faulconer, so what if the pox-ridden bastards do decide to have a go at this flank?" Evans chuckled. "That's why

268

I'm right glad you're here, Colonel."

"Are you saying I'm attached to your brigade?" Faulconer asked.

"I ain't got orders for you, if that's what you mean, but why the hell else were you sent here?"

"I have an appointment with General Beauregard at six in the morning to discover just that," Faulconer said.

There was a pause as Evans evidently uncapped a flask, pulled at it, then screwed the cap back into place. "Colonel," he finally said, "why in hell's name were you put out here? This is the left flank. We're the last sons of bitches that anyone thought to position. We're here, Colonel, in case the god-damned Yankees attack up the Warrenton Pike."

"I have not yet received my orders," Faulconer insisted.

"So what are you waiting for? A choir of goddamned angels? For Christ's sake, Faulconer, we need men on this flank of the army!" Nathan Evans's temper had plainly snapped, but he made an effort to explain matters calmly again. "Beauregard plans to push north on our right, so what if the shit-faced Yankees decided to push south on theirs? What am I supposed to do? Hurl kisses at them? Ask them to delay the war while you fetch your damned orders?"

"I shall fetch those orders from Beauregard," Faulconer said stubbornly, "and no one else."

"Then while you're fetching your goddamned orders why don't you move your goddamned Legion to the wooden bridge? Then if you're needed you can march to the stone bridge over the Run and give my boys a hand."

"I shall not move," Faulconer insisted, "until I receive proper orders."

"Oh, dear God," Adam murmured for his father's obduracy.

The argument went on two minutes more, but neither man would shift. Faulconer's wealth had not accustomed him to taking orders, and least of all from diminutive, ill-smelling, bow-legged, coarse-tongued brutes like Nathan Evans, who, abandoning his attempts to snare the Legion into his brigade, stormed out of the tent and hauled himself into his saddle. "Come on, Meadows," he snarled at his aide, and the two men galloped off into the darkness.

"Adam!" Faulconer shouted. "Pecker!"

"Ah, the second in command is summoned by the great leader," Bird said caustically, then followed Adam into the tent.

"Did you hear that?" Faulconer demanded.

"Yes, Father."

"So you understand, both of you, that whatever that man may order, you ignore. I shall bring you orders from Beauregard."

"Yes, Father," Adam said again.

Major Bird was not so obliging. "Are you ordering me to disobey a direct command from a superior officer?"

"I am saying that Nathan Evans is a lunkhead addicted to stone-jug whiskey," the Colonel said, "and I did not spend a damned fortune on a fine regiment just to see it thrown away in his drink-sodden hands."

"So I do disobey his orders?" Major Bird persisted.

"It means you obey my orders, and no one else's," the Colonel said. "Damn it, if the battle's on the right then that's where we should be, not stuck on the left with the dregs of the army. I want the Legion on parade in one hour. Tents struck, fighting order."

The Legion paraded at half past four by which time the hilltop was bathed in a ghostly twilight and the farther hills were dark shapes receding ever more obscurely until, at last, there was nothing but an opaque darkness in which dimly mysterious points of red light suggested far-off camp fires. There was just enough gray half-light to see that the nearer countryside was littered with carts and wagons, giving the scene an odd resemblance to a camp meeting site on the morning after the preaching had ended, except that among these wagons were the satanic shapes of limbers, portable forges and cannon. The smoke of the dying camp fires clung in the hollows like mist beneath the last fading stars. Somewhere a band was playing "Home, Sweet Home" and a man in B Company tunelessly sang the words until a sergeant told him to be silent.

The Legion waited. Their heavy packs, blankets and ground-sheets had been piled with the tents at the rear of the band so that the men would simply carry their weapons, haversacks and canteens into battle. Around them, mostly unseen, an army took up its positions. Pickets gazed across the stream, gunners sipped coffee beside their monstrous guns, cavalrymen watered horses in the dozen streams that laced the pastureland, and surgeons' assistants tore up lint for bandages or sharpened flesh knives and bone saws. A few officers galloped importantly across the fields, vanishing into the farther darknesses on their mysterious errands.

Starbuck sat on Pocahontas just behind the Legion's color party and wondered if he was dreaming. Was there really to be a battle? The short-tempered Evans had hinted as much and everyone seemed to expect one, yet there was no sign of any enemy. He half-wanted the expectations to be true, and was half-terrified that they would come true. Intellectually he knew that battle was chaotic, cruel and bitter, yet he could not rid himself of the belief that it would turn out to be glorious, plumed and oddly calm. In books, stern-faced men waited to see the whites of their enemies' eyes, then fired and won great victories. Horses pranced and flags whipped in a smokeless wind beneath which the decorous dead lay sleeping and the pain-free dying spoke lovingly of their country and of their mothers. Men died as simply as Major Pelham had died. Oh sweet Jesus, Starbuck prayed as a sudden burst of terror whip-sawed through his thoughts, but don't let me die. I regret all my sins, every one of them, even Sally, and I will never sin again if you will just let me live.

He shivered even though he was sweating under his thick woolen uniform coat and trousers. Somewhere to his left a man

271

shouted an order, but the sound was small and faraway, like a voice heard from a sickbed in a distant room. The sun had still not risen, though the eastern horizon was now suffused with a rosy brilliance and it was light enough for Colonel Faulconer to make a slow inspection of his Legion's ranks. He reminded the men of the homes they had left in Faulconer County, and of their wives, sweethearts and children. He reassured them that the war was not of the South's making, but of the North's choosing. "We just wanted to be left alone, is that so terrible an ambition?" he asked. Not that the men needed the Colonel's reassurance, but Faulconer knew that a commanding officer was expected to rouse the spirits of his men on the morning of battle, and so he encouraged his Legion that their cause was just and that men fighting for a just cause need not fear defeat.

Adam had been supervising the piling of the Legion's baggage, but now rode back to Starbuck's side. Adam's horse was one of the best beasts from the Faulconer stud—a tall, bay stallion, glossily beautiful, a disdainful aristocrat among beasts just as the Faulconers were lords among common men. Adam nodded toward the small house with its dimly glowing windows that stood silhouetted on the hill's flat top. "They sent a servant to ask us whether it would be safe to stay there."

"What did you say?"

"How could I say anything? I don't know what will happen today. But do you know who lives there?"

"How on earth would I know that?"

"The widow of the *Constitution*'s surgeon. Isn't that something? Surgeon Henry, he was called." Adam's voice sounded very stilted, as though it was taking all his self-discipline to contain his emotions. He had put on a soldier's coat for his father's sake, and worn a captain's three metal bars on his collar because to do so was simpler than wearing a martyr's sackcloth, but today he would pay the real price of that compromise, and the thought of it was making him sick to his stomach. He fanned his face with his wide-brimmed hat, then

272

glanced to the east where the cloudless sky looked like a sheet of beaten silver touched with a shimmer of lurid gold. "Can you imagine how hot it will be by midday?" Adam asked.

Starbuck smiled. "'As they gather silver, and brass, and iron, and lead, and tin, into the midst of the furnace, to blow the fire upon it, to melt it; so will I gather you in mine anger and in my fury, and I will leave you there, and melt you.'" He imagined himself writhing in a blast of furnace heat, a sinner burning for his iniquities. "Ezekiel," he explained to Adam, whose expression betrayed that he had not placed the text.

"It isn't a very cheering text for a Sunday morning," Adam said, then shuddered uncontrollably as he imagined what this day might bring. "Do you really feel you might make a good soldier?" he asked.

"Yes." He had failed at everything else, Starbuck thought bitterly.

"At least you look like a soldier." Adam spoke with a touch of envy.

"How does a soldier look?" Starbuck asked, amused.

"Like someone in a Walter Scott novel," Adam answered quickly, "*Ivanhoe*, maybe?

Starbuck laughed. "My grandmother MacPhail always told me I had the face of a preacher. Like my father." And Sally had said he had her father's eyes.

Adam put his hat back on. "I suppose your father will be preaching damnation on all slaveholders this morning?" He was simply wanting to make conversation, any conversation, just noise to divert his thoughts from the horrors of war.

"Perdition and hell fire will indeed be summoned to support the northern cause," Starbuck agreed, and he was suddenly assailed by a vision of his comfortable Boston home where his younger brothers and sisters would just be waking up and readying themselves for early morning family prayers. Would they remember to pray for him this morning? His elder sister would not. At nineteen Ellen Marjory Starbuck already had the

273

pinched opinions of crabbed middle age. She was betrothed to a Congregational minister from New Hampshire, a man of infinite spite and calculated unkindness and, instead of recommending Nathaniel to God's protection, Ellen would doubtless be praying for her older brother James, who, Starbuck supposed, would be in uniform, though for the life of him he could not imagine stuffy, punctilious James in battle. James would be a good headquarters man in Washington or Boston—making fussy lists and enforcing detailed regulations.

The younger children would pray for Nathaniel, though perforce their entreaties would necessarily be silent lest they provoked the wrath of the Reverend Elial. There was sixteen-year-old Frederick George, who had been born with a withered left arm, fifteen-year-old Martha Abigail, who most resembled Nathaniel in looks and character, and last of all was twelve-year-old Samuel Washington Starbuck, who wanted to be a whaling captain. Five other children had died in infancy.

"What are you thinking?" Adam asked abruptly, out of nervousness.

"I was thinking of family history," Starbuck said, "and how congestive it is."

"Congestive?"

"Limiting. Mine, anyway." And Sally's, he thought. Maybe even Ridley's too, though Starbuck did not want to indulge in pity for the man he would kill. Or would he? He glanced across at Ethan Ridley, who sat motionless in the dawn. It was one thing to contemplate a killing, Starbuck decided, but quite another to perform the deed.

A flurry of far musket shots rattled the last shadows of receding dark. "Oh, God." Adam spoke the words as a prayer for his country. He stared eastward, though not so much as a leaf moved in the far wooded hollows where, at last, the creeping light was showing vivid green among the dying grays. Somewhere in those hills and woods an enemy waited, though whether the firing was the first flicker of battle or merely a false alarm, no one could tell.

Another bout of terror rippled through Starbuck. He was frightened of dying, but he was far more terrified of displaying his fear. If he had to die he would prefer it to be a romantic death with Sally beside him. He tried to recall the sweetness of that thunder-laden night when she had lain in his arms and, like children, they had watched the lightning scratch the sky. How could one night change a man so much? Dear God, Starbuck thought, but that one night was like being born again, and that was as wicked a heresy as any he could dream of, but there was no other description that so exactly fitted what he had felt. He had been dragged from doubt into certainty, from misery into gladness, from despair to glory. It was that magical conversion, which his father preached and for which he had so often prayed, and which at last he had experienced, except it was the devil's conversion that had swamped his soul with calmness, and not the Savior's grace that had changed him.

"Are you listening, Nate?" Adam had evidently spoken, but to no avail. "There's Father. He's beckoning us."

"Of course." Starbuck followed Adam to the Legion's right flank beyond Company A where Colonel Faulconer had finished his inspection. "Before I go and find Beauregard," Faulconer spoke awkwardly, as though he was unsure of himself, "I thought I'd make a reconnaissance that way." He pointed northward, out beyond the army's left flank. The Colonel's voice sounded like that of a man trying to convince himself that he was a real soldier on a real battlefield. "Would you like to come? I need to satisfy myself that Evans is wrong. No point in staying here if there's no Yankees out in these woods. Do you feel like a gallop, Nate?"

Starbuck reflected that the Colonel must be in a better mood than he appeared if he called him Nate instead of the colder Starbuck. "I'd like that, sir."

"Come on, then. You too, Adam."

The father and son led Starbuck down the hill to where a

tree-shaded stone house stood beside a crossroads. Two artillery pieces were creaking and jangling eastward along the turnpike, dragged by tired horses. The Colonel galloped between the two guns, then swerved onto the road that led north from the crossroads. The road climbed a long hill between shadowed pastureland, rising to a wooded crest where the Colonel reined in.

Faulconer unholstered and extended a leather-bound telescope, which he trained north toward a far hill crowned by a simple wooden church. Nothing disturbed the fleeting shadows of darkness on that far hill, nor indeed anywhere else in the gentle landscape. A white-painted farm lay in the distance and leafy woods all around, but no soldiers disturbed the pastoral scene. The Colonel stared long and hard at the distant church on its hill, then collapsed the telescope's short tubes. "According to that lunkhead Evans's map, that's Sudley Church. There are some fords beneath there, and no Yankees in sight. Except for you, Nate."

Starbuck took the last words as a pleasantry. "I'm an honorary Virginian, sir. Remember?"

"Not any longer, Nate," Faulconer said heavily. "This isn't a reconnaissance, Nate. The Yankees will never come this far north. I brought you here instead to say goodbye."

Starbuck gazed at the Colonel, wondering if this was some kind of elaborate jest. It seemed not. "Goodbye, sir?" He managed to stammer the iteration.

"This isn't your quarrel, Nate, and Virginia isn't your country."

"But, sir ..."

"So I'm sending you home." The Colonel overrode Starbuck's feeble objection with a firm kindness, just as he might speak to a useless puppy which, despite its potential for amusement, he was about to put down with a single shot to the skull.

"I have no home." Starbuck had meant the words to be defiant, but somehow they came out as a pathetic bleat.

"Indeed you do, Nate. I wrote to your father six weeks ago and he has been good enough to reply to me. His letter was delivered under a flag of truce last week. Here it is." The Colonel took a folded paper from a pouch at his waist and held it out to Starbuck.

Starbuck did not move.

"Take it, Nate," Adam urged his friend.

"Did you know about this?" Starbuck turned fiercely on Adam, fearing his friend's betrayal.

"I told Adam this morning," the Colonel said, intervening. "But this is my doing, not Adam's."

"But you don't understand, sir!" Starbuck appealed to the Colonel.

"But I do, Nate! I do!" Colonel Faulconer smiled condescendingly. "You're an impetuous young man, and there's nothing amiss with that. I was impulsive, but I can't allow youthful impetuosity to lead you into rebellion. It won't do, upon my soul it will not. A man should not fight against his own country because of a youthful mistake. So I have determined your fate." The Colonel spoke very firmly, and once again pushed the letter toward Starbuck who, this time, felt obliged to grasp it. "Your brother James is with McDowell's army," the Colonel continued, "and he's enclosed a laissez-passer that will see you safe through the northern lines. Once past the pickets you should seek out your brother. I fear you'll have to give me your sword and pistol, but I'll let you keep Pocahontas. And the saddle! And that's an expensive saddle, Nate." He added the last words as a kind of enticement that might reconcile Starbuck to his unexpected fate.

"But, sir ..." Starbuck tried to articulate his protest again, and this time there were tears in his eyes. He felt bitterly ashamed of the tears and tried to shake them away, but still one drop brimmed from his right eye and ran down his cheek. "Sir! I want to stay with you! I want to stay with the Legion."

Faulconer smiled. "That's kind of you, Nate, truly kind. I'm

277

obliged, so I am, for your saying as much. But no. This isn't your quarrel."

"The North might think otherwise." Starbuck now attempted defiance, suggesting that the Colonel might be making a fearful enemy in thus sending him away.

"And so they might, Nate, so they might. And if you're forced to fight against us, then I'll pray you live to be reunited with your Virginia friends. Ain't that so, Adam?"

"Indeed it is, Father," Adam said warmly, then held out his hand for Starbuck to shake.

Starbuck did not respond. The sting of the insult was not that he was being ejected from the Faulconer Legion, but that the Colonel held such a low opinion of him, and so he tried to explain his burgeoning hopes of becoming a good soldier. "I really do feel, sir, that soldiering is a profession I can master. I want to be useful to you. I want to return your hospitality, your kindness, by showing what I can do."

"Nate! Nate!" The Colonel interrupted him. "You are not a soldier. You're a theology student who was caught in a snare. Don't you see that? But your family and friends are not going to let you throw your life away because of one conniving woman. You've been taught a hard lesson, but now it's time to go back to Boston and accept your parents' forgiveness. And to make your new future! Your father declares you must abandon your hopes of the ministry, but he has other plans for you, and whatever you do, Nate, I'm sure you'll do well."

"That's true, Nate," Adam said warmly.

"Let me just stay one more day, sir," Starbuck pleaded.

"No, Nate, not even one more hour. I can't brand you traitor in your family's eyes. It wouldn't be a Christian act." The Colonel leaned toward Starbuck. "Unbuckle the sword belt, Nate."

Starbuck obeyed. In everything he had ever done, he thought, he had failed. Now, with his military career a shambles before it had even begun, he unbuckled the clumsy sword and unclipped the heavy pistol in its worn leather holster and handed both weapons back to their rightful owner. "I wish you'd reconsider, sir."

"I have given this matter my weightiest consideration, Nate," the Colonel said impatiently, then, in a less irritated tone, "you're a Boston man, a Massachusetts man, and that makes you a different creature from us southerners. Your destiny doesn't lie here, Nate, but in the North. You'll doubtless be a great man one day. You're clever, maybe too clever, and you shouldn't waste your cleverness on war. So take it back to Massachusetts and follow your father's plans."

Starbuck did not know what to say. He felt belittled. He so desperately wanted to be in control of his own life, but he had always needed someone else's money to survive—first his father's, then Dominique's, and now Colonel Faulconer's. Adam Faulconer was equally as dependent on family as Starbuck, but Adam fitted into his society with a practiced ease, while Starbuck had always felt awkwardly out of place. He so hated being young, yet the chasm between youth and adulthood seemed so wide as to be unjumpable, except that in the last few weeks he had thought he might make a good soldier and thus forge his own independence.

The Colonel pulled Pocahontas's head about. "There are no northern troops out here, Nate. Keep on the road till you come to the fords by the church there, then cross the streams and follow the road toward the rising sun. You'll not find any Yankees for a good few miles, and you'll be coming from their rear, which means you shouldn't run too much risk of being shot by a nervous sentry. And take the coat off, Nate."

"I must?"

"You must. Do you want the enemy to think you're a southerner? You want to be shot for nothing? Take it off, Nate."

Starbuck peeled off the gray frock coat with its single metal bar, which denoted his second lieutenancy. He had never really felt like an officer, not even a lowly second lieutenant, but without the uniform coat he was nothing but a failure being sent home with his tail tucked between his legs. "Where will the battle be fought, sir?" he asked in a small boy's voice.

"Way, way across country." The Colonel pointed east where the sun was at last touching the horizon with its incandescent furnace glow. It was back there, far off on the Confederate right flank, that Washington Faulconer hoped to join the attack that would crush the Yankees. "Nothing's going to happen over here," Faulconer said, "which is why they put that no-good rascal Evans on this flank."

"Allow me to wish you good fortune, sir?" Starbuck sounded very formal as he held out his hand.

"Thank you, Nate." The Colonel managed to sound truly grateful for the wish. "And would you do me the kindness of accepting this?" He held out a small cloth purse, but Starbuck could not bring himself to accept the gift. He desperately needed the money, but he was far too proud to take it.

"I shall manage, sir."

"You know best!" The Colonel smiled and withdrew the purse.

"And God bless you, Nate," Adam Faulconer said vigorously to his friend. "I'll guard your traps and send them on when the war's over. By year's end, certainly. To your father's house?"

"I suppose so, yes." Starbuck shook his best friend's outstretched hand, wrenched the horse's head about and plunged his heels hard back. He went quickly so the Faulconers would not see his tears.

"He took it hard," Colonel Faulconer said when Starbuck was out of earshot, "damned hard!" Faulconer sounded astonished. "Did he really think he might be a success at soldiering?"

"He said as much to me this morning."

Colonel Faulconer shook his head sadly. "He's a northerner, and in times like these you trust your own, not strangers. And who knows where his allegiance lies?"

"It was with us," Adam said sadly, watching Nate canter away down the slope toward the far woods beneath the church. "And he is an honest man, Father."

"I wish I shared your confidence. I can't prove Nate danced a jig with our money, Adam, but I'll just feel happier without him. I know he's your friend, but we were doing him no favors by keeping him away from home."

"I think that is true," Adam said piously, for he genuinely believed Starbuck needed to make peace with his family.

"I had hopes of him," the Colonel said sententiously, "but these preachers' sons are all the same. Once off the leash, Adam, they go hog wild. They commit all the sins their fathers couldn't, or wouldn't or dared not. It's like being brought up in a fancy-cake shop and being told never to touch the candy, and it's no wonder they plunge in up to their snouts the moment they're free." Faulconer lit a cigar and blew a stream of smoke into the dawn. "The whole truth of this matter, Adam, is that blood signifies, and I fear your friend has unreliable blood. He won't stay the course. That family never has. What were the Starbucks? Nantucket Quakers?"

"So I believe, yes." Adam sounded reserved. He was still unhappy at what had happened to Starbuck, even though he recognized it was the best thing for his friend.

"And Nate's father abandoned the Quakers to be a Calvinist, and now Nate wants to flee the Calvinists to be what? A southerner?" The Colonel laughed. "It won't do, Adam, it just won't do. My Lord, he even let that *Tom* company whore run him ragged! He's too unsteady. Altogether too unsteady, and good soldiers need to be steady." The Colonel gathered his reins. "Sun's up! Time to unleash the hounds!" He turned and spurred his horse southward, back to where the Confederate army readied itself for battle beside a small stream called

281

Bull Run that lay twenty-six miles west of Washington, D.C., near the town of Manassas Junction in the sovereign state of Virginia that had once formed a part of the United States of America, which was now two nations, divided under God, and gathering for battle.

Starbuck rode wildly down the long slope to the far woods where he swerved off the dirt road and into the shade of the deep woodland. He yanked too hard on the curb and Pocahontas protested at the pain as she slowed to a stop. "I don't care, damn you," Starbuck growled at the horse, then kicked his right foot out of the stirrup and swung himself down from the saddle. A bird screeched at him from the undergrowth. He did not know what kind of bird it was. He could recognize cardinals, blue jays, chickadees and seagulls. That was all. He had thought he knew what an eagle looked like, but when he had spotted one at Faulconer Court House the men in Company C had laughed at him. That was no eagle, they said, but a sharp-shinned hawk. Any fool could tell that, but not Second Lieutenant Starbuck. Christ, he thought, but he failed at everything.

He looped the horse's reins about a low branch, then slid down the trunk of the tree to sit in the long grass. A cricket chattered at him as he took the creased papers from his pocket. The rising sun was drowning the treetops in light, filtering green brilliance through the summer leaves. Starbuck dreaded reading the letter, but he knew his father's wrath must be faced sooner or later, and better to face it on paper than in the musty, book-lined Boston study where the Reverend Elial hung his canes on the wall like other men hung fishing poles or swords. "Be sure your sin will find you out." That was the Reverend Elial's favorite text, the threnody of Starbuck's childhood and the constant anthem of his frequent beatings with the hook-stemmed sticks. Starbuck unfolded the stiff sheets of paper.

The Reverend Elial Starbuck to Colonel Washington Faulconer, of Faulconer County, Virginia.

My dear Sir.

I am in receipt of yours of the 14th, and my wife unites with me in a Christian appreciation of the sentiments expressed therein. I cannot hide from any man, least of all from myself, my keen disappointment in Nathaniel. He is a young man of the most inestimable privilege, raised in a Christian family, nurtured in a Godly society, and educated as best our means would allow. God granted him a fine intelligence and the affections of a close and intimate family, and it had long been my prayerful wish that Nathaniel would follow me into the ministry of God's word, yet alas, he has instead chosen the path of iniquity. I am not insensible to the high feelings of youth, but to abandon his studies for a woman! And to fall into the ways of a thief! It is enough to break a parent's heart, and the pain Nathaniel has given to his mother is exceeded only, I am sure, by the sadness he has offered to our Lord and Savior.

Yet we are not unmindful of a Christian's duty to the remorseful sinner, and if, as you suggest, Nathaniel is ready to make a full confession of his sins in a spirit of humble and genuine repentance, then we shall not stand in the way of his redemption. Yet he cannot ever again hope that we might rekindle the kind affections we once felt for him, nor must he believe himself worthy for a place in God's ministry. I have repaid the man Trabell of the monies stolen, but will now insist that Nathaniel repay me to the full, to which purpose he must earn his bread by the sweat of his labors. We have secured for him a place with my wife's cousin's practice of law in Salem where, God willing, Nathaniel will reward the liberality of our forgiveness by a diligent attention to his new duties.

Nathaniel's elder brother, James, a good and Christian man, is now with our army embarked upon its present sad duties, and he will, God willing, undertake to see that this missive reaches you safe. I doubt if you and I can ever agree on the tragical events that are presently rending our nation, but I know you will unite with me in reposing a continued hope in the Giver of All Good, the One God, in whose Holy Name we shall yet, I pray, avert fratricidal conflict and bring to our unhappy nation a just and honorable peace.

I render you more thanks for your manifold kindnesses to my son, and pray fervently that you are right in describing his earnestness for God's forgiveness. I pray also for all of our sons, that their lives may be spared in this most unhappy of times.

Respectfully yours,

the Reverend Elial Joseph Starbuck.
Boston, Mass. Thurs. June 20, 1861.

Post scriptum. My son, Captain James Starbuck of the United States Army, assures me he will enclose a "pass" allowing Nathaniel through our army's lines.

Starbuck unfolded the enclosed laissez-passer, which read:

Allow the Bearer Free Ingress
into the Lines of the United States Army,
authorized by the undersigned,
Captain James Elial MacPhail Starbuck,
sous-adjutant to Brigadier General Irvin McDowell.

Starbuck smiled at the pompous subscription to his brother's signature. So James had become a staff officer to the commander of the northern army? Good for James, Starbuck thought, then supposed that he should not really feel any surprise, for his elder brother was ambitious and diligent, a good lawyer and an earnest Christian; indeed James was everything his father wanted all his sons to be, while Starbuck was what? A rebel kicked out of a rebel army. A man who fell in love with whores. A failure.

He rested the two sheets of paper on the grass. Somewhere far away there was a sudden flurry of musketry, but the sound was muffled by the day's close warmth and seemed impossibly remote to ex-Second Lieutenant Nathaniel Starbuck. What did life hold now, he wondered? It seemed he was not to be a minister of the gospel, nor a soldier, but a student lawyer in the offices of cousin Harrison MacPhail of Salem, Massachusetts. Oh dear God, Starbuck thought, but was he to be under the tutelage of that dry, grasping, uncharitable stick of moral rectitude? Was that grim fate what the whisper of illegitimate petticoats could do to a man?

He stood, unlooped Pocahontas's reins, and walked slowly northward. He took off his hat and fanned his face. The horse followed placidly, its hooves falling heavily on the dirt road, which ran gently downhill between unfenced woodland and small pastures. The shadows of the trees stretched hugely long on the summer-bleached meadows. Way off to Starbuck's right was a white farmhouse and a huge hayrick. The farm appeared deserted. The sound of rifle fire faded in the heavy air like a brushfire dying, and Starbuck thought how happy he had been in these last weeks. They had been healthy outdoor weeks, playing at soldiers, and now it was all over. A wave of self-pity engulfed him. He was friendless, unwanted, useless; a victim, just as Sally was a victim, and he thought of the promise to revenge Sally by killing Ridley. So many stupid dreams, he thought, so many stupid dreams.

The road climbed into more woods, then dropped to an unfinished railway embankment beyond which lay the twin Sudley Fords. He mounted Pocahontas and crossed the smaller stream, glanced up at the white-boarded church on the hill above, then turned east across the wider deeper Bull Run. He let the horse drink. The water flowed fast across rounded pebbles. The sun was in his eyes, huge, brilliant, blinding, like the fire of Ezekiel that would melt metal in the furnace.

He urged the horse out of the stream, across a pasture and into the welcome shadow of more woods where he slowed his pace, instinctively rebelling against the life of propriety that his father's letter described. He would not do it, he would not do it! Instead, Starbuck decided, he would join the northern army. He would enlist as a private in some regiment of strangers. He thought of his promise to Sally, that he would kill Ethan, and he was sorry that the promise could not now be kept, and then he imagined meeting Ridley in battle and stabbing forward with a bayonet to pin his enemy to the ground. He rode slowly on, imagining himself a northern soldier, fighting for his own people.

The sound of musketry had changed subtly. The noise had been fading on the summer air, but now the sound became louder again, and more rhythmic and harder edged. He had not given the change any real thought, being too immersed in his own self-pity, but as he turned a slight bend in the road he saw that the new sound was not the sound of musketry at all, but the noise of axes.

Soldiers' axes.

Starbuck stopped the horse and just stared. The axemen were a hundred paces ahead of him. They were stripped to their waists and their axe blades shattered the sunlight into brilliant reflections as chips of wood skittered bright from the blades' hard strokes. They were working on a tangled barricade of felled trees that completely blocked the narrow road. Half the roads of northern Virginia had been so barricaded by

286

patriots trying to impede the northern invasion, and for a moment Starbuck supposed he had come across local men fashioning just such another obstacle, then he wondered why makers of a barricade would assault it with axes? And behind the axemen were teams of horses harnessed with drag chains to pull the sectioned tree trunks off the road, and behind those horse teams and half-hidden by the deep shadows, was a throng of blue-uniformed men above whom a flag showed bright in a slanting shaft of newly risen sunlight. The flag was the Stars and Stripes, and Starbuck suddenly realized these were Yankees, northerners, on a road where there were not supposed to be any northerners, and they were not just a few men, but a whole host of blue-uniformed soldiers who patiently waited for their pioneers to clear the narrow road.

"You there!" A man in officer's braid shouted at Starbuck from behind the half-dismantled barricade. "Stop where you are! Stop, you hear me?"

Starbuck was gaping like a fool, yet in truth he comprehended all that was happening. The northerners had fooled the South. Their plan was not to advance dully on Manassas Junction, nor to wait for the southerners to attack their left flank, but rather to attack here in the undefended Confederate left, and thereby to hook deep into the belly of the secessionist army and so rip it and tear it and savage it that all the vestiges of southern rebellion would die in the weltering horror of one Sabbath day's bloodletting. This, Starbuck grasped instantly, was Brigadier General McDowell's version of Thermopylae, the grand encircling surprise that would give the Yankee Persians victory over the Confederate Greeks.

And Starbuck, understanding all, understood that he no longer needed to become a northern soldier nor break his promise to a southern whore. He was saved.

10

"Faulconer should be here." Major Thaddeus Bird scowled eastward into the rising sun. Bird might have his sharp opinions about how soldiering should be managed, but left alone in notional command of the Faulconer Legion, he was not entirely certain he wanted the responsibility to enact those ideas. "He should be here," he said again. "The men need to know their commanding officer is with them, not lollygagging on his horse. Your future father-in-law," he spoke to Ethan Ridley, "is altogether too fond of excursions by quadruped." Major Bird found this remark amusing, for he raised his angular head and uttered a bark of laughter. "Excursions by quadruped, ha!"

"I presume the Colonel is making a reconnaissance," Ethan Ridley protested. Ridley had watched Starbuck ride away with the Faulconers and was jealous that he had not been invited. In two months Ridley would become Washington Faulconer's son-in-law, with all the privileges that kinship implied, yet still he feared that some other person might usurp his place in the Colonel's affections.

"You presume the Colonel is making a reconnaissance?" Major Bird scoffed at the supposition. "Faulconer's lollygagging, that's what he's doing. My brother-in-law lives under the misapprehension that soldiering is a sporting occupation, like hunting or steeplechasing, but it is mere butchery, Ethan, mere butchery. Our responsibility is to make ourselves into efficient butchers. I had a great uncle who was a pork butcher in Baltimore, so I feel that soldiering might well be in my blood. Do you have any such fortunate ancestry, Ethan?"

Ridley sensibly made no answer. He was sitting on his horse

beside Bird who, as ever, was on foot, while the Legion was lounging on the grass watching the night shadows shrink and fade in the far countryside and wondering what this day would bring. Most of the men were confused. They knew they had spent two days traveling, but where they had come to, or what they were expected to do now that they had arrived, they did not know. Ethan Ridley, seeking answers to the same troubling questions, had sought enlightenment from Thaddeus Bird.

"I doubt anyone knows what will happen today," Thaddeus Bird answered. "History is not marshaled by reason, Ethan, but by the idiocies of lethal fools."

Ethan struggled to elicit a sensible answer. "They reckon we've got twenty thousand men, is that right?"

"Who are 'they'?" Major Bird asked serenely, intentionally infuriating Ridley.

"How many troops do we have, then?" Ridley tried again.

"I have not counted them," Bird said. The rumors at Manassas Junction said that Beauregard's Army of Northern Virginia numbered slightly less than twenty thousand men, but no one could be sure.

"And the enemy?" Ethan asked.

"Who knows? Twenty thousand? Thirty? As the sands of the sea, maybe? A mighty host, perhaps? Shall I guess twenty thousand, will that make you happy?" Again, no one knew how many northern troops had crossed the Potomac into Virginia. Rumor put the number as high as fifty thousand, but no American had ever led an army even half that size so Thaddeus Bird distrusted the rumor.

"And we are attacking on the right? Is that what you hear?" Ridley would normally have avoided Thaddeus Bird altogether, for he found the pedantry of the ragged-bearded schoolteacher annoying in the extreme, but the nervousness that accompanied the anticipation of battle had made even Bird's company acceptable.

"That is the prevailing rumor, yes, indeed." Bird was not

inclined to make life easy for Ridley, whom he considered a dangerous fool, so he did not add that the rumor made a good deal of sense. The Confederate right wing, which was the bulk of Beauregard's army, guarded the direct road from Washington to Manassas Junction. If the federal army captured the rail junction then all of Northern Virginia was lost, so common sense suggested that General Beauregard's best hopes of victory lay in forcing the enemy away from the vulnerable railroads, just as the enemy's best hopes of a swift triumph would seem to be a quick capture of the vital junction. Neither eventuality precluded something cleverer, like a flank attack, but Bird, out on the flank, could see no evidence that either army was risking anything as sophisticated as an attempt to encircle the other, and so he assumed both armies planned to attack in the same place. He jerked his head back and forth at the pleasing notion of two armies mounting simultaneous assaults and of the northern left wing blundering into the advancing rebel right wing.

"But if there is a battle," Ridley said, struggling manfully to keep the discussion within the bounds of sanity, "then our present position is a long way from where it will be fought?"

Bird nodded vigorous assent. "God, if there is such a being, has been merciful to us in that regard. Indeed we are about as far from the army's right wing as it is possible for a regiment to be and still be a part of the army, if indeed we are a part of the army, which we don't seem to be, not unless my brother-in-law receives orders more to his liking than those brought to him by the noxious Evans."

"The Colonel just wants us to take part in the battle." Ethan defended his future father-in-law.

Bird looked up at the mounted Ridley. "I often wondered whether it was possible for my sister to marry beneath herself intellectually, and astonishingly she succeeded." Bird was enjoying himself. "If you want the truth, Ethan, I do not think the Colonel himself knows what he is doing. My own belief is that we should have embraced Evans's orders on the grounds

290

that by staying here on the left we are less likely to risk an heroic death on the right flank. But what does my opinion count? I am merely a humble schoolteacher and a notional second in command." He sniffed.

"You don't want to fight?" Ridley asked with what he hoped was utter scorn.

"Of course I don't want to fight! I shall fight if I have to, and I trust I shall fight intelligently, but the most intelligent desire, surely, is to avoid a fight altogether? Why would any sane man want to fight?"

"Because we don't want the Yankees to win today."

"Nor do we, but neither do I wish to die today, and if I am presented with a choice of becoming worm fodder or else of being governed by Lincoln's Republicans, why then I do believe I would choose to live!" Bird laughed, jerking his head backward and forward. Then, spotting movement in the valley, he abruptly checked the idiosyncratic motion. "Has the great Achilles returned to us?"

Two horsemen had appeared on the Warrenton Turnpike. The sun had not risen high enough to slant its light into the valley and so the two riders were still in shadow, but Ridley, whose eyes were younger and sharper than Bird's, recognized the Faulconers. "That's the Colonel and Adam."

"But where is Starbuck, eh? Do you think he has become a casualty of a reconnaissance, Ethan? You'd like it if young Starbuck was a casualty, wouldn't you? What is it about Starbuck that you dislike so? His good looks? His wits?"

Ethan refused to dignify the cackling questions with any reply, instead he just watched as father and son held a moment's conversation at the crossroads, then parted company. The Colonel ignored his men on the hilltop and rode south, while Adam trotted his horse uphill. "Father's gone to find Beauregard," Adam explained when he reached the plateau where the Legion waited. His horse shivered then nuzzled the nose of Ridley's mare.

"And before that?" Bird enquired. "Ethan claims you were making a reconnaissance, but I decided you were merely lolly-gagging."

"Father wanted to see whether there were any northerners on the Sudley Road," Adam explained awkwardly.

"And are there?" Bird asked in mock solicitude.

"No, Uncle."

"The saints be praised. We may breathe free again. Sweet land of liberty!" Bird raised a hand toward heaven.

"And Father wants you to discharge Nate," Adam continued in his stilted tone. He was carrying Starbuck's sword, pistol and uniform jacket.

"Your father wishes me to do what?" Bird demanded.

"To discharge Nate," Adam insisted. "From the books."

"I understand what the verb 'to discharge' means, Adam. And I will happily scratch Starbuck from the Legion's books if your father so insists, but you must tell me why. Is he dead? Am I to inscribe the name of Starbuck in the honored rolls of southern heroes? Do I enter him as a deserter? Has he expired of a sudden conniption? The demands of accurate bookkeeping require an explanation, Adam." Major Bird peered up at his nephew as he spoke this nonsense.

"He is discharged, Uncle! That's all! And Father would like his name taken off the Legion's books."

Major Bird blinked rapidly, rocked back and forward, then clawed his dirty fingernails through his long straggly beard. "Why do you discharge a man on the verge of battle? I ask merely so that I might understand the subtleties of soldiering?"

"Father decided the matter." Adam wondered why his uncle had to make such a fuss of everything. "He believed Nate should go home."

"Now? Today? At this very instant? Home to Boston?"

"Yes, indeed."

"But why?" Bird insisted.

Ridley laughed. "Why not?"

"A perfectly good question," Bird mocked, "but twice as complicated as mine. Why?" he demanded again of Adam.

Adam said nothing, but just sat with Nate's erstwhile coat and weapons held awkwardly on his saddle's pommel, and so Ethan Ridley chose to fill the silence with a mocking answer. "Because you can't trust a northerner in these days."

"Of course Nate could be trusted," Adam said irritably.

"You are so very loyal," Ridley said with a barely disguised sneer, but added nothing more.

Bird and Adam both waited for Ridley to clarify his sneer. "Beyond complimenting my nephew," Bird finally spoke with heavy sarcasm, "can you elucidate why we should not trust Starbuck? Is it merely the accident of his birth?"

"For the Lord's sake!" Ridley said as though the answer was so obvious that he demeaned himself by even bothering to mention it, let alone explain it.

"For my sake, then?" Bird persisted.

"He arrives in Richmond just as Fort Sumter falls. Does that not indicate something? And he uses your friendship, Adam, to gain the Colonel's trust, but why? Why should a son of that son of a bitch Elial Starbuck come south at this time? Are we really expected to swallow the idea that a goddamn Starbuck would fight for the South? That's like John Brown's family turning against emancipation or Harriet Bitch Stowe attacking her precious niggers!" Ridley, having made what he believed to be an incontrovertible argument, paused to light a cigar. "Starbuck was sent to spy on us," he said, summarizing his case, "and your father's done a kind act in sending him home. If he hadn't, Adam, then we'd have doubtless been forced to shoot Starbuck as a traitor."

"That would have alleviated the boredom of camp life," Bird observed brightly. "We haven't had an execution yet, and doubtless the ranks would enjoy one."

"Uncle!" Adam frowned disapprovingly.

293

"Besides, Starbuck has nigger blood," Ridley said. He was not entirely sure this was true, but his group of cronies had developed the idea as yet another stick with which to beat the despised Starbuck.

"Nigger blood! Oh well! That's different! Thank God he's gone." Major Bird laughed at the absurdity of the charge.

"Don't be a fool, Ethan," Adam said. "And don't be offensive," he added.

"Damned nigger blood!" Ridley's temper drove him on. "Look at his skin. It's dark."

"Like General Beauregard's skin? Like mine? Like yours even?" Major Bird asked happily.

"Beauregard's French," Ridley persisted, "and you can't deny that Starbuck's father is a notorious nigger lover!"

Major Bird's frenetic rocking back and forth indicated the unseemly joy he was deriving from the conversation. "Are you suggesting that Starbuck's mother takes her husband's sermons only too literally, Ethan? That she plays the double-backed beast with contraband slaves in her husband's vestry?"

"Oh, Uncle, please," Adam protested in a pained voice.

"Well, Ethan? Is that indeed what you are suggesting?" Major Bird ignored Adam.

"I'm saying we're well rid of Starbuck, that's what I'm saying." Ridley retreated from his allegations of miscegenation to attempt another attack on Starbuck. "Though I just hope he ain't telling the Yankees all about our battle plans."

"I doubt that Starbuck or anyone else knows about our battle plans," Thaddeus Bird observed dryly. "The plans of this day's battle will be decided in the memoirs of the winning general when the fighting's long over." He cackled at his own wit, then pulled one of his thin dark cigars from a pouch at his belt. "If your father insists that I discharge young Starbuck, Adam, then so I will, but I think it's a mistake."

Adam frowned. "You liked Nate, Uncle, is that it?"

"Did I mention my tastes? Or affections? You never did

294

listen, Adam. I was commenting on your friend's ability. He can think, and that is a distressingly rare talent among young men. Most of you believe that it is sufficient to merely agree with the prevailing sentiment which is, of course, what dogs and churchgoers do, but Starbuck has a mind. Of sorts."

"Well, he's taken his mind north." Adam curtly tried to end the conversation.

"And his cruelty," Major Bird said musingly. "We shall miss that."

"Cruelty!" Adam, who felt he had been insufficiently loyal to his friend all morning, now saw a chance to defend Nate. "He isn't cruel!"

"Anyone raised in the more zealous parts of your church has probably imbibed a God-like indifference to life and death, and that will endow young Starbuck with a talent for cruelty. And in these ridiculous times, Adam, we are going to need all the cruelty we can muster. Wars are not won by gallantry, but by assiduously applied butchery."

Adam, who feared exactly that truth, tried to check his uncle's obvious glee. "So you have frequently told me, Uncle."

Major Bird scratched a match to light his cigar. "Fools usually need repetition to understand even the simplest of ideas."

Adam gazed over the heads of the silent troops to where his father's servants tended a cooking fire. "I shall fetch some coffee," he announced loftily.

"You won't fetch anything without my permission," Major Bird said slyly, "or had you failed to note that in your father's absence I am the regiment's senior officer?"

Adam looked down from his saddle. "Don't be absurd, Uncle. Now, shall I tell Nelson to bring you some coffee?"

"Not unless he serves the men first. Officers are not members of a privileged class, Adam, but merely officials encumbered with greater responsibilities."

Uncle Thaddeus, Adam thought, could twist and convolute

the simplest matter into a tangle of difficulties. Adam found himself wondering just why his mother had insisted on making her brother a soldier, then realized that of course it was to annoy his father. He sighed at the thought, then gathered his reins. "Goodbye, Uncle." Adam turned his horse away and, without seeking permission to leave and with Ridley for company, he raked his spurs back.

The sunlight was at last reaching down the hill's western slope to cast long shadows aslant on the grass. Major Bird unbuttoned his uniform jacket's breast pocket and took out a linen-wrapped *carte de visite* on which was mounted a photograph of Priscilla. Vanity had caused her to take off her spectacles to have the picture made and she consequently looked rather myopic and uncertain, but to Bird she was a paragon of beauty. He touched the stiff pasteboard with its awkward daguerreotype image to his lips, then very reverently wrapped the card in its scrap of linen and placed it back in his breast pocket.

A half mile behind Bird, on a flimsy tower made of lashed branches up which a precarious ladder climbed to a platform thirty feet high, two wig-waggers prepared for their duty. The wig-waggers were signalers who talked to one another with semaphore flags. Four such wig-wagging towers had been constructed so that General Beauregard could stay in touch with the wide-flung wings of his army. One of the wig-waggers, a corporal, uncapped the heavy, tripod-mounted telescope that was used to read the flags from the neighboring towers, adjusted the instrument's focus, then swept it toward the leafy hills that lay northward of the rebel lines. He could see the sun bright on the shingles of the pitched church roof on Sudley Hill and, just beyond it, an empty meadow with a flash of silver showing where the Bull Run stream ran between lush pastures. Nothing moved in that landscape, except for the small figure of a woman who appeared at the church door to shake a mat free of dust. The wig-wagger turned the glass back east to where the sun blazed low over a horizon hazed by the dying smoke of a myriad cooking fires. He was about to turn the glass on toward the next signal tower when he saw some men appear on the summit of a bare knoll that lay about a mile beyond the Run on the enemy's side of the stream. "You want to see some damn Yankees?" the corporal asked his companion.

"Not now, not ever," the second signaler answered.

"I'm looking at the bastards." The corporal sounded excited. "Goddamn! So they are there after all!"

And ready to fight.

The group of men, some on foot, some on horseback, some civilian and some military, stopped on the summit of the bare knoll. The rising sun marvelously illuminated the landscape before them, showing the wooded valleys, fenced pastures and bright glimpses of the stream beyond which the Confederate Army waited for its defeat.

Captain James Elial MacPhail Starbuck was at the center of the small group. The young Boston lawyer sat his horse like a man more accustomed to a leather padded chair than to a saddle, and indeed, if James had to pick the one aspect of soldiering that he most disliked it would be the ubiquitous presence of horses, which he considered to be large, hot, smelly, fly-ridden beasts with yellow teeth, scary eyes and hooves like ungoverned hammers. Yet if riding a horse were necessary to end the slave-holders' revolt, then James would willingly straddle every horse in America for, though he might lack his father's eloquence, he was just as fervent in his belief that the rebellion was more than a blight on America's reputation, but an offense against God himself. America, James believed, was a divinely inspired nation, uniquely blessed by the Almighty, and to rebel against such a chosen people was to do the devil's work. So on this Christian Sabbath, in these green fields, the forces of right-eousness would advance against a satanic rabble, and surely,

James believed, God would not permit the northern army to be defeated? He prayed silently, beseeching God for victory.

"You reckon we can walk down to the battery, Cap'n?" One of the civilians interrupted James's reverie, gesturing at the same time to an artillery battery that was arranging its complicated affairs in a field that lay beside the Warrenton Turnpike at the foot of the knoll.

"It is not permitted," James responded curtly.

"Ain't it a free country, Cap'n?"

"It is not permitted," James insisted in the authoritative voice that always proved so effective in the Commonwealth of Massachusetts's Court of Common Pleas, but which merely seemed to amuse these newspapermen. The civilians accompanying James were reporters and sketch artists from a dozen northern papers who had come to Brigadier General McDowell's headquarters the previous night and had been told to attach themselves to the general's *sous*-adjutant. James already had the responsibility of escorting a half-dozen foreign military attachés who had ridden from their countries' Washington embassies and who were now treating the impending battle as though it were a fine entertainment laid on for their benefit, but at least the foreign military officers treated James with respect while the newspapermen merely seemed to aggravate him.

"What in hell's name is a *sous*-adjutant?" a reporter from *Harper's Weekly* had asked James in the raw small hours after midnight when, all around them, the northern army had been stirring itself ready for its march into battle. "A kind of Indian fighter?"

"*Sous* is French for 'under.'" James suspected that the newspaperman who came from the self-proclaimed "Journal of Civilization" knew full well what *sous* meant.

"Does that mean you're a kind of inferior adjutant, Cap'n?"

"It means I am an assistant to the adjutant." James had managed to keep his temper, despite feeling distinctly out of sorts.

298

He had managed but two hours sleep and had woken to a sharp attack of flatulence that he acknowledged to be entirely his own fault. Brigadier General McDowell was a famous trencherman who had last night encouraged his staff to eat well, and James, despite his conviction that ample nourishment was necessary for both spiritual and bodily health, wondered if a third helping of the general's beef pie had been a plateful too much. Then there had also been the hotcakes and custard, all consumed with the teetotal general's well-sugared lemonade. Such indulgence would not have mattered if James had been able to take a spoonful of his mother's carminative balsam before retiring, but his fool of a servant had forgotten to put James's medicine chest into the headquarters' baggage wagons and so James had been forced to field the inquisitive reporters' questions and, at the same time, hide the exquisite discomfort of a severe attack of indigestion.

The newspapermen, meeting James in the farmhouse at Centreville where he had spent his uncomfortable night, had demanded to know McDowell's intentions, and James had explained, as simply as he could, that the general envisaged nothing less than the wholesale destruction of the rebellion. An hour's march to the south of the Bull Run stream was the small town of Manassas Junction and, once that town was captured, the rail line that linked the two rebel armies in Northern Virginia would be severed. General Johnston could no longer come from the Shenandoah Valley to support Beauregard, so Beauregard's defeated rebel army, cut off from that reinforcement, must retreat to Richmond and there be captured. The war would then peter out as the scattered rebel forces were either defeated or gave up. James had made it all sound very predictable and rather obvious.

"But the rebels gave us a whipping four days ago. Doesn't that worry you?" one of the newspapermen had asked. He was referring to a large northern reconnaissance force that had approached the Bull Run four days before and, in an excess of zeal, had tried to cross the stream, but had instead provoked a withering and deadly hail of bullets from the rebels concealed among the thick foliage on the farther bank. James dismissed the repulse as trivial, and had even tried to gloss it with a coat of victory by suggesting that the accidental contact with the enemy had been designed to convince the rebels that any northern attack would fall in the same place, on their right flank, when in fact the real assault would hook deep around the Confederate left.

"So what's the worst that could happen today, Captain?" another of the newspapermen had wanted to know.

The worst, James conceded, was that General Johnston's forces might have left the Shenandoah Valley and be on their way to reinforce Beauregard's men. That, he admitted, would make the day's fighting much harder, but he could assure the newspapermen that the latest telegraph news from the northern forces in the Shenandoah was that Johnston was still in the valley.

"But if Joe Johnston's rebs do join up with Beauregard's," the newspaperman insisted, "does that mean we're whipped?"

"It means we must work somewhat harder to defeat them." James felt annoyed by the tone of the question, but calmly reiterated his assurance that Johnston was still trapped far to the west, which meant that the great issue of American unity must this day be decided by the men presently gathered either side of the Bull Run. "And it will be a victory," James had confidently predicted. He had taken repeated pains to tell the newspapermen that this northern army was the largest force of troops ever assembled in North America. Irvin McDowell led more than thirty thousand men, over twice as many as George Washington's army at Yorktown. It was, James assured the journalists, an overpowering force and proof of the federal government's resolve to crush the rebellion swiftly and absolutely.

The reporters had pounced on the word *overpowering*. "You

mean we outnumber the rebs, Captain?"

"Not outnumber, exactly." In fact no one knew just how many men the rebels had mustered on the Bull Run's farther bank, the estimates ranging from ten thousand to a most unlikely forty thousand, but James did not want to make the northern victory sound like an inevitability brought about by sheer numbers. There had to be some room for northern heroism, and so he had hedged his answer. "We think," he said grandly, "that the rebels can muster numbers not unlike our own, but in this battle, gentlemen, it will be training, morale, and justice that shall prevail."

And justice would prevail, James still believed, not just to capture a rural railhead, but rather to so defeat and so demoralize the Confederate forces that the victorious northern troops could march unobstructed on to the rebel capital, which lay a mere hundred miles south. "On to Richmond!" the northern newspapers cried, and "On to Richmond!" was sewn in bright cloth letters on the standards of some federal regiments, and "On to Richmond!" the spectators had called to the troops marching across the Long Bridge out of Washington. Some of those spectators had done more than watch the troops leave, but had actually accompanied the army into Virginia. Indeed it seemed to James as though half of Washington's polite society had come to witness the great northern victory for, as the sun now rose above the Bull Run, he could see scores of civilian spectators already mingling with the federal troops. There were elegant carriages parked among the gun limbers, and artists' easels and sketch pads standing amidst the stacks of rifles and muskets. Fashionable ladies sheltered under parasols, servants laid out rugs and picnic hampers, while self-important congressmen, eager to share if not wholly capture the glory of the hour, pontificated to whomever might listen on the army's strategy.

"You reckon we'll make Richmond by Saturday?" the *Harper's Weekly* reporter now asked James Starbuck.

"We devoutly hope so."

"And we'll hang Jefferson Davis on Sunday," the reporter said, then gave a whoop of glee at that happy prospect.

"Not on Sunday, I think." James was too much of a lawyer to let such a careless remark go unchallenged, especially in front of the foreign military attachés, who might conclude from the reporter's words that the United States was not only a nation of Sabbath breakers, but also a pack of uncivilized roughs who did not understand the need for strict legality. "We'll hang Davis after due process," James said for the benefit of those foreigners, "and only after due process."

"The Captain means we'll tie a good knot in the rope first," one of the reporters helpfully explained to the military attachés.

James dutifully smiled, though in truth he found the ways of these newspapermen shockingly dishonest. Many of these journalists had already written their accounts of this day's battle, using their imaginations to describe how the cowardly troops of the slave masters had fled at the first sight of the Stars and Stripes, and how other rebel soldiers had fallen penitent to their knees rather than open fire on the glorious old flag. Northern cavalry had trampled their hooves red in the slavocracy's gore and northern bayonets had become sticky with southern blood. James might be shocked by the dishonesty, but as the stories merely reported an outcome for which he most earnestly prayed, he did not feel comfortable in expressing reproof lest he should be considered defeatist. Defeat, after all, was unthinkable, for this was the day when the rebellion must be broken and the race to Richmond could begin.

There was a sudden flurry at the foot of the hill as the artillery horses were freed from their gun and limber traces. The guns had been placed behind a snake-rail fence and were aimed toward a handsome stone bridge that carried the turnpike over the stream. The bridge was the key to Brigadier

General McDowell's hopes for, by persuading the rebels that his main attack would be an assault straight down the turnpike, he hoped to draw their forces forward in the bridge's defense while his secret flanking column curled about their rear. Other northern troops would demonstrate against the enemy's right wing, but the vital achievement was to hold the rebel left wing hard up against the stone bridge so that the northern flank attack would sweep unopposed and undetected into the Confederate rear. The rebels had thus to be deceived into believing that the feigned attack on the bridge was the main attack of the day, and to add verisimilitude to that deception a massive piece of artillery had been brought forward to open the fake assault.

That artillery piece was a thirty-pounder Parrott rifle with an iron barrel more than eleven feet long and weighing nearly two tons. The gun's metal-rimmed wheels stood as high as a man's shoulders, and the huge weapon had needed nineteen horses to drag it forward during the last hours of darkness. Indeed its slow progress had held up the advance of the whole federal army, and some northern officers thought it madness to maneuver such a giant piece of fortress artillery into the army's forwardmost positions, but every soldier who saw the cumbersome gun roll ponderously past in the first light of dawn reckoned that the beast would be a battle winner all by itself. The bore of the rifled barrel was over four inches across, while its iron-banded black breech was now crammed with nearly four pounds of black powder onto which a conical shell had been rammed. The shell was filled with black powder and was designed to burst apart in a killing explosion of flame and shattering iron that would tear and splinter and flense the rebels on the Bull Run's far bank, though presently the dawn's early light was hardly revealing much in the way of targets on that rebel side of the stream. Once in a while a Confederate officer spurred a horse across a distant field, and some few infantrymen were scattered on a hill that lay at least a mile beyond the stone bridge, but otherwise there was small evidence that the rebels were present in any force.

A friction primer was shoved through the Parrott's touch-hole and deep into the canvas bag of black powder. The primer was a copper tube filled with finely mealed gunpowder. The topmost section of the tube held a small charge of fulminate and was pierced by a serrated metal crosspiece, which when pulled hard by its lanyard would scrape violently across the fulminate and, just like a match head scratched by a file, would detonate the fulminate with friction. A gunner sergeant now grabbed the lanyard's free end while the other crew members stood well clear of the weapon's lethal recoil.

"Ready!" the gunner sergeant called. Some of the crewmen from the other guns in the battery had assembled in a small group to listen to a Bible reading and to say a prayer, but all now turned toward the giant Parrott rifle and covered their ears.

A mounted artillery officer consulted his watch. In the years to come he wanted to tell his children and grandchildren the exact moment at which his great gun had signaled the beginning of the rebellion's end. By his watch it was just approaching eighteen minutes past five in the morning, a mere twelve minutes since the sun had first burst its brilliance across the eastern horizon. The artillery officer, a lieutenant, had entered that moment of sunrise in his diary, though he had also meticulously noted that his watch was liable to gain or lose five minutes in any one day, depending on the temperature.

"Ready!" the gunner sergeant called again, this time with a touch of impatience in his voice.

The artillery lieutenant waited till the watch's hand exactly pointed to the speck that marked the eighteenth minute, then dropped his right hand. "Fire!"

The sergeant snatched the lanyard and the small crosspiece scraped violently across the fulminate. Fire flashed down the copper tube and the powder bag ignited to hurl the shell forward. The base of the shell was a cup of soft brass that expanded to grip the Parrott gun's rifled barrel and start the shell spinning.

The noise exploded violently across the landscape, startling birds up from the trees and thumping the eardrums of the thousands of men who waited for the orders to advance. The gun itself was hurled backward, its trail gouging the soil and its wheels bouncing a clear eighteen inches up from the ground and coming to rest a full seven feet back from where the gun had been fired. In front of the fuming barrel was a scorched patch of turf beneath a roiling cloud of dirty white smoke. Onlookers who had never heard a great gun fired gasped at the sheer fury of the sound, at the appalling crack of the cannon's firing, which promised a horrid destruction on the far side of the stream.

The crew was already feeding the monster's smoking maw with a soaking sponge that would douse the remnants of fire deep in the barrel before the next bag of gunpowder was rammed into the muzzle. Meanwhile the first shell screamed across the meadows, flashed above the bridge, crashed through the wood in a splinter of shattering twigs, then spun hard into the empty hillside beyond the trees. Inside the shell was an ordinary rifle's percussion cap that was fixed to the front of a heavy metal rod which, when the missile struck the hillside, was thrown violently forward to strike against an iron anvil plate in the shell's nose. The copper percussion cap was filled with a fulminate of mercury that was unstable enough to explode under such sudden pressure and which thus ignited the gunpowder crammed into the shell's casing, but the missile had already buried itself three feet into the soft ground and the explosion did little more than quake a few square paces of empty hillside and gout a sudden vent of smoky earth from the riven grass.

"Six and a half seconds." The mounted artillery officer

noted the flight time of the shell aloud, then entered the figure into his notebook.

"You may report that the battle proper began at twenty-one minutes past five," James Starbuck announced. His ears were still ringing from the violence of the cannon's report and his horse's ears were still pricked nervously forward.

"I make it only a quarter past five," the *Harper's Weekly* man said.

"Eighteen minutes past?" The speaker was a French military attaché, one of the half-dozen foreign officers who were observing the battle with Captain James Starbuck.

"Too damned early, whatever the time," one of the newspapermen yawned.

James Starbuck frowned at the oath, then flinched as the heavy gun crashed its second shot toward the stone bridge. The percussive sound of the gun's firing thumped across the green countryside and seemed far more impressive than any effect the shell was having on the distant landscape. James desperately wanted to see havoc and maelstrom beyond the stream. He had thought when he had first seen the huge Parrott that a single shell fired from so massive a weapon might serve to panic the rebels, but alas, everything beyond the stream looked oddly calm, and James feared that lack of carnage might seem ridiculous to these foreign soldiers who had all served in Europe's wars and who, James thought, might therefore be supercilious about these amateurish American efforts.

"A very impressive weapon, Captain." The French attaché soothed all James's worries with the generous remark.

"Entirely manufactured in America, Colonel, at our West Point foundry in Cold Spring, New York, and designed by the foundry's superintendent, Mister Robert Parrott." James thought he heard one of the newspapermen making a birdlike noise behind him, but managed to ignore the sound. "The gun can fire common shell, case shot, and bolts. It has a range of two thousand two hundred yards at five degrees of elevation." Much of James's service had so far consisted of learning just such details so he could keep foreign attachés properly informed. "We would of course be happy to arrange an escorted tour of the foundry for you."

"Ah! So." The Frenchman, a colonel called Lassan, had one eye, a horribly scarred face, and a magnificently ornate uniform. He watched as the huge gun fired a third time, then nodded his approval as the rest of the federal artillery, which had been waiting for the third shot as their signal, opened fire in unison. The green fields to the east of the stream blossomed with smoke as gun after gun crashed back on its trail. A teamhorse, inadequately picketed, bolted in panic from the sky-battering noise, dispersing a group of blackberrying infantrymen behind the gun line. "I never enjoyed artillery fire," Colonel Lassan remarked mildly, then touched a nicotine-stained finger to the patch over his missing eye. "This went to a Russian shell."

"We trust the rebels are sharing your distaste, sir," James said with heavy humor. The strike of the gunshots was now visible beyond the stream where trees shook from the impact of shells and the soil of the farther hillsides was being flecked by ricocheting and exploding missiles. James had to raise his voice to be heard above the loud cannonade. "Once the flanking column reveals itself, sir, I think we can anticipate swift victory."

"Ah, indeed?" Lassan enquired politely, then leaned forward to pat his horse's neck.

"Two bucks says we'll have the bastards on the skedaddle by ten o'clock," a reporter from the *Chicago Tribune* offered the assembled company, though no one took up the wager. A Spanish colonel, magnificent in a red and white dragoon's uniform, unscrewed the cap from a flask and sipped whiskey.

Colonel Lassan suddenly frowned. "Was that a train whistle?" he asked Captain Starbuck.

"I'm sure I couldn't say, sir," James said.

"Did you hear a train whistle?" the Frenchman asked his companions, who shook their heads.

"Is it important, sir?" James asked.

Lassan shrugged. "General Johnston's forces from the Shenandoah Army, surely, would travel here by train, would they not?"

James assured Colonel Lassan that the rebel troops in the Shenandoah Valley were fully occupied by a contingent of northern soldiers and could not possibly have arrived at Manassas Junction.

"But suppose General Johnston has given your covering forces the slip?" Colonel Lassan spoke excellent English in a British accent which James, whose indigestion had not improved with the passing hours, found rather irritating. "You are naturally communicating with your troops in the Shenandoah by telegraph?" Colonel Lassan continued with his needling enquiries.

"We know General Johnston was fully engaged by our forces two days ago," James assured Colonel Lassan.

"But two days is more than sufficient time to sidestep a covering force and ride the trains to Manassas, is it not?" the Frenchman asked.

"I think it most unlikely." James tried to sound coolly dismissive.

"You will recall," Colonel Lassan persisted, "that our great victory over Franz Joseph at Solferino was caused by the speed with which our emperor moved the army by train?"

James, who did not know where Solferino was and knew nothing of any battle there and had never heard of the French emperor's railroad achievements, nodded wisely, but then gallantly suggested that the rebel forces of the Confederacy were hardly capable of imitating the achievements of the French army.

"You had better hope not," Lassan said grimly, then

trained his field glasses on a far hill where a rebel telegraphist was sending a message. "You are confident, Captain, that your flanking force will be on time?" Lassan asked.

"They should be arriving at any moment, sir." James's confidence was belied by the lack of any evidence that fighting had indeed broken out in the rebel rear, though he consoled himself that the intervening distance would surely prevent any such evidence being visible. That proof would come when the Confederate forces defending the stone bridge began their panicked flight. "I've no doubt our flanking force is attacking at this very moment, sir," James said with as much certainty as he could muster, then, because he was so proud of Yankee efficiency, he could not resist adding two words, "as planned."

"Ah! Planned! I see, I see," Colonel Lassan responded gnomically, then shot a sympathetic glance at James. "My father was a very great soldier, Captain, but he always liked to say that the practice of war is much like making love to a woman—an activity full of delights, but none of them predictable and the best of them capable of inflicting grievous injury on a man."

"Oh, I like that!" The Chicago newspaperman scribbled in his notebook.

James was so offended by the tastelessness of the remark that he just stared speechless into the distance. Colonel Lassan, oblivious of the offense he had given, hummed a tune, while the newspapermen scribbled down their first impressions of the war which, so far, were disappointing. War was nothing but noise and smoke, though, unlike the journalists, the skirmishers on both banks of the Bull Run were learning just what that noise and smoke meant. Bullets whickered across the stream as rebel and federal sharpshooters sniped from the trees and edged the watercourse with a wispy lacework of powder smoke that was twitched aside by the screaming passage of the heavy shells that crashed into the timber to explode in gouts of sulfurous black smoke and whistling iron fragments. A branch was struck by a shell, cracked, and splintered down to break a horse's back. The beast screamed terribly while a drummer boy cried for his mother and feebly attempted to stop his guts spilling from the ragged shrapnel gash in his belly. An officer stared in disbelief at the spreading blood that filled his lap from the bullet wound in his groin. A bearded sergeant gripped the ragged stump of his left wrist and wondered how in God's name he was ever to plough a straight furrow again. A corporal vomited blood, then slowly crumpled onto the ground. Gunsmoke sifted among the branches. The cannon were firing more quickly now to make a gigantic drumroll that rose to drown the music of the regimental bands, which still played their jaunting tunes behind the battle lines.

And farther behind the rebel battle line still, back at Manassas Junction, a plume of blue-white woodsmoke streamed back from a locomotive's blackened stack. The first of General Joseph Johnston's men had come from the Shenandoah. They had escaped the northern troops, and eight thousand more rebels had thus begun to reinforce the eighteen thousand that Beauregard had already assembled beside the Run. The armies had gathered, the guns were heating up, and a Sabbath Day's slaughter could begin.

11

"So you're our damned spy, are you?" Colonel Nathan Evans greeted Nathaniel Starbuck who, still mounted on Pocahontas, had his hands tied behind his back and was under the guard of two Louisiana cavalrymen who while scouting the country toward Sudley Church had found and pursued Starbuck, then captured and pinioned him, and now had fetched him back to their commanding officer, who was standing with his brigade staff a short distance behind the stone bridge. "Get the bugger off his horse!" Evans snapped.

Someone took hold of Starbuck's right arm and pulled him unceremoniously out of the saddle so that the northerner fell heavily at Evans's feet. "I'm not a spy," he managed to say. "I'm one of Faulconer's men."

"Faulconer?" Evans barked a brief, humorless noise that might have been laughter or was maybe a growl. "You mean that bastard who thinks he's too good to fight with my brigade? Faulconer doesn't have men, boy, he has white-livered fairies. Milksops. Mudsills. Black-assed, shad-bellied, shit-faced, pussy-hearted trash. And you're one of that scum, are you?"

Starbuck recoiled from the stream of insult, but somehow managed to persevere with his explanation. "I found northern troops in the woods beyond the Sudley Fords. A lot of them, and coming this way. I was on my way back to warn you."

"Bastard's lying like a rug, Colonel," one of the two Louisianan cavalrymen interjected. They were whip-lean, rough-bearded horsemen with weather-darkened faces and wild scary eyes, reminding Starbuck of Sergeant Truslow. They were outrageously armed, each man carrying a carbine, two pistols, a saber and a bowie knife. One of the two cavalrymen had a bleeding cut of freshly slaughtered pork hanging from his saddle bow, while the other, who had efficiently relieved Starbuck of his three dollars and sixteen cents, had two unplucked chickens hanging from his crupper strap by their broken necks. That man had also found the letter from Starbuck's father and his brother's laissez-passer, but, being illiterate, he had taken no interest in the papers which he had carelessly shoved back into Starbuck's shirt pocket. "He weren't weaponed," the laconic cavalryman continued, "and he didn't have no uniform on him. I reckons he's a spy, Colonel, sir. Just listen to the sumbitch's voice. He ain't no southron."

A shell thumped into the meadow a dozen paces in front of the small group. It exploded, jarring a seismic thump through the soil and rooting up chunks of red dirt. The sound, even muffled by the earth, was a violent, scary crack that made Starbuck wince with shock. A scrap of stone or metal whistled close to Evans's shabby brown hat, but the colonel did not even flinch. He just glanced at one of his orderlies who was mounted on a piebald horse. "Intact, Otto?"

"Ja, Colonel, intact."

Evans looked back to Starbuck, who had struggled to his feet. "So where did you see these federal troops?"

"Maybe a half mile beyond the Sudley Fords, sir, on a road that leads east."

"In the woods, you say?"

"Yes, sir."

Evans picked with an opened penknife at his teeth, which were dark and rotten from chewing tobacco. His sceptical eyes looked up and down Starbuck, and did not seem to like what they saw. "So how many federal troops did you see, cuffee?"

"I don't know, sir. A lot. And they've got cannon with them."

"Cannon, eh? I am frightened! Shitting in my pants, I am." Evans sniggered and the men around him laughed. The colonel was famous for the filth of his language, the depth of his thirst and the ferocity of his temper. He had graduated from West Point in 1848, though barely, and now ridiculed the academy's curriculum by claiming that what made a soldier was the talent to fight like a wildcat, not some prinking ability to speak French or to solve fancy problems in trigonometry or to master the complexities of natural philosophy, whatever the hell that was. "You saw the cannon, did you?" he now demanded fiercely.

"Yes, sir." In truth Starbuck had seen no northern guns, but he had watched the federal troops dismantling the barricade and he reasoned they would surely not waste their time clearing the road for infantry. An infantry column could have skirted the felled trees, but guns would need an unobstructed passage, which surely suggested that the concealed flank attack was bringing artillery.

Nathan Evans cut a new slice of tobacco that he plugged into one of his cheeks. "And just what in the name of God were you doing in the woods beyond Sudley Fords?"

Starbuck paused and another shell cracked apart in black smoke and a stab of red flame. The intensity of the explosion was extraordinary to Starbuck, who again flinched as the per-cussive clap shivered the air, though Colonel Nathan Evans appeared entirely unworried by the sound apart from another enquiry of his mounted orderly that all was still well.

"*Ja*, Colonel. All is vell. Don't vorry yourself." The German orderly was a huge man with a woeful face and a curious stoneware barrel that was strapped like a rucksack on his broad back. His master, Colonel Evans, whom Starbuck had gathered from his captors was nicknamed "Shanks," did not look any more prepossessing by daylight than he had in the small hours of the morning; indeed, to Starbuck's jaundiced eye, Evans most resembled one of the bent-backed Boston coal heavers who scuttled with hundredweight sacks of fuel from the street to the kitchen cellars, and it was hardly surprising, Starbuck

313

thought, that the fastidious Washington Faulconer had refused to put himself under the South Carolinian's command.

"Well? You ain't answered my question, boy." Evans glared at Starbuck. "What were you doing on the far side of the Run, eh?"

"Colonel Faulconer sent me," Starbuck said defiantly.

"Sent you? Why?"

Starbuck wanted to salve his pride and say that he had been sent to reconnoiter the woods beyond Bull Run, but he sensed the lie would never hold, and so he settled for the ignominious truth. "He didn't want me in his regiment, sir. He was sending me back to my people."

Evans turned to stare intently at the trees edging the Bull Run stream where his half-brigade was defending the stone bridge carrying the turnpike west from Washington. If the northerners did attack this section of the Run then Evans's defense would be desperate, for his brigade consisted only of a handful of light cavalry, four obsolete smoothbore cannon, an understrength infantry regiment from South Carolina and another, equally undermanned, from Louisiana. Beauregard had left the brigade thus thinly defended because he was certain that the battle would be fought far out on the Confederate right wing. So far, and fortunately for Evans, the northern assault on the brigade had been restricted to harassing rifle and artillery fire, though one of the enemy's cannon delivered a shell so monstrous that the sky seemed to tremble each time one passed overhead.

Evans watched the trees with his head cocked to one side as though he was judging the course of the fighting by the noise of battle. To Starbuck the rifle and musket fire sounded oddly like the fierce crackling of burning dry undergrowth, while above it boomed the artillery fire. The flight of the shells made a noise like ripping cloth, or perhaps bacon frying, except that every now and then the sizzling would swell into a sudden ear-hurting crash as a missile exploded. A few rifle bullets

314

snickered close by Evans's small group, some of them making an eerie whistling. It was all very odd to Starbuck, who was aware of his heart thumping in his chest, yet, in all truth, he was not so frightened of the shells and bullets as he was of the fierce, bow-legged Shanks Evans, who now turned back to the prisoner. "Goddamn Faulconer was sending you to your people?" Evans asked. "What the hell do you mean?"

"My family, sir. In Boston."

"Oh, Boston!" Evans guffawed the name gleefully, inviting his staff to join his mockery. "A shit hole. A piss hole. A city of puling crap. Christ, but I hate Boston. A city of black-assed Republican trash. A city of interfering, hymn-singing, lickbelly women who are no damned good for anything." Evans spat a lavish gob of tobacco-laced spittle onto Starbuck's shoes. "So Faulconer was sending you back to Boston, was he, boy? Why?"

"I don't know, sir."

"Don't know, sir," Evans mimicked Starbuck, "or perhaps you're telling me lies, you miserable twist of shit. Maybe you're trying to drag my men away from the bridge, is that it, you shit-belly?" The Colonel's vehemence was terrifying, over-whelming, blistering, forcing Starbuck to take an involuntary backward step as the Colonel's harangue spattered him with spittle. "You're trying to sell me down the river, you cuffee bastard. You want me to open the pike so the northern bastards can swarm over the bridge and then we'll all be hanging from the trees come nightfall. Ain't that right, you son of a no-good bitch?" There was a few seconds' silence, then Evans repeated his question in a voice that was a high-pitched scream. "Ain't that right, you son of a cuffee bitch?"

"There's a column of northern troops in the woods beyond the Sudley Fords." Starbuck somehow managed to keep his voice calm. He gave his hands a futile jerk, trying to point to the north, but the pinion at his wrists was far too secure. "They're marching this way, sir, and they'll be here in another hour or so."

Another shell crashed into the pasture beyond the turnpike where Evans's two reserve artillery pieces stood waiting in the uncut grass. The resting gunners did not even look up, not even when one of the giant shells fell shorter than usual and tore a branch from a nearby tree before exploding forty yards away in a turmoil of dirt, leaves, iron fragments, and hot smoke.

"How's my barrelito, Otto?" Evans shouted.

"No harm, Colonel. Don't you vorry." The German sounded impassive.

"I vorry," Evans growled, "I vorry about lunkhead pieces of shit from Boston. What's your name, boy?"

"Nathaniel, sir. Nathaniel Starbuck."

"If you're lying to me, Nathaniel Shitface, I'll take you to the woodshed and cut your balls off. If you've got any balls. Have you got balls, Nathaniel?" Starbuck said nothing. He was feeling relieved that this furious, foul-tongued man had not connected his surname to the Reverend Elial. Two more shells screamed overhead and an overshot rifle bullet made its odd whistling noise as it flicked past. "So if I move my men to face your column, fairy-shit"—Evans thrust his face so close to Starbuck that the Bostonian could smell the mephitic mix of whiskey and tobacco on the South Carolinian's breath—"I'll be letting the enemy across the bridge here, won't I, and then there'll be no Confederacy anymore, will there? And then the emancipating shitheads from Boston will come down to rape our women, if that's what the hymn singers from Boston do. Maybe they'd prefer to rape our men? Is that your taste, cuffee-boy? You'd like to rape me, would you?"

Again Starbuck said nothing. Evans spat derision of Starbuck's silence, then turned to see a gray-coated infantryman limping back along the turnpike. "Where in hell are you going?" Evans exploded in sudden fury at the soldier, who just stared back in blank astonishment. "You can still shoot a rifle, can't you?" Evans screamed. "So get back! Unless you want

316

those black-assed Republicans fathering your wife's next bastards? Get back!" The man turned and limped painfully back toward the bridge, using his rifle-musket as a crutch.

A solid shot slapped dust from the turnpike, then ricocheted on without hitting anyone in Evans's headquarters group, but the wind of the shot's passing seemed to stagger the injured infantryman who swayed on his makeshift crutch, then collapsed at the roadside close by the two reserve six-pounder guns. Evans's other two guns were closer to the Bull Run, returning the enemy's fire with shrapnel shells that burst in the distant air like sudden small gray clouds from which fizzing white smoke trails spiraled crazily earthward. Whether the shells were finding their targets no one knew, but in truth Evans was merely firing to keep up his men's morale.

The reserve gunners bided their time. Most lay on their backs, apparently dozing. Two men tossed a ball back and forth while an officer, spectacles perched low on his nose, leaned on a bronze barrel and turned the pages of a book. A shirt-sleeved gunner with bright red suspenders sat with his back against the gun's offside wheel. He was writing, dipping his pen into an ink bottle that rested in the grass by his side. The men's insouciance did not seem out of place for, though the fighting was generating a carapace of noise and smoke, there was no great sense of urgency. Starbuck had expected battle to be more vigorous, like the newspaper accounts of the Mexican War that had told of General Scott's brave troops carrying the American flag through shot and screaming shell into the Halls of Montezuma, but there was almost an abstracted air about this morning's events. The gunner officer slowly turned a page, the letter writer carefully drained ink from his pen's nib before lifting it to the page, while one of the ball players missed a catch and laughed lazily. The wounded infantryman lay in the ditch, hardly moving.

"So what do I do with the sumbitch, Colonel?" one of the Louisiana cavalrymen guarding Starbuck asked.

317

Evans had been frowning toward the mist of smoke that hung above the stone bridge. He turned bad-temperedly back to announce his decision about Starbuck, but was interrupted before he could speak. "A message, sir." The speaker was the lieutenant who had accompanied Evans on his abortive visit to Faulconer's tent that morning. The lieutenant was mounted on a gaunt gray horse and carried a pair of field glasses with which he had been watching the semaphore station on the hill. "From the wig-wag, sir. Our left is turned." The lieutenant spoke without a trace of emotion.

There was a moment's stillness as one of the enemy's monstrous shells ripped overhead. The injured man beside the road was trying to stand, but seemed too feeble to rise. "Say that again, Meadows," Evans demanded.

Lieutenant Meadows consulted his notebook. "'Look out on your left, you are turned.' Those are the exact words, sir."

Evans swiveled fast to stare north, though nothing showed there except the heavy summer trees and a high hawk soaring. Then he turned back to Starbuck, his small eyes wide with shock. "I owe you an apology, boy. By God I owe you an apology. I'm sorry, so I am, sorry!" Evans blurted out the last word, then twisted again, this time to stare toward the stone bridge. His left hand twitched spasmodically at his side, the only evidence of the strain he was enduring. "This is a pretense. They ain't attacking here, they're just stroking our bellies, fooling us, keeping us still while the real attack comes up our backsides. Jesus!" He had been speaking to himself, but suddenly he snapped into a much louder voice. "Horse! Bring my horse! Get on your horse, boy!" This last was to Starbuck.

"Sir!" Starbuck yelped.

"Boy?"

"I'm tied up."

"Release the boy! Otto?"

"*Ja*, Colonel?"

"Give Boston some barrelito. One cup." It seemed that
318

Evans had chosen the name "Boston" for Starbuck's nickname, just as the curious stone barrel on the German orderly's back was called "barrelito."

The big German rode his piebald horse close to Starbuck while another man, hurrying to obey Evans's orders, cut the rope at Starbuck's wrists. Starbuck began massaging the rope burns, then saw that the impassive German orderly had reached behind his back to manipulate a small wooden tap that was let into the base of the stoneware barrel. The German drew a tin cup of liquid from the barrel, then solemnly handed the cup down to Starbuck. "Trink! Come now, quick! I need the cup again. Trink!"

Starbuck accepted the cup that was filled with what appeared to be cold tea. He was thirsty as a dog and eagerly tipped the cup to his lips, then half choked for the liquid was not tea, but whiskey; raw, hard, undiluted whiskey.

"Trink up!" Otto sounded bad-tempered.

"My horse!" Evans yelled. A shell screamed overhead, thumping into the hill behind. At the very same moment a solid shot struck the wounded man beside the road, killing him instantly and flinging his blood ten feet into the air. Starbuck saw what he thought was the man's severed leg spinning through the air, then instantly rejected the sight as unreal. Another solid shot cracked into a tree, splitting a three-foot lance of fresh wood from the trunk and showering leaves onto the raggedly torn leg. Then Lieutenant Meadows, who had repeated the wig-wagger's alarming message, suddenly gulped and widened his eyes. He was staring at Starbuck and his eyes seemed to grow wider and wider as his hand slowly strayed to his throat, where a bead of blood swelled and glistened. His notebook slipped to the ground, its pages fluttering, as the bead of blood grew and split, then suddenly he choked a flood of gore down his tunic's front. He swayed, gargling blood, then his whole body twitched violently as he slid out of the saddle and onto the grass. "I'll take Meadows's horse," Evans snapped, and grabbed the gray's reins. The dying man's foot was caught in the stirrup. Evans jerked it free, then pulled himself up onto the horse's back.

Starbuck drained the tin cup, gasped for breath, then reached for Pocahontas's reins. He clambered awkwardly into the saddle, wondering what he was supposed to do now that he was free.

"Boston!" Evans turned his horse toward Starbuck. "Will that bastard Faulconer listen to you?"

"I think so, sir," Starbuck said, then, more honestly, "I don't know, sir."

Evans frowned as a thought came to him. "Why are you fighting for us, Boston? This ain't your fight."

Starbuck did not know what to say. His reasons were more to do with his father than with America's destiny, still more to do with Sally than with slavery, but this did not seem the time or the place to explain such things. "Because I'm a rebel." He offered the explanation feebly, knowing its inadequacy.

But it pleased Nathan Evans, who had just taken a mug of whiskey from his stern-looking orderly. He drained the mug. "Well, you're my rebel now, Boston, so find Faulconer and tell him I want his precious Legion. Tell him I'm moving most of my troops to the Sudley Road, and I want his Virginians up there too. Tell him to form on my left."

Starbuck, dizzied by the whiskey, his change of fortune and by the sense of panic whirling in the humid air, tried to insert a note of caution into Evans's planning. "Colonel Faulconer was determined to move to the right wing, sir."

"Damn what Faulconer wants!" Evans screamed so loud that the idling gunners across the turnpike were startled. "Tell Faulconer that the Confederacy needs him! Tell the bastard we have to stop the Yankees or else we'll all be doing Lincoln's rope dance tonight! I'm trusting you, boy! Get Faulconer and tell the bastard to fight, damn his eyes! Tell the damp-bellied bastard to fight!" Evans shouted the last words, then savaged his heels back, leaving Starbuck astonished and alone as the staff officers and orderlies streamed after Evans toward the men defending the stone bridge.

Bullets snicked and whimpered in the heavy air. Flies were gathering thick in the ditch to lay their eggs in the gobbets of flesh that had been a man just moments before. Lieutenant Meadows lay on his back with his dead eyes showing surprise and his blood-swilled mouth gaping wide open. Starbuck, the whiskey sour in his belly, gathered the reins, turned Pocahontas's head, and went to find the Legion.

The Faulconer Legion took its first casualty at around five minutes past eight in the morning. A shell came over the hill to the east, skipped once on the reverse slope, tumbled in the air with a horrid shrieking noise, then struck the ground a second time some twelve yards in front of A Company. The shell exploded there, driving a splinter of jagged iron into the skull of Joe Sparrow, the boy who had a scholarship to the university, but who now died as easy a death as any soldier could wish. One moment he was standing upright, grinning at a joke told by Cyrus Matthews, and the next he was on his back. He twitched once, felt nothing, died.

"Joe?" Cyrus asked.

The other men edged nervously away from the collapsed boy, all but his friend George Waters, who had been standing beside Sparrow in the second rank and who now dropped to his knees beside the body. Sparrow's cap had been tugged round by the force of the striking shell fragment and George now tried to pull it straight, but as he tugged at the cap's stiff visor a terrible wash of blood escaped from under the sweatband. "Oh, God!" George Waters recoiled from the horrid sight. "He's dead!"

"Don't be a lunkhead, boy. Skulls bleed like stuck pigs, you know that." Sergeant Howes had pushed through the ranks and now knelt beside Sparrow. "Come on, Runt, wake up!" He pulled the cap straight, trying to hide the blood, then slapped the dead boy lightly on the cheek. This was Blanche and Frank Sparrow's only boy, the pride of their lives. Blanche had tried real hard to persuade the boy not to march to war, but someone had left a scornful petticoat on their front porch, addressed to Joe, and young Joe had wanted to join the Legion anyways and so Blanche had relented, but now Joe was flat on his back in a field.

"Call the doctor! The doctor!" Paul Hinton, captain of A Company, slid out of his saddle and shouted the order.

Major Danson came running with his medical bag from the rear of the regiment where the band was playing "Annie Laurie," the saxhorn tubas embroidering a clever bass line in counterpoint to the plangent melody that was so popular with the men. Danson pushed through the ranks of A Company. "Give him air!" he shouted, which is what he usually shouted whenever he was called to a sick person. Invariably the field hands or the servants or the family members all crowded about the patient, and Danson could not stand working amidst a throng of onlookers all offering suggestions. If they were so knowledgeable, he often wondered, why did they need him? "Stand back, now. Who is it, Dan?"

"Blanche Sparrow's boy, doc," Hinton said.

"Not young Joe! Now come on, Joe, you'll be missing all the fun!" Doctor Danson dropped to his knees. "What's the matter, now? Got hit on the head, did you?"

"He's dead." George Waters had gone white with shock.

Major Danson frowned at this amateur diagnosis, then felt for Joseph Sparrow's pulse. He said nothing for a few seconds, then lifted off the blood-stained forage cap to reveal Joe's hair all soaked and matted red. "Oh, poor Blanche," the doctor said softly, "what are we to tell her?" He unbuttoned the collar of the dead boy's tunic as if to give him air.

Another ricocheted shell whipsawed overhead and crashed to earth a half mile beyond the regiment, its explosion lost in the dense foliage of a stand of trees. Adam Faulconer, who had been standing his horse on the hill crest to watch the cannonade ripple smoke and flame about the distant stream, now realized something was amiss within the Legion's ranks and spurred back to the regiment. "What's happened?" he asked Doctor Danson.

"It's Blanche's boy, young Joe."

"Oh, God, no." There was an awful pain in Adam's voice. The day was already bringing Adam the violence he had feared, and yet, he suspected, the battle had not really begun. The two sides had made contact and were hurling shells at each other, but neither seemed to have launched a real assault.

"Blanche will never live with this," Danson said, struggling to his feet. "I remember when Joe nearly died of the whooping cough and I thought she'd go with him to his grave. Dear God, what a terrible thing." Around him a ring of soldiers stared aghast at the dead boy. It was not that death was so strange to any of them; all had seen sisters or brothers or cousins or parents laid out in the parlor, and all had helped carry a casket into the church or had helped pull a drowned body from the river, but this was different; this was chance death, war's lottery, and it could just as easily have been themselves lying there all bloody and still. This was something they were not really prepared for, because nothing in their training had convinced them that young men ended up open-mouthed, flat on their backs, fly-blown, bloodied and dead.

"Carry him to the back, lads," Captain Hinton now said. "Lift him up! Careful now!" Hinton supervised the removal of the body, then walked back to Adam. "Where's your father, Adam?"

"I don't know."

"He should be here." Hinton gathered his horse's reins and hauled himself laboriously into the saddle.

"I suppose the general's keeping him," Adam suggested lamely. There was a glistening patch of blood beside Joe

Sparrow's fallen cap on the grass. "Poor Blanche," Adam said. "We took Joe out of the color party because we reckoned he'd be safer in the ranks."

But Hinton was not listening. Instead he was frowning eastward to where a horseman had appeared on the brow of the hill. "Is that Starbuck? It is, by God!"

Adam turned and, to his astonishment, saw that it was indeed Starbuck who was galloping toward the Legion and, for a second, Adam thought he must be seeing ghosts, then he saw that it really was his friend who, not three hours before, had been dispatched back north to his own people, but who had now returned coatless, pale, hurried, and urgent. "Where's your father?" Starbuck shouted.

"I don't know, Nate." Adam had ridden to meet his friend. "What are you doing here?"

"Where's Pecker?" Starbuck's voice was curt, ungiving, out of tune with the melancholy mood of Sparrow's death.

"What are you doing here, Nate?" Adam asked again, spurring his horse after Starbuck. "Nate?"

But Starbuck had already kicked his horse down the front of the Legion to where Major Bird stood beneath the Legion's colors that hung limp in the windless air.

"Sir!" Starbuck reined in close to Bird.

Bird blinked up at the horseman. "Starbuck? I was told to discharge you! Are you certain you're meant to be here?"

"Sir." Nathaniel Starbuck sounded stilted and formal. "Colonel Evans sent me, sir. He wants us to advance on the Sudley Road. The enemy has crossed the stream by Sudley Church, and are marching this way."

Pecker Bird blinked up at the young man and noted that Starbuck had sounded remarkably calm, which calmness, he supposed, was a perverse symptom of the boy's excitement, and then Bird thought how astonishingly well everyone was playing their soldierly parts on this unlikely morning. "Aren't those orders more properly addressed to Colonel Faulconer?"

324

Bird heard himself asking, and was amazed that his natural inclination was so to avoid taking the responsibility.

"If I could find the Colonel, sir, I'd tell him. But I don't think there's time, and if we don't move, sir, there won't be anything left of this army."

"Is that so?" Bird also sounded calm, but his hands were clawing through his beard with the stress of the moment. He opened his mouth to speak again, but no sound came. He was thinking that he too would have to play a soldierly part, now that fate had dropped this responsibility into his lap, and then he pusillanimously thought that a soldier's duty was to obey and Colonel Faulconer's orders had been very specific: that he was to ignore any instructions from Colonel Nathan Evans. Faulconer was even now attempting to have the Legion deployed southward to where Beauregard expected the main battle to be fought, but Colonel Nathan Evans wanted the Legion to march northward and was evidently claiming that the Confederacy's entire future depended on Bird's obedience.

"Sir!" Starbuck was evidently not so calm as he seemed for he was pressing Major Bird for a decision.

Bird waved Starbuck to silence. Thaddeus Bird's first impulse had been to avoid all responsibility by blindly obeying Washington Faulconer's instructions, but that very impulse allowed Bird to understand just why his brother-in-law had given in to Miriam's entreaties and appointed him as a major. It was because Washington Faulconer believed that Bird would never dare disobey him. The Colonel evidently dismissed Bird as a safe nonentity who would never detract from his glory. In fact, as Thaddeus Bird suddenly realized, no one was allowed to compete with Washington Faulconer, which was why the Colonel surrounded himself with dullards like Ridley, and why, when a man like Starbuck threatened to show some independence, he was so quickly ejected from the Colonel's entourage. Even Adam's scruples were acceptable to Washington Faulconer because they prevented

325

Adam from rivaling his father. Washington Faulconer would surround himself with dull men just so that he could shine all the brighter, and as Thaddeus Bird understood that truth, so he was determined to thwart it. Damn Faulconer, because Major Thaddeus Bird would not be dismissed as a nonentity! "Sergeant Major Proctor!"

"Sir!" The dignified sergeant major marched stiffly from his place behind the color party.

"The Legion will advance on the crossroads at the foot of the hill, Sergeant Major, in columns of company. Then up the farther road," Bird pointed across the valley. "Give the orders, if you please."

The sergeant major, who knew exactly how much authority Major Bird was supposed to exercise in the Faulconer Legion, drew himself to his full and impressive height. "Are those the Colonel's orders, Major, sir?"

"They are the orders of your superior officer, Sergeant Major Proctor." Now that Bird had made up his mind he seemed to be enjoying himself, for his head was nodding back and forth and his thin mouth was twisted into a sardonic grin. "We shall advance along the Sudley Road, which is that dirt road beyond the crossroads." Bird pointed northward again, then looked at Starbuck for confirmation. "Is that right?"

"Yes, sir. And Colonel Evans requests that we form up on his left when we cross the farther hill." Starbuck guessed that was the exact place where Washington Faulconer had said farewell to him.

"Would it not be better, sir ..." Sergeant Major Proctor said, attempting to subdue Pecker Bird's lunacy.

"Do it!" Bird screamed in sudden rage. "Do it!"

Adam Faulconer had followed Starbuck to Major Bird's side and now intervened to calm things down. "What are you doing, Uncle?"

"The Legion will advance in column of companies!" Major

Bird snapped in a surprisingly loud voice. "Company A will advance first! Companies! 'Shun!"

A very few men shuffled to attention, but most just stayed on the ground, supposing that Pecker had fallen off his perch as he had used to do in the schoolroom after he had been teased or otherwise goaded into a fury. Many of the Legion's officers were having difficulty in suppressing their laughter and some, like Ridley, were jerking their heads back and forth like feeding birds.

"Nate." Adam turned to his friend. "Will you please explain exactly what's happening?"

"The enemy has got round our rear," Nate explained loudly enough for the nearest companies to hear, "and Colonel Evans needs this regiment to help head off their attack. There's no one but us and Colonel Evans's men who can stop them, and if we don't move, the day's lost."

"Like shit." That was Ethan Ridley. "You're a goddamned Yankee and you're doing a Yankee's work. There's no enemy over there."

Adam put a hand on Starbuck's arm to restrain him. Then he stared north across the turnpike. Nothing moved there. Not even a leaf stirred. The landscape was heavy, somnolent, empty.

"I think we'd better stay here," Adam suggested. Sergeant Major Proctor nodded agreement, and Major Bird looked up at Starbuck, appeal in his eyes.

"I saw the northerners," Starbuck said.

"I'm not moving," Ridley announced, and a murmur of agreement supported his stand.

"Why don't we send an officer to have Evans's orders confirmed?" Captain Hinton suggested sensibly. Hinton, like a dozen other officers and sergeants, had come to join the discussion.

"Don't you have written orders, Nate?" Anthony Murphy asked.

327

"There wasn't time to put anything in writing," Starbuck said.

Ridley laughed sourly, while Thaddeus Bird looked uncertain, as though wondering if he had made the right decision.

"Where's Evans now?" Hinton asked.

"He's moving his men from the stone bridge to the Sudley Road." Starbuck was feeling increasingly desperate.

"Is that the Sudley Road?" Thomas Truslow's growl interrupted the proceedings.

"Yes," Starbuck said. Truslow had been pointing north across the shallow valley.

"And you saw Yankees out there?"

"Beyond the fords, yes."

Truslow nodded, but to Starbuck's disappointment said nothing more. Across the turnpike a small group of gray-clad horsemen galloped up to the far crest, their horses leaving dark hoofprints in the turf. The Legion's officers watched until the horsemen disappeared into the far trees. The horsemen were the only sign that anything might be happening beyond the army's left flank, but there were so few of the cavalry that their maneuver was hardly convincing evidence. "It means nothing," Adam said dubiously.

"It means we move to support Colonel Evans"—Bird had decided to stick to his decision—"and the next man to disobey my order will be shot!" Bird drew a Le Mat revolver, which he hefted in his thin right hand, then, as though unsure whether or not he could really carry out his threat, he passed the brutal-looking gun up to Starbuck. "You will shoot, Lieutenant Starbuck, and that is an order. You hear me?"

"Very clearly, sir!" Starbuck realized that the situation had gotten disastrously out of hand, but he did not know what he could do to restore sanity. The Legion was desperate for leadership, but the Colonel was missing and no one seemed adequate to step into his boots. Starbuck himself was a

328

northerner, and a mere second lieutenant if he was anything at all, while Thaddeus Bird was a laughingstock, a country schoolmaster masquerading in a soldier's gaudy uniform, yet only Bird and Starbuck understood what needed to be done, but neither man could impose his will on the regiment and Starbuck, holding the awkward pistol, knew he would never dare use it.

Major Bird took three formal paces forward. He appeared ludicrous as he paced the three giant steps, which he doubtless thought were solemn but which looked more like the gait of a clown clumping upstage on stilts. He turned and stood to attention. "The Legion will come to attention! On your feet!"

Gradually, reluctantly, the men stood. They pulled on their haversacks and lifted their rifles from the grass. Bird waited, then snapped his next orders. "The Legion will advance by column of companies. Company A! By the right! Quick march!"

Not one soldier moved. They had stood up, but they would not move away from their patch of hillside. Company A looked at Captain Hinton for a lead, but Hinton was clearly troubled by the order and made no attempt to enforce it. Thaddeus Bird swallowed hard, then looked up at Starbuck. The pistol felt hugely heavy in Starbuck's hand.

"Lieutenant Starbuck?" Major Bird's voice was a yelp.

"Oh, Uncle Thaddeus, please!" Adam appealed.

The men were on the edge of hysterical laughter, placed there by the ludicrous bathos of Adam's homely appeal, and it would have taken just one more syllable to trigger that laughter when a hard voice, as sudden and grim as the ripsaw sound of the passing shells, turned the Legion's mood into instant apprehension. "Company K! Shoulder arms!"

Truslow had paced back to the Legion's left flank and now shouted the order. Company K snapped to obey him. "On my mark!" he shouted. "Forward march!"

329

Company K crashed out of line, advancing down the hill. Truslow, squat and dark-faced, did not look left or right, but paced ahead with his deliberate, countryman's stride. Captain Roswell Jenkins, the company's commanding officer, galloped after the company, but his remonstrance to Truslow was utterly ignored. We came here to fight, Truslow seemed to be saying, so for God's sake, let us get off our butts and fight.

Captain Murphy, commanding D Company, looked questioningly at Starbuck. Starbuck nodded, and the simple confirmation was enough for Murphy. "Company D!" he shouted, and the men did not even wait for the order to advance, but just started after Truslow's men. The rest of the Legion edged forward. Sergeant Major Proctor looked wildly up at Adam, who shrugged, while Major Bird, at last seeing his orders obeyed, stirred the laggards into motion.

Ridley turned his horse wildly, looking for allies, but the Faulconer Legion was marching west, led by a sergeant, and the officers were left to catch up with their men. Starbuck himself, who had precipitated the move northward, now turned away to shout at Adam. "Where's my coat?"

Adam pushed his horse through the bandsmen, who were making a cacophony of thumps and squawks as they hurried to catch up with the advancing Legion. "Nate!" Adam sounded distressed. "What have you done?"

"I told you. The federals are coming round our rear. Do you know where my jacket is?" Starbuck had dismounted beside Joe Sparrow's dead body. He picked up Sparrow's rifle and tugged off the dead boy's belt with its canteen, cartridge box and cap box.

"What are you doing?" Adam asked.

"Arming myself. I'll be damned if I spend the rest of this day without a gun. People are killing each other here." Starbuck meant the words as a grim joke, but their flippancy made him sound hard:

330

"But Father sent you home!" Adam protested.

Starbuck turned a bitter face on his friend. "You can't dictate my loyalty, Adam. Work out your own, but leave me mine."

Adam bit his lip, then twisted in his saddle. "Nelson! Bring Mister Starbuck's coat and weapons!"

The Colonel's servant, who had been waiting beside the Legion's piled knapsacks, tents and baggage, brought Starbuck his old sword, pistol and coat. Starbuck nodded his thanks, pulled on the coat, then strapped on the sword belt with its heavy pistol. "I seem to be overweaponed," he said, looking at his own revolver, at Joe Sparrow's rifle and at Major Bird's Le Mat revolver. He threw down the rifle, then grimaced at the ugly Le Mat. "It's a nasty-looking brute, isn't it?" The revolver had two barrels, the upper one rifled for bullets, the lower a smoothbore barrel that took a shotgun cartridge. Starbuck broke the gun open and laughed, then showed Adam that the cylinder's nine chambers were all empty. The shotgun barrel was loaded, but the revolving hammer, by which the user could select which barrel to fire, had been twisted upward to fall on one of the empty chambers. "It wasn't loaded," Starbuck said, "Pecker was bluffing."

"He's not bluffing now!" Adam protested and gestured at his father's Legion, which was now halfway down the hill. "Look what you've done!"

"Adam! For Christ's sake, I saw the Yankees. They are coming straight toward us, and if we don't stop them then this war is over."

"Isn't that what we want?" Adam demanded. "One battle, you promised me, then we could talk."

"Not now, Adam." Starbuck had neither the time nor patience for his friend's scruples. He belted his saber and holster belt over his jacket and hauled himself into his saddle just as Ethan Ridley rode back to the hilltop.

"I'm going to find your father, Adam." Ridley ignored Starbuck.

Adam stared downhill to where his neighbors and friends were marching northward. "Nate? Are you sure you saw northerners?"

"I saw them, Adam. After I left you. They were beyond the Sudley Fords and marching this way. They fired at me, Adam, they chased me! I didn't imagine it." The chase had been brief, confused by the woods, and his northern pursuers had given up five minutes before Starbuck had been captured by the two Louisianan cavalrymen who had refused to cross the fords to discover the truth of Starbuck's story for themselves.

"He's lying," Ridley said calmly, then blanched as Starbuck turned toward him.

Starbuck said nothing to Ridley. Instead he was thinking that he was going to kill this man, but not in front of Adam. He would do it in the chaos of battle where no witness could bring a charge of murder. "The Yankees are coming across at Sudley," Starbuck said, turning back to his friend, "and there's no one else who can stop them."

"But ..." Adam seemed wholly unable to grasp the enormity of Starbuck's news—that this left wing of the rebel army really was threatened, and that his confident, wealthy, assured father had been wrong.

"It's Thermopylae, Adam," Starbuck said earnestly, "think of it as Thermopylae."

"It's what?" Ethan Ridley demanded. Ridley had never heard of Thermopylae, where Xerxes's Persians had stolen a flank march on Leonidas's Greeks to snatch victory, nor how the three hundred Spartans had sacrificed themselves so that the other Greeks could escape. Nathan Evans seemed an unlikely Greek hero, but today he was playing the Spartan role and Adam, given a classical context to the emergency, instantly understood that his father's tenants and his father's

332

neighbors had marched off to become heroes and he could not simply let them die alone. A Faulconer had to be there, and if his father was absent, then Adam must be present.

"We have to fight, don't we?" Adam said, though unhappily.

"You should go to your father!" Ridley insisted.

"No. I have to go with Nate," Adam said.

Ridley felt a pulse of victory. The crown prince was siding with the king's enemy, and Ridley would replace them both. Ridley turned his horse. "I'm going for your father," he called back as he spurred away past Joe Sparrow's body.

Adam looked at his friend and shivered. "I'm frightened."

"So am I," Starbuck said, and thought of the severed leg spinning across the road spilling its trails of blood. "But so are the Yankees, Adam."

"I guess they are," Adam said, then clicked his tongue to urge his horse forward. Starbuck followed more clumsily on Pocahontas, and thus the two friends rode down the hill to follow the Legion northward. Above them, in the clear summer air, a howitzer shell drew a trail of smoke across the sky, then fell to earth and exploded somewhere in the woods.

It was still not nine o'clock in the morning.

Advancing in column of companies had not been Major Bird's happiest inspiration, but he had thought it the quickest way to get the Legion moving and so he had ordered it. The formation demanded that the companies march in line abreast, four ranks deep, each rank comprising nineteen or twenty men depending on the company's strength, and the ten companies making a long, broad column with the color party at its center and the band and Doctor Danson bringing up the rear.

The problem was that the Legion had never really rehearsed maneuvers in anything but the flat pastureland at Faulconer Court House, and now they were advancing across a landscape that contained inconvenient ditches, rail fences, bushes, dips, knolls, blackberries, streams and impenetrable thickets of trees. They managed to cross the turnpike successfully enough, but the trees about the stone house and the rail fences of the pastures beyond caused the companies to lose all their cohesion and, naturally enough, the men preferred to use the road and so the column of companies became a long straggling line of men that jostled onto the dirt track before advancing toward the trees at the top of the farther hill.

But at least the men were cheerful. Most were glad to be moving, and happier still to have escaped the bare hillside where the overshot enemy shells fell so randomly, and somehow the morning took on a sportive atmosphere like the sylvan days of training back in Faulconer County. They joked as they climbed the hill, boasting what they would do to the Yankees they only half-expected to meet on the farther slope. Many of the men suspected that Pecker Bird had got everything plain bad wrong and that the Colonel would wring his damned neck as soon as he came back from his meeting with the general, but that was Pecker's problem, not theirs. No one expressed any such suspicions to Truslow, who had begun the whole march and who now stolidly led the Legion north.

Starbuck and Adam galloped their horses up the side of the column until they found Thaddeus Bird striding along with the color party. Starbuck leaned precariously from his saddle to offer Major Bird the big Le Mat revolver. "Your pistol, sir. Did you know it wasn't loaded?"

"Of course it wasn't loaded." Bird took the gun from Starbuck. "Did you really think I wanted you to shoot someone?" Bird chuckled, then turned to look at the straggle of men advancing in shambolic order up the dirt road and into the woods. So this was Washington Faulconer's elite force? Faulconer's Imperial Guard? The thought made Bird laugh aloud.

"Sir?" Starbuck thought Bird had spoken.

"Nothing, Starbuck, nothing. Except I have a suspicion that

334

we should be advancing in more soldierly order."

Starbuck pointed ahead to where a patch of sky promised open country at the far side of the thick belt of woodland which crowned the ridge. "There are fields over the hill crest, sir. You can shake the men into proper line there."

It occurred to Bird that Starbuck had ridden this road when the Colonel had tried to get rid of him. "Why didn't you go when Faulconer gave you the chance?" he asked Starbuck. "Do you really want to fight for the South?"

"I do, yes." But this was hardly the time to explain how quixotic that decision was, nor why the sight of the axemen in the woods had prompted his sudden decision. It was not, he knew, a rational choice, but rather a revulsion against his family, and Starbuck was suddenly amazed at the way in which life presented such choices, and the carelessness with which those choices could be taken even though the resultant decision might utterly change everything that would ever follow, right down to the grave itself. How much history, he wondered, had been made by such flippant choices? How many important decisions were taken from mere pride or from lust or even out of sloth? All Starbuck's religion, all his upbringing, had taught him that there was a plan to life and a divine purpose to man's existence, yet this morning he had taken a shotgun to that idea and had blasted it clean out of God's firmament, and it seemed to Starbuck that his world, as a result, was a better and clearer place.

"Since you are on our side," Thaddeus Bird spoke from beside Starbuck's left stirrup, "would you ride ahead and stop the men at the open land you promised me? I'd rather we didn't stream into battle like a flock of sinners scurrying for repentance." He waved Starbuck forward with a flourish of the Le Mat pistol.

By the time Starbuck reached the column's head Sergeant Truslow had already ordered his men off the road. Company K had reached the crest of the hill where Starbuck had been expelled from the Legion by the Colonel and where the trees

335

gave way to a long, gentle slope of empty pastureland. Truslow was lining his men in two ranks just short of a zigzag rail fence that had been placed to keep cattle from straying out of the grassland and into the trees. K Company's commanding officer was nowhere to be seen, but Truslow did not need officers. He needed targets. "Make certain you're loaded!" he growled at his men.

"Sergeant! Look!" A man at the right flank of the company pointed to the open country where a horde of oddly dressed troops had suddenly appeared from among the trees. The strange troops wore baggy bright red shirts, voluminous black and white pantaloons tucked into white gaiters, and floppy red caps tipped with long blue tassels. It was a regiment in fashionable Zouave uniform that aped the famous light infantry of France.

"Leave 'em alone!" Truslow bellowed. "They're our clowns!" He had spotted the Confederate flag in the center of the weirdly uniformed troops. "Face front!" he shouted. More of the Legion's men were emerging from the road to form on the right of Truslow's company, while the Legion's officers, unsure exactly what was happening or who was commanding this sudden deployment, huddled excitedly at the edge of the trees. Major Bird shouted at the officers to join their companies, then looked to his right to see still more Confederate troops emerging from the trees to fill the wide gap between the Legion and the brightly uniformed Zouaves. The newcomers wore gray, and their arrival meant that a hasty defensive line was forming at the wood's northern edge to face a long wide stretch of open ground that fell softly away from the zigzag fence, past a farmhouse and hayrick, to where a farther belt of woodland hid the distant Sudley Fords. The long open slope seemed designed for the defenders' rifles, a killing ground lit by a merciless sun.

Colonel Evans galloped on his borrowed gray horse to where the Faulconer Legion was still forming its ranks. "Well done,

Boston! Well done!" He greeted Starbuck, then added gesture to the congratulations by swerving his horse close by the northerner and slapping him hard on the back. "Well done! Is Colonel Faulconer here?"

"No, sir."

"Who's commanding?"

"Major Bird. By the colors, sir."

"Bird!" Evans turned his horse hard, slewing soil and grass up from its hooves. "We just have to hold the bastards here. We have to give the bastards hell." His nervous horse had stopped, blowing and shivering as Evans stared northward down the long open slope. "If they're coming," he added the words softly. His left hand was drumming nervously on his thigh. The German orderly with the "barrelito" of whiskey reined in behind the Colonel, as did a dozen staff officers and a mounted standard bearer who carried the palmetto flag of South Carolina. "I've got two guns coming," Evans told Bird, "but no more infantry, so what we've got here will have to do the job until Beauregard wakes up to what's happening. Those gaudy thieves," he nodded toward the far Zouaves, "are Wheat's Louisiana Tigers. I know they look like whores on a picnic, but Wheat says they're mean sons of bitches in a fight. The nearer fellows are Sloan's South Carolinians, and I know they'll fight. I've promised them all Yankee meat for their supper. How are your rogues?"

"Eager, sir, eager." Major Bird, panting and hot after the fast pace of the advance, took off his hat and pushed a hand through his long, thinning hair. Behind him the thirsty men of the Legion were draining their canteens.

"We'll give the shit-eating bastards hell, so we will," Evans said, looking northward again, though nothing moved in that empty landscape, not even a wind to stir the far trees where the road to the fords vanished under the thick canopy of leaves. A small group of men, women and children were standing by the Sudley Church on the hill to the left of the road, and Evans guessed they must be worshipers come to the church only to discover that God's service had been overtaken by war. Behind Evans, dulled by distance now, the sound of the northern cannonade thundered softly in the hot still air. Evans had left just four understrength companies at the stone bridge, a tiny force to hold off any determined Yankee attack down the turnpike, and he suddenly felt a terrible fear that he had been deceived and that this rumored flank attack was a feint, a cheat, a deception to strip the stone bridge of its defenders so that the damned Yankees could end the war in one maneuver. And where the hell was Beauregard? Or General Johnston's men, who were rumored to be arriving from the Shenandoah Valley? Christ on his cross, Evans thought, but this was agony. Evans had fought the Comanches in his years of soldiering, but he had never been forced into taking a decision as momentous as the one he had just made, a decision that had left the northern flank of the Confederate army stripped perilously thin. Would history mock him as the fool whose stupidity had handed an easy victory to the northerners? "Boston!" Evans twitched round in his saddle to glare at Starbuck.

"Sir."

"You didn't lie to me, boy, did you?" Evans remembered the wig-wagger's message and tried to convince himself he had done the right thing, but God in his heaven, just what had he done? Far behind him, out of sight beyond the trees and the turnpike, the shells rumbled and crashed on the empty land he had left virtually unguarded. "Did you lie to me, boy?" he shouted at Starbuck. "Did you lie?"

But Starbuck did not answer. Starbuck was not even looking at the fierce-eyed Colonel. Instead Starbuck was staring down the long pale slope to where, out of the distant trees, the northerners were at last appearing. Rank upon rank of men with the sunlight glinting from their belt buckles and cap badges and rifle butts and saber scabbards and from the polished muzzles of their artillery to make the mirrored lights of a righteous army come to remake God's country.

For the northern trap was sprung. Four full brigades of infantry bolstered by the finest field artillery in North America had hooked into the rebellion's ragged rear to where a scratch southern force led by a whiskey-sucking foulmouth was the only obstacle left to victory. Now all the day needed was one overwhelming charge and the slaveholders' rebellion would become a mere footnote to history, a thing forgotten, a passing summer's madness that would be gone and ended and vanished like smoke in a sudden wind. "God bless you, Boston," Evans said, for Starbuck had not lied after all, and there was going to be a fight.

12

The Yankees came on quick. Their predawn flanking march had taken hours longer than their commanders had expected, and now their task was to thrust hard and fast into the rebel rear before the southerners had time to understand just what was happening.

Drums beat the pace as the first northern regiments spread into their attack lines and as cannon unlimbered at the attackers' flanks. Some guns were deployed on the dirt road, others in the farm at the foot of the slope from where they sent the first shells screaming up toward the wooded ridge where the thin line of Confederate forces waited. The advancing Yankees were confident. They had expected the Sudley Fords would be defended, then had half-feared that the southerners might have fortified an unfinished railway embankment just beyond the fords, but instead they had encountered no resistance as they had steadily advanced into the rebel rear. The surprise of their attack seemed to be total, the ineptness of the southern commanders complete, and all that now stood between the federal forces and victory was this contemptible line of rebel farmboys who edged a wood at the long hill's crest. "On to Richmond, boys!" an officer shouted as the attack started up the gentle slope, and behind the blue-coated infantry a regimental band swung into the tune "John Brown's Body," as though the ghost of that irascible old martyr was personally present to see the two leading regiments, both from Rhode Island, crack the rebel line apart.

More northern troops emerged from the woods behind the advancing Rhode Islanders. Men from New York and New

Hampshire joined the attack as the flanking guns jetted clouds of gray white smoke. Swift fan-shaped patterns of compressed gases rippled the long grass under the guns' smoke as the shells seared up the slope. The explosions were mighty, ear splitting, terrible. Some shells, fired too high, crashed through the branches above the Confederate line, scaring birds out of the trees and showering twigs and leaves down onto the bandsmen and chaplains and servants and medical orderlies who crouched in the rear. A regiment of regular U.S. Army troops marched out from the trees, deployed from column into line, fixed their bayonets, and advanced uphill with the New Yorkers and New Englanders.

Colonel Evans had galloped back to his line's center where Colonel Sloan's South Carolinians were crouching at the wood's edge to make themselves into a difficult target for the enemy artillery. A few rebel skirmishers had advanced beyond the fence and were firing rifles at the advancing Yankees, but Starbuck, watching from horseback at the trees' edge, could see no sign that the rifle fire was causing any casualties. The enemy came steadily on, driven by the music of the distant northern bands and by the beat of the drummers advancing with the companies and by the proximity of glorious victory that waited for the attackers at the hill's crest where the first of Nathan Evans's two ancient cannon had arrived. The gun was hurriedly unlimbered, turned, then fired a roundshot down the slope. The ball bounced on the turf, soared over the Rhode Islanders and plunged harmlessly into the trees beyond. A northern shell exploded short. The sound of the airburst was appalling, as though part of the fabric of the universe itself had been suddenly cracked in two. The air became crazy with smoke and sizzling fragments. Starbuck shuddered. The artillery fire by the stone bridge had been scary, but this was much worse. These gunners were aiming directly at the Legion and their shells screeched like demons as they flashed overhead.

"Skirmishers!" Major Bird called in a cracked voice. He tried again, this time achieving a firmer tone. "Skirmishers! Advance!"

A and K companies, the Legion's two flanking companies, clambered awkwardly over the fence rails and ran into the pastureland. The men were encumbered by their rifles, their sheathed bayonets, their bowie knives and haversacks, and by the canteens, pouches and cap boxes that hung from their belts. They made a loose formation a hundred paces ahead of the Legion. Their task was first to deter the enemy skirmishers, then to snipe at the main line of attackers. The riflemen opened fire, enveloping each kneeling marksman in a small cloud of smoke. Sergeant Truslow walked from man to man, while Captain Roswell Jenkins, still on horseback, fired his revolver at the distant northerners.

"Make sure your weapons are loaded!" Major Bird called to the remaining eight companies. It seemed slightly late to remember such advice, but nothing seemed real this morning. Thaddeus Bird, schoolmaster, was commanding a regiment in battle? He giggled at the thought and earned a disapproving look from Sergeant Major Proctor. The Yankees were still five hundred paces away, but coming on at a smart pace now. The northern officers carried drawn swords. Some carried the blades upright in a stiff attempt at formal dignity, while others slashed at dandelions and thistles as though they were out on a Sunday afternoon stroll. A few were mounted on nervous horses. One horse, scared by the gunfire, had gone out of control and was bolting with its rider across the face of the northern attack.

Starbuck, dry mouthed and apprehensive, remembered that his Savage pistol, which he had earlier returned to Colonel Faulconer and only just retrieved, was still unloaded. He pulled the heavy gun from its long clumsy holster, then released the cylinder lock to expose the empty chambers. He took six paper-wrapped cartridges from the pouch on his belt. Each cartridge contained a conical bullet and its powder charge. He bit the bullet off the first cartridge, tasting the bitter salty gunpowder on his tongue, then carefully poured the powder into one of the cylinder's chambers. Pocahontas, bitten by a horsefly, suddenly whinnied and shifted sideways, causing Starbuck to spill some of the powder onto his saddle.

He swore at the horse, which meant that the bullet in his lips slipped free, bounced on the saddle pommel and fell into the grass. He swore again, tipped the powder from the chamber, and bit off a fresh bullet. This time, as he began to pour the charge, he found his hand was shaking and there seemed to be two chambers under the lip of the torn paper instead of one. His sight was blurred, then he realized his hand was shaking uncontrollably.

He looked up at the advancing enemy. Above them, oddly clear in his otherwise smeared eyesight, was the Stars and Stripes, his own flag, and suddenly Starbuck knew that there were no easy decisions, no turnings in life that could be taken flippantly. He gazed at the distant flag and knew he could not fire on it. His great-grandfather MacPhail had lost an eye on Breed's Hill and later, fighting under Paul Revere at Penobscot Bay, had lost his right hand in the defense of that good flag, and suddenly Starbuck felt a catch in his throat. God, he thought, but I should not be here! None of us should be here! He suddenly understood all Adam's objections to the war, all Adam's unhappiness that this glorious country should find itself riven by battle, and he gazed longingly at the distant flag and was unaware of the first Yankee skirmishers' bullets whipping hard overhead, or of the shell that exploded just short of the fence, or of the hoarse shouts as the Rhode Island sergeants shouted at their men to keep their lines straight as they advanced. Starbuck was oblivious to it all as he sat in the saddle, shaken, his trembling hand dribbling gunpowder down his thigh.

"Are you all right?" Adam joined him.

"Not really."

343

"Now you understand, do you?" Adam asked grimly.

"Yes." Starbuck's hands trembled as he closed up the still-unloaded revolver. His whole life suddenly seemed trivial, wasted, gone to hell. He had thought this morning that war would prove a fine adventure, a defiance to toss into his father's face and an adventure story to describe to Sally, but instead it was proving to be something much more terrible and unexpected, as though a curtain in a frippery theater had lifted to reveal a glimpse of hell's horrors seething with twisted flames. My God, he thought, but I could die here. I could be buried at this wood's edge. "It was a girl," he blurted out.

"Girl?" Adam frowned with incomprehension.

"In Richmond."

"Oh." Adam was embarrassed by Starbuck's admission, but also troubled by it. "Father guessed as much," he said, "but I don't understand why you risk everything for ..." He stopped, maybe because he could not find the right words, or perhaps because a shell had smashed into a tree trunk and ripped a chunk of bright timber clean out of the wood and filled the shadows with its filthy sulfur-laden smoke. Adam licked his lips. "I'm thirsty."

"And me." Starbuck wondered why he had blurted out his confession. The Yankees were coming stolidly on. In minutes, he thought, just minutes, we have to fight. All the posturing and defiance has come to this warm meadow. He watched a northern officer stumble, drop his sword and fall to his knees in the grass. An enemy skirmisher ran forward five paces, knelt to take aim, then realized he had left his ramrod behind and went back to find it in the long grass. A riderless horse cantered across the slope. The drummers' rhythm was more ragged, but still the northerners came on. A bullet whistled close by Starbuck's head. One of the northern bands was playing "The Star-Spangled Banner" and the music prickled at Starbuck's eyes and conscience. "Do you not think about girls?" he asked Adam.

"No." Adam seemed not to be concentrating on the conversation but was staring down the slope. "Never." His fingers were twitching on the reins.

"Are you certain you two should be on horseback?" Major Bird strode over to join Adam and Starbuck. "I'd hate to lose you. You heard that young Sparrow died?" He asked this question of Starbuck.

"I saw his body, yes."

"He should have stayed at home with his mother," Major Bird said. His right hand was clawing at his beard, betraying his nerves. "Blanche was ridiculously overprotective of that boy, as I discovered when I insisted he was ready to imbibe logarithms. Oh, Christ!" Major Bird's imprecation was caused by a sudden volley loosed by the neighboring South Carolinians who were firing over the heads of their own skirmishers. "Actually he mastered logs very quickly," Bird went on, "and he was by far my best pupil for construing Greek. A clever boy, but prone to tears. Highly strung, you see? A waste though, a terrible waste. Why doesn't war take the illiterates first?"

A fresh artillery battery on the enemy's right wing had opened fire and one of its shells struck the slope a hundred paces in front of the Legion and ricocheted up into the trees. Starbuck heard the missile rip through the branches overhead. A second shell plunged into the ground close to the skirmish line and there exploded underground to heave the red soil up in a sudden eruption of brown smoke. Some of the skirmishers edged backward.

"Stand still!" Truslow bellowed, and not only the skirmishers, but the Legion's other eight companies froze like rabbits faced by a wildcat. The eight companies at the trees' edge were in two ranks, the formation suggested by the drill books that Major Pelham and Colonel Faulconer had used in the Legion's training. The books were American translations of French infantry manuals and recommended that riflemen open fire at long range, then sprint forward to finish off the enemy with

345

bayonet thrusts. Major Bird, who had assiduously studied the manuals, believed they were nonsense. In practice the Legion had never proved accurate when firing their rifles at more than one hundred paces, and Bird did not understand how they were supposed to shake an enemy's composure with ill-aimed fire at twice that distance followed by a clumsy charge into the teeth of hostile artillery and rifle fire. The Colonel's airy answer had always been that the men's natural belligerence would overcome the tactical difficulties, but to Major Bird that seemed a prob- lematical and overoptimistic solution.

"Permission to open fire?" Captain Murphy shouted from Company D.

"Hold your fire!" Bird had his own opinions about infantry fire. He was convinced that the first volley was the most destructive and should be saved until the enemy was close at hand. He accepted that he had no experience to bolster that opinion, which clashed with the professional doctrine that was taught at West Point and that had been tested in the war against Mexico, but Major Bird refused to believe that sol- diering demanded that he entirely suspend the exercise of his intelligence, and so he looked forward to this morning's test of his theory. Indeed, as he watched the blue-coated ranks advance toward him through the patches of gunsmoke that hung above the meadow, he found himself hoping that Colonel Faulconer did not suddenly reappear to take back the Legion's command. Major Thaddeus Bird, against all his expectations, was beginning to enjoy himself.

"Time to open fire, Uncle?" Adam suggested.

"I'd like to wait, in fact I will wait."

The Yankees' attacking line was losing its order as the attackers paused to fire and reload, then hurried on again. The minié bullets from the southern skirmishers were causing casualties, and the small roundshots of the two southern guns were slapping horribly through the attackers' files to slash quick bloody swathes on the grass and leave wounded men screaming and writhing in agony. The Yankee skirmishers were sniping at their Confederate opposites, but the battle of skirmishers was a sideshow, a mere sop to military theory that insisted that light infantry range ahead of an attack to weaken the defenders with a galling fire. The main northern attack was coming on too fast and in too much force to need the help of a skirmish line.

Much of the northern artillery had become unsighted by their own men and had fallen silent, though their howitzers, which fired their missiles high into the air, still lobbed shells over the attackers' files. Evans's two guns carried on firing, but Starbuck noted a change in the sound the guns were making and realized they must have changed their ammunition to canister. Canister was a cylindrical tin crammed with musket bullets that burst open at the cannon's muzzle to hurl a spreading cone of bullets at the enemy, and Starbuck could see the effect of the tin cans by the groups of wounded and dead men snatched backward onto the turf from the attackers' lines. Drummers were still beating the attack onward and the northerners were cheering as they advanced, their voices enthusiastic, almost cheerful, as if this whole performance were a sporting contest. The closest American flag was lavishly fringed with gold tassels and so heavy that the standard bearer seemed to wade forward as though he walked in water. The regiment of regular soldiers had caught up with the attack's front line and now hurried forward with fixed bayonets for the honor of being the first federal soldiers to break into the rebel defense.

"Fire!" a South Carolinian officer called, and the gray-coated infantry fired a second volley. A ramrod wheeled through the air as the dirty bank of smoke rolled away from the muskets. The Faulconer Legion's skirmishers were falling back to the regiment's flanks. The Rhode Islanders' bayonets looked wickedly long in the smoke-torn sunlight.

"Take aim!" Major Bird shouted, and the Legion's rifles went into their shoulders.

"Keep your aim low! Keep it low!" Sergeant Truslow shouted from the left flank.

"Aim for the officers!" Captain Hinton, falling back with his skirmishers, shouted.

Starbuck just stared. He could hear a northern officer shouting his men forward. "On, on, on!" The man had long red side-whiskers and gold-rimmed spectacles. "On! On!" Starbuck could now see the individual characters of the northern faces. The men's mouths opened as they shouted, their eyes were wide. A man stumbled, almost dropped his rifle, then regained his balance. The attackers were past the first dead bodies left by the skirmishers. A gold-braided officer mounted on a gray horse dropped his sword to point it straight at the rebels. "Charge!" he shouted, and the attack line quickened into a stumbling run. The northerners were cheering as they came and the drummers lost all cohesion, simply beating their stricks in a frenzy of effort. A fallen color was picked up, its glorious silk stripes a dazzling patch of color in the gray smoke. "Charge!" the northern officer shouted again, and his horse pranced in the gunsmoke's skeins.

"Fire!" Major Bird screamed, then whooped with unfeigned glee as the Legion's whole front disappeared in a gout of filthy smoke.

The fusillade was like the crack of doom at the world's end. It was one sudden, violent, horrifying volley at lethally short range and the shouts and drumming of the attacking northerners were wiped into instant silence, or rather transmuted into screams and shouts.

"Reload!" Murphy shouted.

Nothing could be seen through the bank of powder smoke that twisted above the rail fence. A few enemy bullets whipped through the smoke, but too high. The Legion reloaded, ramming their minié bullets hard down onto powder and wadding.

"Forward!" Major Bird was shouting. "Take them forward! To the fence, to the fence!" He was jumping up and down with excitement and waving his unloaded revolver. "Forward! Forward!"

Starbuck, still lost in a daze, began to load his revolver again. He was not sure why he did it, or whether he could ever use the weapon, but he just wanted to be doing something, and so he fumbled the powder and bullets into the Savage's six chambers, then smeared the bullet cones with grease to seal each chamber and thus prevent the ignited powder in the firing chamber setting off the other charges. His hands still shook. In his mind's eye he could still see that gorgeous banner, all shining red and white, being lifted from the blood-streaked grass to wave again in the sunlight.

"Fire!" Sergeant Truslow shouted from the flank.

"Kill the bastards! Kill the bastards!" That was Major Bird who, only an hour before, had been ridiculing the idea that he wanted to be involved in the day's fighting.

"Aim low! Aim at the bastards' bellies!" That was Captain Murphy, who had abandoned his horse and was firing a rifle like his men. The smoke of the first volley thinned to show that the Yankee officer's gray horse was down in the grass. There were bodies there, puffs of smoke, knots of men.

Adam stayed back at the tree line with Starbuck. He was breathing hard, as though he had just run a race. One of Evans's small smoothbore cannon fired a barrel of canister down the meadow. A northern shell whistled fragments above the Legion's color party. A man reeled back from G Company, blood soaking his left shoulder. He leaned against a tree, breathing hard, and a bullet slapped into the trunk just above his head. The man cursed and pushed himself upright, then stumbled back toward the gun line. Adam, seeing the man's resolve, pulled his revolver from

349

his holster and urged his horse forward.

"Adam!" Starbuck called, remembering his promise to Miriam Faulconer to keep Adam safe, but it was too late. Adam had taken his horse through the bank of bitter gunsmoke, over the fallen fence rails and into the smoke-free air where he was now calmly priming his revolver's chambers with percussion caps in apparent oblivion of the bullets that whipcracked around him. Some of the Legion's men shouted warnings that a man on a horse made a much choicer target than a foot soldier, but Adam ignored them.

Instead he leveled the revolver and fired its full cylinder into the enemy's bank of smoke. He looked almost happy. "Forward! Forward!" he shouted to no one in particular, but a dozen men of the Legion responded by advancing. They knelt close to Adam's horse and fired blindly at the scattered enemy. The Legion's first, overwhelming volley had torn the attackers into small groups of blue-uniformed men who stood in a crude line to exchange shots with the gray-clad southerners. The soldiers' lips were stained by black powder from biting cartridges and their faces were wild with fear or with rage or with excitement. Adam, his revolver empty, was laughing. Everything was in chaos, nothing but a whirl of smoke and stabbing flame and men screaming defiance. A second line of attackers was advancing up the slope behind the ravaged enemy front line.

"Forward!" Major Bird shouted, and groups of men darted a few paces forward, and the enemy edged a few paces backward. Starbuck had joined Adam and was spilling percussion caps from his right hand as he tried to prime the Savage's six cones. Beside him a man knelt and fired, stood up and reloaded. The man was muttering swear words at the northerners, cursing their mothers and their children, cursing their past and all their short futures. A Rhode Island officer waved his sword, urging his men on, and a bullet thumped into his belly, bending him over. Sergeant Truslow, grim-faced and

350

silent, was loading his gun with buck and ball, a combination of a round bullet with three smaller buckshots that achieved something of a shotgun effect. He did not fire the charge blindly, but carefully sought a target then fired deliberately, making sure of his aim.

"Go home! Go home!" Adam was shouting at the northerners, the apparently mild words made almost ludicrous by the note of excitement in his voice. He leveled his revolver again, pulled the trigger, but either he had misloaded or forgotten to prime the gun, for nothing happened, but he went on pulling the trigger as he screamed at the invaders to go home. Starbuck, beside his friend, seemed unable to shoot at the flag he had known all his life.

"Come on, boys! Come on!" The shout came from the far right of the Confederate line where Starbuck saw the gaudily uniformed Louisiana Zouaves charging out of the powder smoke to carry their bayonet-tipped rifles at the enemy. Some of the Louisianans whirled bowie knives as huge as cutlasses. They advanced raggedly, screaming a terrible high-pitched scream that made Starbuck's blood run cold. My God, he thought, but the Zouaves would all be cut down, shot in the open field, but instead the northerners edged back and still farther back, and suddenly the Louisiana infantry were among the blue-coated skirmishers and the northerners were running for their lives. A bowie knife sliced round and a man fell with his skull streaming blood. Another northern skirmisher was pinned to the ground with a bayonet as the whole center of the federal attack line stumbled backward from the bloody Zouave attack, then the rearward movement became a sudden rout as the northerners fled to avoid the heavy blades. But there was only a handful of Louisiana infantry, and their flanks were open to fire, and suddenly a northern volley smashed into their ranks. Colonel Wheat went down, his baggy red shirt soaked with blood.

The Louisianans, hugely outnumbered, came to a halt as

their enemies' bullets drove into them. Their gaudy bodies twitched as the bullets struck, but their mad charge had hurled the heart of the Yankee line a good hundred paces back down the hill. But now it was the Zouaves' turn to go backward and to carry their wounded Colonel toward the trees.

"Fire!" a southern artilleryman shouted and one of the smoothbore cannon belched a belly of canister at the northerners.

"Fire!" Major Bird shouted, and a score of Legion rifles crashed smoke and flame. A boy from Company D rammed a bullet onto a barrel already crammed with three charges of powder and bullets. He pulled the trigger, did not seem to notice that the gun had not fired, and started loading the musket yet again.

"Fire!" Nathan Evans screamed, and the South Carolinians smashed a volley across the fence, and in the pastureland the Rhode Islanders shuffled back to leave their dead and wounded bleeding in the grass.

"Fire!" A Louisiana chaplain, his Bible forgotten, emptied his revolver at the Yankees, pulling the trigger until the hammer fell on empty chambers, yet still he went on pulling, his face a rictus of exaltation.

"Fire!" Truslow shouted at his men. A sixteen-year-old screamed when a cartridge load of powder exploded in his face as he poured it into the hot barrel of his rifle. Robert Decker fired a shotgun into the smoke cloud. The grass of the meadow was flickering with small fires started by the burning wads from the rifle barrels. An injured man crawled back toward the tree line, attempted to clamber over the clutter of fallen fence rails, and there collapsed. His body seemed to shiver, then was still. An officer's horse lay dead, its body shuddering as northern bullets thudded home, but the Yankee fire was sporadic as the Rhode Islanders, too frightened to stand still and reload properly, stepped backward. The rebels screamed defiance and spat bullets into hot barrels, rammed the charges hard home, pulled their triggers, then started the process again. Starbuck watched the Legion fight its first battle and was struck by the atmosphere of glee, of sheer release, of carnival enjoyment. Even their soldiers' screams sounded to Starbuck like the mad whoops of overexcited children. Groups of men were darting forward, emulating the Zouaves' charge, and driving the demoralized Rhode Islanders farther back down the long slope where the first Yankee charge had been stopped cold.

Yet a second Yankee attack line was already halfway up the slope and still more northern troops were coming from the Sudley Road. A U.S. Marine regiment was there, together with three fresh regiments of New York volunteers. More field guns appeared, and the first Yankee cavalry galloped off to the left of their line as the fresh northern infantry marched stoically into the open land to reinforce the ragged remnants of the first attack, which had retreated two hundred paces back from the litter of bodies and the line of slick bloody grass and scorched turf that marked the high-tide line of their first failed assault.

"Form line! Form line!" The shout started somewhere in the center of the Confederate formation, and somehow enough sane officers and sergeants heard the order and echoed it, and slowly the screaming, maddened rebels were brought back to the fence line. They were grinning and laughing, full of pride for what they had done. Every now and then a man would whoop for no apparent reason, or else a man might turn around to blast a bullet at the stalled northern attack. Insults were hurled down the long slope.

"Go back to your mothers, Yankees!"

"Send some real men next time!"

"So how do you like a Virginia welcome, you yellow bastards!"

"Silence!" Major Bird shouted. "Silence!"

Someone began laughing, a hysterical mad laugh. Someone

353

else cheered. At the foot of the slope the northern guns opened fire again, screaming their shells up to the ridge to blast apart in dark-flamed smoke. The short-barreled northern howitzers had never ceased to fire, lobbing spherical case shot high over the Rhode Islanders and New Yorkers to crash raggedly about the edge of the woods.

"Back to the trees! Back to the trees!" The order was repeated down the rebel line and the southerners retreated back into the shadows. In front of them, where the powder smoke cleared slowly from the burnt grass, a handful of bodies lay on either side of the remnants of rail fence while beyond the fence, in the brighter sunlight, a scattering of dead northerners was sprawled in the pasture. The officer with red side-whiskers lay there with his mouth open and his gold-rimmed spectacles half-fallen off his face. A crow flapped down to land near the man's body. A wounded northerner pulled himself toward the trees, asking for water, but no one in the Legion had any water. They had emptied their canteens and now the sun was beating hotter and their mouths were dried by the saltpeter in the gunpowder, but there was no water, and ahead of them were yet more Yankees coming from the far trees to reignite the attack.

"We'll do it to them again, boys! We'll do it to them again!" Major Bird shouted, and even though the chaos of the Legion's first fight had not given him a chance to fully test his theory of musketry, he suddenly knew he had achieved something far more valuable; he had discovered an activity he utterly enjoyed. For all of his adult life Thaddeus Bird had been faced with the classic dilemma of a poor relation, which was whether to show an eternal deferential gratitude or to demonstrate an independency of mind by cultivating a prickly opposition to every prevailing orthodoxy, which latter course had pleased Bird until, in the smoke and excitement of battle, there had been no need to posture. Now he paced behind his men, watching the new northern attack take shape, and felt

354

strangely content. "Load your guns," he called in a firm voice, "but hold your fire! Load your guns, but hold your fire."

"Go for their bellies, boys," Murphy called aloud. "Put them down hard and the rest will go home."

Adam, like his uncle, also felt as though a great weight had gone from his soul. The awful noise of the battle spelt the death of all that he had worked for in the months since Lincoln's election, but the terrible sound also meant that Adam was no longer concerned with the great issues of war and peace, of slavery and emancipation, of states' rights and Christian principle, but only with being a good neighbor to the men who had volunteered to serve his father. Adam even began to understand his father, who had never agonized over morality or wanted to weigh up the balance of his actions in an earnest attempt to guarantee a favorable verdict on the Day of Judgment. Once, when Adam had asked his father about the principles by which he lived his life, Washington Faulconer had simply laughed the question away. "You know your trouble? You think too much. I've never known a happy man who thought too much. Thinking just complicates affairs. Life's like jumping a bad fence on a good horse, the more responsibility you leave to the horse the safer you'll be, and the more you leave to life the happier you are. Worrying about principles is schoolmaster's talk. You'll just find you sleep better if you treat people naturally. It ain't principle, just practicality. I never could stand listening to cant about principle. Just be yourself!" And Adam, in the sudden splintering chaos of a fire-fight, had at last trusted the horse to take the jump, and discovered that all his agony of conscience had evaporated in the simple pleasure of doing his duty. Adam, in a meadow whip-sawed by fire, had behaved well. He might have lost the battle for his country, but he had won the war in his soul.

"Load your guns! Hold your fire!" Major Bird walked slowly behind the Legion's companies, watching the Yankee horde gather for its next attempt. "Shoot low when they come, boys, shoot low! And well done, all of you, well done."

The Legion, in just five minutes, had become soldiers.

"Hey, you!" The voice shouted at Ethan Ridley from the top of the central wig-wag tower. "You! Yes, you! Are you a staff officer?"

Ridley, who had been lost in thought as he galloped his horse southward, reined in. Ridley suspected that being one of Washington Faulconer's aides was not what the signal officer meant by a staff officer, but Ridley was quick-witted enough to realize he needed some excuse to be galloping alone in the rear areas of the Confederate army and so he shouted the affirmative. "Yes!"

"Can you find General Beauregard?" The speaker, an officer wearing captain's bars, clambered down the makeshift ladder. A hand-lettered sign at the foot of the ladder read "Signalers ONLY" while another, in even larger letters, read "KEEP OFF." The officer ran across to Ridley and held up a folded sheet of paper secured by a wafer seal. "Beauregard needs that quick."

"But ..." Ridley had been about to say he had no idea how to find General Beauregard, but then decided such a disclaimer would sound odd from a self-proclaimed staff officer. Besides, Ridley reckoned that Colonel Faulconer would be wherever the general was, so by finding the Colonel he would also discover Beauregard.

"I have wig-wagged the message to Beauregard, if that's what you're about to suggest," the captain said peevishly, "but I'd like to send a written confirmation. You can never be certain a message gets wig-wagged through, not with the fools they give me to work with. I need good men, educated men. I wish you'd make that point to Beauregard for me. With my respects, of course. Half the lunkheads they provide me never learned to spell, and the other half didn't have brains to begin with. Now go on with you, there's a good fellow, quick as you can!"

Ridley kicked back his heels. He was in the army's baggage

area where wagons, limbers, portable forges, ambulances and carriages were parked so tightly that their upturned shafts looked like a winter thicket. A woman shouted as Ridley galloped past, wanting to know what was happening, but he just shook his head and spurred on past cooking fires, past groups of men playing cards and past a child playing with a kitten. What were all these people doing here? he wondered.

He breasted a rise and saw the smoke of battle lying like a river fog in the Bull Run valley to his left. That fog, where the great guns slammed their missiles across the stream, lay around the center and left of the rebel army, while in front of Ridley was the tangle of woods and small pastures that was the Confederate right wing and from where General Beauregard hoped to launch his own attack on the unsuspecting northerners. Colonel Washington Faulconer was somewhere in that tangle and Ridley rested his horse while he tried to make some sense of the landscape. He was tense and angry, fidgeting in his saddle, aware of the enormity of the gamble he was taking, but Ridley would take almost any gamble to fulfill his ambitions. For weeks now Ethan Ridley had played fast and loose with Washington Faulconer's money, but now, as the Legion divided along a line that separated the Colonel's admirers from those who despised him, Ridley would make his choice. He would side whole-heartedly with the Colonel and defeat Starbuck and Bird who, aided by Adam's pusillanimity, had forced the Legion to abandon its obedience to Faulconer.

The reward of loyalty was money, and money was Ridley's god. He had watched his father impoverish a family and seen the pity on his neighbors' faces. He had endured his half-brother's condescension just as he endured Anna Faulconer's cloying attentions, and all because he was poor. He was patronized for his skill with a pencil and paintbrush, as though he could always earn his living as a portrait painter or as an illustrator, but he had no more wish to earn his living as a painter than as a coal heaver or as a lawyer. Instead he wanted to be like Faulconer, to be the possessor of wide acres and fast horses and of a mistress in Richmond and a fine big country house. Of late, since Adam's return, Ridley had doubted that even being Faulconer's son-in-law would be enough to secure an adequate share of the Faulconer wealth, but now the god of battle had played into Ridley's hands. Colonel Washington Faulconer had left one firm order—that the Legion was to ignore Nathan Evans, and Ridley's rivals for the Colonel's gratitude had combined to disobey that order. It was time to betray that disobedience.

But first Ridley had to find Colonel Faulconer, which meant discovering General Beauregard, and so he spurred down from the hill into the undulating landscape of deep woods and small pastures. His horse cleared two fences, running as gamely as though she were following the hounds in the winter hills. He swerved left into a wide path that led under trees where a regiment of southern Zouaves in their distinctive red pantaloons and baggy shirts lolled at their ease. "What's happening?" one of the Zouaves shouted at Ridley.

"We whipping the bastards?" a sergeant called.

"You looking for us?" An officer ran into Ridley's path.

"I'm looking for Beauregard." Ridley curbed his horse. "You know where he is?"

"Go to the end of the wood, turn left, there's a road in your front, and like as not that's where he is. He was there a half hour ago, anyways. You got any news?"

Ridley had no news, so just cantered on, turning left to see a horde of infantrymen resting beside the road at the far end of the clearing. The soldiers were in blue coats and for a second Ridley feared he had galloped clean into the Yankee lines, then he saw the triple-striped Confederate flag over the troops and realized they were southerners in makeshift uniforms of northern blue. "Do you know where the general is?" he called to a blue-coated officer, but the officer just shrugged, then pointed a helpful hand vaguely to the north and east. "Last I heard he was at a farmhouse thataway, but don't ask me where the hell that is."

"He was here," a sergeant offered, "but he ain't here now. You know what's happening, mister? Are we whipping the sumbitches?"

"I don't know." Ridley carried on, coming at last to an artillery battery that was comfortably ensconced on the southern bank of the Bull Run behind a breastwork of wicker baskets filled with dirt.

"This here's Balls Ford," an artillery lieutenant said, taking a pipe from his mouth, "and the general sure was here an hour ago. Can you tell us what's happening out there?" He gestured westward from where the sound of cannon fire grumbled and crackled in the sultry air.

"No."

"Making enough noise about it, ain't they? I thought the war was being held over here, not over there?"

Ridley crossed Balls Ford to the enemy side of the Bull Run. The water came up to his horse's belly, making Ridley lift his boots and stirrups above the quick flow. A company of Virginian infantry lay in the shade on the far bank, waiting for orders. "You know what's happening?" a captain asked.

"No."

"Nor me. An hour back they said as we should wait here, but no one said why. I kind of think we're forgotten."

"Have you seen the general?"

"I ain't seen anything above a major for three hours now. But a sutler said as how we're attacking, mister, so maybe all the generals are that way." The man pointed north.

Ridley rode northward under tall trees, going slow so that his sweating horse did not break a leg in one of the savage ruts cut into the dirt road by artillery wheels. A quarter mile beyond the ford at the edge of a trampled cornfield Ridley found a battery of heavy twelve-pounder cannon. The guns had been unlimbered and deployed to point their lethal barrels across the growing corn, but the battery commander had no idea why he was there or what he was expected to see emerge from the dark green woods at the farther side of the cornfield. "You know what's making all that damned noise?" The artillery major gestured toward the west.

"They seem to be firing at each other over the stream," Ridley said.

"I wish they'd give me something to fire at, because I don't know what in hell's name I'm doing here." He gestured at the cornfield as though it were the dark heart of equatorial Africa. "You're looking at Beauregard's big attack, Captain. Trouble is there ain't no enemy here, nor anyone else. Except maybe some boys from Mississippi who went up the road a while, and God only knows what they're doing."

Ridley wiped the sweat off his face, pulled his slouch hat back on, and spurred his tired horse up the road. He found the Mississippi infantry sheltering under a break of trees. One of their officers, a major whose accent was so thick Ridley could scarce understand him, said that the Confederate advance had come to a halt here, under these cedar trees, and he was not all of a piece sure why, but he was certain, or at least as certain as a man from Rolling Forks could ever be certain, and that was not altogether certain, but it was pretty certain, that General Beauregard had gone back to the other side of the Bull Run, but by a different ford. A ford farther to the east. Or maybe it was farther west. "So do you know what's happening?" the Major asked before taking a bite out of a green apple.

"No," Ridley confessed.

"Nor me!" The Major had a fine feather in his hat, a curved saber and a lavish mustache that had been oiled into sleek elegance. "If you find anyone who does know just what they're doing, mister, then you tell 'em that Jeremiah Colby is right well eager to get this war over and done with. Good luck to you, mister! Fine apples you boys grow here!"

Ridley turned his horse and rode back to the stream, then

360

began quartering the country between the Bull Run and the railroad. The guns thundered in the distance, their bass sound punctuated by the brushfire sound of rifles and muskets. The noise lent urgency to Ridley's quest, except he had no idea how to expedite the urgency. The general, his staff and hangers-on seemed to have been swallowed into this warm huge countryside. He stopped his tired horse at a crossroads beside a small wooden cabin. The vegetables in its trim garden had been torn out, all but for a row of unripe squash. An elderly Negress, smoking a pipe, watched him warily from her cabin door. "Ain't nothing to steal, massa," she said.

"You know where the general is?" Ridley asked her.

"Ain't nothing to steal, massa, all stolen already."

"Stupid cuffee bitch," Ridley said, then louder and slower, as though he were talking to a child. "Do you know where the general is?"

"All stolen already, massa."

"And damn you, too." A shell screamed far overhead, tumbling and wailing as it shrieked across an empty Sunday sky. Ridley swore at the woman again, then chose one of the roads at random and let his weary horse walk at its own slow pace. Dust drifted from the mare's hooves onto a drunken soldier sleeping beside the road. A few paces farther on a black and white farm dog lay dead in the road, shot in the head by some soldier who had presumably resented the dog worrying his horse. Ridley passed the dog by and began to worry that perhaps Beauregard, and Faulconer with him, had ridden north and west to where the battle sounded, for surely no general could stay in this somnolent, buzzing countryside while his men were dying just three miles away? Then, as his horse cleared the margin of a grove of trees, he saw another of the strange lattice signal towers standing beside a farmhouse, and beneath the tower a huddle of horses picketed by the farm's fence, and on the farm's verandah a group of men glinting with gold braid, and so Ridley gave his horse spurs, but, just as he kicked her into reluctant speed, so a

361

single horseman mounted a tall black horse in front of the farm and galloped hard down the drive toward him. It was the Colonel.

"Sir! Colonel Faulconer!" Ridley had to shout to get the Colonel's attention. Washington Faulconer would otherwise have galloped clean past Ridley.

The Colonel glanced at the tired horseman, recognized Ridley, and slowed. "Ethan! It is you! Come with me! What on earth are you doing here? Never mind! I've got good news, wonderful news!"

The Colonel had spent a frustrating morning. He had discovered Beauregard shortly after six o'clock, but the General had not been expecting him and had no time to see him, and so Faulconer had been forced to cool his heels as the hours dragged by. Yet now, wondrously, he had received the orders he had craved. Beauregard, desperate to vivify his attack that had mysteriously stalled in the vacant countryside across the Run, had appealed for fresh troops and Faulconer had seen his chance. He had volunteered the Legion and received orders to march the men across to the right wing. General Johnston's newly arrived men from the Army of the Shenandoah could be left to buttress the rebel left wing, while Beauregard put new impetus into the right. "We need some enthusiasm," Beauregard had grumbled to Faulconer, "some push. It's no good playing kitty-bender on a battlefield, you have to show 'em a touch of whip and spurs." It was all Faulconer wanted; a chance to lead his Legion into a battle-winning charge that would write another glorious page of Virginia history.

"Come on, Ethan!" Washington Faulconer now called back. "We've got permission to attack!"

"But they've gone!" Ridley shouted. His tired horse was much slower than the Colonel's well-rested stallion, Saratoga.

The Colonel curbed Saratoga in, turned him and stared at Ridley.

362

"They've gone, sir." Ridley said. "That's what I came to tell you."

The Colonel swatted at a fly with his riding crop. "What do you mean, gone?" He sounded very calm, as if he had not understood the news Ridley had just fetched across the battle-ground.

"It was Starbuck," Ridley said. "He came back, sir."

"He came back?" the Colonel asked, incredulous.

"He claimed to have orders from Evans."

"Evans!" Faulconer pronounced that name sulfurously.

"So they marched off to Sudley, sir."

"Starbuck brought orders? What the hell did Pecker do?"

"He ordered the men to Sudley, sir."

"Under that ape Evans's command?" The Colonel shouted the question and his horse, unsettled, whinnied softly.

"Yes, sir," Ridley felt the satisfaction of delivering damning news. "That's why I came to find you."

"But there's no damned battle at Sudley! That's a feint! A lure! The General knows all about that!" The Colonel was goaded into a sudden and incandescent fury. "The battle will be here! Christ! On this side of the field! Here!" The Colonel slashed down with his riding crop, whistling the air and frightening an already nervous Saratoga. "But what about Adam? I told him not to let Pecker do anything irresponsible."

"Adam let himself be persuaded by Starbuck, sir." Ethan paused to shake his head. "I opposed them, sir, but I'm only a captain. Nothing more."

"You're a major now, Ethan. You can take Pecker's place. Goddamn Pecker, and goddamn Starbuck! Damn him, damn him, damn him! I'll kill him! I'll feed his guts to the hogs! Now come on, Ethan, come on!" The Colonel slashed his spurs back.

Major Ridley, following as fast as he could, suddenly remembered the wig-wagger's message for Beauregard. He pulled the wafer-sealed paper from his pocket and wondered

363

whether he should mention its existence to the Colonel, but the Colonel was already pounding ahead, his horse kicking up dust, and Ridley did not want to be left too far behind, not now that he was a major and the Colonel's second in command, and so he threw the message away, then galloped after the Colonel toward the sound of the guns.

On the tree-lined crest where Evans's scratch brigade had repelled the first northern attack the battle had become a grim one-sided pounding match. For the Yankee gunners it was little more than a session of unopposed target practice, for both of the small Confederate cannon had been destroyed; the first thrown off its carriage by a direct hit from a twelve-pounder roundshot, while the second had lost a wheel from another plumb hit and, within minutes, another twelve-pound ball had shattered the spokes of its replacement wheel. The two stricken cannon, still loaded with unfired canister, lay abandoned at the edge of the wood.

Major Bird wondered whether there was anything he should be doing, but nothing suggested itself. He tried to analyze the situation and came up with the simple fact that the southern troops were holding off a far greater number of northerners, but that every moment the southerners spent at the tree line the more men they lost and that eventually, by a process as ineluctable as a mathematical equation, there would be no living southerners left and the northerners would march across the rebel corpses to claim the battle and, presumably, the war. Major Bird could not stop that happening because there was nothing clever he could do; no flank attack, no ambush, no manner of out-thinking the enemy. The time had simply come to fight and die. Major Bird regretted it had come to such a hopeless plight, but he saw no elegant way out, and so he was determined to stay where he was. The odd thing was that he felt no fear. He tried to analyze that lack and decided he was privileged by possessing a sanguine temperament. He celebrated that happy realization by sneaking a fond look at his wife's picture.

Nor was Adam Faulconer feeling fear. He could not say he was enjoying the morning, but at least the experience of battle had reduced life's turmoil to simple questions, and Adam was reveling in that freedom. Like all the other officers, he had abandoned his horse, sending it back among the trees. The Legion's officers had learned that the enemy's rifle fire was too high to be of much danger to crouching men, but not so high that the bullets could miss a man on horseback, and so they had abandoned the Colonel's precious orders to stay mounted and had become infantrymen.

Nathaniel Starbuck noted how some men like Truslow and, more surprisingly, Major Bird and Adam, seemed effortlessly brave. They went calmly about their business, stood straight in the face of the enemy, and kept their wits sharp. Most of the men oscillated wildly between bravery and timidity, but responded to the leadership of the brave men. Each time Truslow went forward to shoot at the northerners a dozen skirmishers went with him, and whenever Major Bird stalked along the line of the trees the men grinned at him, took heart from him and were pleased that their eccentric schoolmaster was so apparently unmoved by the dangers. Harness those middling men, Starbuck understood, and the Legion could achieve miracles. There was also a minority of men, the cowards, who huddled far back in the trees, where they pretended to be busy loading or repairing their guns, but who were in fact just cowering from the eerie whistling sound of the minié bullets and the sizzling crack of the shellfire.

The bullets and shellfire had reduced Nathan Evans's Confederate brigade to a ragged line of men crouched in the shadows at the edge of the trees. Every now and then a group of soldiers would dash to the open ground, fire their shots, then scurry back, but the Yankees now had a horde of skirmishers in the pasture and every appearance of a rebel sparked a bitter

365

flurry of rifle fire. The bravest rebel officers strolled at the wood's margin, speaking encouragement and making small jokes, though Adam, determined to be seen by his father's Legion, refused to walk in the shadow but strolled openly in the sunlight, calling aloud as he strolled to warn men not to fire as he passed in front of their guns. The men shouted at him to take cover, to get back in the trees, but Adam would have none of it. He flaunted himself, as though he believed his life was charmed. He told himself he feared no evil.

Major Bird joined Starbuck and watched Adam in the sunlight. "Do you note," Bird said, "how the bullets are going high?"

"High?"

"They're aiming at him, but are shooting high. I've been noting it."

"So they are." Starbuck would probably not have noticed if the Yankees had been firing at the moon, but now that Thaddeus Bird pointed it out he saw that most of the northern rifle fire was indeed clipping at the leaves above Adam's head. "He's a fool!" Starbuck said angrily. "He just wants to die!"

"He's making up for his father," Bird explained. "Faulconer ought to be here, but he's not, so Adam is sustaining the family honor, though if his father had been here, Adam would probably be having a fit of conscience. I've noticed how Adam usually benefits from Faulconer's absence, haven't you?"

"I promised his mother I'd keep him safe."

Bird yelped with laughter. "More fool you. How are you supposed to do that? Buy him one of those ridiculous iron breastplates that the newspapers advertise?" Bird shook his head. "My sister only charged you with that responsibility, Starbuck, to belittle Adam. I assume he was present?"

"Yes."

"My sister, you understand, married into a family of serpents and has been teaching them the secrets of venom ever since." Bird chuckled. "But Adam is the best of them," he allowed, "the very best. And brave," he added.

"Very," Starbuck said, and felt ashamed of himself, for he had done nothing brave in this morning's clash. The confidence that had so filled him in the railroad depot at Rosskill had evaporated, stolen by the sight of his country's flag. He had still not fired the revolver, nor was he sure that he could shoot at his own countrymen, but neither was he willing to desert his friends within the Legion's ranks. Instead he fidgeted at the wood's edge and watched the far-off gouts of smoke spitting from the Yankee guns. He wanted to describe the smoke to Sally and so he had watched it carefully, seeing that it was white at first and how it darkened rapidly into a grayish blue. Once, gazing intently down the slope, Starbuck had sworn he could see the dark trace of a missile in the smoky air, and seconds later he had heard a shell clatter destructively through the branches overhead. One of the northern guns had been placed beside a hayrick in the farmyard at the bottom of the slope and the flame of the gun's firing had set the hay alight. The flames leaped and curled furiously, pumping a darker smoke into the gun-fouled air.

"Did you hear that poor Jenkins is gone?" Major Bird said in the tone of voice he might have used to remark that the spring was early this year, or that the vegetable crop was looking good.

"Gone?" Starbuck asked, because the imprecision of the word had somehow suggested that Roswell Jenkins had simply walked away from the battlefield.

"Vanished. Hit by a shell. Looks like something left on a butcher's slab." Bird's words were callous, but the tone of his voice was regretful.

"Poor Jenkins." Starbuck had not particularly liked Roswell Jenkins, who had distributed bottles of whiskey to ensure his election as an officer and who had left the running of his company to Sergeant Truslow. "So who'll take over K Company?"

"Whoever my brother-in-law wishes, or rather whoever Truslow wants." Bird laughed, then turned the pecking motion of his head into a rueful shake. "If there's any point in anyone taking over at all? Because maybe there'll be no Legion left?" Bird paused. "Maybe there'll be no Confederacy left?" Bird involuntarily ducked as a shell fragment whipped overhead to smack into a tree just six inches above Starbuck's head. Bird straightened up and took out one of his dark cigars. "You'd like one?"

"Please." Since that night with Belvedere Delaney in Richmond, Starbuck had found himself smoking more and more cigars.

"Do you have any water?" Bird asked as he handed the cigar to Starbuck.

"No."

"We seem to have exhausted our water. Doc Billy wanted some for the wounded, but there isn't any and I can't spare anyone to find more. There's so much we overlooked." A crashing volley of musketry sounded to the north, evidence that more Confederate troops had come into action. Starbuck had seen at least two more southern regiments join the right flank of Nathan Evans's makeshift line, but for every fresh man from Alabama and Mississippi there were at least three northerners, and the reinforced Yankees were sending ever more troops up the slope to lay their weight of rifle fire at the thin-scraped rebel line. "It can't be long now," Major Bird said ruefully, "it can't be long."

A South Carolinian officer came running up the tree line. "Major Bird? Major Bird?"

"Here!" Bird stepped away from Starbuck.

"Colonel Evans wants you all to advance, Major." The South Carolinian had a powder-blackened face, a ripped tunic and bloodshot eyes. His voice was hoarse. "The Colonel's going to sound a bugle call, and he wants us all to make a charge." The man paused as though he knew that he was asking the impossible, then he tried a direct appeal to patriotism. "One last real good charge, Major, for the South."

368

For a second it looked as if Major Bird would laugh at such a naked appeal to his patriotism, but then he nodded. "Of course."

For the South, one last mad charge, one last defiant gesture. Before the battle and the cause were lost.

The four companies that Shanks Evans had left guarding the stone bridge were forced away when northerners under a colonel called William Sherman discovered a ford upstream of the bridge and thus outflanked the tiny afterguard. The men fired a ragged volley, then retreated fast as Sherman's men advanced across the Bull Run.

A shell exploded above the abandoned bridge, then a blue-coated officer appeared on its far side and signaled its capture by waving his sword toward the northern gun batteries. "Cease fire!" a battery commander shouted. "Sponge out! Horses up! Look lively now!" The bridge was taken, so now the northern army could pour across the Bull Run and complete the encirclement and destruction of the rebel army.

"It is now safe for you gentlemen to advance to the battery position," Captain James Starbuck announced to the newspapermen, though his announcement was scarcely needed, for groups of excited civilians were already walking or riding toward the captured stone bridge. A congressman waved a smoking cigar at the troops, then stepped aside to let a battery of horse artillery clank and rattle by. "On to Richmond, boys! On to Richmond!" he shouted. "Give the yeller dogs a good whipping, boys! Go on, now!"

A battalion of gray-coated northern infantry followed the horse artillery. The 2nd Wisconsin Regiment wore gray because there had not been enough blue cloth available for their uniforms. "Just hold the good flag high, boys," their colonel had said, "and the good Lord will know we're not rebel scum." Once across the bridge the Wisconsin men swung off the turnpike to march north toward a distant haze of gunsmoke that

showed where a stubborn Confederate line still resisted the federal flanking movement. Captain James Starbuck assumed the
gray-coated Wisconsin troops would lead the assault on the
exposed flank of those rebel defenders, crumpling and destroying them, and thus adding to the God-given victory that the
North was enjoying. Almighty God, James thought piously, had
been pleased to bless his country on this Lord's Day. God's
vengeance had been swift, his justice mighty, and his victory
overwhelming, and even the godless foreign military attachés
were offering congratulations. "This is exactly what Brigadier
General McDowell planned," James said, loyally ascribing
God's doings to the northern general. "We anticipated an initial
resistance, gentlemen, then a sudden collapse and a progressive
destruction of the enemy positions."

The Frenchman, Colonel Lassan, alone seemed sceptical,
wondering why there had been so little evidence of any Confederate artillery fire. "Perhaps they are saving their gunfire?"
he suggested to James.

"I would rather suggest, sir," James bridled at the Frenchman's scepticism, "that the rebels lack the necessary professional skills to deploy their guns efficiently."

"Ah! That must be it, Captain, indeed."

"They're really farmers, not soldiers. Think of it, Colonel, as
a peasants' revolt." James wondered if that was pitching it a bit
strong, but anything that denigrated the rebels was music to
James Starbuck's ears, and so he not only let the insult stand,
but embroidered it. "It is an army of ignorant farmboys led by
immoral slave owners."

"So victory is assured?" Lassan asked diffidently.

"Assured, guaranteed!" James felt the burgeoning happiness
of a man who sees a difficult endeavor triumphantly concluded,
and there was indeed a genuine elation of victory as yet more
federal regiments crossed the stone bridge. Three northern
divisions were crowding the road as they waited to cross the
stream, a dozen bands were playing, women were cheering, the

370

flags were flying, God was in his heaven, Beauregard's flank was turned and the rebellion was being whipsawed into bloody shreds.

And it was still not even midday.

13

"Fix bayonets!" Major Bird shouted the order, then listened as it was echoed out toward the Legion's flanks. The men pulled the heavy, brass-handled sword-bayonets from their scabbards and clicked them over their guns' blackened muzzles. Most of the Legion had never believed they would use the bayonets in an infantry charge, instead, when the war was over and the Yankees had been sent back north, they had thought they would take the bayonets home and use them for pig sticking or hay cutting. Now, though, behind the thinning veil of smoke that hung above the scorched and shattered fence rails, they fixed the bayonets onto the fiercely hot rifle muzzles and tried not to think of what waited in the sunlight.

For a horde of Yankees waited out there—men from Rhode Island, New York and New Hampshire, their volunteer ardor reinforced by the professional fighters from the U.S. Army and Marines. The northern attackers now outnumbered Nathan Evans's men by four to one, yet the Yankee attack had been held for more than an hour by the stubborn southern defense. Those defenders had now been whittled perilously thin and so Evans wanted one last effort to throw the northern attack into chaos and thus buy a few more minutes in which the remainder of the Confederate army could change its alignment to meet the flank attack. Evans would offer one last act of defiance before his rebel line disintegrated and the mighty northern assault rolled irresistibly on.

Major Bird drew his sword. He had still not loaded his Le Mat revolver. He gave the sword an experimental slash, then hoped to God he would not have to use it. To Bird's way of thinking last-ditch bayonet charges belonged in the history books or in romance novels, not in present day actuality, though Bird had to admit the Legion's bayonets looked foully effective. They were long slender blades with a wicked upward curve at their tips. Back in Faulconer County the Colonel had insisted the men practice with their bayonets, and had even hung a cow's carcass from a low branch to make a realistic target, but the carcass had rotted and the men could not be induced to attack it. Now, with the sweat making white channels through the powder stains on their faces, those same men readied themselves for a bout of real bayonet practice.

The northerners, encouraged by the lull in southern rifle fire, began advancing again. A fresh battery of southern artillery had reached the right flank of Evans's line and the newly arrived gunners cracked their canister and roundshot across the face of the federal attack, persuading the northerners to hurry. Three northern bands were now playing in rivalry, driving the heavy fringed flags forward through the smoke wraiths that hung above the meadow that had been so battered by shells and roundshot that the sulfurous stink of the powder smoke was laced with the sweeter smell of new cut hay.

Major Bird looked at his old-fashioned watch, blinked, and looked again. He held the watch to his ear, thinking it must have stopped, yet he could still hear it ticking steadily away. He had somehow thought it was afternoon already, but it was only half past ten. He licked his dry lips, hefted the sword and looked back to the approaching enemy.

The bugle called.

One false note, a pause, then it rang a clean, clear triple of notes, then another triple, a heartbeat's pause, and suddenly the officers and sergeants were shouting at the southern line to get up and go. For a second no one moved, then the gray line at the wood's shell-torn and bullet-stripped edge stirred into life.

"Forward!" Major Bird called, and he walked into the sunlight with his sword held shoulder high and pointing forward.

He somewhat spoilt the heroic posture by stumbling as he crossed the fence rails, but he recovered and walked on. Adam had taken command of Company E whose captain, Elisha Burroughs, was dead. Burroughs had been a senior clerk in the Faulconer County Bank who had not really wanted to volunteer for the Legion, but had feared he might jeopardize his advancement in Washington Faulconer's bank if he had refused. Now he was a corpse, his skin darkening and thick with flies, and Adam had taken his place. Adam walked five paces ahead of E Company with his revolver in his right hand and his saber scabbard in his left. He needed to hold the scabbard away from his legs to stop it tripping him. Starbuck, walking alongside Bird, was having the same trouble with his own scabbard.

"I'm not sure it's worth wearing a sword," Bird commented. "I knew the horses were a bad idea, but it seems that swords are an equal encumbrance. My brother-in-law will be disappointed! I sometimes think his dream is to carry a lance into battle." Bird snuffled with laughter at the thought. "Sir Washington Faulconer, Lord of Seven Springs. He'd like that. I never did understand why our Founding Fathers abolished titles. They cost nothing and give fools a great deal of satisfaction. My sister would dearly love to be the Lady Faulconer. Is your revolver loaded?"

"Yes." Though Starbuck had yet to fire a single shot.

"Mine isn't. I keep forgetting." Bird slashed at a dandelion with his sword. To his right Company E was advancing in good order. At least two of the company's men had slung their rifles and were carrying their long bowie knives instead. Butchers' knives, Thaddeus Bird liked to call them, but the long ungainly blades seemed appropriate enough for this desperate venture. Northern bullets made their odd whistle as they whipped past in the warm air. The Legion's colors twitched as bullets slapped and tugged at the cloth. "Notice how the Yankees are still firing high?" Bird commented.

"Thank God for that," Starbuck said.

The bugle sounded again, urging the rebel line on, and Bird gestured with his sword to encourage the Legion to go faster. The men half-ran and half-walked. Starbuck skirted a patch of smoking earth littered with shell fragments where a mutilated skirmisher lay dead. The shell had ripped out most of the man's belly and half his rib cage, and what was left of him was thick with flies. The corpse had prominent teeth in a face that was already turning black in the heat. "I think that was George Musgrave," Bird said conversationally.

"How could you tell?" Starbuck managed to ask.

"Those rodent teeth. He was a wretched boy. A bully. I wish I could say I'm sorry to see him dead, but I'm not. I've wished him dead a hundred times in the past. A nasty piece of work."

A man in Company K was hit by a bullet and began uttering a succession of panting screams. Two men ran to help him. "Leave him be!" Sergeant Truslow snapped and the wounded man was left writhing on the grass. The Legion's bandsmen, sheltering at the edge of the wood, were the stretcher bearers, and two of them came hesitantly forward to collect the injured soldier.

A howitzer shell screamed down to bury itself in the meadow. It exploded, and was immediately followed by another shell. The northern infantry had stopped their steady advance and were reloading their rifles. Starbuck could see the ramrods rising and falling, and could see the powder-stained faces glancing up from the weapons to eye the approaching rebel line. There seemed so few southerners in the attack, and so many northerners waiting for them. Starbuck forced himself to walk calmly, to show no fear. Funny, he thought, but at this moment his family would be taking their pew in the tall, dark church and his father would be in the vestry, praying, and the congregation would be shuffling out of the sunlight, their pew doors clicking and creaking open beneath the high windows that were left open in the summertime so that the breezes from Boston harbor might cool the worshipers. The stink of horse manure in

375

the street would permeate the church where his mother would be pretending to read her Bible, though in truth her attention would be solely on the gathering congregation; who was present and who absent, who looked well and who queer. Starbuck's older sister, Ellen Marjory, betrothed to her minister, would be ostentatiously displaying her piety by praying or by reading the Scripture, while fifteen-year-old Martha would be catching the eyes of the boys in the Williamses' box across the aisle. Starbuck wondered if Sammy Williams was among the blue-coated enemy waiting three hundred yards away in this Virginian meadow. He wondered where James was, and had a sudden pang as he thought of the possibility of his pompous but kindly older brother lying dead.

The bugle called again, this time more urgently, and the rebel line stumbled into a run.

"Cheer!" Major Bird shouted. "Cheer!"

It seemed to Starbuck that instead of cheering, the men began to scream. Or rather to yelp like the wounded man whom Truslow had left behind on the grass. The sound could have been translated as a screech of terror, except that in unison there was something in the noise that curdled the blood, and the men themselves sensed it and began to reinforce the weird ululating sound. Even Major Bird, running with his clumsy sword, echoed the eerie shriek. There was something bestial in the noise, something that threatened an awful violence.

And then the northerners opened fire.

For a second the whole summer sky, the whole heavy firmament itself, was filled with the wail and scream of the bullets, and the rebel yell hesitated before starting again, only this time there were real screams mingled with the shrill sound. Men were falling. Men were jarred back by the mule-kick force of the striking bullets. Some men staggered as they tried to keep walking. There was fresh blood on the grass. Starbuck could hear a clattering noise and realized it was the sound of northern bullets hitting rifle stocks and bowie knife blades. The southern

376

charge had slowed and men seemed to be wading forward, as if the air had thickened into a resistant treacle in which the ordered lines of the rebel regiments had first broken and then coalesced into shattered groups. The men stopped, fired, then advanced again, but the advance was slow and hesitant.

Another volley came from the federals and more men were plucked back from the rebel charge. Major Bird was screaming at his men to charge, to run, to carry the day, but the Legion had been stunned by the ferocity of the northern counterfire and overwhelmed by the sheer quantity of gunfire that now crackled and flamed and whistled about them. The northern howitzer shells crashed down like thunderbolts, each shell spewing a barrowload of red earth high in the air.

Adam was ten paces ahead of E Company. He walked slowly forward, apparently unmoved by the danger. A sergeant called him back, but Adam, his revolver held low, ignored the call.

"Keep going! Keep going!" Major Bird screamed at his men. So far not one bowie knife nor one bayonet had been reddened, but the men could not keep going. Instead they fell back, silent, and the federals bayed a deep-noted shout of triumph and the noise seemed to spur the rebel retreat into a stumbling run. The Confederates were not panicking yet, but they were close. "No!" Major Bird was livid, trying to force his men back into the attack by sheer force of personality.

"Major!" Starbuck had to shout to make Bird hear. "Look to your left! Your left!" A fresh northern regiment had come up on the Legion's left and now threatened to wrap itself round the open flank of the Virginians. The new attack would not only drive back this failed bayonet attack, but would overlap the wood. Evans's defenders had been outflanked and outfought at last.

"Goddamn!" Bird stared at the new threat. His oath sounded very unconvincing, like a man unused to cursing. "Sergeant Major! Take the colors back." Bird gave the order, but did not yet retreat himself.

"Come back, sir, please! Come back!" Starbuck pulled at Major Bird's sleeve, and this time the major began to withdraw. Bullets screamed in the air as Bird and Starbuck stumbled back, preserved from the northern marksmen by the fog of battle smoke that obscured proper aiming.

Only Adam would not retreat. He was shouting at his men to join him, that there was no danger, that all they had to do was push on to the far side of the meadow, but E Company had seen the retreat of the whole Confederate line, and so they edged backward themselves. Adam stopped and turned toward them, shouting at them to advance, but then he staggered and almost dropped his revolver. He opened his mouth to speak, but no sound came out. He somehow managed to hold his balance as, very slowly and very carefully, like a drunken man pretending to be sober, he pushed the revolver into its holster. Then, with an oddly puzzled look on his face, he fell onto his knees.

"You stupid bastard." Sergeant Truslow had seen Adam fall and now ran across the face of advancing northerners. The rest of the Legion was hurrying back toward the safety of the trees. The whole southern charge had failed utterly and the northerners were in full cry.

"It's my leg, Truslow," Adam said in a puzzled voice.

"Should have been your goddamn brain. Give me your arm." Truslow, even when rescuing Adam, sounded grimly hostile. "Come on, boy. Hurry!"

Adam had been struck in his left thigh. The bullet had hit like a hammer blow, but had not hurt much at the time. Now suddenly there was pain searing white hot from his groin down to his toes. He hissed with the agony and could not resist a half-scream. "Leave me here!" he gasped to Truslow.

"Shut your bleating, for Christ's sake." Truslow half-dragged and half-carried Adam back toward the trees.

Neither Major Bird nor Starbuck had seen Adam's plight. They were hurrying back toward the wood, or rather Starbuck was hurrying and Thaddeus Bird was strolling calmly. "Do you notice," Bird asked yet again, "just how many bullets go high?"

"Yes." Starbuck was trying to run and crouch at the same time.

"We should do something about that," Bird remarked purposefully. "Because we must have been firing high too, wouldn't you say?"

"Yes." Starbuck would have agreed with whatever propositions Bird wanted so long as the Major hurried.

"I mean how many hundreds of bullets have been fired on this pasture this morning," Bird went on, suddenly enthused by his new proposition, "and how many casualties have they caused? Remarkably few, really." He waved with his unblooded sword at the grass where maybe three score of bodies lay where the Legion's charge had failed. "We should look at the tree trunks to see where the bullet scars are, and I'll wager you, Starbuck, that most will be at least eight or ten feet above the ground."

"I shouldn't be surprised, sir. I really shouldn't." Starbuck could see the fence rails ahead now. Just another few paces and they would be among the trees. Most of the Legion was already safe in the woodland, or as safe as any men could be who were crouching among trees that were being shelled by a dozen federal howitzers.

"There, look! You see? Twelve feet up, fifteen. There's another, ten feet high if it's an inch. See?" Major Bird had now stopped altogether and was pointing with his sword at the interesting phenomenon of how high the bullet marks on the trees were. "That one's a little lower, I admit, but look, see? There, on that hickory, Starbuck? Not one bullet strike below ten feet and how many can you see above that height? Four, five, six, and that's just one trunk!"

"Sir!" Starbuck shoved Bird onward.

"Steady!" Bird protested, but did start walking again so that, at last, Starbuck could take shelter under the trees. He saw that most of the men had retreated farther among the trunks, instinctively seeking safety, though a few, the brave few, lingered at the trees' edge to keep steadily firing on the advancing Yankees.

"Go back, lads!" Major Bird realized the southern stand was beaten. "God knows where," he muttered under his breath. "Sergeant Major Proctor?"

"Sir!"

"Make sure the colors are safe!" How ridiculous, Bird thought, that he should think of such things, for what were the colors but two gaudy flags, stitched together from scraps of silk in his sister's bedroom? The northern bullets were ripping and tearing through the leaves. "Starbuck?"

"Sir?"

"Would you mind warning Doc Billy? Tell him we're retreating. He must rescue what wounded he can, and leave the rest. I guess the Yankees will treat them right?"

"I'm sure they will, sir."

"Be off with you, then."

Starbuck ran back through the woods. A shell cracked off to his left and a heavy branch splintered and tore down through the surrounding trees. Groups of men were flitting back through the trees, not waiting for orders, but just making off toward safety. They were abandoning bowie knives, blankets, haversacks, almost anything that might delay their flight. Starbuck found a chaotic press of men about the picketed horses and a corporal trying to lead Pocahontas free of the panicked rabble. "That's mine!" Starbuck shouted, and snatched the reins.

For a second the corporal looked as though he would contest the issue, then he saw Starbuck's grim face and fled. Captain Hinton ran past, shouting for his horse, followed by Lieutenant Moxey, whose left hand was dripping blood. Starbuck hauled himself onto Pocahontas's back and turned her toward the clearing where he had last seen Doctor Danson. Another rush of men ran past, shouting unintelligibly. A crackle of rifle fire sounded from the edge of the trees. Starbuck kicked Pocahontas's flanks. Her ears were pricked back, showing she was nervous. Starbuck ducked under a branch, then almost lost his seat as the mare leaped a fallen trunk. He galloped into the road, planning to turn south toward the casualty station, but suddenly a bullet slashed past his head and he saw a puff of flame-streaked smoke and a blur of blue uniforms in the opposite woods. A man shouted at him to surrender.

Starbuck wrenched the reins, half-falling off the horse. The mare turned, protesting, and Starbuck kicked his heels back. "Come on!" he shouted at her, then cringed as another bullet whipcracked past his head. He still held his heavy pistol and he used its barrel to hit Pocahontas's flank and suddenly the horse jerked forward, almost throwing Starbuck off, but he somehow held on with his left hand as she bolted back into the woods. Starbuck turned her back toward the hillcrest. There seemed no sense in trying to organize an orderly withdrawal of the wounded; instead he needed to find Bird and tell him that the Legion had been deeply outflanked. "Major Bird!" he shouted. "Major Bird!"

Thaddeus Bird had found Sergeant Truslow and was now helping carry Adam back to safety. The three men were with the color party and were the very last of the Legion left in the upper wood. Sergeant Major Proctor was carrying one color, a corporal from Company C had the other, but the heavy flags on their unwieldy staffs were difficult objects to carry through the tangle of thorns and undergrowth. The rest of the Legion, indeed the rest of Nathan Evans's brigade, seemed to have fled, and Bird supposed that this battle was lost. He wondered how the historians would describe the southern revolt. A summer's madness? An aberration of American history to set alongside the Whiskey Rebellion that George Washington had put down so savagely? A shell cracked through the upper trees, showering the color party with leaves.

"Major Bird!" Starbuck shouted. He was galloping madly, blindly through the trees. Fugitives were shouting all around him, but Starbuck's world was a blur of sunlight and green shadow, of a panicked horse running, of sweat and thirst. He could hear a Yankee band off in the meadows and he turned the horse away from the sound. He shouted for Major Bird again, but the only reply was a spatter of shots somewhere to his left. Bullets whistled and slapped close to him, but the northerners were firing in close woodland and could not aim properly. A shell crashed smoke and sizzling fragments off to the right, then Starbuck was in a clearing and he saw the flash of red and white that was the Faulconer Legion colors at the far end of the open space and he turned his horse toward it. He thought he saw Thaddeus Bird with about a dozen other men. "Major Bird!"

But Bird had disappeared into the farther trees. Starbuck hurried after the color party, bursting through a skein of smoke that hung over the clearing. Shots sounded in the woods, a bugle called, and still the Yankee band was playing behind. Starbuck crashed into the trees at the far end of the clearing and ripped through a tangle of low branches that slashed painfully across his face. "Major Bird!"

Bird at last turned, and Starbuck saw Adam was there, dark blood on his thigh. Starbuck was about to shout that there were Yankees on the right flank, but he was too late. A squad of blue-coated men was already running through the trees, coming from the dirt road, and it seemed inevitable that the Legion's colors would fall and that Bird, Adam, Truslow and the other men around the two flags would be captured. "Look out!" Starbuck shouted, pointing.

The color party was running through the trees, desperate to get away, but Bird and Truslow were hampered by Adam. The northerners were shouting at them to stop and put their hands up, while Major Bird was shouting at Sergeant Major Proctor to run. Adam, his leg jolted as he was dragged through the trees, screamed.

Starbuck heard the scream and kicked back. The northerners were whooping and hollering like boys playing games. A rifle fired, the bullet slapping off into the leaves. Major Bird and Sergeant Truslow were staggering under Adam's weight. The northerners shouted again for their surrender and Truslow turned, ready to fight, then saw the bayonets coming straight for him.

And Starbuck struck. He had galloped the mare directly at the pursuing Yankees and now he screamed at them to back away, to leave Adam alone. The northerners swung their bayonet-weighted rifles toward him, but Starbuck was riding too fast. He was screaming at them, all self-control gone, his decision to fight at last made. The Yankees were not backing off but trying to aim their guns as Starbuck straightened his right arm and pulled the Savage's lower trigger, then the upper one, and the gun jarred hard back to his shoulder, smothering him with an instant of smoke that was there and gone. He whooped with joy as though, by firing the gun, he had released his soul to a dark desire. He heard a rifle fire, but no bullet struck him and he screamed defiance.

There were six Yankees in the squad. Five of the six scattered from Starbuck's crazy charge, but the last bravely tried to lunge with his bayonet at the maddened horseman. Starbuck pulled the revolver's lower trigger, revolving the cylinder, then thust the gun's barrel hard down at the man who was challenging him. He had a glimpse of bushy black side-whiskers and tobacco-blackened teeth, then he pulled the trigger and the man's face vanished in a spray of blood-streaked smoke, chips of bone and scarlet drops. Starbuck was keening a terrible sound, a scream of victory and a howl of fury as another Yankee was trampled down by Pocahontas's heavy hooves. A gun crashed terribly loud by his right ear and suddenly the mare was screaming and rearing, but Starbuck kept his balance and urged her on. He tried to fire at a blue-coated man, but the revolver jammed because he pulled both triggers simultaneously, but it did not matter. Major Bird, Adam and Truslow had escaped, the colors had gone safe into the green wood's shelter, and Starbuck was suddenly riding free and clear into a leaf-filled silence.

He was laughing. It seemed that he was filled with a most miraculous happiness, that he had experienced the second most exciting, wonderful moment of his life. He wanted to scream his joy at the heavens as he remembered the Yankee's face exploding away from the gun's muzzle. My God, but he had shown that bastard! He laughed aloud.

While in faraway Boston the dust motes danced and shifted in the shafts of sunlight that streamed down from the high church windows onto the Reverend Elial Starbuck who, his eyes closed and his strong face contorted with the agony of passion, beseeched Almighty God to protect and succor the righteous forces of the United States, to give them the spirit to endure all hardships and the strength to overcome the foul forces of unspeakable evil that had been spewed from the southern states. "And if the cause should come to battle, O Lord, then let thy will be done, and thy victory be gained, and let the blood of thine enemies soak the land and let their pride be trampled beneath the hoofbeats of the righteous!" His appeal was intense, his prayer echoing, his voice as hard as the New Hampshire granite from which the church was built. Elial let the echo of the prayer fade as he opened his eyes, but the congregation, somehow aware that their pastor's angry gray gaze was searching the pews for any evidence of faithlessness, kept their eyes tight shut and their fans quite still. Not one person moved, indeed they hardly dared breathe. Elial lowered his hands to grip the lectern. "In thy holy name we beseech it, Amen."

"Amen," the congregation echoed. Timid eyes opened, hymnals rustled, and Mrs. Sifflard pumped some humid air into the harmonium's bowels. "Hymn number two hundred and sixty-six." The Reverend Elial sounded like a man spent of sudden force, righteously weary. "'There is a fountain filled with blood, Drawn from Emmanuel's veins; And sinners, plunged beneath that flood, Lose all their guilty stains.'"

A loose horse galloped out of the brush and through a row of wounded southern soldiers who had been left to the mercy of the advancing Yankees. One man screamed and convulsed as a hoof struck his thigh. Another man was weeping, calling for his mother. A third man had lost his eyes to a shell's splinters and could not weep. Two of the injured men were already dead, their beards jutting skyward and their skins crawling with flies. The woods slowly filled with northern troops who stopped to rifle the pockets and pouches of the dead. The shellfire had finally stopped, though the fierce fires started by the explosions still burned and crackled in the undergrowth.

To the east of the woods the gray-clad 2nd Wisconsin Regiment, advancing on the Georgia regiment that now formed the right flank of the broken Confederate defense line, was mistaken for southern reinforcements. The northern flag, hanging limp in the windless air, looked very like the Confederate banner, and the Georgians allowed the Wisconsin men to come so close that every southern officer was killed or wounded by the Yankees' opening volley. The surviving Georgians stood for a desperate moment, then broke and fled, and so the last of the makeshift line that Nathan Evans had scraped together was finally vanquished. Yet the line had done its work. It had held an overwhelming attack long enough for a new defense line to be cobbled together on the flat wide summit of the hill where the Faulconer Legion had begun their day.

A battery of Virginian guns commanded by a lawyer turned gunner waited at the plateau's northern crest. The guns looked out across the valley where the men of Evans's shattered brigade now streamed back from the victorious Yankees. Behind the lawyer's guns was a Virginian brigade that had come from the Shenandoah Valley and was led by a godly man of eccentric views and grim demeanor. Thomas Jackson had been an unpopular lecturer at Virginia's Military Institute and afterward an unpopular commander of a militia brigade that he had trained and drilled, drilled and trained until the farmboys in his ranks were sick to the belly of his training and drilling, but now Thomas Jackson's farmboys were on a wide plateau waiting for a victorious Yankee army to attack them, and they were drilled, trained and ready to fight. They were eager for it too.

A second Confederate artillery battery came to the hilltop and deployed its weapons close to where the Faulconer Legion's baggage was piled. The battery commander was an Episcopal minister who ordered his second in command to check and recheck the battery's wormscrews, sponge covers, scrapers, handspikes, and rammers, while he himself prayed aloud that God would have mercy on the Yankees' guilty souls that he intended to send to a better world with his four big guns that he had named for the four evangelists. Thomas Jackson, expecting an enemy cannonade at any moment, ordered his men to lie flat so as not to make themselves a target for the enemy gunners, then he calmly sat in his saddle reading his Bible. He worried that his men might get confused in the smoke of battle, and so all his Virginians had strips of white cloth tied to their arms or tucked into their hatbands, and were under orders to shout a watchword as they fought. "Our Homes!" was their cry, and Jackson expected them to strike their breasts with their left hands as they shouted it. Captain Imboden, the lawyer turned gunner, had long decided that Jackson was mad as a March hare, but he was somehow glad that he was on Jackson's side and not having to face the madman in battle.

A mile to Imboden's right, at the stone bridge where more and more northern troops crossed the Bull Run to continue the crushing attack that had at last begun to roll the rebel army into chaos, General Irvin McDowell sat on his horse

386

beside the turnpike and cheered on his men. "Victory, boys!" he called again and again. "Victory! On to Richmond! Well done, boys, well done!" McDowell was jubilant, ecstatic, so happy that he could forget the dyspepsia that had plagued him ever since his injudiciously large helpings of beef pie at supper the previous night. What did indigestion matter? He had won! He had led the largest army in the history of American warfare to a brilliant victory, and just as soon as the chore of cleaning up the rebel army was completed he would send a sheaf of captured colors back to Washington to be laid as trophies at the president's feet. Not that he had seen any captured colors yet, but he was certain they would soon come in abundance. "Starbuck!" He spotted his *sous*-adjutant surrounded by foreign attachés in their gaudy uniforms. McDowell had gone to college in France and was used to European military fashions, but now, seeing the bright uniforms amid the plain honest coats of his own army, he thought how ridiculously ornate the foreigners appeared. "Captain Starbuck!" he called again.

"Sir?" Captain James Starbuck had been happily beating time to the music of a regimental band that was playing opera selections to the advancing troops. Now he urged his horse closer to the victorious general.

"Scout across the bridge, will you?" McDowell requested genially. "And tell our fellows to send all captured colors back to me. Be sure of that, will you? All of them! And don't worry about your foreign fellows. I'll have a chat with them." The general waved to a passing artillery troop. "Victory, boys, victory! On to Richmond! On to Richmond!" A fat and drunken congressman from New York was riding a limber westward, and the general good-naturedly saluted the politician. The congressman was a rascal, but his good opinion could be useful to a victorious general's career when this short fighting season was done. "A great day, Congressman! A great day!"

"Another Yorktown, General! A veritable Waterloo!" A

387

victorious general could also be of use to a congressman's career, and so the fat politician waved his beaver hat in affable salute to the portly McDowell. "On to glory!" the congressman shouted, and waved his hat so vigorously that he almost lost his balance on the narrow limber seat.

"And Starbuck!" McDowell called after his aide who was already forcing his passage across the crowded bridge. "Don't let too many civilians clutter up the rear. That fellow won't hurt, but we don't want any ladies injured by stray shots, do we?"

"No, sir!" James Starbuck went to hunt for flags.

Colonel Washington Faulconer was also seeking colors, his own, and he found them in the pastureland north of the turn-pike. At first all he could find were the shattered remnants of his precious Legion; a succession of powder-stained, weary men who straggled from the trees, dragging their rifles and scarcely able to recognize their own Colonel. A few men were still in good order, held so by officers or sergeants, but the majority had abandoned their expensive equipment and had lost any idea of where their companies, their officers or even their friends were. Some had retreated with the South Carolinians, some with the Louisianans, just as some men from those regiments now walked back with the Virginians. They were a beaten force, exhausted and stunned, and the Colonel watched them in appalled disbelief. Ethan Ridley, who had at last caught up with Faulconer, dared not even speak for fear of triggering the Colonel's rage.

"This was Starbuck's doing," Washington Faulconer finally said, and Ridley just nodded in mute confirmation. "Have you seen Adam?" the Colonel called to the Legion's survivors, but they just shook their heads. Some glanced up at the beautifully uniformed Colonel who sat his horse so elegantly then turned away to spit dry-mouthed at the meadow.

"Sir?" Ridley had glanced to his right and seen blue Yankee uniforms advancing from the wooden bridge that carried the turnpike across the small tributary of the Bull Run. "Sir!" he repeated more urgently.

But the Colonel was not listening because Faulconer had at last seen his color party emerge from the woods, and he galloped forward to meet them. He was determined that whatever else happened on this awful day, he would not lose the two flags. Even if the Confederacy went down in blazing defeat he would carry those twin colors back to Seven Springs and there hang the flags in his hallway to remind his descendants that their family had fought for Virginia. Ridley followed the Colonel, made silent by the enormity of the defeat.

At first the Colonel did not see Adam, who was now being helped by Sergeant Truslow and Sergeant Major Proctor. The Colonel only saw Thaddeus Bird, who was dragging the Faulconer coat-of-arms in the dirt. "What the hell did you do with my Legion!" Faulconer shouted at his brother-in-law. "What the hell have you done?"

Thaddeus Bird stopped and stared up at the angry Colonel. It seemed to take him a few seconds to recognize Washington Faulconer, but when he did, he just laughed.

"Damn it, Pecker! Damn it!" Faulconer very nearly slashed his riding crop across the schoolmaster's laughing face.

"Adam's wounded." Bird had abruptly ceased laughing and now spoke with an earnest intensity. "But he'll be all right. He fought well. They all fought well, or almost all. We have to teach them to aim low, though, and there are a host of other lessons we have to learn. But we didn't do badly for a first fight."

"Badly! You threw the Legion away! Goddamn you! You threw it away!" The Colonel spurred Saratoga on to where Truslow and Proctor were helping Adam. "Adam!" the Colonel shouted, and was astonished to see his son smiling almost happily.

"Be careful of the woods, Faulconer!" Sergeant Truslow growled. "They're full of goddamned Yankees."

389

The Colonel had intended to snap at Adam, to reprimand him for letting Bird disobey orders, but his son's bloody leg checked his anger. Then he looked up to see a last figure in gray uniform stagger out of the trees. It was Starbuck, and the sight of him made Washington Faulconer's anger surge up so intensely that he shuddered uncontrollably. "I'll come back for you, Adam," he said, then spurred Saratoga on toward Starbuck.

Starbuck was on foot, limping. After Pocahontas had screamed he had pulled her head to the left, raked her sore flanks with his heels and then galloped clear of the stunned and scattered Yankees. He had tried to follow the fleeing color party, but instead he had felt the mare stumble and he saw droplets of blood spraying from her mouth and nostrils. Her stride had faltered, she had blown a great bubbling breath, then half-collapsed onto her knees. Still she had tried to keep going, but the life was roaring out of her punctured lung and so she had fallen to her side, sliding through the leaf mold and thorns, and Starbuck had just managed to kick his feet free of the stirrups and hurl himself out of the saddle before the dying mare crashed into a tree and stopped. She shivered, tried to raise her head, whinnied once, then her hooves beat a dying tattoo on the ground.

"Oh, God." Starbuck was shaking. He was crouching, bruised and frightened, his breath coming in huge gasps. The horse shuddered and a great wash of blood split from her mouth. The bullet wound in her chest seemed very small. Flies buzzed loud, already settling on the dead horse.

The woodland seemed oddly silent. Flames or musketry crackled far away, but Starbuck could hear no footsteps close by. He clambered to his feet and hissed with pain when he put his weight onto his left ankle. His revolver had fallen into the litter of bloody leaves. He picked it up, shoved it into his holster and had been about to start limping away when he remembered how only that morning Colonel Faulconer had stressed

390

how expensive the saddle was, and Starbuck was assailed by the ridiculous conviction that he would be in bad trouble if he did not rescue the saddle and so he had knelt at the belly of the dead horse and scrabbled to unbuckle the girth. Then, half-sobbing and half-panting, he had heaved the heavy saddle free and pulled the stirrups and girth out from under the deadweight of the mare's carcass.

He staggered through the woods, clumsy on his turned ankle and blundering under the weight of the saddle and the heat of the day. He had needed both hands to carry the saddle, so could not keep his sword from tangling in his legs. After the saber had tripped him a third time he stopped, unbuckled the scabbard slings and threw the wretched blade far off into the undergrowth. One small part of his conscious thoughts told him it was stupid to rescue the saddle and throw away the saber, but somehow the saddle seemed more important now. Voices shouted in the far woods, a bugle sounded, a man whooped in triumph and, fearing that he would be ambushed, Starbuck pulled out the revolver, worked the lower lever trigger, then held it in his right hand beneath the heavy saddle. He staggered on, at last emerging from the woodland into a wide pasture scattered with retreating rebels. Ahead of the southerners was the turnpike, then a steep hill climbing to the plateau where the Legion had started its day. He could see the small wooden house on the hilltop and, next to it, some cannon. He wondered if the guns belonged to the North or the South, to the enemy or to friends.

"You bastard!" The shout echoed across the pastureland and Starbuck turned his sweat-stung eyes to see Colonel Faulconer spurring toward him. The Colonel slewed to a stop beside Starbuck, his stallion's hooves slinging up clods of turf. "What in the name of Christ did you do to my Legion? I told you to go home! I told you to go back to your damned father!" And Colonel Faulconer, who was too angry to think what he was doing, or whether a mere second lieutenant could possibly have exercised the power he was now ascribing to Starbuck, brought back his whip hand and slashed it forward so that the riding crop slashed across Starbuck's face. Starbuck flinched, gasped at the pain, then fell as he twisted away. Blood ran salt from his nose.

"I brought your saddle," he was trying to say, but instead he was on all fours, blood dripping from his nose, and the Colonel raised his whip again. "You did your filthy northern work, didn't you? You broke my Legion, you bastard!" He slashed down a second time, then a third. "You bastard!" He screamed, then raised his hand to strike a fourth blow.

The first of the pursuing Yankees had appeared at the edge of the wood. One of them, a corporal, had been with the group of men charged by Starbuck and now, coming into the pastureland, he saw a mounted Confederate not fifty yards away and he thought of his dead comrade as he dropped to his right knee and brought his rifle into his shoulder and snapped off one fast shot. The smoke billowed to hide the Yankee's view, but his aim had been good and the bullet struck the Colonel on his raised right arm, splintering the bone and ricocheting down to score across his ribs and lodge in his belly muscles. Blood poured from his arm that had been thrown back by the bullet's force and his riding crop wheeled through the air. "Oh, God," Washington Faulconer said, astonished rather than hurt. Then the pain stabbed at him and he cried aloud as he tried to force the arm down and to comprehend the sudden mess of torn and blood-soaked cloth and sharp pain.

"Colonel!" Ethan Ridley galloped to the Colonel's side just as a volley of northern shots crackled at the wood's margin. Ridley ducked and hauled on his reins as the minié bullets screamed about his ears. The Colonel was turning away, spurs slashing back, screaming with pain while Ridley was staring down at Starbuck who had brought his right hand out to protect himself from the Colonel's beating. The Savage revolver was in Starbuck's hand and Ridley, seeing it, thought the

392

northerner had tried to kill the Colonel. "You shot him!" Ridley screamed in shocked accusation, then pulled his own revolver free of its holster.

Blood dripped from Starbuck's nose. He was still shocked, still too dazed to understand what was happening, but he saw Ridley's face grimace and saw the revolver spurt smoke, and then the saddle which was still supported by Starbuck's left hand kicked as Ridley's bullet thumped into the wooden tree beneath the leather.

The kick of the bullet hitting the saddle woke Starbuck from his daze. Behind him the northerners were swarming from the trees and Ridley was already turning away, not out of fear of Starbuck but to escape the onrush of Yankees. "Ridley!" Starbuck shouted, but Ridley kicked back with his bloodied spurs as Starbuck raised the heavy gun. He had a promise to keep and just seconds to keep it and so he aimed the big Savage revolver and pulled the upper trigger. Sparks ripped away from the exploding percussion cap as the gun hammered back in Starbuck's hand.

Ridley screamed and arched his back. "Ridley!" Starbuck shouted again, and the air about him whistled with a volley of northern bullets and Ridley's mare reared up, screaming. Ridley was wounded, but he automatically kicked his boots free of the stirrups as he twisted to stare at Starbuck. "This is for Sally, you bastard!" Starbuck shouted hysterically, all sense gone. "For Sally!" He had promised that her name would be the last thing Ridley heard and he shouted it again as he worked the Savage's lower trigger, then pulled the top one again.

Ridley twitched as the second bullet struck and as he fell to earth. He and his horse were both screaming now, but the horse was trying to limp away while Ridley thumped onto the grass.

"You bastard, Ridley!" Starbuck was on his feet, pointing the revolver. He fired again, but his third bullet just drove scraps

393

of soil up from the ground beside the fallen Ridley whose wounded horse was limping away. The Colonel was fifty yards off, but had turned to stare in horror at Starbuck. "This is for Sally," Starbuck said and fired his last bullet into his enemy's body, and suddenly the whole ground in front of Starbuck erupted in dirt and flying blood as a Confederate shell crashed into Ridley's dying body, eviscerating the twitching flesh and throwing up a screen of bloody scraps to hide Starbuck from the retreating Legion.

The warm and bloody blast of the shell threw Starbuck back and soaked his gray tunic with Ridley's blood. More shells screamed across the valley to crack black and red on the meadow where the advancing northerners had appeared from beneath the trees. The crest of the far hill grew a low cloud that pulsed as more smoke poured from the artillery. Starbuck had fallen to his knees again, while Ridley was nothing but a butcher's mess on the grass. Ahead of Starbuck the beaten Confederates were retreating across the turnpike and climbing the farther hill with its crown of gray-white, flame-streaked smoke, but Starbuck stayed in the meadow, staring at the mess of flesh and blood, of white ribs and blue guts, and he knew he had committed murder. Oh dear sweet forgiving Christ, he tried to pray, shivering in the heat, but suddenly a rush of northerners swept past him and one man kicked the revolver out of Starbuck's nerveless fingers and then a brass-bound rifle butt smacked the back of his head and he pitched forward as a northern voice snarled that he should lie still.

He lay facedown in the sweet-smelling grass and remembered Ridley's final despairing backward glance, the whites of his eyes showing, the terror on his dying face the gift of a girl he had betrayed in Richmond. It had taken a second, one short second, to commit murder. Oh God, Starbuck thought, but he could not pray because he felt no remorse. He felt no sense of sin. He just wanted to laugh for Sally's sake, for he had kept her faith and killed her enemy. He had done a friend's duty, and that thought made him start to laugh.

"Over!" A man stirred Starbuck with his bayonet. "Turn over, you crazy bastard!"

Starbuck rolled over. Two bearded men went through his pouches and pockets, but found nothing worth stealing except his cartridge box with its handful of Savage revolver cartridges. "Thinner pickings than a starved dog," one of the two men said, then grimaced at the awful gory mess that had been Ethan Ridley. "You want to search that pile of blood, Jack?"

"Shit, no. On your feet." He prodded Starbuck with the bayonet. "Over there, rebel."

A score of prisoners was assembled at the edge of the trees. Half were from the Legion, the rest were either South Carolinians or Louisianan Zouaves. The Confederate prisoners sat disconsolate, watching as the northern regiments massed on the lower slopes of the opposite hill. More and more northern regiments were appearing from the Bull Run and marching to reinforce the gathering attack. More and more guns wheeled off the turnpike and were aimed toward the Confederate defenders. "What's to happen to us?" one of the Legion prisoners asked Starbuck.

"I don't know."

"You'll be all right," the man spoke resentfully. "You're an officer, they'll exchange you, but not us. They'll keep us right through harvest time."

A Yankee sergeant heard the exchange. "You shouldn't have rebelled then, should you?"

An hour after midday the prisoners were marched down to the red fieldstone house that stood by the crossroads. The northern soldiers were still readying themselves for the attack that would break the last vestiges of southern resistance and, while they gathered themselves, the artillery of each side screamed their shells overhead, battery firing at battery from opposing hilltops and causing a constant trickle of wounded

395

men who limped, staggered or were carried to an aid post that had been established inside the stone house.

Starbuck, limping from his twisted ankle and with his uniform soaked from Ridley's blood, was pushed toward the kitchen door of the house. "I'm not wounded," he protested.

"Shut your mouth, get inside, do what you're told," the sergeant snapped, then ordered the unwounded prisoners to look after the dozen wounded men who had been brought into the open air to recover from their surgery. Inside the house Starbuck found still more men from the Faulconer Legion; one from K Company had lost a leg from a shell burst, two had lungs punctured by bullets, one had been blinded and another had a minié bullet lodged in his lower jaw that now dribbled a mixture of blood and spittle.

A red-bearded doctor was working at a table that had been shoved into the sunlight coming through the kitchen window. He was amputating a man's leg, and his bone saw made a grating noise that set Starbuck's teeth on edge. The patient, a northerner, groaned horribly and the doctor's assistant dripped more chloroform onto the pad he was holding against the man's nose and mouth. Both the doctor and his assistant were dripping with sweat. The room was foully hot, not just with the day's natural warmth, but also because a fierce fire in the kitchen range was being used to boil water.

The doctor discarded the saw and picked up a long-bladed scalpel with which he finished the amputation. The bloody leg, still clad in a boot and sock, thumped to the floor. "A change from treating the pox," the doctor said happily, wiping his forehead with his sleeve. "That's all we've done for the last three months, treat the pox! You southerners needn't have bothered raising an army, you could have just sent all your whores north, then you could have poxed us all to death and saved us a heap of trouble. He's still with us, is he?" This last question was to the assistant.

"Yes, sir."

"Give him a whiff of ammonia, let him know he ain't knocking at the pearly gates yet." The red-bearded surgeon was probing with forceps for the arteries that needed tying off. He had filed the bone stump smooth and now, with the arteries tied, he let the flesh compress over the bone's cut end before drawing the flap of skin round the patient's thigh. He put quick stitches in the newly formed stump, then untied the tourniquet that had constricted the thigh's blood supply during the operation. "Another hero," he said dryly to mark the procedure's end.

"He won't come round, sir." The assistant was holding an open bottle of ammonia spirits next to the patient's nose.

"Give me the chloroform," the doctor ordered, then took a scalpel to the patient's torn trousers and cut back the tattered, bloody cloth to reveal the man's genitals. "Behold a miracle," the doctor announced and poured a trickle of chloroform onto the unconscious man's testicles. The man seemed to go into instant spasm, but then opened his eyes, bellowed with pain and tried to sit up. "Frozen balls," the doctor said happily, "known in the profession as the Lazarus effect." He stoppered the chloroform bottle and stepped away from the table, looking to his unwilling audience for appreciation of his wit. He spotted Starbuck, sheeted with blood from head to foot. "Christ, but why aren't you dead?"

"Because I'm not even wounded. It's someone else's blood."

"If you're not wounded, then get the hell out of here. Go and watch your damned dreams being broken."

Starbuck went into the yard where he leaned against the house wall. The sun shone cruelly bright on a desolate scene of rebel defeat. To the north, where Evans had led his forlorn companies to stem the triumphant Yankee advance, the meadows were empty, all but for a littering of dead men and broken horses.

The battle had swept across those fields and, like a vast wave pushed by a storm surge, now climbed the hill toward the

Henry House, where the attacking line seethed against the second Confederate defense. Nathan Evans had constructed the first barrier out of a flimsy line of men that had stalled the federal attack long enough for Thomas Jackson to make this second line, which the Yankees now set about dismantling. Newly arrived northern cannon were being dragged to the hill's crest while long blue columns of fresh infantry climbed past the guns to reinforce their comrades who were already assaulting the hill's top. The rebel guns that had originally lined the crest had been pushed back by the Yankees' advance. Starbuck, slumped disconsolate beside the kitchen step of the stone house, saw an occasional Confederate round overshoot the plateau and draw a trail of smoke across the sky. Such wasted rounds were evidence that the rebel army still fought, but the turnpike was now so crowded with northern guns and infantry that Starbuck did not see how the fight could ever be sustained.

"What the hell are you doing here?" the officious sergeant demanded of Starbuck.

"The doctor sent me out here."

"You shouldn't be here. You should be over there, with the other prisoners." The sergeant gestured toward the farthest corner of the yard where a small group of unwounded rebels sat under guard.

"The doctor said I should wash this blood off," Starbuck lied. He had just noticed a well beside the road and he hoped the lie would serve to get him a drink of water.

The sergeant hesitated, then nodded. "Hurry, then."

Starbuck crossed to the well and drew up its wooden bucket. He had meant to wash his face clean before drinking, but he was too thirsty to wait and, gripping the pail with both hands, he greedily tipped the water to his face and gulped down great cool mouthfuls. The liquid poured down his face and his bloodied tunic and trousers, and still he drank, slaking a dry thirst stoked by the hours of powder smoke and heat.

He rested the bucket on the well's edge, panting, and saw a

blue-eyed, pretty face watching him. He gaped back. A woman. He must be dreaming. A woman! And a pretty woman, an angel, a vision, a clean, crisp, pretty woman in a lacy white dress and a pink-trimmed bonnet shaded by a white fringed parasol, and Starbuck just stared, wondering if he was going mad, when suddenly the woman, who was sitting in a carriage in the road just beyond the yard's fence, burst out laughing.

"Leave the lady alone!" the sergeant barked. "Back here, rebel!"

"Let him stay!" the woman demanded imperiously. She was sitting with a much older man in an open carriage drawn by two horses. A Negro driver sat on the carriage's box, while a federal lieutenant was attempting to turn the carriage back. They had come too far, the young officer explained to the woman's companion, there was danger here, they should not have crossed the bridge.

"Do you know who I am?" The man was a middle-aged dandy in a colored vest, tall black hat and white silk tie. He carried a gold-topped cane and had a small gray beard elegantly cut to a jutting point.

"Sir, I don't need to know who you are," the northern officer said, "you should not have crossed the bridge, and I must insist—"

"Insist! Lieutenant! Insist! I am Congressman Benjamin Matteson, of the great State of New Jersey, and you do not insist with me."

"But it's dangerous here, sir," the lieutenant protested weakly.

"A congressman can go wherever he finds the Republic endangered," Congressman Matteson answered with lordly scorn, while the truth was that he, like so many others from Washington's society, had merely followed the army so that he could claim a share of the victory's credit and collect some trifling keepsakes like spent rifle bullets or a rebel's bloodstained cap.

"But the woman, sir?" The lieutenant tried again.

"The woman, Lieutenant, is my wife, and a congressman's wife can share any danger." The woman laughed at her husband's absurd compliment, and Starbuck, still dazzled by her, wondered why so young a beauty would marry so pompous a man.

Mrs. Matteson's eyes, blue as the flag's field of stars, were full of mischief. "Are you truly a rebel?" she asked Starbuck. She had bleached gold hair, very white skin and her lace-trimmed dress was smudged with red dust from the summer road.

"Yes, ma'am." Starbuck stared at her as a man dying of thirst might look on a cool, shadowed, clear pool of water. She was so unlike the earnest, plain-spoken, obedient girls who worshiped at his father's church. Instead, this congressman's wife was what the Reverend Elial Starbuck would have called a painted lady, a Jezebel. She was, Starbuck realized, the very image and model of all Sally Truslow wanted to be, and all he himself wanted a woman to be, for his father's biblical austerity had put a taste for just such forbidden fruit into Nathaniel Starbuck. "Yes, ma'am," he said again, "I'm a rebel." He tried to sound defiant.

"Secretly," the woman confided to Starbuck in a voice that carried clean above the cacophony of shells and musketry to reach every prisoner in the yard, "I'm a Lincoln killer too."

Her husband laughed too loudly. "Don't be absurd, Lucy! You're from Pennsylvania!" He gave his wife a reprimanding tap on her knee with his gloved hand. "From the great State of Pennsylvania."

Lucy pushed his hand away. "Don't be obnoxious, Ben. I'm a Lincoln killer through and through." She looked at her driver's stolid back. "Aren't I a rebel, Joseph?"

"You are, missus, you are!" The driver laughed.

"And when we win I shall enslave you, Joseph, won't I?"

"You will, missus, you will!" He laughed again.

Lucy Matteson looked back to Starbuck. "Are you hurt bad?"

"No, ma'am."

"What happened?"

"My horse was shot, ma'am. It fell. I was captured."

"Did you," she said, beginning a question, colored slightly, then a half smile flickered on her face. "Did you kill anyone?"

Starbuck had a sudden memory of Ridley falling backward off his horse. "I don't know, ma'am."

"I feel like killing someone. We slept in the most uncomfortable farm kitchen at Centreville last night, and the Lord only knows where we'll rest tonight. If we rest at all, which I doubt. The rigors of war." She laughed, showing small very white teeth. "Is there a hotel at Manassas Junction?"

"I don't know of one, ma'am," Starbuck said.

"You don't sound like a southerner," the congressman interrupted with a sour note in his voice.

Starbuck, unwilling to explain, merely shrugged.

"You are mysterious!" Lucy Matteson clapped her gloved hands, then held out a cardboard box filled with scraps of tissue paper. "Have one," she said.

Starbuck saw there were pieces of crystallized fruit nestling in the tissues. "Are you sure, ma'am?"

"Go on! Help yourself." She smiled as Starbuck took a piece of the fruit. "Will they send you back to Washington, do you think?"

"I don't know what they plan for the prisoners, ma'am."

"I'm sure they will. They're going to have a mighty victory parade, all honking bands and congratulations, and the prisoners will be marched at gunpoint before being slaughtered in the grounds of the White House."

"Don't be absurd, Lucy. I do beg of you not to be absurd." The Honorable Benjamin Matteson frowned.

"So maybe they'll parole you instead," Lucy Matteson smiled at Starbuck, "and then you'll come to supper. No,

Benjamin, don't argue, I'm quite decided. Give me a *carte de visite*, quick!" She held out her hand until her husband, with obvious reluctance, surrendered a pasteboard card which, with a smile, she passed down to Starbuck. "We rebels shall exchange war stories while these cold northerners frown at us. And if you need anything in prison, you are to ask me. I wish I had something more than scraps of fruit to give you now, but the congressman ate all our cold chicken because he said it would go bad once the pounded ice melted." There was a pure venom in her words that made Starbuck laugh.

The lieutenant who had originally tried to turn the congressman's carriage around now reappeared with a major whose authority was considerably greater. The major would not have cared if half the U.S. Congress had been in the carriage, it still had no business blocking the turnpike in the middle of a battle and so he touched his hat to Lucy Matteson and then insisted that the driver turn the carriage round and take it back across the Bull Run.

"Do you know who I am?" Congressman Matteson demanded, then half ducked as a rebel shell exploded a hundred yards away and a piece of shrapnel rustled overhead and cracked harmlessly against the stone house.

"I don't care if you're the emperor of France. Get the hell out of here! Now! Move!"

Lucy Matteson smiled at Starbuck as the carriage jerked forward. "Come and see us in Washington!"

Starbuck laughed and stepped back. Above him the hill smoked like a volcano and the shells cracked and the rifle fire splintered and the wounded limped back to the crossroads where the prisoners waited for jail and the Yankees waited for victory and the dead waited for burial. Starbuck, ignored now by the sergeant who no longer seemed to care whether he joined the other prisoners or not, sat with his back against the sun-warmed stone of the house and closed his eyes and wondered what his future held. He supposed the whole southern rebellion was being beaten to death in these hot fields, and he thought how much he would regret the premature ending of this war. He had seen the elephant, and he wanted to see more of it. It was not the horror that attracted him; not the memory of the severed leg spinning across the road, nor the man's face disappearing in powder smoke and gore, but rather the rearrangement of all creation that appealed to Starbuck's soul. War, Starbuck had learned this day, took everything that was, shook it, and let the pieces fall where they might. War was a gigantic game of chance, a huge gamble, a denial of all predestination and prudence. War would have saved Starbuck from the fate of family respectability, while peace was duty. War had relieved him of obligation, but peace offered dullness, and Nathaniel Starbuck was young enough and self-confident enough to hate dullness above all other things in the world.

But now he was a prisoner and the battle hammered on while, warmed by the sun and wearied by the day, Starbuck slept.

14

The remnants of the Faulconer Legion had stumbled uphill to where, in a tangle of small woods and fields behind Jackson's Virginia Brigade, the survivors of Nathan Evans's force recovered. The men were exhausted. At Evans's insistence they made a crude line that faced toward the Bull Run, but they were on the flank of the reconstituted southern defense and far enough from the turnpike to be spared the renewed federal attacks. The men sat on the grass, dull-eyed and thirsty, wondering if there would be any food or water.

Doctor Danson extracted the bullet from Adam Faulconer's leg, working fast and without chloroform, "You're lucky, Adam. No major blood vessels hit. You may even have a slight limp to attract the ladies, but that's all. You'll be dancing with the ladies in ten days." He poured lunar caustic into the wound, bandaged it, and moved on to the Colonel. He worked just as swiftly to extract the bullet from Washington Faulconer's belly muscles, sewed up the mangled flesh of his arm, then splinted the broken bone. "You're not quite as lucky as your son, Washington"—the doctor could still not get used to treating his neighbor as a superior officer—"but in another six weeks you'll be back to rights."

"Six weeks?" Colonel Faulconer was still furious that his precious Legion had been decimated under Thaddeus Bird's command and at Nathaniel Starbuck's bidding. He wanted his revenge, not on Bird, whom he had always known was a fool, but on Starbuck, who had become the Colonel's personification for the Legion's failure. Instead of marching to glorious victory under Washington Faulconer's personal command the regiment

404

had been thrown away in some miserable skirmish at the wrong end of the battlefield. The Legion had lost all its baggage and at least seventy men. No one knew the full total, though the Colonel had established that Starbuck was himself among the missing.

Doctor Danson had heard that Starbuck had been captured by the pursuing Yankees, or maybe worse. "A boy in B Company thought Starbuck might have been shot," he told the Colonel as he bandaged the splinted arm.

"Good," the Colonel said with a savagery that might have been excusable in a man suffering from the pain of a newly broken arm.

"Father!" Adam nevertheless protested.

"If the damned Yankees don't shoot him, we shall. He killed Ridley! I saw it."

"Father, please." Adam pleaded.

"For God's sake, Adam, must you always take Starbuck's side against me? Does family loyalty count for nothing with you?" The Colonel shouted the hurt words at his son who, appalled by the accusation, said nothing. Faulconer flinched away from the splints that Danson was trying to put on his upper arm. "I tell you, Adam," Faulconer went on, "that your damned friend is nothing but a murderer. Christ, but I should have known he was rotten when he first told us that tale of thieving and whores, but I trusted him for your sake. I wanted to help him for your sake, and now Ethan's dead because of it and, I promise you, I'll snap Starbuck's neck myself if he has the gall to come back here."

"Not with that arm, you won't," Doctor Danson said dryly.

"Damn the arm, Billy! I can't leave the Legion for six weeks!"

"You need rest," the doctor said calmly, "you need healing. If you exert yourself, Washington, you'll invite the gangrene. Three weeks of exertion and you'll be dead. Let's fashion a sling for that arm."

A thunderous crash of musketry announced that Jackson's Virginians were greeting the enemy. The battle was now being fought on the plateau about the Henry House, a flat hilltop edged with flame and thunder. The waiting Confederate guns tore great gaps in the advancing federal lines, but the northern infantry outflanked the batteries and forced them back, and northern guns unlimbered to take the rebel cannon in the flank. To Captain Imboden, the lawyer turned gunner, the ground around his outnumbered cannon looked as though it was being truffled by a horde of hungry hogs. The northern shells burrowed deep before exploding, but some were finding more solid targets. One of Imboden's limbers exploded from a direct hit and one of his gunners screamed in brief, foul gasps as his guts were sliced open by a jagged-edged scrap of shell casing. More gunners dropped to the marksmanship of northern sharpshooters. Imboden was serving one of his guns, ramming a canister down on top of a roundshot, then stepping back as the lanyard was pulled and the lethal missiles flensed through a northern regiment of infantry that was advancing through the smoke and stench.

The flags were bright squares of color in the gray. Stars and Stripes came forward while the three stripes of the Confederacy edged backward, but then stopped where Thomas Jackson, his well-thumbed Bible safe in his saddlebag, had decreed they would stop. Jackson's men stood hard in the smoke and discovered that the hated hours of drill were transmuted by battle into the unconscious motions of efficiency, and that somehow, despite the flail of northern canister and musketry, and despite the terror of men surrounded by the screaming of the wounded, the sobbing of the dying, the horrors of shattered flesh and of disemboweled friends, their hands still kept ramming bullets and charges, kept feeding percussion caps onto cones, kept aiming, kept firing. Still kept fighting. They were terrified, but they had been trained, and the man who had trained them glowered at them, and so they stayed like a stone wall built across a hilltop.

And the northern attack broke on the wall.

Jackson's Virginians should have been beaten. They should have been swept away like a sand ridge struck by a sea, except they did not know the battle had been lost and so they fought on, even edged forward, and the northerners wondered how you were supposed to beat these bastards, and the fear lodged in the northern hearts and the southerners edged another pace forward over dry grass scorched by burning cartridge wadding. The federals looked behind for reinforcements.

Those northern reinforcements came, but the southerners were being reinforced too as Beauregard at last realized that his whole plan of battle had been wrong. It had been about as wrong as any plan could be wrong, but now he was making amends by plucking men from his unbloodied right and hurrying them toward the plateau about the Henry House. Irvin McDowell, irritated that such a stubborn defense was delaying the sweet moment of victory, was busy ordering more men up the slope and into the sights of Captain Imboden's cannon and into the ghastly carnage of Matthew, Mark, Luke and John's canister, and into range of General Thomas Jackson's rifle-muskets.

And thus the day's real dying had begun.

It began because a battle of motion, of outflanking, advance and retreat, had become a standoff fight. The hilltop was bare of trees, devoid of ditch or wall, just an open space for death, and death grasped at it greedily. Men loaded and fired, fell and bled, cursed and died, and still more men filed onto the plateau to extend death's grip. Twin lines of infantry were stalled just a hundred paces apart and there tried to blast the guts out of each other. Men from New York and New Hampshire, Maine and Vermont, Connecticut and Massachusetts shot at men from Mississippi and Virginia, Georgia and the Carolinas, Maryland and Tennessee. The wounded crawled back to collapse in the grass, the dead were hurled aside, the files closed on the center,

407

the regiments shrank, yet still the firing went on beneath the bright flags. The northerners, firing again and again at the Confederate lines, knew that they only needed to break this small army, capture Richmond, and the whole conceit of a Southern Confederacy would collapse like a rotten pumpkin, while the southerners, returning bullet for bullet, knew that the North, once bloodied, would think twice before they dared invade the sovereign and sacred soil of the South again.

And so, for their twin causes, men fought beneath the colors, though, in the windless heat, the real trophies of the day were the opposing guns, for the side that could silence their enemy's guns was the side likeliest to win the struggle. None of the guns was emplaced behind earthworks, for none of the generals had planned to fight on this bare plateau, and so the gunners were vulnerable to infantry fire because there was not room on the hilltop for men to stand off at a distance. This was a belly-to-belly brawl, a murderous gutter fight.

Men charged at open guns, and the guns, crammed with lethal canister, left swaths of attackers dead in front of their muzzles, yet still the men charged. Then, as the sun passed its dazzling height, a Virginia regiment dressed in blue coats, which had been the only uniforms available to their colonel, came to reinforce the Confederate left and saw a northern battery in front of them. They marched forward. The gunners saw them and waved at them, believing them to be northerners, and in the still, hot smoky air the triple stripes of the Confederate flag hung red, white and blue like the Stars and Stripes. The northern gunners, stripped to their waists and sweating white stripes through powder stains and cursing as they burned their hands on the blazing hot barrels of their guns, did not give a second glance to the blue-coated infantry that marched, as the gunners supposed, to give them support against the infantry in front.

"Take aim!" A whole battalion of Virginia infantry had come to close pistol range on the flank of a northern battery. The rifle muskets went onto blue-uniformed shoulders. There was no time to turn the field guns and so the gunners threw themselves flat, wriggled under their guns and limbers, then covered their heads with their arms.

"Fire!" The flames ripped through the gray smoke and the Virginian officers heard the rattle as hundreds of musket balls beat home on iron gun barrels or wooden limber boxes, and then they heard the screams as forty-nine of the fifty battery horses died. The gunners who had survived the volley turned and fled as the Virginians charged with fixed bayonets and bowie knives. The battery was captured, its guns splashed with blood.

"Turn the guns! Turn the guns!"

"Charge!" More southerners ran forward, bayonets bright in the smoky gloom. "Our homes! Our homes!" they called, and a crash of musketry greeted them, but the northerners here were falling back. A shell exploded somewhere between the lines, streaking the smoke with flame. "Our homes!"

The northerners counterattacked. A regiment swept over the captured guns, forcing the Virginians back, but the recaptured guns were of no use to the federals for the gunners had been shot or else slaughtered by bayonets, and the horse teams were so much dead meat, so the cannon could not even be taken away. Other gunners in other batteries were killed by sharpshooters, and slowly the Confederates edged forward and the northerners heard the strange wailing scream as the rebel line attacked. The shadows lengthened and still more men climbed the hill to enter the stubborn horror.

James Starbuck came to the hilltop. He no longer searched for trophies that his victorious general could lay before the president's feet, instead he came to discover just what had gone wrong on the smoke-wreathed plateau. "Tell me what's happening, Starbuck," Irvin McDowell had ordered his aide. "Off you go!" McDowell had sent six other men on similar errands, but had not thought to visit the plateau himself. In truth

409

McDowell was swamped by the noise and the uncertainty and simply wanted an aide to come back with good news of victory.

James urged his horse up the shell-scarred hillside to where he found hell. His horse, devoid of guidance, ambled slowly forward to where a New York regiment, newly ordered to the hilltop, marched with fixed bayonets toward the enemy line, and it seemed to James that the whole southern army suddenly flowered in flame, a great fence of flame which turned to a rolling bank of smoke, and the New Yorkers just shuddered to a stop, and then another southern volley came from their flank and the New Yorkers stepped backward, leaving their dead and dying, and James saw the ramrods working as the men tried to return the fire, but the New York regiment had attacked alone, without flank support, and they had no chance against the southern volleys that enfiladed and confronted and decimated them. James tried to cheer them on, but his mouth was too dry to make words.

Then James's world obliterated itself. His horse literally jumped beneath him, then reared up its head to scream as it collapsed. A southern shell had exploded dead under its belly, eviscerating the beast and James, stunned, deafened and screaming for help, sprawled clumsily off the collapsing mass of guts and blood and flesh and hooves. He scrambled away on all fours, suddenly throwing up the contents of his distended belly. He stayed on all fours, retching foully, then managed to stagger to his feet. He slipped in a puddle of his horse's blood, then stood again and staggered toward the wooden house that lay at the center of the federal battle line and seemed to offer a kind of refuge, though, as he got closer, he saw how the little building had been splintered and riven and scorched by bullets and shells. James leaned on the springhouse in the yard and tried to make sense of his world, but all he could think about was the welter of horse's blood into which he had fallen. His ears still rang from the explosion.

A Wisconsin soldier, his face a mask of white, was sitting

beside him, and James slowly became aware that the man's head was half-severed by a shell fragment and his brains exposed. "No," James said, "no!" Inside the house a woman was wailing while somewhere in the distance it sounded as though a whole army of women was wailing. James pushed away the spring-house and staggered toward a regiment of infantry. They were Massachusetts men, his own people, and he stood close beside their colors and saw the heap of dead that had been thrown up behind the flags, and even as he watched, another man crumpled down. The flags were a target for enemy marksmen, a bright-starred invitation to death, but as soon as the color bearer fell another man plucked up the staff and held the standards high.

"Starbuck!" a voice shouted. It was a major whom James knew as a dour and canny attorney in Boston, but for some reason, although James must have met the man every week at the Lawyer's Club, he could not place his name. "Where's McDowell?" the major shouted.

"Down by the turnpike." James managed to sound reasonably coherent.

"He should be here!" A shell screamed overhead. The major, a thin and gray-haired man with a neatly clipped beard, shuddered as the missile exploded somewhere behind. "Damn them!"

Damn who, James wondered, then was astonished that he had used the swear word, even silently in his thoughts.

"We're fighting them piecemeal!" The Boston attorney tried to explain the northern army's predicament. "It won't do!"

"What do you mean?" James had to shout to make himself heard over the constant crash of gunnery. What was this man's name? He remembered how the attorney was a terrier in cross-examination, never letting go of a witness till he had shaken the evidence free, and James remembered how, famously, the man had once lost his temper with Chief Justice

Shaw, complaining in open court that Shaw was intellectually and judicially costive, for which contempt Shaw had first fined him, and had then purchased him supper. What was the man's name?

"The attacks should coincide! We need a general officer to coordinate affairs." The major stopped abruptly.

James, who was always made uncomfortable by criticism of constituted authority, tried to explain that General McDowell was undoubtedly aware of what was happening, but then he stopped talking because the major was swaying. James put out a hand, the major gripped it with a demonic force, and then opened his mouth, but instead of speaking he just voided a great flow of blood. "Oh, no," the major managed to say, then he slumped down to James's feet. James felt himself shaking. This was a nightmare, and he felt a most terrible, abject and shameful fear. "Tell my dear Abigail," the dying major said, and he looked pathetically up at James, and James still could not remember the man's name.

"Tell Abigail what?" he asked stupidly, but the major was dead, and James shook the corpse's hand away and felt a terrible, terrible sadness that he was going to die without ever knowing the pleasures of this world. He would die and there was no one who would really miss him, no one who would truly mourn him, and James stared at the sky and howled a self-pitying cry, then he managed to fumble his revolver from its stiff-leather holster and he aimed it vaguely in the direction of the Confederate army and pulled its trigger time and again to spit its bullets into a smoke cloud. Each single shot was a protest and a revenge for his own cautious nature.

The Massachusetts regiment stumbled forward. They were no longer in line but had coalesced into small groups of men that now sidled between the dead and dying. They talked to one another as they fought, cheering one another on, offering praise and small jests. "Hey, reb! Here's a lead pill for your sickness!" a man shouted, then fired.

"You all right, Billy?"

"Gun's all choked up." The minié bullets expanded in the barrels as their hollowed-out backs were swollen by the powder gases to grip the rifling and so give the missile a deadly accurate spin. The friction of the expanded bullet scraping through the barrel was supposed to clean the fouled powder deposits from the rifling, but the theory did not work and the harsh deposits still accreted to make the guns terribly hard for a tired man to load.

"Here, reb! Here's one for you!"

"Christ! That was close."

"No use ducking, Robby, they've gone past before you hear 'em."

"Anyone got a shot? Someone give me a cartridge!"

James took comfort from the quiet words and edged closer to the nearest group of men. The commanding officer of the Massachusetts regiment had started the day as a lieutenant and now shouted at the survivors to advance, and so they tried, shouting a harsh defiance from their raw throats, but then two Confederate six pounders took the regiment's open flank with barrel loads of canister and the musket balls whipped along the survivors, decimating their groups and bloodying the slippery turf with still more blood. The Massachusetts men stepped back. James reloaded his revolver. He was close enough to see the dirty faces of the enemy, to see their eyes showing white through the powder stains on their skin, to see their unbuttoned coats and loose shirts. He saw a rebel fall down, clutching at his knee, then crawl away to the rear. He saw a rebel officer with long fair mustaches screaming encouragement at his men. The man's coat hung open and his trousers were belted with a length of rope. James took careful aim at the man, fired, but his revolver's smoke obscured the effect of his shot.

The rebel guns crashed back, bucking on their trails, smashing down on their wheels, sizzling as the sponges

413

cleaned out their barrels, then firing again to feed the cloud of smoke that thickened like a Nantucket fog. More guns came from Beauregard's right wing. The rebel general sensed that disaster had been averted though it was none of his doing, but rather because his farmhands and college boys and store clerks had withstood the northern assault and were now counterattacking everywhere along Jackson's makeshift line. Two amateur armies had collided and luck was running Beauregard's way.

General Joseph Johnston had brought his men from the Shenandoah Valley, but, now that they were here, he had no duties except to watch them die. Johnston outranked Beauregard, but Beauregard had planned this battle, knew the ground, while Johnston was a stranger, and so he was letting Beauregard finish the fight. Johnston was ready to take over if Beauregard were hit, but till then he would stay silent and just try to understand the flux of the huge event that had come to its terrible climax on the hilltop. Johnston understood clearly enough that the North had wrong-footed Beauregard and turned his flank, but he also saw how the southern forces were fighting back hard and could yet scrape through to victory. Johnston also understood that it was Colonel Nathan Evans, the unregarded South Carolinian, who had probably saved the Confederacy by planting his feeble force across the path of the northern flank attack. Johnston sought out Evans and thanked him, then, working his way back to the east, the general came to where the wounded Washington Faulconer lay on the ground with his back propped against a saddle. Faulconer had been stripped to the waist and his chest was swathed in bandages while his right arm was in its blood-stained sling.

The general reined in and looked sympathetically down at the wounded Colonel. "It's Faulconer, isn't it?"

Washington Faulconer looked up to see a dazzle of yellow braid, but the smoke-diffused sun was behind the horseman and he could not make out the man's face. "Sir?" he answered very warily, already rehearsing the arguments he would use to explain his Legion's failure.

"I'm Joseph Johnston. We met in Richmond four months ago, and of course we had the pleasure of dining together at Jethro Sanders's house last year."

"Of course, sir." Faulconer had been expecting a reprimand, yet General Johnston sounded more than affable.

"You must be feeling foul, Faulconer. Is the wound bad?"

"A six-week scratch, sir, that's all." Faulconer knew how to sound suitably modest, though in truth he was desperately readjusting himself to the wonderful realization that General Johnston was not full of recrimination. Washington Faulconer was no fool, and he knew that he had behaved badly or, at the very least, that it might be imputed that he had behaved unwisely by leaving his Legion and thus not being in place to save them from Starbuck's treachery and Bird's impetuosity, but if Johnston's friendliness was any guide then maybe no one had noticed that dereliction of duty?

"If it hadn't have been for your sacrifice," Johnston said, pouring the balm of Gilead onto Faulconer's self-esteem and making the Colonel's happiness complete, "the battle would have been lost two hours back. Thank God you were with Evans, that's all I can say."

Faulconer opened his mouth to respond, found nothing whatever to say, so closed it.

"The federals had Beauregard completely bamboozled," Johnston went on blithely. "He thought the thing would be decided on the right flank, and all the time the rascals were planning to hit us here. But you fellows got it right, and thank God you did, for you've saved the Confederacy." Johnston was a pernickety, fussy man and a professional soldier of long experience who seemed genuinely moved by the tribute he was paying. "Evans told me of your bravery, Faulconer, and it's an honor to salute you!" In fact Shanks Evans had paid a tribute to the bravery of the Faulconer Legion and had not mentioned Colonel Washington Faulconer's name at all, but it was a simple enough misunderstanding and not one that Washington Faulconer thought needed to be corrected at this moment.

"We merely did our best, sir," Faulconer managed to say, while in his mind he was already rewriting the whole story of the day—how he had, in fact, known all along that the rebel left lay dangerously exposed. Had he not reconnoitered toward the Sudley Fords at daybreak? And had he not left his regiment well placed to meet the enemy's thrust? And had he not been wounded in the subsequent fighting? "I'm just glad we could have been of some small service, sir," he added modestly.

Johnston liked Faulconer's humility. "You're a brave fellow, Faulconer, and I'll make it my business to let Richmond know who are the real heroes of Manassas."

"My men are the real heroes, sir." Just ten minutes ago the Colonel had been cursing his men, especially the bandsmen who had jettisoned two expensive saxhorn tubas, a trumpet and three drums in their desperate efforts to escape the northern pursuit. "They're all good Virginians, sir," he added, knowing that Joseph Johnston was himself from the old dominion.

"I salute you all!" Johnston said, though touching his hat specifically to Faulconer before urging his horse on.

Washington Faulconer lay back and basked in the praise. A hero of Manassas! Even the pain seemed diminished, or maybe that was the morphine that Doctor Danson had insisted he swallow, but even so, a hero! That was a good word and how well it sat on a Faulconer! And maybe six weeks in the Richmond town house would not come amiss, so long, of course, that this battle was won and the Confederacy survived, but granted that proviso, surely a hero stood a better chance of promotion if he dined regularly with the rulers of his country? And what a rebuke to the mudsills like Lee who had been so niggardly in their attitude. Now they would have to deal with a hero! Faulconer smiled at his son. "I think you've earned yourself a promotion, Adam."

"But ..."

"Quiet! Don't protest." The Colonel always felt good when he could behave generously, and this moment was made even better by the burgeoning hopes that his new status as a hero of Manassas made credible. He could surely attain general rank? And he could surely find the time to perfect his Legion, which could then become the jewel and heart of his new brigade. Faulconer's Brigade. That name had a fine ring, and he imagined Faulconer's Brigade leading the march into Washington, presenting arms outside the White House and escorting a conqueror on horseback into a humbled land. He took a cigar from the case beside him and jabbed it toward Adam to emphasize the importance of what he said. "I need you to be in charge of the Legion while I'm convalescing. I need you to make sure Pecker doesn't run wild again, eh? That he doesn't fritter the Legion away in some piddling skirmish. Besides, the Legion should be in family hands. And you did well today, son, very well."

"I did nothing, Father," Adam protested hotly, "and I'm not even sure—"

"Now, now! Quiet!" Washington Faulconer had seen Major Bird approaching and did not want Thaddeus to witness his son's prevarications. "Thaddeus!" The Colonel greeted his brother-in-law with an unaccustomed warmth. "The general asked me to thank you. You did well!"

Major Bird, who knew full well that the Colonel had been furious with him until just a moment before, stopped dead in his tracks then looked ostentatiously about, as though searching for another man called Thaddeus who might be the object of the Colonel's praise. "Are you talking to me, Colonel?"

"You did marvelously well! I congratulate you! You did precisely what I would have expected of you, indeed, exactly

417

what I wanted of you! You held the Legion to its duty till I arrived. Everyone else thought the battle would be on the right, but we knew better, eh? We did well, very well. If my arm wasn't broken I'd shake your hand. Well done, Thaddeus, well done!"

Thaddeus Bird managed to hold his laughter in check, though his head did jerk nervously back and forth as if he was about to burst into a fit of devilish cackles. "Am I to understand," he finally managed to speak without laughing, "that you are also to be congratulated?"

The Colonel hid his anger at his brother-in-law's effrontery. "I think you and I know each other well enough to dispense with an exchange of admiration, Thaddeus. Just be assured I'll put your name forward when I'm in Richmond."

"I didn't come here to offer you admiration," Thaddeus Bird said with tactless honesty, "but to suggest we send a work party to find some water. The men are parched."

"Water? By all means, water. Then you and I should put our heads together and decide what's needed for the future. Mr. Little tells me we've lost some band instruments, and we can't afford to lose as many officers' horses as we did today."

Band instruments? Horses? Thaddeus Bird gaped at his brother-in-law, wondering if the broken bone had somehow drained Faulconer of his wits. What the Legion needed, Thaddeus Bird decided as the Colonel meandered on, was a McGuffey's *Reader* in elementary soldiering, a child's primer in rifle-fire and drill, but he knew it would be no good saying as much. Faulconer's huge complacency had been puffed up by some fool's praise, and he was already seeing himself as the conqueror of New York. Bird tried to sober the Colonel with a small dose of reality. "You'll want the butcher's bill, Faulconer?" He interrupted the Colonel. "The list of our dead and wounded?"

Washington Faulconer again had to hide his irritation. "Is it bad?" he asked guardedly.

"I have nothing with which to compare it, and sadly it's incomplete. We misplaced a lot of men in the course of your brave victory, but we know for sure that at least a score are dead. Captain Jenkins is gone, and poor Burroughs, of course. I assume you'll write to the widow?" Bird paused, but received no answer, so just shrugged and carried on. "Of course there can be other dead ones still out there. We know of twenty-two wounded fellows, some of them atrociously bad—"

"Twenty-three," the Colonel interrupted, and offered Thaddeus Bird a modest smile. "I count myself a member of the Legion, Thaddeus."

"So do I, Faulconer, and had already numbered you among its heroes. As I said, twenty-two, some of them grievously. Masterson won't survive, and Norton has lost both his legs so—"

"I don't need every detail," Faulconer said peevishly.

"And there still appear to be seventy-two men missing," Bird continued stoically with his bad news. "They aren't necessarily lost to us forever; Turner MacLean's boy staggered in five minutes ago having spent the best part of two hours wandering around the battlefield, but he never did have an ounce of sense. Others are probably dead and gone. I hear Ridley was killed."

"Murdered," the Colonel insisted.

"Murdered, was he?" Bird had already heard the story, but wanted to provoke the Colonel.

"He was murdered," the Colonel said, "and I witnessed it, and you will enter that in the regiment's books."

"If we ever find the books," Bird remarked happily. "We seem to have lost all the baggage."

"Murdered! You hear me?" Faulconer thundered the accusation, sending a stab of pain through his wounded chest. "That's what you will enter. That he was murdered by Starbuck."

419

"And Starbuck's missing," Bird went blithely on, "I'm most sorry to say."

"You're sorry?" There was something very dangerous in the Colonel's voice.

"You should be too," Bird said, ignoring the Colonel's tone. "Starbuck probably saved our colors, and he certainly prevented Adam from being taken prisoner. Didn't Adam tell you?"

"I've been trying to tell you, Father," Adam said.

"Starbuck is gone," the Colonel said flatly, "and if he was here you would be required to arrest him for murder. I saw him shoot Ridley. I saw him! Do you hear that, Thaddeus?" In fact half the Legion could hear the Colonel, whose indignation soared as he remembered poor Ridley's death. Good God, Faulconer thought, but did none of these men believe him when he said he had seen Starbuck fire the shots that murdered Ridley! The Colonel had turned in his saddle and watched him fire the revolver! And now Pecker Bird wanted to make out that the Bostonian was some kind of hero? Christ, the Colonel thought, but he was the hero of Manassas! Had not General Johnston said as much? "You say we lost poor Roswell Jenkins?" he asked, deliberately changing the subject.

"He was quite obliterated by shellfire," Bird confirmed, then obstinately changed the subject back. "Are you really ordering me to arrest Starbuck for murder?"

"If you find him, yes!" the Colonel shouted, then winced as a lance of pain shot down his arm. "For God's sake, Thaddeus, why do you always have to make such a damn fuss about things?"

"Because someone has to, Colonel, someone has to." Bird smiled and turned away while behind him, on a plateau edged with fire, the battle came to its breaking point at last.

James Starbuck never quite understood why the northern lines broke, he just remembered a desperate panic suddenly

420

overtaking the federal troops until, all order gone, there was nothing but panic as McDowell's army ran.

Nothing they had done had moved the southern regiments off the plateau. No assault gained enough ground to let supporting troops reinforce success, and so the northern attacks had been beaten back again and again, and each repulse had whelped its litter of dead and dying men who lay in rows like tidal wrack to mark the limits of each federal assault.

Ammunition had run short in some northern regiments. The southerners, pushed back toward their own baggage, were distributing tubs of cartridges to their troops, but the northern supplies were still east of the Bull Run and every wagon or limber or caisson had to be brought through the traffic jam that developed around the stone bridge and too often, even when ammunition was brought to the hilltop, it proved to be the wrong kind and so troops armed with .58 rifles received .69 musket ammunition and, as their rifles fell silent, they retreated to leave a gap in the northern line into which the gray rebels moved.

On both sides the rifles and muskets misfired or broke. The cones through which the percussion cap spat its fire into the powder charge broke most frequently, but as the southerners pressed forward they could pick up the guns of the northern dead and so keep up the slaughter. Yet still the northerners fought on. Their rifle and musket barrels were fouled with the clinker of burnt powder so that each shot took a huge effort to ram home, and the day was hot and the air filled with acrid powder smoke so that the mouths and gullets of the weary men were dry and raw, and their shoulders were bruised black from the recoil of the heavy guns, and their voices hoarse from shouting, their eyes were smarting with smoke, their ears ringing with the hammer blows of the big guns, their arms aching from ramming the bullets down the fouled barrels, yet still they fought. They bled and fought, cursed and fought, prayed and fought. Some of the men seemed dazed, just standing open-eyed and open-mouthed, oblivious to their officers' shouts or to the discordant din of bullets, guns, shells and screams.

James Starbuck had lost all sense of time. He reloaded his revolver, fired and reloaded. He scarce knew what he was doing, only that every shot could save the Union. He was terrified, but he fought on, taking an odd courage from the thought of his younger sister. He had decided that Martha alone would mourn him and that he could not disgrace her affection and it was that resolve which held him to his place where he fought like a ranker, firing and loading, firing and loading, and all the while saying Martha's name aloud like a talisman that would keep him brave. Martha was the sister whose character was most like Nathaniel's, and as James stood amid the litter of wounded and dead, he could have wept that God had not given him Martha and Nathaniel's brazen daring.

Then, just as he manipulated the last of his small percussion caps onto his revolver's cones, a cheer spread along the southern line and James looked up to see the whole enemy front surging forward. He straightened his aching bruised arm and pointed the revolver at what looked like a vast rat-gray army scorched black by powder burns that was charging straight toward him.

Then, just as he muttered his sister's name and half-flinched from the noise his revolver would make, he saw he was utterly alone.

One moment there had been a battle, and now there was rout.

For the federal army had broken and run.

They pelted down the hill, discipline gone to the wind. Men threw away rifles and muskets, bayonets and haversacks, and just fled. Some ran north toward the Sudley Fords while others ran for the stone bridge. A few men tried to stem the charge, shouting at their fellow northerners to form line and stand firm, but the few were swamped by the many. The panicked troops flooded the fields on either side of the turn-pike on which a limbered cannon, its horses whipped into a frantic gallop, ran down screaming infantrymen with its iron-shod wheels. Other men used battle standards as spears with which to fight their way toward the stream.

The rebel pursuit stopped at the plateau's edge. A spatter-ing of musket fire hurried the northerner's retreat, but no one on the rebel side had the energy to pursue. Instead they rev-eled in the slow realization of victory and in the scurrying defeat of the panicked horde beneath them. The rebel gunners brought their surviving cannon to the hillcrest and the south-ern shells screamed away into the afternoon warmth to explode in bursts of smoke along the crowded turnpike and in the farther woods. One of the shots burst in the air plumb above the wooden bridge that carried the turnpike over the deep tributary of the Run just as a wagon was crossing. The wagon's wounded horses panicked and tried to bolt, but the fatal shell had torn off a front wheel and the massive vehicle slewed round, its broken axle gouging timber so that the heavy wagon body was jammed immovably between the bridge's wooden parapets, and thus the northern army's main escape road was blocked and still more shells screamed down to explode among the fleeing northerners. The federal guns, carriages, limbers and wagons still on the Bull Run's western bank were abandoned as their teamsters fled for safety. A shell exploded in the stream, spouting tons of water. More shells smacked behind, driving the panicked mass of men in a mad-dened scramble down the steep slippery bank and into the Run's quick current. Scores of men drowned, pushed under by their own desperate comrades. Others floundered across the deep stream and somehow pulled themselves free and then ran toward Washington.

Nathaniel Starbuck had watched the rout spill over the plateau's edge. At first he had not believed what he saw, then disbelief turned to amazement. The sergeant guarding the prisoners had taken one look at the hillside, then ran. A wounded northerner, recuperating in the yard, had limped away, using his musket as a crutch. The red-bearded doctor came to the door in his blood-spattered apron, took one incredulous look at the whole scene, then shook his head and went back inside to his patients.

"What do we do now?" one of the rebel prisoners asked Starbuck, as if an officer might know the etiquette of handling victory in the middle of a defeated rabble.

"We stay real quiet and polite," Starbuck advised. There were northerners fleeing past the house and some were looking angrily at the southern prisoners. "Stay sitting, don't move, just wait." He watched a northern field gun retreating off the plateau. The gun captain had somehow managed to assemble a team of four horses which, whipped bloody by their frightened drivers, were galloping recklessly down the shell-scarred slope so that the gunners perched on the narrow limber seat were clinging grimly to the metal handles. The horses were white-eyed and scared. The gun itself, attached behind the limber, bounced dangerously as the rig splashed through a streamlet at the hill's foot, then the driver pulled on his reins and the panicked horses turned too fast onto the turnpike and Starbuck watched in horror as first the cannon, then the limber, tipped, rolled and slid hard across the road to crash sickeningly into the trees at the edge of the yard. There was a moment's silence, then the first screams tore the humid air.

"Oh, Christ." A wounded man turned in horror from the carnage. A horse, both rear legs broken, tried to scramble free of the bloody wreckage. One of the gunners had been trapped under the limber and the man clawed feebly at the splintered timbers that impaled him. A passing infantry sergeant ignored the wounded man as he cut the traces of the one uninjured horse, unhooked its chains, then scrambled onto its back. A roundshot from the spilt limber trundled across the road and

424

the wounded horses went on screaming like the dying gunner.

"Oh God, no." One of the prisoners in the tree-shaded yard was a tidewater Virginian who now recited the Lord's Prayer over and over again. The awful screaming went on until a northern officer walked over to the wounded animals and fired into their skulls. It took five shots, but the animals died, leaving only the shrieking, gasping, writhing gunner who was impaled by the mangled spokes of the limber's wheel. The officer took a breath. "Soldier!"

The man must have recognized the tone of authority for he went still for just a second, and that second was all the officer needed. He aimed the revolver, pulled the trigger and the gunner fell back silent. The northern officer shuddered, tossed away the empty revolver then walked away weeping. The world seemed very quiet suddenly. It stank of blood, but it was quiet until the tidewater boy said the Lord's Prayer one more time, as though the repetition of the words could save his soul.

"Are you boys safe?" A gray-coated officer galloped his horse down to the crossroads.

"We're safe," Starbuck said.

"We whipped 'em, boys! Whipped 'em good!" the officer boasted.

"You want an apple, mister?" A South Carolina prisoner, released now, had been searching among the knapsacks that had spilled from the fallen gun limber and now plucked some apples from among the bloody wreckage. He tossed the jubilant officer a bright red apple. "Go whip 'em some more!"

The officer caught the apple. Behind him the first southern infantry was advancing toward the Bull Run. Starbuck watched for a while, then turned away. War's lottery had freed him yet again, and he had one more promise yet to keep.

Tired men collected the wounded, those they could find. Some of the injured were in woodland, and doomed to slow and forgotten deaths in the undergrowth. Thirsty men looked for water while some just drank the fouled liquid in the cannon's sponge buckets, gulping down the gunpowder debris along with the warm, salty liquid. The small wind was brisker now, stirring the camp fires that men made from shattered musket stocks and fence rails.

The rebels were in no state to pursue the federal troops, and so they stayed on the battlefield and stared in dazed astonishment at the plunder of victory—at the guns and wagons and caissons, at the mounds of captured stores and at the hordes of prisoners. A fat congressman from Rochester, New York, was among those prisoners; he had been found trying to hide his vast belly behind a slim sapling and had been brought to the army headquarters where he blustered about the importance of his position and demanding to be released. A rail-thin Georgian soldier told him to shut his damned fat mouth before he had his damned fat tongue cut out to be cooked and served with an apple sauce and the congressman fell instantly silent.

At dusk the rebels crossed the Run to capture the thirty-pound Parrott field rifle that had signaled the federal attack that dawn. The northerners had abandoned twenty-six other guns, along with nearly all their army's baggage. Southern soldiers found full-dress uniforms carefully packed ready for the triumphant entry into Richmond and a North Carolinian soldier paraded proudly about in a Yankee general's finery, complete with epaulettes, sword, sash and spurs. The pockets of the dead were rifled for their pitiful haul of combs, playing cards, testaments, jackknives and coins. A lucky few found wealthier corpses, one with a heavy watch chain hung with golden seals, another with a ruby ring on his wedding finger. Daguerreotypes of wives and sweethearts, parents and children were tossed aside, for the victors were not looking for mementoes of shattered affections, but only for coins and cigars, silver and gold, good boots, fine shirts, belts, buckles or weapons. A brisk market in plunder established itself; fine officers' field glasses were sold for a dollar, swords for three, and fifty-dollar Colt revolvers for five or six. Most prized of all were the posing photographs showing New York and Chicago ladies out of their clothes. Some of the men refused to look, fearing hell's fires, but most passed the pictures around and wondered at the plunder that would come their way if ever they were called upon to invade the rich, plump, soft North that bred such women and such fine rooms. Doctors from North and South worked together in the farm hospitals of the scorched, torn battlefield. The wounded wept, the amputated legs and arms and hands and feet piled in the yards, while the dead were stacked like cordwood for the graves that must wait for morning to be dug.

As evening drew on, James Starbuck was still free. He had hidden himself in a stand of trees, and now he crawled in the bottom of a deep ditch toward the Bull Run. His mind was in chaos. How had it happened? How could defeat have happened? It was so bitter, so terrible, so shameful. Was God so careless of the right that he would allow this awful visitation upon the United States? It made no sense.

"I wouldn't go a foot farther, Yankee," an amused voice suddenly spoke above him, "because that's poison ivy just ahead of you, and you're in enough trouble like it is."

James looked up to see two grinning lads whom he rightly suspected had been watching him for the last few minutes. "I'm an officer," he managed to say.

"Nice to meet you, officer. I'm Ned Potter and that's Jake Spring, and this here's our dog, Abe." Potter gestured at a ragged little mongrel that he held on a length of rope. "We ain't none of us officers, but you're our prisoner."

James stood and tried to brush the dead leaves and stagnant water from his uniform. "My name," he said in his most officious manner, then stopped. What would happen to Elial Starbuck's son in southern hands? Would they lynch him? Would they do the terrible things his father said all southerners did to Negroes and emancipators?

"Don't care what your name is, Yankee, only what's in your pockets. Me, Jake and Abe are kind of poor right now. All we captured so far is two boys from Pennsylvania and they didn't have nothing but cold hoe cakes and three rusty cents between 'em." The musket came up and the grin widened. "You can give us that revolver for a beginnings."

"Buchanan!" James blurted out the name. "Miles Buchanan!"

Ned Potter and Jake Spring stared uncomprehendingly at their prisoner.

"An attorney!" James explained. "I've been trying to remember his name all day! He once accused Chief Justice Shaw of being costive. Intellectually costive, that is ..." His voice died away as he realized that poor Miles Buchanan was dead now, and Abigail Buchanan was a widow, and he himself was taken prisoner.

"Just give us the revolver, Yankee."

James handed over the blackened revolver, then turned out his pockets. He was carrying over eighteen dollars in coin, a New Testament, a fine watch on a seal-heavy chain, a pair of folding opera glasses, a box of pen nibs, two notebooks and a fine linen handkerchief that his mother had embroidered with his initials. Ned Potter and Jake Spring were delighted with their luck, but James felt only a terrible humiliation. He had been delivered into the hands of his bitterest enemies and he could have wept for his country's loss.

One mile away from James, Nathaniel Starbuck searched a meadow that was pockmarked with shell fire and scored with hoofprints. The Yankees were long gone and the meadow was empty except for the dead. It was the pasture where Washington Faulconer had struck him with his riding crop, the place where Ethan Ridley had died.

He found Ridley closer to the tree line than he remembered, but he supposed all his recollections of the battle were confused. The body was a horror of blood and bone, of torn

428

flesh and blackened skin. The birds had already begun their feasting, but flapped reluctantly away as Starbuck walked up to the corpse that was beginning to stink. Ridley's head was recognizable, the small pointed beard being oddly clear of blood. "You son of a bitch," Starbuck said tiredly and without real anger, but he was remembering the scar on Sally's face, and the child she had lost, and the rapes and beatings she had endured just so that this man could be free of her, and so some insult seemed fitting to mark the moment.

The sick-sweet stench of death was thick and nauseous as Starbuck crouched beside the corpse and steeled himself. Then he reached out for what was left of his enemy. There but for the grace of God, he thought, and he pulled the neck of Ridley's jacket to free the remnants of the garment from the bloody corpse, and something deep in the body made a gurgling sound that almost made Starbuck retch. The jacket would not come clear of the bloody mess and Starbuck realized he would have to undo the leather belt that was somehow still in place around the eviscerated mess. He plunged his fingers into the cold, jellylike horror, and found the buckle. He undid it, heaved, and a portion of the corpse rolled away to reveal the revolver that Ridley had fired at Starbuck.

It was the pretty, ivory-handled English gun that Washington Faulconer had shown to Starbuck in his study at Seven Springs. The gun was now choked with Ridley's blood, but Starbuck wiped it on the grass, cuffed more of the blood away with his sleeve, then pushed the beautiful weapon into his empty holster. He then unthreaded the cap box and the cartridge case from Ridley's belt. There were a dozen dollar coins in the case, which he pushed into one of his own blood-soaked pockets.

Yet he had not come here simply to loot his enemy's body, but rather to take back a treasure. He wiped his fingers on the grass, took another deep breath, then went back to the bloody remnants of the gray jacket. He found a leather case which seemed to have held a drawing, though the paper was now so soaked with blood that it was impossible to tell just what the drawing might have shown. There were three more silver dollars in the pocket and a small, blood-wet leather bag, which Starbuck pulled open.

The ring was there. It looked dull in the fading light, but it was the ring he had wanted; the silver French ring that had belonged to Sally's mother and which Starbuck now pushed into his own pocket as he stepped back from the corpse. "You son of a bitch," he said again, then he walked away past Ridley's dead horse. Across the valley the smoke of the camp fires drifted away from the hill to veil the sunset.

Dark was falling as Starbuck climbed the hill to where the southern army made its weary bivouac. A few officers had tried to order their men off the hilltop and down to where the ground did not stink of blood, but the men were too tired to move. Instead they sat around their fires and ate captured hard tack and cold bacon. A man played a fiddle, its notes wondrously plangent in the graying light. The far hills were darkening and the first stars gleaming pale and sharp in a clean sky. A Georgia regiment held a service, the men's voices strong as they sang praises for their victory.

It took Starbuck an hour to find the Legion. It was almost full dark by then, but he saw Pecker Bird's distinctive face in the light of a fire made from a dozen fence rails which radiated out from the flames like spokes. Every man about the fire was responsible for a rail, nudging it into the fire as the rail burned down. The men around the fire were all officers who looked up astonished as Starbuck limped into the flame light. Murphy nodded a pleased greeting to see the Bostonian, and Bird smiled. "So you're alive, Starbuck?"

"So it seems, Major."

Bird lit a cigar and tossed it to Starbuck who caught it, sucked in the smoke, then nodded his thanks.

"Is that your blood?" Murphy asked Starbuck, whose

430

uniform was still thick with Ridley's blood.

"No."

"But it's very dramatic," Bird said in gentle mockery, then twisted himself around. "Colonel!"

Colonel Faulconer, his shirt and jacket now wrapped around his wounded arm, was sitting outside his tent. He had made a huge commotion about the Legion's missing baggage and finally a reluctant search party had discovered Nelson, the Colonel's servant, still guarding as much of the Colonel's baggage as he had managed to carry away from the Yankee attack. Most of the baggage was gone, looted by successive waves of northerners and southerners, but the Colonel's tent had been salvaged and a bed of blankets laid down inside. Adam was lying on the bed while his father sat on a barrel in the tent's door.

"Colonel!" Bird called again, his insistence at last making Washington Faulconer look up. "Good news, Colonel." Bird could hardly keep from grinning as he made his mischief. "Starbuck is alive."

"Nate!" Adam reached for the makeshift crutch that a man had cut from a thicket nearby, but his father pushed him down.

Faulconer stood and walked toward the fire. A mounted staff captain chose that same moment to approach the fire from farther along the plateau, but the captain, who had a message for Colonel Faulconer, sensed the tension around the camp fire and checked his horse to watch what happened.

Faulconer gazed through the flames, flinching from Starbuck's horrid appearance. The northerner's uniform was dark with blood, stiff with it, black in the flame light with the blood that had soaked into every stitch and weave of the gray coat. Starbuck looked like a thing come from a nightmare, but he nodded pleasantly enough as he blew a stream of cigar smoke into the night. "Evening, Colonel."

Faulconer said nothing. Bird lit himself a cigar, then looked

431

at Starbuck. "The Colonel was wondering how Ridley died, Starbuck?"

"Got hit by a shell, Colonel. Nothing left of him but a mess of bones and blood," Starbuck said, his voice careless.

"Is that what you want me to put in the book, Colonel?" Thaddeus Bird asked with a studied innocence. "That Ridley died of artillery fire?"

Still Washington Faulconer did not speak. He was staring at Starbuck with what seemed like loathing, but he could not bring himself to say a word.

Bird shrugged. "Earlier, Colonel, you ordered me to arrest Starbuck for murder. You want me to do that right now?" Bird waited for an answer and when none came he looked back to Starbuck. "Did you murder Captain Ethan Ridley, Starbuck?"

"No," Starbuck said curtly. He stared at Faulconer, daring the Colonel to contradict him. The Colonel knew he was lying, but he did not have the guts to make the accusation to his face. Men had come from the Legion's other camp fires to watch the confrontation.

"But the Colonel saw you commit the murder," Bird insisted. "What do you have to say to that?"

Starbuck took the cigar from his mouth and spat into the fire.

"I assume that expectoration signifies a denial?" Bird asked happily, then looked around the men who were crowding into the flame light. "Did anyone else here see Ridley die?" Bird waited for an answer as sparks whirled upward from the burning rails. "Well?"

"I saw the son of a bitch get filleted by a shell," Truslow growled from the shadows.

"And did Starbuck fire the fatal shell, Sergeant?" Bird asked in a pedantic voice, and the men around the fire laughed aloud at the major's mockery. Faulconer shifted his weight, but still kept his silence. "So I reckon, Colonel, that you were

432

wrong," Bird went on, "and that Lieutenant Starbuck is innocent of murder. And I further reckon you'll be wanting to
thank him for saving the Legion's colors, isn't that right?"

But Faulconer could take no more humiliation from these
men who had fought while he had been swanning across the
countryside in search of fame. He turned away without a
word, only to see the staff captain watching him from horseback. "What do you want?" he snapped bitterly.

"You're invited to supper, Colonel." The staff captain was
understandably nervous. "The president has arrived from
Richmond, sir, and the generals are eager for your company."

Faulconer blinked as he tried to make sense of the invitation, then saw in it his chance of salvation. "Of course." He
strode away, calling for his son. Adam had struggled to his
feet and was now limping to welcome Starbuck back, but his
father demanded his son's loyalty. "Adam! You'll come with
me."

Adam hesitated, then gave in. "Yes, Father."

The two men were helped onto their horses and no one
spoke much as they rode away. Instead the men of the
Faulconer Legion fed their fires and watched the sparks fly
high, but said scarcely a word until the Faulconers had ridden
far beyond the flame light and were just two dark shadows silhouetted against the southern sky. Somehow no one expected
to see Washington Faulconer back again in a hurry. Bird
looked up at Starbuck. "I guess I'm in command now. So
thank you for saving our colors, and more important, for saving me. So now what do I do with you?"

"Whatever you want, Major."

"Then I think I shall punish you for whatever sins you
undoubtedly committed today." Bird grinned as he spoke. "I
shall make you Captain Roswell Jenkins's replacement, and
give you Sergeant Truslow's company. But only if Sergeant
Truslow wants a miserable Boston-bred overeducated beard-
less preacher's son like yourself as his commanding officer?"

"I reckon he'll do," Truslow said laconically.

"So you feed him, Sergeant, not me," Bird said, and raised a dismissive hand.

Starbuck walked away with Truslow. When the two men had gone beyond the earshot of the soldiers gathered around the officers' fire, the sergeant spat a stream of tobacco juice. "'So how does it feel to murder someone?' You remember asking me that? And I told you to find out for yourself, so now you tell me, Captain."

Captain? Starbuck noted, but said nothing of the unwonted respect. "It felt most satisfying, Sergeant."

Truslow nodded. "I saw you shoot the son of a bitch, and I was kind of wondering why."

"For this." Starbuck took the silver ring from his pocket and held it out to the small, dark-bearded Truslow. "Just for this," he said, and dropped the ring into the powder-blackened palm. The silver glinted for an instant in the blood-stinking smoke-darkened night, and then Truslow's hand closed on it fast. His Emily was in heaven, and the ring was back with him where it belonged.

Truslow had stopped dead in the darkness. For a second Starbuck thought the sergeant was weeping, but then he realized it was just the sound of Truslow clearing his throat. The sergeant began walking again, saying nothing, but just gripping the silver ring as if it was a talisman for all his future life. He did not speak again until they were a few yards from the fires of K Company, and then he put a hand on the blood-hardened cloth of Starbuck's sleeve. His voice, when he spoke, was unwontedly meek. "So how is she, Captain?"

"She's happy. Surprisingly happy. She was treated badly, but she came through it and she's happy. But she wanted you to have the ring, and she wanted me to take it from Ridley."

Truslow thought about that answer for a few seconds, then frowned. "I should have killed that bastard myself, shouldn't I?"

"Sally wanted me to do it," Starbuck said, "so I did. And with much pleasure." He could not keep himself from smiling.

Truslow was still for a long, long time, then he thrust the ring into a pocket. "It's going to rain tomorrow," he said. "I can smell it in the air. Most of these bastards have lost their groundsheets and blankets so I reckon in the morning you should let us scavenge a while." He led Starbuck into the light of his company's fires. "New captain" was Truslow's only introduction. "Robert? We'll have some of that fat bacon. John? Break that bread you're hiding. Pearce? That whiskey you found. We'll take some. Sit down, Captain, sit."

Starbuck sat and ate. The food was the most wonderful he had ever tasted, nor could he have asked for better company. Above him the stars shimmered in a sky of dissipating smoke. A fox called from the distant woods and a wounded horse screamed. Somewhere a man sang a sad song, and then a gunshot sounded in the lost darkness like a final echo of this day of battle in which a preacher's son, far from home, had made himself a rebel.

Historical Note

The first battle of Manassas (or Bull Run as northerners call it) was fought much as described in Rebel, though the novel ignores some tough but scrappy fighting that filled the gap between the retreat of Nathan Evans's half-brigade and the first engagement of Thomas Jackson's Virginia Brigade, and it ignores the presence of Jeb Stuart's cavalry on the battlefield, though in this battle, as in most of the big set-piece engagements to come in the War between the States, the cavalry was unimportant to the outcome. First Manassas was won by infantrymen, and it was Shanks Evans, who really did have a "barrelito" of whiskey on constant tap, whose timely maneuver saved the Confederacy, though it was "Stonewall" Jackson whose name became famous that day and whose statue still dominates the hilltop where he earned his nickname. Around nine hundred men died on July 21, 1861, and at least ten times as many were wounded.

The battlefield has been marvelously preserved by the National Park Service. The visitor center on the Henry House hill offers a splendid introduction to a site that is well sign-posted and explained, and is an easy drive from Washington, D.C. There is no Faulconer County in Virginia, nor was there a Faulconer Legion in the state's service.

Copperhead

**Principal Locations
of McClellan's
Peninsular Campaign
April–June 1862**

West
Point Depot

0   10 statute miles

Williamsburg

YORKTOWN

Magruder's
Lines

CHESAPEAKE
BAY

Fort Monroe

Copperhead
is for Bill and Anne Moir

PART ONE

THE INVASION BEGAN AT MIDNIGHT.

It was not truly an invasion, just a heavy raid on a rebel encampment that a patrol had spotted among the thick woods that crowned the high bluffs on the Virginia side of the river, but to the two thousand men who waited to cross the bleak slate-gray swirl of the Potomac River this night's exertions seemed more momentous than a mere raid. This fight across the river was their opportunity to prove their critics wrong. Nursery soldiers, one newspaper had called them; wonderfully trained and beautifully drilled, but much too precious to be dirtied in battle. Yet tonight the despised nursery soldiers would fight. Tonight the Army of the Potomac would carry fire and steel to a rebel encampment and if all went well they would march on to occupy the town of Leesburg, which lay two miles beyond the enemy camp. The expectant soldiers imagined the shamefaced citizens of the Virginia town waking to see the Stars and Stripes flying over their community again, and then they imagined themselves marching south, ever farther south, until the rebellion was crushed and America was reunited in peace and brotherhood.

"You bastard!" a voice shouted loudly from the river's edge where a work party had been launching a boat carried from the nearby Chesapeake and Ohio Canal. One of the work party had slipped in the clay, dropping the boat's stern onto a sergeant's foot. "You no-good son of a bitch goddamn

11

bastard!" The Sergeant hopped away from the boat.

"Sorry," the man said nervously.

"I'll give you sorry, you bastard!"

"Silence! Keep it quiet now!" An officer, resplendent in a new gray overcoat that was handsomely lined in red, clambered down the steep bank and helped lift the skiff toward the river's gray water from which a small mist crept to hide the lower slopes of the far bank. They labored beneath a high moon, no clouds, and a spread of stars so bright and clean they seemed like an augury of success. It was October, the fragrant month when the air smelt of apples and woodsmoke, and when the sweltering dog days of summer gave way to clear sharp weather that held just enough promise of winter to persuade the troops to wear their fine new overcoats that were the same color as the river's drifting mist.

The first boats pushed clumsily off the bank. The oars clattered in the oarlocks, then dipped and splashed as the boats receded into the mist. The men, who a moment before had been cursing and cumbersome creatures clambering down the clay bank into the clumsy boats, were mysteriously transformed into warrior silhouettes, spiky with weapons, who glided silent and noble through the vaporous night toward the misted shadows of the enemy shore. The officer who had remonstrated with the Sergeant stared wistfully across the water. "I suppose," he said softly to the men around him, "that this was how Washington felt on the night he crossed the Delaware?"

"A much colder night, that one, I think," a second officer, a young student from Boston, replied.

"It'll be cold enough here soon," the first officer, a major, said. "There's only two months till Christmas." When the Major had marched to war, newspapers had promised that the rebellion would be over by fall, but now the Major was

12

wondering whether he would be home with his wife and three children for the family rituals of Christmas. On Christmas Eve they sang carols on Boston Common, the children's faces lit by lanterns hung on poles, and afterward there were warm punch and slivers of cooked goose in the church vestry. Then on Christmas Day they went to his wife's parents' farm in Stoughton, where they harnessed the horses and the children laughed in delight as they trotted down country roads in a cloud of snow and a tinkling of sleigh bells.

"And I rather suspect General Washington's organization was superior to ours," the student-turned-lieutenant said in an amused voice. His name was Holmes and he was clever enough to awe his superiors, but usually intelligent enough not to let that cleverness alienate their affections.

"I am sure our organization will suffice," the Major said just a little too defensively.

"I am sure you're right," Lieutenant Holmes said, though he was not sure of that fact at all. Three regiments of northern troops waited to cross, and there were just three small boats to carry them from the Maryland shore to the island that lay close to the river's far bank, upon which island the troops must land before reembarking on two more boats for the final short crossing to the Virginia mainland. Doubtless they were crossing the river at the spot closest to the enemy encampment, but Lieutenant Holmes could not really understand why they did not cross a mile upstream where no island obstructed the river. Maybe, Holmes surmised, this was such an unlikely crossing place that the rebels would never think to guard it, and that seemed the best explanation he could find.

But if the choice of crossing place was obscure, at least the night's purpose was clear. The expedition would climb the Virginia bluffs to attack the rebel camp and capture as

13

many Confederates as possible. Some rebels would get away, but those fugitives would find their flight blocked by a second Yankee force that was crossing the river five miles downstream. That force would cut the turnpike that led from Leesburg to the rebel headquarters at Centreville, and by trapping the defeated rebel forces it would provide the North with a small but significant victory to prove that the Army of the Potomac could do more than just drill and train and mount impressive parades. The capture of Leesburg would be a welcome bonus, but the night's real purpose was to prove that the newly trained Army of the Potomac was ready and able to whip the rebels ragged.

To which end the small boats struggled back and forth in the mist. Each crossing seemed to take forever, and to the impatient men on the Maryland shore the waiting files seemed to get no shorter. The 15th Massachusetts was crossing first, and some men in the 20th Massachusetts feared that their sister regiment would capture the enemy camp long before the few boats succeeded in ferrying the 20th across the river. Everything seemed so slow and clumsy. Rifle butts clattered on gunwales and bayonet scabbards snagged themselves on the bushes at the water's edge as the men clambered into the row boats. At two in the morning a larger boat was discovered upstream and brought down to the crossing place, where it was greeted with an ironic cheer. It seemed to Lieutenant Holmes that the waiting men were making a lot of noise, enough surely to alert any rebels who might be guarding the Virginia bank, but no challenge sounded through the mist and no rifle shots echoed from the high wooded slope that loomed so ominously beyond the island. "Does the island have a name?" Lieutenant Holmes asked the Major who had spoken so wistfully of Christmas.

"Harrison's Island, I think. Yes, Harrison's."

It sounded an undramatic name to Lieutenant Holmes. He would have preferred something nobler to have marked the 20th Massachusetts's baptism of fire. Maybe a name with the iron ring of Valley Forge, or the simple nobility of Yorktown. Something that would ring through history and look fine when it was embroidered on the regiment's battle flag. Harrison's Island sounded much too prosaic. "And the hill beyond it?" he asked hopefully. "On the far bank?"

"That's called Ball's Bluff," the Major said, and that was even less heroic. The battle of Ball's Bluff sounded like a poker game rather than the signal event that would mark the resurgence of northern arms.

Holmes waited with his company. They would be the first of the 20th Massachusetts to cross and so the likeliest of their regiment to be in a fight if the 15th had not already captured the encampment. That possibility of battle made the men nervous. None of them had fought before, though all had heard tales of the battle fought at Bull Run three months before and how the ragged gray-clad rebel ranks had somehow clung together long enough to drive the larger Federal army into panicked retreat, but none of the 20th Massachusetts believed they would suffer a similar fate. They were superbly equipped, well-trained, led by a professional soldier, and confident they could outfight any rebel born. There would be danger, of course – they expected and even wanted some danger – but the night's work would be crowned with victory.

One of the boats coming back from Harrison's Island brought a captain of the 15th Massachusetts who had crossed with the very first troops and who now returned to report to the commanding officers of the waiting regiments. The Captain slipped as he jumped from the boat's bows and would have fallen if Lieutenant Holmes had not reached out a steadying hand. "All quiet on the Potomac?" Holmes asked jocularly.

"All's quiet, Wendell." The Captain sounded disappointed. "Too quiet. There's not even an enemy encampment up there."

"No tents?" Lieutenant Holmes asked in surprise. "Truly?" And he hoped his voice sounded properly disappointed as befitted a warrior denied a chance of battle, and in part he was disappointed because he had been looking forward to the excitement, but he was also aware of a shameful relief that perhaps no enemy waited on the far bluff.

The Captain straightened his coat. "God knows what that patrol thought they saw last night, but we can't find anything." He walked away with his news while Lieutenant Holmes passed the word on to his company. There was no enemy waiting across the river, which meant the expedition would most probably march on to occupy Leesburg. A sergeant wanted to know if there were any rebel troops in Leesburg and Holmes had to confess he did not know, but the Major, overhearing the conversation, volunteered that at best there would be only a handful of the Virginia Militia probably armed with the same guns with which their grandfathers had fought the British. The Major went on to say that their new task would be to capture the harvest that would have been newly gathered into the barns and storerooms of Leesburg, and that while such supplies were a legitimate military target, other private property should be respected. "We're not here to make war on the homes of women and children," the Major said sternly. "We must show the seceshers that northern troops are their friends."

"Amen," the Sergeant said. He was a lay preacher who was trying to rid the regiment of the sins of card-playing, liquor, and womanizing.

16

The last of the 15th Massachusetts crossed to the island and Holmes's gray-coated men shuffled down the bank to wait their turn in the boats. There was a feeling of disappointment among the men. They had anticipated a whooping hunt through the woods, but instead it seemed they would merely be disarming a town's old men of muskets.

In the shadows of the Virginia bank a fox pounced and a rabbit died. The beast's cry was sudden and shrill, gone almost as soon as it had begun, to leave nothing behind but the scent of blood and the echo of death in the dark, sleeping, and unsuspecting woods.

Captain Nathaniel Starbuck reached his regiment's campsite at three in the morning. It was a clear night, star-bright and moonlit, with just a hint of mist showing in the hollows. He had walked from Leesburg and was dog-tired by the time he reached the field where the Legion's tents and shelters were lined in four neat rows. A sentry from C Company nodded companionably at the young black-haired officer. "Hear the rabbit, Captain?"

"Willis? You're Willis, right?" Starbuck asked.

"Bob Willis."

"Aren't you supposed to challenge me, Bob Willis? Aren't you supposed to level your rifle, demand the password, and shoot me dead if I get it wrong?"

"I know who you are, Captain." Willis grinned in the moonlight.

"The way I feel, Willis, you would have done me a favor by shooting me. What did the rabbit say to you?"

"Shrieked like he was dying, Captain. Reckon a fox got him."

Starbuck shuddered at the relish in the sentry's voice. "Good night, Willis, and may sweet angels sing thee to thy rest." Starbuck walked on between the remnants of the

17

night's fires and the handful of Sibley tents where a few men of the Faulconer Legion slept. Most of the regiment's tents had been lost in the chaos of the Manassas battle-field, so now the majority of the regiment slept either in the open air or in neat shelters made of branches and sod. A fire flickered among the shelters of Starbuck's K Company and a man looked up as Starbuck approached.

"Sober?" the man asked.

"Sergeant Truslow is awake," Starbuck declaimed. "Do you never sleep, Truslow? I am perfectly sober. Sober as a preacher, in fact."

"I've known a few drunk preachers in my time," Sergeant Truslow said sourly. "There's a snake-oil Baptist down in Rosskill who can't say the Lord's Prayer without taking a gutful of pine-top whiskey first. He nearly drowned once, trying to baptize a passel of weeping women in the river behind the church. Them all praying and him so full of liquor he couldn't stand up straight. So what were you doing, caterwauling?"

"Caterwauling" was the Sergeant's disapproving word for womanizing. Starbuck pretended to consider the question as he settled beside the fire, then he nodded. "I was cater-wauling, Sergeant."

"Who with?"

"A gentleman does not tell."

Truslow grunted. He was a short, squat, hard-faced man who ruled K Company with a discipline born of pure fear, though the fear was not of Truslow's physical violence, but rather of his scorn. He was a man whose approval other men sought, maybe because he seemed such a master of his own brutal world. In his time he had been a farmer, a horse thief, a soldier, a murderer, a father, and a husband. Now he was a widower and, for the second time in his life, a soldier, who brought to his trade a pure, uncomplicated hatred of

18

Yankees. Which made his friendship with Captain Nathaniel Starbuck all the more mysterious, for Starbuck was a Yankee.

Starbuck came from Boston, second son of the Reverend Elial Starbuck, who was a famous excoriator of the South, a fearsome opponent of slavery, and an impassioned preacher whose printed sermons had shivered guilty consciences throughout the Christian world. Nathaniel Starbuck had been well on the path to his own ordination when a woman had tempted him from his studies at Yale College's seminary. The woman had abandoned him in Richmond, where, too scared to go home and face his father's terrible wrath, Starbuck had joined the army of the Confederate States of America instead.

"Was it the yellow-haired bitch?" Truslow now asked. "The one you met in the prayer meeting after worship service?"

"She is not a bitch, Sergeant," Starbuck said with pained dignity. Truslow responded by spitting into the fire, and Starbuck shook his head sadly. "Did you never seek the solace of female company, Sergeant?"

"Do you mean did I ever behave like a tomcat? Of course I did, but I got it out of my system before I grew a beard." Truslow paused, maybe thinking of his wife in her lonely grave in the high hills. "So where does the yellow bitch keep her husband?"

Starbuck yawned. "With Magruder's forces at Yorktown. He's an artillery major."

Truslow shook his head. "You'll be caught one of these days and have your giblets beaten out of you."

"Is that coffee?"

"So they say." Truslow poured his captain a mug of the thick, sweet, treacly liquid. "Did you get any sleep?"

"Sleep was not the purpose of the evening."

19

"You're just like all preachers' sons, aren't you? Get one smell of sin and you wallow like a hog in mud." There was more than a hint of disapproval in Truslow's voice, not because he disliked womanizers, but because he knew his own daughter had contributed to Starbuck's education. Sally Truslow, estranged from her father, was a whore in Richmond. That was a matter of bitter shame to Truslow, and while he was uncomfortable with the knowledge that Starbuck and Sally had been lovers, he also saw in their friendship his daughter's only chance of salvation. Life could sometimes seem very complicated even for an uncomplicated man like Thomas Truslow. "So what happened to all your Bible reading?" he now asked his officer, referring to the halfhearted attempts at piety that Starbuck still made from time to time.

"I am a backslider, Sergeant," Starbuck said carelessly, though in truth his conscience was not as easy as his flippant tone suggested. At times, assailed by the fears of hell, he felt so trapped in sin that he suspected he could never find God's forgiveness, and at such moments he would suffer agonies of remorse, but come the evening, he would find himself being impelled back to whatever tempted him.

Now he rested against the trunk of an apple tree and sipped the coffee. He was tall, thin, hardened by a season's soldiering, and had long black hair that framed an angular, clean-shaven face. When the Legion marched into a new town or village, Truslow always noticed how the girls looked at Starbuck, always at Starbuck. Just as his own daughter had been drawn to the tall northerner with his gray eyes and quick grin. Keeping Starbuck from sin, the Sergeant reflected, was like keeping a dog out of a butcher's shop. "What time is reveille?" Starbuck now asked.

"Any minute."

"Oh, sweet Jesus." Starbuck groaned.

20

"You should have come back earlier," Truslow said. He threw a billet of wood onto the small fire. "Did you tell the yellow-haired bitch that we're leaving?"

"I decided not to tell her. Parting is such sweet hell."

"Coward," Truslow said.

Starbuck thought about the accusation, then grinned. "You're right. I'm a coward. I hate it when they cry."

"Then don't give them cause to cry," Truslow said, knowing it was like asking the wind not to blow. Besides, soldiers always made their sweethearts cry; that was the way of soldiers. They came, they conquered, and then they marched away, and this morning the Faulconer Legion would march away from Leesburg. In the last three months the regiment had been a part of the brigade that was camped close to Leesburg and guarded a twenty-mile stretch of the Potomac River, but the enemy had shown no signs of wanting to cross, and now, as the fall slipped toward winter, rumors were multiplying of a last Yankee attack on Richmond before the ice and snow locked the armies into immobility, and so the brigade was being weakened. The Legion would go to Centreville, where the main body of the Confederate army defended the primary road that led from Washington to the rebel capital. It had been on that road, three months before at Manassas, that the Faulconer Legion had helped bloody the nose of the North's first invasion. Now, if rumors spoke true, the Legion might be required to do the work all over again.

"But it won't be the same." Truslow picked up the unspoken thought. "I hear there's nothing but earthworks at Centreville now. So if the Yankees come, we'll cut the bastards down from behind good thick walls." He stopped, seeing that Starbuck had fallen asleep, mouth open, coffee spilt. "Son of a bitch," Truslow growled, but with affection, for Starbuck, for all his preacher's-son caterwauling, had

21

proved himself a remarkable officer. He had made K Company into the best in the Legion, doing it by a mixture of unrelenting drill and imaginative training. It had been Starbuck who, denied the gunpowder and bullets needed to hone his men's marksmanship, had led a patrol across the river to capture a Union supply wagon on the road outside Poolesville. He had brought back three thousand cartridges that night, and a week later he had gone again and fetched back ten sacks of good northern coffee. Truslow, who knew soldiering, recognized that Starbuck had instinctive, natural gifts. He was a clever fighter, able to read an enemy's mind, and the men of K Company, boys mostly, seemed to recognize the quality. Starbuck, Truslow knew, was good.

A beat of wings made Truslow look up to see the black squat shape of an owl flit across the moon. Truslow supposed the bird had been hunting the open fields close to the town and was now returning to its roost in the thick stands of trees that grew above the river on Ball's Bluff.

A bugler mishit his note, took a breath, and startled the night with his call. Starbuck jerked awake, swore because his spilt coffee had soaked his trouser leg, then groaned with tiredness. It was still deep night, but the Legion had to be up and doing, ready to march away from their quiet watch on the river and go to war.

"Was that a bugle?" Lieutenant Wendell Holmes asked his pious Sergeant.

"Can't say, sir." The Sergeant was panting hard as he climbed Ball's Bluff and his new gray coat was hanging open to reveal its smart scarlet lining. The coats were a gift from the Governor of Massachusetts, who was determined that the Bay State's regiments would be among the best equipped in all the Federal army. "It was probably one of our buglers," the Sergeant guessed. "Maybe sending out skirmishers?"

Holmes assumed the Sergeant was right. The two men were laboring up the steep and twisting path that led to the bluff's summit where the 15th Massachusetts waited. The slope was about as steep as a man could climb without needing to use his hands, though in the dark many a man missed his footing and slid down to jar painfully against a tree trunk. The river below was still shrouded by mist in which the long shape of Harrison's Island showed dark. Men were crowded onto the island as they waited for the two small boats that were ferrying the troops across the last stretch of river. Lieutenant Holmes had been surprised at the speed of the river's current that had snatched at the boat and tried to sweep it away downstream toward distant Washington. The oarsmen had grunted with the effort of fighting the river, then rammed the small boat hard into the muddy bank.

Colonel Lee, the 20th Massachusetts's commanding officer, caught up with Holmes at the bluff's summit. "Almost sunrise," he said cheerfully. "All well, Wendell?"

"All well, sir. Except I'm hungry enough to eat a horse."

"We'll have breakfast in Leesburg," the Colonel said enthusiastically. "Ham, eggs, cornbread, and coffee. Some fresh southern butter! That'll be a treat. And no doubt all the townsfolk will be assuring us that they aren't rebels at all, but good loyal citizens of Uncle Sam." The Colonel abruptly turned away, startled by a sudden barking cry that echoed rhythmically and harshly among the trees on the bluff's summit. The heart-stopping noise had made the nearest soldiers whip round in quick alarm with rifles raised. "No need to worry!" the Colonel called. "It's just an owl." He had recognized the call of a barred owl and guessed the bird was coming home from a night's hunting with a belly

23

filled with mice and frogs. "You keep going, Wendell" – Lee turned back to Holmes – "down that path till you come to the left-flank company of the 15th. Stop there and wait for me."

Lieutenant Holmes led his company behind the crouching men of the 15th Massachusetts. He stopped at the moon-bright tree line. Before them now was a brief meadow that was dotted with the stark shadows of small bushes and locust trees, beyond which rose another dark stand of trees. It was about there on the previous night that the patrol had reported seeing an enemy encampment, and Holmes guessed that frightened men could easily have mistaken the pattern of moonlight and black shadow in the far woods for the shapes of tents.

"Forward!" Colonel Devens of the 15th Massachusetts shouted the order and his men moved out into the moon-whitened meadow. No one fired at them; no one challenged them. The South slept while the North, unhindered, marched.

The sun rose, glossing the river gold and lancing scarlet rays through the misted trees. Cocks crowed in Leesburg yards where pails were pumped full of water and cows came in for the day's first milking. Workshops that had been closed for the Lord's Day were unlocked and tools picked up from benches. Outside the town, in the encampments of the Confederate brigade that guarded the river, the smoke of cooking fires sifted into the fresh fall morning.

The Faulconer Legion's fires had already died, though the Legion was in no great hurry to abandon its encampment. The day promised to be fine and the march to Centreville comparatively short, and so the regiment's eight hundred men took their time in making ready, and Major Thaddeus Bird, the regiment's commanding officer, did not try to hurry them. Instead he wandered companionably among his men like an affable neighbor enjoying a morning stroll. "My God, Starbuck." Bird stopped in amazement at the sight of K Company's captain. "What happened to you?"

"I just slept badly, sir."

"You look like the walking dead!" Bird crowed with delight at the thought of Starbuck's discomfort. "Have I ever told you about Mordechai Moore? He was a plasterer in Faulconer Court House. Died one Thursday, widow bawling her eyes out, children squalling like scalded cats, funeral on Saturday, half the town dressed in black, grave dug, the Reverend Moss ready to bore us all with his customary inanities, then they hear scratching on the coffin lid. Open it up, and there he is! One very puzzled plasterer! As alive as you or I. Or me, anyway. But he looked like you. Very like you, Nate. He looked half decayed."

"Thank you very much," Starbuck said.

"Everyone went home," Bird went on with his tale. "Doc Billy gave Mordechai an examination. Declared him fit for another ten years and, blow me, didn't he go and die again the very next day. Only this time he was properly dead and they had to dig the grave all over again. Good morning, Sergeant."

"Major," Truslow grunted. Truslow had not been known to address any officer as "sir," not even Bird, the regiment's commanding officer, whom Truslow liked.

"You remember Mordechai Moore, surely, Truslow?"

"Hell yes. Son of a bitch couldn't plaster a wall to save his life. My father and I redid half the Cotton house for him. Never did get paid for it either."

"So no doubt the building trade's better off for having him dead," Bird said blithely. Pecker Bird was a tall, ragged, skeletal man who had been schoolmaster in the town of

Faulconer Court House when Colonel Washington Faulconer, Faulconer County's grandest landowner and Bird's brother-in-law, had established the Legion. Faulconer, wounded at Manassas, was now in Richmond, leaving Bird to command the regiment. The schoolmaster had probably been the least soldierly man in all Faulconer County, if not in all Virginia, and had only been appointed a major to appease his sister and take care of the Colonel's paperwork; yet, perversely, the ragged schoolmaster had proved an effective and popular officer. The men liked him, maybe because they sensed his great sympathy for all that was most fallible in humankind. Now Bird touched Starbuck's elbow. "A word?" he suggested, drawing the younger man away from K Company.

Starbuck walked with Bird into the open meadow that was scarred with the pale round shapes showing where the regiment's few tents had been pitched. Between the bleached circles were smaller scorched patches where the campfires had burned, and out beyond those scars were the large cropped circles marking where the officers' horses had grazed the grass out to the limit of their tethering ropes. The Legion could march away from this field, Starbuck reflected, yet for days afterward it would hold this evidence of their existence.

"Have you made a decision, Nate?" Bird asked. He was fond of Starbuck, and his voice reflected that affection. He offered the younger man a cheap, dark cigar, took one himself, then struck a match to light the tobacco.

"I'll stay with the regiment, sir," Starbuck said when his cigar was drawing.

"I hoped you'd say that," Bird said. "But even so." His voice trailed away. He drew on his cigar, staring toward Leesburg, over which a filmy haze of morning smoke shimmered. "Going to be a fine day," the Major said. A splutter

26

of distant rifle fire sounded, but neither Bird nor Starbuck took any notice. It was a rare morning that men were not out hunting.

"And we don't know that the Colonel really is taking over the Legion, do we, sir?" Starbuck asked.

"We know nothing," Bird said. "Soldiers, like children, live in a natural state of willful ignorance. But it's a risk."

"You're taking the same risk," Starbuck said pointedly.

"Your sister is not married to the Colonel," Bird answered just as pointedly, "which makes you, Nate, a great deal more vulnerable than I. Allow me to remind you, Nate, you did this world the signal service of murdering the Colonel's prospective son-in-law, and, while heaven and all its angels rejoiced at your act, I doubt that Faulconer has forgiven you yet."

"No, sir," Starbuck said tonelessly. He did not like being reminded of Ethan Ridley's death. Starbuck had killed Ridley under the cover of battle's confusion and he had told himself ever since that it had been an act of self-defense, yet he knew he had cradled murder in his heart when he had pulled the trigger, and he knew, too, that no amount of rationalizing could wipe that sin from the great ledger in heaven that recorded all his failings. Certainly Colonel Washington Faulconer would never forgive Starbuck. "Yet I'd still rather stay with the regiment," Starbuck now told Bird. He was a stranger in a strange land, a northerner fighting against the North, and the Faulconer Legion had become his new home. The Legion fed him, clothed him, and gave him intimate friends. It was also the place where he had discovered the job he did best and, with the yearning of youth to discern high purpose in life, Starbuck had made up his mind that he was destined to be one of the Legion's officers. He belonged.

"Good luck to us both, then," Bird said, and they would

27

both need luck, Bird reflected, if his suspicions were right and the order to march to Centreville was part of Colonel Washington Faulconer's attempt to take the Legion back under his control.

Washington Faulconer, after all, was the man who had raised the Faulconer Legion, named it for himself, kitted it with the finest equipment his fortune could buy, then led it to the fight on the banks of the Bull Run. Faulconer and his son, both wounded in that battle, had ridden back to Richmond to be hailed as heroes, though in truth Washington Faulconer had been nowhere near the Legion when it faced the overpowering Yankee attack. It was too late now to set the record straight: Virginia, indeed all the upper South, reckoned Faulconer a hero and was demanding that he be given command of a brigade, and if that happened, Bird knew, the hero would expect his own Legion to be at the heart of that brigade.

"But it isn't certain the son of a bitch will get his brigade, is it?" Starbuck asked, trying in vain to suppress a huge yawn.

"There's a rumor he'll be offered a diplomatic post instead," Bird said, "which would be much more suitable, because my brother-in-law has a natural taste for licking the backsides of princes and potentates, but our newspapers say he should be a general, and what the newspapers want, the politicians usually grant. It's easier than having ideas of their own, you see."

"I'll take the risk," Starbuck said. His alternative was to join General Nathan Evans's staff and stay in the camp near Leesburg where Evans had command of the patchwork Confederate brigade that guarded the riverbank. Starbuck liked Evans, but he much preferred to stay with the Legion. The Legion was home, and he could not really imagine that the Confederate high command would make Washington Faulconer a general.

Another flurry of rifle fire sounded from the woods that lay three miles to the northwest. The sound made Bird turn, frowning. "Someone's being mighty energetic." He sounded disapproving.

"Squabbling pickets?" Starbuck suggested. For the last three months the sentries had faced each other across the river, and while relations had been friendly for most of that time, every now and then a new and energetic officer tried to provoke a war.

"Probably just pickets," Pecker Bird agreed, then turned back as Sergeant Major Proctor came to report that a broken wagon axle that had been delaying the Legion's march was now mended. "Does that mean we're ready to go, Sergeant Major?" Bird asked.

"Ready as we'll ever be, I reckon." Proctor was a lugubrious and suspicious man, forever fearing disaster.

"Then let us be off! Let us be off!" Bird said happily, and he strode toward the Legion just as another volley of shots sounded, only this time the fire had not come from the distant woods, but from the road to the east. Bird clawed thin fingers through his long, straggly beard. "Do you think?" he asked of no one in particular, not bothering to articulate the question clearly. "Maybe?" Bird went on with a note of growing excitement, and then another splinter of musketry echoed from the bluffs to the northwest and Bird jerked his head back and forth, which was his habitual gesture when he was amused. "I think we shall wait awhile, Mr. Proctor. We shall wait!" Bird snapped his fingers. "It seems," he said, "that God and Mr. Lincoln might have sent us other employment today. We shall wait."

The advancing Massachusetts troops discovered the rebels by blundering into a four-man picket that was huddled in a

29

draw of the lower woods. The startled rebels fired first, sending the Massachusetts men tumbling back through the trees. The rebel picket fled in the opposite direction to find their company commander, Captain Duff, who first sent a message to General Evans and then led the forty men of his company toward the woods on the bluff's summit where a scatter of Yankee skirmishers now showed at the tree line. More northerners began to appear, so many that Duff lost count. "There are enough of the sumbitches," one of his men commented as Captain Duff lined his men behind a snake fence and told them to fire away. Puffs of smoke studded the fence line as the bullets whistled away up the gentle slope. Two miles behind Duff the town of Leesburg heard the firing, and someone thought to run to the church and ring the bell to summon the militia.

Not that the militia could assemble in time to help Captain Duff, who was beginning to understand just how badly his Mississippians were outnumbered. He was forced to retreat down the slope when a company of northern troops threatened his left flank, which withdrawal was greeted by northern jeers and a volley of musket fire. Duff's forty men went on doggedly firing as they backed away. They were a ragged company dressed in a shabby mix of butternut-brown and dirty gray uniforms, but their marksmanship was far superior to that of their northern rivals, who were mostly armed with smoothbore muskets. Massachusetts had taken immense pains to equip its volunteers, but there had not been enough rifles for everybody, and so Colonel Devens's 15th Massachusetts regiment fought with eighteenth-century muskets. None of Duff's men was hit, but their own bullets were taking a slow, steady toll of the northern skirmishers.

The 20th Massachusetts came to the rescue of their fellow Bay Staters. The 20th all had rifles, and their more

30

accurate fire forced Duff to retreat still farther down the long slope. His forty men backed over a rail fence into a field of stubble where stooked oats stood in shocks. There was no more cover for a half mile, and Duff did not want to yield too much ground to the Yankees, so he halted his men in the middle of the field and told them to hold the bastards off. Duff's men were horribly outnumbered, but they came from Pike and Chickasaw counties, and Duff reckoned that made them as good as any soldiers in America. "Guess we're going to have to give this pack of black-assed trash a lesson, boys," Duff said.

"No, Captain! They're rebs! Look!" one of his men shouted in warning, then pointed to the tree line where a company of gray-clad troops had just appeared. Duff stared in horror. Had he been firing at his own side? The advancing men wore long gray coats. The officer leading them had his coat open and was carrying a drawn sword that he used to slash at weeds as he advanced, just as though he were out for a casual stroll in the country.

Duff felt his belligerent certainties drain away. He was dry-mouthed, his belly was sour, and a muscle in his thigh kept twitching. The firing all across the slope had died away as the gray-coated company marched down toward the oat field. Duff held up his hand and shouted at the strangers, "Halt!"

"Friends!" one of the gray-coated men called back. There were sixty or seventy men in the company, and their rifles were tipped with long shining bayonets.

"Halt!" Duff tried again.

"We're friends!" a man shouted back. Duff could see the nervousness on their faces. One man had a twitching muscle in his cheek, while another kept looking sideways at a mustachioed sergeant who marched stolidly at the flank of the advancing company.

31

"Halt!" Duff shouted again. One of his men spat onto the stubble.

"We're friends!" the northerners shouted again. Their officer's open coat was lined with scarlet, but Duff could not see the color of the man's uniform because the sun was behind the strangers.

"They ain't no friends of ours, Cap'n!" one of Duff's men said. Duff wished he could feel the same certainty. God in His heaven, but suppose these men were friends? Was he about to commit murder? "I order you to halt!" he shouted, but the advancing men would not obey, and so Duff shouted at his men to take aim.

Forty rifles came up into forty shoulders.

"Friends!" a northern voice called. The two units were fifty yards apart now, and Duff could hear the northern boots breaking and scuffing the oat stubble.

"They ain't friends, Cap'n!" one of the Mississippians insisted, and just at that moment the advancing officer stumbled and Duff got a clear view of the uniform beneath the scarlet-lined gray coat. The uniform was blue.

"Fire!" Duff shouted, and the southern volley cracked like a canebreak burning and a northerner screamed as the rebel bullets slapped home.

"Fire!" a northerner shouted and the Massachusetts's bullets whipped back through the smoke bank.

"Keep firing!" Duff shouted and emptied his revolver into the haze of powder smoke that already obscured the field. His men had taken cover behind the shocks of oats and were steadily reloading. The northerners were doing the same, except for one man who was twitching and bleeding on the ground. There were more Yankees off to Duff's right, higher up the slope, but he could not worry about them. He had chosen to make his stand here, plumb in the middle of the field, and now he would have to fight these bastards till one side could stand no more.

Six miles away, at Edwards Ferry, more northerners had crossed the Potomac and cut the turnpike that led to Centreville. Nathan Evans, thus caught between the two invading forces, refused to show any undue alarm. "One might be trying to fool me while the other one gets ready to rape me, ain't that how it's done, Boston?" "Boston" was his nickname for Starbuck. They had met at Manassas where Evans had saved the Confederacy by holding up the northern attack while the rebel lines reformed. "Lying, thieving, black-assed, hymn-singing bastards," Evans said now, evidently of the whole northern army. He had ridden with an order for the Faulconer Legion to stay where it was, only to discover that Thaddeus Bird had anticipated him by canceling the Legion's departure. Now Evans cocked his ear to the wind and tried to gauge from the intensity of the rifle fire which enemy incursion offered the most danger. The church bell in Leesburg was still ringing, summoning the militia. "So you're not going to stay with me, Boston?" Evans remarked.

"I like being a company officer, sir."

Evans growled in response, though Starbuck was not at all sure the small, foulmouthed South Carolinian had heard his answer. Instead Evans was switching his attention back and forth between the competing sounds of the two northern incursions. Otto, his German orderly, whose main duty consisted of carrying a barrel of whiskey for the General's refreshment, also listened to the gunfire so that the two men's heads twitched back and forth in unison. Evans was the first to stop, clicking his fingers for a drop of whiskey instead. He drained the tin mug, then looked back at Bird. "You'll stay here, Pecker. You're my reserve. I don't reckon there's so many of the bastards, they're not making enough noise for that, so we might as well stay put and see if we

33

can't give the bastards a bloody nose. Killing Yankees is as good a way to start the week as any, eh?" He laughed. "Of course, if I'm wrong we'll all be stone dead by nightfall. Come on. Otto!" Evans put spurs to his horse and galloped back toward the earth-walled fort that was his headquarters.

Starbuck climbed onto a wagon loaded with folded tents and slept as the sun burned the mist off the river and dried the dew off the fields. More northern troops crossed the river and climbed the bluff to mass under the trees. General Stone, the commander of the Federal forces guarding the Potomac, had decided to commit more troops to the crossing and sent orders that the invaders should not just occupy Leesburg but reconnoiter the whole of Loudoun County. If the rebels had gone, Stone commanded, then the Yankees should occupy the area, but if a strong Confederate force opposed the reconnaissance, then the Federal forces were free to withdraw across the river with whatever foodstuffs they might confiscate. Stone dispatched artillery to add firepower to the invading force, but also made plain that he was leaving the decision whether to stay in Virginia to the man he now placed in command of the whole northern operation.

That man was Colonel Ned Baker, a tall, clean-shaven, silver-haired, golden-tongued politician. Baker was a California lawyer, a United States senator from Oregon and one of President Lincoln's closest friends, so close that Lincoln had named his second son after the Senator. Baker was an impetuous, emotional, warmhearted man, and his arrival at the river crossing sent ripples of excitement through those men of the 15th Massachusetts who still waited with the New York Tammany Regiment on the Maryland bank. Baker's own regiment, the 1st Californian, now joined the invasion. The regiment was from New York,

34

but had been recruited from men who had ties to California, and with them came a fourteen-pounder rifled cannon from Rhode Island and a pair of howitzers manned by U.S. Army regulars. "Take everything across!" Baker shouted ebulliently. "Every last man and gun!"

"We'll need more boats," the Colonel of the Tammanys cautioned the Senator.

"Then find them! Build them! Steal them! Fetch gopher wood and build an ark, Colonel. Find a beautiful woman and let her face launch a thousand ships, but let us press on to glory, boys!" Baker strode down the bank, cocking his ear to the staccato crackle of musketry that sounded from the river's far shore. "Rebels are dying, lads! Let's go and kill some more!"

The Tammany Colonel attempted to ask the Senator just what his regiment was supposed to do when it reached the Virginia shore, but Baker brushed the question aside. He did not care if this was a mere raid or a historic invasion marking the beginning of Virginia's occupation, he only knew that he had three pieces of artillery and four regiments of prime, unblooded troops, which gave him the necessary power to offer President Lincoln and the country the victory they so badly needed. "On to Richmond, boys!" Baker shouted as he pushed through the troops on the riverbank. "On to Richmond, and may the devil have no mercy on their souls! On for the union, boys, on for the union! Let's hear you cheer!"

They cheered loud enough to obliterate the splintering sound of musketry that came from the river's far bank where, beyond the wooded bluff, powder smoke lingered among the stooked oats where the day's long dying had begun.

MAJOR ADAM FAULCONER arrived at the Faulconer Legion a few moments after midday. "There are Yankees on the turnpike. They gave me a chase!" He looked happy, as though the hard riding of the last few minutes had been a cross-country romp rather than a desperate flight from a determined enemy. His horse, a fine roan stallion from the Faulconer Stud, was flecked with white foam, its ears were pricked nervously back, and it kept taking small nervous sidesteps that Adam instinctively corrected. "Uncle!" he greeted Major Bird cheerfully, then turned immediately back to Starbuck. They had been friends for three years, but it had been weeks since they had met, and Adam's pleasure at their reunion was heartfelt. "You look as if you were fast asleep, Nate."

"He was at a prayer meeting late last night," Sergeant Truslow interjected in a voice that was deliberately sour so that no one but he and Starbuck would know he made a joke, "praying till three in the morning."

"Good for you, Nate," Adam said warmly, then turned his horse back toward Thaddeus Bird. "Did you hear what I said, Uncle? There are Yankees on the turnpike!"

"We heard they were there," Bird said casually, as though errant Yankees were as predictable a feature of the fall landscape as migrating wild fowl.

"The wretches fired at me." Adam sounded astonished that such a discourtesy might occur in wartime. "But we

36

outran them, didn't we, boy?" He patted the neck of his sweating horse, then swung down from the saddle and tossed the reins to Robert Decker, who was one of Starbuck's company. "Walk him for a while, will you, Robert?"

"Pleased to, Mr. Adam."

"And don't let him drink yet. Not till he's cooled," Adam instructed Decker, then he explained to his uncle that he had ridden from Centreville at dawn, expecting to encounter the Legion on the road. "I couldn't find you, so I just kept going," Adam said cheerfully. He walked with a very slight limp, the result of a bullet he had taken at the battle at Manassas, but the wound was well-healed and the limp hardly noticeable. Adam, unlike his father, Washington Faulconer, had been in the very thick of the Manassas fight even though, for weeks before, he had been assailed by equivocation about the war's morality and had even doubted whether he could take part in the hostilities at all. After the battle, while he was convalescing in Richmond, Adam had been promoted to major and given a post on General Joseph Johnston's staff. The General was one of the many Confederates who was under the misapprehension that Washington Faulconer had helped stem the surprise northern attack at Manassas, and the son's promotion and staff appointment had been intended as a mark of gratitude to the father.

"You've brought us orders?" Bird now asked Adam.

"Just my good self, Uncle. It seemed too perfect a day to be stuck with Johnston's paperwork, so I came for a ride. Though I hardly expected this." Adam turned and listened to the sound of rifle fire that came from the far woods. The gunfire was fairly constant now, but it was nothing like the splintering crackle of battle. Instead it was a methodical, workmanlike sound that suggested the two sides were

37

merely trading ammunition because it was expected of them rather than trying to inflict slaughter upon each other. "What's happening?" Adam demanded.

Major Thaddeus Bird explained that two groups of Yankees had crossed the river. Adam had already encountered one of the invading parties, while the other was up on the high ground by Harrison's Island. No one was quite sure what the Yankees intended by the double incursion. Early on it had seemed they were trying to capture Leesburg, but a single company of Mississippi men had turned back the Federal advance. "A man called Duff," Bird told Adam, "stopped the rascals cold. Lined his fellows up in the stark middle of a field and traded them shot for shot, and damn me if they didn't go scuttling back uphill like a flock of frightened sheep!" The story of Duff's defiance had spread through Evans's brigade to fill the men with pride in southern invincibility. The remainder of Duff's battalion was in place now, keeping the Yankees pinned among the trees at the bluff's summit. "You should tell Johnston about Duff," Bird told Adam.

But Adam did not seem interested in the Mississippian's heroism. "And you, Uncle, what are you doing?" he asked instead.

"Waiting for orders, of course. I guess Evans doesn't know where to send us, so he's waiting to see which pack of Yankees is the more dangerous. Once that's determined, we'll go and knock some heads bloody."

Adam flinched at his uncle's tone. Before he had joined the Legion and unexpectedly became its senior officer, Thaddeus Bird had been a schoolmaster who had professed a sardonic mockery of both soldiering and warfare, but one battle and a few months of command had turned Adam's uncle into an altogether grimmer man. He retained his wit, but now it had a harsher edge, a symptom, Adam thought, of how war changed everything for the worse, though Adam sometimes wondered if he alone was aware of just how the war was coarsening and degrading all it touched. His fellow aides at the army headquarters reveled in the conflict, seeing it as a sporting rivalry that would award victory to the most enthusiastic players. Adam listened to such bombast and held his peace, knowing that any expression of his real views would be met with scorn at best and charges of chickenhearted cowardice at worst. Yet Adam was no coward. He simply believed the war was a tragedy born from pride and stupidity, and so he did his duty, hid his true feelings, and yearned for peace, though how long he could sustain either the pretense or the duplicity, he did not know. "Let's hope no one's head needs to be bloodied today," he told his uncle. "It's much too fine a day for killing." He turned as K Company's cooks lifted a pot off the flames. "Is that dinner?"

The midday dinner was cush: a stew of beef, bacon fat, and cornbread that was accompanied by a mash of boiled apples and potatoes. Food was plentiful here in Loudoun County where the farmland was rich and Confederate troops few. In Centreville and Manassas, Adam said, supplies were much more difficult. "They even ran out of coffee last month! I thought there'd be a mutiny." He then listened with pretended amusement as Robert Decker and Amos Tunney told of Captain Starbuck's great coffee raid. They had crossed the river by night and marched five miles through woods and farmland to raid a sutler's stores on the outskirts of a northern camp. Eight men had gone with Starbuck and eight had come back, and the only northerner to detect them had been the sutler himself, a merchant whose living came from selling luxuries to troops. The sutler, sleeping among his stores, had shouted the alarm and pulled a revolver.

39

"Poor man," Adam said.

"Poor man?" Starbuck protested his friend's display of pity. "He was trying to shoot us!"

"So what did you do?"

"Cut his throat," Starbuck said. "Didn't want to alert the camp, you see, by firing a shot."

Adam shuddered. "You killed a man for some coffee beans?"

"And some whiskey and dried peaches," Robert Decker put in enthusiastically. "The newspapers over there reckoned it was secesh sympathizers. Bushwhackers, they called us. Bushwhackers! Us!"

"And next day we sold ten pounds of the coffee back to some Yankee pickets across the river!" Amos Tunney added proudly.

Adam smiled thinly, then refused the offer of a mug of coffee, pleading that he preferred plain water. He was sitting on the ground and winced slightly as he shifted his weight onto his wounded leg. He had his father's broad face, square-cut fair beard, and blue eyes. It was a face, Starbuck had always thought, of uncomplicated honesty, though these days it seemed Adam had lost his old humor and replaced it with a perpetual care for the world's problems.

After the meal the two friends walked eastward along the edge of the meadow. The Legion's wood and sod shelters were still in place, looking like grass-covered pigpens. Starbuck, pretending to listen to his friend's tales of headquarters life, was actually thinking how much he had enjoyed living in his turf-covered shelter. Once abed he felt like a beast in a burrow: safe, hidden, and secret. His old bedroom in Boston with its oak paneling and wide pine boards and gas mantels and solemn bookshelves seemed like a dream now, something from a different

40

life. "It's odd how I like being uncomfortable," he said lightly.

"Didn't you hear what I said?" Adam demanded.

"Sorry, dreaming."

"I was talking about McClellan," Adam said. "Everyone agrees he's a genius. Even Johnston says McClellan was quite the cleverest man in all the old U.S. Army." Adam spoke enthusiastically, as though McClellan were the new southern commander and not the leader of the north's Army of the Potomac. Adam glanced to his right, disturbed by a sudden crescendo in the sound of musketry coming from the woods above the distant river. The firing had been desultory in the last hour, but now it rose to a sustained crackle that sounded like dry tinder burning fierce. It raged for a half minute or so, then fell back to a steady and almost monotonous mutter. "They must cross back to Maryland soon!" Adam said angrily, as though he were offended by the stubbornness of the Yankees in staying on this side of the river.

"So tell me more about McClellan," Starbuck said.

"He's the coming man," Adam said in a spirited voice. "It happens in war, you know. The old fellows begin the fight, then they get winnowed out by the young ones with new ideas. They say McClellan's the new Napoleon, Nate, a stickler for order and discipline!" Adam paused, evidently worried that he maybe sounded too enamored of the enemy's new general. "Did you really cut a man's throat for coffee?" he asked awkwardly.

"It wasn't quite as cold-blooded as Decker makes it sound," Starbuck said. "I tried to keep the man quiet without hurting him. I didn't want to kill him." In truth he had been scared to death of the moment, shaking and panicked, but he had known that the safety of his men had depended on keeping the sutler silent.

Adam grimaced. "I can't imagine killing a man with a knife."

"It's not something I ever imagined myself doing," Starbuck confessed, "but Truslow made me practice on some ration hogs, and it isn't as hard as you'd think."

"Good God," Adam said faintly. "Hogs?"

"Only young ones," Starbuck said. "Incredibly hard to kill, even so. Truslow makes it look easy, but then he makes everything look easy."

Adam pondered the idea of practicing the skills of killing as though they were the rudiments of a trade. It seemed tragic. "Couldn't you have just stunned the poor man?" he asked.

Starbuck laughed at the question. "I had to make sure of the fellow, didn't I? Of course I had to! My men's lives depended on his silence, and you look after your men. That's the first rule of soldiering."

"Did Truslow teach you that too?" Adam asked.

"No." Starbuck sounded surprised at the question. "That's an obvious rule, isn't it?"

Adam said nothing. Instead he was thinking, not for the first time, just how unlike each other he and Starbuck were. They had met at Harvard, where they had seemed to recognize in each other the qualities each knew he lacked in himself. Starbuck was impetuous and mercurial, while Adam was thoughtful and painstaking; Starbuck was a slave to his feelings, while Adam tried desperately hard to obey the harsh dictates of a rigorous conscience. Yet out of those dissimilarities had grown a friendship that had endured even the strains that had followed the battle at Manassas. Adam's father had turned against Starbuck at Manassas, and Starbuck now raised that delicate subject by asking whether Adam thought his father would be given command of a brigade.

42

"Joe would like him to get a brigade," Adam said dubiously. "Joe" was Joseph Johnston, the commander of the Confederate armies in Virginia. "But the President doesn't listen to Joe much." Adam went on, "He likes Granny Lee's opinion better." General Robert Lee had started the war with an inflated reputation, but had earned the nickname "Granny" after an unsuccessful minor campaign in western Virginia.

"And Lee doesn't want your father promoted?" Starbuck asked.

"So I'm told," Adam said. "Lee evidently believes Father should go as a commissioner to England" – Adam smiled at the notion – "which Mother thinks is a dandy idea. I think even her illnesses would disappear if she could take tea with the Queen."

"But your father wants his brigade?"

Adam nodded. "And he wants the Legion back," he said, knowing exactly why his friend had raised the subject. "And if he gets it, Nate, then he'll demand your resignation. I guess he's still convinced you shot Ethan." Adam was referring to the death of the man who would have married Adam's sister.

"Ethan was killed by a shell," Starbuck insisted.

"Father won't believe that," Adam said sadly, "and he won't be persuaded of it either."

"Then I'd better hope your father goes to England and takes tea with the Queen," Starbuck said carelessly.

"Because you're really going to stay with the Legion?" Adam asked, sounding surprised.

"I like it here. They like me." Starbuck spoke lightly, disguising the fervid nature of his attachment to the Legion.

Adam walked a few paces in silence while the gunfire splintered remote and distant like a skirmish in someone else's war. "Your brother," Adam said suddenly, then paused

43

as though he suspected he was trespassing on a difficult area. "Your brother," he started again, "is still hoping you'll go back north."

"My brother?" Starbuck could not hide his surprise. His elder brother, James, had been captured at Manassas and was now a prisoner in Richmond. Starbuck had sent James gifts of books, but he had not asked for any furlough to visit his brother. He would have found any confrontation with his family too difficult. "You've seen him?"

"Only as part of my duties," Adam said, and explained that one of his responsibilities was to match lists of captured officers who were to be exchanged between the North and the South. "I sometimes visit the prison in Richmond," Adam went on, "and saw James there last week."

"How is he?"

"Thin, very pale, but hoping to be released on exchange."

"Poor James." Starbuck could not imagine his worried and pedantic brother as a soldier. James was a very good lawyer, but had always hated uncertainty and adventure, which were the very things that compensated for the dangerous discomforts of soldiering.

"He worries about you," Adam said.

"I worry about him," Starbuck said lightly, hoping to deflect what he suspected was an imminent sermon from his friend.

"He'll certainly be pleased to hear you're attending prayer meetings," Adam said fervently. "He worries for your faith. Do you go to church every week?"

"Whenever I can," Starbuck said, then decided this was a subject best changed. "And you?" he asked Adam. "How are you?"

Adam smiled, but did not answer at once. Instead he blushed, then laughed. He was clearly full of some piece of

44

news that he was too embarrassed to tell outright, but nevertheless wanted prised out of him. "I'm really fine," he said, leaving the opening dangling.

Starbuck caught the inflection exactly. "You're in love."

Adam nodded. "I really think I might be, yes." He sounded surprised at himself. "Yes. Really."

Adam's coyness filled Starbuck with affectionate amusement. "You're getting married?"

"I think so, yes. We think so, indeed, but not yet. We thought we should wait for the war's end." Adam still blushed, but suddenly he laughed, hugely pleased with himself, and unbuttoned a tunic pocket as though to take out a picture of his beloved. "You haven't even asked what her name is."

"Tell me her name," Starbuck demanded dutifully, then turned away because the sound of rifle fire had swollen again to a frantic intensity. A slight haze of powder smoke was showing above the trees now, a gauzy flag of battle that would thicken into a dense fog if the guns kept up their present rate of fire.

"She's called . . . " Adam began, then checked because hooves thumped loud on the turf behind him.

"Sir! Mr. Starbuck, sir!" a voice hailed, and Starbuck turned to see young Robert Decker galloping across the field on the back of Adam's stallion. "Sir!" He was waving excitedly to Starbuck. "We've got orders, sir! We've got orders! We're to go and fight them, sir!"

"Thank God," Starbuck said, and started running back to his company.

"Her name's Julia," Adam said to no one, frowning at his friend's back. "Her name's Julia."

"Sir?" Robert Decker asked, puzzled. He had slid out of the saddle and now offered the stallion's reins to Adam.

"Nothing, Robert." Adam took the reins. "Nothing at

45

all. Go and join the company." He watched Nate shouting at K Company, seeing the excitement of men stirred from repose by the prospect of killing. Then he buttoned his pocket to secure the leather-cased photograph of his girl before climbing into the saddle and riding to join his father's Legion. Which was about to fight its second battle.

On the quiet banks of the Potomac.

The two Yankee river crossings were five miles apart and General Nathan Evans had been trying to decide which offered his brigade the greater danger. The crossing to the east had cut the turnpike and so appeared to be the bigger tactical threat because it severed his communications with Johnston's headquarters at Centreville, but the Yankees were not reinforcing the handful of men and guns they had thrown over the river there, while more and more reports spoke of infantry reinforcements crossing the river at Harrison's Island and then climbing the precipitous slope to the wooded summit of Ball's Bluff. It was there, Evans decided, that the enemy was concentrating its threat, and it was there that he now sent the rest of his Mississippians and his two Virginia regiments. He sent the 8th Virginians to the near side of Ball's Bluff, but ordered Bird to make for the farther western flank. "Go through the town," Evans told Bird, "and come up on the left of the Mississippi boys. Then get rid of the Yankee bastards."

"With pleasure, sir." Bird turned away and shouted his orders. The men's packs and blanket rolls were to be left with a small baggage guard, while every one else in the Legion was to march west with a rifle, sixty rounds of ammunition, and whatever other weapons they chose to carry. In the summer, when they had first marched to war, the men had been weighed down with knapsacks and haversacks, canteens and cartridge boxes, blankets and groundsheets, bowie knives and revolvers, bayonets and rifles, plus whatever other accoutrements a man's family might have sent to keep him safe, warm, or dry. Some men had carried buffalo robes, while one or two had even worn metal breastplates designed to protect them from Yankee bullets, but now few men carried anything more than a rifle and bayonet, a canteen, a haversack, and a groundsheet and blanket rolled into a tube that was worn slantwise around their chests. Everything else was just impediment. Most had discarded their pasteboard-stiffened caps, preferring slouch hats that protected the backs of their necks from the sun. Their tall stiff boots had been cut down into shoes, the fine twin rows of brass buttons on their long jackets had been chopped away and used as payment for apple juice or sweet milk from the farms of Loudoun County, while many of the skirts of the long coats had been cut away to provide material to patch breeches or elbows. Back in June, when the Legion had trained at Faulconer Court House, the regiment had looked as smart and well-equipped as any soldiers in the world, but now, after just one battle and three months' picket duty along the frontier, they looked like ragamuffins, but they were all far better soldiers. They were lean, tanned, fit, and very dangerous. "They still have their illusions, you see," Thaddeus Bird explained to his nephew. Adam was riding his fine roan horse while Major Bird, as ever, walked.

"Illusions?"

"We think we're invincible because we're young. Not me, you understand, but the boys. I used to make it my business to educate the more stupid fallacies out of youth; now I try to preserve their nonsense." Bird raised his voice so that the nearest company could hear him. "You'll live forever, you rogues, as long as you remember one thing! Which is?"

There was a pause, then a handful of men returned a ragged answer. "Aim low."

"Louder!"

"Aim low!" This time the whole company roared back the answer, then began laughing, and Bird beamed on them like a schoolmaster proud of his pupils' achievements.

The Legion marched through the dusty main street of Leesburg where one small crowd of men was gathered outside the Loudoun County Court House and another, slightly larger, outside Makepeace's Tavern across the street. "Give us guns!" one man shouted. It appeared they were the county militia and had neither weapons nor ammunition, though a handful of men, privately equipped, had gone to the battlefield anyway. Some of the men fell in with the Legion, hoping to find a discarded weapon on the field. "What's happening, Colonel?" they asked Adam, mistaking the scarlet trim and gold stars on his fine uniform as evidence that he commanded the regiment.

"It's nothing to be excited about," Adam insisted. "Nothing but a few stray northerners."

"Making enough noise, ain't they?" a woman called, and the Yankees were indeed much noisier now that Senator Baker had succeeded in getting his three guns across the river and up the steep, slippery path to the bluff's peak, where the gunners had cleared their weapons' throats with three blasts of canister that had rattled into the trees to shred the leaves.

Baker, taking command of the battle, had found his troops sadly scattered. The 20th Massachusetts was posted in the woods at the summit while the 15th had pushed across the ragged meadow, through the far woods and into the open slopes overlooking Leesburg. Baker called the 15th back, insisting that they form a battle line on the left of the 20th. "We'll form up here," he announced, "while

New York and California join us!" He drew his sword and whipped the engraved blade to slash off a nettle's head. The rebel bullets slashed overhead, occasionally clipping off shreds of leaf that fluttered down in the warm, balmy air. The bullets seemed to whistle in the woods, and somehow that odd noise took away their danger. The Senator, who had fought as a volunteer in the Mexican War, felt no apprehension; indeed he felt the exhilaration of a man touched by the opportunity for greatness. This would be his day! He turned as Colonel Milton Cogswell, commander of the Tammany Regiment, panted up to the bluff's summit. "'One blast upon your bugle horn is worth a thousand men!'" Baker greeted the sweating Colonel with a jocular quotation.

"I'll take the goddamn men, sir, begging your pardon," Cogswell said sourly, then flinched as a pair of bullets slapped through the leaves above his head. "What are our intentions, sir?"

"Our intentions, Milton? Our intentions are victory, fame, glory, peace, forgiveness of our enemies, reconciliation, magnanimity, prosperity, happiness, and the assured promise of heaven's reward."

"Then might I suggest, sir," Cogswell said, trying to sober the ebullient Senator, "that we advance and occupy that stand of trees?" He gestured at the woods beyond the patch of ragged meadowland. By pulling the 20th Massachusetts out of those woods Baker had effectively yielded the trees to the rebels, and already the first gray-coated infantry were well-established among the undergrowth.

"Those rogues won't bother us," Baker said dismissively. "Our artillerymen will soon scour them loose. We'll only be here a moment or two, just long enough to assemble, and then we'll advance. On to glory!"

A bullet whipsawed close above both men, causing

Cogswell to curse in angry astonishment. His anger arose not from the near miss, but because the shot had come from a high knoll on the eastern end of the bluffs. The knoll was the highest part of the bluff and dominated the trees where the northern troops were gathering. "Aren't we occupying that height?" Cogswell asked Baker in horror.

"No need! No need! We'll be advancing soon! On to victory!" Baker strolled away, blithe in his self-assurance. Tucked inside the sweatband of his hat, where he had once stuffed his legal notes before going into court, he had pushed the orders he had received from General Stone. "Colonel," the order read in a hurried scribble, "in case of heavy firing in front of Harrison's Island, you will advance the California regiment of your brigade or retire the regiments under Colonels Lee and Devens upon the Virginia side of the river, at your discretion, assuming command on arrival." All of which, in Baker's view, meant very little, except that he was in command, the day was sunny, the enemy lay before him, and martial fame was in his grasp. "'One blast upon your bugle horn,'" the Senator chanted the lines from Sir Walter Scott as he marched through the northern troops gathering under the trees, "'were worth a thousand men!' Fire back, lads! Let the rascals know we're here! Fire away, boys! Give them fire! Let them know the North is here to fight!"

Lieutenant Wendell Holmes took off his gray greatcoat, folded it carefully, then placed it beneath a tree. He drew his revolver, checked that its percussion caps were properly in place over the cones, then fired at the far, shadowy shapes of the rebels. The Senator's fine voice still echoed through the woods, punctuated by the crack and cough of Holmes's revolver. "'Hail to the chief,'" Holmes quietly spoke the line from the same poem Baker was declaiming, "'who in triumph advances.'"

Senator Baker pulled out an expensive watch that had been a gift from his associates and friends of the California bar on the occasion of his appointment to the U.S. Senate. The day was hurrying by, and if he wanted to capture and consolidate Leesburg before nightfall he would need to hurry. "Forward now!" Baker pushed the watch back into his fob pocket. "All of you! All of you! On, my fine boys, on! On to Richmond! On to glory! All for the union, boys, all for the union!"

The colors were lifted, the glorious Stars and Stripes, and beside them the white silk colors of Massachusetts with the arms of the Commonwealth embroidered on one flank and the motto *Fide et Constantia* stitched bright on the other. The silk streamed in the sunlight as the men cheered, broke cover, and charged.

To die.

"Fire!" Two whole regiments of Mississippi men were in the trees now, and their rifles whipped flames across the clearing to where the northerners had suddenly appeared. Bullets splintered the locust trees and shredded the bright yellow leaves of the maples. A dozen northerners went down in the volley. One, a man who had never sworn in his life, began cursing. A Boston furniture maker stared astonished at the blood spreading on his uniform, then called for his mother as he tried to crawl back to cover.

"Fire!" Colonel Eps of the 8th Virginia had the high ground that dominated the Yankees' eastern flank and his riflemen poured a slaughtering fusillade down onto the northerners. So many bullets whined and sang off the bronze barrels of the Yankee howitzers that the gunners fled down the precipice of the bluff to where they were safe from the hornets' whine and hissing slash of the rebel bullets.

"Fire!" More Mississippians opened fire. They lay flat

51

among the trees, or knelt behind trunks and peered through the powder smoke to see that their volleys had sent the northern attack reeling back. Scattered among the Mississippians were men from Leesburg and from the surrounding farms who fired fowling pieces and shotguns at the faltering Yankees. A New York sergeant cursed at his men in Gaelic, but the curses did no good and a bullet shattered his elbow. The northerners were retreating back into the trees, seeking shelter behind trunks and fallen logs where they reloaded their muskets and rifles. Two of the Massachusetts companies had been recruited from German immigrants, and their officers shouted in that language, exhorting them to show the world how Germans could fight. Other northern officers feigned indifference to the storr. of bullets that whipped and hissed across the bluff's crest. They strolled among the trees, knowing that a display of insouciant bravery was the quality necessary for rank. They paid for the display with blood. Many of the men from the 20th Massachusetts had hung their fine new scarlet-lined coats from branches and the garments twitched as the bullets plucked and tore at the rich gray cloth. The sound of the battle was constant now, like calico tearing or a canebreak burning, but under that splintering crackle came the sobbing of wounded men and the screams of hurt men and the rattle of dying men.

Senator Baker shouted at his staff officers to man one of the abandoned howitzers, but none of them knew how to prime a vent and the hail of Virginia bullets drove the officers back into the shadows. They left a major dead and a lieutenant coughing up blood as he staggered back from the gun. A bullet slashed a shard of wood from a howitzer's wheel spoke, another smacked on the muzzle's face, and a third punctured the water bucket.

A group of Mississippi men, enraged because their

Colonel had been shot, tried to charge across the patch of rough meadowland, but as soon as they showed themselves at the tree line the frustrated northerners poured fire at them. It was the rebels' turn to pull back, leaving three men dead and two wounded. At the right flank of the Massachusetts line the fourteen-pound cannon was still firing, but the Rhode Island gunners had used up their small stock of canister and now had nothing to fire but solid iron bolts. The canister, tearing itself apart at the cannon's muzzle to scatter a lethal spray of musket balls into the enemy ranks, was ideal for close-range killing work, but the solid bolts were intended for long-range accurate fire and were no good for scouring infantry out of woodland. The bolts, which were elongated iron cannonballs, screamed across the clearing and either vanished into the distance or else struck slivers of freshly splintered timber from tree trunks. The smoke from the cannon pumped its foul-smelling cloud twenty yards in front of the muzzle, forging a smokescreen that hid the right flank companies of the 20th Massachusetts. "Come on, Harvard!" an officer shouted. At least two-thirds of the regiment's officers had come from Harvard, as had six of its sergeants and dozens of its men. "Come on, Harvard!" the officer shouted again and he stepped forward to lead his men by example, but a bullet took him under the chin and jerked his head sharply back. Blood misted around his face as he slowly crumpled to the ground.

Wendell Holmes, dry-mouthed, watched the stricken officer kneel and then slump forward. Holmes ran forward to help the man, but two other soldiers were closer and dragged the body back into the trees. The officer was unconscious, his bloodied head twitching, then he made a harsh rattling sound and blood bubbled at his throat. "He's dead," one of the men who had pulled the body back to cover said. Holmes stared at the dead man and felt a sour surge of vomit rise in his throat. Somehow he kept the vomit down as he turned away and forced himself to stroll with apparent carelessness among his company. He really wanted to lie down, but he knew he needed to show his men that he was unafraid and so he paced among them, his sword drawn, offering what help he could. "Aim low, now. Aim carefully! Don't waste your shots. Look for them now!" His men bit cartridges, souring their mouths with the salty taste of the gunpowder. Their faces were blackened with the powder, their eyes red-rimmed. Holmes, pausing in a patch of sunlight, suddenly caught the sound of rebel voices calling the exact same advice. "Aim low!" a Confederate officer called. "Aim for the officers!" Holmes hurried on, resisting the temptation to linger behind the bullet-scarred trunks of the trees.

"Wendell!" Colonel Lee called.

Lieutenant Holmes turned to his commanding officer. "Sir?"

"Look to our right, Wendell! Maybe we can outflank these rogues." Lee pointed to the woods beyond the field gun. "Find out how far the rebel line extends. Hurry now!"

Holmes, thus given permission to abandon his studied and casual air, ran through the trees toward the open right flank of the northern line. To his right, below him and through the trees, he glimpsed the bright, cool surprise of the river, and the sight of the water was oddly comforting. He passed his gray greatcoat folded so neatly at the foot of a maple tree, ran behind the Rhode Islanders manning their cannon and on toward the flank, and there, just as he emerged from the smoke and could see that the far woods were indeed empty of rebel enemy and thus offered a way for Colonel Lee to hook around the Confederate left flank, a bullet struck his chest.

He shuddered, his whole frame shaken by the bullet's whipsaw strike. The breath was knocked hard out of him, leaving him momentarily unable to breathe, yet even so he felt oddly cool and detached, so that he was able to register just what he was experiencing. The bullet, he was sure it was a bullet, had struck him with the impact he imagined equal to the kick of a horse. It had left him seemingly paralyzed, but when he tried to take a breath he was pleasantly surprised to discover his lungs were working after all, and he realized it was not true paralysis, but rather an interruption of his mind's control over physical motion. He also realized that his father, Professor of Medicine at Harvard, would want to know of these perceptions, and so he moved his hand toward the pocket where he kept his memorandum book and pencil, but then, helpless to stop himself, he began to topple forward. He tried to call for assistance, but no sound would come, and then he tried to raise his hands to break his fall, but his arms seemed suddenly enfeebled. His sword, which he had been carrying unsheathed, fell to the ground, and he saw a drop of blood splash on the mirror-bright blade and then he fell full-length across the steel and there was a terrible pain inside his chest so that he cried aloud in pity and agony. He had a vision of his family in Boston and he wanted to weep.

"Lieutenant Holmes is down!" a man shouted.

"Fetch him now! Take him back!" Colonel Lee ordered, then went to see how badly wounded Holmes was. He was delayed a few seconds by the Rhode Island artillerymen who shouted for the infantry to stand clear as they fired. Their cannon crashed back on its trail, jetting smoke and flame far out into the sunlit clearing. Each time the gun fired it recoiled a few feet farther back so that its trail left a crudely plowed furrow in the leaf-covered dirt. The gun's crew was too busy to haul the weapon forward again and each shot was fired a few feet farther back than the one before.

Colonel Lee reached Holmes just as the Lieutenant was being lifted onto a stretcher. "I'm sorry, sir," Holmes managed to say.

"Be quiet, Wendell."

"I'm sorry," Holmes said again. Lee stopped to retrieve the Lieutenant's sword and wondered why so many men assumed that being wounded was their own fault.

"You've done well, Wendell," Lee said fervently, then a burst of rebel cheering turned him around to see a rush of new rebel troops arriving in the woods opposite, and he knew he had no chance now of hooking around the enemy's open flank. Indeed, it looked as if the enemy might hook around his. He swore softly, then laid Holmes's sword beside the wounded Lieutenant. "Take him down gently," Lee said, then flinched as a corporal began screaming because a bullet had plowed into his bowels. Another man reeled back with an eye filled with blood, and Lee wondered why in God's name Baker had not ordered a retreat. It was time to get back across the river before they all died.

On the far side of the clearing the rebels had begun making the demonic sound that northern veterans of Bull Run claimed had presaged the onset of disaster. It was a weird, ulullating, inhuman noise that sent shivers of pure terror up Colonel Lee's spine. It was a prolonged yelp like a beast's cry of triumph, and it was the sound, Lee feared, of northern defeat. He shuddered, gripped his sword a little tighter, and went to find the Senator.

The Faulconer Legion climbed the long slope toward battle. It had taken longer than anyone expected to march through the town and find the right track toward the river, and now it was late afternoon and some of the more confident men were complaining that the Yankees would all be dead and looted before the Faulconer Legion could get its share of the spoils, while the timid noted that the battle still crackled on unabated. The Legion was close enough to smell the bitter stench of gunpowder carried on the small north wind that sifted the gunsmoke through the green leaves like a winter fog shifting through branches. At home, Starbuck thought, the leaves would all have changed color, turning the hills around Boston into a glorious surprise of gold, scarlet, flaming yellow, and rich brown, but here, on the northern edge of the southern Confederacy, only the maples had turned gold and the other trees were still heavy with green leaves, though their greenness was being plucked and twitched by the storm of bullets being fired from somewhere deep inside the woods.

The Legion marched across the leprous scatter of scorched stubble that showed where Duff's company of Pike and Chickasaw County men had fought the advancing Yankees to a standstill. The burning wads of their rifles, coughed out with the bullets, had started the small fires that had burned and died away to leave ashy scars in the field. There were a couple of patches of blood too, but the Legion was too distracted by the fight at the hilltop to worry about those signs of earlier battle.

More detritus of battle showed at the woodland's edge. A dozen officers' horses were picketed there, and a score of wounded men were being tended by doctors. A mule loaded with fresh ammunition was led into the trees while another, its panniers empty, was brought out. A slave, come to the battle as his master's servant, ran uphill with canteens he had refilled at the wellhead in the nearest farm. At least a score of children had come from Leesburg to watch the battle and a Mississippi sergeant was attempting to chase them out of range of the northern bullets. One small boy had fetched his father's huge shotgun to the field and was pleading to be allowed to kill one Yankee before bedtime. The boy did not even flinch as a fourteen-pound solid bolt streaked out from the trees and slapped close overhead. The shot appeared to fly halfway to the Catoctin Mountain before it fell with a mighty splash into a stream just beyond the Licksville Road. The Legion had now come to within sixty yards of the trees, and those officers who still rode horses dismounted and hammered iron picket pins into the turf while Captain Hinton, the Legion's second-in-command, ran ahead to establish exactly where the left flank of the Mississippi boys lay.

Most of Starbuck's men were excited. Their relief at surviving Manassas had turned to boredom in the long weeks guarding the Potomac. Those weeks had hardly seemed like war, but instead had been a summer idyll beside cool water. Every now and then a man on one or other riverbank would take a potshot across the water and for a day or two thereafter the pickets would skulk in the shadows, but mostly the two sides had lived and let live. Men had gone swimming under the gunsights of their enemies, they had washed their clothes and watered their horses, and inevitably they had struck up acquaintances with the other side's sentries and discovered shallow places where they could meet in midstream to exchange newspapers or swap southern tobacco for northern coffee. Now, though, in their eagerness to prove themselves the best soldiers in all the world, the Legion forgot the summer's friendliness and swore instead to teach the lying, thieving, bastard Yankees to come across the river without first asking for rebel permission.

Captain Hinton reappeared at the edge of the trees and cupped his hands. "A Company, to me!"

"Form on A Company's left!" Bird shouted to the rest of the Legion. "Color party to me!"

One of the cannon bolts slashed through the trees, showering the advancing men with leaves and splinters. Starbuck could see where an earlier shot had ripped a branch from a trunk, leaving a shocking scar of fresh clean timber. The sight gave him a sudden catch in the throat, a pulse of fear that was the same as excitement.

"Color party to me!" Bird shouted again and the standard-bearers raised their flags into the sunlight and ran to join the Major. The Legion's own color was based on the Faulconer family's coat-of-arms and showed three red crescents on a white silken field above the family motto "Forever Ardent." The second color was the national flag of the Confederacy, two red horizontal stripes either side of a white stripe, while the upper quadrant next to the staff showed a blue field on which was sewn a circle of seven white stars. After Manassas there had been complaints that the flag was too similar to the northern flag and that troops had fired on friendly units believing them to be Yankees, and rumor had it that a new design was being made in Richmond, but for today the Legion would fight beneath the bullet-torn silk of its old Confederate color.

"Dear sweet Jesus save me, dear sweet Jesus save me," Joseph May, one of Starbuck's men, prayed breathlessly as he hurried behind Sergeant Truslow. "Save me, O Lord, save me."

"Save your breath, May!" Truslow growled.

The Legion had been advancing in column of companies and now it peeled leftward as it turned itself from a column of march into a line of battle. A Company was first into the trees and Starbuck's K Company would be the last. Adam Faulconer rode with Starbuck. "Get off that horse, Adam!" Starbuck shouted up to his friend. "You'll be killed!" He needed to shout for the crackle of musketry was loud, but the sound was filling Starbuck with a curious elation.

59

He knew as well as Adam that war was wrong. It was like sin, it was terrible, but just like sin it had a terrible allure. Survive this, Starbuck felt, and a man could take anything that the world might hurl at him. This was a game of unimaginably high stakes, but also a game where privilege conferred no advantages except the chance to avoid the game altogether, and whoever used privilege to avoid this game was no man at all, but a lickspittle coward. Here, where the air was foul with smoke and death whipped among green leaves, existence was simplified to absurdity. Starbuck whooped suddenly, filled with the sheer joy of the moment. Behind him, their rifles loaded, K Company spread among the green leaves. They heard their Captain's whoop of joy and they heard the rebel yell sounding from the troops on the right, and so they began to make the same demonic wailing screech that spoke of southern rights and southern pride and southern boys come to make a killing.

"Give them hell, boys!" Bird shouted. "Give them hell!"

And the Legion obeyed.

Baker died.

The Senator had been trying to steady his men whose nerves were being abraded by the whooping, vengeful, southern fiends. Baker had made three attempts to break out of the woods, but each northern advance had been beaten bloodily back to leave another tide mark of dead men on the small meadow that lay like a smoke-palled slaughter field between the two forces. Some of Baker's men were abandoning the fight; hiding themselves on the steep escarpment that dropped down to the riverbank or sheltering blindly behind tree trunks and outcrops of rock on the bluff's summit. Baker and his aides rousted such timid men out from their refuges and sent them back to where the brave still attempted to keep the rebels at bay, but the timid crept back to their shelters just as soon as the officers were gone.

The Senator was bereft of ideas. All his cleverness, his oratory, and his passion had been condensed into a small tight ball of panic-stricken helplessness. Not that he showed any fear. Instead he strolled with drawn sword in front of his men and called on them to aim low and keep their spirits high. "There are reinforcements coming!" he said to the powder-stained men of the 15th Massachusetts. "Not much longer, boys!" he encouraged his own men of the 1st Californian. "Hot work now, lads, but they'll tire of it first!" he promised the men of New York Tammanys. "If I had one more regiment like you," he told the Harvards, "we'd all be feasting in Richmond tonight!"

Colonel Lee tried to persuade the Senator to retreat across the river, but Baker seemed not to hear the request and when Lee shouted it, insisting on being heard, Baker merely offered the Colonel a sad smile. "I'm not sure we have enough boats for a retreat, William. I think we must stand and win here, don't you?" A bullet spat inches above the Senator's head, but he did not flinch. "They're only a pack of rebels. We won't be beaten by such wretches. The world is watching and we have to show our superiority!"

Which was probably what an ancestor of Baker's had said at Yorktown, Lee reflected, but wisely did not say aloud. The Senator might have been born in England, but there was no more patriotic American. "You're sending the wounded off?" Lee asked the Senator instead.

"I'm sure we are!" Baker said firmly, though he was sure of no such thing, but he could not worry about the wounded now. Instead he needed to fill his men with a righteous fervor for the beloved union. An aide brought him news that the 19th Massachusetts had arrived on the river's far bank and he was thinking that if he could just bring that fresh regiment across the Potomac he would have enough men to throw an attack against the knoll from which the rebels were decimating his left flank and preventing his howitzers from doing their slaughtering work. The idea gave the Senator instant hope and fresh enthusiasm. "That's what we'll do!" he shouted to one of his aides.

"We'll do what, sir?"

"Come on! We have work!" The Senator needed to get back to his left flank and the quickest route lay in the open where the gunsmoke offered a fogbank in which to hide. "Come on," he shouted again, then hurried down the front of his line, calling to the riflemen to hold their fire until he had passed. "We're being reinforced, boys," he shouted. "Not long now! Victory's coming. Hold on there, hold on!"

A group of rebels saw the Senator and his aides hurrying in the shifting smoke, and though they did not know Baker was the northern commander, they knew that only a senior officer would carry a tasseled sword and wear a uniform so tricked out with braid and glitter. A gold watch chain hung with seals was looped on the Senator's coat and caught the slanting sun. "There's their gang boss! Gang boss!" a tall, stringy, redheaded Mississippian called aloud, pointing to the striding figure who marched so confidently across the battle's front. "He's mine!" the big man shouted as he ran forward. A dozen of his companions scrambled after him in their eagerness to plunder the bodies of the rich northern officers.

"Sir!" one of Baker's aides called in warning.

The Senator turned, raising his sword. He should have retreated into the trees, but he had not crossed a river to flee a rabble of seceshers. "Come on then, you damn rebel!" he shouted, and he held the sword out as though ready to fight a duel.

But the red-haired man used a revolver and his four

bullets thudded into the Senator's chest like axe blows hitting softwood. The Senator was thrown back, coughing and grasping at his chest. His sword and hat fell as he tried to stay on his feet. Another bullet ripped his throat open and blood spilt in a scarlet wash down the brass-buttoned tunic of his double-breasted coat and clogged in the links of the gold watch chain. Baker was trying to breathe and was shaking his head as though he could not believe what was happening to him. He looked up at the lanky killer with a puzzled expression, then collapsed onto the grass. The red-haired rebel ran to claim his body.

A rifle shot spun the red-haired man around, then another bullet put him down. A volley drove the other Mississippians back as two of the Senator's aides dragged their dead master back into the trees. One of the men retrieved the Senator's hat and took out the sweaty, folded message that had launched this madness across a river.

The sun was low in the west. The leaves might not have turned, but the nights were drawing on and the sun would be quite gone by half past five, but darkness could not save the Yankees now. They needed boats, but there were only five small craft, and some of the wounded had already drowned as they tried to swim back to Harrison's Island. More wounded were climbing clumsily down the bluff to where the northern casualties already filled the small area of flatland that lay between the base of the steep hill and the riverbank. Two aides carried the Senator's body through the press of moaning men to one of the boats and ordered a space cleared for the corpse. The Senator's expensive watch fell from his pocket as his carcass was manhandled down the bank. The watch swung on its bloody chain, first dragging in the mud, then striking hard against the boat's timbers. The blow broke the watch's crystal and scattered small sharp scraps of glass into the bilges. The

Senator's bloody corpse was rolled on top of the glass. "Take him back!" an aide ordered.

"We're all going to die!" a man screamed on the hilltop, and a Massachusetts sergeant told him to shut his damn noise and die like a man. A group of rebels tried to cross the clearing and were hurled back by a crescendo of musket fire that twisted them around and plucked scraps of wood from the trees behind them. A Massachusetts color bearer was hit and his great, beautiful, bullet-beaten silk flag fluttered down toward the dirt, but another man seized its tasseled fringe and lifted the stars back toward the sun before the stripes had touched the ground.

"What we'll do," said Colonel Cogswell, who had finally established that he was the senior officer alive and thus had command of the four Yankee regiments stranded on the Virginia shore, "is fight our way downstream to the ferry." He wanted to take his men out of the murderous shadows and into the open fields where their enemies would no longer be able to hide behind trees. "We'll march fast. It means we'll have to abandon the guns and the wounded."

No one liked that decision, but no one had a better idea, and so the order was relayed back to the 20th Massachusetts, who lay at the right-hand flank of the Yankee line. The fourteen-pounder James rifle would have to be abandoned anyway for it had recoiled so far that at last it had toppled back over the bluff. As it had fired its final shot a gunner had shouted in alarm, then the whole heavy cannon had tilted over the escarpment's crest and crashed sickeningly down the steep slope until it smashed against a tree. Now the gunners gave up their attempts to haul the gun back to the crest and listened instead as Colonel Lee explained to his officers what the regiment was about to do. They were to leave their wounded to the mercy of the rebels and gather at the left-hand flank of the northern line. There they would make a mass charge through the rebel forces and so down to the water meadows which led to where the second Yankee force had crossed the river to cut the turnpike. That second force was covered by artillery on the Maryland bank of the river. "We can't cross back into Maryland here," Lee told his officers, "because we don't have enough boats, so we'll have to march the five miles downstream and fight the rebels off all the way." He looked at his watch. "We'll move in five minutes."

Lee knew it would take that long for the orders to reach all his companies and for the casualties to be gathered under a flag of truce. He hated leaving his wounded, but he knew none of his regiment would reach Maryland this night if he did not abandon the casualties. "Hurry now," he told his officers and tried to sound confident, but the strain was telling now and his sanguine appearance was fraying under the constant whip and whistle of the rebel bullets. "Hurry now!" he called again, then he heard a terrible screaming noise from his open right flank and he turned, alarmed, and suddenly knew that no amount of hurrying could help him now.

It seemed the Harvards would have to fight where they were. Lee drew his sword, licked dry lips, then committed his soul to God and his beloved regiment to its desperate end.

"WE'RE TOO FAR LEFT," Truslow had growled at Starbuck as soon as K Company reached the battle line. "Bastards are that way." Truslow pointed across the clearing to where a veil of smoke hung in front of the trees. That smoke lay well to the right of K Company, while directly across from Starbuck's men there was no gunsmoke, just empty trees and long, darkening shadows among which the maple trees looked unnaturally bright. Some of K Company had begun firing into those empty trees, but Truslow snarled at them to stop wasting powder.

The company waited expectantly for Starbuck's orders, then turned as another officer came running through the brush. It was Lieutenant Moxey, who had reckoned himself a hero ever since taking a slight wound in his left hand at Manassas. "The Major says you're to close on the center." Moxey was filled with the moment's excitement. He waved a revolver toward the sound of musketry. "He says you're to reinforce Murphy's company."

"Company!" Truslow shouted at his men, anticipating Starbuck's orders to move.

"No! Wait!" Starbuck was still gazing directly across the clearing to the undisturbed trees. He looked back to his right again, noting how the Yankee fire had momentarily died down. For a few seconds he wondered if that lull in the firing signified that the northern forces were retreating, but then a sudden charge by a yelping group of rebels triggered a furious outburst of northern rifle fire. For a few seconds the gunfire splintered in a mad tattoo, but the moment the rebels retreated the fusillade died away. Starbuck realized that the northerners were holding their fire until they could see targets while the southerners were keeping up a steady fusillade. Which meant, Starbuck decided, that the Yankees were worried about having enough ammunition.

"The Major says you're to move at once," Moxey insisted. He was a thin, pale-faced youth who resented that Starbuck had received a captaincy while he remained a lieutenant. He was also one of the few men in the Legion who begrudged Starbuck's presence, believing that a Virginia regiment had no need of a renegade Bostonian, but it was an opinion he kept to himself, for Moxey had seen Starbuck's temper and knew the northerner was more than willing to use his fists. "Did you hear me, Starbuck?" he demanded now.

"I heard you," Starbuck said, yet still he did not move. He was thinking that the Yankees had been fighting in these woods nearly all day, and presumably they had just about used up all the cartridges in their pouches, which meant they were now relying on whatever small amounts of ammunition could be brought across the river. He was also thinking that troops worried about having sufficient cartridges were troops that could be panicked very quickly. He had seen panic at Manassas and reckoned it could bring a victory just as swift and complete here.

"Starbuck!" Moxey insisted on being heard. "The Major says you're to reinforce Captain Murphy."

"I heard you, Mox," Starbuck said again, and still did nothing.

Moxey made a great play of pretending that Starbuck had to be particularly stupid. He tapped Starbuck's arm and pointed through the trees to the right. "That way, Starbuck."

"Go away, Mox," Starbuck said, and he looked back across the clearing. "And on your way tell the Major we're crossing over here and we'll be rolling the bastards up from the left. Our left, got that?"

"You're doing what?" Moxey gaped at Starbuck, then looked up at Adam who was on horseback a few paces behind Starbuck. "You tell him, Adam," Moxey appealed to higher authority. "Tell him to obey orders!"

"We're crossing the field, Moxey," Starbuck said in a kind, slow voice, as though he addressed a particularly dull child, "and we're going to attack the nasty Yankees from inside the trees over there. Now go away and tell that to Pecker!"

The maneuver seemed the obvious thing to do. The two sides were presently blazing away from either side of the clearing, and though the rebels had a clear advantage, neither side seemed capable of advancing straight into the concentrated rifle fire of the other. By crossing the clearing at this open flank Starbuck could take his men safe into the northerners' trees and then advance on their undefended wing. "Make sure you're loaded!" Starbuck shouted at his men.

"You can't do this, Starbuck," Moxey said. Starbuck took no notice of him. "Do you want me to tell the Major you're disobeying his orders?" Moxey asked Starbuck cattily.

"Yes," Starbuck said, "that's exactly what I want you to tell him. And that we're attacking their flank. Now go away and do it!"

Adam, still on horseback, frowned down at his friend. "Do you know what you're doing, Nate?"

"I know, Adam, I really do know," Starbuck said. In truth the opportunity to turn the Yankee flank was so straightforward that the dullest fool might have seized it, though a wise man might have sought permission for the maneuver first. But Starbuck was so certain he was right and so confident that his flank attack would finish the Yankee defense that he reckoned seeking permission would simply be a waste of time. "Sergeant!" he called for Truslow.

Truslow once again anticipated Starbuck's order. "Bayonets on!" he called to the company. "Make sure they're fixed firm! Remember to twist the blade when you drive home!" Truslow's voice was as calm as though this were just another day's training. "Take your time, lad! Don't fumble!" He spoke to a man who had dropped a bayonet in his excitement, then he checked that another man's bayonet was firmly slotted onto the rifle's muzzle. Hutton and Mallory, the company's two other sergeants, were similarly checking their squads.

"Captain!" one of Hutton's men called. It was Corporal Peter Waggoner, whose twin brother was also a corporal in the company. "You staying or going, Captain?" Peter Waggoner was a big, slow man of deep piety and fierce beliefs.

"I'm going over there," Starbuck said, pointing across the clearing and deliberately misunderstanding the question.

"You know what I mean," Waggoner said, and most of the other men in the company knew too for they stared apprehensively at their Captain. They knew Nathan Evans had offered him a job, and many of them feared that such a staff appointment might be attractive to a bright young Yankee like Starbuck.

"Do you still believe that people who drink whiskey will go to hell, Peter?" Starbuck asked the Corporal.

"That's the truth, isn't it?" Waggoner demanded sternly. "God's truth, Mr. Starbuck. Be sure your sins will find you out."

"I've decided to stay here until you and your brother get drunk with me, Peter," Starbuck retorted. There was a second's silence as the men understood just what he had meant and then there was a cheer.

"Quiet!" Truslow snapped.

Starbuck looked back at the enemy side of the clearing. He did not know why his men liked him, but he was hugely moved by their affection, so moved that he had turned away rather than betray his emotion. When he had first been made their Captain he knew the men had accepted him because he had come with Truslow's approval, but they had since discovered that their Yankee officer was a clever, fierce, and combative man. He was not always friendly, not like some of the officers who behaved just like the men they commanded, but K Company accepted Starbuck's secretive and cool manner as the trait of a northerner. Everyone knew that Yankees were queer cold fish and none were stranger or colder than Bostonians, but they had also learned that Starbuck was fiercely protective of his men and was prepared to defy all the Confederacy's authorities to save one of his company from trouble. They also sensed he was a rogue, and that made them think he was lucky, and like all soldiers, they would rather have a lucky leader than any other kind. "You're really staying, sir?" Robert Decker asked.

"I'm really staying, Robert. Now get yourself ready."

"I'm ready," Decker said, grinning with pleasure. He was the youngest of the fifty-seven men in the company, almost all of whom came from Faulconer County, where they had been schooled by Thaddeus Bird and doctored by Major Danson and preached at by the Reverend Moss and employed, like as not, by Washington Faulconer. A handful were in their forties, a few were in their twenties and thirties, but most were just seventeen, eighteen, or nineteen years old. They were brothers, cousins, in-laws, friends, and enemies, not a stranger to each other among the lot of them, and all were familiar with each other's houses and sisters and mothers and dogs and hopes and weaknesses. To a stranger's eye they looked as fierce and unkempt as a pack of winter hounds after a wet day's run, but Starbuck knew them better. Some, like the Waggoner twins, were deeply pious boys who witnessed nightly with the other soldiers and who prayed for their captain's soul, while others, like Edward Hunt and Abram Statham, were rogues who could not be trusted a short inch. Robert Decker, who had come from the same high Blue Ridge valley as Sergeant Truslow, was a kind, hardworking, and trusting soul, while others, like the Cobb twins, were lazier than cats.

"You're supposed to reinforce Murphy's company!" Lieutenant Moxey still lingered close to Starbuck.

Starbuck turned on him. "Go and give Pecker my message! For God's sake, Mox, if you're going to be a message boy, then be a good one. Now run!" Moxey backed away and Starbuck looked up at Adam. "Will you please go and tell Pecker what we're doing? I don't trust Moxey."

Adam spurred away and Starbuck turned back to his men. He raised his voice over the noise of the musketry and told the company what he expected of them. They were to cross the clearing at the double, and once on the far side they would wheel to their right and make a line that would sweep up through the far woods like a broom coming at the open edge of the Yankees' line. "Don't fire unless you have to," Starbuck said, "just scream as loud as you can and let them see your bayonets. They'll run, I promise you!" He knew instinctively that the sudden appearance of a pack of screaming rebels would be sufficient to send the Yankees packing. The men grinned nervously. One man, Joseph May, who had been praying as he climbed the hill, peered at his bayonet's fixture to make sure it was properly secure. Starbuck saw the boy squint. "Where are your spectacles, Joe?"

"Lost 'em, Captain." May sniffed unhappily. "Got broke," he finally admitted.

"If any of you see a dead Yankee with specs, bring them to Joseph!" Starbuck instructed his men, then put his own bayonet onto his rifle's muzzle. At Manassas, at Washington Faulconer's insistence, the Legion's officers had gone into battle with swords, but those officers who survived had learned that enemy sharpshooters liked nothing better than a sword-bearing target and so they had exchanged their elegant blades for workmanlike rifles and their braid-encrusted sleeves and collars for undecorated cloth. Starbuck also carried an ivory-handled, five-shot revolver that he had taken as plunder from the battlefield at Manassas, but for now he would leave that expensive English-made revolver in its holster and depend on his sturdy Mississippi rifle with its long, spikelike bayonet. "Are you ready?" Starbuck called again.

"Ready!" the company answered, wanting to get the battle over with.

"No cheering as we go across!" Starbuck warned them. "We don't want the Yankees knowing we're coming. Go fast and be real quiet!" He looked around at their faces and saw the mixture of excitement and nervous anticipation. He glanced at Truslow, who nodded curtly as though adding his approval to Starbuck's decision. "So come on!" Starbuck called and led the way into the dappled golden-green sunlight that slanted across the clearing and shimmered through the pearly gunsmoke that rested like layered skeins of misty veils between the trees. It was turning into a lovely fall evening and Starbuck felt a sudden and terrible fear that he would die in this sweet light and he ran harder, fearing a blast of canister from a cannon or the sickening mulekick of a bullet's strike, but not one northerner fired at the company as they pounded over to the inner stand of trees.

They trampled their way into the undergrowth on the Yankees' side of the clearing. Once he was safe under the trees Starbuck could see a glint of water where the river turned away from the bluff, and beyond that bright curve he could see the long, green, evening-shadowed fields of Maryland. The sight gave him a moment's pang, then he called to his men to swing right and form a line and he swung his left arm around to show how he wanted them to form the new line of battle, but the men were not waiting for orders; instead they were already pounding through the trees toward the enemy. Starbuck had wanted them to advance on the Yankee flank in a steady line, but they had chosen to race forward in small excited groups, and their enthusiasm more than made up for the raggedness of their deployment. Starbuck ran with them, unaware that he had begun to scream the high-pitched banshee scream. Thomas Truslow was to his left, carrying his bowie knife with its nineteen-inch blade. Most of the Legion's men had once owned such wicked-looking blades, but the weight of the ponderous knives had persuaded almost all of the soldiers to abandon them. Truslow, out of perversity, had kept his and now carried it as his weapon of choice. Alone in the company he made no noise, as if the job at hand was too serious for shouting.

Starbuck saw the first Yankees. Two men were using a fallen tree as a firing position. One was reloading, working the long ramrod down his rifle while his companion aimed across the trunk. The man fired and Starbuck saw the kick of the rifle on the man's shoulder and the puff of spark-lit smoke where the percussion cap exploded. Beyond the two men the woods suddenly seemed thick with blue uniforms and, more oddly, gray coats that hung from trees and twitched as rebel bullets struck home. "Kill them!" Starbuck screamed, and the two men by the fallen tree turned to stare in horror at the rebel charge. The man who had reloaded his rifle swung it to face Starbuck, aimed, then pulled the trigger, but in his panic he had forgotten to prime his rifle. The hammer fell with a click onto bare steel. The man scrambled to his feet and ran past an officer who stood with drawn sword and a look of appalled bewilderment on his whiskered face. Starbuck, seeing the officer's expression, knew he had done the right thing. "Kill them," he screamed, completely unaware that he was uttering anything so bloodthirsty. He just felt the elation of a man who has outwitted an enemy and so imposed his will on a battlefield. That feeling was intoxicating, filling him with a manic elation. "Kill them!" he screamed again, and this time the words seemed to spur the whole Yankee flank into disintegration.

The northerners fled. Some threw themselves off the bluff's edge and slithered down the slope, but most ran back along the line of the summit and, as they ran, more men joined the flight, and the retreat became ever more crowded and chaotic. Starbuck tripped on a wounded man who screamed foully, then ran into the clearing where the Rhode Island cannon had plowed its ragged furrow back and over the bluff's crest. He jumped a box of ammunition, still screaming his challenge at the men running ahead.

Not all the northerners ran. Many of the officers reckoned that duty was more important than safety and, with a bravery that was close to suicide, stayed to fight the rebels' flanking attack. One lieutenant calmly aimed his revolver, fired once, then went down under two bayonets. He tried to fire the revolver even as he was dying, then a third rebel put a bullet into his head and there was a spray of blood as the shot struck home. The Lieutenant died, though the men with the bayonets still savaged his corpse with the ferocity of hunting dogs rending a fallen buck. Starbuck shouted at his men to let the dead man alone and hurry on. He did not want to give the Yankees time to recover.

Adam Faulconer was riding his horse in the sunlit clearing, shouting for the rest of the Legion to cross over and support Starbuck's company. Major Bird led the color party across into evening woods full of the shrill sound of rebels attacking, of gunshots and of northern officers shouting orders that stood no chance of being obeyed in the panic.

Truslow told a northerner to drop his rifle, the man either did not hear or decided to defy the demand, and the bowie knife chopped down once with a horrid economy of effort. A group of Yankees, their retreat blocked, turned and ran blindly back toward their attackers. Most stopped when they saw their mistake and raised their hands in surrender, but one, an officer, sliced his sword in a wild blow at Starbuck's face. Starbuck checked, let the blade hiss by, then rammed his bayonet forward and down. He felt the steel hit the Yankee's ribs and cursed that he had stabbed down instead of up.

"Nate!" the Yankee officer gasped. "No! Please!"

"Jesus!" The blasphemy was torn from Starbuck. The man he was attacking was a member of his father's church, an old acquaintance with whom Starbuck had endured an eternity of Sunday school lessons. The last news Starbuck had heard of William Lewis was that he had become a student at Harvard, but now he was gasping as Starbuck's bayonet scored down his ribs.

"Nate?" Lewis asked. "Is it you?"

"Drop your sword, Will!"

William Lewis shook his head, not out of obstinate

refusal, but out of puzzlement that his old friend should appear in the unlikely guise of a rebel. Then, seeing the look of fury on Starbuck's face, he let the sword drop. "I surrender, Nate!"

Starbuck left him standing over the fallen sword and ran on to catch his men. The encounter with an old friend had unnerved him. Was he fighting a Boston battalion? If so, how many more of this beaten enemy would recognize him? What familiar households would he plunge into mourning by his actions on this Virginia hilltop? Then he forgot his qualms as he saw a giant bearded man howling at the rebels. The man, dressed in shirtsleeves and suspenders, was using one hand to swing an artillery rammer like a club, while in his other he held a short Roman-pattern stabbing sword that was standard issue to gunners. His retreat had been cut off, but he was refusing to surrender, preferring to die like a hero than yield like a coward. He had already felled one of Starbuck's men; now he challenged the others to fight him. Sergeant Mallory, who was Truslow's brother-in-law, fired at the huge man, but the bullet missed and the bearded gunner turned like a fury on the wiry Mallory.

"He's mine!" Starbuck shouted and pushed Mallory aside, lunged forward, then swayed back as the huge man whirled the rammer. This, Starbuck reckoned, was his duty as an officer. The company must see that he was the least afraid, the most ready to fight. Besides, today he felt unbeatable. The scream of battle was in his veins like a splash of fire. He laughed as he lunged with the bayonet, only to have the blade knocked hard aside by the short sword.

"Bastard!" the gunner spat at Starbuck, then slashed the short sword in quick vicious sweeps, trying to keep Starbuck's attention on the blade while he swung the rammer. He thought he had tricked the rebel officer and bellowed with a kind of joy as he anticipated the clublike wooden head smashing his enemy's skull, but Starbuck ducked hard down so that it hissed over his slouch hat and the momentum of the great swing was sufficient to sway the big man off-balance. Then it was Starbuck's turn to shout in triumph as he rammed the bayonet up, hard up, pushing against the astonishing resistance of skin and flesh, and he was still screaming as the big man jerked and fell, twitching on the blade's long shank like a gaffed fish dying.

Starbuck was breathless as he tried to pull his bayonet free, but the gunner's flesh had closed tight on the steel and the blade would not move. The man had dropped his own weapons and was clawing feebly at the rifle in his gut. Starbuck also tried to twist the steel free, but the flesh's suction gripped like stone. He pulled the rifle's trigger, hoping to blast the bayonet loose, but still it would not move. The gunner gasped horribly as the bullet struck, then Starbuck abandoned the weapon and left the gunner dying on the forest floor. He unholstered his fine ivory-handled revolver instead and ran after his company only to discover that K Company was no longer alone in the woods, but was merely a small part of a gray and butternut tide that was overwhelming the northern defenders and driving the survivors in a terrible stampede off the bluff's summit and down to the narrow, muddy ledge beside the river. A New York sergeant screamed as he lost his precarious footing and tumbled down the slope to break his leg on a rock.

"Nate!" Adam had spurred his stallion into the trees. "Call them off!"

Starbuck stared uncomprehendingly at his friend.

"It's over! You've won!" Adam said and gestured at the mass of rebels who had begun firing down the bluff's steep slope at the Yankees trapped beneath. "Stop them!" Adam said, as if he blamed Starbuck for this display of gleeful, vengeful victory, then he turned his horse savagely away to find someone with the authority to finish the killing.

Except no one wanted to end the killing. The northerners were trapped beneath the bluff and the southerners poured a merciless fire into the writhing, crawling, bleeding mass below. A rush of Yankees tried to escape the slaughter by trampling over the wounded to the safety of a newly arrived boat, but the weight of the fugitives overturned the small craft. A man called for help as the current dragged him away. Others tried to swim the channel, but the water was churning and spattering with the strike of bullets. Blood soured the stream and was carried seaward. Men drowned, men died, men bled, and still the remorseless, unending slaughter went on as the rebels loaded and fired, loaded and fired, loaded and fired, jeering all the while at their beaten, cowed, broken enemy.

Starbuck edged his way to the bluff's edge and stared down at a scene from the inferno. The base of the bluff's escarpment was like a wriggling, sensate mass; an enormous beast dying in the gathering dusk, though it was not yet a fangless beast for shots still came up the slope. Starbuck pushed his revolver into his belt and cupped his hands and shouted downhill for the Yankees to cease fire. "You're prisoners!" he shouted, but the only answer was a splintering of rifle flames in the shadows and the whistle of a fusillade past his head. Starbuck pulled his revolver free and emptied its chambers down the hill. Truslow was beside him, taking loaded rifles from men behind and firing at the heads of men trying to swim to safety. The river was being beaten into a froth, looking just as though a school of fish were churning frantically to escape a tidal shallow. Bodies drifted downstream, others snagged on branches or lodged on mudbanks. The Potomac had become a river of death, blood-streaked, bullet-lashed, and body-filled. Major Bird grimaced at the view, but did nothing to stop his men firing.

"Uncle!" Adam protested. "Stop them!"

But instead of stopping the slaughter, Bird gazed down on it like some explorer who had just stumbled upon some phenomenon of nature. It was Bird's view that war involved butchery, and to engage in war but protest against butchery was inconsistent. Besides, the Yankees would not surrender but were still returning the rebel fire, and Bird now answered Adam's demand by raising his own revolver and firing a shot into the turmoil.

"Uncle!" Adam cried in protest.

"Our job is to kill Yankees," Bird said and watched as his nephew galloped away. "And their job is to kill us," Bird went on, even though Adam had long since gone from earshot, "and if we leave them alive today then tomorrow their turn might come." He turned back to the horror and emptied his revolver harmlessly into the river. All around him men grimaced as they fired and Bird watched them, seeing a blood lust raging, but as the shadows lengthened and the return fire stuttered to nothing and as the fear and passion of the long day's climax ebbed away, so the men ceased firing and turned away from the twitching, bloodied river.

Bird found Starbuck pulling a pair of spectacles from a dead man's face. The lenses were thick with clotted blood that Starbuck wiped on his coat hem. "Losing your vision, Nate?" Bird asked.

"Joe May lost his glasses. We're trying to find a pair that suits."

"I wish you could find him a new brain. He's one of the dullest creatures it was ever my misfortune to teach," Bird said, holstering his revolver. "I have to thank you for disobeying me. Well done." Starbuck grinned at the compliment, and Bird saw the feral glee on the northerner's face and wondered that battle could give such joy to a man. Bird supposed that some men were born to be soldiers as others were born to be healers or teachers or farmers, and Starbuck, Bird reckoned, was a soldier born to the dark trade. "Moxey complained about you," Bird told Starbuck, "so what shall we do about Moxey?"

"Give the son of the bitch to the Yankees," Starbuck said, then walked with Bird away from the bluff's crest, back into the trees where a company of Mississippi men was gathering prisoners. Starbuck avoided the sullen-looking northerners, not wanting to be recognized by a fellow Bostonian. One Mississippi soldier had picked up a fallen white banner which he paraded through the twilight, and Starbuck saw the handsome escutcheon of the Commonwealth of Massachusetts embroidered on the blood-flecked silk. He wondered whether Will Lewis was still on the bluff's summit or whether, in the chaos of the defeat, the Lieutenant had sneaked off down to the river and made a bid for the far bank. And what would they say in Boston, Starbuck wondered, when they heard that the Reverend Elial's son had been screaming the rebel yell and wearing the ragged gray and shooting at men who worshipped in the Reverend's church? Damn what they said. He was a rebel, his lot thrown in with the defiant South and not with these smart, well-equipped northern soldiers who seemed like a different breed to the grinning, long-haired southerners.

He left Bird with the Legion's own colors and went on hunting through the woods, looking for spectacles or any other useful plunder that the corpses might yield. Some of the dead looked very peaceful, most looked astonished. They lay with their heads tipped back, their mouths open, and their outreaching hands contracted into claws. Flies were busy at nostrils and glazed eyes. Above the dead the discarded, bullet-torn gray coats of the northerners were still suspended from branches to look like hanged men in the fading light. Starbuck found one of the scarlet-lined coats neatly folded and placed at the bole of a tree and, thinking it would be useful in the coming winter, picked it up and shook out the folds to see that it was unscarred by either bullet or bayonet. A nametape had been neatly sewn into the coat's neck, and Starbuck peered to read the letters that had been so meticulously inked onto the small white strip. "Oliver Wendell Holmes Jr.," the label read, "20th Mass." The name brought Starbuck a sudden and intense memory of a clever Boston family, and of Professor Oliver Wendell Holmes's study with its specimen jars on high shelves. One such jar had held a wrinkled, pallid human brain, Starbuck remembered, while others had strange, big-headed homunculi suspended in cloudy liquid. The family did not worship at Starbuck's church, but the Reverend Elial approved of Professor Holmes, and so Starbuck had been allowed to spend time in the doctor's house where he had become friendly with Oliver Wendell Junior, who was an intense, thin, and friendly young man, quick in debate and generous in nature. Starbuck hoped his old friend had survived the fight. Then, draping Holmes's heavy coat about his shoulders, he went to find his rifle and to discover just how his men had fared in the battle.

In the dark, Adam Faulconer vomited.

He knelt in the soft leaf mold beneath a maple tree and retched till his belly was dry and his throat sore, and then he closed his eyes and prayed as though the very future of mankind depended on the intensity of his petition.

Adam knew that he had been told lies, and, what was worse, knew that he had willingly believed those lies. He had believed that one hard battle would be a sufficient bloodletting to lance the disease that beset America, but instead the single battle had merely worsened the fever, and today he had watched men kill like beasts. He had seen his best friend, his neighbors, and his mother's brother kill like animals. He had seen men descend into hell, and he had seen their victims die like vermin.

It was dark now, but still a great moaning came from the foot of the bluff where scores of northerners lay bleeding and dying. Adam had tried to go down and offer help, but a voice had screamed at him to get the hell away and a rifle had fired blindly up the slope toward him, and that one defiant shot had been sufficient to provoke another rebel fusillade from the bluff's crest. More men had screamed in the dark and wept in the night.

Around Adam a few fires burned, and around those fires the victorious rebels sat with grinning devil faces. They had looted the dead and rifled the pockets of the prisoners. Colonel Lee of the 20th Massachusetts had been forced to surrender his fine braided jacket to a Mississippi muleskinner who now sat wearing it before a fire and wiping the grease from his hands on the coat's skirts. There was the raw smell of whiskey in the night air and the sour stench of blood and the sweet-sick odor of the rotting dead. A handful of southern casualties had been buried in the sloping meadow that looked south toward Catoctin Mountain, but the northern bodies were still unburied. Most had been collected and stacked like cordwood, but a few undiscovered corpses were still hidden in the undergrowth. In the morning a work party of slaves would be fetched from the nearby farms and made to dig a trench big enough to hold the Yankee dead. Near the stack of bloody corpses a man played a fiddle beside a fire and a few men sang softly to his mournful tune.

God, Adam decided, had abandoned these men, just as

they had abandoned Him. Today, on the edge of a river, they had arrogated God's choice of life and death. They were, Adam decided in his wrought state, given to evil. It did not matter that some of the victorious rebels had prayed in the dusk and had tried to help their beaten enemy; they were all, in Adam's view, scorched by the devil's breath.

Because the devil had taken America in his grip and was dragging the fairest country on earth down to his foul nest, and Adam, who had let himself be persuaded that the South needed its one moment of martial glory, knew he had come to his own sticking point. He knew he had to make a decision, and that the decision involved the risk of severing himself from his family and his neighbors and his friends and even from the girl he loved, but it was better, he told himself as he knelt in the death- and vomit-scented air of the bluff's crest, to lose his Julia than to lose his soul.

The war must be ended. That was Adam's decision. He had tried to avert the conflict before the fighting ever began. He had worked with the Christian Peace Commission and he had seen that band of pious worthies swamped by the fervent supporters of war, so now he would use the war to end the war. He would betray the South because only by that betrayal could he save his country. The North must be given all the help he could give it, and as an aide to the South's commanding general Adam knew he could give the North more help than most other men.

He prayed in the dark and his prayer seemed to be answered when a great peace descended on him. The peace told Adam that his decision was a good one. He would become a traitor and would yield his country to its enemy in the name of God and for America.

Bodies floated downstream in the dark, carried toward the Chesapeake Bay and the distant ocean. Some of the corpses were trapped on the weirs by Great Falls where the river turned south toward Washington, but most were carried through the rapids and floated through the night to snag on the piles of the Long Bridge that carried the road south from Washington into Virginia. The river washed the corpses clean so that by the dawn, when the citizens of Washington walked beside the waters and looked down at the mudshoals by its banks, they saw their sons all clean and white, their dead skins gleaming, though the bodies were now so swollen with gas that they strained the buttons and stretched the seams of their lavish new uniforms.

And in the White House a president wept for the death of Senator Baker, his dear friend, while the rebel South, seeing the hand of God in this victory by the waters, gave thanks.

The leaves turned and dropped, blowing gold and scarlet across the new graves at Ball's Bluff. In November the rebel troops moved away from the river, going to winter quarters nearer Richmond where the newspapers warned of the swelling northern ranks. Major General McClellan, the Young Napoleon, was said to be training his burgeoning army to a peak of military perfection. The small fight at Ball's Bluff might have filled northern churches with mourners, but the North consoled itself with the thought that their revenge lay in the hands of McClellan's superbly equipped army, which, come the springtime, would descend on the South like a righteous thunderbolt.

The North's navy did not wait for spring. In South Carolina, off Hilton Head, the warships blasted their way into Port Royal Sound and landing parties stormed the forts that guarded Beaufort Harbor. The North's navy was blockading and dominating the southern coast and though the southern newspapers tried to diminish the defeat at Port Royal, the news provoked cheers and singing in the

Confederacy's slave quarters. There was more celebration when Charleston was almost destroyed by fire – a visitation from the angel of revenge, the northern preachers said – and the same preachers cheered when they learned that a Yankee warship, defying the laws of the sea, had stopped a British mail ship and removed the two Confederate commissioners sent from Richmond to negotiate treaties with the European powers. Some southerners also cheered that news, declaring that the snub to Britain would surely bring the Royal Navy to the American coast, and by December Richmond's jubilant newspapers were reporting that redcoat battalions were landing in Canada to reinforce the permanent garrison in case the United States chose to fight Britain rather than return the two kidnapped commissioners.

Snow fell in the Blue Ridge Mountains, covering the grave of Truslow's wife and cutting off the roads to the western part of Virginia that had defied Richmond by seceding from the state and joining the Union. Washington celebrated the defection, declaring it to be the beginning of the Confederacy's dissolution. More troops marched down Pennsylvania Avenue and so out to the training camps in occupied northern Virginia where the Young Napoleon honed their skills. Each day new guns arrived on trains from the northern foundries to be parked in giant rows in fields close to the Capitol Building that gleamed white in the winter sun beneath the spidery scaffolding of its unfinished dome. One good hard push, the northern newspapers claimed, and the Confederacy would collapse like a dead, rotted tree.

The rebel capital felt no such confidence. The winter had brought nothing but bad news and worse weather. Snow had come early, the cold was bitter, and the Yankee noose seemed to be tightening. That prospect of imminent northern victory at least cheered Adam Faulconer who, two weeks before Christmas, rode his horse down from the city to the stone quay at Rockett's Landing. The wind was chopping the river into short, hard, gray waves and whistling in the tarred rigging of the truce ship which sailed once a week from the Confederate capital. The ship would journey down the James River and under the high guns of the rebel fort on Drewry's Bluff and so through the low, salt-marsh fringed meanders to the river's confluence with the Appomattox and from there eastward along a broad, shallow fairway until, seventy miles from Richmond, it reached the Hampton Roads and turned north to the quays of Fort Monroe. The fort, though on Virginia soil, had been held by Union forces since before the war's beginning and there, under its flag of truce, the boat discharged captured northerners who were being exchanged for rebel prisoners released by the North.

The cold winter wind was stinging Rockett's Landing with snatches of thin rain and souring the quay with the smell of the foundries that belched their sulfurous coal-smoke along the riverbank. The rain and smoke turned everything greasy; the stones of the quay, the metal bollards, the lines berthing the ship, and even the thin, ill-fitting uniforms of the thirty men who waited beside the gangplank. The waiting men were northern officers who had been captured at Manassas and who, after nearly five months in captivity, were being exchanged for rebel officers captured in General McClellan's campaign in what now styled itself the state of West Virginia. The prisoners' faces were pale after their confinement in Castle Lightning, a factory building which stood on Cary Street next to the two big storage tanks that held the gas supply for the city's street lighting. The clothes of the released prisoners hung loose, evidence of the weight

they had lost during their confinement in the commandeered factory.

The men shivered as they waited for permission to board
the truce boat. Most carried small sacks holding what few
possessions they had managed to preserve during their
imprisonment: a comb, a few coins, a Bible, some letters
from home. They were cold, but the thought of their imminent release cheered them and they teased each other
about their reception at Fort Monroe, inventing ever more
lavish meals that would be served in the officers' quarters.
They dreamed of lobster and beefsteak, of turtle and oyster
soup, of ice cream and apple butter, of venison steak with
cranberries, of duck and orange sauce, of glasses of Madeira
and flagons of wine, but above all they dreamed of coffee, of
real, good, strong coffee.

One prisoner dreamed of no such things, but instead
paced with Adam Faulconer up and down the quay. Major
James Starbuck was a tall man with a face that had once
been fleshy, but now looked pouchy. He was still a young
man, but his demeanor, his perpetual frown, and his thinning hair made him look old far beyond his years. He had
once boasted a very fine beard, though even that had lost its
luster in Castle Lightning's damp interior. James had been a
rising Boston lawyer before the war and then a trusted aide
to Irvin McDowell, the General who had lost the battle at
Manassas, and now, on his way back north, James did not
know what was to become of him.

Adam's duty this day was to make certain that only those
prisoners whose names had been agreed between the two
armies were released, but that duty had been simply discharged by a roll call and head count, and once those duties
were done he had sought James's company and asked to talk
with him privately. James, naturally enough, assumed
Adam wanted to talk about his brother. "There is no

chance, you think, that Nate could change sides?" James asked Adam wistfully.

Adam did not like to answer directly. In truth he was bitterly disappointed with his friend Nathaniel Starbuck, who, he believed, was embracing war like a lover. Nate, Adam believed, had abandoned God, and the best he could hope for was that God had not abandoned Nate Starbuck, but Adam did not want to state that harsh judgment, and so he tried to find some shard of redeeming goodness that would buoy James's hopes for his younger brother. "He told me he attends prayer meeting regularly," he answered lamely.

"That's good! That's very good!" James sounded unusually animated, then he frowned as he scratched his belly. Like every other prisoner held in Castle Lightning he had become lousy. At first he had found the infestation terribly shaming, but time had accustomed him to lice.

"But what will Nate do in the future?" Adam asked, then answered his own question by shaking his head. "I don't know. If my father resumes command of the Legion, then I think Nate will be forced to look for other employment. My father, you understand, is not fond of Nate."

James jumped in alarm as a sudden eruption of steam hissed loudly from a locomotive on the nearby York River Railroad. The machine jetted another huge gout of steam, then its enormous driving wheels screamed shrilly as they tried to find some traction on the wet and gleaming steel rails. An overseer bellowed orders at a pair of slaves who ran forward to scatter handfuls of sand under the spinning wheels. The locomotive at last found some purchase and jerked forward, clashing and banging a long train of boxcars. A great gust of choking, acrid smoke wafted over Adam and James. The locomotive's fuel was resinous pinewood that left a thick tar on the rim of the potlike chimney.

"I had a particular reason for seeing you today," Adam said clumsily when the locomotive's noise had abated.

"To say farewell?" James suggested with an awkward misunderstanding. One of his shoe soles had come loose and flapped as he walked, making him stumble occasionally.

"I have to be frank," Adam said nervously, then fell silent as the two men skirted a rusting pile of wet anchor chain. "The war," Adam finally explained himself, "must be brought to a conclusion."

"Oh, indeed," James said fervently. "Indeed, yes. It is my prayerful hope."

"I cannot describe to you," Adam said with an equal fervor, "what tribulation the war is already bringing to the South. I dread to think of such iniquities being visited on the North."

"Amen," James said, though he had no real idea what Adam was talking about. In prison it had sometimes seemed as if the Confederacy were winning the war, an impression that had been heightened when the disconsolate prisoners from Ball's Bluff had arrived.

"If the war continues," Adam said, "then it will degrade us all. We shall be a mockery to Europe; we shall lose whatever moral authority we possess in the world." He shook his head as if he had not managed to express himself properly. Beyond the quay the train was picking up speed, its boxcar wheels clattering over the rail joints and the locomotive's smoke showing white against the gray clouds. A guard jumped onto the platform of the moving caboose and went inside out of the cold wind. "The war is wrong!" Adam finally blurted out. "It is against God's purpose. I've been praying on this matter and I beg you to understand me."

"I do understand you," James said, but he could say no more because he did not want to offend his new friend by saying that the only way God's purpose could be fulfilled was by the Confederacy's defeat, and though Adam might be voicing sentiments very close to James's heart, he was still wearing a uniform of rebel gray. It was all very confusing, James thought. Some of the northern prisoners in Castle Lightning had openly boasted of their adultery, they had been blasphemers and mockers, lovers of liquor and of gambling, Sabbath-breakers and libertines; men who James had deemed to be of the crudest stamp and vilest character, yet they were soldiers who fought for the North while this pained and prayerful man Adam was a rebel.

Then, to James's astonishment, Adam proved that supposition wrong. "What is necessary," Adam said, "and I beg for your confidence in this matter, is for the North to gain a swift and crushing victory. Only thereby can this war be halted. Do you believe me?"

"I do, I do. Of course." James felt overwhelmed by Adam's sentiments. He stopped and looked down into the younger man's face, oblivious to a bell that had begun ringing to summon the prisoners aboard the truce ship. "And I join my prayers to yours," James said sanctimoniously.

"It will take more than prayers now," Adam said, and he took from his pocket an India-paper Bible that he handed to James. "I am asking you to take this back to the North. Hidden behind the endpapers is a full list of our army's units, their strength as of this week, and their present positions in Virginia." Adam was being modest. Into the makeshift slipcase made by the Bible's leather cover he had crammed every detail concerning the Confederate defenses in northern Virginia. He had listed the ration strengths of every brigade in the rebel army, and discussed the possibility of conscription being adopted by the Richmond government in the spring. His staff job had enabled Adam to reveal the weekly total of newly manufactured artillery reaching the army from the Richmond foundries, and to betray how many of the cannons facing the northern pickets from the rebel redoubts around Centreville and Manassas were fakes. He had sketched the Richmond defenses, warning that the ring of earth forts and ditches was still under construction and that every passing month would render the obstacles more formidable. He told the North of the new ironclad ship being secretly built in the Norfolk dockyard, and of the forts which protected the river approaches to Richmond. Adam had included all that he possibly could, describing the South's strengths and weaknesses, but always urging the North that one strong attack would surely crumble secession like a house of cards.

Adam desperately hoped this one inclusive betrayal would be sufficient to end the war, yet he was sensible enough to know that whoever received this letter might well demand more information. Now, pacing the greasy quay in the cold rain, Adam told James precisely how a message could reach him from the North. Adam had worked hard on his scheme, attempting to foresee every liability that might reveal his identity to the southern authorities, and he knew that the greatest danger would be posed by northern messages coming south. "Which is why I'd rather you never contacted me," he warned James, "but if you must, then I beg you never to use my name on the letters."

"Of course." James closed his cold hands over the Bible's leather cover, guiltily aware of an unseemly happiness. It was right and proper that he should be glad of Adam's espousal of the North's cause, yet he felt it shameful that he should see in that espousal an advantage for himself, for he was guiltily aware that the letter concealed in the Bible could well assist his military career. Instead of returning North as the humbled aide of a failed general, he was suddenly the carrier of northern victory. His prayers had been answered a hundredfold.

"If necessary I can send you more information," Adam went on, "but only to you. Not to anyone else. I cannot trust anyone else." Both sides were riddled with informers who would betray anyone for the price of a bottle of whiskey, but Adam was certain he could trust this Boston lawyer who was as pious and godly a man as any in either army. "Will you give me your Christian word that you will keep my identity secret?"

"Of course," James said, still dazed by this stroke of good fortune.

"I mean a secret from everyone," Adam insisted. "If you reveal my identity to General McClellan I have no faith he will not tell someone else, and that someone else could be my ruin. Promise me this. No one but you and I must ever know."

James nodded again. "I promise." He turned as the ship's bell rang again. His fellow prisoners were climbing the gangway, but still James made no move to join them. Instead he delved into an inside pocket of his faded, dirty jacket and brought out an oilcloth-covered packet. The oilcloth was loosely wrapped and James let it fall away to reveal a small, much-thumbed pocket Bible with a worn cover. "Will you give this to Nate? Ask him to read it?"

"With pleasure." Adam took the thick Bible and watched as James wrapped his new Scriptures in the patch of oilcloth.

"And tell him," James added in a heartfelt voice, "that if he returns north I will do my best to reconcile him to Father and Mother."

"Of course," Adam said, though he could not imagine Starbuck responding to his brother's generosity.

"You want to stay here, mister?" a sailor called to James from the ship.

"Remember your promise," Adam said. "Tell no one who gave you that letter."

"You can trust me," James assured Adam. "I'll tell no one."

"God bless you." Adam felt a sudden great warmth for this good, clumsy man who was so obviously a brother in Christ. "And God bless the United States."

"Amen to that," James responded, then held out his hand. "I shall pray for you."

"Thank you," Adam said, and he shook James's hand before walking the northerner to the waiting ship.

The gangplank was heaved inboard and the warps cast off. James stood at the rail, the new Bible clutched tight in his hands. As the last warp dropped away and the boat perceptibly moved into the river's current, the freed prisoners cheered. The sidewheels began to turn, their great paddles churning the greasy water white. The motion of the paddles made the released prisoners cheer again, all but James, who stood silent and apart. A plume of dirty smoke sagged from the ship's tall funnel to blow across the river.

Adam watched as the ship dropped past the navy yard, its progress helped by a cold, wind-fretted current. He gave James a last wave, then looked down at the pocket Bible to see that its margins were smothered in tightly written notes. It was the Bible of a man who wrestled with God's will, the Bible of a good man. Adam closed and held the book tightly, as though he could take strength from the word of God, and then he turned and limped back toward his tethered horse. The wind gusted fresh and cold, but Adam felt an immense calm because he had done the right thing. He had chosen the course of peace, and by so doing he would bring nothing but blessings on his country; it would be one country again, North and South, united in God's purpose.

Adam rode toward the city. Behind him the truce boat splashed and smoked its way around the bend and so headed south carrying its cargo of treachery and peace.

PART TWO

GEORGE WASHINGTON'S BIRTHDAY was fixed as the day of Jefferson Davis's formal inauguration as President of the Confederate States of America. He had been inaugurated once before, in Montgomery, Alabama, but that ceremony had only made Davis into the President of a provisional government. Now, hallowed by election and properly installed in the Confederacy's new capital, he would be inaugurated a second time. The choice of Washington's birthday as the date of this second ceremony was intended to invest the occasion with a symbolic dignity, but the auspicious day brought nothing but miserable and incessant rains which drove the huge crowd gathered in Richmond's Capitol Square to shelter beneath a host of umbrellas so densely packed that it seemed as if the speechmakers orated to a spread of glistening black lumps. The drumming of the rain on carriage roofs and tightly stretched umbrella skins was so loud that no one except the platform party could hear any of the orations, prayers, or even the solemn presidential oath of office. After taking the oath President Davis invoked God's help to the South's just cause, his prayer punctuated by the sneezing and coughing of the dignitaries around him. Gray February clouds scudded low over the city, darkening everything except the new battle flags of the Confederate's eastern army. The flag, which was hanging on staffs behind the platform and from every rooftop within sight of Capitol Square, was a fine red banner, slashed with

97

a blue St. Andrew's cross on which were sewn thirteen stars to represent the eleven rebellious states as well as Kansas and Missouri, whose loyalty both sides claimed. Southerners who looked for auguries were pleased that thirteen states founded this new country, just as thirteen had founded a different country eighty-six years before, though some in the crowd perceived the number as unlucky, just as they perceived the drenching rain as an omen of ill fortune for the newly inaugurated president.

After the ceremony a procession of bedraggled notables hurried along Twelfth Street to attend a reception in the Brockenborough House on Clay Street which had been leased by the government to serve as the presidential mansion. The house was soon crowded with dripping people who draped wet coats on the twin statues of Comedy and Tragedy that graced the entrance hall, then edged their way from one room to another to appraise and criticize the new President's taste in furniture and pictures. The President's slaves had placed protective covers over the expensive carpets in the reception rooms, but the visitors wanted to inspect the patterns and pulled the cotton sheets aside, and soon the beautifully patterned carpets were trodden filthy with muddy boots, while the twin arrays of peacock feathers on the mantel of the ladies' drawing room were ravaged by people wanting souvenirs of the day. The President himself stood frowning beside the white marble fireplace in the state dining room and assured everyone who offered him congratulations that he conceived of the day's ceremony as a most solemn occasion and his presidency as a mighty heavy duty. Some army musicians were supposed to be entertaining the guests, but the crowd was so tightly pressed that the violinist did not even have room to draw his bow, and so the soldiers retired to the kitchen where the cooks regaled them with good Madeira wine and cold jellied chicken.

Colonel Washington Faulconer, resplendent in an elegant Confederate uniform that was made even more dashing by the black sling supporting his right arm, congratulated the President, then went through the small fuss of not being able to shake hands with his wounded right arm and offering his left instead.

President Davis finally managed a limp, awkward handshake, then muttered that he was honored by Faulconer's presence on this solemn occasion which was ushering in these days of heavy duty.

"Heavy duties call for great men, Mr. President," Washington Faulconer responded, "which means we are fortunate indeed in you."

Davis's thin mouth twitched to acknowledge the compliment. He had a piercing headache that made him seem even more remote and cold than usual. "I do regret," he said stiffly, "that you did not feel able to accept the duty of commissioner."

"Though I certainly saved myself some inconvenience thereby, Mr. President," Faulconer responded lightly, before realizing that in war all men were supposed to welcome inconvenience, even if that inconvenience did mean being kidnapped by the U.S. Navy from the comfortable staterooms of a British mail ship. The two commissioners had now been released, thus saving the North from battling the British as well as the Confederacy, but their arrival in Europe had not fetched good news. France would not support the South unless the British made the first move, and the British would not intervene unless the South gave clear signs of being able to win the war without outside help, which all added up to meaningless nonsense. The President, reflecting on the diplomatic failure, had concluded that the wrong men had been chosen as commissioners. Slidell and Mason were raw-mannered and blunt men, accustomed to the homespun texture of American politics, but hardly slippery enough for the sly chanceries of a suspicious Europe. A more elegant commissioner, the President now believed, might have achieved a greater success.

And Washington Faulconer was certainly an impressive man. He had flaxen hair and a frank, honest face that almost glowed with handsomeness. He had broad shoulders, a trim waist, and one of the greatest fortunes in all Virginia; a fortune so large that he had raised a regiment with his own money and then equipped it to a standard equal to the best in either army, and rumor claimed that he could have repeated that generosity a dozen times over and still not have felt the pinch. He was, by any man's standard, a fortunate and striking man, and President Davis once again felt irritation that Faulconer had turned down diplomatic office to pursue his dream of leading a brigade into battle. "I'm sorry to see you're not recovered, Faulconer." The President gestured at the black sling.

"Some small loss of dexterity, Mr. President, but not sufficient to prevent me from wielding a sword in my country's defense," Faulconer said modestly, though in truth his arm was entirely mended and he wore the sling only to give an impression of heroism. The black sling was especially inspiring to women, an effect that was made more convenient by the absence from Richmond of Faulconer's wife, who lived an invalid's nervous existence on the family's country estate. "And I trust the sword will be so employed soon," Faulconer added in a heavy hint that he wanted the President's support for his appointment as a brigadier.

"I suspect we shall all soon be fully employed in our various duties," the cadaverous President answered vaguely. He wished his wife would come and help him deal with these eager people who wanted more enthusiasm than he felt able to give. Varina was so good with small talk, while on these social occasions the President felt the words shrivel on his tongue. Was Lincoln similarly afflicted by office seekers? Davis wondered. Or did his fellow President have a greater ease of manner with importunate strangers? A familiar face suddenly appeared beside Faulconer, a man who smiled and nodded at the President, demanding recognition. Davis scrabbled for the man's name which, thankfully, came in the very nick of time. "Mr. Delaney," the President greeted the newcomer unenthusiastically. Belvedere Delaney was a lawyer and gossip whom Davis did not remember inviting to this reception, but who had typically come anyway.

"Mr. President." Delaney inclined his head in recognition of Jefferson's high office. The Richmond lawyer was a small, plump, smiling man whose bland exterior concealed a mind as sharp as a serpent's tooth. "Allow me to extend my sincere felicitations on your inauguration."

"A solemn occasion, Delaney, leading to heavy duties."

"As the weather seems to intimate, Mr. President," Delaney said, appearing to take an unholy glee in the day's damp character. "And now, sir, if I might, I have come to request Colonel Faulconer's attention. You cannot monopolize the company of our Confederate heroes all day, sir."

Davis nodded his grateful assent for Delaney to take Faulconer away, though the release only permitted a plump congressman to heartily congratulate his fellow Mississippian on being inaugurated as the Confederacy's first President.

"It is a heavy duty and solemn responsibility," the President murmured.

The Mississippi Congressman gave Jefferson Davis's shoulder a mighty slap. "Heavy duty be damned, Jeff," the Congressman bellowed in his President's ear. "Just send our boys north to cut the nuts clean off old Abe Lincoln."

"I must leave strategy to the generals." The President tried to move the Congressman on and accept the more limpid good wishes of an Episcopalian clergyman instead.

"Hell, Jeff, you know as much 'bout war as any of our fine soldier boys." The Congressman hawked a tobacco-rich gob toward a spitoon. The stream of brown spittle missed, spattering instead on the rain-soaked hoop skirt of the clergyman's wife. "Time we settled those chicken-shit Yankees once and forever," the Congressman opined happily, then offered the new President a pull on his flask. "Finest rotskull whiskey this side of the Tennessee River, Jeff. One slug will cure whatever ails you!"

"You're demanding my company, Delaney?" Faulconer was irritated that the short, sly lawyer had taken him away from the President.

"It ain't me who wants you, Faulconer, but Daniels, and when Daniels calls, a man does best to respond," Delaney said.

"Daniels!" Faulconer said in astonishment, for John Daniels was one of the most powerful and reclusive men in Richmond. He was also famously ugly and foulmouthed, but important because it was Daniels who decided what causes and men the powerful Richmond *Examiner* would support. He lived alone with two savage dogs that it was his pleasure to make fight while he cackled from the vantage point of a high barber's chair. He was no mean fighter himself; he had twice faced his enemies on the Richmond dueling ground in Bloody Run and had survived both fights with his malevolent reputation enhanced. He was also regarded by many southerners as a first-rate political theorist, and his pamphlet, "The Nigger Question," was widely admired by all those who saw no need to modify the institution of slavery. Now, it seemed, the formidable John Daniels waited for Faulconer on the elevated back porch of the new Executive Mansion where, horsewhip in hand, he stared moodily at the rain.

He gave Faulconer a sideways glance, then flicked his whip toward the water dripping off the bare trees. "Is this weather an augury for our new President, Faulconer?" Daniels asked in his grating, hard voice, eschewing any more formal greeting.

"I hope not, Daniels. You're well, I trust?"

"And what do you think of our new President, Faulconer?" Daniels ignored Faulconer's courtesy.

"I think we are fortunate in such a man."

"You sound like an editorial writer on the *Sentinel*. Fortunate! My God, Faulconer, the old U.S. Congress was full of mudsills like Davis. I've seen better men drop out the backside of a hog. He impresses you with his gravity, does he? Oh, he's grave, I'll grant you that, because there's nothing alive inside him, nothing but notions of dignity and honor and statesmanship. It ain't notions we need, Faulconer, but action. We need men to go and kill Yankees. We need to soak the North in Yankee blood, not make fine speeches from high platforms. If speeches won battles we'd be marching through Maine by now on our way to taking Canada. Did you know Joe Johnston was in Richmond two days ago?"

"No, I didn't."

"Know what Johnston calls you, Faulconer?" Daniels asked in his unpleasant voice. It did not matter to Daniels that Faulconer was one of the South's richest men, so rich that he could have bought the *Examiner* a dozen times over; Daniels knew his own power, and that power was the ability to mold public opinion in the South. That same power gave him the right to lounge in the President's wicker rocking

103

chair with his shabby boots up on the President's back rail while Faulconer, in his gaudy colonel's uniform, stood beside him like a supplicant. "He calls you the hero of Manassas," Daniels said sourly. "What do you say to that?"

"I'm most grateful," Faulconer said. In truth the soubriquet was a mistake, for General Johnston had never discovered that it was not Faulconer who had led the Legion against the North's surprise flank attack at Manassas, but the unsung Thaddeus Bird, nor had Johnston ever learned that Bird had made that decision in deliberate disobedience of Faulconer's orders. Instead, like so many other folk in the Confederacy, Johnston was convinced that in Washington Faulconer the South had a brilliant and fitting hero.

That belief had been carefully nurtured by Washington Faulconer himself. The Colonel had spent the months since Manassas lecturing on the battle in halls and theaters from Fredericksburg to Charleston. He told his audiences a tale of disaster averted and victory snatched from certain defeat, and his tale was given drama and color by a small group of wounded musicians who played patriotic songs and, at the more dramatic moments of the narration, played imitation bugle calls that gave the audience the impression that ghostly armies maneuvered just outside the lecture hall's dark windows. Then, as the story reached its climax and the whole fate of the Confederacy hung in history's balance, Faulconer would pause and a snare drum would rattle a suggestion of musketry and a bass drum crash the echoes of distant cannon fire before Faulconer told of the heroism that had saved the day. Then the applause would ring out to drown the drummers' simulated gunfire. Southern heroism had defeated dull-witted Yankee might, and Faulconer would smile modestly as the cheers surrounded him.

Not that Faulconer had ever actually claimed to be the hero of Manassas, but his account of the fight did not specifically deny the accolade. If asked what he had done personally, Faulconer would refuse to answer, claiming that modesty was becoming to a warrior, but then he would touch his right arm in its black sling and he would see the men straighten their backs with respect and the women look at him with a melting regard. He had become accustomed to the adulation; indeed, he had been making the speech for so long now that he had come to believe in his own heroism, and that belief made his memory of the Legion's rejection of him on the night of Manassas hard to bear.

"Were you a hero?" Daniels now asked Faulconer directly.

"Every man at Manassas was a hero," Faulconer replied sententiously.

Daniels cackled at Faulconer's answer. "He should have been a lawyer like you, eh, Delaney? He knows how to make words mean nothing!"

Belvedere Delaney had been cleaning his fingernails, but now offered the editor a swift, humorless smile. Delaney was a fastidious, witty, clever man whom Faulconer did not wholly trust. The lawyer was presently in Confederate uniform, though quite what his martial duties entailed, Faulconer could not guess. It was also rumored that Delaney was the owner of Mrs. Richardson's famous brothel on Marshall Street and of the even more exclusive house of assignation on Franklin Street. If true, then the collected gossip of the two brothels doubtless provided Delaney with damaging knowledge about a good number of the Confederacy's leaders, and doubtless the sly lawyer passed all that pillow talk on to the scowling, diseased, twisted-looking Daniels.

"We need heroes, Faulconer," Daniels now said. He stared sourly down at the flooded paths and muddy vegetable beds of the soaking garden. A wisp of smoke twisted up from the presidential smokehouse where a dozen Virginia hams were being cured. "You heard about Henry and Donelson?"

"Indeed," Faulconer said. In Tennessee Forts Donelson and Henry had been captured and now it looked as if Nashville must fall, while in the east the Yankee navy had again struck from the sea; this time to capture Roanoke Island in North Carolina.

"And what would you say, Faulconer" – Daniels shot an unfriendly look at the handsome Virginian – "if I were to tell you that Johnston is about to abandon Centreville and Manassas?"

"He can't be!" Faulconer was genuinely aghast at the news. Too many acres of northern Virginia were already under enemy occupation, and yielding more of the state's sacred turf without a fight appalled Faulconer.

"But he is." Daniels paused to light a long black cheroot. He spat the cheroot's tip over the railing, then blew smoke into the rain. "He's decided to pull back behind the Rappahannock. He claims we can defend ourselves better there than in Centreville. No one's announced the decision yet, it's supposed to be a secret, which means Johnston knows, Davis knows, you and I know, and half the goddamn Yankees probably know too. And can you guess what Davis proposes doing about it, Faulconer?"

"I trust he'll fight the decision," Faulconer said.

"Fight?" Daniels mocked the word. "Jeff Davis doesn't know the meaning of the word. He just listens to Granny Lee. Caution! Caution! Caution! Instead of fighting, Faulconer, Davis proposes that a week tomorrow we should all have a day of prayer and fasting. Can you believe that? We are to starve ourselves so that Almighty God will take note of our plight. Well, Jeff Davis can tighten his belt, but

106

I'll be damned if I shall. I shall give a feast that day. You'll join me, Delaney?"

"With enormous pleasure, John," Delaney said, then glanced around as the door at the end of the verandah opened. A small boy, maybe four or five years old and carrying a hoop, appeared on the porch. The boy smiled at the strangers.

"Nurse says I can play here," the boy, whom Washington Faulconer guessed was the President's oldest son, explained himself.

Daniels shot a venomous look at the child. "You want a whipping, boy? If not, then get the hell out of here, now!"

The boy fled in tears as the editor turned back to Faulconer. "Not only are we withdrawing from Centreville, Faulconer, but as there isn't sufficient time to remove the army's supplies from the railhead at Manassas, we are torching them! Can you credit it? We spend months stocking the army with food and ammunition and at the very first breath of spring we decide to burn every damn shred of material and then scuttle like frightened women behind the nearest river. What we need, Faulconer, are generals with balls. Generals with flair. Generals not afraid to fight. Read this." He took from his vest pocket a folded sheet of paper that he tossed toward Faulconer. The Colonel needed to grovel on the porch's rush matting to retrieve the folded sheet, which proved to be the galley proof of a proposed editorial for the Richmond *Examiner*.

The editorial was pure balm to Faulconer's soul. It declared that the time had come for bold action. The spring would surely bring an enemy onslaught of unparalleled severity and the Confederacy would only survive if it met that onslaught with bravery and imagination. The South would never prevail by timidity, and certainly not by digging trenches such as those with which General Robert

107

Lee seemed intent upon surrounding Richmond. The Confederacy, the editorial proclaimed, would be established by men of daring and vision, not by the efforts of drainage engineers. The writer grudgingly allowed that the Confederacy's present leaders were well-meaning men, but they were hidebound in their ideas and the time had surely come to appoint new officers to high position. One such man was Colonel Washington Faulconer, who had been unemployed since Manassas. Let such a man loose on the North, the article concluded, and the war would be over by summer. Faulconer read the editorial a second time and pondered whether he should go to Shaffers this very afternoon and order the extra braid for his sleeves and the gilded wreaths that would surround the stars on his collar wings. Brigadier General Faulconer! The rank, he decided, sat well on him.

Daniels took the editorial back. "The question is, Faulconer, do we publish this?"

"Your decision, Daniels, not mine," Faulconer said modestly, hiding his elation as he shielded a cigar from the wind and struck a light. He wondered if publication would offend too many senior officers, then realized he dared not express such a timid reservation to Daniels or else the editorial would be changed to recommend that some other man be given a brigade.

"But are you our man?" Daniels growled.

"If you mean, would I attack and attack and go on attacking, yes. If you mean, would I abandon Manassas? No. If you mean, would I employ good men to dig drainage ditches around Richmond? Never!"

Daniels was silent after Faulconer's ringing declaration. Indeed he was silent for so long that Washington Faulconer began to feel rather foolish, but then the small, black-bearded editor spoke again. "Do you know the size of

McClellan's army?" He asked the question without turning to look at Faulconer.

"Not precisely, no."

"We know, but we don't print the figure in the newspaper because if we did we might just cause people to despair." Daniels twitched the long whip as his voice rumbled just a little louder than the seething and incessant rain. "The Young Napoleon, Faulconer, has over a hundred and fifty thousand men. He has fifteen thousand horses, and more than two hundred and fifty guns. Big guns, Faulconer, slaughtering guns, the finest guns that the northern foundries can pour, and they're lined up wheel to heavy wheel to grind our poor southern boys into bloody ruin. And how many poor southern boys do we have? Seventy thousand? Eighty? And when do their enlistments run out? June? July?" Most of the southern army had volunteered for just one year's service, and when that year was over the survivors expected to go home. "We'll have to conscript men, Faulconer," Daniels went on, "unless we beat this so-called genius McClellan in the spring."

"The nation will never stand for conscription," Faulconer said sternly.

"The nation, Colonel, will damn well stand for whatever brings us victory," Daniels said harshly, "but will you lead those conscripted men, Faulconer? That's the proper question now. Are you my man? Should the *Examiner* support you? After all, you're not the most experienced officer, are you now?"

"I can bring new ideas," Faulconer suggested modestly. "New blood."

"But a new and inexperienced brigadier will need a good and experienced second-in-command. Ain't that right, Colonel?" Daniels looked malevolently up at Faulconer as he spoke.

Faulconer smiled happily. "I should expect my son Adam to serve with me. He's on Johnston's staff now, so he has the experience, and there isn't a more capable or honest man in Virginia." Faulconer's sudden sincerity and warmth were palpable. He was desperately fond of his son, not just with a father's love, but also out of a gratified pride in Adam's undoubted virtues. Indeed, it sometimes seemed to Faulconer that Adam was his one undoubted success, the achievement that justified the rest of his life. Now he turned smilingly to the lawyer. "You can vouch for Adam's character, can't you, Delaney?"

But Belvedere Delaney did not respond. He just stared down into the sopping garden.

Daniels hissed in a dubious breath, then shook his ugly head warningly. "Don't like it, Faulconer. Don't like it one goddamn little bit. Stinks of favoritism to me. Of nepotism! Is that the word, Delaney?"

"Nepotism is the very word, Daniels," Delaney confirmed, not looking at Faulconer, whose face was like that of a small boy struck brutally hard.

"The *Examiner* could never stand for nepotism, Faulconer," Daniels said in his grating voice, then he threw a curt gesture toward Delaney, who obediently opened the verandah's central door to admit onto the porch a gaunt and ragged creature dressed in a wet, threadbare uniform that made the newcomer shiver in the day's raw cold. The man was in his early middle age and looked as though life had served him ill. He had a coarse black beard streaked with gray, sunken eyes, and a tic in his scarred cheek. He was evidently suffering from a cold for he cuffed his dripping nose, then wiped his sleeve on his ragged beard that was crusted with flakes of dried tobacco juice. "Johnny!" this unprepossessing creature greeted Daniels familiarly.

"Faulconer?" Daniels looked up at the Colonel. "This is Major Griffin Swynyard."

Swynyard gave Faulconer a brisk nod, then held out his left hand, which, Faulconer saw, was missing its three middle fingers. The two men made an awkward handshake. The spasm in Swynyard's right cheek gave his face a curiously indignant look.

"Swynyard," Daniels said to Faulconer, "served in the old U.S. Army. He graduated from West Point, when?"

"Class of twenty-nine, Johnny." Swynyard clicked his heels together.

"Then served in the Mexican and Seminole wars. Is that right?"

"Took more scalps than any white man alive, Colonel," Swynyard said, grinning at Faulconer and revealing a mouthful of rotted yellow teeth. "I took thirty-eight headpieces in one day alone!" Swynyard boasted. "All with my own hands, Colonel. Squaws, papooses, braves! I had blood to my elbows! Spattered to the armpits! Have you ever had the pleasure of taking a scalp, Colonel?" Swynyard asked with a fierce intensity.

"No," Faulconer managed to say. "No, I haven't." He was recovering from Daniels's refusal to countenance Adam's appointment, and realizing that promotion would carry a price.

"There's a knack to it," Swynyard went on. "Like any other skill, there's a knack! Young soldiers always try to cut them off and, of course, it don't work. They end with something which looks like a dead mouse." Swynyard believed this was funny, for he opened his gap-toothed mouth to breathe a sibilant laugh at Faulconer. "Cutting don't work for a scalp, Colonel. No, you have to peel a scalp off, peel it like the skin of an orange!" He spoke lovingly, demonstrating the action with his wounded, clawlike hand. "If you're ever in the Tidewater I'll show you my collection. I've three cabin trunks full of prime scalps, all cured and tanned proper." Swynyard evidently felt he had made a good impression on Faulconer for he smiled ingratiatingly while the tic in his cheek trembled fast. "Maybe you'd like to see a scalp now, Colonel?" Swynyard suddenly asked, pawing at the button of his top pocket as he spoke. "I always keep one about my person. As a good-luck charm, you understand? This one's from a Seminole squaw. Noisy little bitch she was, too. Savages can squeal, I tell you, how they can squeal!"

"No, thank you." Faulconer managed to prevent the trophy from being produced. "So you're a Virginia man, Major?" he asked, changing the subject and disguising his distaste for the wretched-looking Swynyard. "From the Tidewater, you say?"

"From the Swynyards of Charles City Court House," Swynyard said with evident pride. "The name was famous once! Ain't that so, Johnny?"

"Swynyard and Sons," the editor said, staring into the rain, "slave traders to the Virginia gentry."

"But my daddy gambled the business away, Colonel," Swynyard confided. "There was a time when the name Swynyard meant the selfsame thing as nigger trading, but Daddy lost the business with the sin of gambling. We've been poor men ever since!" He said it proudly, but the boast suggested to Washington Faulconer exactly what proposition was being made to him.

The editor drew on his cigar. "Swynyard's a cousin of mine, Faulconer. He's my kin."

"And he has applied to you for employment?" Faulconer guessed shrewdly.

"Not as a newspaperman!" Major Swynyard intervened. "I don't have skill with words, Colonel. I leave that to the

112

clever fellows like cousin Johnny here. No, I'm a soldier through and through. I was weaned on the gun's muzzle, you might say. I'm a fighter, Colonel, and I've got three cabin trunks crammed full of heathen topknots to prove it."

"But you are presently unemployed?" Daniels prompted his cousin.

"I am indeed seeking the best place for my fighting talent," Swynyard confirmed to Faulconer.

There was a pause. Daniels took the editorial from his pocket and pretended to cast a critical eye over its paragraphs. Faulconer took the hint. "If I should find employment for myself, Major," he told Swynyard hastily, "I should count it as a great honor and a privilege if you would consider being my right-hand man?"

"Your second-in-command, don't you mean?" John Daniels interjected from the President's rocking chair.

"My second-in-command indeed," Faulconer confirmed hurriedly.

Swynyard clicked his heels. "I'll not disappoint you, Colonel. I might lack the genteel graces, by God, but I don't lack fierceness! I ain't a soft man, my God, no. I believe in driving soldiers like you drive niggers! Hard and fast! Bloody and brutal, no other way, ain't that the truth, Johnny?"

"The entire truth, Griffin." Daniels folded the editorial, but did not yet return it to his vest pocket. "Unfortunately, Faulconer," Daniels went on, "my cousin impoverished himself in the service of his country. His old country, I mean, our new enemies. Which also means he has come to our new country with a passel of debts. Ain't that so, Griffin?"

"I'm down on my luck, Colonel," Swynyard confessed gruffly. A tear appeared at one eye and the tic in his cheek quivered. "Gave my all to the old army. Gave my fingers

113

too! But I was left with nothing, Colonel, nothing. But I don't ask much, just a chance to serve and fight, and a grave of good Confederate soil when my honest labors are done."

"But you are also asking for your debts to be settled," John Daniels said pointedly, "especially that portion of the debt which is owed to me."

"I shall take great pleasure in establishing your credit," Faulconer said, wondering just how much pain that pleasure would cost him.

"You're a gentleman, Colonel," Swynyard said, "a Christian and a gentleman. It's plain to see, Colonel, so it is. Moved, I am. Touched deep, sir, very deep." And Swynyard cuffed the tear from his eye, then straightened his back as a sign of respect to his rescuer. "I'll not disappoint you. I ain't a disappointer, Colonel. Disappointing ain't in the Swynyard nature."

Faulconer doubted the truth of that assertion, yet he guessed his best chance of being named a general was with Daniels's help, and if Daniels's price was Swynyard, then so be it. "So we're agreed, Major," Faulconer said, and held out his left hand.

"Agreed, sir, agreed." Swynyard shook Faulconer's offered hand. "You move up a rank, sir, and so do I." He smiled his decayed smile.

"Splendid!" Daniels said loudly, then delicately and pointedly inserted the folded editorial back into his vest pocket. "Now if you two gentlemen would like to improve upon each other's acquaintance, Mr. Delaney and I have business to discuss."

Thus dismissed, Faulconer and Swynyard went to join the throng which still crowded the President's house, leaving Daniels to flick his whip out into the rain. "Are you sure Faulconer's our man?"

"You heard Johnston," Delaney said happily. "Faulconer was the hero of Manassas!"

Daniels scowled. "I heard a rumor that Faulconer was caught with his pants around his ankles? That he wasn't even with the Legion when it fought?"

"Mere jealous tales, my dear Daniels, mere jealous tales." Delaney, quite at his ease with the powerful editor, drew on a cigar. His stock of precious French cigarettes was exhausted now, and that lack was perhaps the most pressing reason why he wanted this war to end quickly. To which end Delaney, like Adam Faulconer, secretly supported the North and worked for its victory by causing mischief in the South's capital, and today's achievement, he thought, was a very fine piece of mischief indeed. He had just persuaded the South's most important newspaperman to throw his paper's massive influence behind one of the most foppish and inefficient of the Confederacy's soldiers. Faulconer, in Delaney's caustic view, had never grown up properly, and without his riches he would be nothing but an empty-headed fool. "He's our man, John, I'm sure of it."

"So why has he been unemployed since Manassas?" Daniels asked.

"The wound in his arm took a long time healing," Delaney said vaguely. The truth, he suspected, was that Faulconer's inordinate pride would not allow him to serve under the foulmouthed, lowborn Nathan Evans, but Daniels did not need to know that.

"And didn't he free his niggers?" Daniels asked threateningly.

"He did, John, but there were extenuating reasons."

"The only extenuating reason for freeing a nigger is because the bastard's dead," Daniels declared.

"I believe Faulconer freed his slaves to fulfill his father's dying wish," Delaney lied. The truth was that Faulconer

115

had manumitted his people because of a northern woman, an ardent abolitionist, whose good looks had momentarily enthralled the Virginia landowner.

"Well, at least he's taken Swynyard off my hands," Daniels said grudgingly, then paused as the sound of cheering came from inside the house. Someone was evidently making a speech and the crowd punctuated the oration with laughter and applause. Daniels glowered into the rain that still fell heavily. "We don't need words, Delaney, we need a goddamn miracle."

The Confederacy needed a miracle because the Young Napoleon was at last ready, and his army outnumbered the southern troops in Virginia by two to one, and spring was coming, which meant the roads would be fit once more for the passage of guns, and the North was promising its people that Richmond would be captured and the rebellion ended. Virginia's fields would be dunged by Virginia's dead and the only way the South could be saved from an ignominious and crushing defeat was by a miracle. Instead of which, Delaney reflected, he had given it Faulconer. It was enough, he decided, to make a sick cat laugh.

Because the South was doomed.

Just after dawn the cavalry came galloping back across the fields, their hooves splashing bright silver gouts of water from the flooded grass. "Yankees are at Centreville! Hurry it up!" The horsemen spurred past the earthen wall that was notched with gun embrasures, only instead of cannon in the embrasures there was nothing but Quaker guns. Quaker guns were tree trunks painted black and then propped against the firing steps to give the appearance of cannon muzzles.

The Faulconer Legion would be the last infantry regiment to leave the Manassas positions, and the last, presumably, to march into the new fortifications that were being dug behind the Rappahannock River. The retreat meant ceding even more Virginia territory to the northerners, and for days now the roads south through Manassas had been crowded with refugees heading for Richmond.

The only defenses left behind at Manassas and Centreville would be the Quaker guns, the same fake weapons that had brooded across the landscape all winter to keep the Yankee patrols far from Johnston's army. That army had been wondrously supplied with food that had been painstakingly hauled to the Manassas depot by trains all winter long, but now there was no time to evacuate the depot and so the precious supplies were being burned. The March sky was already black with smoke and rich with the smell of roasting salt beef as Starbuck's company torched the last rows of boxcars left in the rail junction. The cars had already been primed with heaps of tinder, pitch, and gunpowder, and as the burning torches were thrust into the incendiary piles, the fire crackled and bellowed fiercely upward. Uniforms, bridles, cartridges, horse collars, and tents went up in smoke, then the boxcars themselves caught fire and the flames whipped in the wind and spewed their black smoke skyward. A barn full of hay was torched, then a brick warehouse of flour, salt pork, and dry crackers. Rats fled from the burning storehouses and were hunted down by the Legion's excited dogs. Each company had adopted at least a half-dozen mongrel mutts that were lovingly cared for by the soldiers. Now the dogs seized the rats by their necks and shook them dead, scattering blood. Their owners cheered them on.

The boxcars would burn till there was nothing left but a pair of blackened wheels surrounded by embers and ash. Sergeant Truslow had a work party pulling up rails and stacking them on burning piles of wooden ties soaked in pitch. The burning stacks generated such a fierce heat that the steel rails were being bent into uselessness. All about the regiment were the pyres of other fires as the rearguard destroyed two months' worth of food and a winter's worth of stored equipment.

"Let's be moving, Nate!" Major Bird strode across the scorched depot, jumping in alarm as a box of ammunition caught fire in one of the boxcars. The cartridges snapped like firecrackers, forcing an incandescent blaze in one corner of the burning wagon. "Southward!" Bird cried dramatically, pointing in that direction. "You hear the news, Nate?"

"News, sir?"

"Our behemoth was met by their leviathan. Science matched wits with science, and I gather that they fought each other to a standstill. Pity." Bird suddenly checked and frowned. "A real pity."

"The Yankees have a metal ship too, sir?" Starbuck asked.

"It arrived the day after the *Virginia's* victory, Nate. Our sudden naval superiority is all for naught. Sergeant! Leave those rails, time to be on our way unless you wish to be a guest of the Yankees tonight!"

"We lost our ship?" Starbuck asked in disbelief.

"The newspaper reports that it floats still, but so does their monstrous metal ship. Our queen is now matched by their queen, and so we have stalemate. Hurry up, Lieutenant!" This injunction was to Moxey, who was using a blunt knife to cut through the hemp rope of a well bucket.

Starbuck's spirits sank. It was bad enough that the army was yielding Manassas Junction to the Yankees, but everyone had been cheered by the sudden news that a southern secret weapon, an iron-sided ship impervious to cannon fire, had sailed into the Hampton Roads and decimated the northern blockading squadron of wooden warships. The U.S. Navy's ships had turned and fled, some going aground, others sinking, and the rest simply making what desperate speed they could to escape the clanking, smoke-dark, plodding, but vengeful *Virginia*, the ironclad fashioned from the hulk of an abandoned U.S. Navy ship, the *Merrimack*. The victory had seemed compensation for Manassas's abandonment and promised to destroy the strangulation of the U.S. Navy's blockade, but now it seemed that the North had a similar beast which had succeeded in fighting the CSS *Virginia* to a standstill.

"Never mind, Nate. We'll just have to settle the war on land," Bird said, then clapped his hands to encourage the last of the men to leave the burning railyard and form up on the road leading south.

"But how in God's name did they know we had an iron ship?" Starbuck asked.

"Because they have spies, of course. Probably hundreds of them. You think everyone south of Washington suddenly changed their patriotism overnight?" Bird asked. "Of course they didn't. And some folks undoubtedly believe that any accommodation with the Yankees is better than this misery." He gestured toward another group of pitiful refugees and was suddenly assailed by an image of his own dear wife being forced from her home by the invading Yankees. That was hardly a likely fate, for Faulconer County lay deep in the heart of Virginia, yet Bird still touched the pocket in which Priscilla's portrait was carefully wrapped against the rain and damp. He tried to imagine their small house with its untidy piles of music and its scatter of violins and flutes being burned by jeering Yankee troops.

"Are you all right?" Starbuck had seen the sudden grimace on Bird's face.

"Enemy horse! Look lively!" Sergeant Truslow shouted at his company, but he also intended the sudden bellow to startle Major Bird out of his reverie. "Yankees, sir." Truslow pointed north to where a group of horsemen was silhouetted against the pale trunks of a far wood.

"March on!" Bird shouted toward the head of the Legion's column, then he turned back to Starbuck. "I was thinking of Priscilla."

"How is she?" Starbuck asked.

"She says she's very well, but she wouldn't say anything else, would she? The dear girl isn't one to worry me with complaints." Bird had married a girl half his age and, in the manner of a confirmed bachelor falling at last to the enemy, regarded his new bride with an adoration that verged on worship. "She says she's planted onions. Is it too early to plant onions? Or maybe she means she planted them last year? I don't know, but I am so impressed that the dear thing knows about onions. I don't. Lord knows when I'll see her again." He sniffed, then turned to look at the distant horsemen who seemed very wary of the lavish display of wooden guns that threatened their approach. "Onward, Nate, or backward rather. Let us yield this field of ashes to the enemy."

The Legion marched past the burning storehouses, then through the small town. A few of the houses were empty, but most of the inhabitants were staying behind. "Hide your flag, man!" Bird called to a carpenter who was defiantly flying the new Confederate battle flag above his shop. "Fold it away! Hide it! We'll be back!"

"Is anyone behind you, Colonel?" The carpenter inadvertently gave Bird a promotion.

"Just some cavalry. After that it's all Yankees!"

"Give them bastards a good whipping, Colonel!" the carpenter said as he reached for his flag.

"We'll do our best. Good luck to you!"

The Legion left the small town behind and marched stolidly along a wet and muddy road that had been torn apart by the passage of refugee wagons. The road led to Fredericksburg, where the Legion would cross the river, then destroy the bridge before joining the bulk of the southern army. Most of that army was retreating on a road farther west which went direct to Culpeper Court House where General Johnston had his new headquarters. Johnston was assuming that the Yankees would swing wide in an attempt to turn the river line and that a great battle would therefore need to be fought in Culpeper County; it would be a battle, Bird observed to Starbuck, which would make the fight at Manassas look like a skirmish.

The Legion's retreat took them through that old battle-field. To their right was the long hill down which they had fled in disorder after stalling the Yankees' surprise attack, and to their left was the steeper hill where Stonewall Jackson had finally held, turned, and repelled the northern army. That battle was eight months in the past, yet still the steep hill showed the scars of artillery strikes. Close by the road was a stone house where Starbuck had watched the surgeons slash and saw at wounded flesh, and in the yard of the house was a shallow grave trench that had been washed thin by the winter's rain so that the knobbly-headed stumps of bones showed white above the red soil. There was a well in the yard where Starbuck remembered slaking his thirst during the day's terrible, powder-exacerbated heat. A group of stragglers, sullen and defiant, now squatted beside the well.

The stragglers, all of them from regiments that were marching ahead of the Legion, annoyed Truslow. "They're supposed to be men, ain't they? Not women." The Legion passed more and more such laggards. A few were sick and could not help themselves, but most were simply tired or suffering from blistered feet. Truslow snarled at them, but even Truslow's savage scorn could not persuade the stragglers to ignore the blood filling their boots and to keep on marching. Soon some of the men from the Legion's leading companies began dropping back. "It ain't right," Truslow complained to Starbuck. "Go on like this and we'll lose half the army." He saw three men from the Legion's A Company and he stormed over to them, bellowing at the chicken-hearted bastards to keep walking. The three men ignored him, so Truslow punched the tallest of the three, dropping him to the ground. "Get up, you son of a bitch!" Truslow shouted. The man shook his head, then squirmed in the mud as Truslow kicked him in the guts. "Get up, you slime-bellied bastard! Up!"

"I can't!"

"Stop it!" Starbuck called the order to Truslow, who turned in astonishment at receiving a direct reprimand from his officer.

"I ain't letting these sons of bitches lose the war because they're gutless weaklings," Truslow protested.

"I don't intend to allow that to happen either," Starbuck said. He walked over to the man from A Company, watched by a score of other stragglers who wanted to see just how the tall, dark-haired officer could succeed where the squat, fierce sergeant had failed.

Truslow spat into the mud as Starbuck approached. "You plan on talking reason to the sumbitch?"

"Yes," Starbuck said, "I do." He stood above the fallen man, watched by the whole of K Company, who had paused to enjoy the confrontation. "What's your name?" Starbuck asked the straggler.

"Ives," the man said warily.

"And you can't keep up, Ives?"

122

"Reckon I can't."

"He always was a useless sumbitch," Truslow said. "Just like his pa. I tell you, if the Ives family were mules you'd have shot the whole damn lot at birth."

"All right, Sergeant!" Starbuck said reprovingly, then smiled down at the wet, miserable Ives. "You know who's following us?" he asked.

"Some of our cavalry," Ives said.

"And behind the cavalry?" Starbuck asked gently.

"Yankees."

"Just hit the no-good bastard," Truslow growled.

"You leave me alone!" Ives shouted at the Sergeant. Ives had been emboldened by Starbuck's gentle and considerate manner and by the support of the other stragglers, who murmured their resentment of Truslow's brutality and their appreciation of Starbuck's reasonable tone.

"And do you know what the Yankees will do to you?" Starbuck asked Ives.

"Reckon it can't be worse than this, Captain," Ives said.

Starbuck nodded. "So you can't go on?"

"Reckon I can't."

The other stragglers murmured their agreement. They were all too tired, too pained, too wet, too desperate, and too unhappy even to think of continuing the march. All they wanted was to collapse beside the road, and beyond that thought of immediate rest they had no cares or fears.

"You can stay here then," Starbuck told Ives.

Truslow growled in protest. The other stragglers grinned with pleasure as Ives, his battle apparently won, struggled to his feet.

"There is just one other thing," Starbuck said pleasantly.

"Captain?" Ives was eager to please now.

"You can stay here, Ives, but I can't let you keep any equipment that belongs to the government. That wouldn't be fair, would it? We don't want to give the Yankees our precious guns and uniforms, do we now?" He smiled.

Ives was suddenly wary. He shook his head very cautiously, but clearly he did not really understand what Starbuck was saying.

Starbuck turned to his company. "Amos, Ward, Decker, come here!" The three men ran over to Starbuck, who nodded toward Ives. "Strip the gutless bastard naked."

"You can't . . . " Ives began, but Starbuck took one pace and thumped him in the belly, then brought his other hand up to slap his head hard back. Ives collapsed in the mud again.

"Strip him!" Starbuck said. "Cut the bastard's clothes clean off."

"Jesus Christ," one of the other stragglers blasphemed in disbelief as Starbuck's men ripped and tore Ives's clothes away. Truslow, grinning now, had taken the man's rifle and ammunition. Ives was screaming that he wanted to stay with the Legion, but Starbuck knew he needed to make an example of one man, and it was Ives's misfortune to be that man. Ives thrashed and fought, but he was no match for Starbuck's men who pulled off his boots, his pack, and his blanket roll, dragged his pants down, and cut away his jacket and shirt. Ives was left in nothing but a grimy pair of frayed drawers. He staggered to his feet, blood oozing from the blow Starbuck had given his nose.

"I'll keep going, Captain!" Ives pleaded. "Really I will!"

"Take your drawers off," Starbuck said harshly.

"You can't!" Ives backed away, but Robert Decker tripped him, then leaned over and ripped the frayed undergarment away to leave Ives stark-naked in the rain and mud.

Starbuck looked at the other stragglers. "If any one of you wants to stay here and get acquainted with the

Yankees, then get undressed now! If you don't, then get walking."

They all began walking. Some exaggerated their limps to show that they had genuine cause to be laggards, but Starbuck shouted that he could strip a cripple far faster than he could rip the clothes off a whole man, and that encouragement made the stragglers walk faster. Some even half ran as they hurried to get clear of Starbuck and Truslow, spreading the word as they went that there was no mercy to be had at the rear of the Legion's column.

·Ives pleaded for his clothes. Starbuck drew his pistol. "Get the hell away from here!"

"You can't do this!"

Starbuck fired. The bullet splashed mud onto Ives's fish-belly-white calves. "Run!" Starbuck shouted. "Go to the Yankees, you son of a bitch!"

"I'll kill you!" Ives shouted. He was running now, splashing jaybird-naked down the road toward Manassas. "I'll kill you, you Yankee bastard!"

Starbuck holstered the revolver and grinned at Truslow. "You see, Sergeant? Sweet reason always works, every time."

"You're a smart son of a gun, ain't you?"

"Yes, Sergeant, I am. Forward now!" Starbuck called to the company and they marched on, grinning, while Truslow handed out Ives's ammunition. The number of stragglers dropped to a handful, and that handful seemed composed of men who were genuinely crippled. Starbuck had his men take their weapons and cartridges, but otherwise left them alone. There were no more malingerers.

In the early afternoon the Legion trudged past what had once been the largest meat-curing factory in the Confederacy, but was now an inferno of yellow and blue flames. Fat hissed and crackled and sent molten streams pouring down through the hovels where the factory's slaves lived. The Negroes watched the soldiers pass and betrayed not a flicker of emotion. Soon, they knew, the northerners would come, but they dared show no pleasure at that prospect. Children clung to their mothers' aprons, the men watched from shadows, while behind them the burning meat roasted and fried to send a tantalizing aroma of beef and bacon across a wide swath of damp country.

The smell of bacon stayed with the Legion right into the middle of the afternoon when the cavalry rearguard at last caught up with the retreating infantry. The troopers dismounted and led their tired, sweat-whitened horses by the reins. Some of the troopers had no saddles and were using folded squares of heavy cloth instead, while others had bridles made of knotted ropes. The men scanned the road verges as they walked south, looking for anything useful among the equipment that had been thrown aside by the infantry battalions ahead. There were coats, tents, blankets, and weapons, all of them taken from the stores abandoned at Manassas, but then found to be too heavy to carry and so simply thrown away. The Legion's dogs gorged themselves on food that had been snatched from the burning depots but that now was being jettisoned as the men's weariness increased. "It feels more like a defeat than a retreat," Starbuck grumbled to Thaddeus Bird.

"I believe the textbooks describe it as a tactical withdrawal," Bird said with relish. He was enjoying the day. The sight of so much material being burned was proof of the essential idiocy of mankind and especially that portion of mankind which was in authority, and Bird always enjoyed such proofs of general stupidity. Indeed his enjoyment was so great that he sometimes felt guilty for it. "Though I don't suppose you ever feel guilty, do you, Starbuck?"

"Me?" Starbuck was startled by the question. "All the time."

"For enjoying the war?"

"For being a sinner."

"Ha!" Bird liked that confession. "You mean that blacksmith's wife in Manassas? What a fool you are! To feel guilty for doing what is natural? Does the tree feel guilty for growing? Or the bird for flying? Your fault is not the commission of sins, Starbuck, but your fear of loneliness."

That cut too close to the bone, so close that Starbuck ignored the comment altogether. "Your conscience is never tender?" he asked Bird instead.

"I never allowed my conscience to be confused by the bleating of God's ministers," Bird said. "I never listened long enough, you understand. Good Lord, Starbuck, if it had not been for this war you might well be an ordained man of God by now! You'd be marrying people instead of killing them!" Bird laughed, jerking his head back and forth, then suddenly turned as a rifle fired far behind the Legion. A bullet whipped through the trees and the dismounted rebel cavalry immediately turned to meet the threat. A troop of Yankee horsemen had appeared in the distance. The rain made the enemy difficult to see, though every now and then a puff of white smoke betrayed the spot where a carbine had been fired. The sound of the gun would come flat and dull a few seconds later, just after the bullet had slapped into the wet road or flicked harmlessly through the pine needles. The northern cavalry was firing at very long range, relying on luck rather than marksmanship for any effect.

"This calls for your fellows, Nate," Major Bird said with an unholy relish. Bird had firm beliefs about musketry. He liked to hold his regimental volleys until the very last moment and he believed his skirmishing companies should be sharpshooters, and Starbuck's insistence on constant practice had made K Company into the Legion's most lethal skirmishers. A handful of the men, like Esau Washbrook and William Tolby, were natural marksmen, but even the most inept members of the company had improved in the months of training. Joseph May was one of the inept men, though in his case the improvement in his marksmanship was owed to the pair of gold-rimmed spectacles that had been taken from a dead Yankee captain at Ball's Bluff.

Major Bird now stared down the long road that led straight between dark evergreen trees. "One well-aimed volley, Nate. The rascals won't risk coming close, and once they know we can shoot they'll drop even farther back, so the omnipotent, all-seeing God is only giving us one chance to send their miserable souls to hell." He rubbed his thin hands. "Would you be offended if I gave the orders, Nate?"

Starbuck, amused by Bird's bloodthirsty enthusiasm, assured his commanding officer that no offense would be taken, then told his company to find themselves firing positions and to load their rifles. There were about a dozen Yankee cavalrymen in sight, but more were probably hidden by the ruins of a clapboard tavern which stood at the bend in the road where the enemy had appeared. The northerners were firing their carbines from their saddles in the evident belief that they were too far from the rebel rearguard to be in real danger. Their fire was not so much a threat as a mockery, a parting, derisive gesture to the retreating rebels. The Confederate cavalry were firing back, but their makeshift collection of revolvers, sporting guns, and captured carbines were proving even more inaccurate than the northern gunfire.

"A quarter mile!" Truslow shouted. That was very long range for the Legion's rifles. As a rule Starbuck reckoned that shots fired at distances greater than two hundred yards were probably wasted unless one of the company's best marksmen was firing, but a quarter mile was not an impossible distance. He loaded his own rifle, first biting the bullet off the top of the paper-wrapped cartridge, then pouring the powder down the barrel. He stuffed the empty paper into the barrel as wadding, then spat the bullet into the muzzle. The bitter, salty taste of gunpowder lingered in his mouth as he pulled out the rifle's steel ramrod. He thrust the cone-shaped bullet hard down onto the wadding and powder, then slotted the ramrod back into its place. Finally he fished out a small copper percussion cap that he fumbled over the rifle's breech cone. The cap was filled with a pinch of fulminate of mercury, a chemical unstable enough to explode when struck sharply. The rifle's hammer, cracking on the cap, would cause the fulminate to explode and so lance a needle of fire down through the pierced cone into the gunpowder he had rammed into the rifle's breech.

An enemy bullet spat into a puddle thirty yards short of the company and spewed up a splash of dirty water. Ned Hunt, ever the company's clown, jeered at the distant cavalry until Truslow told him to curb his damn tongue. Starbuck knelt beside a tree on which he could steady his aim. He lifted the rear leaf sight to four hundred yards, then, because cold rifles fired short, added an extra hundred for good measure.

"Give us room, boys!" Major Bird called out to the rebel cavalry, and the gray-coated, long-haired horsemen pulled their horses back past Starbuck's company.

"You won't hit a thing, boys!" one of the horsemen shouted good-naturedly. "You might as well chuck rocks at the bastards."

There were more Yankees visible at the bend in the road now, maybe a score altogether. Some had dismounted to kneel beside the tavern while others still aimed and fired from the saddle. "We'll shoot at the group on the right!" Bird called. "Remember to aim off for the wind, and wait for my order!"

Starbuck edged his barrel leftward, so allowing for the wind that gusted out of the east. Rain beaded the rifle's barrel as he laid the foresight on a horseman in the center of the Yankee group. "I'll count to three, then give the order," Major Bird announced. He was standing in the very center of the roadway and staring at the enemy through one half of a pair of field glasses he had taken from a corpse at Manassas. "One," he sang out, and Starbuck tried to control the wavering of his rifle's muzzle. "Two!" Major Bird called, and the rain stung Starbuck's eyes, making him blink as he raised the stock so that the leaf sight framed the foresight. "Three," Bird cried, and the company held their collective breath and tried to freeze their muscles into rigidity. Starbuck held the foresight exactly over the blurred figure of a mounted man a quarter mile away and kept it there until at last Bird shouted the order. "Fire!"

Fifty rifles cracked almost in unison, spitting a ragged cloud of white powder smoke across the wet road. The butt of Starbuck's rifle slammed into his shoulder while a bitter spew of exploding fulminate seared his nostril. Major Bird ran clear of the powder smoke and trained his broken glass at the far bend in the road. A horse was galloping loose there, a man was down on the road, a second was limping toward the wood, while a third crawled in the mud. Another horse was down, kicking and thrashing, while beyond the dying beast a score of Yankees scattered like chaff. "Well done!" Bird shouted. "Now form up and march on!"

"How did we do?" Starbuck asked.

"Three men and a horse," Bird said. "Maybe one of the three men dead?"

"Out of fifty shots?" Starbuck asked.

"I read somewhere," Bird said happily, "that it took two hundred musket shots to cause one casualty in Napoleon's wars, so three men and a horse from fifty bullets doesn't seem a bad tally to me." He gave an abrupt bark of laughter, jerking his head back and forth in the mannerism that had earned him his nickname. He explained his merriment as he put the broken field glass away. "Just six months ago, Nate, I was full of scruples about killing. Now, dear me, I seem to regard it as a measure of success. Adam is right, war does change us."

"He had that conversation with you, too?"

"He allowed his conscience to leak all over me, if that's what you mean. It was hardly a conversation as he regarded any contribution of mine as irrelevant. Instead he moaned at me, then asked me to pray with him." Bird shook his head. "Poor Adam, he really should not be in uniform."

"Nor should his father," Starbuck said grimly.

"True." Bird walked in silence for a few paces. A small farm had been cut from the trees by the side of the road and the farmer, a white-bearded man with a tall ragged hat and hair that fell past his shoulders, stood in his door and watched the soldiers pass. "I keep fearing that Faulconer will reappear among us," Bird said, "full of bluster and dignity. Yet every day that passes and he is not reappointed or, God help us, given a brigade, serves to astonish me that perhaps there is some common sense in our high command after all."

"But none in our newspapers?" Starbuck observed.

"Don't remind me, please." Bird shuddered to recall the editorial in the Richmond *Examiner* that had called for Washington Faulconer's promotion. Bird wondered how newspapers could get things so utterly wrong, then pondered how many of his own prejudices and ideas had been

131

shaped by similarly mistaken journalism. But at least no one in Richmond seemed to have heeded the editorial. "I've been thinking," Bird said after a while, then promptly fell silent.

"And?" Starbuck prompted the Major.

"I've been wondering why we call ourselves the Faulconer Legion," Bird said. "After all, we're no longer in his lordship's pay. We are charges on the Commonwealth of Virginia, and I think we should find ourselves a new name."

"The 45th? The 60th? The 121st?" Starbuck suggested sourly. State regiments were given numbers according to their seniority, and somehow being the 50th Virginia or the 101st Virginia was not quite the same as being the Legion.

"The Virginia Sharpshooters," Bird suggested proudly.

Starbuck thought about the name, and the more he thought the more he liked it. "And what about the colors?" he asked. "You want the Virginia Sharpshooters to go into battle under the Faulconer coat of arms?"

"A new color, I think," Bird said. "Something bold, bloody, and resolute. Maybe with the state motto? *Sic semper tyrannis!*" Bird declaimed the words dramatically, then laughed. Starbuck laughed too. The motto meant that anyone who tried to oppress the Commonwealth of Virginia would meet the same humiliating defeat as King George III, but the threat could equally well refer to the Colonel who had abandoned his own Legion when it marched against the enemy at Manassas. "I like the idea," Starbuck said, "very much."

The company breasted a small rise in the road to see the smoke of a bivouac rising from a ridge half a mile away. The rain and clouds were masking the setting sun to bring on an early dusk in which the campfires on the ridge showed bright. The ridge was where the division's rearguard would spend the night, protected by a stream and two batteries of artillery that stood silhouetted on the far skyline. Most of the Legion had already reached the encampment, far ahead of Starbuck's company, which had been delayed by its encounter with the stragglers and its brush with the Yankee cavalry. "Home comforts in sight," Bird said happily.

"Thank God," Starbuck said. The sling of his rifle was chafing through his soaking uniform, his boots squelched with rain, and the prospect of resting by a fire was like a foretaste of heaven.

"Is that Murphy?" Bird squinted through the rain at a horseman who was galloping down the road from the ridge. "Looking for me, I daresay," Bird said, and he waved to attract the Irishman's attention. Murphy, a fine horseman, spurred through a shallow ford, galloped up to K Company, then turned his horse in a flurry of hooves and mud to rein in beside Bird. "There's a man waiting for you in the encampment, Pecker. He's kind of demanding you hurry up and see him."

"Does his rank make his demand important to me?"

"I reckon it does, Pecker." Murphy curbed his excited horse. Mud splashed up from the beast's hooves to spatter Bird's trousers. "His name's Swynyard. Colonel Griffin Swynyard."

"Never heard of him," Bird said cheerfully. "Unless he's a Swynyard of the old slaver family? They were a nasty set. My father always reckoned you needed to stay well upwind of a Swynyard. Does this fellow smell, Murphy?"

"No worse than you or me, Pecker," Murphy said. "But he wants you on the chop, he says."

"You can tell him to boil his head, perhaps?" Bird suggested happily.

"Reckon not, Pecker," Murphy said sadly. "Reckon not. He's got new orders for us, you see. We're changing brigades."

"Oh God, no," Bird said, guessing the awful truth. "Faulconer?"

Murphy nodded. "'Fraid so, Pecker. Faulconer himself isn't here, but Swynyard's his new second-in-command." Murphy paused, then looked at Starbuck. "He wants you too, Nate."

Starbuck swore. But swearing would do no good. Washington Faulconer had secured his brigade, and with it he had taken back his Legion.

And suddenly the day really did feel like defeat.

A group of men, some in civilian clothes and some in uniforms, walked slowly along the line of abandoned fortifications north of the rail depot at Manassas. The day was ebbing fast, draining a wet land of what small gray light had illuminated its misery. The rain was helping to reduce the fires set by the retreating Confederates into damp smoking piles of evil-smelling ash through which the newly arrived northern troops raked in hopes of salvaging souvenirs. The townspeople looked sourly on these invading Yankees who were the first free northerners seen in Manassas since the war had begun. A few free blacks offered a better welcome to the Federal troops, bringing out plates of hoecakes and dodgers, though even that generosity was offered cautiously for the town's northern sympathizers could not be certain that the wind of battle would not turn south once more and bring the Confederate army back.

Yet for now the northern army controlled the rail junction and the commander of that army was inspecting the earthworks abandoned by the retreating Confederates. Major General George Brinton McClellan was a small man, stoutly built, with a full, fresh-colored, and boyish face. He was just thirty-five years old, but made up for his youthfulness with a stiff dignity and a permanent scowl that helped compensate for his diminutive stature. He also cultivated a small mustache that he mistakenly supposed added authority to his looks, but which only made his youth more apparent. Now, in the smoky air of the rail junction, he stopped to examine one of the black-painted logs that jutted like a cannon's muzzle across the wet embrasure.

A dozen staff officers paused behind the Major General and stared with him at the dripping, black-painted log. No one spoke until a weighty civilian broke the portentous silence. "It's a log, General," the civilian said in heavy sarcasm. "What we folk back in Illinois call a tree trunk."

Major General George Brinton McClellan did not dignify the remark with a reply. Instead, and taking fastidious care to avoid placing his polished boots in the deeper puddles, he walked to the next embrasure, where he gave an almost identical log another earnest examination. A rebel had chalked two small words on the fake gun's muzzle: "Ho Ho."

"Ho ho," the man from Illinois said. He was middle-aged, red-faced, and a Congressman known to be close to President Lincoln. Such a relationship would have inhibited most officers from offending the politician, but McClellan despised the Congressman for being one of the Republican mudsills who had spent the winter mocking the Army of the Potomac for its inactivity. "All quiet on the Potomac," the mockers sang, demanding to know why the most expensive army in America's history had waited somnolent throughout the winter before advancing on the enemy. It was men like this Congressman who were nagging the President to find a more combative soldier to lead the northern armies, and McClellan was tired of their criticism. He showed his contempt by pointedly turning his back on the Congressman and glaring at one of his staff officers instead. "The Quakers were placed here this morning, you think?"

The staff officer, an engineer colonel, had examined the Quaker guns and deduced from the rotted state of their butt ends that the logs had been in place since the previous summer at least, which meant that the Federal Army of the United States, the largest force ever assembled in America, had spent the last few months being scared away by a bunch of felled trees smeared with pitch. The Colonel, however, knew better than to confirm such a view to General McClellan. "Maybe they were emplaced yesterday, sir," he said tactfully.

"But there were real guns here last week?" McClellan demanded fiercely.

"Oh, undoubtedly," the Colonel lied.

"For sure," another officer added, nodding sagely.

"We saw them!" a third northern officer claimed, though in truth he was wondering whether his patrolling cavalry had been fooled by these painted logs which, from a distance, did look astonishingly like real cannon.

"These tree trunks" – the Illinois Congressman put a derisive spin on the words – "look pretty well-established to me." He clambered over the muddy embrasure, streaking his clothes with dirt, then slid heavily down beside the Quaker gun. There must have been real guns in the embrasures once, for the fake guns rested on gently ramped earth slopes that had been faced with wooden planks up which a firing gun would have recoiled before rolling gently back into position. The Congressman almost lost his footing on the old wooden planks that were slick with a greasy, damp mold. He kept his balance by holding on to the Quaker's barrel, then hacked down with his right foot. The heel of his shoe broke clean through the rotted planks of the platform to disturb a colony of sowbugs that crawled desperately away from the daylight. The Congressman took a wet chewed stump of a cigar from his mouth. "Don't see as how a real gun could have stood here in months, General. I reckon you've been wetting your pants because of a bunch of sawn-off tree trunks."

"What you are witnessing, Congressman" – McClellan wheeled fiercely on the politician – "is a victory! Maybe an unparalleled victory in the annals of our country! A magnificent victory. A triumph of scientifically employed arms!" The general threw a dramatic hand toward the pyres of smoke and the scattered pairs of blackened boxcar wheels and the tall brick chimney stacks that had been left gaunt among the smoldering embers. "Behold, sir," McClellan said, waving his arm at the dispiriting landscape, "a defeated army. An army that has retreated before our victorious advance like hay falling before the scythe."

The Congressman obediently surveyed the scene. "Precious few bodies, General."

"A war won by maneuver, sir, is a merciful war. You should fall to your knees and thank Almighty God for it." McClellan made that his parting shot and strode briskly away toward the town.

The Congressman shook his head, but said nothing. Instead he just watched as a lean man wearing a threadbare and tarnished French cavalry uniform climbed over the embrasure to look at the Quaker gun. The Frenchman wore a monstrous straight sword at his side, had a missing eye disguised with a patch, and displayed a cheerful demeanor. His name was Colonel Lassan and he was a French military observer who had been attached to the northern army since before the previous summer's battle at Bull Run. Now he jabbed his toe against the planks of the gun platform. His spurs jingled as the rotted wood broke apart under his half-hearted kick. "Well, Lassan?" the Congressman demanded. "What do you make of it?"

"I am but a mere guest in your country," Lassan said

137

tactfully, "a foreigner and an observer, and so my opinion, Congressman, is of no importance."

"You've got eyes, ain't you? Well, one anyway," the Congressman added hastily. "You don't have to be an American to decide whether this piece of lumber was put in place just yesterday."

Lassan smiled. His face was foully scarred, but there was something indomitable and mischievous in his expression. He was a sociable man who spoke perfect English with a British accent. "I've learned one thing about your wonderful country," he said to the Congressman, "which is that we mere Europeans should keep our criticisms to ourselves."

"Patronizing frog son of a goddamn bitch," the Congressman said. He liked the Frenchman, even though the one-eyed bastard had taken two months' salary off him at a poker game the night before. "So you tell me, Lassan. Were these logs put here yesterday?"

"I think the logs have been here somewhat longer than General McClellan assumes," Lassan said tactfully.

The Congressman glowered at the General's party which was now a hundred paces off. "I reckon he doesn't want to get his nice clean army dirty by getting into a brawl with some nasty, ill-mannered southern boys. Is that what you reckon, Lassan?"

Lassan reckoned the war could be over in a month if the northern army just marched straight ahead, took some casualties, and kept on marching, but he was far too diplomatic to pick sides in the disagreements that were argued so fiercely in Washington's offices and across the capital's well-stocked dining tables. So Lassan simply shrugged off the question, then was saved from further interrogation by the arrival of a newspaper sketch artist who began making a drawing of the rotted planks and the decaying log.

"You're seeing a victory, son," the Congressman said

sarcastically, peeling off the damper parts of his cigar before thrusting it back into his mouth.

"It sure ain't a defeat, Congressman," the artist said loyally.

"You think this is victory? Son, we didn't throw the rebels out, they just strolled away in their own sweet time! They're getting their wooden guns ready someplace else by now. We won't have real victory till we string Jeff Davis up by his scrawny heels. I tell you, son, these here guns have been rotting here since last year. I reckon our Young Napoleon's just been humbugged again. Wooden guns for a timberhead." The Congressman spat into the mud. "You make a sketch of these wooden cannon, son, and be sure to show the wheelmarks where the real guns were towed away."

The artist frowned at the mud beyond the decaying firing ramps. "There ain't any wheelmarks."

"You got it, son. And that means you're one long jump ahead of our Young Napoleon." The Congressman stumped away, accompanied by the French observer.

A hundred paces away another man in civilian dress stood frowning at another of the Quaker guns. This man had a tough, squat, thick-bearded face out of which a blackened pipe jutted belligerently. He wore a shabby riding coat, tall boots, and a round, narrow-brimmed hat. He carried a small horsewhip that he suddenly cut viciously across the fake muzzle of one of the wooden guns, then turned and shouted for an assistant to bring his horse.

Later that night the bearded man received a visitor in the parlor of the house that was his quarters. Houses were scarce in Manassas, so scarce that most men beneath the rank of lieutenant general were forced to live in tents, so the fact that this civilian had a whole house for his own use was proof of his importance. The chalk inscription on the

139

house door read "Major E. J. Allan," though the man was neither a soldier nor bore the surname Allan, but instead was a civilian who liked to use pseudonyms and disguises. His true name was Allan Pinkerton and he had been a detective in Chicago's police force before General McClellan had appointed him as head of the Army of the Potomac's Secret Service Bureau. Now, in the guttering light of candles, Pinkerton looked up at the tall, nervous officer who had been fetched from the tail of the army into his presence. "You're Major James Starbuck?"

"Yes, sir," James Starbuck responded in the cautious manner of a man who expects any summons to presage trouble. These days James looked a disconsolate soul. From being a lofty staff officer, privy to the secrets of the army's commander, he had been relegated to a job with the commissary department of the 1st Corps. His new duties were concerned with the supply of dried vegetables, flour, jerked beef, salt pork, hardtack, and coffee beans, duties he discharged conscientiously, but however much food he managed to supply it was never enough, so that officers from every regiment and battery and troop felt free to swear at him as a useless, black-assed son of a pious bitch. James knew he should ignore such insults, but instead they overwhelmed and humiliated him. He had rarely felt so miserable.

Now, to James's astonishment, he saw that the man called Allan was studying Adam's long letter which James had sent to Major General McClellan's headquarters back in the old year. As far as James was aware, the letter had been utterly ignored by the army's high command, and since James had neither the authority nor the character to persuade anyone of the letter's importance, he had assumed the letter was long forgotten, yet now this unprepossessing Major Allan had finally realized its value. "So who gave you this letter, Major?" Pinkerton demanded.

"I promised not to say, sir." James wondered why he was calling this shabby little man "sir." It was not as though Allan outranked James, yet something in the man's pugnacious demeanor brought out James's natural subservience, though at the same time it also triggered a tiny streak of stubbornness as he decided he would not use the honorific again.

Pinkerton stabbed at the tobacco in his pipe with a callused finger, then placed the bowl by a candle flame and sucked it alight. "You've got a brother with the rebels?"

James blushed, and no wonder, for Nate's treason was a matter of immense shame to the Starbuck family. "Yes, si- . . . Major. I do, alas."

"Did he write this letter?"

"No, si- . . . Major. No, he didn't. I wish he had."

Pinkerton's pipe bubbled as he sucked on the short stem. Wind gusted at the window and howled in the short chimney, driving a billow of thick smoke back into the room. "If I assure you that I can be trusted, Major," Pinkerton said, his voice retaining the soft burr of his native Scotland, "and if I cross my heart and hope to die, and if I swear to you upon my dear departed mother's soul and upon the soul of her own dear mother and upon all the Bibles in all of North America as well, and if by so swearing I promise you that I will never, not ever, reveal your informant's name to any man, will you tell me?"

James felt the temptation. Maybe, if he gave Adam's name, he might be relieved of his foul commissary duty, but he had given his word and he would not break it, and so he just shook his head. "No, Major, I would not tell you. I would trust you, but I could not break my word."

"Good for you, Starbuck. Good for you." Pinkerton hid his disappointment and frowned at Adam's letter again.

141

"Your man was right," he went on, "and all the rest were wrong. Your man told us the truth, or something close to it. He got Johnston's numbers wrong, we know for a fact the rebel army's at least twice the size he told you, but everything else here is spot on the mark, straight on the target, good as gold!" What had impressed Pinkerton was Adam's description of the wooden Quaker guns. He had given their exact number and location, and Pinkerton, coming on the guns in the rainy twilight, had remembered the discarded report and had ordered it dug out of his files. There were hundreds of such discarded reports, many the work of imaginative patriots, some mere suppositions based on newspaper stories, while others undoubtedly were sent by southerners attempting to mislead the North. So much information flowed north that Pinkerton was forced to throw much away, yet now he realized he had discarded some gold with the dross. "Has your man sent you any other letters?"

"No, Major."

Pinkerton leaned back in his chair, making its legs creak ominously. "Do you think he would be willing to supply us with more information?"

"I'm sure he would, yes." James's greatcoat dripped water on the parlor floor. He was shivering with cold, despite the small fire that spat angrily but gave precious little warmth to the shabby room. A bare patch on the plaster above the fireplace betrayed where a picture had been hastily removed prior to the northern army's arrival; maybe a portrait of Jeff Davis or perhaps of Beauregard, who was the victor of Manassas and the South's favorite general.

Pinkerton peered closely at the letter again, wondering why he had not taken it seriously before. He noted that the writing paper was of high quality, plainly from a stock left over from before the war and of much better manufacture than the discolored, fibrous, and paltry stuff the South now made. The writer had used capital letters, thus disguising his handwriting, but the grammar and vocabulary betrayed him to be a well-educated man, and the information revealed him to be a man at the very heart of the rebel army. Pinkerton knew he had made a mistake when he had first ignored this letter, yet he consoled himself that some nuggets were bound to be lost in the chaos. "Remind me how your man got this letter to you?" Pinkerton demanded.

James had explained the circumstances in a covering letter that he had attached to Adam's long screed, but apparently that explanation had long disappeared. "He gave it to me in Richmond, Major, when I was exchanged."

"And how would you communicate with him now?"

"He said letters should be left in the vestibule of St. Paul's Church in Richmond. There's a bulletin board in that vestibule, criss-crossed with tape, and if a letter is placed under the tapes addressed to the Honorary Secretary of the Confederate Army Bible Supply Society, then he will collect it. I don't think there is any such society," James said, then paused. "And I have to confess I wouldn't know how to get a letter to Richmond." He added the admission humbly.

"Nothing to it, man. We do it almost every day," Pinkerton said heartily, then he pulled open a leather valise and took out a traveling writing case. "We're going to need your friend's help, Major, in these coming weeks." He took a sheet of paper from the case, added an ink bottle and pen, and pushed them all across the table. "Sit yourself down."

"You want me to write to him now, Major?" James asked in astonishment.

"No time like the present, Starbuck! Strike while the iron's still steaming, isn't that what they say? Tarry not! Tell your friend that his intelligence is of the greatest value, and that it was appreciated at the very highest levels of the Federal army." Pinkerton had discovered that a little flattery went a long way with secret agents. He paused as James pulled a candle near his paper and began to write in a swift, efficient hand. The pen had a split nib that spattered small droplets of ink as it scratched fast across the paper. "Write something personal," Pinkerton went on, "so he'll know it's you."

"I already have," James said. He had expressed the hope that Adam had found an opportunity to pass on the Bible to Nate.

"Now write that we would be obliged to your friend if he could help us with the enclosed request."

"Enclosed request?" James asked in puzzlement.

"You won't tell me who he is," Pinkerton said, "so I'm hardly going to tell you what we want of him."

James rested the pen on the edge of the table. He frowned. "Will he be at risk, sir?"

"Risk? Of course he'll be at risk! There's a war on! Risk is the very air we breathe!" Pinkerton scowled and sucked his tobacco pipe at the candle's flame again. "Is your man doing this for money?"

James stiffened at the implication. "He's a patriot, Major. And a Christian."

"Then the reward of heaven is surely all the more reason for him to run a risk?" Pinkerton demanded. "But do you think I want to lose your man? Of course not! I promise you I'll not ask him to do anything which I would not expect my own son to do, of that you can be sure, Major. But let me tell you something else." Pinkerton, as though demonstrating how important his next words were, removed the pipe from his mouth and cuffed the spittle from his lips. "What I'll be asking of your man could well win us this war. That's how important it is, Major."

James dutifully took up the pen. "You simply want me to ask him to fulfill the enclosed request."

"Aye, Major, that's what I want. Then I'll bother you to address the envelope for me." Pinkerton leaned back and sucked on his pipe. He would be asking Adam for information about the rebel defenses to the east of Richmond, for it was in that damp and empty landscape, any day now, that General McClellan planned to spring his surprise attack on the rebel capital. This present slow advance toward the ruins of Manassas had only ever been intended to keep the Confederate army pinned north of their capital while McClellan secretly launched the greatest fleet of history to carry his real attack force around to the rebels' eastern flank. Richmond by May, Pinkerton told himself, peace by July, and the rewards of victory for the rest of his life.

He took the letter and envelope from James. The envelope was made of lumpy brown paper that one of Pinkerton's agents had brought back from a secret visit to the Confederacy and James had addressed it to the Honorable Secretary of the Confederate Army Bible Supply Society care of St. Paul's, Grace Street, Richmond. Pinkerton found one of the cheap-looking green five-cent stamps showing Jefferson Davis's sunken face and gummed it onto the envelope. "This informant, I suppose, will only trust you?" Pinkerton asked.

"Indeed," James confirmed.

Pinkerton nodded. If this strange spy would only trust James, then Pinkerton wanted to make certain James was always close at hand. "And before the war, Major," he asked, "what was your trade?"

"It was a profession," James corrected Pinkerton sternly. "I was a lawyer in Boston."

"A lawyer, eh?" Pinkerton stood and went close to the

feeble fire. "It was my dear mother's wish that I should be a lawyer, what in Scotland they call a writer to the signet, but alas, there was never the money for the schooling. But I like to think I would have made a fine attorney had I been given the chance."

"I'm sure you would," James said, sure of no such thing.

"And as a lawyer, Major, you're accustomed to sifting evidence? To winnowing truth from falsehood?"

"Indeed," James said.

"I ask you," Pinkerton explained, "because of late this bureau has been suffering from lack of good order. We've been too busy to keep our files as neat as I'd like, and I need a chief of staff, Major, someone who can make judgments and marshal evidence. I assure you that General McClellan will authorize the move instantly, so there'll be no problems with your present commanding officer. Is it presumptuous of me to offer you such a job?"

"It's most generous, sir, most generous," James said, quite forgetting his sturdy resolve not to call this man "sir." "I should be honored to join you," he went on hurriedly, hardly daring to believe that he was truly being rescued from the echoing, damp store sheds of the commissary department.

"In that case, welcome aboard, Major." Pinkerton held out a hand of welcome. "We don't stand on ceremony here," he said when he had given James's hand a sturdy grip and a vigorous pumping, "so from now on you can call me Bulldog."

"Bulldog?" James stuttered the word.

"Just a nickname, Major," Pinkerton assured James.

"Very good," James hesitated, "Bulldog. And I should be honored if you were to know me as James."

"I intended to, Jimmy, I intended to! We'll start work in the morning, so we shall. You'll want to fetch your traps

146

tonight? You can sleep in the scullery here if you don't mind a rat or two?"

"I became accustomed to rats while in prison," James said, "and worse."

"Then be on your way, Major! We need to start work early in the morning," Pinkerton said, and then, once James had gone, the head of the Secret Service sat and wrote a brief letter that would go south inside James's covering note. The letter asked for detailed information on the rebel defenses east of Richmond, and particularly asked how many troops manned those defenses. Pinkerton then requested that this information be delivered to a Mr. Timothy Webster, care of the Ballard House Hotel on Richmond's Franklin Street.

Timothy Webster was Pinkerton's most brilliant spy, a man who had already made three forays into the Confederacy and was now in the middle of his fourth. This time Webster had established himself as a blockade-running merchant seeking business in Richmond, while in truth he was using the Secret Service's funds to make friends with indiscreet rebel officers and politicians. Webster's mission was to discover and betray the defenses of Richmond, a job that involved horrible risks, but now, with the advent of James Starbuck's informant, Pinkerton felt certain of Webster's success. He sealed the two sheets of paper into the envelope, uncorked a bottle of his precious Scotch whisky and offered himself a toast. To victory.

COLONEL GRIFFIN SWYNYARD was greedily eating a plate of fried cabbage and potato when Bird and Starbuck reached his tent. It had begun to rain and the heavy clouds had brought a premature dusk so that the Colonel's tent needed to be lit with two lanterns that hung from the ridge pole. The newly promoted Colonel sat beneath the twin lamps wearing a voluminous gown of gray wool over uniform trousers and a dirty shirt. He flinched whenever a bite provoked a twinge of agony from one of his yellowed, decayed teeth. His servant, a cowed slave, had announced Major Bird and Captain Starbuck and then scuttled back into the night where the rearguard's fires struggled against the wind and rain. "So you're Bird," Swynyard said, pointedly ignoring Starbuck.

"And you're Swynyard," Bird responded with a matching curtness.

"Colonel Swynyard. West Point, class of twenty-nine, late U.S. Army, 4th Infantry." Swynyard's bloodshot eyes had a sickly yellow cast in the lamplight. He chewed a spoonful of his dinner, then helped it down with a mouthful of whiskey. "Now appointed second-in-command to the Faulconer Brigade." He pointed his spoon at Bird. "Which makes me your superior officer."

Bird acknowledged the relationship with a curt nod, but refused to call Swynyard "sir," which was presumably what the Colonel wanted. Swynyard did not press the point;

148

instead he scored across his supper plate with a sharp knife, then spooned up another mouthful of the unappetizing mixture. His tent had a newly sawn pinewood floor, a folding table, a chair, a camp bed, and a sawhorse that was being used as a stand for his saddle. The furniture, like the saddle and the tent, was all brand-new. It would have been expensive before the war, but what such equipment must have cost in this time of shortage, Bird did not like to guess. There was a wagon parked just outside the tent that Bird guessed was being used to transport Swynyard's comforts and was yet more evidence of the money that had been expended on the Colonel's accoutrements.

Swynyard bolted down his mouthful of food, then took another pull of his whiskey. Rain pattered on the tent's tight-stretched canvas, while in the dark a horse whinnied and a dog howled. "You are now in the Faulconer Brigade," Swynyard announced formally, "which consists of this Legion, the Izard County Volunteer Battalion from Arkansas, the 12th and 13th Florida Regiments, and the 65th Virginia. All of which are now under the orders of Brigadier General Washington Faulconer, God bless him, who is awaiting our arrival on the Rappahannock tomorrow. Questions?"

"How is my brother-in-law?" Bird asked politely.

"Military questions, Bird. Military."

"Is my brother-in-law's wound recovered sufficiently to allow him to fulfill his military duties at last?" Bird asked sweetly.

Swynyard ignored the mocking question. A tic throbbed in his right cheek as he used his maimed left hand to claw at his gray-streaked beard where a scatter of cabbage scraps had lodged. The Colonel had placed a wad of damp chewing tobacco to one side of his plate, and now he put the tobacco back into his mouth and sucked hard on it as he stood and edged around the sawhorse that served as his saddle stand. "Ever taken a scalp?" he challenged Bird.

"Not that I can recall, no." Bird managed to hide his surprise and distaste at the sudden question.

"There's a knack to it! Like any other skill, Bird, there's a knack! The trouble with young soldiers is that they always try to cut them off and that won't do. That won't do at all. No, you have to peel them off, peel them! Help the peel with a knife, if you must, but only to trim the edges, that way you get something fine and furry! Something like this!" Swynyard had taken a hank of black hair from the pocket of his gown and he waved it to and fro in front of Bird's face. "I've taken more savages' hairpieces than any white man alive," Swynyard went on, "and I'm proud of that, proud of it. I served my country well, Bird, none served it better, I daresay, yet my reward was to watch it elect that black-assed chimpanzee Lincoln, so now we must fight for a new country." Swynyard made this speech emotionally, leaning close enough so that Bird could smell a mix of cabbage, tobacco, and whiskey on his breath. "We shall get on, Bird, you and I. Man to man, eh? How is the regiment? Tell me that."

"They're well," Bird answered curtly.

"Let's hope it is well, Bird. Good and well! The General's not sure it should be commanded by a major, you understand me?" Swynyard held his face close to Bird's as he spoke. "So you and I had better get along, Major, if you want my good opinion to help sway the General's mind."

"What are you suggesting?" Bird asked quietly.

"I don't make suggestions, Major. I ain't clever enough to make suggestions. I'm just a blunt soldier who was weaned on the gun's black muzzle." Swynyard breathed a gust of hoarse laughter over Bird, then dragged the woolen gown tight around his thin chest before going unsteadily back to his chair. "All that matters to me," Swynyard continued after he had sat down, "is that the Legion is ready to fight and knows exactly why it is fighting. Do the men know that, Bird?"

"I'm sure they do," Bird said.

"You don't sound sure, Bird. You don't sound sure at all." Swynyard paused to take some more whiskey. "Soldiers are simple folk," he went on. "There ain't nothing complicated about a soldier, Bird. Point a soldier in the right direction, boot his backside, and tell him to kill, that's all a soldier needs, Bird! Soldiers are nothing more than white niggers, that's what I say, but even a nigger does better if he knows why he's doing it. Which is why, tonight, you will distribute these booklets to the men. I want them to know the nobility of the cause." Swynyard tried to lift a wooden box filled with pamphlets onto the table, but the box's weight defeated him, and so he used his foot to nudge the crate toward Bird instead.

Bird stooped for one of the booklets, then read the title page aloud. "'The Nigger Question,' by John Daniels." Bird's voice betrayed his distaste for John Daniels's virulent opinions. "You really want me to give this to the men?" he asked.

"You must!" Swynyard declared. "Johnny's my cousin, you see, and he sold those pamphlets to General Faulconer just so the men would read them."

"How generous of my brother-in-law," Bird said acidly.

"And how useful these pamphlets will be." Starbuck spoke for the first time since entering the tent.

Swynyard stared suspiciously at Starbuck. "Useful?" he asked in a dangerous voice after a long silence.

"Fires are terrible hard things to get started in this wet weather," Starbuck said blandly.

The tic in Swynyard's cheek began to flutter. He said

151

nothing for a long while, but just fidgeted with his bone-handled knife as he contemplated the young officer.

"Daniels is your cousin?" Bird broke the silence suddenly.

"Yes." Swynyard took his eyes off Starbuck and laid the knife back on the table.

"And your cousin, I presume," Bird said slowly as the light dawned on him, "wrote the editorial encouraging the army to promote Washington Faulconer?"

"What of it?" Swynyard asked.

"Nothing, nothing," Bird said, though he could hardly hide his amusement as he realized just what price his brother-in-law had paid for Daniels's support.

"You find something comical?" Swynyard demanded malevolently.

Bird sighed. "Colonel," he said, "we have marched a long way today, and I possess neither the energy nor the desire to stand here and explain my amusements. Is there anything else you want of me? Or might Captain Starbuck and I get some sleep?"

Swynyard stared at Bird for a few seconds, then pointed with his ravaged left hand at the tent's flap. "Go, Major. Send a man for the pamphlets. You stay here." The last three words were directed at Starbuck.

Bird did not move. "If you have business with one of my officers, Colonel," he said to Swynyard, "then you have business with me. I shall stay."

Swynyard shrugged as if to suggest he did not care if Bird stayed or went, then looked at Starbuck again. "How is your father, Starbuck?" Swynyard asked suddenly. "Still preaching brotherly love for the niggers, is he? Still expecting us to marry our daughters to the sons of Africa?" He paused for Starbuck's reply. One of the lamps flared suddenly, then its flame settled again. The sound of men's singing came from the rainy darkness. "Well, Starbuck!" Swynyard demanded. "Is your father still wanting us to give our daughters to the niggers?"

"My father never preached marriage between the races," Starbuck said mildly. He had no love for his father, but in the face of Swynyard's mockery he felt driven to defend the Reverend Elial.

The tic in Swynyard's cheek quivered, then he shot out his wounded left hand and pointed at the two stars that decorated the collar of his brand-new uniform jacket that hung from a nail hammered into one of the tent poles. "What does that insignia mean, Starbuck?"

"It means, I believe, that the jacket belongs to a lieutenant colonel," Starbuck said.

"It belongs to me!" Swynyard said in a rising voice.

Starbuck shrugged as though the jacket's ownership were of small consequence.

"And I outrank you!" Swynyard screamed the words, spewing a mist of spittle and tobacco juice across the remains of his cabbage and potato, "so you will call me 'sir'! Won't you!"

Starbuck still said nothing. The Colonel glared at him, his maimed hand scratching at the table's edge. The silence stretched. The singing in the near darkness had checked when the men first heard the Colonel screaming at Starbuck, and Major Bird guessed that half the Legion was now listening to the confrontation that was taking place inside the yellow-lit tent.

Colonel Swynyard was oblivious of that silent, unseen audience. He was losing his temper, goaded to the loss by the look of amusement on Starbuck's handsome face. The Colonel suddenly seized a short-handled riding whip that lay on his camp bed and snapped its woven thong toward the Bostonian. "You're a northern bastard, Starbuck, a

153

nigger-loving piece of black Republican trash, and there's no place for you in this brigade." The Colonel lurched to his feet and cracked the whip again, this time flicking the tip just inches from Starbuck's cheek. "You are hereby dismissed from the regiment, now and forever, you hear me? Those are the Brigadier General's orders, signed, sealed, and entrusted to me." Swynyard used his left hand to fumble through the papers on his folding table, but the dismissal order eluded him and he abandoned the search. "You will remove yourself now, this minute!" Swynyard flicked the whip's lash toward Starbuck a third time. "Get out!"

Starbuck caught the lash. He had planned to do nothing but ward the blow off, but as the whip's thong curled around his hand a more devilish course suggested itself. He half smiled, then tugged, thus pulling Swynyard off-balance. The Colonel clawed at the table for support, then Starbuck pulled harder and the folding table collapsed beneath Swynyard's weight. The Colonel sprawled on the floor in a splintering mess of broken wood and spilt cabbage. "Guard!" Swynyard screamed as he fell. "Guard!"

A bemused Sergeant Tolliver of A Company pushed his head through the tent's flaps. "Sir?" He looked down at the Colonel, who was lying amid the wreckage of the broken camp table, then shot a despairing look at Bird. "What do I do, sir?" Tolliver asked Bird.

Swynyard struggled to his feet. "You will place this piece of northern scum under arrest," he shouted at Tolliver, "and you will hand him to the provost marshals and order him sent to Richmond, there to be interred as an enemy of the state. You understand me?"

Tolliver hesitated.

"Do you understand?" Swynyard screamed at the hapless Sergeant.

"He understands you," Major Bird intervened.

"You are dismissed from the army," Swynyard shouted at Starbuck. "Your commission is ended, you are finished, you are dismissed!" Spittle landed on Starbuck's face. The Colonel's self-control was gone utterly, eroded by alcohol and Starbuck's subtle goading. He lurched toward Starbuck, fumbling suddenly at the strap of his holster, which hung with his jacket on the tent pole. "You are under arrest!" Swynyard hiccuped, still trying to pull the revolver free.

Bird took hold of Starbuck's elbow and pulled him out of the tent before any murder took place. "I think he's mad," Bird said as he hurried Starbuck away from Swynyard's tent. "Stark, plain mad. Addled. Demented. Moon-touched." Bird stopped a safe distance from the tent and stared back as though he could not really credit what he had just witnessed. "He's drunk too, of course. But he lost his wits long before he ever drowned his tonsils in rotgut. My God, Nate, and he's our new second-in-command?"

"Sir?" Sergeant Tolliver had followed the two officers out of the Colonel's tent. "Am I to arrest Mr. Starbuck, sir?"

"Don't be ridiculous, Dan. I'll look after Starbuck. You just forget about all this." Bird shook his head. "Crazed!" he said in wonderment. There was no movement in the Colonel's tent now, just the glow of the lamplit canvas showing through the rain. "I'm sorry, Nate," Bird said. He still held Daniels's pamphlet, which he now tore into scraps.

Starbuck swore bitterly. He had expected Faulconer's revenge, but somehow he had still hoped he could stay with K Company. That was his home now, the place where he had friends and purpose. Without K Company he was a lost soul. "I should have stayed with Shanks," Starbuck said. "Shanks" was Nathan Evans, whose depleted brigade had long gone south.

Bird gave Starbuck a cigar, then plucked a brand from a

155

nearby fire to light the tobacco. "We have to get you out of here, Nate, before that lunatic decides to have you arrested properly."

"Arrested for what?" Starbuck asked bitterly.

"For being an enemy of the state," Bird spoke softly. "You heard what the befuddled idiot said. I suspect Faulconer put that idea into his head."

Starbuck stared at the Colonel's tent. "Where the hell did Faulconer find that son of a bitch?"

"From John Daniels, of course," Bird said. "My brother-in-law has just bought himself a brigade, and the price of it was whatever Daniels demanded. Which presumably included a job for that drunken maniac."

"I'm sorry, Pecker," Starbuck said, ashamed of his self-pity. "The bastard threatened you too."

"I shall survive," Bird said confidently. He knew well enough that Washington Faulconer despised him and would like to demote him, but Thaddeus Bird also knew he had the Legion's respect and affection and just how hard it would be for his brother-in-law to fight that attachment. Starbuck was a much easier target for Faulconer. "It's more important, Nate," Bird went on, "to get you safely away from here. What do you want to do?"

"Do?" Starbuck echoed. "What can I do?"

"You want to go back north?"

"Christ, no." Going back north meant facing his father's bitter wrath. It meant betraying his friends in the Legion. It meant crawling home as a penitent failure, and his pride would not let him do it.

"Then go to Richmond," Bird said, "find Adam. He'll help you."

"His father won't let him help me." Starbuck sounded bitter again. He had heard nothing from Adam all winter, and he suspected his erstwhile friend had abandoned him.

"Adam can be his own man," Bird said. "Go tonight, Nate. Murphy will take you to Fredericksburg and you can take a train from there. I'll give you a furlough pass that should see you through to Richmond." No one could travel in the Confederacy without a passport issued by the authorities, but soldiers were allowed to go on leave using furlough slips issued by their regiments.

The news of Starbuck's dismissal had spread like gunsmoke through the Legion. K Company wanted to protest, but Bird persuaded them that this argument could not be won by appealing to Swynyard's sense of justice. Ned Hunt, who regarded himself as the company's jester, wanted to saw through the spokes of Swynyard's wagon or else burn down the Colonel's tent, but Bird would entertain no such nonsense and even placed a guard over the Colonel's tent to stop it. The important thing, Bird maintained, was to get Starbuck safely away from Swynyard's malice.

"So what will you do?" Truslow asked Starbuck while Captain Murphy readied two horses.

"See if Adam can help."

"In Richmond? So you'll see my Sally?" Truslow asked.

"I hope so." Starbuck, despite the night's disasters, felt a small pang of anticipation.

"Tell her I think about her," Truslow said gruffly. It was as close to an admission of love and forgiveness as he was able to make. "If she lacks for anything," Truslow went on, then shrugged because he doubted that his daughter could possibly lack for money. "I wish," Truslow began, then faltered into silence again, and Starbuck supposed that the Sergeant was wishing that his only child was not earning her living as a whore, but then Truslow surprised him. "You and she," he explained, "I'd like to see that."

Starbuck blushed in the dark. "Your Sally needs someone with better prospects than me," he said.

157

"She could do a lot worse," Truslow said loyally.

"I don't see how." Starbuck let the self-pity well up inside him again. "I'm homeless, penniless, jobless."

"But not for long," Truslow said. "You won't let that son of a bitch Faulconer beat you."

"No," Starbuck said, though in truth he suspected he was already beaten. He was a stranger in a strange land, and his enemies were wealthy, influential, and implacable.

"So you'll be back," Truslow said. "Till then I'll keep the company good and smart."

"You don't need me to do that," Starbuck said. "You never needed me to do that."

"You're a fool, boy," Truslow growled. "I ain't got your brains, and you're a fool not to see that." A curb chain jingled as Captain Murphy led two saddled horses through the rain. "Say your farewells," Truslow ordered Starbuck, "and promise the boys you'll come back. They'll need that promise."

Starbuck said his farewells. The men of the company possessed nothing but what they could carry, yet still they tried to press gifts on him. George Finney had plundered a silver Phi Beta Kappa key from a dead officer's watch chain at Ball's Bluff and wanted Starbuck to take the seal. Starbuck refused, just as he would not accept an offer of cash from Sergeant Hutton's squad. He just took his furlough pass and then strapped his blanket onto the back of his borrowed saddle. He pulled Oliver Wendell Holmes's scarlet-lined greatcoat around his shoulders and hauled himself onto the horse's back. "I'll see you all soon," he said as though he believed it and then rammed back his heels so that none of the Legion would see how close he was to despair.

Starbuck and Murphy rode into the night, passing Colonel Swynyard's darkened tent. Nothing moved there.

The Colonel's three slaves crouched under the wagon and watched the horsemen ride into the black rain. The hooves faded into the darkness.

It was still raining when morning came. Bird had slept badly and felt older than his years as he crawled out of his turf-covered shelter and tried to warm his bones beside a feeble fire. He noted that Colonel Swynyard's tent had already been struck and that the three slaves were roping the load onto the Colonel's wagon ready for the day's journey to Fredericksburg. A half mile north, on the far ridge, two Yankee horsemen were watching the rebel encampment through the rain. Hiram Ketley, Bird's half-witted but willing orderly, brought the Major a mug of coffee adulterated with dried sweet potato, then tried to agitate the fire into stronger life. A handful of officers shivered about the miserable fire, and it was when those officers looked past Bird with alarm on their faces that he was aware of someone approaching him. He turned and saw the ragged beard and bloodshot eyes of Colonel Swynyard, who, astonishingly, smiled a yellow smile and held out a hand for Bird to shake. "Morning! You're Bird, yes?" Swynyard asked in an energetic voice.

Bird nodded cautiously but did not accept the hand.

"Swynyard." The Colonel appeared not to recognize Bird. "Meant to talk to you last night, sorry I was unwell." He took his hand back awkwardly.

"We did talk," Bird said.

"We talked?" Swynyard frowned.

"Last night. In your tent."

"Malaria, that's the trouble," Swynyard explained. The tic throbbed in his cheek, making his right eye appear to wink constantly. The Colonel's beard was damp from washing, his uniform was brushed, and his hair had been slicked down with oil. He had retrieved his whip and now held it in his maimed hand. "The fever comes and goes, Bird," he explained, "but it generally strikes at night. Knocks me flat, you see. So if we did talk last night, then I won't remember a thing. Fever, see?"

"You were feverish, yes," Bird said faintly.

"But I'm all right now. Nothing like some sleep to drive off the fever. I'm Washington Faulconer's second-in-command."

"I know," Bird said.

"And you're now in his brigade," Swynyard went on blithely. "There's you, some ragamuffins from Arkansas, the 12th and 13th Florida Regiments, and the 65th Virginia. General Faulconer sent me to introduce myself and to give you the new orders. You won't be manning the Fredericksburg defenses, but joining the rest of the brigade farther west. It's all written down." He gave Bird a folded piece of paper that had been sealed with Washington Faulconer's signet ring.

Bird tore open the paper and saw it was a simple movement order directing the Legion to march from Fredericksburg to Locust Grove.

"We're in reserve there," Swynyard said. "With any luck we'll have a few days to pull ourselves into shape, but there is one delicate matter we have to deal with first." He took Bird's elbow and moved the startled Major away from the inquisitive ears of the other officers. "Something very delicate," Swynyard said.

"Starbuck?" Bird ventured.

"How did you guess?" Swynyard sounded astonished, but also impressed by Bird's acuity. "Starbuck indeed, Bird. A bad business. I hate to disappoint a man, Bird, it ain't my style. We Swynyards have always been forthright, to a fault I sometimes think, but we're too long in the tooth to change now. Starbuck exactly. The General won't abide him, you know, and we have to get rid of him. I promised I'd do it tactfully, and thought you might know best how to do that?"

"We've done it already," Bird said bitterly. "He went last night."

"He did?" Swynyard blinked at Bird. "He did? Good! First chop! Your doing, I assume? Well done! Then there's no more to be said, is there? Good to meet you, Bird." He raised the whip in a farewell salute, then suddenly turned back. "There was one other thing, Bird."

"Colonel?"

"I've some reading matter for your men. Something to cheer them up." Swynyard gave Bird a yellow grin. "They look a bit sullen, as if they need something to enthuse them. Send a man to collect the booklets, will you? And order any man who can't read to have a friend read it aloud. Good! Well done! Carry on!"

Bird watched the Colonel walk away, then closed his eyes and shook his head as if verifying that the damp morning was not an awful dream. It seemed it was not and that the world really was quite irretrievably insane. "Maybe," he said to no one in particular, "the Yankees have got one just like him. Let's hope so."

Over the valley the mounted Yankee pickets turned and vanished into the damp woods. The southern artillery limbered its guns and followed Colonel Swynyard's wagon south, leaving the Legion to extinguish its fires and pull on its damp boots.

The retreat went on, and it felt like defeat.

The great mass of the Army of the Potomac did not advance beyond Manassas. Instead, in a maneuver designed to throw the rebel forces off balance, the troops returned to Alexandria, just across the river from Washington, where a fleet waited to carry them down the Potomac and out into the Chesapeake Bay and so south to the Union stronghold of Fort Monroe. The fleet had been chartered by the U.S. government and the masts of the waiting ships made a forest above the river. There were sidewheelers from as far north as Boston, ferryboats from the Delaware, schooners from a score of ports on the Atlantic seaboard, and even transatlantic passenger boats with needle-sharp bows and elegant gilt scrollwork handsome about their poops. The steam from a hundred engines hissed into the air while the scream of a hundred whistles frightened the horses that waited to be loaded into the bowels of the vessels. Steam derricks lifted nets of cargo aboard as lines of soldiers climbed the sloping gangplanks. Guns and caissons, limbers and portable forges were tied down on the steamers' decks. McClellan's staff reckoned it would take twenty days for the whole expedition to be transported, all one hundred and twenty-one thousand men with their three hundred cannons, and eleven hundred wagons, and fifteen thousand horses, and ten thousand beef cattle, and the seemingly endless bales of forage and pontoon boats and drums of telegraph wire and barrels of powder, all of which needed to be protected during the voyage by the battleships and frigates and gunboats of the U.S. Navy. The fleet of the Army of the Potomac was the largest ever assembled, proof of the Union's resolve to end the rebellion with one massive stroke. Those mudsills who had complained of McClellan's supine nature would now see how the Young Napoleon could fight! He would take his army to the lightly guarded tongue of land that stretched seventy miles southeastward from Richmond and like a thunderbolt, strike west to capture the rebels' capital and destroy their resolve.

"I have held you back that you might give the deathblow to the rebellion that has distracted our once happy country," McClellan's printed proclamation explained to his troops, then it promised that their General would look over his soldiers "as a parent over his children; and you know that your General loves you from the depths of his heart." The proclamation warned the troops that there would be desperate combats, but also assured them that when they carried their victory home they would regard their membership in the Army of the Potomac as the greatest honor of their lives.

"Fine sentiments," James Starbuck said when he read the proclamation that had been produced on the printing press that traveled with the army headquarters, and he was not alone in admiring the fine words and noble feelings. The northern newspapers might call McClellan the Young Napoleon, but the soldiers of the Army of the Potomac knew their general as "Little Mac" and declared there was no finer soldier in all the world. If any man could bring swift victory it was Little Mac, who had persuaded the Army of the Potomac that they were the best-equipped, best-drilled, and best-trained soldiers in the Republic's history, if not in all the world's history, and though Little Mac's political enemies might complain of his caution and sing sarcastically that all was quiet on the Potomac, the soldiers knew their General had just been waiting for the perfect moment to strike. That moment had now come as hundreds of paddlewheels and propellers churned the Potomac white and hundreds of smokestacks vented coalsmoke to a blue spring sky. The first ships dropped downriver, bands playing, to dip their ensigns as they steamed past George Washington's home at Mount Vernon.

"They'll need more than sentiments," Allan Pinkerton remarked darkly to James. General McClellan's Secret Service Bureau was waiting in a commandeered house close to the Alexandria quays until the General himself was ready to sail, and this morning, as James and his chief stared across the rail lines to the busy quays, Pinkerton was waiting for the arrival of visitors. The rest of the bureau was employed collating the latest scraps of information that had arrived from the South. Every day brought an indigestible mass of such information from deserters or from escaping slaves or in letters from northern sympathizers that were smuggled across the Rappahannock, yet Pinkerton trusted none of it. He wanted to hear from his best agent, Timothy Webster, and through Webster from James's mysterious friend, but for weeks now there had been an ominous silence from Richmond. The good news in that silence was that there had been no mention in the Richmond newspapers of any arrests and no gossip had come north about high-placed southern officers being accused of treason, but Webster's silence worried Pinkerton. "We need to give the General the best intelligence possible," he told James repeatedly. Pinkerton never referred to General McClellan as Little Mac, not even as the Young Napoleon, but always as the General.

"We can certainly reassure the General that the peninsula is lightly defended?" James remarked. He was working at a small camp table that he had set up on the verandah.

"Ah, ha! But that's precisely what the southerners want us to believe," Pinkerton said, turning excitedly to see if a clatter of hooves presaged the arrival of his visitors. A horseman rode past and Pinkerton subsided. "But until I hear further news from your friend, then I'll believe nothing!"

Adam had already sent one reply through the good offices of Timothy Webster, and that one reply had been astonishingly detailed. Except in guns, Adam had written, the defenses facing Fort Monroe were very lightly held. Major General Magruder was screening the fort with four weak brigades, comprising just twenty under-strength battalions. In infantry, at the last count, those battalions had contained just ten thousand men, most of whom Magruder had concentrated in earth-walled forts on Mulberry Island on the southern side of the peninsula and in similar fortifications at Yorktown on the northern side. Some of the Yorktown defenses, Adam had added pedantically, were relics from the unsuccessful British defense of 1783. The fourteen miles between Yorktown and Mulberry Island were guarded by a mere four thousand men and a scatter of dirt forts. Magruder's weakness in numbers was partly compensated by a concentration of artillery, and Adam reported ominously that no fewer than eighty-five pieces of heavy artillery and fifty-five lighter field guns were incorporated in the rebels' defenses. Nevertheless, Adam stressed, even all those guns could not cover every path or track on the peninsula.

Ten miles behind the Yorktown line, Adam reported, close to the small college town of Williamsburg, Magruder had prepared some more earth forts, but these were presently unmanned. Otherwise, Adam said, there were no defenses between Fort Monroe and the new trenches and redoubts being dug around Richmond by General Robert E. Lee. Adam had added apologetically that his information was a week or so out of date and that he understood some further reinforcements were soon to be sent to General Magruder, and he promised to send details of those reinforcements just as soon as he learned of them.

Those further details had never come; indeed no news of any kind had come either from Adam or from Timothy Webster. Their sudden silence was worrying, though James did not believe the silence had any military significance, for every single report that came out of rebel Virginia served to confirm the accuracy of Adam's first detailed account of the peninsula's defenses. The consensus of those reports suggested that Magruder's lines were very thinly held and the last thing the rebels expected was a massive attack from the sea, and James could not understand why Pinkerton was not reassured by that intelligence. Now, waiting on the porch of the Alexandria house, James pleaded with his chief to trust the news coming from beyond the rebel lines. "Magruder, even with his reinforcements, can't have more than fourteen thousand men," James said firmly. He had read every scrap of intelligence coming from the South, and only a handful of the reports contradicted Adam's figures, and that handful James suspected were planted reports intended to mislead the Federal high command. Every instinct in his soul told James that the Young Napoleon would brush the enemy aside with a contemptuous ease. The one hundred and ten thousand men shipping out of the Alexandria quays would meet just fourteen or fifteen thousand rebels, and James, for the life of him, did not understand Pinkerton's qualms.

"They just want us to think they're weak, Jimmy!" Pinkerton now explained his worries. "They want to suck us in before they hit us!" He feinted like a man playing fisticuffs. "Think about your figures!"

James had been thinking about precious little else for two weeks now, but still he humored the small Scotsman. "You know something I don't, Major?"

"In war, James, not every man fights." Pinkerton had been sorting through newspapers at another table on the verandah, but now, after weighting the papers against the day's small wind, he began to stride up and down the wooden deck. On the river, in a pale sunlight, a great transatlantic steamer was maneuvering herself into the wharf where three New Jersey regiments waited. The ship's massive paddlewheels churned mightily and a small tugboat thumped angry puffs of black smoke as it butted its padded bow against the steamer's elegant bows. One of the regimental bands was playing "Rally Round the Flag, Boys!" and Pinkerton was beating time to the music as he paced the porch. "In war, Jimmy, only a handful of men actually carry a rifle and bayonet to the enemy, yet thousands more serve, and serve nobly! You and I are fighting for the union, yet we do not march in the mud like common rankers. You'll grant me the point?"

"Of course," James said cautiously. He could not bring himself to call Pinkerton "Bulldog," though other members of the department cheerfully used the small Scotsman's nickname.

"So!" Pinkerton turned at the end of the verandah. "We agree that not every man is counted in the ranks, only those who actually carry a rifle, you grasp my point? Yet behind those weapon-carrying heroes, Jimmy, are a host of cooks and clerks, of signalmen and teamsters, of staff men and generals, of bandsmen and doctors, of orderlies and provosts, of engineers and commissary clerks." Pinkerton accompanied this catalog of men by expansive gestures which summoned an imaginary host from the air. "My point, Jimmy, is that behind the fighting men are thousands of other souls who are feeding and supplying, supporting and directing, and all pushing forward to make the fighting possible. You grasp my argument?"

"Up to a point, yes," James said cautiously, his tone suggesting that while he grasped his chief's argument, he was not yet persuaded by it.

"Your friend himself said that reinforcements were being sent to Magruder's lines," Pinkerton declared vigorously. "How many men? We don't know! Where are they? We don't know! And how many are uncounted? We don't know!" Pinkerton stopped beside James's table and seized a

167

pencil and sheet of paper. "We don't know, James, but let us make some educated estimates. You reckon that Magruder has fourteen thousand men? Very good, let us start with that figure." He scribbled the number at the top of the sheet of paper. "Those, of course, are only the men present at roll call, so we have to add in those at sick call and those on furlough, and you can be sure that those fellows will rally round their filthy flag as soon as the fighting begins. So how many would that be? Six thousand? Seven? Call it seven." He scribbled the new number beneath the first. "So now we have deduced that General Magruder has at least twenty-one thousand men, and those twenty-one thousand need feeding and supplying, and those duties must add at least another ten thousand troops, and we should not forget the bandsmen and hospital men and all the ancillaries who make an army work, and they must surely total a further ten thousand men." Pinkerton added that figure to his column. "And then we must reckon that the enemy are almost certainly trying to mislead us by undercounting their numbers, so a prudent man would add fifty percent to our final figure to compensate for their lying deceptions, and what do we have?" He spent a few seconds scribbling his calculations. "There! Sixty-one thousand, five hundred men! Some of the spies give a figure close to that, don't they?" Pinkerton leafed through the piles of paper, looking for some of the reports James had discarded as being too carefully contrived. "There!" He flourished one such letter. "And that's just at Yorktown, James! Who knows how many are garrisoned in the towns behind Yorktown?"

James rather thought the number was zero, but he did not like to contradict the small Scotsman who was so energetically sure of himself.

"My report to the General," Pinkerton proclaimed, "will say that he can expect to fight at least sixty thousand men in the Yorktown entrenchments. Where, remember, even the great General Washington chose to starve his enemies rather than attack them, even though he did outnumber them by two to one. And we face at least the same odds, Jimmy, and who knows how many more rebels will swarm out of Richmond to support Magruder's lines? It's a desperate task, desperate! You see now why we need another report from your friend?" Pinkerton still did not know Adam's identity and had abandoned his attempts to prise the name out of James. Not that James's reticence in any way disappointed Pinkerton, who regarded James's appointment as a brilliant success, for the lawyer had brought the Secret Service Bureau some desperately needed organization.

James sat unhappily at his table. He was unconvinced by Pinkerton's mathematics and knew that had this been a Massachusetts courtroom and Pinkerton a hostile witness, he would have enjoyed picking at that farrago of dubious assumptions and unlikely arithmetic, but now he forced himself to suppress his doubts. War made all things different, and Pinkerton, after all, was Major General McClellan's personal choice as Secret Service chief and presumably understood these matters in a way that was impossible for James to comprehend. James still felt himself to be a military amateur and so patriotically hushed his doubts.

Pinkerton turned as a buggy came rattling over the rail lines that lay between the house and the Alexandria quays. The buggy's horses pricked their ears and showed the whites of their eyes as a locomotive hissed a sudden gust of steam, but the driver calmed the beasts down as he hauled on the reins. Pinkerton recognized the buggy's driver and passenger and waved a hand in greeting. "It's time," he told James mysteriously, "for desperate measures."

The two men climbed down from the buggy. They were young men, both clean-shaven, both dressed in civilian clothes, but otherwise as different as chalk and cheese. One was tall with lank fair hair falling over a thin and rather melancholy face, while the other was short and rubicund, with tightly curled black hair and a cheerful expression. "Bulldog!" the smaller man exclaimed as he ran up the verandah steps. "It's grand to see you again, so it is!"

"Mr. Scully!" Pinkerton was equally delighted to greet his visitors. He embraced Scully, then shook the other man's hand before introducing both to James. "Be pleased to meet John Scully, Major, and Price Lewis. This is Major Starbuck, my chief of staff."

"It's a grand day, Major!" John Scully said. He had an Irish accent and a quick smile. His companion, altogether more reserved, offered James a limp handshake and a reserved, almost suspicious nod.

"Mr. Scully and Mr. Lewis," Pinkerton declared with palpable pride, "have volunteered to travel south."

"To Richmond!" Scully responded happily. "I hear it's a grand wee city."

"It smells of tobacco," James said, really for want of anything else to say.

"Like myself, eh, Bulldog?" Scully laughed. "A right wee tobacco stinker I am too, Major. The last woman I took to bed said she didn't know whether to make love to me or smoke me!" Scully laughed at this display of his own wit, Price Lewis looked bored, Pinkerton beamed with delight, and James struggled not to show his shocked disapproval. These men, after all, were about to attempt something extraordinarily brave, and he felt he should endure their coarseness.

"Major Starbuck is a God-fearing churchman."

170

Pinkerton had detected James's embarrassment and offered the explanation to John Scully.

"As I am myself, Major," Scully assured James hurriedly, and matched action to words by making the sign of the cross. "And if I made a confession, doubtless I'd be told what a wicked boy I've been, but what the hell? You have to make a laugh or two, don't you, or else you'll end up with a face as miserable as this Englishman here." He grinned good-naturedly at Price Lewis, who pointedly ignored the jibe and watched the New Jersey soldiers file on board the transatlantic steamer instead.

"Europeans," Pinkerton explained to James, "can travel the Confederacy more easily than Yankees. Mr. Lewis and Mr. Scully will pose as blockade runners seeking business."

"And it will all be dandy as long as no one recognizes us," Scully said cheerfully.

"Would that be possible?" James asked worriedly.

"A wee chance, but hardly one to fret over," Scully said. "Price and I spent some time ferreting out southern sympathizers in Washington and throwing the rascals back across the border, but we're about as certain as a man could ever be that none of those bastards are in Richmond. Isn't that a fact, Price?"

Price bowed his head in grave acknowledgment.

"It seems you put yourselves in great danger," James said in fervent tribute to the two men.

"Bulldog pays us to endanger ourselves, don't you now?" Scully said cheerfully. "And I hear the women of Richmond are as beautiful as they are desperate for real Yankee money. And Price and I do love obliging the ladies, ain't that God's honest truth, Price?"

"If you say so, John, if you say so," Lewis said airily, still gazing loftily at the activity on the quay.

"I can't wait to get my hands on one of those southern

girls," Scully said lasciviously. "All airs and graces, eh? All frills and furbelows. Too good for the likes of us until we chink a few good northern coins, and then we'll watch the skirt hoops roll away, eh, Price?"

"If you say so, John, if you say so," Price Lewis said, then put a hand to his mouth as though disguising a yawn.

Pinkerton moved to end the small talk, explaining to James that Lewis and Scully were traveling south to discover what had happened to Timothy Webster. "He's not been a well man," Pinkerton said, "and there's always the risk that he could be in his sickbed or worse, in which case Mr. Lewis and Mr. Scully will need to get the information direct from your friend. Which means, Jimmy, that they need a letter from you claiming they can be trusted."

"Which we can be, Major," John Scully said happily. "Except with the ladies, isn't that a fact, Price?"

"If you say so, John, if you say so."

James sat at the table and wrote the requisite letter. It would be used, he was assured, only if Timothy Webster had disappeared, otherwise the letter would stay securely hidden inside John Scully's clothing. James, writing at Pinkerton's dictation, assured Adam that the need for information about the defenses on the peninsula behind Fort Monroe was as urgent as ever, and that he should trust whatever instructions accompanied this covering letter, which came with prayerful good wishes from his brother in Christ Jesus, James Starbuck. He then addressed the envelope to the Honorary Secretary of the Confederate Army Bible Supply Society, and Pinkerton sealed the envelope with a common gummed seal before handing it with a flourish to Scully. "There's a message board in the vestibule of St. Paul's Church, and that's where you put it."

"St. Paul's now, would that be a prominent church?" Scully asked.

"In the very center of the city," Pinkerton assured him.

Scully kissed the envelope, then put it in a pocket. "We'll have your news within the week, Bulldog!"

"You'll cross tonight?"

"And why not?" The Irishman grinned. "The weather looks fine, and there's a good wee wind for us."

James had learned enough to know that Pinkerton's preferred method of infiltrating the Confederacy was for his men to travel across the wide mouth of the Potomac by night, leaving from one of the deserted lonely creeks on the Maryland shore and running silent under a dark sail to the Virginia coast. There, somewhere in King George County, a northern sympathizer provided the agents with horses and papers. "Allow me to wish you well," James said very formally.

"Just pray the women are glad to see us, Major!" Scully said happily.

"And send us news as soon as you can!" Pinkerton added sternly. "We need numbers, John, numbers! How many thousands of troops are stationed in the peninsula? How many guns? How many troops in Richmond stand ready to support Magruder?"

"Worry not, Major, you'll have your numbers," John Scully answered cheerfully as the two agents went back to their waiting buggy. "Two days to Richmond!" John Scully cried happily. "Maybe we'll wait for you there, Bulldog! Celebrate victory in Jeff Davis's wine cellar, eh?" He laughed. Price Lewis raised a hand in solemn farewell, then clicked his tongue at the horse. The buggy rattled back across the rail tracks.

"Brave men," Pinkerton said with a hint of a sniff. "Very brave men, Jimmy."

"Yes, indeed," James said.

On the quays the steam derricks lifted boxes and bales of

artillery ammunition: cannonballs and bolts, canister rounds and case shot, shells, and grape. Another great ship was turning in the river, its spadelike paddles slapping the water white as it fought against the Potomac's swift current. More men arrived on the quay, pouring out of a newly stopped train to form in ranks and wait their turn on the river. Their regimental band began to play while the Stars and Stripes, hanging from a dozen jackstaffs, cracked like whips in the fresh spring wind. The army of the North, the greatest army in all American history, was on the move.

To where just ten thousand rebels guarded a peninsula.

Belvedere Delaney arranged for Nate Starbuck to work in the Confederate Passport Bureau. Starbuck's first reaction had been disgust. "I'm a soldier," he told the lawyer, "not a bureaucrat."

"You're a pauper," Delaney had responded icily, "and people are willing to pay very large bribes for a passport."

The passports were required not just to travel beyond Richmond, but even to be on the city's streets after dark. Civilians and soldiers alike needed to make applications for passports at the filthy, crowded office which stood on the corner of Ninth and Broad Street. Starbuck, arriving with Delaney's patronage, was given a room to himself on the third floor, but his presence was as superfluous as it was tedious. A Sergeant Crow did all the real work, leaving Starbuck to stare out of the window or else read a novel by Anthony Trollope that some former occupant of the dusty office had used to prop up the broken leg of the table. He also wrote letters to Adam Faulconer at the army headquarters at Culpeper Court House, begging his friend to use his influence to get him restored to Company K of the Faulconer Legion. Starbuck knew that Washington Faulconer had never been able to resist his son's entreaties,

174

and for a few days he let his hopes stay high, but no reply came from Adam, and Starbuck, after two more importunate appeals, abandoned his attempts.

It was a full three weeks before Starbuck realized that no one expected him to be in the office, and that as long as he paid his respects to Sergeant Crow once or twice a week, he was free to enjoy whatever pleasures Richmond offered. Those pleasures were given a dangerous air by the continuing arrival of northern troops at Fort Monroe. A small panic had swept through the city at the first news of those landings, but when the Yankees made no attempt to break out of their lines, the received opinion became that the northerners were merely pausing on their way to reinforce the Federal garrison at Roanoke. Belvedere Delaney, with whom Starbuck lunched often, scorned that idea. "Why land them at Fort Monroe?" Delaney asked at one such luncheon. "No, my dear Starbuck, they'll be marching on Richmond soon. One battle and the whole fuss will be over. We shall all be prisoners!" He sounded rather pleased at the prospect. "At least the food can't be worse. I'm learning that the worst thing about war is its effect on luxuries. Half the things that make life worth living are unobtainable, and the other half are ruinously expensive. Isn't this beef awful?"

"It tastes better than salt pork."

"I keep forgetting you have served in the field. Maybe I should hear the sound of a bullet once before the war ends? It will make my war memoirs so much more convincing, don't you think?" Delaney smiled, showing off his teeth. He was a vain man and proud of his teeth, which were all his own, unchipped and clean, almost unnatural in their whiteness. Starbuck had met Delaney the year before, when he had first been stranded in Richmond, and the two had struck up a cautious friendship. Delaney was amused that

175

the Reverend Elial Starbuck's prodigal son was in Richmond, though his liking for Starbuck ran deeper than that of mere curiosity, while Starbuck's affection for Delaney arose partly because the lawyer was so ready to be helpful, and partly because Starbuck needed the friendship of men like Delaney and Bird who would not judge his actions by the standards of his father's unforgiving faith. Such men, Starbuck thought, had traveled a mental road he wanted to follow himself, though sometimes, in Delaney's company, he wondered if he was clever enough to free himself of guilt. Starbuck knew that Delaney, for all his carefully cultivated exterior of Pickwickian affability, was both clever and ruthless; qualities the lawyer was presently using to amass a fortune from the sale of what Delaney liked to describe as the twin necessities of warriors: women and weapons. Now the lawyer took off his glasses and polished their lenses on his napkin. "People say bullets whistle, is that true?"

"Yes."

"In what key?"

"I've never noticed."

"Maybe different bullets sound different notes? A skilled marksman might be able to play a tune," Delaney suggested, then happily sang the opening line of a song that had been popular in Richmond all winter long: "'What are you waiting for, Tardy George?' though he's not waiting any longer, is he? Do you think the war's climacteric shall be reached on the peninsula?"

"If it is," Starbuck said, "I want to be there."

"You are foolishly bloodthirsty, Nate." Delaney grimaced, then held aloft a gruesome morsel of gristle for Starbuck's inspection. "Is this food, do you think? Or something that died in the kitchen? No matter, I shall have something at home instead." He pushed his plate to one side. They were lunching in the Spotswood House Hotel, and when his own meal was done Starbuck produced a sheaf of blank passports that he pushed across the table. "Well done," Delaney said, pocketing the passes. "I owe you four hundred dollars."

"How much?" Starbuck was shocked.

"Passports are valuable, my dear Starbuck!" the small sly lawyer said with delight. "Northern spies pay a fortune for these scraps of paper." Delaney laughed to show that he was teasing. "And it is only right and proper that you should share in my ill-gotten gains. Believe me, I sell these for a rare fortune. I assume you would like payment in northern money?"

"I don't care."

"You do, believe me you do. A northern dollar is worth at least three of our southern ones." Delaney, careless of the stares of other diners, counted out a stack of the newfangled dollar bills that were replacing much of the north's coinage. Southern money was supposed to be of equal value, but the whole system of value and price seemed to have gone mad. Butter was fifty cents a pound in Richmond, firewood eight dollars a cord, coffee unobtainable at almost any price, while even cotton, the supposed staple of southern prosperity, had doubled in price. A room which a year before would not have rented for fifty cents a week was now fetching ten dollars a week.

Not that Starbuck cared. He had a room in the stable block of the huge house on Franklin Street where Sally Truslow and her two companions now lived with their servants, cooks, and dressmaker. The house was one of the finest residences in the city and had belonged to a tobacco merchant whose fortunes had been hard-hit by the northern blockade. The man had been forced to sell, and Belvedere Delaney had then transformed the house into

Richmond's most exclusive and expensive place of assignation. The furniture, pictures, and ornaments were, if not of the very highest quality, at least fine enough to pass a candle-lit inspection, while the food, liquor, and entertainment were as lavish and elegant as wartime privations allowed. The ladies held receptions in the evening, and by day were at home to callers, though only those visitors who had made arrangements beforehand were allowed beyond the sculpted newel post at the foot of the grand staircase. Money changed hands, but so discreetly that the rector of St. James's had visited the house three times before discovering the nature of its business, after which he never visited again, though the same knowledge did not deter three of his fellow clergymen. Delaney's rule was that no officer below the rank of major was to be admitted and no civilian whose clothes betrayed a vulgar taste. The clientele, in consequence, was wealthy and on the whole civilized, though the necessary admission of members of the Confederate Congress depressed the house's sophistication far below Delaney's extravagant hopes.

Starbuck had a small, damp stable room that lay at the end of a dank and abandoned garden. In lieu of rent he provided Delaney with passes, while to the women his presence was a deterrent to the crime which preyed on Richmond. Burglaries were so common as to go almost unremarked while street robberies were flagrant and frequent. Which made Starbuck an even more welcome guest in the house, for he was always happy to escort one of the women to Ducquesne's, the Parisian hairdresser on Main Street, or else to one of the dress shops that somehow discovered enough material to go on manufacturing luxury goods.

He was idling outside Ducquesne's one morning, waiting for Sally and reading one of the *Examiner*'s usual demands for the Confederacy to abandon its supine stance and end the war by invading the north. It was a sunny morning, the first in almost three weeks, and the taste of spring warmth had given the city a jaunty air. The two veterans of Bull Run who guarded Ducquesne's salon were teasing Starbuck about the state of his uniform. "With a girl like that, Captain, you shouldn't be wearing rags," one of the two said.

"Who needs clothes with a girl like that?" Starbuck asked.

The men laughed. One had lost a leg, the other an arm; now they stood guard over a hairdresser's shop with a pair of shotguns. "Say anything in that paper about the Young Napoleon?" the one-armed man asked.

"Not a word, Jimmy."

"So he ain't at Fort Monroe?"

"If he is then the *Examiner* hasn't heard about it," Starbuck said.

Jimmy spat a long stream of tobacco juice into the gutter. "If he ain't there, they ain't comin' here, and we'll know they're comin' here when he gets there." He sounded gloomy. The Virginia newspapers might mock McClellan's pretensions, but there was nevertheless a feeling that the North had found its military genius and the South had no one who would prove his equal. At the war's beginning the name of Robert Lee had filled Virginia with optimism, but Lee's bright reputation had been dulled in the early fighting in western Virginia, and now he spent his time digging endless trenches around Richmond, earning himself the nickname "King of Spades." He still had his supporters, chief among them Sally Truslow, who reckoned Lee to be the greatest general since Alexander, but that opinion was based solely on the fact that the courtly Lee had once raised his hat to Sally in the street.

Starbuck gave the newspaper to Jimmy, then glanced at a clock in a shop window to gauge how much longer Sally would fuss with her hair. He reckoned she would be at least another quarter hour and so he tipped his hat back, lit a cigar, and leaned against one of the gilded pillars that framed Ducquesne's entrance. It was then that the voice hailed him.

"Nate!" The call came from across the street, and for a second Starbuck could not see who had shouted because a wagon team rolled past with a load of cut timber, and after the wagon a smart buggy with painted wheels and fringed cushions rattled by, then Starbuck saw it was Adam who was now hurrying between the traffic with an outstretched hand. "Nate! I'm sorry, I should have written. How are you?"

Starbuck had been feeling bitter about his friend, but there was such a wealth of affection and remorse in Adam's voice that the bitterness vanished immediately. "I'm well," he said lamely. "And you?"

"Busy, horribly busy. I spend half my time here and half at the army headquarters. I have to liaise with the government and it isn't easy. Johnston doesn't like the President overmuch, and Davis ain't the biggest admirer of the General, so I tend to get bitten by both sides equally."

"Whereas I just got bitten by your father," Starbuck said, some of his bitterness returning.

Adam frowned. "I'm sorry, Nate, truly." He paused, plainly embarrassed, then shook his head. "I can't help, Nate. I wish I could, but father's set against you and he won't listen to me."

"Have you asked him?" Starbuck asked.

Adam paused, then his innate honesty conquered his temptation to prevaricate. "No, I haven't. I haven't seen him for a month, and I know it won't do any good writing

180

to him. Maybe he'll soften if I ask him directly? To his face? Can you wait till then?"

Starbuck shrugged. "I'll wait," he said, knowing how little choice he had in the matter. If Adam could not change his father's mind, no one could. "You look well," he said to Adam, changing the subject. The last time Starbuck had seen his friend was at Ball's Bluff, where Adam had been hag-ridden with the horrors of battle, but now he had regained all his good looks and enthusiasm. His uniform was clean, his saber scabbard shone in the sun, and his spurred boots gleamed.

"I am well," Adam said very emphatically. "I'm with Julia."

"The fiancee?" Starbuck asked teasingly.

"Unofficial fiancee," Adam offered the correction. "I wish it was official." He smiled shyly. "But we all agree it would be better to wait until hostilities are concluded. Wartime is no time for marriage." He gestured across the road. "You'll come and meet her? She's with her mother in Sewell's."

"Sewell's?" Starbuck thought he knew every dress shop and milliner in Richmond, but he had not heard of Sewell's.

"The Scripture shop, Nate!" Adam chided his friend, then explained that Julia's mother, Mrs. Gordon, had opened a Bible teaching class for the free blacks who had come to find work in Richmond's wartime economy. "They're looking for simple testaments," Adam explained, "maybe a child's version of Luke's Gospel? Which reminds me, I have a Bible for you."

"A Bible?"

"Your brother left it here for you. I've been meaning to send it to you for months. Now come and meet Mrs. Gordon and Julia."

Starbuck hung back. "I'm with a friend," he explained, and gestured at Ducquesne's window with its elaborate display of lotions and tortoiseshell combs and beribboned wigs, and just as he made the gesture the door opened and Sally walked out. She offered her arm to Starbuck and smiled prettily at Adam. She knew Adam from Faulconer County, but it was evident that Adam did not recognize Sally. The last time he had seen her she had been a ragged girl in a faded cotton shift who had been lugging water and herding animals on her father's smallholding, whereas now she was in a hooped silk skirt and wore her hair looped and curled beneath a beribboned bonnet.

"Ma'am," Adam acknowledged her with a bow.

"Adam, you know . . . " Starbuck began.

Sally interrupted him. "My name is Victoria Royall, sir." That was her professional name, bestowed on Sally in the brothel on Marshall Street.

"Miss Royall," Adam said.

"Major Adam Faulconer," Starbuck completed the introduction. He could see the delight that Sally was taking in Adam's ignorance and resigned himself to endure her mischief. "Major Faulconer is a very old friend of mine," he told Sally as if she did not know.

"Mr. Starbuck has mentioned your name to me, Major Faulconer," Sally said, behaving in her most demure fashion. She looked demure too, for her dress was of a very dark gray and the red, white, and blue ribbons in her bonnet were more a patriotic gesture than a display of luxuries. No one flaunted jewels or finery on Richmond's streets, not when crime was so prevalent.

"And you, Miss Royall, you come from Richmond?" Adam asked, but before Sally could offer any answer Adam saw Julia and her mother emerge from the Scripture shop on the opposite side of the road, and he insisted that

182

Starbuck and Sally come and be introduced.

Sally had her arm in Starbuck's. She giggled as they trailed Adam over the road. "He didn't know me!" she whispered.

"How could he? Now, for God's sake, be careful. These are church people." Starbuck offered the warning and then composed his face into a stern respectability. He handed Sally up the curb, politely throwing away what was left of his cigar, then turned to face Mrs. Gordon and her daughter.

Adam made the introductions and Starbuck lightly touched the gloved fingers of the ladies' outstretched hands. Mrs. Gordon proved to be a thin, shrewish woman with a pinched nose and eyes as sharp as a hungry hawk, but her daughter was altogether more surprising. Starbuck had expected a mousy church girl, timid and pious, yet Julia Gordon had a forthright air that immediately destroyed his misconception. She was black-haired and dark-eyed and had a face that was almost defiant in its strength. She was not beautiful, Starbuck thought, but she was certainly handsome. She carried character, strength, and intelligence in her looks, and Starbuck, meeting her gaze, felt oddly jealous of Adam.

Sally was introduced, but Mrs. Gordon immediately turned back to Starbuck, wanting to know if he was related to the famous Reverend Elial Starbuck of Boston. Starbuck confessed the famous abolitionist was his father.

"We know him," Mrs. Gordon said disapprovingly.

"You do, ma'am?" Starbuck asked, holding his scruffy hat in his hand.

"Gordon" – Mrs. Gordon spoke of her husband – "is a missioner of the ASPGP."

"Indeed, ma'am," Starbuck said respectfully. Starbuck's father was one of the trustees of the American Society for

183

the Propagation of the Gospel to the Poor, a mission that carried salvation into the darkest corners of America's cities.

Mrs. Gordon gave Starbuck's poor uniform a glance. "Your father cannot be pleased that you are wearing a Confederate uniform, Mr. Starbuck?"

"I'm sure he's not, ma'am," Starbuck said.

"Mother has judged you before she knows the facts," Julia intervened with a light touch that made Starbuck smile, "but you shall be given a chance to make a plea of mitigation before her sentence is passed."

"It's a very long story, ma'am," Starbuck said respectfully, knowing he dared not describe how he had fallen in hopeless and unrewarded love with an actress for whose sake he had abandoned the North, his family, his studies, and his respectability.

"Too long to be heard now, I daresay," Mrs. Gordon said in a voice made brusque by years of chivvying reluctant churchgoers into some semblance of enthusiasm. "But nevertheless I am delighted to see you defending states' rights, Mr. Starbuck. Our cause is noble and just. And you, Miss Royall" – she turned to Sally – "you are from Richmond?"

"From Greenbrier County, ma'am," Sally lied, naming a county in the far western part of the state. "My father didn't want me staying on there with all the fighting going on, so he sent me to a relative here." She was doing her best to smooth out the country roughness of her speech, but an echo of it remained. "An aunt," she explained, "on Franklin Street."

"Would we know her, perhaps?" Mrs. Gordon was appraising the fineness of Sally's dress and the expense of her parasol and the delicacy of the lace collar that made a distinct contrast to the darned, simple clothes that mother and daughter wore. Mrs. Gordon must also have noted that

Sally was wearing powder and paint, accoutrements that would never have been allowed in Mrs. Gordon's house, but there was an innocence about Sally's youth that maybe softened Mrs. Gordon's disapproval.

"She's real sick." Sally tried to evade further inquiry about her notional aunt.

"Then I'm sure she would like a visit." Mrs. Gordon responded to the mention of a sickbed like a vigorous old warhorse hearing the trumpet. "And where does your aunt worship, Miss Royall?"

Starbuck sensed that Sally had run out of invention. "I was introduced to Miss Royall at the Grace Street Baptist Church," he said, deliberately naming one of the city's lesser-known congregations. Starbuck was aware of Julia Gordon's grave gaze, and aware too of trying to make a good impression on her.

"Then I'm sure we must know your aunt," Mrs. Gordon persisted to Sally. "I think Gordon and I are familiar with all the evangelical families in Richmond. Is that not so, Julia?"

"I'm sure that is so, Mother," Julia said.

"Your aunt's name, Miss Royall?" Mrs. Gordon insisted upon an answer.

"Miss Ginny Richardson, ma'am," Sally said, using the name of the madame of the brothel on Marshall Street.

"I'm not sure I know any Virginia Richardson." Mrs. Gordon frowned as she tried to place the name. "Of Grace Street Baptist, you say? Not that we are Baptists, Miss Royall." Mrs. Gordon made the disclaimer in much the same tone with which she might have assured Sally that she was not a cannibal or a Papist, "but of course we know of the church. Perhaps sometime you would like to hear my husband preach?" The invitation was made to both Starbuck and Sally.

"I most surely would," Sally said with an enthusiasm that stemmed from her relief at not having to invent any more details about her imaginary aunt.

"You could take tea with us?" Mrs. Gordon suggested to Sally. "Come on a Friday. We offer divine service to the wounded in Chimborazo Hospital on Fridays." The hospital was the largest army hospital in Richmond.

"I would like that," Sally said sweetly and eagerly, as though Mrs. Gordon's proposal would enliven her otherwise dull evenings.

"And you too, Mr. Starbuck," Mrs. Gordon said. "We always need healthy hands to assist in the wards. Some of the men cannot hold their Scriptures."

"Of course, ma'am. It would be a privilege."

"Adam shall arrange it. No crinolines, Miss Royall, there's not enough room between the cots for such frills. Now come, Julia." Mrs. Gordon, having got in her lick against Sally's costume, bestowed a smile on Sally and a nod to Starbuck, then swept away down the street. Adam hastily promised he would leave a letter for Starbuck at the Passport Bureau, then, after touching his hat to Sally, ran to catch up with the Gordons.

Sally laughed. "I was watching you, Nate Starbuck. You like that Bible girl, don't you?"

"Nonsense," Starbuck said, but in truth he had been wondering just what it was about the plain-dressed Julia Gordon that had attracted him. Was it, he wondered, because the missioner's daughter represented a world of piety, intelligence, and innocence that he had forever lost by his backsliding?

"She looked a bit like a school miss to me," Sally said, putting her hand through his arm.

"Which is probably what Adam needs," Starbuck said.

"Hell, no. She's much too strong for him," Sally said

186

scathingly. "Adam was always a ditherer. Never could make up his mind to jump one way or the other. But he never recognized me, did he?"

Starbuck smiled at the pleasure in her voice. "No, he didn't."

"He was looking at me real strange, like he thought he should know me, but he never did manage to place me!" Sally was delighted. "You reckon they'll invite us for tea?"

"Probably, but we won't go."

"Whyever not?" Sally asked as they began walking toward Franklin Street.

"Because I spent my whole damn life in respectable evangelical houses and I'm trying to get away from them."

Sally laughed. "You wouldn't go for your Bible girl?" she teased Starbuck. "But I'd like to go."

"Of course you wouldn't."

"I would too. I like to see how folks live and how they do things proper. I ain't never been invited to a respectable house. Or are you ashamed of me?"

"Of course I'm not!"

Sally stopped and made Starbuck turn to face her. There were tears in her eyes. "Nate Starbuck! Are you ashamed to take me into a proper house?"

"No!"

"Because I earn a living on my back? Is that it?"

He took her hand and kissed it. "I am not ashamed of you, Sally Truslow. I just think you'll be bored. It's a dull world. A world without crinolines."

"I want to see it. I want to see how to be respectable." She spoke with a pathetic obstinacy.

Starbuck guessed this perverse ambition of Sally's would pass, and thus he decided there was small need to oppose it. "Sure," he said, "if they ask us, we'll go. I promise you."

"I don't get asked anywhere," Sally said, still close to

187

tears as they walked on. "I want to be asked somewhere. I can take a night off."

"Then we'll go," Starbuck said soothingly, and he wondered what would happen if the missioner discovered that his wife had invited a whore to take tea, and that thought made him laugh aloud. "We'll surely go," he promised. "We surely will."

Julia teased Adam about Sally. "Was she not a little gaudy?"

"Decidedly. Indeed."

"But you seemed fascinated by her?"

Adam was too blunt a character to detect Julia's teasing. Instead he blushed. "I assure you . . . "

"Adam!" Julia interrupted him. "I think Miss Royall is a remarkable beauty! A man would have to be made of granite to remain unaware of her."

"It was not that," Adam said truthfully, "but the feeling I'd seen her somewhere before." He was standing in the parlor of the Reverend Mr. Gordon's small house on Baker Street. It was a dark room, heavy with the smell of furniture wax. The glass-fronted bookshelves held commentaries on the Bible and tales of mission life in heathen countries while the room's one window looked out across the pious headstones of Shockoe Cemetery. The house was in a very humble area of Richmond, built in close proximity to an almshouse, a charity hospital, the city poorhouse, and the cemetery. Nor could the Reverend Mr. Gordon afford a better house, for it was the rule of the American Society for the Propagation of the Gospel to the Poor that its missioners live among their flock, and to ensure that the rule was followed, the society's trustees kept their missioners' salaries at a pitiably low level. Those trustees were all northerners, and it was their parsimony which explained Mrs. Gordon's avid adhesion to the southern cause. "I'm sure I know Miss Royall." Adam frowned. "But for the life of me I can't place her!" He was annoyed with himself.

"Any man who can misplace a beauty like Miss Royall must be hard-hearted," Julia said, then laughed at Adam's evident confusion. "Dear Adam, I know you are not hard-hearted. Tell me about your friend Starbuck. He looks interesting."

"Interesting enough to need our prayers," Adam said and explained as best he could how Starbuck had been studying for the ministry, but had been tempted away. Adam did not describe the nature of the temptation and Julia was too clever to ask. "He took refuge here in the South," Adam explained, "and I fear that it is not just his political allegiances that have changed."

"You mean he's a backslider?" Julia asked gravely.

"I fear so."

"Then we shall certainly pray for him," Julia said. "Has he backslid so far that we should not invite him to tea?"

"I hope not," Adam said, frowning.

"Then do we invite him or not?"

Adam was not entirely sure, then he remembered how his friend had been attending prayer meetings at Leesburg, and he decided that Starbuck must have retained enough respectability to earn an invitation from the missioner's family. "I think you may," Adam said gravely.

"Then you shall write and invite them both for this Friday. I have a feeling that Miss Royall needs a friend. Now, will you stay for luncheon? I fear it is a poor soup only, but you are welcome. Father would like it if you stayed."

"I have business. But thank you."

Adam walked back into town. Miss Royall's identity still nagged at him, but the more he thought about it, the more elusive the identification became. He finally managed to dismiss the puzzle from his mind as he climbed the steps of the War Department.

His duties meant that Adam spent one or two days each week in Richmond, from where he kept General Johnston informed of political opinion and professional gossip. He also acted as Johnston's liaison with the headquarters of the Confederate Commissary Department which requisitioned supplies and directed where they should be sent.

It was that duty which gave Adam an intimate knowledge of where the army's brigades and battalions were posted, which knowledge he had been so careful to pass to Timothy Webster. Adam assumed that his two recent letters had long ago been forwarded to McClellan's headquarters and he often wondered why the northern troops were taking so long to take advantage of the peninsula's weak defenses. The North was pouring men into Fort Monroe, yet only a handful of rebels opposed them and still the North made no move to destroy that handful. At times Adam wondered whether Webster had forwarded his letters, then he would suffer an attack of sheer terror at the thought that maybe Webster had been secretly arrested, and Adam would only regain his composure after reminding himself that Webster did not know and could not possibly discover the identity of his mysterious correspondent.

Adam now settled in his office and wrote his daily dispatch to Johnston. It was a dull document listing the numbers of men released from the hospital fever wards in Richmond and describing what supplies were newly available in the capital's armories and storehouses. He finished with a summary of the latest intelligence, which reported that Major General McClellan was still in Alexandria and that the forces in Fort Monroe were showing no signs of aggression, then he bundled the latest editions of the newspapers to make one large packet that a dispatch rider would carry to Culpeper Court House. He sent the package down-stairs, then opened the letter from his father that had been waiting on his desk. The letter, as Adam expected, was yet another plea that Adam should leave Johnston's staff and join the Faulconer Brigade. "I think you should take com-mand of the Legion from Pecker," Washington Faulconer had written, "or, if you'd prefer, you could be my chief of staff. Swynyard is difficult, doubtless he will show his finer qualities in battle, but till then he is overfond of the bottle. I need your help." Adam crumpled the letter, then walked to the window and stared uphill to where the fine white pillars of the noble Capitol Building were touched by the afternoon sun. He turned as his office door opened suddenly. "You might have to add some news to your dispatch, Faulconer," a shirtsleeved officer called to Adam.

Adam had to hide his sudden excitement. "They're moving from Fort Monroe?" he asked.

"Oh Lord, no. The damn Yankees have taken root there. Maybe they never plan to move? You'd like some coffee? It's the real thing, fetched from Liverpool on a blockade runner."

"Please."

The officer, a captain called Meredith from the Signal Department, shouted for his orderly to bring the coffee, then came into the room. "The Yankees are idiots, Faulconer. Plumb crazy! Fools!"

"What have they done?"

"They are half-wits! Rattleheads, numskulls!" Meredith sat in Adam's swivel chair and put his mud-stained boots up on the leather-topped desk. He lit a cigar, chucking the match into a spitoon. "They are know-nothings, dunderheads, blockheaded lubberlouts. In brief they are northerners. You know who Allan Pinkerton is?"

"Of course I know."

191

"Harken then, and I shall amuse you. Over here!" This last was to the orderly who had edged into the room with the two mugs of coffee. Meredith waited till the orderly was gone, then took up his tale. "It seems that Pinkerton wished to send some secret agents to spy on us. They were sent to discover our darkest desires and innermost secrets, and who does he send? Does he send some secretive fellow plucked from obscurity? No, he sends two fools who, not six months ago, were employed as plug-uglies evicting southern sympathizers from Washington! Lo and behold, one of the men they evicted walks into them on Broad Street. 'Hello,' says he, 'I know you two beauties. You're Scully and Lewis!' Our heroes deny it, but the fools are carrying papers with their real names on them. Price Lewis and John Scully, large as life! How featherbrained can you be? So now the North's two finest spies are clapped in irons in Henrico Jail. Isn't that splendid?"

"It's certainly foolish," Adam said. His heart was suddenly racing as fear whipsawed through him. Scully and Lewis? Was Webster using one of those names as a disguise? Was the truth being beaten out of the two men even now? There were terrible rumors about the punishments given to traitors in the secret cells of the Confederate prisons, and Adam almost whimpered as another pang of terror soured his gut. He forced himself to look calm and to take a sip of the hot coffee, all the while reminding himself that he had not signed the two long documents he had sent to Webster, and had taken pains to disguise the handwriting on both detailed reports. Even so, the shadow of the noose suddenly seemed very close. "They'll hang, I suppose?" he asked casually.

"The bastards certainly deserve to, but Lewis is English and the wretched Scully is Irish, and we need London's goodwill more than we need to watch two of the Queen's

192

subjects twitching at the end of a pair of ropes." Meredith sounded disgusted at the leniency. "The bastards won't even get ten kinds of hell beaten out of them in case the British government objects. And they know it, which is why the two bastards aren't admitting anything."

"Maybe they have nothing to admit?" Adam suggested lightly.

"Of course they do. I'd make the clods squeal," Meredith said darkly.

"I won't trouble Johnston with the news," Adam said. "I'll wait till they have something to say."

"I just thought you'd like to know," Meredith said. He clearly felt that Adam's response had been too muted, but Major Faulconer had the reputation of being an odd fish around the headquarters. "Can't tempt you to Screamersville tonight?" Meredith asked. Screamersville was the black section of Richmond and held the city's wildest brothels, gambling houses, and liquor dens. Liquor was officially banned in Richmond in an attempt to cut the crime rate, but no provost patrol would dare go into Screamersville to enforce the law, any more than they would try to confiscate the champagne from the city's expensive *maisons d'assignation*.

"I have other engagements tonight," Adam said stiffly.

"Another prayer meeting?" Meredith asked mockingly.

"Indeed."

"Say one for me, Faulconer. I plan to need a prayer or two tonight." Meredith swung his boots off the desk. "Take your time with the coffee. Just put the mug back in our room when you're done."

"Surely. Thank you."

Adam drank the coffee and watched the shadows lengthen across Capitol Square. Clerks were scurrying with bundled documents from the government offices to the

193

Capitol Building while a patrol of provosts, their bayonets fixed, paced slowly down Ninth Street past the Bell Tower, which rang the alarm for fires and other city emergencies. Two small children walked hand in hand with one of their family's slaves, going uphill toward the statue of George Washington. Two years ago, Adam thought, this city had seemed as homely and friendly as Seven Springs, his family's estate in Faulconer County, but now it reeked of danger and intrigue. Adam shuddered, thinking of the trapdoor falling open beneath his feet and the void swallowing him and the roughness of a rope around his neck and the snatch as the noose jerked taut, then he told himself he had no need to worry, for James Starbuck had given his word never to reveal Adam's name, and James was a Christian and a gentleman, so it was quite impossible for Adam to be betrayed. The arrest of Scully and Lewis, whoever they were, need not concern Adam. Thus reassured, he sat at his desk, drew a piece of notepaper toward him, and wrote an invitation for Captain Nathaniel Starbuck and Miss Victoria Royall to take tea at the Reverend Mr. Gordon's home on Friday.

194

JOHN SCULLY AND PRICE LEWIS admitted nothing, not even when documents that might have incriminated a saint were found sewn into their clothing. Lewis, the Englishman, had a map of Richmond on which had been sketched an outline of the new defenses dug by General Lee with hatched marks suggesting where the existence of redoubts and star forts was merely surmised. A memorandum attached to the sketch map demanded confirmation of the assumptions and an assessment of the artillery contained in the new works. John Scully, the small Irishman, carried an unstamped letter addressed to the Honorary Secretary of the Confederate Army Bible Supply Society which had been signed by a Major James Starbuck of the U.S. Army who described himself as "brother in Christ" to the letter's unnamed addressee. The letter said that the enclosed instructions could be trusted, and those instructions begged for a complete and up-to-date enumeration of the Confederate troops under General Magruder's command with especial care taken to report the total number of troops available in the towns, garrisons, and forts between Richmond and Yorktown.

John Scully, confronted with the letter that had been discovered sewn into the lapel of his jacket, swore he had bought his clothes from a sutler outside the city and had no idea what the letter meant. He smiled at the Major conducting the interrogation. "I'm sorry,

Major, so I am. I'd help you if I could."

"Damn your help." Major Alexander was a tall fleshy man with bushy sidewhiskers and an expression of perpetual indignation. "If you don't talk," he threatened Scully, "we'll hang you."

"That you won't, Major," Scully said, "seeing as how I'm a citizen of Great Britain."

"Damn Britain."

"And ordinarily I'd agree with you, so I would, but as of this moment, Major, this is one Irishman who would go on his knees and thank the Almighty God for making him British." Scully smiled like a cherub.

"Being British won't protect you. You'll hang!" Alexander threatened, but still Scully would not talk.

Next day came news that the Yankees had at last broken out of their lines at Fort Monroe. General McClellan had arrived on the peninsula, and all Virginia now knew from where the thunderbolt would fall. A mighty army was advancing against the slender defenses strung between Yorktown and Mulberry Island. "Another month," Price Lewis assured John Scully, "and we'll be rescued. We'll be heroes."

"If they don't hang us first," John Scully said, making the sign of the cross.

"They won't. They daren't."

"I'm not so sure." Scully's confidence was weakening.

"They won't!" Price Lewis insisted. But the very next day a military tribunal was summoned to the jail and presented with the map of Richmond's defenses and the letter addressed to the Honorary Secretary of the Confederate Army Bible Supply Society. The evidence overcame whatever scruples the tribunal might have felt for the prisoners' nationality, and less than an hour from the moment when the court had convened, the president sentenced the two prisoners to death. Scully shuddered in fear, but the tall Englishman simply sneered at his judges. "You won't dare do it."

"Take them away!" The Lieutenant Colonel who had presided over the tribunal slammed his hand on the table. "Hanged by the neck, you dogs!"

Scully suddenly felt the wings of death's angel very close above him. "I want a priest!" he pleaded with Major Alexander. "For the love of God, Major, bring me a priest!"

"Shut your face, Scully!" Price Lewis called.

The Englishman was hurried down the corridor to his cell while John Scully was put into a different room where Major Alexander brought him a bottle of rye whiskey. "It's illegal, John. But I thought it might help your last hours on earth."

"You won't dare do it! You can't hang us!"

"Listen!" Alexander said, and in the silence Scully could hear the sound of hammering. "They're building the scaffold ready for the morning, John," Alexander said softly.

"No, Major, please."

"Lynch, his name is," Alexander said. "That should please you, John."

"Please me?" Scully asked, bemused.

"Doesn't it please you to be hanged by another Irishman? Mind you, old Lynch is no craftsman. He bungled his last two. One was a black fellow who took twenty minutes to die and it wasn't a pretty sight. Dear me, no. Twitching he was, and pissing himself, and the breath scraping in his throat like sandpaper. Terrible." Alexander shook his head.

John Scully crossed himself, then closed his eyes and prayed for strength. He would be strong; he would not betray Pinkerton's trust. "All I want is a priest," he insisted.

"If you talk, John, you won't hang in the morning," Alexander tempted him.

"I've nothing to say, Major, except to a priest," Scully insisted bravely.

That night a priest came to John Scully's new cell. The priest was a very old man, though he still had a fine head of long white hair that flowed well below the collar of his soutane. His face was a dark brown, as if his life had been spent in the tropical mission fields. It was an ascetic, kindly face, touched with a hint of abstract intellectualism that suggested his thoughts had already gone to a higher and better world. He settled on Scully's bed and took an old, threadbare scapular from his case. He kissed the embroidered strip of cloth and placed it around his thin neck, then made the sign of the cross toward the prisoner. "My name is Father Mulroney," he introduced himself, "and I'm from Galway. I'm told you want to make a confession, son?"

Scully knelt. "Forgive me, Father, for I have sinned." He crossed himself.

"Go on, my son." Father Mulroney's voice was deep and fine, the voice of a man who has preached sad things to great halls. "Go on," Mulroney said again, his marvelous voice low and comforting.

"It must be ten years since my last confession," Scully began, and then the dam broke and he poured out the list of all his transgressions. Father Mulroney closed his eyes as he listened, the only sign of wakefulness being the slight beat of one of his long, bony fingers on a delicate ivory crucifix that hung on a simple iron chain about his neck. He nodded once or twice as Scully listed his pathetic sins: the whores cheated, the oaths made, the trifles stolen, the lies told, the religious duties ignored. "My mother always said I'd come to a bad end, so she did." The small Irishman was almost weeping as he finished.

"Peace, my son, peace." The priest's voice was dry and

whispery, yet very comforting. "You repent of these sins, my son?"

"I do, Father, oh God, I do." Scully had begun to weep. He had fallen forward so that his head rested on his hands, which, in turn, were supported by the old man's knees. Father Mulroney's face showed no reaction to Scully's terror and remorse; instead he lightly stroked the Irishman's head with long fingers and stared around the white-painted cell with its lantern and its grim barred window. The tears ran down Scully's face to make a damp patch on Mulroney's faded and threadbare soutane. "I don't deserve to die, Father," Scully said.

"Then why are they hanging you, my son?" Mulroney asked, and went on stroking Scully's short black hair. "What have you done that's so bad?" the priest asked in his sad, kind voice, and Scully told how Allan Pinkerton had asked Lewis and Scully to travel south to look for the missing agent, the best agent the North possessed, and how Pinkerton had assured them that as British subjects they would be safe from any rebel recriminations, yet how, despite that assurance, they had been condemned to hang by the military tribunal.

"Of course you don't deserve to die, my son," Mulroney said with indignation in his voice, "for all you ever did was try to help your fellowman. Isn't that the truth of it?" His fingers still soothed Scully's fears. "And did you ever find your man?" Father Mulroney's own Irish accent seemed to have grown stronger during the confession.

"We did, Father, and the reason he disappeared is that he's ill. Sick as a dog, he is. He's got the rheumatism fever. He was supposed to be in the Ballard House Hotel, only he moved, and it took us a day or so to find him, but the poor man's in the Monumental Hotel now, and one of Pinkerton's ladies is looking after him there."

Mulroney calmed Scully, who was gabbling the words desperately. "The poor man," Mulroney said. "You say he's ill?"

"He can hardly move. He's terrible sick, so he is."

"Give me his name, my son, so I can pray for him," Mulroney said softly, then the priest sensed a hesitation in Scully, and so he tapped his fingers in very mild reproof. "This is a confession you're making, my son, and the secrets of the confessional go to the grave with a priest. What you say here, my son, is a secret between you, me, and God Almighty. So tell me the name so I can pray for the poor man."

"Webster, Father, Timothy Webster. And he was always the real spy, not us. Price and I are just doing a favor for Pinkerton by coming to look for him! Webster's the real spy. He's the best one there is!"

"I shall pray for him," Mulroney said. "And the woman who's looking after the poor man, what would her name be, my son?"

"Hattie, Father, Hattie Lawton."

"I shall pray for her too," Mulroney said. "But the Major in the prison here, what was his name? Alexander? He said you were carrying a letter?"

"We were only to deliver the letter if we never found Webster, Father," Scully said, then described the bulletin board in the vestibule of St. Paul's where the letter would have been tucked beneath the criss-crossed tape. "What's the harm in delivering a letter to a church, Father?"

"None at all, my son, none at all," Mulroney said, then assured the frightened man that it had been a good confession. He gently lifted Scully's head and told the Irishman he must make a good contrition and say four Hail Marys, then he absolved him in solemn Latin, and afterward he promised that he would seek mercy for Scully from the

Confederate authorities. "But you know, my son, how little they listen to us Catholics. Or to us Irishmen, indeed. These southerners are as bad as the English, so they are. They've small love for us."

"But you'll try?" Scully looked desperately up into the kindly eyes of the priest.

"I shall try, my son," Mulroney said, then gave the blessing and made the sign of the cross above Scully's head.

Father Mulroney walked slowly back to the jail's main office where Major Alexander waited with a thin, bespectacled lieutenant. Neither of the officers spoke as Father Mulroney took off the scapular, then lifted the soutane over his head to reveal an old but finely cut black suit. There was a bowl of water on the table, and the old man began washing his hands as though he wanted to rid his fingers of the lingering touch of Scully's hair. "The person you want," the man who had called himself Mulroney now said in an accent that had nothing of Ireland in it at all, but only Virginia, "is a Timothy Webster. You'll find him in the Monumental Hotel. He's sick, so he shouldn't give you any trouble. He has a female attendant called Hattie Lawton. She's another of the scum, so take her as well." The old man took a silver case from his pocket and extracted a slender, fragrant cigar. The bespectacled Lieutenant leaped forward and snatched up a candle from the table and offered it to the cigar. The old man sucked on the flame and then offered the Lieutenant a jaundiced look. "You're Gillespie?"

"Yes, sir, indeed, sir."

"What's in the bag, Gillespie?" The old man nodded at a leather bag that hung from the Lieutenant's shoulder. Gillespie opened the bag to reveal a brass funnel and a six-sided bottle made of dark blue glass.

"My father's oil," Gillespie said proudly.

The old man's mouth twisted. "You were planning on

administering the oil to the prisoners, perhaps?"

"It works wonders with lunatics," Gillespie said defensively.

"I don't care about your damn lunatics," the old man snapped. "You can try it on another prisoner, one who doesn't matter to anyone. But Lewis and Scully have to be spared." His thin, ascetic face twitched with a spasm of disgust, then he smoothed his long silver hair back over his collar and looked at Alexander. "I fear political considerations dictate that the scum will have to live, just in case their deaths dissuade the British from helping us. But even the British won't expect us to keep them in any comfort. Put them in the Negro section, let them break stone for a few months." He drew on the cigar, frowning, then gave orders that the letter addressed to the Honorary Secretary of the Confederate Army Bible Supply Society was to be put in the vestibule of St. Paul's where it was to be watched night and day in case the spy came to collect it. "But arrest Webster first."

"Of course, sir," Alexander said.

The old man took a fine gold ring from his pocket. It was engraved with an ancient coat of arms, testimony to the man's long pedigree. "Is it still raining?" he asked as he slipped the ring on a finger.

"It is, sir, yes," Alexander said.

"That will obstruct the Yankees' approach, will it not?" the old man said grimly. The northerners' advance on Yorktown was being slowed by mud and rain, but even so the old man knew what terrible danger the Confederacy faced. So little time, but at least this night's work had uncovered one more spy and might even yield the traitor who skulked behind the mask of being the Honorary Secretary of the Confederate Army Bible Supply Society. The old man looked forward to finding that man and watching him swing on a rope's looped end. He took a derringer pistol from his jacket pocket and checked that it was loaded, then picked up his cloak and hat. "I shall come in the morning to see this Webster for myself. Good day, gentlemen." He crammed the hat on his long hair, then went out to where an antique carriage with varnished panels and gilded axle bosses waited in the slashing rain. A slave opened the door and folded down the carriage steps.

Alexander let out a breath when the old man was gone, almost as though he sensed that a sinister presence had passed from the prison. Then he drew his revolver and checked that its percussion caps were firmly in place. "To work," he told Gillespie. "To work! Let's go and find Mr. Webster! To work!"

The rain turned the roads leading inland from Fort Monroe into strips of slick yellow dirt. The pale strips looked firm enough, but as soon as a horse put a hoof to the surface the sandy crust broke to expose a quagmire of glutinous red mud beneath.

A troop of northern cavalry abandoned the road to ride southward under a low, gray sky and a spitting rain. It was April, and the trees were in bud and the meadows a lovely green, yet the wind was cold and the troopers rode with their collars turned up and their hats pulled low. Their commander, a captain, peered through the rain in case the enemy cavalry should suddenly appear like gray-clad devils in the murk, but to his relief the land seemed empty.

A half hour after they had left the road the patrol emerged from the shelter of some skinny pine trees to see the red scars of freshly turned earth marking the line of rebel fortifications that stretched from Yorktown to Mulberry Island. The earthworks were not continuous, but consisted rather of earthen forts with heavy guns that enfiladed the intervening stretches of flooded water meadow. The Captain led his patrol southward, stopping every few hundred yards to examine the enemy works with a small telescope. The Colonel had been particular in his demand that all his cavalry patrols should attempt to determine whether the enemy cannons were real or made of wood, and the Captain sourly wondered how in the name of God he was supposed to attempt that piece of research. "You want to ride up to the rampart and give one of those guns a rap with your knuckles, Sergeant?" the Captain asked the man riding beside him.

The Sergeant chuckled, then disappeared beneath his greatcoat to light a cigar.

"The guns look real to me, Captain!" one of the men called.

"So did the guns at Manassas," the Captain said, then jumped with astonishment as one of the distant cannons suddenly fired. The smoke from the gun jetted thirty yards out from the embrasure to shroud the tongue of fire in the smoke's heart. The missile, evidently a solid ball or a shaped bolt of iron, crashed through the newly green trees just behind the patrol.

"Bastards," the Sergeant said, and rammed his spurs back. None of the cavalry had been hurt, but their sudden acceleration provoked a jeer from the distant rebel gunners.

A half mile farther on the Captain came upon a small knoll that protruded a few feet above the flat, water-laced landscape. He led his men to the knoll's summit where they dismounted and where the Captain discovered a tree that had a convenient crutch in which he could rest his telescope's barrel. From here he had a view between two of the rebel redoubts, a view across a stretch of marshland where hyacinths grew bright and deep into the rebel rear where he could just make out a road running among some shadowed pine trees. There were troops marching on the road, or at least struggling along the muddy road's verges. He counted them, company by company, and realized he was seeing a whole rebel battalion marching south.

"Listen, sir." The Sergeant had come to stand beside the Captain. "Can you hear it, sir?" The Captain turned down his collar and, by listening hard, caught the sound of distant trumpets carried on the cold wind. The sound was thin and far away. One trumpet sounded, another answered the call, and now that the Captain had turned his ears to those elfin noises it seemed as though the whole of this damp land was filled with the calls. "There are enough of the bastards," the Sergeant said with a shudder, as though the ghostly noise presaged a mysterious enemy.

"We've only seen the one battalion," the Captain said, but then another column of gray-clad troops appeared on the far road. He watched through the telescope and counted another eight companies. "Two battalions," he said, and no sooner had he spoken than a third regiment came into view.

The cavalry stayed on the knoll for two hours, and in that time the Captain saw eight rebel regiments marching south. One hopeful rumor had claimed that the rebels only had twenty battalions to guard all the Yorktown defenses, yet here, five miles south of the famous town, the Captain had watched regiment after regiment march by. The enemy was plainly in far greater strength than the optimists had hoped.

The cavalry remounted their horses in midafternoon. The Captain was the last to leave the knoll. He turned at the last moment and saw yet another rebel regiment appearing in the far trees. He did not stay to count heads, but instead carried his news eastward through the water-logged meadows of rich clover and past sullen farmhouses where unsmiling people watched their enemy pass.

205

The northern cavalry patrols all returned to tell identical stories of massive troop movements behind the rebel lines, of hidden units signaling with trumpets, and of real guns packed in newly dug earthworks. McClellan listened to the reports and shuddered. "You were right," he told Pinkerton. "We're facing at least seventy thousand men, maybe a hundred thousand!" The General had taken over the commandant's comfortable quarters in Fort Monroe from where he had a view of the massed shipping that had brought his army south from Alexandria. That army was ready for action now and McClellan had hoped to use it in a lightning-fast lunge toward Richmond, a maneuver that would have cracked through the eggshell defenses anchored on Yorktown, but today's cavalry reconnaissances meant there could be no sudden lunge after all. The capture of Yorktown and Richmond would have to be done the old-fashioned way, the hard way, with siege guns and patience and counter-trenching. His one hundred and twenty-one thousand men would have to wait while the besieging redoubts were constructed and the massive siege guns were dragged from Fort Monroe along the nightmare roads. The delay was a pity, but Pinkerton had cautioned him that the rebel defenses were manned in far greater strength than anyone supposed, and now the General thanked the head of his Secret Service Bureau for that timely and accurate intelligence.

Meanwhile, behind the rebel earthworks, the single battalion of Georgia troops that had marched nine times along the same stretch of muddy road, and had doubled back nine times through the trees before trudging the road again, shivered in the dusk and grumbled that their time was being wasted. They had joined the army to beat the living hell out of Yankees, not to march around and around in damn circles listening to scattered buglers serenade the

206

empty trees. Now, in the lonely woods, they lit fires and wondered if the rain would ever stop. They felt very lonely, and no wonder, for there were no other infantry battalions within three miles. Indeed, there were only thirteen thousand men stretched across the whole damp peninsula, and those thirteen thousand troops were supposed to stop the largest army ever assembled in America. It was no wonder that the Georgia men shivered and grumbled about having played the damn fool all day in the rain.

In the twilight the trees were filled with the screeching call of birds. The sound was subtly different from the call of the same bird in Georgia, but the men who had marched around in circles all day were country boys and knew well enough what bird made such a racket in the evening trees.

General Magruder knew too, and he at least smiled at the sound because he had spent these days trying to fool the Yankees into thinking that they faced a host when in truth the defensive line was pitiably manned. Magruder had marched and countermarched his men all day, putting on a show of force, and now in the evening rain he prayed that the birdsong was for McClellan and not for him.

Because in the dusk the mockingbirds sang.

It seemed it would never cease raining. Water poured down the gutters of Richmond to where the river frothed white with the effluents pumped from the ironworks and the tobacco factories and the tanyards and the slaughteryards. The few people in the streets hurried beneath somber black umbrellas. Even at midday coal-gas lamps were lit in the chamber where the Confederate Congress debated a measure that would encourage the development of a synthetic saltpeter for the manufacture of gunpowder. The voices in the chamber had to fight against the sound of rain outside. A handful of the Congressmen listened, some slept, while others sipped whiskey that had been sold by pharmacies as medicine and was thus free of the liquor ban imposed on the city. One or two of the Congressmen worried that the Yankee army closing on Yorktown would make all these discussions futile, but no one dared articulate such a thought. There had been too much defeatism lately, and too many good reasons for it; too many coastal forts captured by the U.S. Navy and too many hints that the Confederacy was encompassed by an implacable enemy.

Sally Truslow, arm in arm with Nate Starbuck, did not care about the Yankees seventy miles away, or about the rain. Sally was elated at the thought of taking tea in a respectable house, to which end she had dressed in a dark, high-necked dress with long sleeves and a skirt barely plumped by a mere two petticoats. She had forsworn all cosmetics other than a brushing of powder and a hint of black about her eyes.

Sally and Starbuck ran down Franklin Street, half protected by the umbrella Starbuck held, then sheltered in the doorway of a bakery on the corner of Second Street until a horsecar came into sight. They crowded aboard and paid the fare to Shockoe Cemetery. "Maybe they won't go to the hospital in this weather?" Sally said. She pushed close against Starbuck in the damp, crowded bus and peered through a filthy glass window at the rain.

"Bad weather doesn't stop good works," Starbuck said dourly. He was not looking forward to the afternoon or evening, for not even Sally's ebullient company could reconcile him to this encounter with a world he thought he had left far behind in Boston. Yet he could not deny Sally her happiness, and so he had decided to endure whatever discomfort the day presented even though he still did not understand why Sally had been so pleased when Adam's invitation arrived.

Sally herself hardly knew, though she did understand that the Gordons were a family and she dimly perceived that in all her life she had never been a member of a family, at least not of an ordinary, unexciting, simple, plain family. She had been the daughter of a horse thief and his woman, two fugitives who farmed a hard patch in the high mountains, and now she was a whore and shrewd enough to know she could climb as high as any ambition desired if she just understood the true value of the services she offered, but she also knew she could never have the satisfactions of belonging to plain, ordinary, straightforward folk. Sally, unlike Starbuck, had a sentimental idea that the commonplace was the reward of success. She had grown up an outcast and yearned for respectability, while Starbuck had grown up respectable and reveled in being a rebel.

Julia and Mrs. Gordon greeted them in the narrow hallway where there was scarcely room to take off the wet cloak and coat and pile them on a mirrored hallstand around which Sally and Starbuck edged to enter the parlor. The spring day was cold enough to justify a fire in the small cast-iron hearth, though the pile of glowing coals was so small that the heat barely reached beyond the plain iron fender. The floor was covered in strips of painted cotton-canvas, poor man's carpet, but everything was scrupulously clean, smelling of lye and polish, and suggesting to Starbuck just why Adam would be attracted to a daughter of this house with its suggestion of honest poverty and simple values. Adam himself stood by a piano, a second young man was standing in the window, while the Reverend John Gordon, the missioner, warmed himself before his tiny heap of smoking coals. "Miss Royall!" he greeted Sally, though with a mouth obstructed by cake. "Excuse me, my dear." He wiped one hand on the skirt of his frock coat, placed the cup and saucer on the mantel, and at last held out a welcoming hand. "It is a pleasure to meet you."

"Sir," Sally said, and dropped a flustered curtsey instead of shaking the offered hand. In her own house she knew how to greet generals and senators, she could tease the city's most eminent doctors and scorn the witticisms of its lawyers, but here, faced with respectability, she lost all her assurance.

"It is a pleasure to meet you," the Reverend John Gordon repeated with what seemed to be a genuine affability. "I believe you know Major Faulconer? So allow me to introduce Mr. Caleb Samworth. This is Miss Victoria Royall." Sally smiled, curtseyed again, then moved aside to make room for Starbuck, Mrs. Gordon, and Julia. More introductions were made, and then a pale and timid maid brought in another tray of teacups and Mrs. Gordon busied herself with the pot and strainer. Everyone agreed the weather was terrible, quite the worst springtime in Richmond's memory, and no one mentioned the northern army that was somewhere out on the city's eastern flank.

The Reverend John Gordon was a small, thin man with a very pink face and a scalp rimmed with wispy white hair. He had a weak chin that another man might have disguised with a full beard, but the missioner was clean-shaven, suggesting that his wife did not like beards. Indeed, the missioner looked so small and defenseless, while Mrs. Gordon appeared so very formidable, that Starbuck concluded that it was she and not he who ruled this deliberately cramped roost. Mrs. Gordon handed out the tea and inquired after the health of Miss Royall's aunt. Sally replied that her aunt was neither better nor worse, and there, much to Sally's relief, the matter of her aunt's sickness rested.

Mrs. Gordon explained Caleb Samworth's presence by revealing that he was the possessor of a wagon in which they would all travel to Chimborazo Hospital. Samworth smiled when his name was mentioned, then stared at Sally like a man dying of thirst might gaze on a distant but unreachable stream of cool water. The wagon, he explained haltingly, belonged to his father. "You may have heard of us? Samworth and Son, Embalmers and Undertakers?"

"Alas, no," Starbuck said.

Adam and the wilting Samworth invited Sally to sit with them in the window. Adam moved a great heap of empty cloth bags that the ladies of the house, like almost all the ladies in Richmond, were stitching out of whatever scraps of old material they could spare. The bags were being taken to Granny Lee's new earthworks to be filled with sand, though how much good such ramparts would prove against the northern horde that pressed forward from Fort Monroe no one could tell. "You sit here, Mr. Starbuck," the Reverend John Gordon said, drawing up a chair beside his own, then he launched into a long lamentation for the problems secession imposed on the American Society for the Propagation of the Gospel to the Poor. "Our headquarters, you understand, are in Boston."

"Mr. Starbuck knows well enough where the Society's headquarters are, Gordon," Mrs. Gordon interjected from her throne behind the tea tray. "He is a Bostonian. Indeed his father is a trustee of the Society, is that not so, Mr. Starbuck?"

"Indeed he is," Starbuck said.

"One of the trustees," Mrs. Gordon added pointedly, "who has depressed the missioners' emoluments these many years."

"Mother," the Reverend John Gordon chided his wife timidly.

"No, Gordon!" Mrs. Gordon would not be deflected. "While God gives me tongue I shall speak, indeed I shall.

211

One of the blessings of the South's secession has been to free us of our northern trustees! God clearly intended it to be so."

"We have heard nothing from headquarters in nine months!" the Reverend John Gordon explained in a worried voice to Starbuck. "Fortunately the mission's expenses are being met locally, praise God, but it is worrying, Mr. Starbuck, most worrying. There are accounts missing, reports half finished, and visitations undone. It is irregular!"

"It is a providence, Gordon," Mrs. Gordon corrected her husband.

"Let us pray so, Mother, let us pray so." The Reverend John Gordon sighed and took a bite from his slice of dry and mealy fruitcake. "Your father, then, is the Reverend Elial Starbuck?"

"Yes, sir, he is." Starbuck sipped his tea and managed to stop himself from grimacing at the bitter taste.

"A great man of God," Gordon said rather glumly. "Strong in the Lord."

"But blind to the needs of the Society's missioners!" Mrs. Gordon observed tartly.

"I find it strange, forgive me, that you should be wearing southern uniform, Mr. Starbuck?" the Reverend John Gordon inquired diffidently.

"I'm sure Mr. Starbuck is doing the Lord's work, Gordon." Mrs. Gordon, who had found Starbuck's loyalty equally inexplicable when she had met him outside the Scripture shop, now chose to defend her guest against her husband's quieter curiosity.

"Indeed, indeed," the missioner said hurriedly. "Even so, it is tragic."

"What is tragic, sir?" Starbuck asked.

The Reverend John Gordon waved his hands in a helpless gesture. "Families divided, a nation divided. So sad."

212

"It would not be sad if the North would simply withdraw its troops and allow us to live in peace," Mrs. Gordon said. "Don't you agree, Miss Royall?"

Sally smiled and nodded. "Yes, ma'am."

"They won't withdraw," Adam said gloomily.

"Then we'll just have to beat the hell out of them," Sally said unthinkingly.

"I was wondering" – Julia played a tinny note on the pianoforte to cut across the sudden surprise that had filled the room after Sally's words – "that perhaps we should not use such mournful hymns in the ward tonight, Father?"

"To be sure, my dear, to be sure," her father said. He explained to Sally and Starbuck that he began his ward services with a selection of hymns and a prayer, and afterward one of the party would give a reading from God's word. "Perhaps Miss Royall would like to read the Scriptures?" he suggested.

"Oh no, sir, no." Sally, aware that she had blundered once already, blushed as she declined the offer. She was learning to read and, in the last year, had progressed so far that she could actually open a book for pleasure, but she had no faith in her ability to read aloud.

"You are saved, Miss Royall?" Mrs. Gordon asked suspiciously as she peered hard at her guest.

"Saved, ma'am?"

"You have been washed in the blood of the Lamb? You have accepted Jesus into your heart? Your aunt, surely, has introduced you to your Savior?"

"Yes, ma'am," Sally said timidly, not having a clue as to what Mrs. Gordon meant.

"I should be happy to read for you," Starbuck interjected to the Reverend John Gordon.

"Mr. Samworth reads Scripture very well," Mrs. Gordon said.

213

"Perhaps, Caleb, you would read from God's word?" the Reverend John Gordon asked, "and after that" – he turned to his guests again to explain the form of service – "we have a time for prayer and testimony. I encourage the men to witness to the power of God's saving grace in their lives, and then we sing another hymn and I make a few remarks before we close our worship with a last hymn and a blessing. We then give the patients some time for private conversation or prayer. Sometimes they need us to write letters for them. Your assistance" – he smiled first at Sally, then at Starbuck – "will be very greatly appreciated, I'm sure."

"And we shall need help distributing the hymnals," Mrs. Gordon said.

"It'll be a pleasure," Sally said warmly, and to Starbuck's amazement she really did seem to be enjoying herself, for when the conversation became general once more her laughter sounded clear and often across the small room. Mrs. Gordon frowned at the sound, but Julia was plainly enjoying Sally's company.

At five o'clock the sallow maid collected the tea plates, and afterward the Reverend John Gordon said a word of prayer in which he begged Almighty God to shower blessing upon their worship this evening, and then Caleb Samworth fetched the wagon which was kept in a yard just around the corner in Charity Street. The wagon was painted black and had a black canvas cover supported by hoops. Two benches ran on either side of the wagon's bed, while a pair of shining steel rails were fixed down its center. "Is that where they put the casket?" Sally asked as Caleb helped her up the steps built into the folded-down backboard.

"Indeed, Miss Royall," he said.

Sally and Julia shared a bench with Adam, Starbuck sat with the Reverend and Mrs. Gordon, while Caleb

214

Samworth perched on the driver's box swathed in an oil-skin cape. It took the hearse twenty minutes to reach the hill where the newly constructed hospital sheds spread across the grass of Chimborazo Park. It was dusk and a dim yellow lamplight was showing through scores of tiny windows. A haze of coalsmoke lingered in the rain over the shed's tarred roofs. The mission party alighted outside the ward chosen for this night's service, then Caleb and Adam took the wagon to fetch the hospital's harmonium while Julia and Sally distributed copies of the mission's hymnal.

Starbuck went with Adam. "I wanted a word in private," he confided to his friend as the undertaker's cart jolted over the wet ground. "Have you spoken to your father?"

"I haven't had a chance," Adam said. He did not look at Starbuck but stared into the wet night.

"All I want is to be back with my company!" Starbuck appealed.

"I know."

"Adam!"

"I'll try! But it's difficult. I have to choose the right moment. Father's touchy, you know that." Adam shook his head. "Why are you so keen to fight? Why don't you just sit the war out here?"

"Because I'm a soldier."

"A fool, you mean," Adam said with a touch of exasperation, then the wagon lurched to a halt, and it was time to carry the harmonium back to the ward.

There were sixty sick men in the wooden shed. Twenty of their cots were arranged against each long wall while another twenty cots were set in a double row in the hut's center. A potbellied stove occupied a central position, its hot plate crowded with coffeepots. The nurse's table was pushed aside to make room for the harmonium. Julia pumped the carpeted pedals, then played a few wheezy chords as though clearing the cobwebs out of the instrument's reeds.

The Reverend and Mrs. Gordon went around the cots shaking hands and saying words of comfort. Sally did the same, and Starbuck noted how her presence cheered the wounded men. Her laughter filled the shed with brightness and Starbuck thought that he had never seen Sally so happy. Water buckets were placed about the ward so that the patients' wound dressings could be kept damp, and Sally found a sponge and gently moistened the dark-stained bandages. The ward stank of decaying flesh and human waste. It was cold and damp despite the stove, and dark despite the half-dozen lanterns that hung from the rough-sawn rafters. Some of the men were unconscious, most were fevered, only a few had battle wounds. "Once the fighting starts proper again," a sergeant who had lost an arm told Starbuck, "that's when you'll see the wounded arrive." The Sergeant had come for the service with a score of other patients from neighboring sheds, bringing chairs and extra lanterns. The Sergeant had been injured in a train accident. "Fell onto the rails," he told Starbuck, "when I was drunk. My own fault." He looked appreciatively at Sally. "There's a rare-looking girl, Captain, a girl to make a man's life worth living."

The sound of the hymn singing brought yet more patients to the ward, together with some unwounded officers who had been visiting friends and who now crowded at the back of the shed. Some of the wounded were Yankees, but all the voices swelled in melody, filling the shed with a sentimental comradeship that made Starbuck suddenly yearn for the company of his soldiers. One man alone seemed unaffected by the singing; a bearded, pale, gaunt creature who had been sleeping, but who suddenly woke and began to scream in terror. The voices faltered, then

Sally crossed to the man's side and pulled his head into her arms and stroked his cheek, and Starbuck saw the man's fluttering hands calm down on the threadbare gray blanket that was his cot's covering.

The gaunt man stayed silent as the voices sang on. Starbuck watched Julia at the harmonium, then suddenly felt the pull of his old faith tug at him. Maybe it was the yellow light, or the faces of the wounded who looked so pathetically pleased to have God's word brought to them, or maybe it was Julia's absorbed beauty, but Starbuck was suddenly assailed with a sinner's guilt as he listened to the Reverend John Gordon pray that God's blessings would shower upon these wounded souls. The missioner proved to have a gentle and effective manner that seemed far more suitable than the strong rant that Starbuck's father would have employed. The Scripture was from Ecclesiastes chapter twelve and Samworth read it in a high, nervous voice. Starbuck followed the passage in his brother's Bible, which Adam had sent with the invitation to take tea.

The words of Scripture struck sharp at Starbuck's soul. "Remember now thy Creator in the days of thy youth," the passage began, and James had written beside it in his tiny handwriting, "Easier to be a Christian in later life? Years bring wisdom? Pray for grace now," and Starbuck knew he had fallen from grace, that he was a sinner, that the doors of hell gaped as wide as the flaming maw of the blast furnaces down by Richmond's river, and he felt the trembling terror of a sinner come face to face with God. "'Because man goeth to his long home,'" Samworth read, "'and the mourners go about the street. Or ever the silver cord be loosed, or the golden bowl be broken, or the pitcher be broken at the fountain, or the wheel broken at the cistern,'" and the words filled Starbuck with the sudden premonition that he would die an untimely death: flensed by a Yankee shot, disemboweled by a vengeful, righteous shell, a sinner gone to his long and fiery home.

He did not hear much of the sermon, or many of the testimonies in which the wounded men gave praise to God for His blessings on their lives. Instead Starbuck was lost in the dark pit of remorse. After the service, he decided, he would seek a word with the Reverend John Gordon. He would lay his sins before God and, with the missioner's help, seek to return his soul to its proper place. But how could he ever take his proper place? He had quarreled with Ethan Ridley because of Sally, and he had killed Ethan Ridley because of the quarrel, and that one act alone would surely damn his soul forever. He told himself the killing had been self-defense, but his conscience knew it was murder. Starbuck blinked back tears. All was vanity, but what use was vanity in the face of eternal damnation?

It was well past eight o'clock when the Reverend John Gordon pronounced his blessing on the patients, and then the missioner moved from bed to bed, praying and offering encouragement. The wounded seemed so young; even to Starbuck they seemed like mere boys.

One of the hospital's senior surgeons arrived, still in his bloody apron, to thank the Reverend John Gordon. With the surgeon was a clergyman, the Reverend Doctor Peterkin, who was the hospital's honorary chaplain as well as one of the city's more fashionable ministers. He recognized Adam and went to talk with him, while Julia, her music put away, crossed to Starbuck. "How did you find our little service, Mr. Starbuck?"

"I was moved, Miss Gordon."

"Father is good, isn't he? His sincerity shines." She was worried by Starbuck's expression, mistaking his sinner's guilt as a distaste for the ward's horrors. "Does it deter you from soldiering?" Julia asked.

"I don't know. I hadn't thought about it." He looked at Sally, who was now devoting herself to the ragged, frightened man who gripped her hands as though she alone could keep him alive. "Soldiers don't think they'll end up in places like this."

"Or worse," Julia said drily. "There are wards here for the dying, for men who can never be helped. Though I'd like to help them." She spoke wistfully.

"I'm sure you do," Starbuck said gallantly.

"I don't mean by visiting and playing hymns, Mr. Starbuck, I mean by nursing them. But Mother won't hear of it. She says I will contract a fever, or worse. Nor will Adam permit it. He wants to protect me from the war. You know he disapproves of it?"

"I know," Starbuck said, then glanced at Julia. "And you?"

"There's nothing here to merit approval," Julia said. "Yet I confess I am too proud to want the North to triumph over us. So maybe I am a warmonger. Is that what makes men fight? Mere pride?"

"Mere pride," Starbuck said. "On the battlefield you want to prove you're better than the other side." He recalled the joy of hitting the Yankees' open flank at Ball's Bluff, the panic in the blue ranks, the screams as the enemy were tumbled off the crest and down to the bloody, bullet-lashed river. Then he felt guilty at that remembered pleasure. The gates of hell, he thought, would surely gape especially wide for him.

"Mr. Starbuck?" Julia asked, concerned for the horror that showed on his face, but before he could respond and before Julia could say another word, Sally suddenly hurried across the ward and took Starbuck's elbow.

"Take me away, please." Her voice was low and urgent.

"Sal –" Starbuck checked himself, realizing that Julia

knew Sally as Victoria. "What is it?"

"That man," Sally just breathed the words, not even bothering to indicate which man she spoke of, "recognizes me. Please, Nate. Take me away."

"I'm sure it doesn't matter," Starbuck said softly.

"Please!" Sally hissed. "Just take me out of here!"

"Might I help?" Julia asked, puzzled.

"I think we should go," Starbuck said, though the trouble was that Sally's cloak and his coat were piled at the end of the shed where the bloody-aproned surgeon was standing, and it was the surgeon who had recognized Sally and spoken with the Reverend Doctor Peterkin, who, in turn, now talked to Mrs. Gordon. "Come," Starbuck said, and he pulled Sally by the hand. He would abandon the coats, even though he regretted losing the fine gray coat that had belonged to Oliver Wendell Holmes. "You will forgive me?" he asked Julia as he edged past her.

"Mr. Starbuck!" Mrs. Gordon called imperiously. "Miss Royall!"

"Ignore her," Starbuck said to Sally.

"Miss Royall! Come here!" Mrs. Gordon called and Sally, stung by the tone, turned toward her. Adam hurried down the ward to see what was the matter while the Reverend John Gordon looked up from where he knelt beside a fevered man's cot.

"I will speak with you outside," Mrs. Gordon declared, and she turned onto the small porch where, on fine days, the patients could take the air under the shelter of a sloping roof.

Sally plucked up her cloak. The surgeon smirked and offered her a bow. "Son of a bitch," Sally hissed at him. Starbuck extricated his coat and went onto the porch.

"Words fail me," Mrs. Gordon greeted Sally and Starbuck in the rainy darkness.

"You wanted words with me?" Sally confronted her.

"I cannot believe it of you, Mr. Starbuck." Mrs. Gordon ignored the defiant Sally and looked at Starbuck instead. "That you, raised in a godly home, should have the ill manners to introduce a woman like this into my house."

"A woman like what?" Sally demanded. The Reverend John Gordon had come onto the porch and, in obedience to his wife's sharp command, closed the door, though not before Adam and Julia had crowded onto the small porch.

"You will go inside, Julia," her mother insisted.

"Let her stay!" Sally said. "A woman like what?"

"Julia!" Mrs. Gordon glared at her daughter.

"Mother, dear," the Reverend John Gordon said, "might you tell us what this is all about?"

"Doctor Peterkin," Mrs. Gordon said indignantly, "has just informed me that this, this, woman is a . . . " She paused, unable to find a word she could decently use in front of her daughter. "Julia! Inside this instant!"

"My dear!" the Reverend John Gordon said. "What is she?"

"A Magdalen!" Mrs. Gordon shouted the word.

"She means I'm a whore, Reverend," Sally said sourly.

"And you brought her to my house!" Mrs. Gordon shrieked at Starbuck.

"Mrs. Gordon," Starbuck began, but he could not interrupt the tirade that now poured on his head like the rain that was drumming on the porch's tarpaper roof. Mrs. Gordon wondered if the Reverend Elial Starbuck knew to what depths of iniquity his son had sunk, and how far from God's grace he had fallen, and how evil was his choice of companions. "She is a fallen woman!" Mrs. Gordon screamed, "and you brought her to my house!"

"Our Lord consorted with sinners," the Reverend John Gordon said feebly.

"But He didn't give them tea!" Mrs. Gordon was beyond argument. She turned on Adam. "And you, Mr. Faulconer, I am shocked by your friendships. There is no other word. I am shocked."

Adam looked remorsefully at Starbuck. "Is it true?"

"Sally is a friend," Starbuck said. "A good friend. I'm proud to know her."

"Sally Truslow!" Adam said, the identity of Miss Royall at last yielding to his memory.

"Are you saying you know this woman?" Mrs. Gordon challenged Adam.

"He don't know me," Sally said tiredly.

"I am forced to wonder if you are a fit companion for my daughter, Mr. Faulconer." Mrs. Gordon pressed her advantage on Adam. "This night has been a providence of God; maybe it has revealed your true self!"

"I said he don't know me!" Sally insisted.

"Do you know her?" the Reverend John Gordon asked Adam.

Adam shrugged. "Her father was one of my family's tenants once. A long time ago. Beyond that I don't know her."

"But you do know Mr. Starbuck." Mrs. Gordon had not wrung a full measure of remorse from Adam yet. "Are you telling me you approve of the company he keeps?"

Adam looked at his friend. "I'm sure Nate didn't know Miss Truslow's nature."

"I knew it," Starbuck said, "and as I said, she is a friend." He put an arm around Sally's shoulder.

"And you approve of your friend's choice of companion?" Mrs. Gordon demanded of Adam. "Do you, Mr. Faulconer? For I cannot have my daughter attached, however respectably, to a man who consorts with the friends of scarlet women."

"No," Adam said, "I don't approve."

"You're just like your father," Sally said. "Rotten to the core. If you Faulconers didn't have money you'd be lower than dogs." She pulled herself free of Starbuck's arm and ran into the rain.

Starbuck turned to follow Sally, but was checked by Mrs. Gordon. "You're making a choice!" she warned him. "This is the night you choose between God and the devil, Mr. Starbuck!"

"Nate!" Adam added his voice to Mrs. Gordon's warning. "Let her go."

"Why? Because she's a whore?" Starbuck felt the rage rise in him, a filthy rage of hatred for these sanctimonious prigs. "I told you, Adam, she's a friend, and you don't abandon friends. God damn you all." He ran after Sally, catching up with her at the edge of the sheds where the muddy slope of Chimborazo Park fell steeply down into the Bloody Run, where the city's dueling ground was set beside a stream. "I'm sorry," he told Sally, taking her arm again.

She sniffed. The rain made her hair dank and straggling. She was crying and Starbuck pulled her into his body, covering her with the scarlet lining of his coat. The rain stung his face. "You were right," Sally said, her voice muffled. "We shouldn't have gone."

"They shouldn't have behaved like that," Starbuck said.

Sally cried softly. "I sometimes just want to be ordinary." She managed to speak through the tears. "I just want a house and babies and a rug on the floor and an apple tree. I don't want to live like my father and I don't want to be what I am now. Not forever. I just want to be plain. Do you know what I mean, Nate?" She looked up at him, her face lit by the fires of the forges that burned day and night beside the river on the far side of the run.

He stroked her rain-dampened face. "I know," he said.

"Don't you want to be ordinary?" she asked.

223

"Sometimes, yes."

"Jesus," Sally swore. She pulled away from him, cuffed her nose, and pushed her wet hair off her forehead. "I thought if the war ends I'd have enough money to buy a small store. Nothing fancy, Nate. Dry goods, maybe? I'm saving my money, you see, so I can be ordinary. No one special. Not Royall anymore, just plain ordinary. But my father's right," she said with a new note of vengeance, "there are two kinds of folk in this world. There are sheep and wolves, Nate, sheep and wolves, and you can't change your nature. And they're all sheep." She jerked a contemptuous thumb toward the hospital sheds. "Including your friend. He's like his father. He's frightened of women." It was a scathing judgment.

Starbuck held her close again and stared across the shadows of Bloody Run to where the ironwork fires shimmered their reflections on the rain-pocked river. He had not understood till this moment just how alone in the world he was, an outcast, a wolf running alone. Sally was the same, rejected by polite society because in her desperation for escape and independence she had broken its rules, and for that she would never be forgiven, any more than Starbuck would be forgiven. Which meant he must make it alone, he would spit on these people for rejecting him, and he would do it by being the best soldier he could be. He had always known that his salvation in the South lay in the army, for there no man cared what he was as long as he proved a fighter.

"You know what, Nate?" Sally said. "I was thinking in there that maybe I had a chance. Like a real chance? That I could be good." She said the last word fervently. "But they don't want me in their world, do they?"

"You don't need their approval to be a good person, Sally."

224

"I don't care anymore. One day I'll have the likes of them begging to stand on my carpet, just you watch and see."

Starbuck smiled in the dark. They were a whore and a failed soldier, declaring war on the world. He stooped and kissed Sally's rain-wet cheek. "I must take you home," he said.

"To your room," Sally said. "I don't feel like working."

Beneath them a train pulled out of the city, the light of its firebox throwing a lurid glow along the damp grass beside the stream. The locomotive was hauling cars of ammunition bound for the peninsula where a thin line of playacting rebels was holding off a horde.

Starbuck walked Sally home, then took her to his bed. He was a sinner and this night, after all, was not for repentance.

Sally left Starbuck just after one o'clock in the morning, so he was alone in the narrow bed when the troops came. He was sleeping soundly, and the first he knew of the incursion was the splintering sound of the outside stable door being broken down. There was no light in the room. He fumbled for his revolver as feet pounded on the stairs and he had just succeeded in pulling the ivory-handled weapon out of its holster when the door crashed open and a wash of lantern light flared bright in the small dingy attic room. "Put the gun down, lad! Down!" The men were all in uniforms and carried rifles with fixed bayonets. Throughout Richmond a fixed bayonet was the mark of "plug-ugly," a provost of General Winder's martial police force, and Starbuck sensibly let the revolver fall back onto the floor. "Your name's Starbuck?" the man who had ordered him to lay the gun down now asked.

"Who are you?" Starbuck shielded his eyes. Three

lanterns were in the room now and what seemed to be a whole platoon of soldiers.

"Answer the question!" the voice roared. "Is your name Starbuck?"

"Yes."

"Take him! Quick now!"

"Let me dress, for God's sake!"

"Hurry, lads!"

Two men seized Starbuck, dragged him naked from the bed, and thumped him hard and painfully against the flaking plaster wall.

"Put a blanket round him, boys. We don't want to frighten the horses. Manacle him first, Corporal!" Starbuck's eyes had adjusted and he could see that the commanding officer was a broad-chested, brown-bearded captain.

"What the hell . . . " Starbuck began to protest as the Corporal produced chains and wristbands, but the soldier holding Starbuck pushed him hard against the wall.

"Silence!" the Captain roared. "Take everything, lads, everything! I'll take that bottle as evidence, thank you, Perkins. All papers to be cased up properly; that's your responsibility, Sergeant. And that bottle too, Perkins, to me." The Captain put the whiskey bottles in his uniform's capacious pockets, then led the way down the stairs. Starbuck, his wrists chained and his body loosely swathed in a rough gray blanket, stumbled after the Captain through the empty coach house and out into Sixth Street where a black carriage with four horses waited under the streetlight. It was still raining, and the horses' breath steamed in the gaslight. A church clock struck four and a window at the back of the main house rattled up. "What's going on?" a woman's voice cried. Starbuck thought it might be Sally, but he could not tell.

226

"Nothing, ma'am! Back to your bed!" the Captain called, then he pushed Starbuck up the carriage steps. The Captain and three soldiers followed. The rest of the party were still searching Starbuck's lodgings.

"Where are we going?" Starbuck asked as the carriage jolted away from the sidewalk.

"You are now a prisoner of the Provost Guard," the Captain responded very formally. "You will speak when you are spoken to and at no other time."

"You're speaking to me now," Starbuck said, "so where are we going?"

It was dark in the carriage so Starbuck did not see the fist that suddenly smacked him hard across the eyes and banged his head against the carriage's backboard. "Shut the hell up, you Yankee bastard," a voice said, and Starbuck, his eyes involuntarily streaming with the effects of the blow, did as the man suggested.

The journey was short, no more than half a mile, and then the iron-rimmed wheels screeched in protest as the carriage slewed around a tight corner before jolting to a stop. The door was thrown open and Starbuck saw the torchlit gates of Lumpkin's Jail, known now as Castle Godwin. "Move!" the Corporal shouted, and Starbuck was pushed down the carriage steps and through a wicket entrance cut into Castle Godwin's larger gates.

"Number fourteen!" a turnkey bawled as the arresting party came through the gate. A uniformed guard led the way through a brick arch and down a stone-flagged corridor lit by two oil lamps until he reached a stout wooden door marked with a stenciled "14." He opened the door with a heavy key made from gleaming steel. The Corporal unlocked the manacles from Starbuck's wrists.

"In there, cuffee," the guard said, and Starbuck was pushed inside the cell. He saw a wooden bed, a metal pail, and a large puddle. The room stank of sewage. "Shit in the bucket, sleep on the bed, or the other way round, cuffee." The guard laughed, then the door crashed shut with an echoing din and the cell was plunged into an absolute darkness. Starbuck, exhausted, lay on the wooden bed and shivered.

They gave him a pair of coarse gray trousers, square leather brogans, and a shirt from which the bloodstains of its last owner had not been removed. Breakfast was a cup of water and the heel of a stale loaf. The city's clocks were striking nine when two guards came and ordered him to sit on the bed and extend his feet toward them. They chained a pair of iron anklets on his feet. "They stay till you leave," one of the guards said, "or till they hang you." He stuck out his tongue and contorted his face into the grotesque leer of a hanged man.

"On your feet!" the second guard said. "Move!"

Starbuck was pushed into the corridor. The chains on his feet forced him into an awkward shuffle, but the guards were evidently used to the slow pace for they did not try to hurry him, indeed they encouraged him to linger as they passed through a courtyard that reminded Starbuck of the lurid tales he had heard of medieval torture chambers. Chains hung from the wall, while in the yard's center was a wooden horse that consisted of a plank mounted sideways on a pair of trestles. The punishment was to sit a man on the plank's edge and weight his feet so that the wood would drive into his groin. "This ain't for your kind, cuffee," one of the two guards said. "They're trying something new on you. Keep walking."

Starbuck was taken to a room with brick walls, a flagged floor with a drain in its center, a table, and a chair. A barred window looked east toward the open sewer of Shockoe

228

Creek, which flowed through the city. One of the small panes was open and the smell of the creek soured the room. The guards, whom Starbuck could observe properly now, stacked their muskets against the wall. They were both big men, as tall as Starbuck, with pale, coarse, clean-shaven faces and the vacant expressions of men who asked and received little of life. One spat a viscous stream of tobacco juice toward the open drain. The discolored spittle landed dead center. "Good one, Abe," the other guard said.

The door opened and a thin, pale man entered. He had a leather bag hanging from one shoulder and a small fair beard that merely fringed his chin. His cheeks and upper lip still gleamed from his morning shave and his lieutenant's uniform was immaculate, brushed spotless and pressed to knife-crease edges. "Good morning," he said in a diffident voice.

"Answer the officer, you Yankee scum," the guard called Abe said.

"Good morning," Starbuck said.

The Lieutenant brushed the seat of the chair, sat down, took a pair of spectacles from a pocket, and hooked them over his ears. He had a very thin and rather earnest face, like a new minister coming to an old congregation. "Starbuck, isn't it?"

"Yes."

"Call the officer 'sir,' scum!"

"Peace, Harding, peace." The Lieutenant frowned in evident disapproval of Harding's rudeness. He had placed the leather bag on the table and now he took a folder from it. He untied the folder's green ribbons, opened its covers, and examined the papers inside. "Nathaniel Joseph Starbuck, yes?"

"Yes."

"Presently residing at Franklin Street, the old Burrell house, yes?"

"I don't know who lived there."

"Josiah Burrell, a tobacco factor. The family fell on hard times, like so many these days. Now, let me see." The Lieutenant leaned back, making his chair creak ominously, then took off his glasses and tiredly rubbed his eyes. "I'm going to ask you some questions, Starbuck, and your role, as you might surmise, is to answer those questions. Normally, of course, these things are subject to law, but there's a war on and I fear the necessity of eliciting the truth cannot wait upon the rigmarole of lawyers. Do you understand?"

"Not really. I'd like to know what the hell I'm doing here."

The guards behind Starbuck growled a warning for his truculence, but the Lieutenant held up a placatory hand. "You shall find out, Starbuck, I do promise you." He fixed the glasses back on his nose. "I forgot to introduce myself. How remiss. My name is Lieutenant Gillespie, Lieutenant Walton Gillespie." He spoke the name as though he expected Starbuck to recognize it, but Starbuck merely shrugged. Gillespie took a pencil from his uniform pocket. "Shall we begin? You were born where?" Gillespie asked.

"Boston," Starbuck said.

"Where exactly, please?"

"Milk Street."

"Your parents' home, yes?"

"Grandparents. My mother's people."

Gillespie made a note. "And your parents live where now?"

"Walnut Street."

"Do they now? How very pleasant for them! I was in Boston two years ago and had the privilege of hearing your father expound the gospel." Gillespie smiled in evident pleasure at the memory. "On we go," he said, and he took Starbuck through a series of questions about his schooling and Yale Theological College and how he had come to be in the South when the war started and what service he had seen in the Faulconer Legion.

"So far, so good," Gillespie said when he had finished hearing about Ball's Bluff. He turned a page and frowned at whatever was written there. "When did you first meet John Scully?"

"Never heard of him."

"Price Lewis?"

Starbuck shook his head.

"Timothy Webster?"

Starbuck simply shrugged to show his ignorance.

"I see," Gillespie said in a tone which suggested that Starbuck's denial was particularly puzzling. He made a pencil mark, still frowning, then took off his spectacles and massaged the bridge of his nose momentarily. "Your brother's name is what?"

"I've got three brothers. James, Frederick, and Sam."

"Their ages?"

Starbuck had to think. "Twenty-six or -seven, seventeen, and thirteen."

"The oldest. His name is?"

"James."

"James." Gillespie repeated the name as though he had never heard it before. In the courtyard a man suddenly screamed and Starbuck heard the distinct sound of a whip slashing through the air, then the crack of the lash slapping home. "Did I shut the door, Harding?" Gillespie asked.

"Tight shut, sir."

"So noisy, so noisy. Tell me, Starbuck, when you last saw James?"

Starbuck shook his head. "It has to be long before the war."

"Before the war," Gillespie said as he wrote it down. "And the last time you received a letter from him?"

"Again, before the war."

"Before the war," Gillespie repeated again slowly, then took a small penknife from his pocket. He opened the blade and sharpened the point of his pencil, fussily brushing the shards of wood and lead into a neat pile at the table's edge. "What does the Confederate Army Bible Supply Society mean to you?"

"Nothing."

"I see." Gillespie laid his pencil down and leaned back in the rickety chair. "And just what information did you send to your brother about the disposition of our forces?"

"None!" Starbuck protested, at last beginning to understand what this whole farrago was about.

Gillespie once again took off his spectacles and rubbed them against his sleeve. "I mentioned to you earlier, Mr. Starbuck, that we are forced, regrettably forced, to extreme measures in our attempts to elicit the truth. Usually, as I said, we would have recourse to a process of law, but extreme times demand extreme measures. Do you understand?"

"No."

"Then let me ask you again. Do you know John Scully and Lewis Price?"

"No."

"Have you been in communication with your brother?"

"No."

"Have you received letters care of the Confederate Army Bible Supply Society?"

"No."

"And did you deliver a letter care of Mr. Timothy

Webster at the Monumental Hotel?"

"No," Starbuck protested.

Gillespie shook his head sadly. When Major Alexander had arrested Timothy Webster and Hattie Lawton he had also discovered a letter written in tight block capitals that described the entire disposition of Richmond's defenders. The letter was addressed to Major James Starbuck, the same name that appeared on the communication taken from John Scully. The letter would have been a disaster to the South's cause for it had even offered a description of the playacting with which General Magruder had been attempting to deceive McClellan's patrols. All that had prevented Webster from delivering the letter was a terrible rheumatic fever that had kept the man in bed for weeks.

Starbuck, questioned again about the letter, shook his head. "I've never heard of a Timothy Webster."

Gillespie grimaced. "And you insist upon those answers?"

"They're the truth!"

"Alas," Gillespie said, and he pulled open the leather bag and took out a funnel of bright brass and a bottle made of blue-colored glass. He unstoppered the bottle, letting a thin, sour smell fill the room. "My father, Starbuck, like yours, is a man of some eminence. He is the medical superintendent of the Chesterfield Lunacy Asylum. You know it?"

"No." Starbuck gazed at the bottle apprehensively.

"There are two schools of opinion governing the treatment of lunacy," Gillespie said. "One theory claims that madness can be coddled out of patients by fresh air, good food, and kindness, but the second opinion, to which my father adheres, insists that lunacy can be shocked out of the sufferer's system. In essence, Starbuck" – Gillespie looked up at the prisoner and his eyes seemed oddly bright – "we must punish the lunatic for his aberrant behavior and so drive him back into the company of civilized men. This" – he held up the blue-glass bottle – "has been declared the finest coercive substance known to science. Tell me about Timothy Webster."

"There's nothing to tell!"

Gillespie paused, then nodded at the two guards. Starbuck turned to resist the nearest man, but he was too slow. He was hit from behind and thrown down to the floor, and before he could twist around he was pinned onto the stone. The chains around his ankle clanked as his hands were pinioned behind his back. He swore at the two guards, but they were big men accustomed to subduing prisoners and they ignored his oaths, instead turning him onto his back. One of them took the brass funnel and rammed it into Starbuck's mouth. When he resisted by gritting his teeth the man threatened to hammer the funnel down and so break his teeth, and Starbuck, knowing when he was beaten, released his jaw.

Gillespie knelt beside him with the blue bottle. "This is croton oil," he told Starbuck, "you know of it?"

Starbuck could not speak, so he shook his head.

"Croton oil is drawn from the seeds of the *Croton tiglium* plant. It's a purgative, Mr. Starbuck, and a very violent one. My father employs it whenever a patient exhibits offensive behavior. No madman can be violent or perverse, you see, when he is having a score of bowel movements every ten minutes." Gillespie smiled. "What do you know about Timothy Webster?"

Starbuck shook his head, then tried to twist his way out of the guards' grip, but the two men were far too strong for him. One of them pushed Starbuck's head hard back onto the flagstones while Gillespie poised the bottle over the funnel. "In times past the treatment of lunacy depended upon simple physical punishments," Gillespie explained, "but my father's contribution to medicine was the discovery that an application of this cathartic is far more efficient than any amount of whipping. A small taste first, I think." He poured a thin stream of the oil into the funnel. It tasted fatty and rank in Starbuck's mouth. He choked on it, but one of the guards clamped a hand around his jaw and Starbuck had no choice but to swallow the oil. It left a burning sensation in his mouth.

Gillespie eased the bottle away and motioned for the guards to free Starbuck. Starbuck gasped for breath. His mouth burned and his gullet seemed raw. He sensed the thick oil hitting his stomach as he struggled to his knees.

Then the purgative hit. He doubled over, spewing vomit onto the floor. The spasm left him breathless, but before he could recover, another spasm ripped up from his belly, then his bowels opened uncontrollably and the room filled with his terrible stink. He could not stop himself. He groaned and rolled on the floor, then jerked as another spasm of vomit tore up his body.

The guards grinned and stepped back from him. Gillespie, careless of the awful smell, watched avidly through his spectacles and made an occasional note in a small book. Still the spasms racked Starbuck. Even when there was nothing left in his belly or bowels he kept on gasping and twitching as the awful oil scoured through his guts.

"Let us talk again," Gillespie said after a few minutes, when Starbuck was calmer.

"Bastard," Starbuck said. He was filthy, lying in filth, his clothes smeared with filth; he was humiliated and helpless and degraded by the filth.

"Do you know a Mr. John Scully or a Mr. Lewis Price?" Gillespie asked in his precise voice.

"No. And to hell with you."

"Have you been in communication with your brother?"

"No. Damn you."

"Have you received letters care of the Confederate Army Bible Supply Society?"

"No!"

"And did you deliver information to Timothy Webster at the Monumental Hotel?"

"I'll tell you what I did, you bastard!" Starbuck raised his face and spat a dribble of vomit toward Gillespie. "I carried a gun into battle for this country, which is more than you ever did, you shit-faced son of a bitch!"

Gillespie shook his head as though Starbuck was peculiarly recalcitrant. "Again," he said to the guards and lifted the bottle from the table.

"No!" Starbuck said, but one of the guards threw him down and both men pinioned him to the floor. Gillespie brought the croton oil.

"I'm curious to discover just how much oil one person can endure," Gillespie said. "Move him this way, I don't want to kneel in his droppings."

"No!" Starbuck moaned, but the funnel was thrust into his mouth once more and Gillespie, half smiling, poured another stream of the viscous yellowish liquid into the brass maw.

The spasms hit again. The pain was much worse this time, a terrible flaying raw agony that burned in Starbuck's belly and spread outward as he twisted in his own filth. Twice more Gillespie poured the purgative down his throat, but the extra liquid yielded no more information. Starbuck still insisted he knew no one called Scully or Lewis or Webster.

At midday the guards threw buckets of cold water over him. Gillespie watched expressionless as the inert and stinking body of the northerner was carried out of the room to be dumped in his cell and then, annoyed with himself for being late, he hurried away to the regular Bible class that met at lunchtime in the nearby Universalist church.

While Starbuck lay in the damp and whimpered.

Reluctantly, like a heavy beast rousing itself from a long sleep, the rebel army took itself away from its positions around Culpeper Court House. It moved slowly and cautiously, for General Johnston could not yet be certain that the North was not attempting a giant piece of deception. Maybe the much-advertised voyage of the great ships from Alexandria to Fort Monroe was merely an elaborate charade to make him move his troops to Richmond's blind side? Such a ruse would open the roads of northern Virginia to the real Federal attack and, fearing just such a deception, Johnston sent cavalry patrols deep into Fauquier and Prince William counties, then still farther north into Loudoun County. The men of the partisan brigades, the ragged riders whose job was to stay behind and harass any northern invaders, crossed the Potomac into Maryland, yet all the patrols came back with the same news. The Yankees were gone. The defenses around Washington were fully manned, and the forts that guarded the northern enclave in Virginia's Fairfax County were strongly garrisoned, but the North's field army had vanished. The Young Napoleon was attacking in the peninsula.

The Faulconer Brigade was among the first to be ordered to the outskirts of Richmond. Washington Faulconer summoned Major Bird to receive the orders. "Isn't Swynyard supposed to be your errand boy?" Bird demanded of Washington Faulconer.

"He's resting."

"You mean he's drunk."

237

"Nonsense, Pecker." Washington Faulconer wore his new uniform jacket that bore the wreathed stars of a brigadier general on its collars. "He's bored. He's fretting for action. Man's a warrior."

"Man's a dipsomaniac lunatic," Bird said. "He tried to arrest Tony Murphy yesterday for not saluting him."

"Captain Murphy has a rebellious streak," Faulconer said.

"I thought we were all supposed to have a rebellious streak," Bird observed. "I tell you, Faulconer, the man's a souse. You've been cheated."

But Washington Faulconer was not about to admit a mistake. He knew as well as anyone that Griffin Swynyard was a liquor-sodden disaster, but the disaster would need to be endured until the Faulconer Brigade had made its reputation in battle and thus provided its commander with the freedom to defy the power of the Richmond *Examiner*. Which paper was now open on Faulconer's camp table. "You see the news about Starbuck?"

Bird had not even seen the paper, let alone heard any news of Starbuck.

"He's been arrested. It is believed he traded information with the enemy. Ha!" Faulconer made the explanation with evident satisfaction. "He never was any good, Pecker. God only knows why you champion him."

Bird knew his brother-in-law was looking for an argument so he refused to offer him the satisfaction. "Anything else, Faulconer?" he asked coldly instead.

"One other thing, Pecker." Faulconer, his coat buttoned and belt buckled, drew his curved saber and cut it through the air with a deliberately casual motion. "The elections," Faulconer said vaguely, as if he had only just thought of the topic.

"I've arranged for them."

238

"I don't want any nonsense, Pecker." Faulconer pointed the saber's tip at Bird. "No nonsense, you hear me?"

In two weeks the Legion was required to hold new elections for company officers. The requirement had been imposed by the Confederate government, which had just introduced conscription and, at the same time, had extended the terms of service of those men who had originally volunteered one year's service. From now on the one-year men must serve till death, disability, or peace discharged them from the ranks, but thinking that the bitter pill needed a candy coating, the government had also ruled that the one-year regiments be given another chance to select their own officers. "What nonsense could there be?" Thaddeus Bird asked innocently.

"You know, Pecker, you know," Faulconer warned.

"I have not the first, the faintest, the slightest idea what you mean," Bird said.

The saber tip slashed around to quiver just inches from Bird's ragged beard. "I don't want Starbuck's name on the ballot."

"Then I shall make sure it isn't there," Bird said in all innocence.

"And I don't want the men writing his name in."

"That, Faulconer, is beyond my control. It's called democracy. I believe your grandfather and mine fought a war to establish it."

"Nonsense, Pecker." Faulconer felt the usual frustrations of dealing with his brother-in-law, and his usual regret that Adam so mulishly refused to leave Johnston and take over the Legion's command. Faulconer could think of no other man whom the Legion would accept as a replacement for Pecker, and even Adam, Faulconer conceded, would have a difficult time replacing his uncle. Which meant, Faulconer privately conceded to himself, that Bird would probably have to be given the colonelcy of the regiment, in which case why could he not demonstrate just a hint of gratitude or cooperation? Washington Faulconer believed himself to be a man of charitable and kind instincts, and all he really wanted was to be liked in return, yet so often he seemed to engender resentment instead. "The men certainly wouldn't be tempted to vote for Starbuck if there was a good officer leading K Company," Faulconer now suggested.

"Who, pray?"

"Moxey."

Bird rolled his eyes. "Truslow would eat him alive."

"Then discipline Truslow!"

"Why? He's the best soldier in the Legion."

"Nonsense," Faulconer said, but he had no other candidate to suggest. He sheathed his saber, the blade hissing against the scabbard's wooden throat. "Tell the men that Starbuck's a traitor. That should cool their enthusiasm. Tell them he'll be hanged before the month's out, and tell them that's exactly what the son of a bitch deserves. And he does deserve it! You know damn well he murdered poor Ethan."

In Bird's opinion the killing of Ethan Ridley had been the best day's work Starbuck had ever done, but he kept that opinion to himself. "Have you any other orders, Faulconer?" he asked instead.

"Be ready to leave in an hour. I want the men to look smart. We'll be marching through Richmond, remember, so let's put on a show!"

Bird stepped outside the tent and lit a cheroot. Poor Starbuck, he thought. He did not believe in Starbuck's guilt for a single instance, but there was nothing Bird could do about it, and the schoolmaster turned soldier had long decided that what he could not affect he should not allow to affect him. Still, he thought, it was sad about Starbuck.

Yet, Bird reflected, Starbuck's tragedy was doubtless

240

about to be swallowed in the greater disaster posed by McClellan's invasion. When Richmond fell the Confederacy would stagger on for a few defiant months, but bereft of its capital, and shorn of the Tredegar Iron Works which were the largest and most efficient in all the South, the rebellion could hardly be expected to survive. It was odd, Bird thought as he strolled along the brigade's camp lines, but it was just about one year to the day since the rebellion had begun with the guns firing on Fort Sumter. One year, and now the North was curling around Richmond like a great mailed fist about to crack tight shut.

Drums beat, and the shouted orders of the drill sergeants echoed back across the damp campground as the brigade got ready to march. The sun actually appeared from behind the clouds for the first time in weeks as the Faulconer Legion left, marching south and east to where America's fate would be decided in battle.

On one point only did Lieutenant Walton Gillespie trap Starbuck into some kind of admission of wrongdoing, and having found that weakness Gillespie worked on it with a desperate enthusiasm. Starbuck had admitted selling passports for gain and Gillespie pounced on the admission. "You admit signing passports without verifying their validity?"

"We all do."

"Why?"

"For money, of course."

Gillespie, already pale, actually seemed to blanch at this confession of moral turpitude. "You mean you accepted bribes?"

"Of course I did," Starbuck said. He was as weak as a kitten, his gullet and belly a mass of raw pain while his face had erupted into weeping pustules wherever the croton oil had splashed on his skin. The weather was warming, but he shivered all the time and feared he was catching a fever. Day after day he had been questioned, and day after day he had ingested the filthy oil until now he no longer knew how long he had been in jail. The questions seemed unending, while the vomit and the dysentery racked him day and night. It hurt him to swallow water, it hurt him to breathe, it hurt him to be alive.

"Who bribes you?" Gillespie asked, then grimaced as Starbuck spat a bloody scrap of dribble onto the floor. Starbuck was sitting slumped in a chair for he was too weak to stand and Gillespie did not like to interview men crumpled on the floor. The two guards leaned on the wall. They were bored. In their own private opinions, which they accepted counted for nothing, this damn northerner was innocent, but Gillespie still kept at him. "Who?" Gillespie insisted.

"All kinds of damn people." Starbuck was so weary, so hurt. "Major Bridgford came once with a stack of forms, so did –"

"Nonsense!" Gillespie snapped. "Bridgford wouldn't do such a thing."

Starbuck shrugged as though he did not care one way or the other. Bridgford was the Provost Marshal of the army, and he had indeed brought Starbuck a sheaf of blank passports for signature and afterward had dropped a bottle of rye whiskey on Starbuck's desk as payment for the favor. A score of other senior officers and at least a dozen Congressmen had done the same, usually paying more than an illegal bottle of liquor, and Starbuck, at Gillespie's bidding, named them all. The only man he did not name was Belvedere Delaney. The lawyer was a friend and a benefactor and the least Starbuck could do in return was to protect him.

"What did you do with the money?" Gillespie asked.

242

"Lost it at Johnny Worsham's," Starbuck answered. Johnny Worsham's was the city's largest gambling den, a riotous place of women and music guarded by two black men so tall and powerful that even the armed provosts dared not tangle with them. Starbuck had lost some of the money there, but most of it was safely locked away in Sally's room. He dared not reveal that hiding place for fear that Gillespie would go after Sally. "Played poker," he added. "No damn good at poker." He gave a dry heave, then groaned as he tried to restore his breath. Gillespie had abandoned the croton oil these last few days, yet still Starbuck was half bent double because of the pains in his belly.

The next day Gillespie reported to Major Alexander, who grimaced when he saw how little had been learned from Starbuck. "Maybe he's innocent?" Alexander suggested.

"He's a Yankee," Gillespie said.

"He's guilty of that, certainly, but is he guilty of writing to Webster?"

"Who else could it be?" Gillespie demanded.

"That, Lieutenant, is what we are supposed to determine. I thought your father's scientific methods were infallible? And if they are infallible, then Starbuck must be innocent."

"He takes bribes."

Alexander sighed. "We might as well arrest half the Congress for that crime, Lieutenant." He leafed through the reports of Gillespie's interrogation, noting with distaste the huge amounts of oil that had been forced down the prisoner's throat. "I have a suspicion we're wasting our time," Alexander concluded.

"Another few days, sir!" Gillespie said urgently. "I'm sure that he's ready to break, sir. I know he is!"

"You said that last week."

"I've withheld the oil these last few days," Gillespie said enthusiastically. "I'm giving him a chance to recover, then I plan to double the dose next time."

Alexander closed Starbuck's file. "If he had anything to tell us, Lieutenant, he'd have confessed it by now. He's not our man."

Gillespie bridled at the implication that his interrogation had failed. "You do know," he asked Alexander, "that Starbuck had quarters in a brothel?"

"You'd condemn a man for being lucky?" Alexander asked.

Gillespie blushed. "One of the women has been asking for him, sir. She visited the prison twice."

"Is she the pretty whore? The one called Royall?"

Gillespie's blush deepened. In truth Victoria Royall had been more beautiful than his dreams, but he dared not admit that to Alexander. "She was called Royall, certainly. And she was royally insolent. She wouldn't tell me what her interest in the prisoner was, and I think she should be questioned."

Alexander shook his head wearily. "Her interest in the prisoner, Lieutenant, is that her father served in his infantry company, and she probably served in Starbuck's bed. I talked to the girl and she knows nothing, so there's no need for you to question her further. Unless you had a different entertainment in mind?"

"Of course not, sir." Gillespie bridled at the suggestion, though in truth he had been hoping that Major Alexander would deputize him to question Miss Victoria Royall.

"Because if you did have something different in mind," Alexander went on, "then you should know that the *nymphs du monde* in that house are the most expensive in all the Confederacy. You might find the ladies in the establishment opposite the YMCA more to your purse's taste."

"Sir! I have to protest . . ."

"Be quiet, Lieutenant," Alexander said tiredly. "And in case you have a mind to visit Miss Royall privately, then do reflect on just how many high-ranking officers are among her clients. She can probably make a great deal more trouble for you than you can for her." Some of those clients had already protested Starbuck's imprisonment, which Alexander himself was finding increasingly hard to justify. God in his heaven, the Major thought, but this case was proving difficult. Starbuck had seemed the obvious candidate, but he was admitting nothing. Timothy Webster, bedridden in his cell, had yielded no information in his interrogations, while the man set to watch the notice board in St. Paul's was patently wasting his time. A false letter had been placed under the tapes of the message board in the church vestibule, but no one had appeared to collect it.

"If you'd just let me administer my father's purgatives to Webster," Gillespie suggested eagerly.

Alexander cut off the suggestion. "We have other plans for Mr. Webster." Alexander also doubted whether the ailing Webster knew the identity of the man who had written to Major James Starbuck. Maybe only James Starbuck knew.

"The woman captured with Webster?" Gillespie suggested.

"We are not going to have the northern newspapers claiming that we purge women," Alexander said. "She'll be sent back north unharmed." The sound of a military band prompted Alexander to cross to his office window and stare down at a battalion of infantry that was marching eastward on Franklin Street. Johnston's army, stirred at last from its positions around Culpeper Court House, was arriving to defend the Confederacy's capital. The very first regiments

245

to arrive had already gone to thicken Magruder's defenses at Yorktown, while the later arrivals were now making their encampments east and north of Richmond.

The infantry band was playing "Dixie." Children with sticks instead of muskets swaggered beside the troops who all wore daffodils in their hats. Even from the third floor Alexander could see how ragged and ill-uniformed the soldiers were, but they marched steadily enough and their morale seemed high. They tossed daffodils to the prettier girls. A mulatto girl standing among the spectators on the far pavement had a whole armful of the flowers and laughed as the soldiers piled on yet more blooms. The infantry was being deliberately routed through the city so that Richmonders would know an army had come to their defense, though the soldiers themselves needed defending from the city, or rather from its diseased whores, and so the marching column was escorted by lines of provosts with fixed bayonets who made sure that no man slipped away into the crowds.

"We can't just release Starbuck," Gillespie complained. He had gone to stand at the second window.

"We can accuse him of bribery, I suppose," Alexander conceded, "but we can't haul him in front of a court-martial looking like he's on his deathbed. Clean him up, let him recover, then we'll decide whether to put him on trial for taking bribes."

"So how do we find our real traitor?" Gillespie asked.

Alexander thought of an old man with long hair and gave an involuntary shudder. "I guess we'll have to sup with the devil, Gillespie." Alexander turned from the window and stared morosely at a map of Virginia that hung on his office wall. Once past Yorktown, he thought, there was nothing to stop the Yankees. They would burst against the defenses of Richmond like a spring tide pushed by an onshore gale. They would surround the city, then strangle it, and what of the Confederacy then? In the west, despite the southern newspapers' attempts to paint a victory, Beauregard had retreated after taking massive casualties at a place called Shiloh. The North was claiming victory there and Alexander feared their claims would prove true. How soon before the North claimed victory here in Virginia as well? "Have you ever thought," he asked Gillespie, "that maybe this is all a waste of effort?"

"How can it be?" Gillespie was puzzled by the question. "We have the moral right. God won't desert us."

"I was forgetting God," Alexander said, then put on his hat and went to find the devil.

TWO SOLDIERS FETCHED STARBUCK from his cell. They woke him in the darkness, making him cry aloud in sudden fear as they pulled the blanket off his cot. He was still not properly awake as they hurried him into the corridor. Expecting another interrogation, Starbuck instinctively turned to his right, but one of the soldiers pushed him in the other direction. The prison was sleeping, its corridors smoky from the small flames of the tallow candles that burned every few paces. Starbuck shivered despite the palpable warmth in the spring air. It had been days since Gillespie had last administered croton oil to him, but he was still painfully thin and cemetery-pale. He was no longer retching and he had even managed to eat some prison gruel without his stomach immediately voiding the coarse food, but he felt kitten-weak and hog-filthy, though the ending of his interrogation had at least given him a sliver of hope.

Starbuck was taken to the prison guardroom where a slave was ordered to knock the anklets off his feet. On the guardroom table was a perpetual calendar made of pasteboard cards in a wooden frame. The cards recorded that it was Monday, April 29, 1862. "How are you feeling, boy?" the Sergeant behind the table asked. He was cradling a tin mug in his big hands. "How's your stomach?"

"Empty, raw," Starbuck said.

"Best thing for it today." The Sergeant laughed and

248

sipped at the cup before making a wry face. "Parched goober-pea coffee. Tastes like Yankee shit."

The soldiers ordered Starbuck into the prison yard. The absence of the leg chains caused him to lift his feet unnaturally high, making his gait grotesque and clumsy. A black-painted prison coach waited in the yard with its single rear door open and a swaybacked, blinkered horse in the shafts. Starbuck was pushed into the vehicle. "Where am I going?" he asked.

There was no answer. Instead the coach door was slammed on him. There was no handle inside the door and there were no windows in the coach. It was just a felon's van; a wooden box on wheels with a slatted bench on which he sat and groaned. He heard the guards climbing onto the back step of the vehicle as the driver cracked his whip.

The coach lurched forward. Starbuck heard the prison gates creak open, then the clumsy vehicle jolted over the gutter and into the street. He shivered in the lonely darkness, wondering what new indignities were about to be heaped on him.

It was a half hour before the coach stopped and the door was pulled open. "Out, cuffee," one of the guards said, and Starbuck stepped down into the crepuscular dawn and saw he had been fetched to Camp Lee, Richmond's old Central Fair Grounds that lay west of the city. The camp was now the biggest troop depot in the capital. "That way," the guard said and pointed toward the rear of the coach.

Starbuck turned and for a second or two he could not move. At first it was incomprehension that kept him motionless, then, as he realized just what he looked at in this dawn, a wave of terror froze him.

For there, in the ghost light, was a scaffold.

The gibbet was newly built of raw, clean wood. It was a

249

monstrous thing, gaunt in the gray remnants of night, with a platform twelve feet above the ground. Two posts on the platform supported a square beam ten feet higher still. A rope hung from the beam, its noosed end presumably coiled on the trapdoor. A ladder led from the grass to the platform on which there waited a bearded man in black shirt, black trousers, and stained white jacket. He leaned on one of the posts, smoking a pipe.

A small crowd of uniformed men waited at the foot of the scaffold. They smoked cigars and made small talk, but when Starbuck appeared they fell silent as one by one they turned to watch him. Some of them grimaced, and no wonder, for Starbuck was dressed in a filthy shirt, dirty ragged trousers held up with a frayed piece of knotted string, and clumsy leather brogans that flapped on his feet like butter boxes. His ankles had been worn to bloody scabs by the irons, his hair was matted and filthy, and his new beard was a mess. He stank.

"You're Starbuck?" a mustachioed major barked at him.

"Yes."

"Stand and wait there," the Major said, pointing to a space apart from the small crowd. Starbuck obeyed, then turned in alarm as the coach that had fetched him from the city suddenly lurched away. Was he to leave here in the pine coffin that waited beside the ladder? The Major saw the terror on Starbuck's face and frowned. "It ain't for you, you fool." Relief coursed through Starbuck. It made him feel shaky, almost wanting to cry.

A second carriage arrived as the prison coach pulled away. The newly arrived carriage was an elegant, old-fashioned vehicle with dark varnished panels, gilded axle bosses, and four matching horses. The coach's Negro driver reined in on the far side of the scaffold, pulled on the brake, then climbed down to open the carriage's door. An old man appeared. He was tall and thin, with a great mane of white hair that framed a darkly tanned and deeply lined face. He was not in uniform, but was instead dressed in an elegant black suit. The dawn's light reflected from the man's watch chain and its pendant seals, and from the silver head of his cane. It also glittered from his eyes, which seemed to be staring straight at Starbuck in a fixed gaze that was oddly disturbing. Starbuck stared back, fighting the discomfort of the old man's inspection, and just when it seemed that he was locked into a childish competition to discover who would look away first, a commotion behind Starbuck announced the arrival of the scaffold's victim.

Camp Lee's commandant led the small procession, and after him came the Episcopal chaplain who read aloud from the Twenty-third Psalm. The prisoner followed, helped along by two soldiers.

The prisoner was a big man, fine-looking, with a strong mustache, a clean-shaven chin, and a head of thick dark hair. He was dressed in shirt, trousers, and shoes. His hands were tied in front of him, his legs bore no chains or ropes, yet even so he seemed to be having trouble walking. He limped, and each step was plainly an agony. The crowd fell silent again.

The embarrassment and pain of watching a crippled man walk to his death was made worse when the prisoner tried to climb the ladder. His pinioned hands would have made the climb difficult at the best of times, but the pain in his legs made the ascent almost impossible. The two soldiers helped him as best they could, and the white-jacketed executioner tapped the sparks from his pipe, then leaned down to help the prisoner up the last few rungs. The prisoner had made small noises of agony with each step. Now he limped forward to the trapdoor, and Starbuck saw the executioner duck down to pinion the victim's feet.

The chaplain and the commandant had followed the prisoner to the platform. The sun's first rays were touching the scaffold's crossbeam with a lavish golden light as the commandant unfolded the warrant of execution. "'In accordance with the sentence passed on you by the Court-Martial lawfully assembled here in Richmond on the sixteenth day of April . . . '" the camp's commandant began to read.

"There is no law by which you may do this," the prisoner interrupted the commandant. "I am an American citizen, a patriot, a servant of this country's lawful government!" The prisoner's protest was given in a husky voice that still managed to generate a startling power.

"'You, Timothy Webster, were sentenced to death for the crime of espionage, carried on unlawfully within the borders of the sovereign Confederate States of America . . . '"

"I am a citizen of the United States!" Webster roared his defiance, "which alone has authority over this place!"

"'Which sentence shall now be carried out according to the provisions of law.'" The commandant finished in a hurry, then stepped away from the trapdoor. "Have you anything to say?"

"God bless the United States of America!" Timothy Webster said in his harsh, deep voice. Some of the watching officers had taken off their hats, others half looked away. The hangman had to stand on tiptoe to put the black hood over Webster's head and the noose around his neck. The chaplain's voice was a murmur as he began to recite the Psalm again. The sunlight crept down the upright posts toward the condemned man's hood.

"God save the United States of America!" Webster cried aloud, his voice muffled by the hood, and then the hangman kicked back the bolt that held the trapdoor in its place and there was a gasp from the spectators as the pinewood hatch swung hard away and the prisoner hurtled downward.

It all happened so quickly that Starbuck did not recall the details until later, and even then he was not certain that his mind had not embellished the events. The rope seemed to tighten, the prisoner even checked momentarily, but then the noose seemed to ride up over his hooded face and suddenly, with hands and feet tied like a hog, Webster fell to the ground to leave the hanging rope swinging in the dawn with the black hood caught in its empty noose. Webster screamed with pain as he landed on his fragile, rheumatic ankles. Starbuck shuddered at the sound of the man's pain, while the old white-haired man with the silver-topped cane just stared fixedly at Starbuck.

One of the watching officers turned away, a hand to his mouth. Another braced himself by leaning on a tree. Two or three pulled on flasks. One man crossed himself. The hangman just gaped down through the open hatch.

"Again! Do it again!" the commandant called. "Hurry. Pick him up! Leave him, Doctor." A man, evidently a doctor, had knelt beside Webster, but now backed away uncertainly as two soldiers ran to pick up the fallen man. Webster was sobbing, not from fear, but because of the awful pain in his joints.

"Hurry!" the commandant shouted again. One of the watching officers vomited.

"You will kill me twice!" Webster protested in a voice made tremulous with agony.

"Hurry!" The commandant seemed close to panic.

The soldiers pulled Webster to the ladder. They had to untie his feet and place them one by one on the rungs. Webster inched up, still sobbing with the pain, as the hangman retrieved the noose. One of the spectators reached up with a drawn sword to push the trapdoor shut once more.

The hood had fallen off the noose and the hangman was complaining he could not do his job without the black bag. "It doesn't matter!" the commandant snapped. "Get on with it, for Christ's sake!"

The chaplain was shaking so hard that he could not hold the Bible still. The hangman retied the prisoner's feet, placed the noose back about his neck, then grunted as he tightened the knot beneath the victim's left ear. The chaplain began to say the Lord's Prayer, gabbling the words as though he feared he might forget them if he said the prayer too slowly.

"God bless the United States!" Webster called aloud, though in a voice that was a sob of hurt. He was bent over in pain, but then, in the full wash of the morning sun, he made a supreme effort to beat the agony and to show his killers that he was stronger than they. Inch by inch he forced his crippled, hurt body until he at last stood upright. "God bless the United –"

"Do it!" the commandant screamed.

The hangman hit the bolt and once again the trapdoor banged open and once again the prisoner shot through, only this time the rope snapped taut and the body danced for a second as the neck stretched and snapped. One of the watching officers gasped in shock as the body bounced on the rope's end. Webster had been killed instantly this time, his neck snapped clean so that his canted face seemed to gaze up at the swinging trapdoor that creaked in the early light. Dust sifted down from the platform. The dead man's tongue showed between his lips and then a liquid began to drip from his right shoe.

"Get him down!" the commandant shouted.

The officers turned away, all but a doctor who hurried under the platform to certify the spy's death. Starbuck, wondering why he had been fetched through the city to witness the barbarous execution, turned to stare at the rising sun. He had not seen an open sky for so long. The air felt fresh and clean. A cockerel called in the camp, its cry counterpointing the sound of hammer and nails as soldiers coffined the spy's broken body.

A bony hand fell hard on Starbuck's shoulder. "Come with me, Starbuck, come with me." It was the old white-haired man who had spoken and who now led Starbuck toward his carriage. "Now that our appetite is whetted," the old man said happily, "let us go for breakfast."

A few yards from the gibbet a grave had been dug. The coach rattled by the empty hole, then jolted south across the parade ground and headed toward the city. The old man, hands clasped on his silver cane, smiled all the way. His day, at least, had started well.

Hyde House, where the old man lived, occupied a tri-angular lot where Brook Avenue cut diagonally across Richmond's grid of streets. The lot was hemmed in by a tall brick wall that was capped with a course of white pitted stone above which a profusion of trees and blossoms showed. Deep inside the unkempt trees, and approached through a metal gate topped with spikes, was a three-story house, grand once, railed around with verandahs on every floor and fronted with an ornate carriage porch. It was not raining, but in the early morning air everything about the house seemed damp. Even the fine blossomed creepers that were draped from the verandah rails drooped disconso-lately, while the verandahs themselves had peeling paint and broken balustrades. The wooden front steps up which the old man led Starbuck seemed green and rotted. A slave snatched the varnished front door open an instant before the old man would have walked straight into its heavy panels.

"This is Captain Starbuck," the old man snarled at the

pretty young woman who had opened the door. "Show him to his room. His bath is drawn?"

"Yes, massa."

The old man pulled out his watch. "Breakfast in forty-five minutes. Martha will show you where. Go!"

"Sir?" Martha said to Starbuck and beckoned him toward the stairs.

Starbuck had not uttered a single word during the journey, but now, surrounded by the sudden and fading luxuries of this old mansion, he felt his self-assurance drain away. "Sir?" he said to the old man's back.

"Breakfast in forty-four minutes!" the old man said angrily, then disappeared through a door.

"Sir?" Martha said again, and Starbuck let the girl lead him upstairs to a wide and lavish bedroom. The room had been elegant once, but now its fine wallpaper had been spotted and stained by damp, and its lavish carpet was moth-eaten and faded. The bed was draped with threadbare tapestries on which, laid out as carefully as though they were a suit of the finest evening clothes, Starbuck's own Confederate uniform lay. The coat had been laundered and darned, the belt was polished, and his boots, which stood fitted with trees at the bed's foot, had been mended and waxed. Even Oliver Wendell Holmes's overcoat was there. The slave threw open a door that led to a small dressing room where a hip bath stood steaming in front of a coal fire. "You want me to stay, massa?" Martha asked timidly.

"No. No." Starbuck could scarcely believe what was happening to him. He walked into the dressing room and put a tentative hand into the water. It was so hot he could scarcely bear its touch. A pile of white towels waited on a cane chair, while a straight razor, soap, and a shaving brush stood beside a white china bowl on a washstand.

"If you leave your old clothes outside the door . . . "

Martha said, but did not finish the sentence.

"You'll burn them?" Starbuck suggested.

"I'll come back for you in forty minutes, massa," she said, and dropped a curtsey before backing through the door and closing it behind her.

One hour later Starbuck was shaved, scrubbed, dressed, and filled with eggs, ham, and good white bread. Even the coffee had been real, while the cigar that he smoked after the meal was fragrant and mild. The richness of the food had threatened to provoke another spasm of sickness, but he had taken the meal slowly at first, then ravenously when his stomach did not rebel. The old man had scarcely spoken throughout breakfast, except to mock and deride paragraphs in the morning newspapers. He was, to Starbuck's curious gaze, a creature as extraordinary as he seemed malevolent. His house slaves were plainly frightened of him. Two girls served the meal, both as light-skinned and attractive as Martha. Starbuck wondered whether he was just in a state to find all women desirable, but the old man saw him look at one of the two slaves and confirmed his judgment. "I can't abide ugly things round the house, Starbuck. If a man has to own women, he might as well possess the prettiest, and I can afford them. I sell them when they're twenty-five. Keep a woman too long and she fancies she knows your life better than you do yourself. Buy them young, keep them docile, sell them sharp. There lies happiness. Come into the library."

The old man led the way through double doors into a room that was pure magnificence, though a magnificence that had been allowed to decay horribly. Beautifully carved bookcases reached from the hardwood floor to the decorated plaster ceiling twelve feet above, but the plaster was crumbling and the gold leaf on the bookcases was worn away, and the leather-bound books had spines hanging loose. Old tables were littered with books swollen with moisture and the whole sad room reeked of damp. "My name is death," the old man said in his beguiling voice.

"Death?" Starbuck could not hide his surprise.

"Small D, E, apostrophe, A, T, H. French origin: de'Ath. My father came here with Lafayette, never went home. Nothing to go back to. He was a bastard, Starbuck, born to the wrong side of an aristocratic whore's blanket. Whole family got what they deserved in the French terror. Heads chopped off by Doctor Guillotine's splendid device. Ha!" De'Ath settled behind the largest table, which was a mess of books, papers, inkwells, and pens. "The excellent Doctor Guillotine's machine made me the Marquis of something or other, except under the wisdom of our former country we are not allowed to use titles. Do you believe in that Jeffersonian nonsense that all men are created equal, Starbuck?"

"I was brought up to believe it, sir."

"I am not interested in what nonsenses were thrust into your infant head, but rather what nonsenses are lodged there. Do you believe all men are created equal?"

"Yes, sir."

"Then you are a fool. It is obvious to the meanest intelligence that some men are created wiser than others, some stronger, and a fortunate few more ruthless than the rest, from which we might fairly deduce that our Creator intended us to live within the comfortable confines of a hierarchy. Make all men equal, Starbuck, and you elevate foolishness into wisdom and lose the ability to tell the one from the other. I told Jefferson that often enough, but he never listened to other men's sense. Sit down. Tap your ash onto the floor. When I die it will all rot away." He waved a thin hand to show that he was talking about the house and its glorious but decaying contents. "I don't believe in

258

inherited wealth. If a man can't make his own money, then he should not have the disposition of another man's fortune. You have been ill-treated."

"Yes, I have."

"It was your misfortune to be considered a Confederate. If we capture a northerner and think him a spy we don't beat him in case the northerners beat our spies. We don't mind hanging them, but we won't beat them. Foreigners we treat according to what we desire from their countries, but our own people we treat abominably. Major Alexander is a fool."

"Alexander?"

"Of course, you did not meet Alexander. Who questioned you?"

"A little bastard called Gillespie."

De'Ath grunted. "A pale limpid thing who learned his techniques from his father's lunatics. He still believes you're guilty."

"Of taking bribes?" Starbuck asked scornfully.

"I should hope you did take bribes. How else can anything ever get achieved in a republic of equals? No, Gillespie thinks you're a spy."

"He's a fool."

"For once I agree with you. Did you enjoy the hanging? I did. They botched the job, didn't they? That's what happens when you entrust responsibility to cretins. They're supposed to be our equals, but they can't even hang a man properly! How difficult can it be? I daresay you or I would get it right first time, Starbuck, but you and I were endowed by our Creator with brains, and not with a skullful of stale semolina. Webster suffered from rheumatic fever. The worst punishment would have been to let him live in a damp place, but we were merciful and strung him up. He was reputed to have been the North's best and brightest spy, but

259

he can't have been very bright if we managed to catch him and bodge him to death, eh? Now we have to catch another one and bodge him to death as well." De'Ath climbed to his feet and walked to a grimy window through which he stared at the thick damp vegetation that screened the house. "President Davis has appointed me, *ex officio*, to be his witch-finder general or rather to be the man who rids our country of traitors. You think the task is possible?"

"I wouldn't know, sir."

"Of course it isn't possible. You can't draw a line on the map and say henceforth everyone on this side of the line will be loyal to a new country! We must have hundreds of people who secretly wish for the North to win. Hundreds of thousands if you count the blacks. Most of the white ones are women and preachers, that kind of harmless fool, but a few of them are dangerous. My job is to cull the truly dangerous and use the rest to send false messages to Washington. Read this." De'Ath crossed the room and tossed a piece of paper into Starbuck's lap.

The paper was very thin and covered with block capitals that had been written very small, but with a huge ambition to betray. Even Starbuck, who knew nothing of the army's dispositions, realized that if this message reached McClellan's headquarters it would be of immense use. He said as much.

"If McClellan believes it, yes," de'Ath allowed, "but our job is to make sure he doesn't get the chance. You see who it's addressed to?"

Starbuck turned the page over and read his brother's name. For a few seconds he stared at the ascription in sheer disbelief, then he cursed softly as he understood just why he had spent the last few weeks in jail. "Gillespie believed I wrote this?"

"He wants to believe it, but he's a fool," de'Ath said. "Your brother was a prisoner here in Richmond, was he not?"

"Yes."

"Did you see him when he was here?"

"No," Starbuck said, but he was thinking that Adam had seen James during his imprisonment, and he lifted the letter again and looked closely at the handwriting. It was disguised, but even so he felt a sinking fear that this was his friend's writing.

"What are you thinking?" De'Ath sensed something in Starbuck's manner.

"I was thinking, sir, that James is ill-suited for matters of deception and guile," Starbuck lied smoothly. In truth he had been wondering if Adam was his friend anymore. Adam could surely have visited him in jail, could even have stopped Gillespie's torture, yet as far as Starbuck knew Adam had not tried to do either of those things. Was Adam so horrified by Starbuck introducing Sally into a respectable home that he had cut off his friendship? Then Starbuck imagined Adam being pushed up the scaffold's ladder and standing on the trapdoor while the hangman clumsily pinioned his ankles and tugged the hood over his head and, however strained the friendship, Starbuck knew he could not countenance that sight. He told himself that just because Adam had talked to James did not make Adam a traitor. A score of Confederate officers must have visited the prisoners in Castle Lightning.

"Who does your brother know here in Richmond?" De'Ath's voice was still suspicious.

"I don't know, sir. James was a prominent lawyer in Boston before the war, so I guess he must have met plenty of southern attorneys?" Starbuck made his voice sound innocent and speculative. He dared not reveal Adam's name, else his friend would be taken to the damp cells at Castle Godwin and stuffed with Gillespie's croton oil.

De'Ath glowered silently at Starbuck for a few seconds, then lit a cigar, tossing the spill into the dirt that littered the grate. "Let me tell you what is about to happen, Starbuck. Let me tell you the war's grim news. McClellan pours men and guns into his siege works at Yorktown. Within a day or two we shall retreat. We have no choice. That means the northern army will be free to advance on Richmond. Johnston believes he can stop them at the Chickahominy River. We shall see." De'Ath sounded dubious. "By this time next week" – de'Ath blew a plume of smoke toward an oil painting so darkly varnished that Starbuck could hardly see the picture beneath – "Richmond may well be abandoned."

That made Starbuck sit up straight. "Abandoned!"

"You think we're winning this war? My God, man, do you believe those tales of victory at Shiloh? We lost that battle. Thousands of men dead. New Orleans has surrendered, Fort Macon is taken, Savannah is threatened." De'Ath growled the list of Confederate reverses, astonishing and dispiriting Starbuck. "The North has even closed its recruiting offices, Starbuck, and sent their recruiters back to their battalions. You know why? Because they know the war is won. The rebellion is over. All that remains for the North to do now is to take Richmond and mop up the pieces. That's what they think and maybe they're right. How long do you think the South will survive without Richmond's factories?"

Starbuck did not reply. There was nothing to say. He had not dreamed that the Confederacy was so precarious. In prison he had heard rumors of defeats at the southern and western extremities of the Confederate States, but he had never guessed that the North was now so close to victory

262

that it had closed its recruiting offices and returned the recruiting officers to their regiments. All the North needed to do now was capture Richmond's hellish tangle of blast furnaces and molten metal, of slave quarters and coal dumps, of shrieking whistles and crashing steam hammers, and the rebellion was history.

"But maybe we can yet win." De'Ath broke into Starbuck's gloomy thoughts. "Though not if spies like that bastard are betraying us." He gestured toward the letter on Starbuck's lap. "We found that letter hidden in Webster's hotel room. He never had a chance to send it north, but sooner or later another man will get the news across the lines."

"So what do you want of me?" Starbuck asked. Not a name, he prayed, anything but a name.

"Why are you fighting?" de'Ath suddenly asked.

Starbuck, taken aback by the question, just shrugged.

"Do you believe in slavery as an institution?" de'Ath challenged him.

It was a question Starbuck had never really considered because growing up in the Reverend Elial Starbuck's house meant that he had never needed to consider it. Slavery was plain evil and that was the end of the matter, and that attitude was so deeply ingrained in Starbuck that even after a year in the Confederacy he felt uncomfortable in the company of slaves. They made him feel guilty. Yet he was also sure that the real argument was not about whether slavery was right or wrong; most people knew it was wrong, but just what the hell could be done about it, and that dilemma had baffled the best and most benign minds of America for years. The question was simply too deep for a glib answer and, once again, Starbuck merely shrugged.

"Were you unhappy with the government of the United States?"

Before the war Starbuck had never given the govern-

263

ment of the United States a moment's thought. "Not particularly," he said.

"Do you believe there are vital constitutional principles at stake?"

"No."

"So why are you fighting?"

Again Starbuck just shrugged. It was not that he did not have an answer, but rather that his answer seemed so very inadequate. He had begun fighting for the South as a gesture of his own independence from an overpowering father, but in time it had become something more than mere rebellion. The outcast had found a home, and that was enough for Starbuck. "I've fought well enough," he answered belligerently, "not to need to say why I fight."

"And you still want to fight for the South?" de'Ath asked in a skeptical voice. "Even after what Gillespie did to you?"

"I'll fight for K Company, the Faulconer Legion."

"Maybe you won't get a chance to. Maybe it's all too late." De'Ath drew on his cigar. A nub of ash fell from its tip to smear his coat. "Maybe this war is over, Starbuck, but on the chance that we might yet see these bastards off our land, then will you help?"

Starbuck nodded cautiously.

De'Ath blew smoke across the room. "Tomorrow's newspapers will report that the charges against you are dropped and that you have been released from prison. You need that in print so that your brother believes your story."

"My brother?" Starbuck was confused.

"Think about it, Starbuck." De'Ath lowered himself into a porter's chair that stood beside the hearth. The chair's capacious hood shrouded his face in shadows. "There is a spy, a very capable spy, who has been in contact with your brother. He has been sending intelligence through Webster, but Webster's illness cut the flow of information and so the

North sent two fools called Lewis and Scully to restore it. Lewis and Scully are now captured, Webster is bodged to death, and the North must be wondering just how in the name of God they are to get in touch with their man again. Then, out of the blue, you turn up in their lines carrying the spy's message. Or rather you turn up with a false message that I shall concoct. You will tell your brother that you are disenchanted with the South, that your experiences in jail have disabused whatever romantic notions you once had about supporting the rebellion. You will tell him that you allowed your disenchantment to be known in Richmond, which is why some person unknown passed you a letter in the hope that you would deliver it to your brother. You will then volunteer to return to Richmond to serve as a messenger for any further communications. You will convince your brother that your newfound passion for the North has persuaded you to take Webster's place. It's my belief that your brother will believe you and that he will tell you how you may get in touch with this spy, and you, if you are truthful about serving the Confederacy and not your native North, will then tell me. Thus we shall set a trap, Mr. Starbuck, and give ourselves the exquisite pleasure of watching a fool bodge another spy to death."

Starbuck thought of Adam hanging, his golden head canted at the rope's stark angle, his tongue swollen between parted teeth, his urine dripping from his swinging boots. "Suppose my brother doesn't trust me?" Starbuck asked.

"Then you will still have delivered some false information that will help our cause and you can slip back here in your own good time. Conversely you can betray us, of course, by persuading your brother's superiors that we are a beaten force reduced to cavilling tricks of intelligence in an effort to survive. I must confess, Mr. Starbuck, that the North so outnumbers us at present that we shall probably not survive, but I would like to think we shall play our hand to the very last card." De'Ath paused, drawing on his cigar so that its tip glowed bright in the dark of the chair's hood. "If we are to be beaten," he went on softly, "then let us at least give the bastards a mauling that will give them nightmares for years to come."

"How do I cross the lines?"

"There are men called pilots who escort travelers through the lines. I'll provide you with one of the best, and all you have to do is deliver to your brother a letter I shall write. It will be in the same disguised handwriting as the letter Webster was carrying, only this letter will be a tissue of lies. We shall weave fantasies of imaginary regiments, of cavalry sprung like seeded dragons' teeth from the soil, of guns innumerable. We shall convince McClellan that he faces a vengeful horde of serried thousands. We shall, in brief, attempt a deception. So will you be my deceiver, Mr. Starbuck?" De'Ath's eyes glittered from under the hood of the porter's chair as he waited for Starbuck's answer.

"When will you want me to go?" Starbuck asked.

"Tonight." De'Ath offered Starbuck a skull smile. "You may enjoy the amenities of this house till then."

"Tonight!" Starbuck had somehow imagined he would have a few days to prepare.

"Tonight," de'Ath insisted. "It will take two or three days to get you safely through the lines, so the quicker you leave the better."

"There's something I want first," Starbuck said.

"Of me?" De'Ath sounded dangerous, like a man unaccustomed to making bargains. "Gillespie? Is that it? You want revenge on that pathetic creature?"

"I'll work my revenge on him in my own time," Starbuck said. "No, I need to make some visits in the city."

"Who?" de'Ath demanded.

Starbuck offered the ghost of a smile. "Women."

De'Ath grimaced. "You don't like Martha?" He gestured irritably toward the back of the house where, presumably, his slaves were quartered. Starbuck said nothing and de'Ath scowled. "And if I let you make your visits, will you carry my message to your brother?"

"Yes, sir."

"Then you may see your doxies tonight," de'Ath said sourly, "and afterward ride eastward. Agreed?"

"Agreed," Starbuck said, though in truth he intended to play a much more difficult game, a game he did not intend should lead to a dawn gibbet with a friend twitching at the rope's end. "Agreed," he lied again, then waited for the night.

It had taken the northern troops four weeks to build the siege works needed to destroy the rebel earthworks at Yorktown. Major General McClellan was an engineer by training and a siege enthusiast by avocation, and he planned to use the siege as a demonstration of his country's implacable efficiency. The eyes of the world were on his campaign; newspapermen from Europe and America were attached to his army while military observers from all the great powers rode with his headquarters. At Yorktown, where the United States had first made itself free, the world would witness the flowering of a continent's military prowess. It would see a siege of ruthless ferocity, engineered by the world's new Napoleon.

First the roads from Fort Monroe to Yorktown had needed to be corduroyed so that the army's vast train of wagons could reach the siege ground opposite the Yorktown defenses. Hundreds of axemen felled and trimmed thousands of trees. Teamsters then dragged the trunks out of the woods to where the logs were laid lengthwise on the treacherous mud roads. A second layer of logs was laid crosswise to form the roadway itself. In some places the new log roads still sank beneath the glutinous red mud and yet more layers of newly cut trunks needed to be added until at last the guns and ammunition could be dragged forward.

Fifteen artillery batteries were built. The early part of the work was done at night when the laborers were safe from rebel sharpshooters. At each of the fifteen sites the workmen threw up an earth bank six feet high, then faced its steep sides with mats of woven wood that would stop the earth sliding away in the incessant rain. The walls of each battery were fifteen feet thick, a depth necessary to stop and smother an exploding rebel shell. Protecting the front of each battery was a ditch from which the material for the massive wall had been excavated, and in front of each ditch the engineers laid abatis of tangled branches. Any rebel attack trying to assault a battery would first have to force a way through the chest-high, thorn-infested tangles, then wade through the quagmire in the bed of the flooded ditch before climbing the wall's slick face to where a line of sand-bags formed the parapet, and all that time the attackers would be under the fire of the battery's guns and enfiladed by the cannon fire from the flanking batteries north and south.

Once the walls, ditches, and abatis were finished the batteries were readied for the guns. The smaller guns, the twelve-pounders and four-inch rifles, merely needed a timber-faced ramp up which they could recoil after each shot, but the large guns, the great cannons that would blast the rebel defenses into bloody ruin, needed more careful work. Foundations were dug behind the embrasures, then filled with rubble stone brought from Fort Monroe in heavy wagons. The engineers then laid an aggregate of stone, sand, and cement that was leveled to make a rock-hard platform, though before the concrete could set hard a great curve of metal rail was sunk into its surface. The rail formed a semicircle, its open side facing the enemy. Just inside the embrasure a metal post was sunk into the gun platform so that the curved rail described an arc like a compass line around the post's protruding stud.

The post's stud and the curved rail were now ready to take a gun carriage. The base of the carriage was simply a pair of cast-iron beams that sloped upward from front to back. Beneath the rear of the twin beams was a pair of metal wheels which fitted into the curved rail, while at the front was the socket that slid over the post's greased stud, so that now the whole gun carriage could be swung around on the hinge of the post. Mounted on top of the beams was the gun carriage itself which, when the gun was fired, slid back along the beams. The friction of the tons of metal crashing back along the twin beams was sufficient to soak up the massive recoil. Last of all the huge guns themselves were brought to the batteries. The biggest guns were too heavy for the corduroyed roads and had to be fetched from Fort Monroe on flat-bottomed boats that crept up the peninsula's creeks at the top of the spring tides. The guns were transferred from the barges onto sling carts that consisted of little more than a pair of wheels so vast that the heavy gun barrels could be suspended from their axle. The weird, gaunt vehicles rolled up to the batteries and the mighty cannon were winched carefully down until their trunnions dropped into the sockets of the waiting carriages. The job had to be done at night, yet even so the rebels detected the activity and sent shell after shell screaming across the waterlogged ground in an effort to frustrate the Yankee progress.

The biggest guns were monsters more than thirteen feet long and over eight tons in weight. They fired a shell that was eight inches in width and weighed two hundred pounds. A dozen more guns fired shells a hundred pounds in weight, and even those smaller guns were larger than any of the cannon concealed behind the rebel embrasures. Yet still McClellan was not satisfied and he decreed that the siege bombardment could not commence until he had brought up the North's largest mortars, the largest over ten tons in weight. The mortars were short-barreled, wide-mouthed guns that squatted on their wide wooden bases like monstrous cooking pots and could blast shells weighing two hundred and twenty pounds into a high looping trajectory that would drop the tumbling missiles almost vertically into the Confederate lines. The big guns on their traversing carriages were designed to batter down the rebel ramparts with direct fire while the mortar bombs exploded behind the crumbling walls to fill the rebel bastions with high-explosive death. McClellan planned to keep up the bombardment for twelve terrible hours, and only when the great guns had finished their awful work would the northern infantry be asked to cross the spring grass that grew between the lines.

The guns were at last emplaced. Each of the batteries had been equipped with stone-lined underground chambers and day by day those magazines were filled with six hundred wagonloads of ammunition brought from the ships at Fort Monroe. Other engineers sapped forward to dig the parallel, a trench placed ahead of the fifteen batteries that would serve as the launching point for the infantry attack. None of this was achieved without loss. Rebel sharpshooters sniped from their lines, mortar fire sometimes fell among the diggers, cannon fire might rip away the thin wicker shield protecting a working party from the enemy's sight, yet inch by inch and yard by yard the Federal siege lines took shape. Bombproof shelters were dug for the gunners so that they might survive the Confederate counter-battery fire, ranges were measured precisely and the heavy guns laid with a mathematical exactitude. If all the guns fired together, and McClellan was determined that they should, then each northern volley would throw more than three tons of explosive shells into the rebel lines. "We shall keep that weight of fire going for twelve hours, gentlemen," McClellan informed the eager foreign observers on the night before the bombardment. McClellan reckoned he could soak the rebel lines with more than two thousand tons of fiery metal and that at the end of that sky-borne slaughter the surviving rebel defenders would be reeling and dizzy, easy meat for the northern infantry. "We shall give the seceshers a half day's medicine, gentlemen," McClellan boasted, "then see what kind of defiance they can show. We shall see them beaten by tomorrow afternoon!"

That night, almost as if they knew what fate was being planned for them in the morning, the rebel guns opened fire on the completed northern lines. Shot after shot screamed through the rainy darkness, the burning fuses scratching red lines of fire against the night. Most of the shells exploded harmlessly in the waterlogged ground, but a few found targets. A tethered mule team screamed in pain, a tent in the lines of the 20th Massachusetts was hit and two of its occupants were killed, the first men of the battalion to die in action since their disastrous baptism of fire on Ball's Bluff. And still the rebel shells whipped through the night until, as suddenly as the bombardment had begun, the guns fell silent and left the darkness to barking dogs, whinnying horses, and the calls of the mockingbirds.

The next day dawned clear. There were clouds in the north and the local farmers swore that rain would come soon, yet the early sun shone bright. Smoke from ten thousand cooking fires rose from the tented encampments of the northern infantry. The men were cheerful, anticipating an easy victory. The gunners would wreck the enemy defenses, then the infantry would stroll across the intervening ground to dig the survivors out of the smoking rubble. It would be a textbook assault, proof that an American general and an American army could achieve in twelve hours what Europeans had bungled in as many weeks in the Crimea. McClellan had been an observer of the Crimean sieges and was determined that the French and British officers with his army would be taught a quiet but unmistakable lesson this day.

Deep in the brand-new gun emplacements the Yankee gunners made their last preparations. The big cannon were loaded, friction primers were pushed into touchholes, and artillery officers examined their targets through telescopes. Over a hundred heavy guns waited for the signal to launch their terrible destruction on the Confederate defenses. A month's hard work had been invested in this moment, and to many northerners waiting in their bastions it seemed as if the world held its breath. In the York River the gunboats edged nearer the shore, ready to add their own cannon fire to the slaughtering weight of the army's bombardment. A small wind lifted the ships' ensigns and carried the smoke of their steam engines east across the water.

A half mile behind the Yankee gun emplacement, hidden by a grove of pine trees that had somehow escaped the axes of the road builders, a curious yellow form took monstrous shape. Men struggled to pour carboys of sulfuric acid into vats half filled with iron turnings and still more men worked the giant pumps that pushed the hydrogen formed in those vats along rubberized canvas hoses that led to the great, yellow-skinned balloon that slowly swelled to its full bulbous shape above the trees. The balloon's inflation had begun in the dark so that it would be ready soon after sunrise, and by dawn the huge device needed a crew of thirty men to keep it earthbound. Two men climbed into the balloon's wicker basket. One was Professor Lowe, the famous aeronaut and balloonist whose skills had made the vehicle possible, the other was General Heintzelman, who was being carried aloft so that his seasoned military eye could spy on the destruction wrought by the guns. Heintzelman was looking forward to the experience. He would watch the guns work, then he would telegraph to McClellan when he saw the rebel lines break apart and flee westward in panic. Professor Lowe tested the telegraph equipment, then shouted for the crew to let the vehicle go.

Slowly, like a stately yellow moon rising above the trees, the balloon lifted. Fifteen hundred feet of cable tethered the vehicle to a massive winch that slowly unwound as the aeronauts climbed higher and higher into the clear patch of sky. The sight of the balloon normally provoked a flurry of long-range cannon fire from the rebel lines, but this morning there was only silence. "Saying their prayers, maybe?" Professor Lowe suggested happily.

"They need to," General Heintzelman answered. He drummed his fingers on the edge of the balloon's basket. He had made a wager with his chief of staff that the rebel defenders would break in six hours, not twelve. The basket swayed and creaked, but it was not, Heintzelman decided, an unpleasant sensation. Better than most sea voyages, that was certain. As the balloon passed eight hundred feet the General trained his telescope on the western horizon where he could see the dark smoky smear that was the rebel capital. He could even see the scars of earth where fresh defenses had been carved into the hills around the city. "The serpents' lair, Professor!" Heintzelman proclaimed.

"Indeed, General, and we shall scour the vipers soon enough!"

Heintzelman abandoned his sightseeing and instead stared down at the enemy lines that lay so clear beneath him. He felt hugely powerful, granted a godlike view of his enemies' secrets. He could see their batteries, and the trenches leading from their bombproof shelters, and the tents hidden behind earth walls. War would never be the same again, Heintzelman thought, not when there was no hiding place left. He trained his telescope on one of the bigger enemy gun batteries. None of the Yankee guns would open fire until Heintzelman was ready to report on the effects of their fire and that moment, he decided, had now come. "I think we're ready to communicate, Professor," the General said.

"Not many cooking fires, General," Lowe said, nodding toward the rebel encampments where a handful of shabby tents showed among the ragged, turf-covered shelters. A few fires smoked in the lines, but very few, and no smoke at all showed from the tin chimneys sticking out of the earth shelters by the batteries.

Heintzelman stared into the gun battery. A rebel flag stirred on its flagstaff, but no gunners were visible. Were they expecting the bombardment and already under shelter? He raised the telescope to search the encampment. He could see where horses had been tethered and where limbers had left the imprint of their wheels on the grass, but he could see no men.

"What shall we tell them?" Lowe asked. The Professor had a hand poised over the balloon's telegraph machine which communicated to the ground by a wire that ran down the tethering cable. A second telegraph machine waited at the balloon's earthbound station to relay the aeronauts' news to General McClellan's headquarters.

McClellan himself had stayed in bed, content to let his gunners do their work without his presence.

An aide woke the Young Napoleon two hours after sunrise. "We have a report, sir, from the balloon."

"So?" The General resented being woken.

"The enemy, sir, is gone."

McClellan peered at his watch on the bedside table, then leaned over and pulled back a shutter. He flinched from the bright sunlight, then turned again to the aide. "What did you say?"

"The enemy lines, sir, they are deserted." The aide was Louis Philippe Albert d'Orleans, the Count of Paris, come to America in the spirit of Lafayette to help restore America's unity, and for a moment he wondered whether his English was at fault. "The rebels have retreated, sir," he said as clearly as he could. "The lines are empty."

"Who says?" McClellan asked angrily.

"General Heintzelman is in the balloon's gondola, sir, with Professor Lowe."

"They're dreaming. Dreaming!" The General could not abide such stupidity. How could the rebels have retreated? Only last night they had lit up the sky with their cannonade! The gun flashes had flickered like summer lightning on the western horizon, the fuses had seared the sky with lines of airborne fire, and the explosions had echoed dark across the waterlogged fields. The General slammed the shutter hard against the light and waved his aristocratic aide back toward the door. Downstairs the telegraph machine clattered with more news from the balloonists, but the General did not want to know. He wanted another hour's sleep. "Wake me at eight o'clock," he ordered. "And tell the guns to open fire!"

"Yes, sir, of course, sir." The Count of Paris backed quietly from the room, closed the door, then allowed himself to sigh in disbelief at the General's obtuseness.

The gunners waited. Behind them, high in the sky, the yellow balloon tugged at its tether. The sun went behind cloud and the first spots of rain pattered on the balloon's rubberized skin. A dozen foreign military attaches and a score of newspapermen waited in the largest Federal batteries for the order to open fire, but though the guns were laid and loaded and the primers ready, no order came from the balloon.

Instead a small cavalry picket rode forward from the Federal lines. The dozen horsemen were spread out in a long skirmish line in case an enemy gun crammed with grapeshot or canister was fired at them. They advanced very cautiously, stopping every few paces while their officer gazed at the enemy works through his telescope. The horses lowered their heads to crop at the luscious long grass that had grown undisturbed in the space between the two armies.

The cavalry moved on again. Here and there a sentry was visible on the enemy redoubts, but the sentries did not move even when hit by the bullets of northern sharpshooters. The sentries were men of straw, guarding abandoned earthworks, for in the night General Johnston had ordered Magruder's defenders to retreat toward Richmond. The rebels had gone silently, abandoning their guns, their tents, their fires, abandoning whatever could not be carried on their backs.

General McClellan, awake at last to the truth of the day, ordered a pursuit, but no one in the northern army was prepared for sudden action. The cavalry horses were grazing, while the cavalrymen were playing cards and listening to the rain drum on the sides of their tents. The only troops ready for action were the artillerymen, and their targets had melted away in the night.

The rain fell harder as the northern infantry took possession of the abandoned lines. The cavalry at last saddled their horses, but the detailed orders for the pursuit were lacking and so the horsemen did not move. McClellan, meanwhile, was composing his dispatch to the northern capital. Yorktown, the General told Washington, had fallen in a brilliant display of northern soldiering. He claimed that a hundred thousand rebels with five hundred guns had been evicted from their lines, enabling the march upon the enemy capital to be resumed. There would be more desperate battles, he warned, but for this day at least, God had smiled upon the North.

Magruder's men, unpursued and unmolested, marched west while the Young Napoleon sat down to his belated lunch. "We have a victory," he told his aides. "Thank God Almighty, we have a victory."

De'Ath gave Starbuck his last instructions in the hallway of the decaying Richmond house. Rain streamed from broken gutters and cascaded off the porch roof; it dripped from the thick foliage in the garden and puddled on the sandy driveway where de'Ath's ancient carriage waited. The coach's gilded axle bosses reflected the dim light cast by the flickering lanterns on the porch. "The coach will take you to your ladies," de'Ath said with a sour twist on the last word, "but you will not keep the coachman waiting beyond midnight. At that time he will take you to a rendezvous with a man named Tyler. Tyler is the pilot who will take you through the lines. This is the pass to get you out of the city." De'Ath handed Starbuck one of the familiar brown paper passports. "Tyler's the man to pilot you back too. If you come back."

"I shall come back, sir."

"If there's anything to come back to. Listen!" The old man gestured toward the road which lay beyond his garden's high, stone-capped wall, and Starbuck heard the sound of wheels and hooves. The traffic had been thick ever since the news of Yorktown's abandonment had reached the city and plunged Richmond into panicked flight. Those who had the money had hired carts or carriages, piled them with their luggage, and set off for the state's southern counties, while those people unable to carry their treasures to safety were burying them in their back yards. The hallways of the government offices were stacked high with boxes of official papers addressed to Columbia, South Carolina, which would be the next capital of the Confederacy should Richmond fall, while in the Byrd Street depot of the Richmond and Petersburg Railway there was a locomotive waiting with a full head of steam and a train of armored boxcars, ready to evacuate the Confederacy's stack of gold. Even the President's wife, it was rumored, was readying to take her children away from the advancing Yankees. "Though she would," de'Ath had commented sourly when that news was brought to Hyde House. "The woman has the breeding of a fishwife."

Now, in the rainy darkness, de'Ath made certain that Starbuck had the false letter which the old man had concocted that afternoon. The letter, in a handwriting that imitated the block capitals of the document found in Webster's hotel room, reported a massive concentration of rebel troops in Richmond. The letter was sewn into a waterproof oilcloth pouch that was concealed in the waistband of Starbuck's trousers. "I have it, sir," Starbuck said.

"Then God be with you," de'Ath said abruptly, and turned away.

Starbuck guessed he would get no other farewell than that brief benediction and so he pulled Oliver Wendell Holmes's coat around his shoulders, crammed on his slouch hat, and ran through the rain to the waiting carriage. He

278

wore no weapons. He had abandoned carrying a sword after his first battle, he had left his rifle with Sergeant Truslow, and the fine ivory-handled revolver which he had taken from Ethan Ridley's corpse at Manassas had been stolen while he was in prison. Starbuck would have liked to carry a revolver, but de'Ath had advised against it. "Your object is to get through the lines, not to be mistaken for an infiltrator. Go unarmed, keep your hands held high, and tell lies like a good lawyer."

"How does a lawyer lie?"

"With passion, Mr. Starbuck, and with a self-inflicted belief, albeit temporary, that the facts he is reciting are the very stuff of God's own truth. You have to believe in a lie, and the way to believe is to convince yourself that the lie is a shortcut to the good. If telling the truth will not help a client, then don't tell the truth. The good is the client's survival, the lie is the servant of the good. Your lies are the servants of the Confederacy's survival, and I pray God you desire that survival as much as I do myself."

De'Ath's Negro driver was on the coach's box, swathed there in a multiplicity of coats and with his head covered by a canvas hood. "Where to, massa?" the man called.

"Just go down Marshall. I'll tell you when to stop," Starbuck said, then climbed inside as the great vehicle lurched forward. The coach's seats were of cracked hide and were leaking horsehair. Starbuck lit himself a cigar from the shielded lantern that dimly illuminated the coach's interior, then he eased up one of the leather roller blinds. The coach's progress was slow, for the coming of night had scarcely diminished the evacuation traffic. Starbuck waited till they had passed Thirteenth Street and then he pulled down the window and shouted at the driver to stop outside the Medical College of Virginia. He had deliberately stopped a good distance away from his destination so that the driver could not report to de'Ath which house he had visited.

"Just wait here," he ordered, then jumped down to the roadway and hurried two blocks down Marshall before turning up Twelfth Street. The house he wanted lay on the far side of Clay Street, a big house, one of the most lavish in all Richmond, and Starbuck slowed down as he approached the house for he was uncertain how best to approach this business.

He understood well enough the trap that de'Ath was laying, but he was unwilling to let Adam walk into that trap. If indeed the traitor was Adam. Starbuck had no proof, only a suspicion that his erstwhile friend's distaste for the war could easily have been transformed into betrayal, and that Adam's friendship with James could easily have provided a means for that betrayal to be carried out.

If, indeed, "betrayal" was the right word. Because if the spy was Adam, then he was only being loyal to the country of his birth, just as Starbuck was now being loyal to a friendship. That friendship might have been tested, it might even have been broken, but even so Starbuck could not cold-bloodedly allow the trap to be sprung. He would give Adam his warning.

And so he crossed the street and climbed the steps of the Faulconer town house. He pulled the big brass handle and heard the house bell jangle deep in the servants' quarters. Starbuck had lived in this house once, back when he had first come to Richmond and when Washington Faulconer had been his ally and not his enemy.

The door opened. Polly, one of the maids, gaped at the soaking wet figure on the top step. "Mr. Starbuck?"

"Hello, Polly. I was hoping young Mr. Faulconer was at home."

"He's not here, massa," Polly said, and then, as Starbuck

moved to step in out of the rain, she raised a frightened hand to stop him.

"It's all right, Polly," Starbuck tried to soothe her fears. "I just want to write a note and leave it here for Mr. Adam."

"No, massa." Polly obstinately shook her head. "You're not to be let in. Mr. Adam's orders."

"Adam said that?" Starbuck would have believed it if the prohibition had come from Washington Faulconer, but not of Adam.

"If you ever come, you're to be turned away. Mr. Adam said so," Polly insisted. "I'm sorry."

"It's all right, Polly," Starbuck said. He looked past her to see that the pictures which had graced the famous curving staircase had all been taken down. There had been a fine portrait of Adam's sister Anna on the wall facing the door, but now there was just a square of lighter-colored wallpaper. "Can you tell me where Mr. Adam is, Polly? I only want to talk with him. Nothing else."

"He's not here, massa." Polly tried to close the door, but then a new voice spoke from behind her.

"Adam has been ordered back to the army," the voice said. It was a woman's voice and Starbuck peered into the shadowy recesses of the hall to see a dark, tall figure standing silhouetted in the doorway of the downstairs parlor.

"I'm obliged to you, ma'am," Starbuck said. "Is he with his father's troops? Or with General Johnston?"

"With General Johnston." The speaker came out of the shadows and Starbuck saw it was Julia Gordon. He pulled off his hat. "It seems," Julia went on, "that since Yorktown's abandonment, it is a case of all hands to the pumps. Do you think we are about to be overrun by vengeful northerners, Mr. Starbuck?"

"I'm sure I don't know, Miss Gordon." The rain beat on his head and trickled down his cheeks.

"Nor do I know. And Adam does not write to tell me, so it is all a great mystery. Why don't you come in out of the rain?"

"Because I've been forbidden to enter the house, Miss Gordon."

"Oh, stuff and nonsense. Let him in, Polly. I won't tell anyone if you don't."

Polly hesitated, then grinned and opened the door wide. Starbuck stepped over the threshold, dripping water onto the plain dust-sheet that protected the hardwood floor by the front door. He let Polly take his coat and hat, which she draped over a stepladder that had been used to lift down the paintings. Almost everything was gone from the hall: the fine European furniture, the pictures, the Turkish rugs, even the splendid gilded chandelier that had hung in the staircase well from fifty feet of chain. "All of it sent packing to Faulconer Court House," Julia said, seeing Starbuck gaze about the room. "General Faulconer believed his belongings would be safer in the country. Things must be truly desperate, don't you think?"

"The North has stopped recruiting soldiers," Starbuck said, "if that denotes anything."

"Surely it denotes that we have lost?"

Starbuck smiled. "Maybe we haven't even begun to fight?"

Julia liked the bravado and beckoned toward the lit parlor. "Come into the parlor so Polly doesn't have to be terrified that someone will see you and report her to the General." Julia led him into the downstairs parlor that was lit by two overhead gasoliers. Most of the furniture was gone, though the bookshelves were still crammed with volumes and a plain kitchen table stood next to some open crates. As Starbuck entered the familiar room he thought how odd it was to hear Washington Faulconer described as

282

the General, yet so he was, and an even more powerful enemy because of it. "I'm sorting out the family's books," Julia said. "The General didn't want to send all his volumes to the country, only the valuable ones, and he trusts me to tell him which those are."

"Aren't they all valuable?"

Julia shrugged. "Some nice bindings, perhaps, but most of the books are fairly commonplace." She plucked one at random. "Motley's *Rise of the Dutch Republic*? Hardly a rare volume, Mr. Starbuck. No, I'm putting aside the very best bindings, the books with especially fine plates, and a handful of others."

"You know about books?" Starbuck asked.

"I know more about books than General Faulconer does," Julia said with a hint of amusement. She was wearing a dress of dark blue cotton with a high collar and looped panniers at her waist. The arms of the dress were protected by a pair of white linen dust sleeves. Her black hair was piled high and pinned, though some strands had come loose to hang over her forehead. She looked, Starbuck thought, oddly attractive, and he felt guilty for that thought. This was Adam's fiancee.

"You're not removing yourself to safety, Miss Gordon?" Starbuck asked her.

"Where could we go? My mother's people live in Petersburg, but if Richmond falls then Petersburg cannot be far behind. The General murmured an invitation for us to take ourselves to Faulconer Court House, but he made no provisions for our furniture and poor Mr. Samworth's hearses have been taken for the army's use, which means our belongings must stay here. And where Mother's furniture is, there is Mother, so it seems that for the lack of a cart we must stay in Richmond and endure the Yankee invasion. If it happens." She glanced at a plain tin-cased clock that looked as if it had been borrowed from the servants' quarters. "I don't have long, Mr. Starbuck, as my father is coming to escort me home in a few moments, but I did want to apologize to you."

"To me?" Starbuck asked in surprise.

Julia offered him a solemn look. "About the night at the hospital," she explained.

"I doubt if you have anything to apologize for," Starbuck said.

"I think we do," Julia insisted. "You would have thought, would you not, that a mission to the poor would be accustomed to dealing with girls like your friend?"

Starbuck smiled. "Sally's not very poor."

Julia liked that remark and smiled back. "But she is your friend?"

"Yes, she is."

Julia turned back to the table and began sorting through the books as she spoke. "We are enjoined, are we not, to imitate Christ in all things? Yet on that night I think our Savior would have been more pleased with your behavior than with ours."

"Oh, no," Starbuck said awkwardly.

"I think so. Adam has forbidden me to mention that night ever again. Forbidden me, Mr. Starbuck!" She had plainly been piqued by the order. "Adam is very embarrassed by it. He is afraid of offending my mother, you see? More afraid of that, I think, than of offending me." She wiped dust from the spine of a book. "Macauley's *Essays*? I think not. Was your friend very hurt?"

"Not for long."

"Baynes's *Christian Life*. I doubt that would have been of much guidance to us that night. Look, the pages aren't even cut, but even so it's not of any value. Except for its spiritual advice, but I doubt the General would thank me for that."

284

She tossed the book back onto the table. "Would your friend be offended if I called on her?"

The request startled Starbuck, but he managed to conceal his surprise. "I think she would be pleased, yes."

"I ventured to suggest as much to Adam, but he was very definitely not pleased at the idea. He informed me that pitch defiles, and I'm sure I was grateful for the information but I could not resist thinking that such pitch is more likely to defile a man than a woman. Wouldn't you agree?"

"I think that may well be true, Miss Gordon," Starbuck said with a straight face.

"Mother would disapprove if she thought I was contemplating such a visit, and her disapproval I can understand. But why should Adam mind so very much?"

"Shouldn't Caesar's wife be above suspicion?"

Julia laughed. She had a very quick laugh that animated her face and stung Starbuck's heart. "You think Adam is Caesar?" she asked mockingly.

"I think he wants what is best for you," Starbuck said tactfully.

"Do you think he knows?" Julia asked vehemently. "I'm sure I don't know what's best for me. I would like to be a nurse, but Mother says that isn't a suitable occupation and Adam agrees with her." She threw a book onto the table, then seemed to regret the violence of the throw. "I am not entirely sure Adam knows what is best for himself," Julia added, half to herself, then picked up a slim book bound in dark red leather. "Lambarde's *Eirenarcha*. Over two hundred years old and well worth keeping. Do you think Adam knows what is best for me, Mr. Starbuck?"

Starbuck was obscurely aware of deep, dark waters that might be best unplumbed. "I should hope he does, if you're to marry."

"Are we to marry?" Her dark eyes were defiant. "Adam wants to wait."

"Till the war's over?"

Julia laughed, breaking the odd intimacy that had existed for a few seconds. "That's what he says and I'm sure he must be right." She blew dust off a book, peered at the title, and tossed it into one of the open crates. The gaslights suddenly dimmed, then brightened again. Julia grimaced. "They keep doing that. Is it a sign of civilization's ending? Did I hear you tell Polly that you wanted to see Adam?"

"Yes. Rather urgently."

"I wish I could help you. General Johnston demanded his presence and Adam flew to obey. But where General Johnston is, I cannot tell, though I suppose if you were to march toward the sound of the guns you would find him. Might I pass on a message? I'm sure he'll be back in the city soon and if not, then I can always send him a letter."

Starbuck thought for a few seconds. He could not simply go to the army and search for Adam. His pass was only good for this one journey out of the city and the provosts would never let him roam the army's back areas searching for a headquarters aide. He had planned on leaving a message here for Adam, but then he decided that the message might just as easily be delivered by Julia. "But not," he begged her, "by letter."

"No?" Julia was intrigued.

Letters, Starbuck knew, could be opened and read, and this message, with its implication of a traitorous correspondence, must not be read by men like Gillespie. "When you next see him," he asked Julia, "would you tell him that he would be well advised to suspend his correspondence with my family?" He almost said "brother," but decided he did not need to be specific. "And if he finds that advice mysterious, then I will explain it as soon as I can."

Julia gazed very gravely at Starbuck for a few seconds. "I find it mysterious," she said after a while.

"I fear it must remain a mystery."

Julia picked up a book and glanced at its spine. "Adam said you were in jail?"

"I was released today."

"An innocent man?"

"As driven snow."

"Really?" Julia laughed, evidently unable to be stern for long. "The newspaper said you took bribes. I'm glad you didn't."

"I did, though. Everyone does."

Julia put the book down and gave Starbuck a speculative look. "You are at least honest about your dishonesty. But not about your friendships. Adam tells us we are not to talk to you or to your friend, and you say he is not to talk to your family? We are all to take vows of silence? Well, despite all, I shall talk to your friend Miss Royall. What would be the best time to call?"

"Late morning, I think."

"And what name does she prefer?"

"I suspect you had better ask for Miss Royall, though her real name is Sally Truslow."

"Truslow. With a W?" Julia wrote it down, then copied out the address on Franklin Street. She glanced at the clock again. "I must see you out before my father arrives and worries that I am being defiled by the touch of pitch. Maybe, one day, we shall have the pleasure of meeting again?"

"I would like that, Miss Gordon."

In the hallway Starbuck pulled on his coat. "You have the message, Miss Gordon?" he asked.

"Adam is not to correspond with your family."

"And please don't tell anyone else. Just Adam. And not by letter, please."

287

"I ceased needing to be told everything twice when I was an infant, Mr. Starbuck."

Starbuck smiled at the reproof. "My apologies, Miss Gordon. I'm used to dealing with men, not women." With those words he left her smiling, and was smiling himself as he walked into the rain. He carried a memory of her face that was so strong that he almost walked into the path of a wagon carrying another fugitive's furniture eastward. The Negro driving the team shouted a protest, then flicked his whip over the heads of the skittish horses. The wagon was heaped high with furniture that was half protected from the rain by an inadequate tarpaulin.

Starbuck walked on from one pool of gaslight to another, assailed by a sense of sudden loss. He had been defiant to Julia, claiming that the South had yet to begin fighting, but the truth was surely otherwise. The war was over, the rebellion lost, the North triumphant, and Starbuck, his wagon hitched to a dying star, knew he had to turn his life about and strike off anew. He stopped to turn and stare at the Faulconer House. It was, he thought, a moment of farewell. A portion of his life that had begun with a friendship at Yale was ending in a night of panicked defeat, but at least in its ending Starbuck could afford a feeling of self-denying nobility. His friend had rejected him, but he had been true to his friend. He had delivered Adam the warning, and thus snatched his friend from the gallows at Camp Lee. Adam would survive, would marry, would doubtless prosper.

Starbuck turned away from the house and walked on toward de'Ath's waiting coach. The streets echoed with iron-shod wheels and the shouts of teamsters. Lights burned late. Down in the valley a train banged and clashed, its steam whistle mournful in the long rain. Slaves and servants heaped cabin trunks and carpetbags onto wagons; children cried. Somewhere to the east, cloaked by the night, a vengeful army came to claim back a city and Starbuck went to save himself.

He went in through the back door, going into the kitchen where Grace and Charity were broiling venison on the black-leaded stove. The two slaves screamed when Starbuck came through the door, then greeted him with a chorus of questions about where he had sprung from and exclamations at the state of his clothes and health. "You've gone skinny!" Grace said. "Look at you!"

"I missed your cooking," Starbuck said, then managed to tell them that he needed to see Miss Truslow. "Is she busy?"

"Busy? Busy with the dead!" Grace said ominously, but would not explain more. Instead she took off her apron, patted her hair into a rough order, then climbed the stairs. She came back five minutes later and told Starbuck to use the back staircase to Sally's room.

The bedroom was on the third floor and looked across the wet, tangled garden toward the stable block where the window of his old room showed as a black rectangle. The walls of the bedroom were papered in an elegant pale green stripe and her bed was canopied in green cloth. Dried flowers stood in a gilded vase on the mantel and landscapes hung in lacquered frames on the walls. The room was lit by two gas mantles, but candles stood on a table in case the city's gas supply should fail. The furniture was waxed and polished, the draperies were clean, the rugs well beaten and aired. It was a room that suggested solid American virtue, clean and prosperous, a room of which Starbuck's mother would have been proud.

The door clicked open and Sally hurried in. "Nate!" She ran across the room and threw her arms around his neck. "Oh, God! I was so fretting for you!" She kissed him, then brushed at his coat. "I tried to find you. I went to the city

289

jail, then down to Lumpkin's, and I asked people to help, but it was no good! I couldn't get to you. I wanted to, but . . . "

"It's all right. I'm fine," he told her. "I'm really fine."

"You're thin."

"I'll grow back," he said, smiling, then cocked his head toward the open door through which the sound of laughter came from downstairs.

"They're raising the dead," Sally said wearily. She took the chignon from her hair and laid it carefully on her dressing table. Without the false curls she looked younger. "They're having a fake seance," she explained. "All of them drunk as Indians and trying to get advice off General Washington. It's because the Yankees are coming, so everyone's high on whiskey."

"But not you?"

"Honey, you want to make money in this business, you stay cold stone sober." She crossed the room and was about to push the door shut, but paused. "Or did you want to go downstairs? Join in?"

"No. I'm going away."

She sensed the portentousness in his voice. "Where?"

He showed her the pass. "I'm going across the lines. Back to the Yankees."

Sally frowned. "You going to fight for them, Nate?"

"No. There'll be no more fighting soon. It's going to be over, Sally. The bastards have won. They're so damn cocky that they've even closed their recruiting stations. Think what that means!"

"It means they're confident," Sally said scornfully, then banged the door shut. "And so what? Have you ever known a Yankee who wasn't confident? Hell, that's why they're Yankees. All strut and flurry, Nate, and showing the rest of the world how to suck eggs, but I don't see any of them marching down Franklin Street yet. It's like my pa says. It ain't over till the hog stops squealing." She crossed to a table and took two cigars from a humidor. She lit both from a gaslight and brought one to Starbuck, then crouched opposite him on the hearthrug. Her hooped skirts rustled as she crouched. She was dressed in an elaborate white silk dress, wide-skirted and narrow-waisted, with bare shoulders beneath a shawl of pearl-studded lace. There were more pearls at her neck and on her ears. "Did you come to say goodbye?" she asked him.

"No."

"For what then? That?" She jerked her head toward the bed.

"No." He paused. The sound of a bottle breaking came from downstairs, followed by an ironic cheer. "Some seance," he said with a smile. Spiritualism was rife in Richmond, condemned from the city's pulpits, but succored by the families of men killed on the battlefield who wanted reassurance that their sons and husbands were safe on the far side of death.

"It ain't a proper seance. They're just sitting around the table kicking its legs." Sally paused and offered Starbuck a cautious smile. "So what is it, Nate?"

He took the plunge. Adam was safe, now it was his turn. "Do you remember that night at the hospital?" he asked her. "How you told me you wanted to be ordinary? Just to be plain ordinary. Maybe to run a store? So come with me. This pass will get us both across the lines." He was not entirely sure of that, but he was quite certain that he would not go without Sally if she agreed to accompany him. "I've got permission to go," he told her, "because I'm doing something for the government."

Sally frowned. "For our government?"

"I have to deliver a letter," Starbuck said, and he saw

that she still suspected he was going back to fight for the North, and so he explained more. "There's a spy here in Richmond," he told her, "a dangerous one, and they want me to trap him, see? And to do it I have to take this letter to the Yankees."

"And they don't expect you to come back?" Sally asked.

"They want me to come back," Starbuck admitted, but he did not explain any further. He had already revealed as much as he dared, and he did not know how to tell her the rest; how he believed Adam was the spy and how by coming back to Richmond he would entrap his friend. Instead he had planned to carry the false letter and let that undo the damage Adam had already caused, and then he would go away with Sally and leave the armies to fight out the ragged end of the war. At best, he reckoned, there could only be a month or two's fight left in the Confederacy and it would be better to strike out of the wreckage now than be destroyed in the final catastrophe. "Bring your money," he urged Sally, "and we'll go north. Maybe to Canada? Maybe Maine? We'll start your dry goods store. Maybe we'll go west?" He frowned, knowing he was expressing himself badly. "I'm saying you can start again. I'm saying come with me, I'll look after you."

"On my money?" Sally smiled.

"You've got some money of mine. I know it isn't much, but between us we can manage. Hell, Sally, we can settle wherever we want! Just you and me."

She drew on the cigar, watching him. "Are you offering to marry me, Nate Starbuck?" Sally asked after a while.

"Of course!" Had she not understood that?

"Oh, Nate." Sally smiled. "You're a great one for running away."

"I'm not doing that," he said, nettled by the accusation.

She did not notice his hurt. "Sometimes I want to marry,

Nate, and sometimes I don't. And when I do, honey, God knows I'd marry you before anyone else." She smiled sadly at him. "But you'd tire of me."

"No!"

"Sh!" She put a finger to his lips. "I saw you look at that Bible girl at the hospital. You'd always want to know what it would be like to marry your own kind."

"That's not fair," Starbuck protested.

"But it's true, honey." She drew on the cigar. "You and me are friends, but we'd make a rotten marriage."

"Sally!" Starbuck protested.

She shushed him. "I'll see this war through, Nate. If the Yankees come I'll spit on them, then make money out of the bastards. I don't know what else I'll do, but I do know I won't run away."

"I'm not running away," he protested, but too weakly.

She thought for a second. "You haven't had things hard, Nate. I know lots of boys like you. You like your comforts." This time she saw she had hurt him and so she reached out a hand and touched his cheek. "Maybe I'm wrong. I keep forgetting this ain't your country, but it is mine." She fell silent for a while, thinking, then she gave him a swift smile. "There comes a time when you have to stand on your own feet, not on your father's shoulders. That's what my pa taught me. I ain't a quitter, Nate."

"I'm not . . ."

"Sh!" She touched his lips again. "I do know that the Yankees ain't won yet, and you told me yourself that it takes five of them to beat one of our boys."

"I was boasting."

"Just like a man." She smiled. "But the hog's still squealing, honey. We ain't beat yet."

Starbuck sucked on the cigar. He had convinced himself that Sally would come with him. He had never for one moment imagined that she would prefer to stay and risk the Yankee victory. He had thought they would run away together and make a small refuge far from the world's troubles. Her refusal left him confused.

"Nate?" Sally asked. "What is it you want?"

He thought about the question. "I was happy last winter," he said. "When I was with the company. I like being a soldier."

"Then if you want something, honey, go get it. Like my pa says, the world don't owe no one a damn thing, which means you have to go out there and grow it, make it, buy it, or steal it." She smiled at him. "You being honest about this spy business?"

He looked up at her. "Yes. I promise."

"Go catch the bastard, honey. You promised to deliver that letter, so do it. And if you want to run away after that, that's your business, but you do it on your own feet, not mine." She leaned forward and kissed him. "But if you do come back here, honey, I'll still be here. I owe you still." It was for Sally's sake that Starbuck had murdered Ethan Ridley, and Sally's gratitude for that act was heartfelt and deep. Now she threw what remained of her cigar onto the tiles of the hearth. "You want me to give you the money that's yours?"

He shook his head. "No." His certainties were vanishing, leaving him confused again. "Would you do something for me?" he asked Sally.

"If I can, sure."

"Write to your father."

"My pa!" She sounded alarmed. "He doesn't want a letter from me!"

"I think he does."

"But I can't write proper!" She was blushing, suddenly ashamed of her lack of education.

294

"He doesn't read too good either," Starbuck said. "Just write to him and tell him I'm coming back. Tell him I'll be with the company before the spring finishes. Promise him that."

"I thought that bastard Faulconer wouldn't have you in the Legion?"

"I can beat Faulconer."

Sally laughed. "A minute ago, Nate, you were all for running away and hiding yourself in Canada, now you're taking on General Faulconer? Sure, I'll write my pa. You certain about your money?"

"Keep it for me."

"So you are coming back?"

He smiled. "Hog's still squealing, honey."

She kissed him, then climbed to her feet and crossed to her dressing table where she carefully fixed the chignon on her brushed-back hair. She made sure the curls fell naturally, then gave him a smile. "I'll see you, Nate."

"You will, too." He watched her walk to the door. "The Bible girl," he suddenly remembered.

"What about her?" Sally paused with her hand on the door's edge.

"She wants to come and talk to you."

"To me?" Sally grinned. "What about? Jesus?"

"Maybe. Do you mind?"

"If Jesus don't mind, why the hell should I?"

"She feels bad about that night."

"I'd forgotten it," Sally said, then shrugged. "No, I didn't forget. I kind of hoped to forget. But maybe I can teach her a thing or two."

"Such as?"

"What a real man is, honey." She grinned at him.

"Don't upset her," Starbuck said and was surprised by that sudden impulse of protection toward Julia, but Sally

295

had not heard him. She had already gone out of the door. He finished his cigar. It seemed there was no easy way out, which meant he had a promise to keep and a spy to betray. Somewhere in the night a clock struck the hour and Starbuck went into the dark.

"WHAT IS THIS?" Belvedere Delaney held a bank note between his finger and thumb as though the crumpled thing held a contagion. "'Parish of Point Coupee,'" he read aloud from the note's inscription, "'two dollars.' My dear Sally, I do hope that isn't what you charge for your services?"

"Real funny, ain't you," Sally said, then took the note from the lawyer's hand and added it to one of the piles on the cherrywood table. "Gambling winnings," she explained.

"But what am I to do with it?" Delaney inquired fastidiously, taking up the offending bank note again. "Am I to travel to Louisiana and demand that the Parish Clerk of Point Coupee pay me two dollars?"

"You know well enough that they'll discount it at the Exchange Bank," Sally said briskly, taking back the note and adding it to the week's takings. "That's four hundred and ninety-two dollars and sixty-three cents from downstairs." "Downstairs" meant the tables where poker and euchre were played, and where the house took a straight percentage of the winnings. The policy was that any kind of money agreeable to the players could be used at the tables, but upstairs the only acceptable currencies were the newfangled northern dollar bills, gold and silver coinage, and Virginia Treasury Notes.

"And how much of the four hundred and ninety-two dollars is in useful money?" Delaney asked.

"Half," Sally admitted. The rest was in fancy bills issued

by a variety of southern banks, merchants, and municipal governments who had harnessed their printing presses to replace the dearth of northern money.

"The Bank of Chattanooga," Delaney said derisively, riffling through the bank notes. "And what in the name of Jehovah is this?" He dangled a scrap of faded paper. "A twenty-five-cent note from the Inferior Court of Butts County, Jackson, Georgia? My God, Sally, we're rich! A whole quarter!" He tossed the note onto the table. "Why don't we just print up some notes for ourselves?"

"Why don't we?" Sally asked. "It'd be a damn sight easier than the work I do upstairs."

"We could invent whole parishes! Whole counties! We could devise our own banks!" Delaney was quite taken with the idea. Anything that sabotaged the Confederacy appealed to Belvedere Delaney, and destroying the currency would certainly hasten the demise of the rebellion. Not that the South's currency needed much debasement; prices were rising every day and the whole financial system was based upon loose promises that depended for their fulfillment on final Confederate victory. Even the government's official bank notes admitted as much, promising to pay the bearer the face value of the note but only six months after peace had been declared between the warring sides. "We could put a printing press in the coach house," Delaney suggested. "Who's to know?"

"The printer?" Sally suggested sourly. "You'd need too many people, Delaney, and sure as eggs they'd end up blackmailing you. Besides, I've got a better idea for the coach house."

"Tell me."

"Black it out, carpet it, put in a table and a dozen chairs, and I'll guarantee you a bigger profit than you can ever make out of my bedroom."

Delaney shook his head, not understanding. "You're going to serve meals?"

"Hell no. Seances. Set me up as Richmond's best medium, feed me gossip, charge five bucks a general session and fifty bucks for a private consultation." The idea had come to Sally the previous night when the house's clients had conducted their fake seance in the darkened parlor. It had been a game, but Sally had noted how some of the participants had still expected a supernatural intervention, and she reckoned that superstition could be harnessed to profit. "I'll need a helper to rap on walls and wave around the cheesecloth," she told a fascinated Delaney, "and we'll have to develop some other tricks."

Delaney liked the idea. He waved a vague hand toward the upper floors. "And you'd leave the bedroom business?"

"So long as I'm making more money, hell yes. But I'll need you to invest some cash first. We can't gammon the city with a cheap room. It's got to be done proper."

"You're brilliant, Sally. Quite brilliant." Delaney's praise was genuine. He enjoyed his weekly meetings with Sally, whose business acumen impressed him and whose sturdy good sense amused him. It was Sally who ran the financial side of the house, doing it with a brisk efficiency and a tough honesty. The whorehouse, with its luxuries and air of exclusivity, was a gold mine to the lawyer, but it was also a place where he picked up gossip about southern politicians and military commanders, and all that gossip was passed on to Delaney's contact in Washington. How much of the information was true or useful Delaney did not always know, nor did he particularly care. It was enough that he was siding with the North and could thus anticipate profiting from that allegiance when, as he saw it, the inevitable northern victory occurred. Now, still mulling over Sally's proposal to turn the house's back premises into a spiritualist shrine, Delaney took his share of the week's money. "So tell me the news?"

Sally gestured through the window to where refugees' carts and coaches still jammed the street. "That's the news, ain't it? We'll soon have no customers left."

"Or a new set arriving?" Delaney suggested delicately.

"And we'll charge them double," Sally sniffed, then asked if it was true that the northern recruiting offices had been closed down.

"I'd not heard as much," Delaney said, taking care not to show how elated he was by the news.

"The Yankees must be pretty cock-a-hoop," Sally said with a grimace.

And with good reason, Delaney thought, for the northern army was just a day's march from the city now. "Which client told you about the recruiting offices?" he asked Sally.

"Wasn't no customer," Sally said. "It was Nate."

"Starbuck?" Delaney asked in surprise. "He was here?"

"Last night. They'd just let him out of jail."

"I saw he'd been released," Delaney said. The news had been in both the *Examiner* and the *Sentinel*. "Is he in his old room? I should say hello."

"Silly bastard's being a damn fool." Sally lit herself a cigar. "God knows where he is."

"Meaning what?" Delaney asked. Sally had been trying to disguise the anxiety in her voice, but Delaney was far too acute to miss her tone and he knew just how fond of Starbuck she was.

"Because he's risking his damn life," Sally said, "that's what. He's taking a letter across the lines and he wanted me to go with him."

Delaney scented a rich morsel here, but he dared not be too eager in his questioning lest he rouse Sally's suspicions. "He wanted you to go to the Yankees? How odd."

"He wanted me to marry him," Sally corrected her employer.

Delaney smiled at her. "What sophisticated taste our friend Starbuck has," he said gallantly. "And yet you turned him down?" He teased her very gently with the question.

Sally grimaced. "He reckoned we could set up a dry goods store in Maine."

Delaney laughed. "My dear Sally, you would be wasted! And you'd hate Maine. They live in icehouses, suck on salt fish for their subsistence, and sing Psalms for entertainment." Delaney gave a rueful shake of his head. "Poor Nate. I shall miss him."

"He says he's coming back," Sally said. "He didn't want to come back, not if I'd run off with him, but since I ain't moving he says he'll deliver his letter, then get himself back here."

Delaney pretended to hide a yawn. "What sort of letter?" he asked innocently.

"He never said. Just a letter from the government here." Sally paused, but then her worry for Starbuck drove her to explain further and she never once suspected that her explanations might endanger Starbuck. Sally trusted Delaney wholly. The lawyer was a friend, a uniformed Confederate officer, and a man of gentle kindness. Other whores put up with beatings and scorn, yet Belvedere Delaney always behaved with consideration and courtesy to the women he employed; indeed he seemed as concerned for the happiness and health of his employees as for the profits they made him, and so Sally felt free to pour her worries into his sympathetic ear. "Nate reckons there's a spy," she said, "a real dangerous one who's telling the Yankees everything our army plans on doing, and if he can deliver the letter safe then that'll finish off the spy. He didn't tell me more than that, but it's enough. He's an idiot. He don't

301

want to be mixed up in that nonsense, Delaney. He'll end up hanging like that man they strung up at Camp Lee." Webster's end had made a rich story for the newspapers, which had depicted the hanging as the deserved fate of a spy.

"We certainly don't want poor Nate to hang," Delaney said gravely, and he saw that his right hand was trembling slightly, just enough to make the smoke from his cigar shiver as it rose toward the molded ceiling. His first reaction was that Starbuck was on a mission to entrap him, then he dismissed that fear as self-indulgent nonsense. Richmond was full of spies, ranging from the open and eccentric like the rich and crazy Betty Van Lew, who stumped about the city muttering treason and carrying gifts to northern prisoners, to the subtle and secretive like Delaney himself. Yet Delaney was privy to remarkably few military secrets, and Sally's words suggested that the spy Starbuck was hunting was a military man and one who had access to all the Confederacy's secrets. "So what do you want me to do?" Delaney asked Sally.

Sally shrugged. "I reckon Nate'll only be happy if he can get back into the Legion. He likes being there. Can't you fix it? If he gets back from seeing the Yankees, of course."

"And if there's still a Confederacy," Delaney said dubiously.

"Of course there'll be a Confederacy. We ain't whipped yet. So can't you talk to General Faulconer?"

"Me!" Delaney shuddered. "Faulconer doesn't like me, my dear, and he positively hates Nate. I can tell you now that Faulconer won't let Nate back into his precious Legion."

"Then can you get Nate into another regiment? He likes being a soldier."

More fool him, Delaney thought, but kept that opinion

to himself. "I can try," he said, then he glanced at an ormolu clock that graced the mantel. "I think I should be going, my dear."

"You ain't staying for breakfast?" Sally sounded surprised.

Delaney stood. "Even lawyers have to do some work from time to time, my dear," he said. Delaney was a legal adviser to the War Department, an appointment that entailed less than an hour's work a month, but which paid Delaney an annual salary of $1560, though admittedly the dollars were in southern scrip. He pulled his jacket straight. "I'll do my best for Nate, I do promise."

Sally smiled. "You're a good man."

"Is that not an astonishing truth?" Delaney kissed Sally's hand with his customary politeness, put his cash into a leather case, and hurried out into the street. It had begun to rain again; the drops brought on an unseasonably chill wind.

Delaney hurried one block north to his apartment on Grace Street, where he unlocked his rolltop desk. There were times when the lawyer suspected that the hundreds of northern informants in Richmond were all competing to provide the best intelligence, and that the winner of that secret competition would reap the biggest rewards when the North took over the city. His pen scratched swiftly across the notepaper and he reflected that this small nugget of gossip should garner a top prize when that victory came. He wrote down all that Sally had told him. He wrote swiftly, warning the North that Nathaniel Starbuck was a traitor, and then he sealed his letter inside an envelope that he addressed to Lieutenant Colonel Thorne in the Inspector General's Department in Washington, D.C. He sealed that envelope within another which he addressed to the Reverend Ashley M. Winslow in Canal Street, Richmond, then he handed the packet and three northern dollars to his house slave. "This is urgent, George. It is for our mutual friends."

George knew and shared his master's loyalty. He carried the letter to Canal Street and gave it to a man named Ashley who was owned by a supervisor on the Central Virginia Railroad. George gave Ashley two dollars. By nightfall a train had carried the letter and one of the two-dollar coins to Catlett's Station in northern Virginia, where a free black who owned a small cobbler's shop took charge of the envelope.

While in Richmond, meanwhile, the exodus went on. The President's wife took her children away from the city. The price of haulage tripled. When the wind was in the east there was sometimes an odd muffled percussion in the air, barely detectable, but there all the same. It was the sound of guns. Belvedere Delaney heard the distant gunfire and laid a northern flag in his parlor ready to hang from the window as a greeting to the victorious Yankees. He wondered if his letter would reach Washington in time, or if the war would end before Starbuck's treachery was uncovered. In some ways he hoped the young northerner would live, for Starbuck was an attractive rascal, but a rascal all the same, which probably meant he was doomed to the noose anyway. It would be a death Delaney would regret, but in this season of death one more corpse could not make that much difference. It would be a pity, but scarcely more. The lawyer listened to the sound of faraway guns and prayed it signified rebellion's defeat.

The first Yankees to take notice of Starbuck were men of the 5th New Hampshire Infantry, who mistook him for a rebel straggler and marched him at bayonet point to their adjutant, a gaunt, wild-bearded captain with pebble-lensed spectacles who sat astride a piebald horse and peered through the rain at the bedraggled prisoner. "Have you searched the miserable bastard?" the Captain asked.

"He's got nothing," one of Starbuck's captors answered. "Poor as an honest lawyer."

"Take him to brigade," the Captain ordered. "Or if that's too much trouble just shoot the bastard when no one's looking. That's what deserters deserve, a bullet." He gave Starbuck a crooked grin as if daring him to object to the verdict.

"I'm not a deserter," Starbuck said.

"Never thought you were, reb. I just reckon you're a footsore bastard who couldn't keep up. Reckon I'd be doing the seceshers a favor just by killing you, which is maybe why I'll let you live." The Captain gathered his reins and gave a dismissive jerk of his head. "Take the bastard away."

"I'm carrying a message," Starbuck said desperately. "I'm not a deserter and I'm no straggler. I'm carrying a message for Major James Starbuck of the Secret Service. I brought it from Richmond two nights ago!"

The Captain gave Starbuck a long jaundiced look. "Son," he said at last, "I'm bone-weary, I'm dog-hungry, I'm wet through, and I just want to be home in Manchester, so if you're wasting my time I might just get so goddamn tired of you that I'll bury your miserable carcass without even wasting a bullet on it first. So convince me, son."

"I need to borrow a knife."

The Captain looked at the two burly men who had captured Starbuck and grinned as he thought of the prisoner trying to fight them. "You feeling heroic, reb, or just plain lucky?"

"A small knife," Starbuck said tiredly.

The Captain fumbled through layers of damp clothing. Behind him the New Hampshire infantry trudged along the muddy road, rain dripping from greatcoats worn like capes over their haversacks. Some gave Starbuck an inquiring look, trying to see in this captured rebel's frayed gray jacket and patched baggy pants the lineaments of devilry that the northern preachers had described.

The Captain produced a small scrimshaw penknife which Starbuck used to pick at the stitches of his waistband. He brought out the oilcloth pouch, which he handed up to the horseman. "It shouldn't get wet, sir," Starbuck said.

The Captain unfolded the pouch, then slit its stitching to reveal the sheets of onionskin paper. He swore as a raindrop splashed on the top page to dissolve a word into instant oblivion, then hunched forward to shelter the papers from the weather. He pulled the rain-smeared spectacles down on his nose and peered close over their rims at the tight handwriting, and what he read plainly convinced him of Starbuck's truthfulness, for he carefully folded the papers back inside their oilcloth pouch, which he handed back to Starbuck. "You're putting me to a world of trouble, son, but I reckon Uncle Sam would want me to exert myself. You need anything?"

"A cigar."

"Give the man a cigar, Jenks, and take your bayonet out of the poor bastard's ribs. Looks like he's on our side after all."

Horses were found, and an escort formed of two lieutenants who welcomed a chance to ride to Williamsburg. No one was entirely sure where the Army of the Potomac's headquarters was, but Williamsburg seemed the obvious place, and one of the lieutenants had seen a girl there the previous day whom he swore was the prettiest thing he could ever hope to see this side of paradise, and so to Williamsburg they rode. The Lieutenant wanted to know if the girls of Richmond were just as pretty, and Starbuck assured him this was so. "I sure can't wait to get there," the Lieutenant said, but his companion, a much less optimistic man, asked Starbuck how formidable the rebel defenses around the city were.

"Pretty formidable," Starbuck said.

"Well I guess our cannon boys can't wait to chew 'em up. Not since the seceshers skedaddled from Yorktown without waiting to be killed first."

The lieutenants assumed, and Starbuck did not disillusion them, that he was a northern patriot who had risked his life for his country and they were naturally curious about him. They wanted to know where he came from, and when Starbuck told them he was a Bostonian they said they had gone through Boston on their way to the war and what a fine city it was, better than Washington, which was all windy avenues and half-finished buildings and scalpers trying to make a buck or two out of honest country soldiers. They had met President Lincoln there, and he was a good kind of man, plain and straight, but for the rest of the city, they said, there were hardly words bad enough.

The lieutenants were in no particular hurry and stopped at a tavern where they asked for beer. The tavern keeper, a surly man, said he had been drunk dry of beer and offered instead a bottle of peach wine. It was sweet and thick, sickly to the tongue. Starbuck, sitting on the tavern's back porch, saw hatred for the invaders on the tavern keeper's face. In turn the two lieutenants derided the tavern keeper as a long-haired ignoramus in desperate need of northern enlightenment. "It isn't a bad-looking country!" The more cheerful of the two lieutenants gestured at the scenery. "If it was drained proper and cultivated scientifically, a man could make money here."

In truth the rainy landscape looked desperately uninviting. The tavern was built in a clearing of trees just north of

307

the swamps which edged the Chickahominy River. The river itself was no wider than Richmond's Main Street, but it was fringed by broad strips of dank and flooded marshland that gave off a heavy, rank smell. "Looks a sick kind of place to me," the more pessimistic Lieutenant observed. "That kind of swamp breeds illness. It isn't a land for white men."

The lieutenants, disappointed in the thick sweet wine, decided to ride on. Their journey took the three horsemen against a tide of oncoming infantry and Starbuck noted how well the northern soldiers were equipped. None of these men had shoe soles held to uppers with lengths of string, none wore frayed rope belts, none carried flintlock smoothbore muskets like those that had been used by George Washington's men when they had marched these same roads to pin the British against the sea at Yorktown. These troops did not have uniforms patched with butternut, nor did they need to grind roasted goober peas and smoke-dried apples to make a substitute coffee. These northerners looked well-fed, cheerful, and confident, an army trained and equipped and determined to end a sad business swiftly.

A mile or two short of their destination they passed an artillery park where Starbuck paused to gape in sheer amazement. He had not imagined there were so many guns in all the world, let alone in one small Virginia field. The cannon were lined wheel to wheel, all with newly varnished limbers, all polished, and beyond them were lines of brand-new covered wagons which held the gunners' supplies and spare ammunition. He tried to count the guns, but it was dusk and he could not see clearly enough to make even a rough estimate. There were rows of workmanlike twelve-pounder Napoleons, and lines of Parrott guns with their bulbous breeches, and acres of three-inch rifles with their slender barrels. Some of the guns had blackened muzzles, reminders that the rebels had fought a brisk and bloody delaying action in Williamsburg to slow the Federal advance. Groups of artillerymen gathered around cooking fires among the parked guns, and the smell of roasting meat made the three riders urge their horses on toward the comforts of the nearby town.

The first lantern lights were showing through windows as they trotted into Williamsburg with its fine spread of ancient college buildings. They approached the college along a street of shingled houses. Some of the houses were pristine and neat, but others, presumably those abandoned by their owners, had been rifled by the Yankees. Torn curtains hung at broken windows and smashed china littered the yards. A doll lay in the mud of one yard, and a torn mattress was draped over the splintered remains of a cherry tree. One house had burned to the ground so that all that remained were two gaunt and blackened brick chimney stacks and some twisted, half-melted bed frames. Troops were billeted in all the houses.

The College of William and Mary had suffered just as much as the town itself. The lieutenants tied their horses to a hitching post in the main yard and explored the Wren Building in search of the Secret Service headquarters. A sentry on the college gate had assured them that the bureau was in residence, but he was not certain just where, and so the three men wandered lantern-lit corridors littered with broken books and torn papers. To Starbuck it looked as if a barbarian horde had come to destroy learning. Every bookshelf had been emptied and the books tipped into piles, or burned in grates or simply kicked aside. Paintings had been slashed and old documents taken from chests that had been broken up for firewood. In one room the linenfold paneling had been prised from the plaster walls by bayonets and splintered into so much matchwood that was now just ash in a wide grate. The corridors stank of urine. A crude effigy of Jefferson Davis with a devil's horns and forked tail had been painted in limewash on a lecture-room wall. Troops were encamped in the high-ceilinged rooms. Some had found professors' gowns hanging in a cupboard and now swooped up and down the corridors swathed in the black silk robes.

"You're looking for headquarters?" A New York captain, his breath stinking of whiskey, pointed the three men toward some houses that lay a short distance away in the darkness. "Faculty houses." He hiccuped, then grinned when a woman's laughter sounded from the room behind him. Someone had chalked "Amalgamation Hall" over the room's doorway. "We have captured the college's liquor and are presently amalgamating its liberated kitchen girls," the Captain announced. "Come and join us."

A New York sergeant offered to escort Starbuck to the house where he believed the Secret Service had its quarters while the two New Hampshire lieutenants, their duty discharged, went to join the New Yorkers' celebrations. The Sergeant was angry. "They've no notion of duty," he said of his officers. "We're on a righteous crusade, not a drunken debauch! They're just kitchen maids, scarce out of childhood! What do we want those poor innocent blacks to think? That we're no better than southerners?"

But Starbuck could spare no sympathy for the Sergeant's unhappiness. He was too consumed by nervous apprehension as he walked down a puddled path toward the row of elegant, lamplit houses. He was just seconds away from meeting his brother and discovering for certain whether his erstwhile friend was a traitor. Starbuck also had to play a deceiver's game and he was not sure he could continue to play it. Maybe, seeing James's face, he would lose his resolve? Maybe this whole deception was God's way of restoring him to righteousness? His heart felt flabby and loud in his chest; his belly, still soured by Gillespie's mistreatment, felt raw. Unto thine own self be true, he told himself, but that just threw up Pilate's question. What is truth? Did God want him to betray the South? For a pittance he would have turned and fled from this confrontation, but instead the Sergeant gestured at a house that was brightly lit by candles and guarded by two blue-coated sentries who huddled from the wind against the red brick wall. "That's the house," the Sergeant said, then called to the two sentries. "He's got business inside."

The house door was marked in chalk "Major E. J. Allan and Staff, KEEP OUT." Starbuck half expected the sentries to bar him entry, but instead they unquestioningly let him into the entrance hall that was hung with etchings of European cathedrals. A hallstand made from stag antlers was thickly draped with blue coats and sword belts. Men's voices and the sound of cutlery scraping on china came from a room that opened off the hall to Starbuck's left. "Is someone there?" a voice shouted from the dining room.

"I'm looking for . . ." Starbuck began, but his voice was slightly cracked and he needed to start again. "I'm looking for Major Starbuck," he called again.

"And who in the name of holy hell are you?" A short, bearded man with a hard voice appeared in the open doorway. He had a napkin tucked into his collar and a piece of chicken speared onto a fork in his right hand. He gave Starbuck's bedraggled uniform a scornful look. "Are you a miserable rebel? Eh? Is that what you are? Come to beg a decent meal, have you, now that your miserable rebellion has collapsed? Well? Speak up, you fool."

"I'm Major Starbuck's brother," Starbuck said, "and I have a letter from Richmond for him."

The belligerent man stared at him for a few seconds.

"Christ on His cross," he said at last in astonished blasphemy. "You're the brother from Richmond?"

"Yes."

"Then come in, come in!" He gestured with his speared chicken morsel. "Come in!"

Starbuck walked into a room where a dozen men sat around a well-laden table. Candles burned in three candelabras along the polished board, a score of plates held fresh bread, green vegetables, and roasted meat, while red wine and heavy silverware glinted in the flamelight. Starbuck, hungry though he was, noticed none of it; instead he saw only the bearded man on the table's far side who had begun to stand up, but who now seemed frozen motionless halfway up from his chair. He stared at Starbuck, his eyes showing incredulity.

"Jimmy!" the man who had accosted Starbuck in the hallway said. "He says he's your brother."

"Nate," James, still crouched half in and half out of his chair, said in a faint voice.

"James." Starbuck suddenly felt a great rush of affection for his brother.

"Oh, thank God," James said, and he collapsed backward onto his chair as if the moment were too much for him. "Oh, thank God," he said again, touching a napkin to his closed eyes as he prayed his thanks for his brother's return. The other men about the table stared at Starbuck in a still silence.

"I've brought you a message," Starbuck interrupted his brother's silent prayer.

"From?" James said in a tone of eager hope, almost adding the name, but then remembering his promise to keep Adam's identity a secret. He checked his question and even placed a finger to his lips as though warning his brother not to say the name aloud.

312

And Starbuck knew then. His brother's warning motion intimated that he would indeed know the spy's identity, and that could only mean that the traitor was Adam. It had always had to be Adam, though that inevitability had not stopped Starbuck from hoping and praying that the spy might turn out to be some total stranger. He felt a sudden and immense sadness for Adam, and a despair because he would now need to use this new certainty. James was still waiting for an answer and Starbuck nodded. "Yes," he said, "from him."

"Thank God for that too," James said. "I feared he might be captured."

"Jimmy's at his prayers again," the short, bearded man broke cheerfully into the brothers' conversation, "so you'd better sit and eat something, Mr. Starbuck. You look fair famished. You have the message on you?"

"That is Mr. Pinkerton," James introduced the short man. "The chief of the Secret Service Bureau."

"And honored to meet you," Pinkerton said, thrusting out a hand.

Starbuck shook hands, then gave Pinkerton the square of oilcloth. "I guess you've been waiting for this, sir," he said.

Pinkerton unfolded the sheets and looked at the carefully disguised handwriting. "It's the real thing, Jimmy! From your friend! He's not let us down! I knew he wouldn't!" He stamped a foot on the rug as a sign of happiness. "Sit down, Mr. Starbuck! Sit! Eat! Make room for him! Next to your brother, yes?"

James stood as Nate approached. Nate was so happy to see James again that for a second he was tempted to offer an embrace, but the family had never been demonstrative and so the brothers merely shook hands. "Sit," James said. "I'll trouble Lieutenant Bentley for some chicken? Thank you.

313

And some bread sauce. You always liked bread sauce, Nate. Sweet potato? Sit, sit. Some lemonade?"

"Wine, please," Starbuck said.

James looked horrified. "You drink ardent spirits?" Then, unable to spoil this moment with pious disapproval, he smiled. "Some wine, then, of course. For your stomach's sake, I'm sure, and why not? Sit, Nate, sit!"

Starbuck sat and was assailed by questions. It seemed that every man about the table knew who he was, and all had seen the reports in the Richmond newspapers announcing his release. Those papers had made the journey to Williamsburg a good deal faster than Starbuck, who now assured his brother's colleagues that his imprisonment had all been a mistake. "You were accused of taking bribes?" James scorned the suggestion. "What nonsense!"

"A trumped-up charge," Starbuck said through a mouthful of chicken and bread sauce, "and merely an excuse to hold me while they tried to make me confess to espionage." Someone poured him more wine and wanted to know exactly how he had escaped from Richmond, so Starbuck told of journeying north to Mechanicsville and there turning east into the tangle of small roads that lay above the Chickahominy. He made it sound as though he had made the journey alone, though in truth he would never have reached the northern lines without de'Ath's pilot who had led him safely through quiet back lanes and ghostly forests. They had traveled by night, first to Mechanicsville, then to a farm just east of Cold Harbor, and on the last night through the rebel picket line by the York and Richmond Railroad and so down to a pine wood close to St. Peter's Church where George Washington had married. It was there that the taciturn Tyler had left Starbuck. "You walk from here," Tyler had said.

"Where are the Yankees?"

"We passed them two mile back. But from here on, boy, the bastards are everywhere."

"How do I get back?"

"Go to Barker's Mill and ask for Tom Woody. Tom knows how to find me, and if Tom's not there, you're on your own. Go on, now."

Starbuck had stayed under the cover of the pines for most of the morning, then had walked south until he reached the road where the New Hampshire regiment had captured him. Now, satiated with a meal richer than any he had eaten in months, he pushed his chair back from the table and accepted the gift of a cigar. His brother frowned at his use of tobacco, so Starbuck assured James it was merely to alleviate a bronchial condition caught in the rebel dungeons. He then described his treatment in prison and horrified the company with his graphic account of Webster's hanging. He could give Pinkerton no news of Scully or Lewis, nor of the woman, Hattie Lawton, who had been captured with Webster.

Pinkerton, busy stuffing a pipe with James River tobacco captured along with the faculty house in which they were quartered, frowned at Starbuck. "Why did they let you witness poor Webster's death?"

"I think they expected me to betray myself by recognizing him, sir," Starbuck said.

"They must think we're fools!" Pinkerton said, shaking his head at this evidence of southern stupidity. He lit his pipe, then tapped the sheets of onionskin paper on which de'Ath's false message was written. "Am I to assume you know the man who wrote this?"

"Indeed, sir."

"A family friend, eh?" Pinkerton glanced from the lean Starbuck to the plumper James, then back to Starbuck again. "And I assume, Mr. Starbuck, that if this friend asked

315

you to deliver the letter he must have known of your northern sympathies?"

Starbuck assumed the question was meant as a clumsy test of his loyalty and for a second it actually was, for he understood this was the moment where he must begin telling lies. Either that or confess the truth and see his friends in K Company and in Richmond ground down beneath the northern army. For one blinding instant he felt the temptation to truthfulness, if only for the sake of his soul, but then the thought of Sally made him smile at the expectant Pinkerton. "He knew my sympathies, sir. For some time now I've been helping him collect the information he sends you."

The lie came smoothly. He had even made it sound modest, and for a second or two he was aware of the room's silent admiration, then Pinkerton slapped the table in approbation. "So you did deserve imprisonment, Mr. Starbuck!" He laughed to show it was a jest, then slapped the table again. "You're a brave man, Mr. Starbuck, there's no doubting it." Pinkerton spoke feelingly and the men around the table murmured their approbation of their chief's sentiments.

James touched Starbuck's arm. "I always knew you were on the right side. Well done, Nate!"

"The North owes you a debt of gratitude," Pinkerton said, "and I'll make it my business to see it's paid. Now, if you're through with your victuals, maybe you and I can talk privately? And you, Jimmy, of course. Come. Bring your wine, Mr. Starbuck."

Pinkerton led them into a small and elegantly furnished parlor. Theology books lined the shelves while a sewing machine stood on a walnut table with a half-finished shirt still trapped beneath its foot. Silver-framed family portraits were lined up on a side table. One, a daguerreotype of a small child, had its frame draped with a strip of crepe to signify that the child had died recently. Another showed a young man in Confederate artillery uniform. "Pity that one's not swathed in black, eh, Jimmy?" Pinkerton said as he sat down. "Now, Mr. Starbuck, what are you called? Nathaniel? Nate?"

"Nate, sir."

"You can call me Bulldog. Everyone does. Everyone except Jimmy here because he's too much of a cold Boston fish to use nicknames, ain't that so, Jimmy?"

"Quite so, Chief," James said, gesturing for Starbuck to sit opposite Pinkerton beside the empty fireplace. Wind gusted in the chimney and rattled rain on the curtained windows.

Pinkerton took de'Ath's forged message from his vest pocket. "The news is bad, Jimmy," the detective said gloomily. "It's just as I feared. There must be a hundred and fifty thousand rebels facing us now. See for yourself." James fixed some reading glasses on the bridge of his nose and placed the proffered letter directly under an oil lamp. Starbuck wondered if his brother would spot the counterfeit handwriting, but instead James tutted at the news and shook his head in evident sympathy with his chief's pessimism.

"It's bad, Major, very bad."

"And they're sending reinforcements to Jackson in the Shenandoah, you see that?" Pinkerton pulled on his pipe. "That's how many men they've got! They can afford to send troops away from the Richmond defenses. It's what I've been fearing, Jimmy! For months now the rascals have been trying to convince us their army is small. They want to draw us in, you see? Suck us in. Then they would have hit us with everything!" He shadowboxed two punches. "My God, if it hadn't been for this message, Jimmy, it might have worked too. The General will be grateful. 'Pon my soul he'll be grateful. I shall visit him in a moment or two." Pinkerton seemed obscurely pleased at the bad news, almost energized by it. "But before I go, Nate, tell me what's happening in Richmond. Don't pull your punches, lad. Tell me the worst, spare us nothing."

Starbuck, thus enjoined, described a rebel capital thronged with soldiers from every part of the Confederacy. He reported that the Tredegar Iron Works had been forging cannon day and night since the war's beginning and that the guns were now pouring from the factory gates toward the newly dug defenses that ringed Richmond. Pinkerton leaned forward as though eager for every word and winced at each new revelation of rebel strength. James, sitting to one side, made notes in a small book. Neither man challenged Starbuck's inventions, but instead swallowed his outrageous inventions whole.

Starbuck finished by saying he had seen trains steam into the Richmond depot of the Petersburg railroad loaded with crates of British rifles that had been smuggled through the U.S. Navy's blockade. "They reckon every rebel soldier has a modern rifle now, sir, and ammunition enough for a dozen battles," Starbuck said.

James frowned. "Half the prisoners we've taken in the last week were armed with old-fashioned smoothbores."

"That's because they're not letting their newest weapons leave Richmond," Starbuck lied smoothly. He was suddenly enjoying himself.

"You see, Jimmy? They're sucking us in! Luring us!" Pinkerton shook his head at this evidence of rebel perfidy. "They'll pull us in, then hit us. My God, but it's clever." He puffed on his pipe, deep in thought. A clock ticked on the mantel, while from the wet darkness came the sound of men's voices singing. Pinkerton finally threw himself back in his chair as though he had been unable to see a way through the thicket of enemies that sprang up around him. "Your friend, now, the fellow who writes these letters," Pinkerton said, pointing his pipe at Starbuck, "how is he planning to send us further letters?"

Starbuck drew on his cigar. "He suggested, sir, that I go back to Richmond and that you use me as you would have used Webster. Ad –" He stopped himself from saying Adam's name just in time. "Admittedly I'm not ideal, perhaps, but it could be done. No one in Richmond knows I've crossed the line."

Pinkerton stared hard at Starbuck. "What is your status with the rebels, Nate? They let you out of prison, but are they fool enough to expect you back in their army?"

"I asked for some furlough, sir, and they agreed to that, but they'll want me back in the Passport Bureau by the end of the month. That's where I was working when I was arrested, you see."

"My word, but you could be mighty useful to us in that bureau, Nate! My word, but that would be useful!" Pinkerton stood and paced the small room excitedly. "But you're running a fearful risk by going back. Are you really willing to do it?"

"Yes, sir, if it's necessary. I mean if you don't finish the war first."

"You're a brave man, Nate, a brave man," Pinkerton said, and he went on pacing up and down while Starbuck relit his cigar and sucked the smoke deep into his chest. De'Ath, he thought, would have been proud of him. Pinkerton stopped his pacing and stabbed the stem of his pipe toward Starbuck. "The General might want to see you. You'll hold yourself ready?"

Starbuck hid his alarm at the thought of facing the northern commander. "Of course, sir."

"Right!" Pinkerton scooped up the false letter from the table in front of James. "I'm away to see his lordship. I'll leave the two of you to talk." He swept out of the room, shouting for an orderly to bring his coat and hat.

James, suddenly embarrassed, sat in the chair Pinkerton had vacated. He shyly caught his brother's eye, then smiled. "I always knew you weren't a copperhead at heart."

"A what?"

"Copperhead," James said. "It's an insult for northerners who sympathize with the South. Journalists use the word."

"Nasty beasts, copperheads," Starbuck said lightly. One of his men had almost been bitten by a copperhead the previous year and he remembered Truslow barking a warning and then slashing the snake's brown head clean off with his bowie knife. The snake had smelt, Starbuck remembered, of honeysuckle.

"How is Adam?" James asked.

"Earnest. In love, too. She's the daughter of the Reverend John Gordon."

"Of the ASPGP? I've never met him, but I've heard good things of him." James took the reading glasses off his nose and polished them on the skirt of his coat. "You're looking thin. Did they really use purgatives on you?"

"Yes, they did."

"Terrible, terrible." James frowned, then offered his brother a smile of wry sympathy. "Now we've both been in prison, Nate. Who would ever have thought it? I must confess that when I was in Richmond I took great comfort from the Acts of the Apostles. I believed that if the Lord could deliver Paul and Silas from the dungeon then He would surely deliver me. And He did!"

"Me too," Starbuck said, squirming with embarrassment. There was a certain pleasure in deceiving Pinkerton, but none in hoodwinking James.

James smiled. "Adam encouraged me to believe you might come back to our side."

"He did?" Starbuck asked, unable to hide his surprise that his erstwhile friend should have so misunderstood him.

"He told me you'd been attending prayer meetings," James said, "so I knew you must have been laying your burden before the Lord and I thanked God for it. Did Adam give you the Bible?"

"Yes, thank you. It's here," Starbuck said, tapping his breast pocket. The Bible had been waiting with his uniform at de'Ath's house. "Would you like it back?"

"No! No. I would like you to have it, as a gift." James breathed on his glasses and polished their lenses again. "I asked Adam to persuade you to come home. Once I knew his real feelings on the war, of course."

"He did encourage me," Starbuck lied.

James shook his head. "So there really are that many rebel soldiers? I must confess I had my doubts. I thought Pinkerton and McClellan were seeing dangers where none existed, but I was wrong! Well, with God's help we shall prevail, but I admit the fighting will be hard. But at least you have done your duty, Nate, and I shall make it my business to let Father know that."

Starbuck gave a quick embarrassed smile. "I can't see Father forgiving me."

"He's not given to forgiveness," James agreed, "but if I tell him how valuable your services have been, who knows? Maybe he will see his way to restoring his affections." He busied himself by polishing his spectacles yet again. "He's still angry, I must confess."

"About the girl?" Starbuck asked brutally, referring to the days when he had fled from both Yale and his father's wrath. "And about the money I stole?"

"Yes." James colored, then smiled. "But even Father

can't deny the parable of the prodigal son, can he? And I shall tell him that it is time to forgive you." He paused, trapped between his desire to confess an emotion and an upbringing that had taught him to hide all such revelatory feelings. Desire won. "It wasn't till you were gone that I realized how much I missed you. You were always the rebellious one, weren't you? I think I needed your mischief more than I knew. After you'd gone I decided we should have been better friends, and now we can be."

"That's kind of you," Starbuck said, acutely embarrassed.

"Come!" James suddenly slid forward off his chair and knelt on the hooked rug. "Shall we pray?"

"Yes, of course," Starbuck said, and for the first time in months, he went to his knees. His brother prayed aloud, thanking the Lord for the return of this prodigal brother and praying God's blessing on Nate and Nate's future and the North's righteous cause. "Maybe," James finished, "you'd like to add a word of prayer, Nate?"

"Just amen," Starbuck said, wondering what betrayals he would need to make in the next few days if he was to keep the promise he had made to Sally's father. "Just amen."

"Then amen and amen," James said. He smiled, replete with happiness, because righteousness had triumphed, a sinner had come home, and a family disgrace could be ended at last.

The CSS *Virginia*, the ironclad built on the hull of the old USS *Merrimack*, was run aground and burned when Norfolk, her home base, was abandoned. The loss of the rebel ironclad opened the James River to the northern navy, and a flotilla of warships crept upstream toward Richmond. Rebel batteries on the riverbanks were overwhelmed by naval gunfire; the huge missiles of the flask-shaped Dahlgren guns ripping the rain-sodden parapets apart and the screaming hundred-pound shells of the Parrott rifles tearing up the damp-rotted fire platforms and shattering the gun carriages. Mile by mile the northern squadron of three ironclads and two wooden gunboats churned upstream, confident that there was no secessionist ship left afloat on the James capable of challenging them and discovering no shore battery strong enough to stop their inexorable progress.

Six miles south of Richmond, just where the squadron's course turned through a right angle to run straight north toward the heart of the city, one last rebel fort remained. It stood high on Drewry's Bluff, a great hill on the James's southern bank, and its heavy guns pointed east toward the river's mouth. To the north of Drewry's Bluff, where the river ran so invitingly into the heart of rebellion, a barricade of stone-filled barges had been sunk against great pilings. The water heaped above the barricade and flowed white through its sluices, while a tangled mat of driftwood and floating trees was trapped upstream to make the obstacle look even more formidable.

The northern squadron came upon the last fort and its barricade just after dawn one morning. The five warships had been anchored in midstream all night, harassed by rifle fire from the enemy banks, but now, with the rising sun behind them, they cleared their turrets and gundecks for the decisive battle. First they would subdue the fort, then blast a gap through the barricade. "Richmond by nightfall, boys!" an officer on the leading ironclad called to his gun crews. Through his telescope he could see the distant city in the new day's light, could see the sun shining on white spires and on a pillared temple and on the roofs that climbed the city's seven hills. He could see the wretched rebel flags flying and he swore that before this day was through his ship would land a raiding party to take one of those rags from its Richmond staff. First they would destroy this last obstacle, then they would steam upstream into the city's heart and shell its citizens into submission. The army would thus be saved the need to mount a siege. Victory by nightfall.

The five ships loaded their guns, hauled their anchors from the river's mud, and steamed toward battle with their ensigns bright in the rising sun. The rebels fired first, shooting downriver when the leading warship was just six hundred yards away. The rebel shells screamed down from the hill's crest, each missile trailing a whip-thin wisp of fuse-smoke. The first shots plunged into the river, exploding great fountains of water that streamed away into mist. Then the first shells struck home and the rebel gunners cheered. "Save your breath! Reload! Look lively now!" a gun captain shouted.

The ironclad USS *Galena* led the attack, enduring the rebel cannonade as she maneuvered herself into a firing position. First she threw out a stern anchor, then, with her propeller stopped, she let the current swing her around so that the ship's full broadside could be brought against the small fort on its high bluff. The *Galena*'s Captain intended to check the current's swing by letting a bow anchor go when he was broadside to the rebel guns, but no sooner had the makeshift ironclad begun to swing than the rebel shells began to tear her armored sides apart. The iron plates bolted over the *Galena*'s wooden hull were no match for the fort's big guns. The armor plates buckled and fell, then the enemy shells ripped through the unprotected wooden skin to turn the gundeck into a sudden slaughterhouse of fire and white-hot steel. Screams echoed under low beams, smoke billowed through hatches, and fire exploded out of gunports. The warship cut her anchor cable and, leaking blood from her scuppers, limped downstream to safety.

The *Monitor*, a purpose-built ironclad with a deck and turret of solid metal, thumped up to the point of danger with her nine-foot-wide propeller churning the river brown with bottom mud. The fort's gunners paused to let the smoke from their eight guns dissipate, then turned the quoins and levered their guns' carriages to sharpen their aim. The *Monitor* was an altogether harder target, for she was little more than a flat metal deck flush with the river on which was mounted a circular turret twenty feet across. To the men in the fort she looked like a cake tin afloat on a waterlogged metal tray, then a puff of smoke showed as her auxiliary steam engine engaged the drive that would revolve the ship's gun turret and so bring her two monstrous cannons to bear.

"Fire!" the rebel gun commanders shouted and the flames whipped out of the guns that crashed back on their barbette carriages. The shells and shot cracked down on the ironclad. Some drove great gouts of water from the river, others hit their target square on, but only to bounce off the deck armor and wail above the riverbanks in tumbling flight.

The *Monitor*'s sailors cranked open the gun ports. The whole boat shivered as an enemy shot struck the deck, then again as another shell made the turret reverberate like a giant drum. "Fire!" the turret's officer called the command.

"They won't go high enough!" a gun captain shouted back. "The guns! They can't elevate any higher!" Another enemy shell cracked on the turret, starting dust from every rivet and join in the inner armor. Water splashed across the guns from a near miss, then another shell screamed off the armor plate.

The officer squinted along the gun sights and saw that the weapon's barrel was pointed at the slope below the fort.

"They won't go higher!" the gun captain shouted over

the terrible noise of solid shot cracking against the turret's eight layers of one-inch armor plates. The ironclad's main engine thumped in the boat's deep belly, holding her against the current while every few seconds a whipcrack of sound announced the strike of a sharpshooter's bullet fired from the rifle pits that lined the riverbank.

"Fire anyway!" the officer shouted.

The *Monitor* fired, but her huge twin shells merely buried themselves on the damp hill slope and churned a small avalanche of wet dirt away from the rock. Enemy shells banged and bounced off the one-inch armor of her deck and drowned the engines' intake vents with water splashes. The ironclad's helmsman, fighting against the sideways pull of the monstrous propeller, peered through slits in the solid iron blocks of the pilothouse to see nothing but water and gunsmoke. The ironclad fired again, the boat's whole stern momentarily settling a foot lower in the water as the two big guns recoiled, but again the shells fell far short of the earth-walled fort that was built so high above the river. "Go astern!" the ship's captain shouted up to the helmsman. The *Monitor*, its guns unable to hurt the enemy batteries, drifted downstream after the defeated *Galena* and the helmsman listened to the mocking jeers of the rebel infantry on the riverbanks.

The third ironclad, the USS *Naugatuck*, edged past the frustrated *Monitor* to take the lead position in the narrow river. Her first salvo went low, her next broadside screamed above the fort to splinter the tall trees beyond, then her gunners reckoned they had the proper elevation and rammed a one-hundred-pound shell into the twelve-foot barrel of their big Parrott gun. They stood back, the gunner yanked the lanyard to scrape the friction fuse and fire the gun, but instead the whole barrel, over four tons of iron, exploded in a blinding crack. Men whipped away in sprays of blood as jagged fragments of the burst breech whistled across the gundeck. Fire licked the deck, exploding a ready charge at the next gun. That smaller explosion laid open a man's ribs as cleanly as if they'd been cut with a knife and spilt his intestines like a dribble of butcher's offal across a rope-hauled ammunition hoist. An enemy shell added to the horror, coming through the open gun port to kill two men who were dragging a firehose aft. Flames roared along the gundeck, driving the gun crews up onto the poop where they made easy targets for the rebel sharpshooters on the banks. The ship's pumps brought the fire under control, but not until the *Naugatuck*, like the *Galena* and the *Monitor*, had drifted on the current out of range of the enemy guns. The two smaller gunboats fired on at long range, but neither dared take her fragile wooden hull close to the unscathed heavy guns on Drewry's Bluff and inch by inch, as though unwilling to admit defeat, the wounded flotilla fell back downstream.

In Richmond the guns sounded like summer thunder, rattling casements and shivering the colored water that filled the long-necked flasks in the windows of Monsieur Ducquesne's hairdressing salon. The twelve hundred slaves who labored in the hellish five acres of the Tredegar Iron Works silently cheered the unseen attackers while their overseers glanced nervously through grimy windows as if they expected to see a monstrous fleet of Yankee ironclads come steaming around the river bend at Rockett's Landing with their smokestacks blackening the sky and their great guns raised to tear the heart from the secessionist capitol. But nothing moved on the bend except the wind-stirred water. The guns cracked on, their sound muffled in the long, hot morning.

The sound gave urgency to a meeting of the free citizenry that had been summoned to assemble at the foot of the great steps of the State House. At the top of the steps, framed and given nobility by the soaring columns of Jefferson's architecture, the Mayor of Richmond and the Governor of Virginia both swore that the city would never surrender as long as there was breath in their bodies and pride in their hearts. They vowed to fight street to street, house to house, and promised that the James would run crimson with Yankee blood before Virginia's city yielded to northern tyranny. The crowd, encumbered with weapons, cheered the sentiments.

Julia Gordon, walking home with a pair of skinned rabbits that she had bartered at the Union Street market for a fine damask tablecloth that had formed a part of her mother's wedding goods, paused at the edge of the crowd and listened to the speakers. She noted in the pauses between the cheers how the guns' sound seemed to rise, fall, fade, and echo like some far-off thunderstorm. A famous Confederate congressman had begun speaking, using as his text a copy of the New York *Herald* which told how the citizens of Albany, the capital of New York State, were celebrating the imminent victory of the North over secession. They were dancing in the northern streets, the Congressman claimed, because the overweening Yankees reckoned their war was won. And why do they reckon thus? the orator asked. Because the great McClellan was marching on Richmond. "And shall McClellan win?" the orator roared the question.

"No!" the crowd roared back.

The Young Napoleon, the speaker said, would meet his Waterloo and the capering in Albany's streets would turn into the shuffle of mourning. The dancing bands would give way to muffled drums and the harlequins to grieving widows. For every brave hero buried in Richmond's Hollywood cemetery, the orator promised, twenty corpses

328

would be interred in the North, and for every teardrop shed by a southern widow, a bucketful would flow in the hated union. Richmond would not surrender, the South would not yield, the war was not lost. The crowd cheered and the far guns echoed.

Julia walked slowly on, the two bloody carcasses dripping from her hand. She skirted the crowd and took the path that led down to the Bell Tower. Crippled beggars sat by the railings that edged the tower, all of them wounded at the battle of Manassas. Beyond the tower, parked beside St. Paul's in Ninth Street, a hearse waited behind a team of horses wearing tall plumes of black feathers. The Negro postilions wore white gloves and black frock coats. Behind the hearse a small military band with black armbands waited for the casket to be brought from the church.

Julia crossed the road in front of the plumed horses, climbed the steps to the War Department, and asked the clerk in the hall office whether Major Adam Faulconer of General Johnston's staff was in the building. The clerk did not even need to examine his book. "All the General's staff are out of the city, miss. We haven't seen Major Faulconer for a month now."

"Did he send a letter for me?" Julia asked. Sometimes staff officers circumvented the postal service by using the army's messengers to carry their private mail into the city. "For Miss Gordon?" Julia said.

The clerk sorted through the letters on his table, but there was nothing for Julia. She thanked him and walked slowly uphill, turning into Franklin Street and trying to decide whether she was disappointed by Adam's silence or whether, in an odd way, it was a relief. Julia had written to tell Adam she had a message for him, but she had received no reply and was beginning to suspect that Adam's silence was perhaps a symptom of his change of heart.

329

Julia had been surprised when Adam first courted her, but she had also been flattered, for he was a remarkably handsome man and known to be both honorable and honest. Adam was also – and Julia was not so dishonest to pretend to be blind to the advantage – sole heir to one of Virginia's greatest fortunes, and while Julia constantly told herself that her affection for Adam was in no wise altered by that circumstance, she also knew that the circumstance must have an effect as marked and constant as the unseen pull of the sun on the earth's tides. Julia's mother lived with the constant shame of poverty, which shame made her husband's life a misery, and by marrying into the Faulconer family, Julia knew she could alleviate the unhappinesses of both her parents.

Yet, and Julia fell into a reverie as she walked slowly through the city, there was something which did not ring true about her feelings for Adam. The word "love," she thought, was so imprecise. Did she love Adam? She was sure she did, and she anticipated a married life of good and charitable works that would stretch far ahead, even into the next century, and whenever she thought about that useful good life she saw it in terms of being briskly busy, but never in terms of being happy. Not unhappy, certainly, but not happy either, and then she would chide herself for an un-Christian selfishness in even wanting happiness. Happiness, she told herself, was not a product of pleasurable pursuits, but an effect brought about by being engaged in ceaseless good works.

Yet sometimes, in the middle of the nights when she awoke to the sound of the wind sighing across the roofs and the rain bubbling in the gutters, she felt melancholy because she sensed a lack of joy. Did Adam, she wondered, ever worry about joy? He seemed so gloomy, so full of high purpose and deep troubles. He said it was the war that oppressed his soul, but Julia was not blind to other young people whose love and happiness transcended the fighting.

Julia realized she was walking west on Franklin Street, which meant she must soon pass the house where Sally Truslow lived. Julia had not yet summoned the courage to make that call and was ashamed of that failure. She walked past the house on the far side of the road and felt intimidated by its grandeur. A hazy sun glossed the windows, but could not quite hide the chandeliers that hung in the rooms beyond. The front door gleamed in the unfamiliar sunlight. She had a sudden impulse to cross the road and pull the polished brass bellpull, but then decided that carrying two bloody rabbits into a house, even a house of ill repute, was hardly the best way to save a soul. And that, she assured herself, was why she wanted to visit Sally.

She walked on home, passing houses tightly shuttered and locked because their inhabitants had fled the Yankee approach. The city was safer because of that evacuation for the army had increased the provost patrols in an effort to protect the otherwise unguarded property. Other patrols had searched the city's poorer quarters to root out deserters, while the newspapers also proclaimed that the authorities were hunting down northern spies who sought to betray the Confederacy. The city was full of rumors and fear, and now it shivered to the sound of gunfire. The enemy was at the gates.

Julia reached her parents' house. She stood for an instant and listened to the muffled percussion of the heavy guns firing on the river and she closed her eyes and said a prayer that all the young men would come home safe. Unbidden, she had an image of Starbuck and was so surprised at that incursion that she burst into laughter. Then she carried the rabbits indoors and closed the house against the sound of war.

*

331

Belvedere Delaney's letter to Lieutenant Colonel Thorne stayed hidden for a whole week in the cobbler's shop in Catlett's Station. Each day the cobbler added more letters to the hiding place until, at last, he had enough to make his journey worthwhile. Then, with sixteen letters to Colonel Thorne all resealed into one large envelope, he locked his shop and told his friends he was delivering finished shoes to distant customers. Then, carrying a heavy bag of patched shoes with the clandestine mail hidden in its lining, he walked north. Once out of his own district he traveled only at night, taking care to avoid the partisan patrols of horsemen who had been known to string up a free Negro on the nearest hanging tree, passport or no passport.

It took him two nights' travel to reach the Federal lines south of the Potomac, where he simply strolled into a camp of Pennsylvania infantry. "You looking for work, Sambo?" a sergeant challenged him.

"Just the mail clerk, sir." The cobbler pulled off his hat and bobbed his head respectfully.

"There's a mail wagon by the sutler's shed, but I'm watching you! You thieve anything, you black bastard, and I'll have my men use your hide for target practice."

"Yes, sir! I'll behave, sir! Thank you, sir!"

The postal service clerk took the one large envelope, franked it, then pushed the change across the counter and told the cobbler to make himself scarce. Next day the sixteen letters were placed on Lieutenant Colonel Thorne's desk in the Inspector General's Department in Washington, D.C., where they waited with over a hundred other letters that needed the Colonel's attention. The Colonel's office was woefully undermanned, for, in the rapid expansion of the U.S. Army, the Inspector General's Department had perforce become a convenient place to delegate tasks that no other department seemed competent or willing to perform. Among those tasks was the appreciation of intelligence received from the Confederacy, a job which might have been more properly performed by the Secret Service Bureau, but not everyone in the U.S. government shared General McClellan's faith in Detective Pinkerton, and so a separate intelligence service had sprung up in Washington, which, like every other orphaned responsibility, had landed in the Inspector General's Department.

It was that haphazard delegation of responsibility which had first guided Belvedere Delaney's original offer of help to Lieutenant Colonel Thorne's desk. Ever since that day Delaney, like a score of other northern sympathizers in the Confederacy, sent his material to Thorne, who added such correspondence to the great flood of information that threatened to overwhelm an office already overburdened with extraneous duties. Thus, when Delaney's latest letter reached his office, Thorne was nowhere near Washington, but was in Massachusetts conducting an inspection tour of northern seacoast forts, which tour was expected to last for much of the month of May, and so Delaney's letter waited in Washington while Colonel Thorne enumerated Fort Warren's fire buckets and latrines. It was not, Thorne told himself, why he had joined the army, but he still lived in hope that one day he might gallop across a smoke-torn field and save his country from disaster. Colonel Thorne, for all his ramrod-straight back and hardened face and unyielding eye, could still dream a soldier's dreams and pray a soldier's prayer, which prayer was that he would get to fight at least one battle for his country before the Young Napoleon brought America a lasting peace.

And the letter gathered dust.

*

The land torpedo had been left so that the commander of the Army of the Potomac could see for himself to just what abject depths the rebel forces had sunk. "It's only by the grace of Almighty God we discovered this one before it blew, though God knows too many others have exploded without warning." The speaker was a short, brusque major of the Corps of Engineers who was dressed in shirtsleeves and suspenders and had an air of competent efficiency that reminded Starbuck of Thomas Truslow.

Major General McClellan alighted from his horse and walked stiffly across to examine the land torpedo that had been concealed in a barrel stenciled with the misspelled legend "Dried Oisters, Messrs Moore and Carline, Mt Folly, Va." McClellan, immaculate in a blue frock coat with twin rows of brass buttons and a fine gilded belt, approached the barrel gingerly.

"We've made it safe, sir, as you'll see." The Major must have noticed the General's nervousness. "But it was a most ungodly device, upon my soul it was, sir."

"A disgrace," McClellan said, still keeping his distance from the oyster barrel. "A thorough disgrace."

"We found it on yon house." The Major gestured toward a small farmhouse that stood abandoned a hundred yards from the road. "We brought it down here for you to see, sir."

"And so you should, for all the world to see!" McClellan stood very erect, one hand slipped into an unbuttoned opening of his coat and with a concerned frown on his face. That frown, Starbuck had noted, seemed to be the young General's perpetual expression. "I would not have believed," McClellan said loudly and slowly so that the horsemen gathered beside the road could hear every word, "that men born and raised in the United States of America, even men bitten by the envy of secessionism, should stoop to stratagems so low and devices so evil." Many of the mounted officers nodded gravely while Pinkerton and James, who were accompanying Starbuck on this ride westward with the General, tutted loudly. The foreign newspaper reporters, to whom McClellan was really aiming his remarks, scribbled in their notebooks. The only man who seemed unsurprised and unshocked by the booby-trapped barrel was a scarred, one-eyed French military observer who, Starbuck had noted, seemed roundly amused by much of what he saw, even by this evil device.

The oyster barrel had been half filled with sand in which a three-and-a-half-inch shell had been stood upright. The copper fuse plug had been unscrewed from the shell's nose to leave a narrow shaft running into the missile's explosive belly. That shaft had been filled with gunpowder, but not before a crude, old-fashioned flintlock had been soldered onto the shell's nose. The Major demonstrated how a string attached to the underside of the barrel's lid should have tripped the flintlock so that it would have struck a spark that would have ignited the powder and so exploded the main charge buried deep inside the shell. "It would have killed a man easily," the Major said solemnly. "Two or three men if they'd been close enough."

The retreating Confederates had left scores of such land torpedoes. Some were buried in the roads, some by wells, others in deserted houses; so many that by now the advancing Yankees had learned to search for tripwires or other trigger mechanisms, but every day one or two of the implements still found their victims, and every such victim added to the outrage felt by the northerners. "Tactics," McClellan announced to the newspapermen accompanying his headquarters staff, "that even heathen savages might hesitate before employing. You would think, would you not, that with the preponderance of men enjoyed by the rebels they

335

would scarcely need to use such desperate measures? Yet such devices are, I suppose, a mark of their spiritual and moral degradation."

Murmurs of agreement sounded as the General remounted his horse and spurred away from the lethal barrel. The other horsemen jostled into place behind the army's diminutive commander, struggling to get the great man's attention, but McClellan, seeking a companion for the next portion of his journey, gestured to Pinkerton. "Bring your man, Pinkerton!" McClellan called, and Pinkerton urged Starbuck forward. They had waited days for this meeting with the General, a meeting that Starbuck had no enthusiasm for, but which Pinkerton insisted must happen. "So this is your messenger, Pinkerton?" McClellan said fiercely.

"It is, sir, and a brave man."

McClellan glanced at Starbuck, his face giving nothing away. They were riding through a flat country, past worn-out fields and dark sloughs and dripping pine trees. Hyacinths grew on the margins of the small streams, but little else in the scenery looked attractive or cheerful. "Your name?" McClellan barked at Starbuck.

"Starbuck, sir."

"His brother, sir, is one of my most valuable men." Allan Pinkerton gestured toward James with the stem of his pipe. "He's behind us, sir, if you'd like to greet him?"

"Quite so, good," McClellan said unhelpfully, then went silent again. Starbuck looked surreptitiously at the Yankee commander, seeing a short, stoutly built man with light brown hair, blue eyes, and a fresh complexion. The General was chewing tobacco and every now and then spat a stream of juice onto the road, taking care to lean well out of his saddle so that none of the spittle would soil his uniform or spatter on his highly polished boots.

"Did you know what was in the message you delivered?" McClellan suddenly demanded of Starbuck.

"Yes, sir."

"And? And? What of it? You agree with it?"

"Of course, sir."

"It's a bad business," McClellan said, "a bad business." He fell silent again and Starbuck noticed that the sardonic French officer had ridden close so he could listen to their conversation. McClellan also saw the Frenchman. "You see, Colonel Lassan, just what we are fighting?" The General twisted in his saddle to confront the Frenchman.

"Exactly what is that, *mon General?*"

"An overwhelming enemy, that is what! An enemy that can match us two soldiers to one, and what does Washington do? You know what they do? They prevent McDowell's Corps from reinforcing us. In all the annals of warfare, Colonel, in all military history do you know another piece of treachery to match that? And why? Why? To preserve Washington, which is under no attack, none! They are fools! Cowards! Traitors! Apes!" The sudden passion astonished Starbuck, though he was hardly surprised by it. Most of the army knew of Major General McClellan's anger that President Lincoln had prevented the 1st Corps from sailing to reinforce the men on the peninsula. McClellan, the President said, must make do with the hundred and twenty thousand men he already possessed, but McClellan declared that the missing thirty-five thousand were the key to northern victory. "If I just had those men I might achieve something. As it is we can only hope for a miracle. Nothing else will save us now, only a miracle."

"Indeed, *mon General,*" Colonel Lassan said, though with what Starbuck took to be an extraordinary lack of conviction.

McClellan turned back to Starbuck and wanted to know

337

what units he had seen marching through the streets of Richmond, and Starbuck, who had by now become accustomed to telling monstrous lies, detailed unit after unit that he had neither seen nor heard of. He invented a whole Florida brigade, made up a cavalry regiment from Louisiana, and described batteries of heavy artillery that he conjured from the warm Virginia air. To his astonishment and amusement McClellan listened as avidly as Pinkerton had done, taking Starbuck's word as proof that a mighty enemy did indeed wait to ambush him in the environs of Richmond. "It's what we feared, Pinkerton!" McClellan said when Starbuck's invention had run its course. "Johnston must have a hundred and fifty thousand men!"

"At least that many, sir."

"We must be cautious. If I lose this army, then the whole war is done," McClellan said. "We need to know the exact deployments of these new rebel brigades." This last requirement was addressed to Pinkerton, who assured the General that Starbuck would be ready to travel back to Richmond just as soon as he was given the list of questions which McClellan wanted answered by the prized, mysterious spy who seemed to lie at the very heart of the Confederate high command. "You'll get your questions," McClellan assured Starbuck, then raised a hand in response to a cheering group of Negroes who stood beside the road. A woman in a ragged dress and torn apron ran forward with a bunch of hyacinths that she offered to the General. McClellan hesitated, plainly hoping that one of his aides would take the flowers for him, but the woman thrust the blossoms up into his hands. He took them with a forced smile. "Poor people," he said when they were out of earshot. "They believe we've come to liberate them."

"You haven't?" Starbuck could not resist the question.

"This is not a war to divest United States citizens of

their lawful property, not even those citizens foolish enough to make armed rebellion against their government." The General sounded peeved at having to make the explanation. "This is a conflict about preserving the union, and if I believed for one moment that we were risking white men's blood to free slaves I would resign my commission. Isn't that so, Marcy?" He hurled the request for confirmation over his shoulder and Marcy, a gloomy-looking staff officer, confirmed that was indeed the General's firm opinion. McClellan suddenly scowled at the hyacinths in his hand and tossed them to the side of the road, where the blossoms scattered across a puddle. Starbuck turned in his saddle and saw that the Negroes were still watching the horsemen. He felt a sudden temptation to dismount and gather up the flowers, but just as he twitched his reins Pinkerton's horse trod the blossoms into the mud.

The sight of the Negroes provoked Colonel Lassan, who spoke perfect English, to tell of a slave girl he had met in Williamsburg. "Only nineteen, and a pretty thing. She had four sons already and each one of them whelped off a white man. She reckoned that made her boys more valuable. She was proud of that. She said a good half-breed male infant could sell for five hundred dollars."

"A pretty half-breed girl would fetch a deal more," Pinkerton offered.

"And some are damn near white," a staff officer observed. "Damned if I could tell the difference."

"Buy a white one, Lassan, and take her home," Pinkerton suggested.

"Why just one?" the Frenchman asked with mock innocence. "I could manage a boatload if they were all pretty enough."

"Is it true," McClellan broke into the conversation in a tone which suggested he disapproved of such idle and lascivious talk, "is it true," he repeated as he stared intently at Starbuck, "that Robert Lee is made second-in-command to Johnston?"

"I'd not heard as much, sir," Starbuck said truthfully.

"I pray it is true," McClellan said with a thoughtful frown. "Lee's always been too cautious. A weak man. He doesn't like responsibility. He lacks moral firmness, and men like that prove timid under fire. I've noticed it. What do they call Lee in the South?" he asked Starbuck.

"Granny, sir."

McClellan gave a short bark of a laugh. "I suspect a young Napoleon can manhandle a grandmother, eh, Lassan?"

"Indeed, *mon General.*"

"But can he handle a hundred and fifty thousand rebels?" McClellan asked, then fell silent as he pondered that question. They were riding through an area where infantry was encamped and the northern troops, discovering that their General was in the vicinity, ran to the road and began cheering. Starbuck, dropping back from McClellan's side, noted how the small General was immediately encouraged by the troops' adulation and how genuine that adulation was. The men were invigorated by McClellan's presence just as the General was vivified by their cheers. There were even greater cheers when he stopped his horse and begged a soldier to lend him his smoking pipe so he could light himself a cigar. That homely touch seemed especially moving to the infantrymen who crowded around to touch the General's big bay horse.

"Tell us when we're going to beat the rebs, General!" a man shouted.

"In good time! All in good time! You know I won't risk your lives unnecessarily! All in good time!" One of the men offered the General a piece of hardtack and McClellan raised huge cheers by disingenuously inquiring whether you were supposed to eat the thing or use it to shingle a roof.

"He's a wonderful man," James confided to his brother.

"Isn't he!" Starbuck said. In these last few days he had discovered that the best way to handle James was to offer a bland agreement to everything his brother said, yet even that small gesture was sometimes hard. James's relief and pleasure at the prodigal's return were heartfelt and he wanted to make Starbuck happy as a reward for that change of heart, but his attentions could be cloying. James might believe, like his father, that tobacco was the devil's weed, but if Starbuck wanted to smoke then James was happy to buy cigars from the army's sutlers whose wagons acted as trading posts wherever a regiment was encamped. James even pretended to believe Starbuck's claim that he needed wine and whiskey to settle his dyspeptic stomach and used his own money to buy the so-called medicine.

James's tender assiduity only increased Starbuck's guilt, a guilt that was worsened when he saw how much his brother liked having his company. James was proud of his brother, envied him indeed, and took pleasure in spreading the story that his brother, far from having been a copperhead this past year, had in fact been an agent for the North ever since the war's first shots. Starbuck did not deny the story, but James's pleasure in it only made the younger brother's conscience more tender as he contemplated betraying the trust. Though, perversely, the prospect of that betrayal became ever more inviting because it meant returning to Richmond and so escaping James's attentions. All that was delaying Starbuck's return was the list of questions which he was supposed to deliver to Adam. Those questions were being devised by McClellan and Pinkerton, but as each day brought fresh rumors of rebel reinforcements, so each day added more questions and amended those already on the list.

Another rush of eager soldiers came to surround the General, so many that James and Starbuck were driven apart by the press of bodies. Starbuck's horse edged sideways and began cropping at the grass growing between the muddy ruts cut into the road's verge. General McClellan delivered his customary speech about leading his precious boys to victory, but only when the time was right and the circumstances propitious. The men cheered the words as the General rode on westward.

"They will follow him anywhere," a sardonic voice spoke softly from just behind Starbuck. "Unfortunately he never wants to lead them anywhere."

Starbuck turned to see that the speaker was the savage-looking French military attache, Colonel Lassan, whose ruined eye was covered with a mildewed patch. The Frenchman's uniform was one of faded glory, the metallic thread of his tunic tarnished and his epaulettes ragged. He wore a massive, steel-hilted, straight-bladed sword, and had two revolvers holstered on his saddle. He lit a cigar and offered it to Starbuck. The gesture allowed the other staff officers to ride on by, which was evidently what the Frenchman desired. "A hundred and fifty thousand men?" Lassan asked skeptically.

"Maybe more." Starbuck had taken the cigar. "Thank you."

"Seventy thousand?" The Frenchman lit a cigar for himself, then clicked his tongue to make his horse walk obediently on.

"Sir?"

"I'm guessing, monsieur, that General Johnston has seventy thousand men. At the most, and that your mission is to deceive General McClellan." He smiled at Starbuck.

"The suggestion, sir, is outrageous," Starbuck protested hotly.

"Of course it's outrageous," Lassan said in an amused tone, "but also true, yes?" Ahead of them, dimly visible through a squall of rain that was sweeping toward the party of horsemen, the bulbous yellow shape of one of Professor Lowe's balloons swayed in the gray sky. "Let me tell you my position, Mr. Starbuck," Lassan continued suavely. "I am an observer, sent by my government to watch the war and to report to Paris what techniques and weapons might be useful to our own army. I am not here to take sides. I am not like the Count of Paris or the Prince de Joinville" – he gestured at two elegant French staff officers who rode close behind the General – "who have come here to fight for the North. I frankly do not care which side wins. It is not my business to care, only to observe and to write reports, and it seems to me that perhaps it is time I watched the fighting from the southern side."

Starbuck shrugged, as if to suggest that Lassan's decisions were none of his business.

"Because I would very much like to see how seventy thousand men plan to outwit a hundred and twenty thousand," Lassan said.

"The rebels' one hundred and fifty thousand men," Starbuck said doggedly, "will dig in and see the northerners off with cannon fire."

"Not so," Lassan said. "You can't afford to have so many Yankees sitting on your doorstep, nor can you afford to match McClellan at siege warfare. The man may be a bombast, but he knows his engineering. No, you rebels have to outmaneuver him and the battle will be fascinating. My problem, of course, is that I am not allowed to cross the lines. My choices are either to sail to Bermuda and pay a blockade runner to smuggle me into one of the

343

Confederacy's ports, or else to go west and work my way back overland through Missouri. Either way I shall miss this spring's fighting. Unless, that is, you will consent to allow me to accompany you when you go back to the rebel side?"

"If I go back to the rebel side," Starbuck said with as much haughtiness as he could muster, "I shall do so as a servant of the United States."

"Nonsense!" Lassan said equably. "You're a rogue, Mr. Starbuck, and one rogue can always recognize another. And you're an inventive liar. The 2nd Florida Brigade! Very good, Mr. Starbuck, very good. Yet surely there are not enough white men living in Florida to make one brigade, let alone two! Do you know why General McClellan believes you?"

"Because I'm speaking the truth."

"Because he wants to believe you. He desperately needs to be outnumbered. That way, you see, no disgrace attaches to his defeat. So when will you be going back?"

"I cannot say."

"Then let me know when you can say," Lassan said. Somewhere ahead of the horsemen there sounded the bark of artillery fire, the noise dimmed by the damp air. The sound seemed to be coming from the left-hand side of the road beyond a distant belt of trees. "Watch now," Lassan said to Starbuck. "We shall stop our advance at any moment. You see if I'm not right."

The guns cracked again, and suddenly General McClellan raised a hand. "We might pause here," the General announced, "just to rest the horses."

Lassan offered Starbuck an amused look. "Are you a betting man?"

"I've played some poker," Starbuck said.

"So do you think the rebels' pair of deuces will beat the Young Napoleon's royal flush?"

344

"Nothing can beat a royal flush," Starbuck said.

"It depends on who is holding it, Mr. Starbuck, and whether they dare play it. Maybe the General doesn't want to get his nice new cards dirty?" The Frenchman smiled. "What are they saying in Richmond? That the war is lost?"

"Some are," Starbuck said, and felt himself coloring. He had said that himself, and had tried to persuade Sally of it.

"It isn't," Lassan said, "not as long as the Young Napoleon is the South's enemy. He's frightened of shadows, Mr. Starbuck, and I suspect your job is to make him see shadows where there are none. You're one of the reasons why seventy thousand men might well beat a hundred and twenty."

"I'm just a northerner who has come to his senses," Starbuck retorted.

"And I, monsieur, am the King of Timbuctoo," Lassan said. "Let me know when you want to ride home." He touched his hat and spurred on, and Starbuck, watching the Frenchman ride toward the sound of the guns, suddenly knew he was wrong and Sally was right. The hog was still squealing, and the war was not lost.

"You think the war's lost, you bastard?" Sergeant Truslow grabbed hold of Izard Cobb's ear, ignoring the man's yelp of pain. "If I tell you to hurry, you towheaded piece of shit, you hurry. Now hurry!" He kicked Cobb in the rear. A bullet whistled overhead, making Cobb duck. "And hurry upright!" Truslow shouted, "you goddamn son of a pregnant bitch!"

A burst of smoke showed as a cannon fired from the far tree line. The fuse smoke of the shell traced a tiny gray streak in the air, visible only to the men almost directly in line with the missile's trajectory. Sergeant Truslow, seeing the shell coming, knew there was no time to take cover and

345

so pretended insouciance. The missile slammed into the railroad embankment behind him just a heartbeat before the cannon's noise cracked over the river and marshes.

"Corporal Bailey!" Truslow shouted almost as soon as the dirt thrown up by the striking shell had subsided.

"Sergeant!"

"Dig that shell out!" The shell had failed to explode, which meant there could be a perfectly usable missile buried in the soft dirt of the embankment. If there had been a Confederate artillery battery nearby Truslow would have offered the gunners the salvaged shell to be returned to its senders, but lacking any gunners who might appreciate the gift, he reckoned he would rig it as a land torpedo.

The Legion was on the southern bank of the Chickahominy River, hard by the trestles of the Richmond and York Railroad bridge. The last Confederate locomotive to cross the bridge had steamed by three hours before, dragging behind it all the rolling stock from the depot at White House and the sidings of Tunstall's Station. The engineers had then set charges to the bridge, lit the fuses, and watched as nothing happened. The Faulconer Legion, the nearest infantry unit to the bridge, had then been ordered to hold off the enemy's skirmishers while the engineers determined just what had gone wrong with their explosives.

The bridge was no great piece of engineering. It did not have to fly across a cavernous gorge or carry the rails between two mighty hills; instead it was little more than a low trestled pier that plodded through the marshes, splashed across the river, then went stolidly on for another wet quarter mile until the rails again reached solid ground on the Chickahominy's far bank. It was on that solid ground that the Yankees had unlimbered two field guns beside a dense grove of moss-hung trees, and now the northern artillery fire was crashing across the grassy marsh with its stagnant pools, stunted bushes, and reed beds. Some dismounted northern cavalrymen were also on the far ground, adding their carbine fire to the cannonade, while yet another group of dismounted cavalrymen was advancing along the trestle bridge in the hope of driving the southern engineers away.

"Sergeant Hutton!" Truslow shouted. "Bring your squad! Hurry now!"

Carter Hutton shouted at his men to close on the embankment where Truslow formed them in two ranks. For a few seconds they made a tempting target for the gunners, but Truslow had been timing the cannon fire and knew he had a half minute while the artillerymen reloaded. "Aim at those bastards! Straight down the rails! Sights at three hundred yards." He glanced at the advancing cavalrymen who had not recognized the danger and still advanced along the dry rails instead of using the marshy ground on either side of the trestles. "Fire!" Truslow shouted. "Now get down, off the rails, hurry!"

Five seconds later a shell screamed just above the place where Truslow's twin files had been standing and exploded harmlessly in the trees behind the Legion's position. The smoke from Truslow's volley cleared to show that the advancing cavalrymen had scattered into the rain-filled pools on either side of the bridge. "Keep their heads down!" Truslow shouted, then turned as Andrew Bailey walked up with the excavated shell cradled in his arms. It was a ten-pound shell, just under three inches across, with a zinc plug in its nose. Truslow placed the shell on a rail tie and used the back blade of his bowie knife to unscrew the plug. Two men crouching nearby edged fearfully away, earning a look of scorn from Truslow.

The zinc plug had sealed the shaft sunk into the shell. In the shaft was a sliding plunger tipped with a brass percussion cap that should have been thrown forward by the shell's impact to explode on the underside of the plug. The sliding plunger was held in place by two thin and brittle metal projections that were designed to stop the detonator slipping forward and exploding when the shell was being transported or manhandled. Only the violent impact of a landing shell should have sufficient force to snap the metal projections, but this shell, landing in the soft earth of the embankment, had stayed intact.

Truslow used the knife blade to break the twin projections, then turned the shell upside down to shake the plunger loose. The plunger, topped with its percussion cap, had a narrow hole drilled down its center and filled with explosive. That powder was supposed to carry the fire down to the main charge that was protected from damp by a paper diaphragm. Truslow used a stick to pierce the diaphragm, then half filled the shell's empty fuse shaft with gunpowder taken from rifle cartridges. Lastly he put the plunger back into its tube, but now, instead of dropping to the bottom of the shaft, the plunger protruded an inch above the shell's nosecone. If anyone were to strike the exposed plunger the fire would lance down into the shell, explode the gunpowder Truslow had put in the shaft, and so ignite the main charge.

Now he needed to place the shell. Once the last train had passed the engineers had pulled up the steel rails and loaded them on the train's wagons for transport to Richmond, but they had left the wet wooden ties sunk in the ground. Truslow had two men dig up one of the ties, then excavate a hole in the coffin-shaped space the tie had left imprinted in the railbed. He placed the shell in the hole, its point uppermost, then put a stone next to it and carefully balanced the rail tie on the stone. He very gently rocked the tie, moving it an inch up and down, then stepped back to admire his work. The tie seemed to be raised an inch or so from its position, but with any luck the Yankees would not notice and a man would step on the tie and so bang the wood down onto the percussion cap.

"Enjoying yourself, Sergeant?" Major Bird had walked forward from the tree line where most of the Legion waited.

"Pity to waste a good shell," Truslow said, detecting a slight note of disapproval in Bird's otherwise innocent question.

Bird was not certain that land torpedoes were an entirely sporting method of waging war, yet he also knew that to wage a war on sporting lines was a ridiculous notion, the sort of notion his brother-in-law would entertain. War was about killing, not about obeying arcane rules of chivalry. "A letter's just arrived for you," he told Truslow.

"For me?" Truslow asked, astonished.

"Here." Bird took the letter from his pocket and handed it over, then used his half binocular to see how the engineers were progressing. "What's taking all the time?"

"Damp fuses," Truslow said, then brushed his hands against his coat before opening the delicate pink envelope and taking out the single pink sheet that must have come from a prewar stock of gilded and deckled paper. Truslow peered at the signature first. "It's from my Sally!" He sounded surprised. A bullet whistled past his ear and a shell tumbled overhead, making an eerie wail as it passed.

"Oh good," Major Bird said, not at Truslow's news, but because the engineers were at last scrambling back toward the southern bank.

"Give them cover!" Truslow shouted, and the skirmishers' rifles snapped angrily across the river. "I didn't know my Sally could even write."

Judging from the envelope, Bird thought, she could not.

It was a miracle the letter had arrived at all, except the army was good at trying to work that particular miracle. Few things benefited morale as much as letters from home. "What does she say?" Bird asked.

"Can't rightly tell," Truslow growled.

Bird gave the Sergeant a shrewd glance. Truslow was, without doubt, the toughest man in the Legion, indeed he was probably the toughest man Bird had ever met, yet there was a look of embarrassed shame in Truslow's eyes now. "Can I help?" Bird asked casually.

"It's the girl's writing," Truslow said. "I can make out her name, just about, but not much else."

"Let me," Bird said, who knew full well that Truslow was no great reader. He took the letter, then looked up as the engineers ran past him. "Fall back!" Bird shouted at the men of K Company, then he looked down at the letter again. "My God," Bird exclaimed. The handwriting was truly appalling.

"Is she all right?" Truslow immediately asked, his voice full of anxiety.

"It's just her handwriting, Sergeant, nothing else. Let me see now. You'll be surprised to hear from her, she says, but she is indeed well and she reckons that she ought to have written a long time ago, but says she's just as stubborn as you are which is why she didn't write," Bird paraphrased. He and Truslow, left alone on the embankment, were suddenly the target for a flurry of carbine shots. An engineer shouted at the two men to get back before the fuse was lit and so they began walking slowly toward the safety of the trees. "She says she's sorry for what happened," Bird went on reading the letter as the cavalry bullets whistled around them, "but she's not sorry for what she did. Does that make sense?"

"Never could make hide or hair out of what that girl

said," Truslow commented gruffly. In truth he missed Sally. She was a stubborn little bitch, but the only kin he had.

Bird hurried on, not wanting to embarrass Truslow by noticing the Sergeant's tears. "She says that she saw Nate Starbuck! This is interesting. He came to her when they let him out of prison and he asked her to write to you and promise that he'll be coming back to the Legion. So that's why she's writing. I must say," Bird said, "that Starbuck has a curious way of announcing his return."

"So where is he?" Truslow demanded.

"She doesn't say." Bird turned the letter over. The engineers had lit the fuse and the spark-spitting trail hissed unnoticed past the two men. Bird frowned as he tried to decipher the second page. "She said that's why she wrote, because Nate asked, but she's glad he asked because it's time you and she became friends. And she also says she has a new job, one you'd approve of, but she doesn't say what it is. There, that's it." Bird handed the letter back to Truslow. "I'm sure you can make it out for yourself now that I've described it."

"Reckon I can," Truslow said, then sniffed again. "So Mr. Starbuck's coming back!"

"According to your daughter, yes." Bird sounded dubious.

"So you won't need to appoint an officer to K Company?"

"I wasn't going to," Bird said.

"Good," Truslow said. "After all, we elected Starbuck, didn't we?"

"I'm afraid you did." And much against General Faulconer's will, Bird reflected happily. Over seven hundred men had placed votes in the election of field officers and Starbuck's name had been written onto more than five hundred of the slips.

"And if elections mean anything," Truslow said, "then Starbuck should be here, shouldn't he now?"

"I suppose he should," Bird said, "but I confess I can't see General Faulconer allowing it. Or Colonel Swynyard." Not that Swynyard was much in evidence these days. So far as Bird could determine the brigade's second-in-command was lost in a perpetual stupor brought on by an unending supply of four-dollar-a-gallon skull-rot whiskey.

"A dollar of my money says that Starbuck can whip the General," Truslow said. "He's a smart one, Starbuck."

"A dollar?" Bird asked. "Done." He shook Truslow's grimy hand just as the bridge exploded behind them. Three hundred pounds of gunpowder shattered the stilts and sent the old timbers spinning into the air. Smoke and noise boiled across the marshes, startling a hundred fowl up from the reed beds. The river water seemed to recoil from the explosions, then washed back with a great rush to send a plume of steam billowing after the smoke. Where there had been a bridge there was now just a line of rotted, blackened stumps in the churning water, while up and downstream the debris splashed into the Chickahominy or else slapped down into the stagnant marsh pools where the cotton-mouths and moccasins squirmed away.

One piece of wood flew high into the air and then tumbled down with an unerring aim to smack direct onto the tie that Truslow had balanced with such care on the stone. The impact of the wood banged the tie onto the per-cussion cap and the shell beneath exploded, biting a small crater into the rain-weakened embankment. "Son of a bitch," Truslow said, evidently speaking of the wasted effort he had expended on the land torpedo, but Major Bird saw that the Sergeant was smiling anyway. Such happiness, he decided, was something to be prized in wartime. Today might be filled with laughter, yet tomorrow could bring what the preachers called the long dark home in the dirt. And the thought of such graves filled Bird with a sudden terror. Suppose Truslow did not live to see his Sally again? Or suppose his own dear Priscilla were widowed? That thought filled Thaddeus Bird with the dread that he was not tough enough to be a soldier. Because war, to Bird, was a game, despite all his caustic preaching to the contrary. War, to Bird, was a game of wits in which the unregarded schoolteacher would prove he was wittier and cleverer and faster and better than all the rest. Yet when the wax-skinned dead were lined in sepulchral judgment, and their bruised, dirt-clotted eyes asked clever Bird to explain why they had died, he had no answer.

The two Yankee guns fired a last futile time and their shells skipped and slapped across the marsh. The river's turmoil subsided until the water once again slid slow and gray past the blackened remnants of the bridge to carry its dead cargo of white-bellied fish toward the sea. A mist crept off the wetland to mingle with the gunsmoke. The woods were filled with whippoorwills, and Major Bird, who did not believe in God, suddenly wished to Almighty God that this goddamn war was over.

PART THREE

THE ARMIES CAME TO A STOP IN A CURVE which ran around Richmond's northeastern flank. General Johnston had now retreated so far that the northern soldiers could hear the hours being tolled on Richmond's church bells and, when the wind was in the west, smell the city's rich stench of tobacco and coalsmoke.

Richmond's newspapers grumbled that the Yankees had been allowed too close to the city and the doctors of both armies complained because so many troops were stationed in the disease-ridden marshes of the Chickahominy River. The hospitals filled with men dying of the river's fever, an ailment that, even as the days warmed toward summer's stifling heat, made its victims shake with uncontrollable fits of shivering. Doctors explained that the fever was a natural consequence of the invisible miasma that crept from the river with the sepulchral mists which whitened the marshes at dawn and dusk, and if the armies could but move to higher ground then the fever would disappear, but General Johnston insisted that the fate of Richmond depended on the river and that his men must therefore endure the mist-borne miasma. There was a strategy, Johnston insisted, and in the face of that military word the doctors could do nothing but abandon their arguments and watch their patients die.

At the end of May, on a Friday afternoon that was sultry and still, Johnston assembled his aides and explained that strategy. He had pinned a map to the parlor wall of the house that served as his headquarters and was using a walnut-handled toasting fork as a pointer. "You see, gentlemen, how I have forced McClellan to straddle the Chickahominy? The northern army is a divided force, gentlemen, a divided force." He emphasized the remark by rapping the map north and south of the river with the toasting fork. "One of the first rules of war is never to divide your force in the face of the enemy, but that is just what McClellan has done!" Johnston was in one of his didactic moods, treating his aides as though they were a group of new cadets at West Point. "And why should a general never divide his force?" he now asked, peering expectantly at his aides.

"Because it can be defeated in detail, sir," one of the aides replied smartly.

"Precisely. And tomorrow morning, gentlemen, at dawn, we shall obliterate this half of the northern army." Johnston tapped the toasting fork on the map. "Obliterate, gentlemen, obliterate."

He had indicated that portion of the map which lay east of Richmond and south of the Chickahominy River. The river's source lay northwest of the city, then, widening swiftly, the watercourse ran slantwise across the city's northern approaches and down through the lowlands that lay to the east of Richmond before it joined the wider flow of the James. Johnston's Confederate army was all south of the river, but McClellan's larger force was divided; half the troops were north of the Chickahominy's malarial swamps and half were south. It was Johnston's intention to crash out of the dawn mists and tear that southern half into bloody ruin before the Yankee troops north of the river could march over their replacement bridges to rescue their beleaguered colleagues. "And we shall do it tomorrow morning, gentlemen, at dawn," Johnston said, and could not resist a satisfied smile when he saw their astonishment.

He was pleased because their surprise was exactly the response he wanted. Johnston had informed no one of his plans; neither his second-in-command, General Smith, nor even his President, Jefferson Davis. There were too many spies in Richmond, and too many men who might be tempted to desert to the enemy with the news, and to prevent that betrayal Johnston had hatched his plans in secret and kept them hidden until now, the afternoon before battle, when his aides must carry his orders to the divisional commanders.

Daniel Hill's division would lead the attack, striking at the center of the enemy lines. "Hill must fight alone for a while," Johnston explained to his aides, "because we want to suck the Yankees in, embroil them, then we'll hit their flanks, here and here." The toaster rapped on the map, tearing it each time and showing how, like the outer tines of a trident, the twin attacks would slam into an enemy who would have conveniently impaled himself on the trident's central spike. "Longstreet strikes their northern flank," Johnston continued, "while General Huger's division hits their southern, and by midday, gentlemen, the Yankees will be dead, prisoners, or fugitives in the White Oak Swamp." Johnston could taste the victory already; he could hear the cheers as he rode into Richmond's Capitol Square and see the envy on the faces of his rival generals like Beauregard and Robert Lee. The plan, he knew, was brilliant. All that lay between this moment and glory was the battle that would begin when his gray-clad troops swarmed out of the dawn mists, and if those troops had surprise on their side, then victory, Johnston believed, was assured.

Three aides were given the sealed orders to carry to the three generals of division. Adam Faulconer was ordered to ride to General Huger's headquarters, which lay on the very edge of Richmond. "One set of orders," Johnston's chief of staff, an affable man called Morton, said as he handed the sealed packet to Adam, "and your signature here, Adam." Colonel Morton held out a receipt which acknowledged that Adam had indeed taken possession of the envelope. "You get Huger to sign the receipt here, see? Old Huger will probably invite you to supper, but be back here by midnight. And for God's sake, Adam, make sure he knows what he's supposed to be doing tomorrow." That was why Johnston had taken such care to demonstrate his strategy to his aides; so that they, in turn, could answer his generals' questions. Johnston knew that if he had fetched the generals to his headquarters the army would have smelt the imminent excitement and some wretched man would have been bound to slip over to the enemy in the night and warn them that trouble was brewing.

Adam signed the receipt, thus acknowledging that he had taken responsibility for one set of orders, then he put the paper into a leather pouch on his belt. "I'd be on your way," Colonel Morton advised, "before the rain comes. And make sure Huger signs that paper, Adam! Either him or his chief of staff. No one else."

Adam waited on the house verandah as his horse was saddled. The air was motionless and stagnant, heavy and dark, matching his brooding and despondent mood. He fingered the precious order, wondering if the destruction of all his hopes lay inside the sealed envelope. Perhaps, he thought, the envelope was the key to southern victory, and he imagined the northern army fleeing as they had at Bull Run, and in his fears he saw panicked men floundering in the chest-high sloughs of White Oak Swamp and being shot down by malicious, gleeful rebels like the cackling fiends who had fired from the summit of Ball's Bluff. He saw the Chickahominy spilling blood-reddened waters into the James and shuddered at the realism of his imaginings, and for a mad second he was tempted to take his horse and gallop it across the lines, roweling its flanks bloody as he spurred past the astonished Confederate pickets and so to the northern army. Then he thought of the grief that such a desertion would cause his father, and he thought of Julia in Richmond, and all the old turmoil surged up inside Adam. The war was wrong, yet he was a Faulconer and so heir to a family that had ridden into battle beside George Washington. Faulconers did not disgrace their lineage by deserting to the enemy.

Except how could the country founded by Washington be the enemy?

Adam fingered the orders in his belt pouch and wondered for the thousandth time why the Young Napoleon had proved so hesitant. Adam had betrayed the South's weakness on the peninsula and as a consequence had expected McClellan to break out of Fort Monroe like an avenging angel, but instead the northern commander had chosen a stately, cautious approach that had given the rebels ample time to stiffen and thicken the defenses of Richmond. And now, just when the North was within an easy afternoon's walk of Richmond, the rebels were planning an onslaught that could tear the heart from the northern army, and Adam, standing on the verandah and watching clouds black as night heap ominously above the stagnant forests, knew that he was incapable of stopping the disaster. He did not have the courage to desert.

"Young Adam! Don't move!" Colonel Morton pushed his head through the muslin curtains of a window at the verandah's far end. "We've got another letter for you!"

"Very good, sir," Adam acknowledged. An orderly had just brought Adam's horse to the front of the house and

Adam told the man to tie the reins to the balustrade. The horse lowered its head and grazed a patch of grass that grew thick by the verandah steps. A slave who belonged to the owner of the commandeered house was digging at the hoof-trampled remains of a vegetable garden. The man was tired and kept pausing, but then he would remember Adam's presence on the verandah and so he would wipe his brow and bend again to his work. Adam, watching the man, felt an impulse of irrational and unfair anger at the whole black race. Why in God's name had anyone imported them to America, for without them the country would surely be the happiest, most peaceful land on earth. That unbidden thought made him feel ashamed of himself. It was not the fault of the slaves, but of the slavocracy. It was not the black race, but his own kind who had disturbed the peace and soured the land's content. "It's too hot to work, isn't it?" he called to the slave, trying to make open amends for his private thoughts.

"Too hot, massa. Certain too hot."

"I'd rest if I were you," Adam said.

"Plenty rest in heaven, Lord Jesus be praised, massa," the slave said and thrust the spade's broad blade back into the reddish, dull soil.

"Here you are, Adam." Colonel Morton strode onto the verandah, his spurs clinking as he walked. "We're lending Pete Longstreet some of Huger's men. Huger won't like it, but Longstreet will be advancing closer to the Yankees, so he needs the extra rifles. For God's sake be politic with Huger."

"Of course, sir." Adam took the proffered envelope. "Will you be requiring . . . " He had begun to ask whether Colonel Morton would want another signature from General Huger acknowledging receipt of this second set of orders, but then Adam checked his words. "Very good, sir."

"Back by midnight, young Adam, we all need our beauty sleep tonight. And be gentle with old Huger. He's a prickly beast."

Adam rode west. Where the road passed through the woods the air seemed even more oppressive. Leaves hung motionless, their stillness oddly threatening. The day felt unnatural, but so much of Adam's world seemed unreal these days, even Julia, and that thought reminded him that he should make an effort to see her soon. She had written with her mysterious summons, and even though she had insisted that her message was not of a personal nature Adam could not shake a suspicion that Julia wanted to end the engagement. Of late Adam had begun to think that he did not really understand Julia, and to apprehend that her desires were altogether more complicated than he had ever supposed. On the surface she was a conventional, pious, and dutifully gracious young lady, but Adam was subtly aware of a quicksilver vivacity that Julia kept hidden, and it was that quicksilver quality that made Adam feel unworthy of her. He suspected his mother had possessed the same quality and that it had been crushed out of her by his father.

Adam stopped his horse in a stretch of woods where no army camps were visible. His journey had taken him through a score of regimental camps, but suddenly he was alone in a heavy, dark, and still forest and able to tease into the light an idea that had been flickering in the back of his mind. He opened his pouch and brought out the two messages. They were wrapped in identical light brown envelopes, sealed with identical blobs of scarlet wax, and addressed in the same spiky black handwriting. The battle orders were thicker than the second set of instructions, but otherwise there was nothing to distinguish one envelope from the other.

He brought out the receipt. It mentioned one set of orders only.

Adam looked back at the envelopes. Suppose, he thought, he simply forgot to deliver the battle orders? Suppose Huger did not march in the morning. Suppose then that the North won tomorrow's battle and took Richmond; who would then care about a missing set of orders? And if, by some outlandish chance, the South won tomorrow without Huger's troops, who would care? And even if his dereliction were discovered – and Adam was not so foolish as to presume that it would not eventually be found out – then it need not be construed as an act of treason, but rather as one of simple forgetfulness or, at worst, of carelessness. The dereliction would doubtless cost him his job on Johnston's staff, but it would not bring disgrace, merely an unfortunate reputation for carelessness. And maybe, he told himself, he should spend this war sheltering beneath his father's wing. Maybe he would be happier as his father's chief of staff where, if nothing else, he could at least try to preserve his father's tenants and neighbors in the Legion from the worst rigors of war. "Oh, dear God," he murmured aloud, and it was really a prayer for his own happiness and not for guidance because he already knew what he was going to do.

Slowly, deliberately, and with due ceremony, Adam tore the battle orders across, and then across again, and then he tore the ragged pieces into further shreds. He tore them as though he were rending the very fabric of history, and when the orders were reduced to a handful of scraps, he scattered the specks of paper into the black waters of a ditch beside the road. And with that act of treacherous destruction there came a sudden leaping happiness. He had sabotaged victory! He had done the Lord's work on a black day and he felt as though a wearisome burden of guilt and indecision had rolled away from him. He spurred his horse westward.

A half hour later Adam came to the small house that served as Huger's headquarters where, with a punctiliousness that verged on insubordination, Adam insisted on receiving the General's signature before he handed over the single remaining envelope. He then stood respectfully aside while Huger opened and read the single sheet of orders. The General, proud of his French ancestry, was a fussy, cautious man who had enjoyed a successful career in the old U.S. Army and now relished making unfavorable comparisons between his old employer and his new. "I don't understand!" he told Adam after reading the order a second time.

"I'm sorry, sir?" Adam was standing with Huger's aides on a verandah that looked down on Gillies Creek. The house was so close to Richmond that Adam could see the sprawl of roofs and chimneys that lay behind Rockett's Landing where the masts and yards of a dozen ships trapped by the barricade at Drewry's Bluff showed in the evening's gloom. Beneath the house, at the end of a long meadow dotted with the wagons and guns belonging to Huger's artillery, the Richmond and York Railroad ran beside the creek, and in the fading light that was made worse by the mass of dark cloud, a train steamed slowly toward the city. The train drew a curious collection of flatcars on which was mounted the Confederacy's balloon unit. The balloon itself was a fine confection made from the best silk dresses donated by Richmond's ladies and was raised and lowered by means of a giant winch that was bolted to one of the flatcars. Other flatcars housed the chemical apparatus that manufactured the hydrogen. The balloon, which had been observing the enemy lines beyond the torn-up railhead at Fair Oak Station, was still being winched down as the train clanked and crashed and puffed beneath General Huger's headquarters. "Am I to understand" – the white-haired Huger now peered over a pair of reading glasses at Adam — "that some of my men are being given over to General Longstreet's command?"

"I believe that is so, sir, yes," Adam said.

Huger gave a series of small snuffling snorts that were evidently intended to denote sarcastic laughter. "I suppose," Huger finally observed, "that General Johnston is aware, even dimly aware, that I am senior to General Longstreet?"

"I am sure he is, sir."

Huger was working his dudgeon into a fine display of wounded vanity. "General Longstreet, I seem to remember, was a paymaster in the old army. A mere major. I don't believe he was ever made more than a major or entrusted with any duty more onerous than distributing the troops' wages. Yet now he is to give men under my command their orders?"

"Only a few of your men, sir," Adam observed tactfully.

"And why?" Huger demanded. "Surely Johnston has his reasons? Has he thought to explain those reasons to you, young man?"

Johnston had, but it would have defeated Adam's purpose to have passed on the explanation, so he contented himself with the lame observation that General Longstreet's division was camped closer to the enemy and that therefore it had been thought prudent to beef up his brigades with the extra men. "I'm sure it's only a temporary expedient, sir," Adam finished, then stared past the unhappy Huger to where the train had come to a complete halt while the balloon was winched down the last few feet. The smoke from the locomotive looked oddly white and bright against the black cloud.

"I am not complaining," Huger said indignantly. "I am above such petty considerations, and in the exigencies of this army such insults are to be expected. But it would have been civil of Johnston to have asked if I minded my troops being yielded to the orders of a mere paymaster. Would it not have been civil?" he inquired of his own aides, who both nodded their eager agreement.

"I am certain General Johnston means you no slight, sir," Adam said.

"You may be certain of what you like, young man, but I am more experienced in these matters." Huger, who reckoned himself to be something of a natural aristocrat, drew himself erect so he could look down his nose at Adam. "Perhaps General Johnston needs my men to guard the army's wages, is that it?" This joke was again signaled by a series of snorting snuffles that caused Huger's aides to smile in companionable appreciation. "There was a time," Huger said, folding the orders into a tight square, "when military matters were performed properly in North America. When such things were done in a soldierly fashion. As in a well-organized army." He tossed the folded orders onto a bench suspended by chains hanging from the verandah's beams. "Very well, young man, tell Johnston I've received his orders, even if I cannot understand them. I'm sure you'll want to return to your master before the rain comes, and so I'll bid you good day." This curt dismissal, delivered without even offering Adam as much as a glass of water, was a deliberate snub, but Adam did not mind. He had taken his huge risk and he had played his part well, but he did not think he could go on parrying the General's questions. My God, Adam thought with a pang of terror, but there would be hell to pay when Johnston discovered what had happened. Then, once again, Adam reassured himself that he was guilty of nothing worse than forgetfulness.

He put the signed receipt into his pouch and went back to his horse. It was a Friday evening and he knew he would find Julia in the nearby Chimborazo Hospital. He was feeling guilty about her letter, and knowing that he had this whole evening free, he rode to meet his fiancee. His route took him past one of General Lee's new star-shaped forts that ringed the city. The earthwork was crowned with rows of freshly filled sandbags donated by the sewing circles of Richmond. The ladies had used every spare scrap of available fabric so that the newly placed ramparts looked like a quilt of flowery chintzes, deep velvets, and gaily patterned cottons, and in the sinister light of the storm-threatening dusk, that patchwork effect was oddly cheerful, a domestic touch in a warlike scene. The air, which had been sultry and still all day, suddenly stirred as an unexpected gust of wind lifted the folds of the Confederate battle flag above the gaily colored bastions. The country to the south, beyond the river, was lit by some last slanting rays of sunshine that reached far beneath the clouds so that the land seemed brighter than the sky. Adam, his new act of treachery completed, tried to read into that distant shaft of golden sunlight an augury of happiness and success.

He had to show his headquarters pass to one of the sentries at the guardpost that barred the road into the city. A far-off rumble of thunder sounded like gunfire coming from the land between the rivers. The sentry grimaced. "Reckon there'll be a storm tonight, Major. Right big one, too."

"It looks bad," Adam agreed.

"Never known a spring like it," the sentry said, then paused as a second clap of thunder rolled ominously over the sky. "Maybe it'll drown a Yankee or two. That'll save us having to kill all the sumbitches."

Adam did not respond, but just took his pass back and spurred onward. Lightning stuttered in the northern sky. He urged the horse into a trot, racing against the rain that began to fall in huge and ominous drops just as he turned into the hospital grounds. An orderly told Adam which ward was having the missioner's service and he galloped the horse through the sudden gusting wind that snatched at the smoke dribbling from the thin metal chimneys jutting from each hut. The rain began to fall harder, drumming on the tin roofs and quivering the taut canvas of the tents which had been erected as supplementary wards. He found the right hut, tied his horse to the porch upright, then plunged inside just as an explosion of thunder seemed to tear the heart out of the skies and trigger a veritable cloudburst of rain that rattled so loud on the ward roof that the Reverend John Gordon's voice was quite drowned out. Julia, seated at the wheezing little harmonium, smiled her pleasure at Adam's unexpected arrival. Adam, closing the door behind him, saw that this was one of the Friday nights when Julia's mother had chosen not to come to the hospital. There were just Julia, her father, and the inevitable Mr. Samworth, who looked nervously up at the roof as another crash of thunder bellowed over the sky.

The service limped on, interrupted by thunder and muted by the noise of the rain. Adam, standing by a window, watched the night fall across Richmond and saw the new darkness punctuated by slivers of lightning that offered a hellish luminosity to the city's spires. The storm seemed to intensify like the echoes of a war in heaven, while the rain pounded the roof with such a malevolent force that the Reverend Mr. Gordon gave up the unequal struggle and called for a hymn. Julia pumped the small instrument and led the ward in "Praise God From Whom All Blessings Flow." Once the singing was done the missioner pronounced an inaudible blessing and so abandoned the storm-racked service.

"This must pass over soon!" The Reverend Mr. Gordon had to shout at Adam to make himself heard, yet the storm seemed fixed above the city and relentless in its fury. The ward's roof leaked in a dozen places and Adam helped move the cots away from the cold streams. Julia wanted to see the storm for herself, and wrapping her coat about her, went to stand on the small verandah at the back of the ward where, under the shelter of the shingled lean-to roof, she and Adam watched the great storm shudder the skies above Virginia. Bolt after bolt of lightning cracked down to earth, and crash after crash of thunder echoed in the clouds. Night had fallen, but it was a night riven by fire and made huge by the sky's explosions. A dog howled somewhere in the hospital, while rivers of water ran and gurgled and poured into the black depths of the Bloody Run.

"Mother has a headache. She can always tell when a storm's coming by her headaches," Julia told Adam in an unsuitably cheerful voice, but Julia had always liked storms. She apprehended something very special in nature's fury, believing that she was witnessing a feeble echo of the chaos out of which God had created the world. She clutched her coat tightly about her and, in the lightning flashes, Adam saw that her eyes were bright with excitement.

"You wanted to see me?" Adam asked her.

"I hope you wanted to see me too!" Julia said teasingly, though inwardly she yearned for him to offer a passionate declaration that he would have ridden through a dozen such storms just to be beside her.

"Of course I did, yes," Adam said. He stood decorously apart from Julia though, like her, he had his back pressed hard against the shed's wall, where he gained most benefit from the verandah's small roof. Water poured off the shingles to make a curtain that was lit by a silver sheen whenever lightning flickered from the clouds. "But you wrote to me," Adam reminded her.

Julia had almost forgotten the letter with its hint of an important message and now, so long after, she suspected that the message had probably lost most of its urgency. "It was about your friend Nate Starbuck," she explained.

"Nate?" Adam, half expecting to be told that his engagement was ended, could not hide his surprise.

"He came to call on you just after he'd been released from prison," Julia said. "I happened to be at your father's house and I know I shouldn't have invited him inside, but it was raining almost as hard as it is now and he seemed so desolate that I took pity on him. You don't mind, do you?" She stared up at Adam.

Adam had almost forgotten the impulse that had made him warn his father's servants to turn Starbuck away from the house. At the time and in the wake of the appalling introduction of a fallen woman into the missioner's house, the ban had seemed a just precaution, but Adam's outrage had cooled since that terrible night. "What did he want?" Adam now asked.

Julia paused as a torrent of thunder cracked and faded above the city. Lightning backlit the clouds, flickering across the hidden sky like misted rivers of airborne silver. One lightning bolt had started a fire somewhere in the town of Manchester across the James River, for there was a dull red stuttering glow that lasted a few seconds before the rain drowned it out. "He had a message for you," Julia said. "I thought it was all very mysterious, but he wouldn't explain it to me. He just said you'd understand. He says you're to stop corresponding with his family."

Adam felt a chill run through him. He said nothing, but just stared into the dark river valley where the rain hammered at the sullen water.

"Adam?" Julia inquired.

Adam was suddenly besieged by the image of a noose hanging from a high beam. "He said what?" he managed to ask.

371

"He said that you were to cease corresponding with his family. Does that seem strange to you? It seemed very odd to me. After all, the Starbuck family is in Boston, so how can you correspond with them? I'm told people do get letters through to the North, but I'm sure I can't imagine you going to that kind of trouble just to write to the Reverend Elial Starbuck. And Nate also said that he would explain as soon as he was able, but he was equally mysterious about when that might be."

"Oh, dear God," Adam said and shivered as all the terror came whipping back. He thought of the shame if his father were to discover that his son had betrayed Virginia. And how had Starbuck found out? Had James written to him? There could be no other explanation. How else could Starbuck have discovered it? And if Starbuck knew, who else did? "Where is Nate?" he now asked Julia.

"I don't know. How would I know?" In truth Julia had the strangest idea that Starbuck had crossed the lines, but as her source for that belief was Sally Truslow she did not think it wise to make any mention of it. Julia had finally summoned the courage to visit Sally, going to the house armed with a Bible and a bag full of tracts describing the fearsome terrors of hell awaiting all sinners, but the visit had unexpectedly turned into a joyous morning of laughter in which, instead of attempting to lead the younger woman to the Lord, Julia had found herself admiring Sally's collection of gowns and shawls. They had talked of cambric and chambray, and whether tarlatan could replace tulle as a material for veils, and Julia had fingered Sally's silks and satins, and after the city's damp fears, such talk of baubles and frills had been nothing but relief. Julia's religious beliefs had been offended only by Sally's enthusiastic plans to establish a spiritualist shrine in the house's back quarters, but Sally's evident cynicism and her honest description of how she planned to deceive the clients had ended up sparking Julia's amusement rather than her disapproval. Julia had also been touched by the concern Sally had shown for Starbuck and flustered when Sally had claimed how much Starbuck liked Julia. It had all been very odd, much too odd to explain to Adam, who would surely have exploded in righteous anger at the mere thought of his fiancee visiting one of Richmond's courtesans, though in truth Sally's house had outwardly appeared to be as respectable as any in the city and a good deal cleaner than most. Yet Julia could no more tell Adam of that visit than she could have told her mother. "Does it matter where Nate is?" Julia now asked Adam.

"I suppose not." Adam shifted uneasily, his spur chains and scabbard links clinking softly beneath the roar of the rain and the howl of the wind.

"So what does the message mean?" Julia asked directly. Her curiosity had been piqued by Adam's reaction, which, to her mind, looked startlingly like guilt.

Adam shook his head, but then did offer a halting explanation. "It goes back," he said slowly and not altogether articulately. "Back to when Nate first arrived here. I have been trying. Father anyway tried to restore Nate's family connections. It seemed important." Adam was a bad liar, and to cover his embarrassment he pushed away from the hut's wall and rested his hands on the balustrade. "I think Nate resents our efforts," he finished lamely.

"So it isn't so very mysterious after all?" Julia said, not believing a word Adam had said.

"No," Adam said, "not really."

Julia listened to the dogs howling and the horses whinnying and the tent canvas flogging in the wind. "What did Nate do?" she asked after a long pause.

"What do you mean?"

373

"I mean what did Nate do to lose his family's affections?"

For a long time Adam did not answer, then he shrugged. "He ran away."

"Is that all?"

Adam was certainly not going to tell Julia that there had been a woman involved, an actress who had used Starbuck as her foil, then dropped him in Richmond. "He behaved very badly," Adam said pompously, knowing it to be an inadequate explanation and also an unfair one. "Nate isn't a bad man," he added, but did not know how to finish his qualification.

"Just passionate?" Julia asked.

"Yes," Adam said, "just passionate," then fell silent as a massive explosion of thunder tore the sky apart. A sheet of lightning crashed down on the river's far bank to illuminate the naval yard with a stark white corpse light that was set off with jet-black shadows. "When the Yankees come" – he changed the subject from Nate Starbuck's character – "you should stay at home."

"Did you think I was planning to welcome them to Richmond?" Julia asked tartly.

"You have a flag? I mean a United States flag?" Adam asked.

"No."

"I'm sure there's one in my room in Clay Street. Ask Polly to give it to you. Hang it out of a window at home."

That sounded very supine advice to Julia. "You seem very sure that they will enter Richmond," she said.

"They will," Adam said fervently. "It's God's will."

"It is?" Julia was surprised. "Then why, I wonder, did God allow this war to happen at all?"

"We declared war," Adam said. "Man did that, not God, and it was the South that made the declaration." He fell silent for a while, examining his own conscience and finding it wanting. "I believed everything my father said back then. He told me America just needed a little bloodletting, like a doctor leeching a disease. One sharp battle and we would all learn the wisdom of peaceful negotiations. Now look at it!" He waved a hand out toward the storm and Julia dutifully stared across the valley to where a blue-white splinter of lightning silhouetted the tracery of ships' rigging on the river and spilt white fire along the waterway. The rain drummed the earth and splashed off the ward's roof and poured out of gutters and flooded in the run below the hospital. "We're going to be punished," Adam said.

Julia remembered Starbuck's bravado, quoting John Paul Jones's fine defiance. "I thought we hadn't begun to fight?" She echoed Starbuck's words and rather surprised herself by her belligerence. She had never thought of herself as a supporter of the war party, but she was too engaged in the discussion to realize that she was using a political allegiance as a means of arguing about a personal relationship. "We can't just admit defeat without fighting!" she insisted.

"We're going to be punished," Adam said again. "We unleashed the evil, you see. I saw that today." He fell silent and Julia, thinking he must have witnessed some appalling injury, did not probe, but then Adam offered a quite different explanation, saying how he had found himself blaming a slave for the war. "Don't you see how war brings out the worst in all of us?" he asked her. "All the ropes that bind us to decency and to God are being cut away and we're drifting on a rotten tide of anger."

Julia frowned. "You think the South deserves to lose because you were uncharitable to a slave?"

"I think America is one country," Adam said.

"It sounds to me," Julia said, doing her best to curb a rising anger, "that you're fighting for the wrong side."

"Maybe I am," Adam said quietly, but not so quietly that

Julia could not hear him over the seething rain.

"Then you should go north," Julia said coldly.

"Should I?" Adam asked in an oddly meek voice, as if he really did want her advice.

"You must surely fight for what you believe in," Julia said bluntly.

Adam nodded. "And you?" he asked.

Julia remembered something Sally had said, something that had surprised her: that men, for all their boasts and show, were as weak as newborn kittens. "Me?" Julia asked as though she had not immediately understood what Adam was implying.

"Would you abandon the South?"

"Would you want me to?" Julia asked, and in truth it was an invitation for Adam to woo her and to declare that great love deserved extravagant gestures. Julia did not want love to be commonplace, she wanted it to hold the same life-changing mysteries as religion and to be as tempestuous as the storm that now racked its anger across the whole peninsula.

"I would want you to do whatever your heart and soul tells you to do," Adam said stiffly.

"Then my heart tells me to stay in Virginia," Julia responded just as coldly. "It tells me I should work here, in the hospital. Mother doesn't approve, but I might have to insist. Would you object if I were to become a nurse?"

"No," Adam said, but without the slightest conviction. He seemed bereft, like a traveler marooned in a strange land, then he was saved from saying anything more because the door from the ward opened and the Reverend John Gordon peered anxiously onto the verandah.

"I was fearing the two of you had been washed away," Julia's father said in as strong a reproof as he was capable of delivering. His wife would have protested at the impropriety of Adam and Julia being alone in the darkness, but the Reverend Mr. Gordon could not bring himself to discern anything sinful in their behavior.

"We're quite dry, Father," Julia said, deliberately misconstruing her father's gentle reprimand. "We were just watching the storm."

"'The winds blew, and beat upon that house; and it fell not: for it was founded upon a rock,'" the Reverend John Gordon quoted happily from Matthew's gospel.

"'I came not to send peace,'" Julia quoted from the same gospel, "'but a sword.'" She was looking at Adam as she spoke, but Adam was unaware of her gaze. He was staring across a dark void split by fire and remembering the scraps of white paper shred in a black ditch. That was a trail of treason that should bring northern victory, and in that victory's blessed wake, peace. And surely, Adam told himself, in peace all would be made whole again.

Tomorrow.

The rain-soaked earth steamed in the morning sun. The attack should have been two hours old by now, it should already have ripped the heart from the Yankee lines and be driving the northerners back toward the White Oak Swamp, but nothing moved on the three roads that led from the rebel lines into the Yankee positions.

General Johnston had planned to use the three roads like a trident. Hill's division would advance in the center first, attacking down the Williamsburg Stage Road to assail the northern troops massed behind Fair Oaks Station. Johnston hoped that the Yankee infantry would then close on Hill's advancing troops like swarming bees, only to be struck from the north by Longstreet's division and from the south by Huger's. All that was needed for Hill's division to begin its attack was a message that Longstreet and Huger's

377

troops had advanced from their camps close to Richmond. Longstreet's men should be on the Nine Mile Road, close to Old Tavern, while Huger's division should be on the Charles City Road near White's Tavern.

Except both roads were empty. They were puddled deep by the night's tempestuous rain, but otherwise deserted. The morning mists cleared away to reveal a waterlogged landscape rippled by a brisk cold wind that was strong enough to keep the Yankees' two observation balloons grounded and to snatch at the smoke of the cooking fires that struggled to consume the rain-soaked wood. "Where the hell are they?" Johnston demanded, and sent his aides splashing through the soaked meadows and along the ominously empty roads in search of the missing divisions. "Find them, just find them!" he shouted. By now, according to his timetable, the attacks should already have broken through the Yankee lines and be driving a mass of panicked refugees toward the treacherous White Oak Swamp. Instead the Yankees were oblivious of their fate and the eastern horizon was misted with the smoke of their cooking fires.

An aide came back from General Huger's headquarters to say that he had discovered the General in bed, fast asleep.

"He was what?" Johnston demanded.

"Asleep, sir. All his staff were asleep too."

"After sunup?"

The aide nodded. "Fast asleep, sir."

"Good God Almighty!" Johnston stared in disbelief at the aide. "Didn't he get any orders?"

The aide, a friend of Adam's, hesitated as he looked for a way to spare his friend.

"Well?" Johnston demanded angrily.

"His chief of staff says not, sir," the aide said, with an apologetic shrug in Adam's direction.

378

"Goddamn it!" Johnston snapped. "Morton!"

"Sir?"

"Who took Huger his orders?"

"Major Faulconer did, sir, but I can assure you the orders were delivered. I've got the receipt with the General's signature. Here, sir." Colonel Morton produced the receipt and handed it to the General.

Johnston glanced at the paper. "He did get the orders! Which means he just overslept?"

"So it would seem, sir," the aide who had woken General Huger answered.

Johnston seemed to quiver with a suppressed fury that he was quite unable to express in words. "And where the hell is Longstreet?" he asked instead.

"We're still trying to find him, sir," Colonel Morton reported. He had sent an aide to the Nine Mile Road, but the aide had disappeared as thoroughly as Longstreet's division.

"For the love of God!" Johnston shouted, "find me my goddamn army!"

Adam had hoped to spread confusion by his destruction of Huger's orders, but he could never have dared to hope that the confusion would have been so thoroughly compounded by General Longstreet, who had airily decided that he did not want to advance along the Nine Mile Road and had elected to use the Charles City Road instead. The decision meant that his division had to march clean through the encampments of General Huger's troops. General Huger, rudely woken with orders that he should have been advancing eastward on the Charles City Road, discovered that it was choked solid with Longstreet's troops. "Damn the paymaster," Huger said and ordered breakfast.

A half hour later the paymaster himself came to Huger's headquarters. "Hope you don't mind me using your road,"

Longstreet said, "but my road was too wet for marching. Knee-deep in mud."

"You'll take some coffee?" Huger suggested.

"You're damn cool, Huger, for a man facing battle," Longstreet said, glancing at the generous plate of ham and eggs that had just been served to his fellow General.

Huger knew nothing of any battle, but he was certainly not going to reveal his ignorance to a jumped-up paymaster. "So what are your orders today?" he asked, masking his growing alarm that he might have missed something important.

"Same as yours, I imagine. March east till we find the Yankees, then attack. Is that fresh bread?"

"Help yourself," Huger said, wondering if the world had gone mad. "But I can't advance if you're on my road."

"I'll step aside for you," Longstreet offered generously. "I'll get my fellows over the creek, then give them a rest while you march past us. Will that do?"

"Why not have some ham and eggs too?" Huger asked.

"I'm not sure I'm hungry." He stood and shouted for his chief of staff. He had a division to move and a battle to fight. Good God, he thought, but these things had been arranged better in the old army! So much better.

Back at the army's headquarters General Johnston opened his watch for the hundredth time. The battle should have been four hours old and still not a shot had been fired. The wind rippled the puddles but did little to stir the day's humidity. The muskets would choke up today, Johnston thought. A dry day meant that gunpowder burned clean while wet weather promised fouled rifle barrels and hard ramming for the men. "Where in God's name are they?" he cried in frustration.

General Hill's division had been ready since daybreak. His men, sheltering in woods where great trees had been split apart by the night's lightning strikes, clutched their rifles and waited for the signal to advance. The foremost ranks could see the Yankee picket posts at the far side of a damp clearing. Those guardposts were rough shelters made from felled branches behind which the northern pickets took what cover they could from the weather. Some of the enemy had hung coats and shirts to dry on their crude windbreaks. One Yankee, not suspecting that the woods across the clearing were crammed with an enemy waiting to attack, took a shovel and walked along the tree line. He waved toward the rebels, assuming that he was merely being observed by the same southern pickets with whom, just the day before, he had exchanged coffee for tobacco and a northern newspaper for a southern.

General Hill opened his watch. "Any news?"

"None, sir." The general's aides had ridden to White's Tavern and Old Tavern and seen nothing.

"Have you heard anything from Johnston?"

"Nothing, sir."

"Goddamn it. This ain't no way to win a war." Hill rammed his watch into his coat pocket. "Give the signal!" he shouted at an artillery battery whose three spaced shots would be the agreed signal for the attack to begin.

"You'll advance unsupported?" an aide asked, aghast at the thought of the division taking on half the northern army without any flanking reinforcements.

"They're only goddamn Yankees. Let's see the bastards run. Fire the signal!"

The dull, harsh, soulless sounds of the three signal shots broke the noontime peace. The first shot splintered through the far woods, scattering droplets and pine needles, the second skipped up from the wet meadow to smack into a tree trunk, while the third and last brought on the battle.

*

"Johnston won't attack," James Starbuck assured his brother.

"How do we know?"

"McClellan knew him before the war. Knew him well, so he knows his mind," James explained, oblivious of the irony that the United States Secret Service might be expected to discover a slightly more reliable indicator of enemy intentions than the mind-reading abilities of the commanding General. James reached for the plate of bacon and helped himself. He had always been a healthy eater, and though this was lunchtime and the cooks had provided him with a lavish plate of fried chicken, James had demanded that the bacon left over from breakfast be served as well. "Have some bacon," he invited his brother.

"I've eaten enough." Starbuck was leafing through the enormous pile of newspapers that were brought to wherever the Secret Service had its field headquarters. This pile contained the Louisville *Journal*, the Charleston *Mercury*, the Cape *Codman*, the New York *Times*, the New York *Herald*, the *Mississippian*, the *National Era*, *Harpers Weekly*, the Cincinnati *Gazette*, the Jacksonville *Republican*, the Philadelphia *North American*, and the Chicago *Journal*. "Does anyone read all these papers?" Starbuck asked.

"I do. When there's time. There never is enough time. We don't have enough staff, that's the trouble. Just look at that pile!" James looked up from the newspaper he was reading and gestured at the telegraph messages that needed decoding and that lay untranslated for lack of sufficient clerical help. "Maybe you could join us, Nate?" James now suggested. "The chief likes you."

"When I get back from Richmond, you mean?"

"Why not?" James was delighted with the idea. "Sure you don't want some bacon?"

"Very sure."

382

"You take after Father," James said, cutting a piece of newly baked bread and slathering it with butter, "whereas I've always been fleshy like Mother." He turned a page of the newspaper, then looked up as Pinkerton came into the room. "How's the General?" James asked.

"Sick," Pinkerton said. He paused to steal a rasher of bacon from James's plate. "But he'll live. The doctors have wrapped him in flannel and are dosing him with quinine." General McClellan had gone down with the Chicka-hominy fever and was alternately sweating and shivering in a commandeered bedroom. Pinkerton's Secret Service had taken over a neighboring house, for the General never liked to be far from his best source of information. "But the General's thinking clearly," Pinkerton went on, "and he's agreed it's time you should go back." He pointed what was left of his rasher of bacon at Starbuck.

"Oh, dear God," James said and glanced at his younger brother in consternation.

"You don't have to, Nate," Pinkerton said, "not if you think it's too dangerous." He put the rest of the bacon into his mouth and went to the window to peer up at the sky. "Too damn windy for balloons. Never seen a storm like last night's. Did you sleep?"

"Yes," Starbuck said, hiding the pulse of excitement that fluttered inside him. He had begun to suspect that he would never be given the list of questions and never get back to the southern side and never see Sally or her father again. In truth he was bored, and if he were honest he was most bored with the company of his brother. James was as good a soul as any that walked on earth, but he had no conversa-tion beyond food, family, God, and McClellan. When Starbuck had first come to the Yankee lines he had feared his loyalties would be tested and his reverence for the Stars and Stripes would be resurrected so strongly that it would break his rebel allegiances, but the tedium of James's company had served as a barrier to that renewal of patriotism.

Besides, he had nurtured the image of himself as an outcast, and in the rebel army Starbuck had a reputation as a renegade, a daredevil, a rebel indeed, while in this bigger army with its tighter organization he could only ever be just another young man from Massachusetts who would forever be bounded by his family's expectations. In the South, Starbuck thought, he himself defined what he wanted to be and the only limits to that ambition lay within himself, but in the North he would forever be Elial Starbuck's son. "When?" he asked Pinkerton a little too eagerly.

"Tonight, Nate?" Pinkerton suggested "You'll say you've been traveling." Pinkerton and James had concocted a story to explain why Starbuck had stayed away from Richmond so long. The story claimed that Starbuck had recovered from his prison experience by traveling through the lower Confederacy where he had been delayed by bad weather and unpunctual trains. Pinkerton, like James, had no idea that such a story was unnecessary, that all Starbuck needed was the paper that Pinkerton now produced and that he would deliver to de'Ath, his powerful protector in Richmond. "Putting the General to bed at least made him concentrate on our business," Pinkerton said happily, "so now you can take these questions to your friend." McClellan's questions, just like the false message that de'Ath had provided Starbuck, were sealed inside a sewn oilcloth pouch.

Starbuck took the packet and thrust it into his pocket. He was wearing one of his brother's cast-off Yankee coats, a voluminous double-breasted blue uniform jacket that hung from Starbuck's lean body in great folds.

"We need to know a lot more about Richmond's defenses," Pinkerton explained. "It's going to become a siege, Nate. Our guns against their earthworks, and we want your friend to tell us which forts are the weakest." Pinkerton looked back to James. "Is that bread fresh, Jimmy?"

"Good God." James ignored his chief's question and instead stared wide-eyed at a newly secured copy of the Richmond *Examiner* that lay beside his plate. "Well, I never," he added.

"Bread, Jimmy?" Pinkerton tried again.

"Henry de'Ath's dead," James said, oblivious of his chief's hunger. "Well, I never."

"Who?" Pinkerton demanded.

"Eighty years old, too! A good age for a bad man. Well, I never."

"Who in the name of hell are you talking about?" Pinkerton demanded.

"Henry de'Ath," James said. "That's the end of an era, and no mistake." He peered closely at the newspaper's smudged ink. "They say he died in his sleep. What a rogue, what a rogue!"

Starbuck felt a shiver pass through him, but he dared not betray his sudden worry. Maybe Henry de'Ath was not the man who had sent Starbuck across the lines, but some other man with the same surname. "What sort of rogue?" he asked.

"He had the principles of a jackal," James said, though not without a note of admiration. As a Christian he had to disapprove of de'Ath's reputation, but as a lawyer he felt envy for the man's effectiveness. "He was the only man Andrew Jackson refused to fight in a duel," James went on, "probably because de'Ath had killed six men by then, maybe more. He was lethal with a sword or pistol. And lethal in a courtroom too. I remember Judge Shaw telling me that de'Ath had once boasted to him of knowingly

385

sending at least a dozen innocent men to the scaffold. Shaw naturally protested, but de'Ath claimed that the tree of liberty was irrigated by blood and told Shaw not to be so particular whether the blood was innocent or guilty." James shook his head in reproof at such wickedness. "He always claimed to be half French, but Shaw was certain he was a natural son of Thomas Jefferson." James actually blushed at retelling this scrap of lawyer's gossip. "I'm sure that wasn't true," he added hastily, "but the man attracted that kind of exaggeration. Now he's gone to his final judgment. Jeff Davis will miss him."

"Why?" Pinkerton demanded.

"They were thick as thieves, sir," James said. "De'Ath was an *eminence grise*. Must have been one of Davis's closest advisers."

"Then thank God the bastard's cold in his bed," Pinkerton said cheerfully. "Now is that bread fresh?"

"It is, Chief," James said, "very fresh."

"Carve me a piece, if you would. And I'll thank you for a leg of chicken too. What I thought we'd do" – Pinkerton turned back to Starbuck when he had secured his luncheon – "is send you over the James River tonight. We'll have to put you two or three hours' walk from Petersburg and you'll have to get yourself north from there. You think you can manage that?"

"I'm sure of it, sir," Starbuck said and was astonished that his voice sounded so normal, because inside he was consumed with a stomach-churning terror. De'Ath dead? Then who in Richmond would speak for Starbuck? Who in the Confederacy could guarantee that he was not a deserter? Starbuck shook suddenly. He could not go back! That realization flooded cold into his consciousness. Only de'Ath could vouch for him, and without de'Ath he was friendless in Richmond. Without de'Ath he appeared a double turncoat, doubly despicable, and without de'Ath he could surely never return to the South, let alone rejoin the Legion.

"You're looking nervous, Nate!" Pinkerton said robustly. "Are you worried about going back? Is that it?"

"I shall be fine, sir," Starbuck said.

"I'm sure you will. All my best agents are nervous. Only fools don't show a touch of nerves at the thought of going south." The Scotsman turned in puzzlement as a rumble of gunfire sounded in the long distance. "Is that gunfire?" he asked, "or more thunder?" He crossed the room and opened a window wide. The unmistakable sound of gunfire rolled along the horizon, faded, then swelled again as another battery joined in. Pinkerton listened, then shrugged. "Maybe a gun crew exercising?"

"Can I borrow a horse to take a look?" Starbuck asked. He wanted to be alone to decide his future now that his sponsor was dead. He imagined de'Ath lying in the crumbling mansion with a sardonic smile on his dead lips. Would the old man have left a note exonerating Starbuck? Somehow Starbuck doubted it and he shivered again despite the heat.

"Take my horse," James offered.

"But be back here before six!" Pinkerton warned Starbuck. "I have a man coming to take you down to the river at six!"

"Six o'clock," Starbuck promised and then, in a daze of uncertainty and fear, he went to the stables.

Pinkerton took Starbuck's chair and helped himself to more chicken. "He's a fine young man, your brother. But high-strung, Jimmy, very high."

"He always suffered from nervous debility," James said. "And he doesn't help himself by using tobacco and alcohol."

387

Pinkerton smiled. "I've been known to use those myself, Jimmy."

"But you're a well-set man," James explained, "and my brother's thin. People like you and I, Major, suffer in the belly and bowels, but men like my brother will always suffer in their nerves. He takes after my father in that."

"It must be a great thing to be educated," Pinkerton said, settling himself to his plate. The sound of gunfire increased, but he ignored it. "Now my own dear grandmother, God rest her soul, always claimed there was no disease on God's earth that a wee dram of good whiskey would not cure. I doubt you'll agree with her, Jimmy, but she lived a good long while and scarce knew a day's sickness."

"But she only recommended a wee dram," James said, delighted to have scored the point, "not a hog's bellyful, Major, and no sensible person will dispute whiskey's curative powers, but sadly it is not usually imbibed as a medicine."

"Your brother likes his drop," Pinkerton pointed out wickedly.

"Nate is a sore disappointment," James admitted. "But I look at it this way, Major. He has forsworn his political mistake, so he is well started on the hard road to redemption. He backslid a long way, but with God's grace he'll come back every step of that path and then go on toward full salvation."

"I daresay you're right," Pinkerton grumbled. He was never comfortable when his chief of staff fell into a preaching mode, but he was sensible of James's solid virtues and knew that the odd sermon was well worth the rigorous order that James brought to the affairs of the Secret Service.

"And maybe we can help Nate's salvation," James persisted, "by offering him a post in the Bureau? We're grievously understaffed, Chief. Just look at that!" He gestured at the pile of telegraphs and interrogations.

"When he's back from Richmond," Pinkerton said, "we'll think on it, I promise you." He twisted toward the window, frowning. "Those guns are lively. You think the seceshers are attacking us?"

"We have no intimation of a rebel attack," James said, thus implying that no assault could possibly be happening. Whenever an attack did take place there was always a trickle of deserters bringing news of the enemy's preparations, but the front between the armies had been unusually quiet these last few days.

"You're right, Jimmy, you're right." Pinkerton turned back to the table. "It's probably just a gunboat exercising its crew. And doubtless we'll hear soon enough if it's anything more remarkable." He picked up a one-week-old copy of the Jacksonville *Republican* and began reading a boastful account of how a blockade runner had evaded the northern warships off the South Carolina coast. The ship had been carrying canvas cloth from Genoa, French-made shoes, British percussion caps, gutta-percha from Malaya and eau de cologne. "Why would they want cologne water?" Pinkerton asked. "Why in God's name would they want that?"

James did not answer. He was applying himself to his lunch plate and had just helped himself to another serving of chicken when the door to the parlor was rudely thrown open and a tall, gaunt-faced colonel stepped into the room. The Colonel was wearing riding boots and carried a crop, while his uniform was spattered with red mud, evidence of how hard he had been riding. "Who the devil are you?" Pinkerton looked up from his newspaper.

"Name's Thorne. Lieutenant Colonel Thorne. Inspector General's Department in Washington. Who the devil are you?"

"Pinkerton."

"Well, Pinkerton, where's Starbuck?"

"Sir? I'm Starbuck, sir," James said, plucking the napkin from his neck and standing up.

"You're Nathaniel Starbuck?" Colonel Thorne asked grimly.

James shook his head. "No, sir, I'm his brother."

"Then where the devil is Nathaniel Starbuck? Have you arrested him?"

"Arrested him?" Pinkerton asked.

"I wired you yesterday. Does no one attend to business here?" Thorne asked the question in a bitter voice, conscious that Delaney's letter revealing Starbuck to be a traitor had lain unopened on his own desk for far too long. "So where the devil is he?"

James fluttered a feeble hand toward the back of the house. "In the stables, I believe."

"Then take me there!" Thorne drew a revolver from a holster at his waist and slipped a percussion cap onto one of the chamber's cones.

"Might I ask . . ." James began nervously.

"No you damn well may not ask! Take me to the stables!" Thorne shouted. "I haven't come all the way from Washington to watch you dithering like a virgin in her wedding bed. Now move!"

James ran to the stables.

The door of the stall where his horse had been cribbed swung creaking in the wind. The stall was empty. "He was going to see what the firing was about," James said weakly, frightened of Thorne's savage expression.

"He'll be back here by six," Pinkerton assured Thorne.

"You had better pray he is," Thorne said. "Where's McClellan? He'll have to find me some cavalry and we'll pursue the treacherous bastard."

"But why?" James asked. "Why? What's he done?"

But the Colonel had already gone. The guns cracked on the horizon where now a film of white smoke showed pale above the trees. Nate was gone west, something terrible was adrift in the universe, and James felt his heart sink hard. He prayed his fears were wrong, then went to find a horse.

The Confederate infantry half trotted and half walked across ground that was hard in places and like a morass in others. The Yankee pickets saw the line of gray and brown uniforms emerge from the woods and ran back to warn their comrades that the rebels were advancing.

Bugles sounded the alarm in the Federal encampments spread across the farms south of Fair Oaks Station. General McClellan had trained these men well and would have been proud of the way they stood to their arms. Whole regiments dropped the letters they were writing and the coffee they were brewing, they dropped their baseballs and playing cards, and they snatched up the rifles that were stacked like tepee poles as they ran to form ranks behind the waist-high abatis that protected their camps. The skirmishers ran out to a line of rifle pits that had been dug a hundred paces ahead of the abatis where a slight rise in the ground supposedly kept the soil above the floodline, but the night's storm had flooded the pits anyway and so the skirmishers knelt beside the waterlogged holes and pulled out the muzzle stoppers which had kept the rain from rusting their rifle barrels. The rest of the newly alerted regiments formed two long ranks which now stood in the warm, hard wind and watched the trees from which the pickets had just come running. Men loaded their weapons and placed percussion caps on their rifles' cones.

The abatis in front of the waiting infantry was a tangled barrier of felled trees. It was interrupted by gaps that let the skirmishers through and by the earth ramparts of artillery emplacements. The cannons, mostly twelve-pounder Napoleons but with a handful of ten-pound Parrotts, were already loaded with shell. Gunners pulled tarpaulins off ammunition limbers, rammed friction primers into touch-holes, and ordered rounds of canister stacked in readiness for the second and third shots. Birds were flapping up from the trees, disturbed by the advancing rebels, then a pair of deer bolted from the woods and galloped across the front of a new battalion of unblooded New Yorkers. "Hold your fire!" a sergeant snarled at a man tracking the deer with his rifle. "Aim low when they come, look for their officers! Steady now!" The Sergeant paced along the front of his nervous men. "They're just a bunch of ragged-assed farm-boys, no different from you miserable lot. There ain't nothing magical in rebs. They can be killed like anyone else. Aim low when you see them."

One boy was muttering Christ's name over and over again. His hands were shaking. Some of the men had pushed their ramrods into the wet turf so they would be more readily at hand for reloading. "Wait, lads, wait," the Sergeant said, seeing the nervousness on the young faces. The Colonel galloped behind their rear rank, his horse's hooves kicking up sprays of water and dirt.

"Where are they?" a man asked.

"You'll see 'em soon enough," another man said. In the line's center the colors looked bright against the dull sky.

Somewhere off to the right a blast of musketry sounded like a burning canebrake. A cannon fired with a noise that made the men jump. Over on that flank men were scream-ing like demons and smoke was drifting above the wet ground, but there was still no enemy visible in front of the New York boys. A second cannon fired, spewing a plume of smoke thirty yards along the ground. A shell burst in the air behind the New York regiment, evidence that a rebel battery was in action somewhere in the vicinity. One of the waiting New Yorkers suddenly buckled over and vomited a bellyful of hardtack and coffee onto the grass. "You'll feel better when you see them," the Sergeant growled. Another deer burst from the trees and galloped north toward the smoke and noise, then reversed itself and ran across the regiment's front. There were shapes moving among the trees now and the flicker of dull light reflecting from weapons and the splash of bright color where a rebel battle flag showed among the pines.

"Ready! Aim!" the Colonel of the New Yorkers shouted, and seven hundred rifles came up into seven hundred shoulders. The skirmishers had already opened fire from beside the flooded rifle pits, dotting the rough ground with patches of smoke that were whipped northward on the wind.

"Wait for it! Wait for it!" the Sergeant called. A lieutenant slashed at a weed with his sword. He tried to swallow, but his throat was too dry. For days now he had been constipated, but suddenly his bowels felt like water. "Steady now! Wait for it!" The Sergeant stepped back into the front rank.

And then, quite suddenly, they were there; the enemy they had all read about and had been told about and had joked about, and a poor, tattered enemy they looked too, nothing but a scattered line of ragged men in dirt-brown and rat-gray uniforms who emerged from the shadows of the far trees.

"Fire!" The Colonel had drawn his sword and now whipped it down. The New York regiment's front rank vanished behind the gouts of smoke.

"Fire!" the gun captains shouted and the artillery shells screamed into the edge of the woods and exploded in sudden small smoke clouds. Men swabbed out barrels and rammed canisters down onto powder charges.

"You're stopping them, boys! You're holding them!" The New Yorker's chaplain strode up and down behind the companies, his Bible in one hand and a revolver in the other. "Send their souls to the Lord, boys, translate the rascals to glory. Well done! Praise the Lord, aim low!"

"Fire!" The canisters split apart at the guns' muzzles to fan like duckshot across the rough ground. Rebels were snatched backward, their blood stippling the puddles left by the night's rain. Steel ramrods clattered in rifle barrels as the New Yorkers reloaded. The smoke of their opening volley had thinned and they could see the enemy was still advancing, though now they came forward in small groups of men who stopped, knelt, fired, then came on again, and all the time they made the weird, ululating scream that was the famous rebel yell. Their new battle flag looked bloodred against the trees. "Fire!" the Sergeant shouted and watched as one of the rebel groups was stopped cold. Two men in gray went down. A ramrod, fired in error, wheeled through the smoke. Rebel bullets smacked into the logs at the heart of the abatis while others whistled overhead. The New York skirmishers were falling back, yielding the useless rifle pits to the rebel skirmishers. Smoke was beginning to hide the battlefield and make a patchy screen behind which the rebels were mere shapes punctuated by rifle flames.

The cannon cracked back on their carriages and dug their trails deep into the waterlogged turf. There had been no time to make proper embrasures with hardened floors, only time to erect a rough wall in front of the guns that now choked out the killing blasts of canister. Each twelve-pounder was now being double-shotted with two full canisters rammed on top of a bag containing two-and-a-half pounds of gunpowder so that every barrel fired fifty-four musket balls, each musket ball a full one-and-a-half inches across. The canisters themselves were made from tin that tore apart, and the balls were packed in sawdust that vanished in flame at the cannons' muzzles. The balls cracked on the tree trunks beyond the attacking rebels, splashed into the wet soil, and tore into Confederate bodies. Each time the guns fired they recoiled farther, digging their trails deeper into the soft ground, and the gunners had neither the strength nor the time to haul the heavy weapons out of the sucking mud. Barrels had to be lowered to compensate for the sinking trails, but still the gunfire was doing its job and holding the rebel attack. The unsettling sound of the rebel yell had stopped, replaced by the swishing noise of canister tearing through the far woods.

"You're beating them! You're beating them!" The New York Colonel stood in his stirrups to shout at his men. "You're doing just bully," he said, then gave a stifled gasp as a bullet slapped into his lower throat. The Colonel began to twitch his head in the manner of a man whose stiff collar was too tight. He tried to speak, but no words came, just a mix of blood and spittle. He slumped back hard onto his saddle, a look of astonishment on his bearded face as his sword slipped out of his hand to quiver point first in the mud.

"Boys are doing real well, sir, real well!" A major rode up beside the Colonel, then watched appalled as his commanding officer toppled slowly out of the saddle. The Colonel's horse whinnied and trotted forward, dragging the Colonel by his left foot, which was trapped in its stirrup.

"Oh, Christ," the Major said. "Doctor! Doctor!" Then another cannon crashed its hollow-sounding noise of canister, only this time the canister balls flickered into the New York ranks, crackling in the abatis and sending four men reeling back. Another field gun cracked and the Major saw that the rebels had put two guns on his forward left flank and were unlimbering two more. He turned his horse to ride toward the threatened flank, but already the wing company was edging backward from the rebel threat. There were other northern troops on that flank, but they were too far away to help, and besides, those men were fighting off their own surge of rebel attackers.

"Hold them! Hold them! Hold them!" the Major shouted, but the arrival of the rebel artillery had given heart to the southern attack and now the gray-brown figures were coming closer to the abatis and their musketry was becoming ever more deadly. Wounded men limped and crawled away from the New York ranks, going to find help from the bandsmen who served as medical orderlies. The Yankee dead were pushed out of the ranks and the living closed on the center. Their mouths were dry from the salt in the gunpowder that leaked whenever they bit a cartridge open, and their faces were blackened by the powder. Sweat ran clean lines through the black faces. They rammed and fired, rammed and fired, flinching when the heavy rifles punched back into bruised shoulders, then they rammed and fired again. The ground behind the rebels was heaped with dead and wounded, with groups of the casualties concentrated wherever the canister blasts had cut through the advancing ranks. The new rebel color, with its starred blue cross on a bright red field, had been torn by canister, but a man picked up the staff and ran forward until a Yankee bullet shattered his leg and put the flag down again. Another man plucked it up and a dozen New York riflemen fired at him.

A New York sergeant watched a boy ram a bullet home and saw that the ramrod only went twenty inches into the barrel before being stopped. The Sergeant pushed through the ranks and seized the gun. "You have to fire the goddamn bullet before you shove another one on top." The Sergeant reckoned the boy had put at least four or five charges into the rifle and had forgotten to prime the cone with a percussion cap each time. The Sergeant tossed the rifle aside and picked up a dead man's gun. "That's why God gave you percussion caps, lad, to kill rebels. Now get on with it."

The New York Major turned and galloped past the body of his Colonel back to the nearest Yankee battery, where his horse slid to a stop in a slurry of wet mud. "Can't you bear on those guns?" he asked, pointing with his drawn sword to the rebel artillery that was pumping smoke into the killing ground.

"We can't move the guns!" an artillery lieutenant called back. The northern guns were dug so deep in the mud that the combined strength of men and horses could not unglue them. A shell moaned overhead to explode just beyond the New Yorkers' tents. Two of the Yankee guns fired, but their trails were now dug in so deep that their canister just whistled eerily over the heads of the rebels.

Then the weird screaming began again, the shrill, blood-curdling yelp that somehow suggested insanity as well as a perverse enjoyment of killing, and it was that sound, rather than the musketry or the rebel artillery, that persuaded the New Yorkers that they had done their duty. They stepped back from the abatis, still firing as they went, but eager to escape the hell of canister and rifle fire that ripped through the abatis and drove men down from the ranks. "Steady now, boys, steady!" the Major called as his troops backed away. The wounded begged to be taken with the retreating battalion, but every unwounded man who slung his rifle to help save a casualty was one less gun to help stave off the attack. The rebel fire was growing in intensity while the New York fire slackened, yet even so the green New Yorkers were putting on a brave display. They kept firing as they went and they did not panic.

"Proud of you, boys! Proud of you!" the Major shouted dry-mouthed, then yelped as a pain like a sledgehammer's hit struck his left arm. He stared in disbelief at the blood that suddenly dripped thick from his sleeve. He tried to move his hand from under the dripping blood, but only his little finger would move, so he crooked his arm upright, and that stopped the dripping blood. He felt oddly faint, but dismissed the sensation as unworthy. "You're doing well, boys, real well!" His voice lacked conviction and blood was puddling in the elbow of his sleeve.

The rebels were at the abatis now, using it as a breast-work for their rifles. Some men began dragging parts of the barricade aside, while others discovered the gaps left for the pickets and darted through. Puffs of smoke appeared from the rebel lines and were shredded away. The New Yorkers were going back faster now, panicked by the sight of the gunners who were abandoning their mired cannon and flee-ing on the backs of their team horses. One artillery officer stayed and tried to spike the weapons by hammering soft metal nails into their touchholes, but he was first shot, then bayoneted by a rebel who eagerly rifled his victim's pockets.

The Major at last managed to put a tourniquet above his left elbow. His horse trotted unguided through the regi-ment's tents, which were still immaculate from the morning inspection. The tents' side flaps and doors were all properly brailed up, the groundsheets were swept, and the men's bed-ding was folded neatly. Campfires burned. On one a pot of untended coffee boiled away. Playing cards fluttered in the wind. The rebels were coming on faster now and the New Yorkers began running for the shelter of the tree line behind their camp. Somewhere beyond those trees, around the road junction where seven tall pine trees stood in an isolated clump, there were more northern troops and larger gun redoubts and a sturdier abatis. That was where salvation lay and so the Yankees fled and the Confederates took over their camp with its treasure troves of food and coffee and comforts sent by loving families to men engaged upon the great and sacred business of holding the union together.

Four miles away, on a glutinous mud road that stretched between gloomy woods, General Huger's division waited while its commanding officer tried to determine just where he was supposed to be. Some of his men were entangled with the rear units of General Longstreet's division and were further confused because Longstreet had just ordered his brigades to about turn and march back the way they had come. The muggy warm air played tricks with the sound waves, sometimes muffling them so the battle seemed to be miles away and at other times making it seem as though the conflict had moved farther east. The two divisions that should have closed like steel jaws on the Yankee army milled in bad-tempered confusion while General Johnston, oblivious that his wings had become entangled and ignorant that his center had started an attack without them, waited at the Old Tavern for the arrival of Longstreet's troops. "Do we have any news of Longstreet?" the General asked for the twentieth time that hour.

"None, sir," Morton said unhappily. Longstreet's division had vanished. "But Huger's men are advancing," Morton said, though he did not like to add that they were advancing so slowly that he doubted any of them would reach the battlefield before nightfall.

"There's going to be a full inquiry into this, Morton," Johnston threatened. "I want to know who disobeyed what orders. You'll arrange it."

"Of course, sir," Morton said, though the chief of staff was more concerned by the rumble of gunfire that sounded from the direction of Hill's division. The rumble was not loud, for once again the layers of warm and sultry air were baffling the sound waves so that the battle's nearby clamor was being muted to the timbre of far-off thunder.

Johnston dismissed his chief of staff's fears about the muffled sound. "An artillery duel on the river," he suggested. "Hill wouldn't attack without support. He's not a fool."

Six miles away, in Richmond, the sound of the guns was much clearer, echoing through streets washed clean by the night's cloudburst. People clambered to rooftops and church belfries to get a view of the gunsmoke rising from the eastern woods. The President had not been informed that any battle was imminent and sent plaintive messages to his army's commander demanding to be told what was happening. Were the Yankees attacking? Should the government's reserves of gold be loaded on the waiting train and carried south to Petersburg? General Robert Lee, as ignorant of Johnston's intentions as President Davis, advised the President to be cautious. It would be better to wait for news, he said, before starting another evacuation panic in the capital.

Not everyone waited nervously for news. Julia Gordon distributed New Testaments in Chimborazo Hospital while across town, in Franklin Street, Sally Truslow used the absence of clients to organize a thorough spring cleaning of the whole house. Sheets were scrubbed and hung to dry in the garden, drapes and rugs were beaten free of dust, delicate glass light shades were washed clean of lampblack, wooden floors were waxed, and windows were polished with newspapers soaked in vinegar. In midafternoon a teamster's wagon brought the great round mahogany table that would be the centerpiece of Sally's seance room, and that had to be waxed. The kitchen steamed with vats of hot water and smelt of lye and washing soda. Sally, her arms and hands reddened, her hair pinned up and her face glistening with sweat, sang as she worked. Her father would have been proud of her, but Thomas Truslow was fast asleep. The Faulconer Brigade was held in reserve, guarding the Chickahominy crossings northeast of the city where the men listened to the noise of distant battle, played cards, pitched horseshoes, and counted their blessings that their presence was not required this day upon the killing ground.

Starbuck rode south and west, following the road that led to the nearest crossing of the Chickahominy. He hardly knew where he was going, or what he could do. De'Ath had been his sponsor, his protector, and now Starbuck was on his own. For days Starbuck had been terrified that a genuine message from Adam might reach James and thus unmask his treachery, but he had never anticipated this danger, that he would be left friendless on the wrong side of the battle-lines. He felt like a hunted animal driven from cover, then he remembered the document that Pinkerton had just given him and wondered if there was enough power in that scrap of paper to see him safe home to the Legion. He was sure that was where he wanted to go, but now he would have to prise the Legion's ranks open without de'Ath's help, and that prospect made him feel close to despair again. Perhaps, he thought, he should just volunteer for a northern infantry regiment. Change his name, pick up a rifle, and so disappear into the blue ranks of America's biggest army.

Starbuck's horse ambled along the verge while its rider tried to find some hope in the whirl of fear and fancy that assailed him. The road had been cut and churned into a morass of deep red mud while the ruts left by the wheels of guns and wagons had filled with stormwater that now rippled under the wind. The countryside here was flat farm-land interrupted by swaths of forest and stretches of bog amid which slow streams meandered between rushes, though not far ahead there were low hills that promised firmer footing for his borrowed horse.

The cannon fire was incessant now, suggesting that one side or the other was making a determined effort to dislodge its enemy, yet even so there was remarkably little urgency being displayed in the camps that were uncomfortably pitched in these wet meadows. Men idled away the after-noon as though the battle across the river belonged to some other army or some other nation. A line of soldiers waited at a sutler's store to buy what small luxuries the merchant offered, and a still larger line trailed away from a tent that advertised dried oysters. One of the men winked at Star-buck and tapped his canteen, suggesting that the oyster seller was, in truth, offering illicit whiskey. Starbuck shook his head and rode on. Maybe he should run away? Go to the badlands in the west? Then he remembered Sally's scorn and knew he could not just cut and run. He had to fight for what he wanted!

He passed a Baptist church that was being used as a hospital. Parked beside the church was an undertaker's encampment with its owner's slogan painted in raw vermil-lion letters on the canvas hood of a covered wagon: "Ethan Cornett and Sons, Newark, New Jersey, Embalming, Cheap and Thorough, Warranted Free of Odor and Infection." A second wagon was piled with pine caskets, each one labeled with the address to which it must be delivered. The embalmed corpses would be taken home to Philadelphia and Boston, Newport and Chicago, Buffalo and St. Paul, and there buried to the accompaniment of sobbing families and the high-flown rhetoric of bloodthirsty parsons. Most bodies were buried where they fell, but some men, dying in hospital, paid to have their corpses carried home. Even as Starbuck watched, a body was brought out of the church and laid on a table beside one of the embalmer's tents. The toes of the corpse's stockings had been pinned together and a label was tied to one ankle. A shirtsleeved man wearing a stained canvas apron and carrying a broad-bladed knife came from a tent to inspect the new body.

Starbuck urged the horse on through the rank smell of embalming chemicals, then up a slight gradient that climbed through a thick belt of woodland beyond which was a small poor farm with fields that had once been fenced with snake rails, though all that was left of the fences were zigzag traces in the grass, for the rails had been stolen for cooking fires. A log cabin sat by the road with a homemade Stars and Stripes hanging from the eaves of its sod roof. The stripes had been made of dark and light colored sacking, while the stars were thirty-four limewash blobs daubed onto a faded scrap of pale blue canvas. The log house was evidently home to a family of free blacks, for an old, white-haired Negro came out of the tiny cabin as Starbuck rode past. The man walked toward his vegetable patch carrying a fork that he hefted in salute to Starbuck. "Go give them hell, master!" he called. "Do the Lord's work now, sir, you hear me, sir."

Starbuck raised a hand in silent acknowledgment. Ahead now he could see a sliding shiny stretch of river and beyond it, far beyond it, a great patch of smoke that looked as though a vast area of woodland was afire. That was the mark of a battle, and the sight of it made Starbuck check his horse and think of K Company, and he wondered if Truslow was under that smoke, and if Decker and the Cobb twins and Joseph May and Esau Washbrook and George Finney were fighting there. God, he thought, but if they were fighting he wanted to be with them. He inwardly cursed de'Ath for dying, then looked beyond the smoke, far beyond, to where a smear of darker vapor betrayed where the foundries and mills of Richmond pumped their noxious smoke into the windy sky, and that evidence of the distant city made him homesick for Sally.

He took a cheroot from his pocket and scratched a match alight. He inhaled the smoke greedily. Putting the matches back into his pocket he felt the cigar shape of the oilskin packet that was his only weapon left. The paper inside would have to be his passport to the Legion, yet if the list of damning questions was found by a rebel provost it could mean the noose. Once again Starbuck felt a tremor of fear and the temptation to run away from both armies.

"Do the Lord's work now, master, go give them hell, sir," the old black man said, and Starbuck turned, thinking it was to him that the old man had spoken again, but instead he saw another horseman spurring up the road toward him. A quarter mile behind that newcomer a group of northern cavalry were roweling their horses through the sticky red mud, the first sign of urgency Starbuck had seen this side of the Chickahominy River.

He looked back to the battle smoke as a hard, percussive drumroll of cannon fire rumbled cruel across the landscape. Then a half-familiar voice hailed him urgently and Starbuck turned back with a panicked start to realize he was in still more trouble.

THE REBEL ATTACK STALLED among the abandoned tents of the New York regiment. It was not northern resistance that held up the advance, but northern affluence, for within the tents, which themselves were made from stout white canvas of a quality forgotten by the southerners, were boxes of food, knapsacks stuffed with good shirts, spare trousers, and proper leather shoes made to fit either the right or the left foot, unlike the square-toed Confederate-issue brogans which were rigid boxes of stiff leather that could be worn on either foot indiscriminately and promised equal damage to both. Then there were the parcels of food sent from loving northern homes: boxes of chestnuts, jars of green-pepper pickles, bottles of apple butter, paper-wrapped slabs of ginger cake, tins of fruitcake, cans of sugarplums, cloth-wrapped cheeses, and best of all, coffee. Real coffee. Not coffee adulterated with dried and ground goober peas, or coffee made from parched corn pounded into powder, or coffee made from desiccated dandelion leaves mixed with dried apple powder, but real fragrant dark coffee beans.

At first the rebel officers tried to keep their troops moving through the snares of enemy wealth, but then the officers themselves became seduced by the easy pickings within the abandoned tents. There were fine hams, smoked fish, dried oysters, new butter, and fresh-baked bread. There were thick blankets and, in some tents, quilts that had been made by womenfolk for their hero sons and husbands. One

405

quilt displayed a union flag on which a legend had been sewn in letters of golden silk. "Avenge Ellsworth!" the quilt read.

"Who the hell's Ellsworth?" a rebel asked his officer.

"A New Yorker who got himself killed."

"That's a habit of Yankees these days, ain't it?"

"He was the first. Got himself shotgunned when he tried to take one of our flags off a hotel roof in Virginia."

"Son of a bitch should have stayed in New York then, shouldn't he?"

In the officers' tents there were fine German field glasses, family photographs framed in silver standing on folding hardwood tables, elegant traveling writing cases filled with engraved notepaper, leather-bound books, hairbrushes backed with polished tortoiseshell, fine steel razors in leather cases, boxes of Roussell's Shaving Cream, well-thumbed stacks of intimate daguerreotypes of undressed ladies, stone jars of good whiskey, and bottles of fine wine stored in sawdust-filled crates. A Confederate major, coming across one such cache of bottles, fired his revolver into the chest so that the liquor could not tempt his men. The crate's sawdust became discolored with wine as the heavy bullets drove down into the bottles. "Keep the men moving!" the Major shouted at his officers, but the officers were like the men and the men were like children in a toy store and would not be shifted on to the day's proper business.

In the battalion's wagon park, behind the headquarters tents, a sergeant discovered a hundred brand-new Enfield Rifles packed in rope-handled crates stenciled with the rifle manufacturer's name, "Ward & Sons, Birmingham, England." The Enfield was a prized gun and a far more accurate and sturdy rifle than the weapon this regiment of rebels was using, and soon a clamor of men jostled about the wagon to get hold of one of the precious guns.

Slowly the chaos was sorted out. Some officers and sergeants slashed the guy ropes of the tents, collapsing the canvas on the contents to persuade the men to abandon the plunder and keep pressing after the defeated Yankees. On either flank, where no campground served to delay the attack, the rebel lines already pushed on through a wide belt of woodland where windflowers, bloodroot, and violets blossomed, and then the attackers emerged into an open stretch of waterlogged grassland where the wind shivered the puddles and lifted the heavy flags of the Yankee troops who were making their stand just west of the junction where the three roads on which the rebel attacks were supposed to be advancing came together. The crossroads was marked by seven tall pines and two gaunt farmhouses, landmarks of this killing ground where Johnston had planned his annihilation of the Yankees south of the river.

The crossroads was also protected by an elaborate earth-walled fort that was studded with cannon and crowned by old Glory on a staff made of a trimmed pine trunk. The approaches to the fort were traversed by abatis and rifle pits. It was here that Johnston had planned to surround the Yankees, first hitting them in the center, then breaking them from north and south and so driving them whimpering into the snake-haunted marshes of the White Oak Swamp, but instead one rebel division alone advanced from the trees. That division had already broken one northern line and now, across the wind-shivered morass, they saw a second line waiting beneath its bright flags and so the gray and brown troops began to scream their shrill, eerie yell of attack.

"Fire!" a northern officer standing on the fort's rampart called. The northern cannon slammed back on their trails.

Shells burst in the far air, white smoke lancing scraps of white-hot steel down onto the rebel line. The minie bullets whistled over the marsh, striking home in misty sprays of blood. The colors fell and were lifted again as the rebels waded on through sodden ground.

General Huger heard the renewed cannonade, but refused to translate it as a summons for urgency. "Hill knows his business," he claimed, "and if he needed our help he'd have sent for us." In the meantime he pushed a brigade cautiously down an empty road, claiming it was a reconnaissance in force. The brigade found nothing. Longstreet, meanwhile, frustrated first in one direction and then in the other, ordered his men to countermarch one more time. Both generals cursed the lack of maps and a drifting afternoon fog that was just thick enough to hide the battle's telltale plume of gunsmoke that would otherwise have told them just where the baffling and muffled sound of guns came from.

President Davis, frustrated by his commanding general's silence, rode from Richmond toward the battlefield. He asked every officer he met what news there was, but no one knew what happened in the marshy fields south of the river. Even the President's military adviser could not discover the truth. Robert E. Lee had no standing in the army's affairs and could only surmise that an attack had been launched from the Confederate lines, though with what aim and with what success he could neither say nor guess. The President asked if anyone knew where Johnston's headquarters was, but no one was certain of that either, but the President decided he must find Johnston anyway, and so his party worked its way eastward in search of news about a battle that flared into life again as Hill's unsupported columns crashed into the Yankees' hard-dug defenses around the seven pines.

Where the guns grew hot as, fed by confusion and succored by pride, the killing kept on.

The man who had hailed Starbuck was the French military observer, Colonel Lassan, who now spurred over the brow of the hill and seized the bridle of Starbuck's horse, dragging him on down the road and so out of sight of the Yankee cavalry. "You know you're in trouble?" the Frenchman asked.

Starbuck was trying to jerk his horse's head out of the Frenchman's grasp.

"Don't be such a bloody fool!" Lassan snapped in his perfect English. "And follow me!" He let go of the bridle and pricked his horse's flanks with his spurs, and such was the authority in his voice that Starbuck instinctively followed as the Frenchman swerved sharply right off the road and across a boggy patch of ground into the sudden cover of some broad-leaved trees. The two men forced a path through grasping undergrowth and low, soaking wet branches, at last reaching a clearer patch of woodland where the Frenchman turned his horse and raised a hand ordering Starbuck to silence.

The two men listened. Starbuck could hear the solid, ear-thumping bang of big guns across the river, and the lighter, sharper crackle of musketry, and he could hear the rustle and moan of the wind in the high trees, but he could hear nothing else. Yet the Frenchman still listened and Starbuck looked with renewed curiosity at his rescuer. Lassan was a tall man, maybe in his forties, with a black mustache and a thin face made singular by the scars of war. Starbuck saw the scars where a Russian saber had laid open the Frenchman's right cheek, a Cossack's bullet had taken his left eye, and an Austrian rifle bullet had mangled his left jawbone, yet despite the injuries there remained such an air

409

of confident enjoyment about the Frenchman that it was hard to call the horribly scarred face ugly. Rather it was superbly battered; a face on which life had left a tale of adventure that had been met with panache. Lassan rode his tall black horse with the same innate grace as Washington Faulconer, while his uniform, which had once been gaudy with lace and gold chain and gilt froggings, was now sunbleached and darned, and its fine metal embellishments were either tarnished or missing altogether. He must once have had a splendid uniform hat, maybe in lustrous fur or shining brass and towering with plumes or a scarlet crest, but now he wore a floppy farm hat that looked as if it had come from a scarecrow. "It's all right." Lassan broke his silence. "They're not following us."

"Who's they?"

"The leader of the pack is a fellow called Thorne. Comes from Washington." Lassan paused to pat his horse's neck. "Claims to have evidence that you were sent across the lines to mislead the Yankees. Worse, that you were sent over to discover who their best spy in Richmond is." Lassan took a compass from his pocket and let its needle settle before gesturing northwest. "We'll go this way." He turned his horse and started it at a walk through the trees. "What it boils down to, my friend, is that they want to measure your neck for a rope. I got involved because the energetic Thorne came to McClellan demanding the use of cavalry. I overheard, and here I am. At your service, monsieur." Lassan offered Starbuck a rakish grin.

"Why?" Starbuck demanded ungraciously.

"Why not?" Lassan responded cheerfully, then went silent as his horse descended the bank of a small stream and scrambled up the far side. "All right, I shall tell you why. It's just as I told you before. I need to get to the rebel side, simple as that, and preferably before this campaign is over, which means I can't spend weeks traveling halfway around the damn world to get from Yorktown to Richmond. I prefer to make a run across the lines, and I guessed you'd be doing the same thing this afternoon and so I thought to myself, why not? Two heads are better than one, and when we get to the other side you will be my guarantor so that instead of arresting and shooting me as a spy they will accept your word that I am, indeed, Patrick Lassan, Chasseur Colonel of the Imperial Guard." He grinned at Starbuck. "Does that make sense?"

"Patrick?" Starbuck asked, his curiosity piqued by the name that did not seem at all French.

"My father was English and his closest friend was Irish, and thus the name. My mother is French and I took her surname because she never found time to marry her Englishman, and what that makes me, *mon ami*, is a mongrel bastard." Lassan had spoken with evident affection for his parents, an affection that made Starbuck envious. "It also makes me a bored mongrel bastard," Lassan continued. "The Yankees are a fine, hospitable people, but they are increasingly beset by a Teutonic discipline. They wish to hedge me in with regulation and rules. They want me to stay a decorous distance from the fighting as befits an observer and not a participant, but I need to smell the killing, otherwise I can't tell how this war is being won and lost."

"We have rules and regulations too," Starbuck said.

"Ah, ha!" Lassan twisted in his saddle. "So you are a rebel?"

For a second the ingrained habit of the last weeks tempted Starbuck to a denial, then he shrugged. "Yes."

"Good for you. So maybe your rules and regulations are as bad as those of the Yankees, I shall see. But it will be an adventure, yes? A fine adventure. Come on!" He led

Starbuck out of the trees and across a meadow that was being used as an artillery park. Another road lay ahead and beside it were ranks of resting Yankee infantry. Lassan proposed that if anyone challenged their presence he would explain that he was an official observer riding to the battle and that Starbuck was his orderly. "But our biggest obstacle is crossing the river. Your pursuers will stay on the road behind us, but there's a chance they've telegraphed to all the bridges warning the sentries to keep a lookout for you."

Starbuck felt the sour pulse of fear in his belly. If the Yankees caught him they would hang him, and if the rebel provosts found Pinkerton's paper then they would do the same. Yet by crossing the lines there was still a chance that he could bluff his way back into the Legion. "You're taking a risk, aren't you?" he asked Lassan.

"Not at all. If they apprehend us I shall disclaim all knowledge of your criminal soul. I shall say you tricked and deceived me, then I shall smoke a cigar while you hang. Though don't worry, I shall say a prayer for your soul."

The thought of his damned soul made Starbuck think of all his brother's wasted prayers. "Did you see my brother?" Starbuck asked as he and the Colonel threaded the parked guns toward the infantrymen who rested by the road.

"He was proclaiming your innocence. Your brother, I think, is not a born soldier." It was a delicately kind judgment. "I spent most of the battle at Bull Run in your brother's company. He's a man who likes the confinement of rules and regulations. Not a rogue, I think. Armies could not survive without such careful men, but they need rogues even more."

"James is a good lawyer," Starbuck said in his brother's defense.

"Why do you Americans take such pride in your attorneys? Lawyers are merely the symptoms of a quarrelsome

society and every cent given to a lawyer is a sip less champagne, a woman unconquered, or a cigar unsmoked. Damn
the bloodsucking lot of them, I say, though I'm sure your
brother is a very angel compared to the rest. Sergeant!"
Lassan shouted at one of the infantrymen, "what unit are
you?"

The Sergeant, persuaded by Lassan's obvious authority,
said that his unit was the 1st Minnesota in General
Gorman's brigade. "You know what's happening, sir?" the
Sergeant asked.

"Damned rebels are twitching, Sergeant. You'll be
marching to give them a hiding soon enough. Good luck to
you!" Lassan rode on, trotting between the road's deep
muddied ruts and the waiting infantry. "This is General
Sumner's Corps," he told Starbuck. "Sumner must have
closed up to the bridge, which means he's waiting for orders
to attack, but I doubt he'll get them very quickly. Our
Young Napoleon doesn't seem entirely seized of the day's
urgency. He's ill, but even so he should be slightly
animated."

"You don't like McClellan?" Starbuck asked.

"Like him?" The Frenchman considered the question for
a moment. "No, not much. He's a drill sergeant, not a general. Nothing but a pompous little man with too high an
opinion of himself. It wouldn't matter if he could win
battles, but he doesn't seem capable of fighting them, let
alone winning them. So far all he's done in this campaign is
lean on the rebels, using his weight to push them back, but
he hasn't fought them. He's scared of them! He believes
you've got two hundred thousand men!" Lassan gave a bark
of laughter, then pointed up to a shiny telegraph wire that
had been strung on makeshift poles alongside the road.
"That's our problem, Starbuck. Suppose our friend Thorne
has telegraphed ahead, eh? They might be waiting for you

413

at the bridge. They'll probably hang you on the gallows in Fort Monroe. Last cup of coffee, a cigar, a quick trot through the Twenty-third Psalm, then they'll put on the hood and wallop you down through the hatch. A quick way to go, they say. Much better than shooting. Have you ever seen a firing squad?"

"No."

"You will. I'm always astonished how often a firing squad misses. You line the dumb buggers up at ten paces, pin a piece of paper over the poor man's heart, and still they'll pepper his liver and elbows and bladder; anywhere, in fact, that won't put the poor bastard out of his misery, which means that the officer then has to go and give the quivering wretch a coup de grace in the skull. I'll never forget my first. I had a hand shaking like a leaf and the poor bastard twitching like a landed fish. It took me three pistol bullets and a whole fortnight to get his blood out of the stitching in my boots. Messy business, firing squads. You feeling all right?"

"I'm fine," Starbuck said, and in truth Lassan's conversation was diverting him from his worries about de'Ath's death.

Lassan laughed at Starbuck's aplomb. The road had entered a gloomy, dank stretch of forest where creepers trailed from trees and sour pools of water stretched under the branches. The road had been corduroyed, which made the going hard for the horses, so hard that after a while Lassan suggested they dismount and lead the horses by the reins. He talked of the Crimea and of the idiocy of generals, then of the days when he had joined the French army as an officer cadet in 1832. "My father wanted me to join the British army. Be a rifleman, he told me, best of the best, and my mother wanted me to be a French cavalryman. I chose the French."

"Why?"

"Because I was in love with a girl whose parents lived in Paris and I thought if I went to St. Cyr I'd be able to seduce her, while if I moved to England I should never see her again."

Starbuck thought of Mademoiselle Dominique Demarest of New Orleans, cheap actress and cheaper whore, who had tempted him to leave Yale and run away with a traveling band of showmen. He wondered where Dominique was now and whether he would ever meet to settle accounts with her. Then, quite suddenly, he realized he had no grudge against Dominique. She had only made him do what he had wanted to do, which was to flee from his family's stultifying bonds. "What happened to the girl?" Starbuck asked.

"She married a draper in Soissons," Lassan said. "And now I can hardly remember what she looked like."

"Was your father angry?"

"Only about my taste in women. He said he'd seen a prettier face on a bullock." Lassan laughed again. "But I made my choice for love, you see, and I don't regret it. And maybe if I'd chosen the other way I wouldn't have regretted that either. There isn't an optimum of life, just one hell of a good time waiting for those who have the courage to take it. And courage is what we must now have, *mon ami*." Lassan gestured at the bridge that had just come into view. "Cross this bridge and we only have the bullets and shells of two armies to survive."

The bridge was a miserable-looking contraption. The mud-covered corduroy road led straight through a stagnant marsh, then seemed to elevate itself a foot or two above the mephitic, rank river before sliding down to another distasteful stretch of bog on the water's southern bank. The slight elevation was caused by four pontoons, tin-covered wooden punts that carried the corduroyed roadway across the river. The pontoons were held in place by enormously long ropes that had been carried back to the forests and tied to trees, but it was evident that there was a problem with the complicated arrangement of ropes, pontoons, pulleys, and roadway. The storm of the previous night had raised the river's level and brought down a mass of floating debris that had become trapped against the bridge, so stretching the mooring lines that the road now bulged dangerously downstream. There was plainly a danger that the pressure of water and flotsam would snap the lines and destroy the bridge, to prevent which disaster a score of unhappy engineer troops were standing up to their chests in the swirling, muddy water as they tried to clear the bridge and secure new mooring lines.

"You can't cross!" A shirtsleeved engineer accosted Lassan and Starbuck as the two men led their horses out from the cover of the forest. The engineer was middle-aged, his pants were smeared with mud, and his whiskered face dripped with sweat that had also turned his white shirt dark with damp. "I'm Colonel Ellis, Engineer Corps," he introduced himself to Lassan. "The bridge isn't safe. The storm gave it a hell of a beating." Ellis gave Starbuck a glance, but showed no other interest in him. "There's another bridge a mile upriver."

Lassan grimaced. "How do we reach this other bridge?"

"Go back the way you've come. After half a mile there's a turning to the left, take it. Another half mile there's a T junction, turn left again." Ellis slapped at a mosquito. Out in the river a line of men hauled on a cable and Starbuck saw the fragile bridge dip and quiver as the big rope tightened. The line came up from the water, looped with dripping vegetation, then one of the men in the river screamed as he saw a snake clinging to the newly tautened rope. He let go of the line and the panic spread to his fellows, who all released their grip and fled toward the bank. The bridge creaked as it surged downstream again.

A sergeant bellowed at the troops, cursing them for chicken-livered bastards. "It's only a goddamn moccasin! It won't kill you! Now take hold! Haul, you bastards, haul!"

"You know there's a corps waiting to cross this bridge?" Lassan asked Colonel Ellis sternly, as though the Engineer Colonel was personally responsible for delaying the advance of the corps. "They're waiting on the far side of the woods."

"They're not crossing anything till the bridge is repaired," Ellis said bad-temperedly.

"I think we should discover for ourselves whether the bridge is safe," Lassan said airily. "The future of the union might depend on it. In war, Colonel, there are risks that should be taken which would be unthinkable in peace, and if a fragile bridge is the only route to victory then it must be risked." He declaimed this nonsense as he marched resolutely on toward the bridge, which was quivering under the force of the water's onslaught. Starbuck could see how the stormwater had tugged two of the pontoons out of their alignment and as a result the corduroy road had fanned apart to reveal ankle-wide gaps between its top layer of logs.

"Who are you?" The mud-spattered Engineer Colonel hurried after the Frenchman. Lassan ignored him, instead glancing into a small tent that was precariously pitched close to a stagnant pool and inside which a telegraph machine chattered unattended. "I demand to know who you are!" the Colonel, red-faced, insisted.

"I am General Lassan, Viscount Seleglise of the Duchy of Normandy and a Chasseur of the Emperor's Imperial Guard, presently attached to Major General George McClellan's staff." Lassan strode on with Starbuck beside him.

417

"I don't care if you're the King of Siam," Ellis insisted. "You still can't cross."

"Maybe not, which means I shall die trying," Lassan said very grandly. "If my body is recovered, Colonel, pray have it sent back to Normandy. My companion, on the other hand, is from Boston, so you may allow his body to rot in whatever noxious swamp it comes to rest. Come on, boy!" This last encouragement was to his horse, which was bridling nervously at the uncertain footing of the bridge's approach. The corduroyed logs sank beneath the weight of the horses and a bubbling ooze of watery mud seeped up between the chinks.

"Get the hell back!" the Sergeant, standing to his waist in water and with the bitter end of a rope in his hands, shouted at Lassan and Starbuck.

"I'm going on. My risk, not yours!" Lassan called back to the Sergeant, then he gave Starbuck a mischievous grin. "Onward, ever onward!"

"General! Please?" Colonel Ellis tried a last appeal, but Lassan simply ignored the engineers and paced resolutely out across the logs to where the damaged bridge inched up above the river's swirling, swollen, hard-running waters. The roadway creaked and dipped as they ventured onto the ramp. Starbuck, passing the first pontoon, saw that it was half flooded with rainwater, then he encountered the bridge's inadvertent bend and his horse tried to shy away from the seethe of the water where it swirled against the driftwood and the pontoons. Starbuck dragged the horse on, but painfully slowly, for the beast needed time to place its hooves on the shaking logs. "Stay on the upstream side," Lassan advised. "The logs are closer together." The second pontoon was almost awash, and under the weight of Lassan's horse the roadway dipped perilously close to the red muddy swirl of the river. "Colonel Ellis!" Lassan

418

shouted back to the working party.

"What is it?"

"You'd find the work easier if you pumped the pontoons out."

"Why don't you mind your own damn business!"

"A good question," Lassan said happily to himself. He and Starbuck were halfway across now, their weight depressing the heavy roadway to within inches of the river's surface. "You have very good engineers in this country," the Frenchman told Starbuck. "Better than ours. The French love being cavalrymen, at worst they will accept being turned into light infantrymen, but anything else is believed demeaning. Yet I have a horrible suspicion that future wars will be decided by the artillerymen and engineers, the mathematical drudges of warfare, while we splendid horsemen will be reduced to mere errand boys. Still, I can't imagine good women falling in love with engineers, can you? That's the good thing about being a cavalryman, it does make the important conquests of life somewhat easier."

Starbuck laughed, then gasped as one boot slid out from beneath him on a greasy patch of log. He managed to keep his balance, though the sudden movement seemed to stretch the nearest pontoon's guy ropes so that the whole bridge lurched under the assault of the river water that bubbled and surged between a crack in the logs. Starbuck and his horse both stood motionless until the worst of the bridge's shaking subsided and they could step cautiously on. "Are you really a viscount?" Starbuck asked the Frenchman, and he remembered that de'Ath too had claimed a French title, though if James's gossip was right, then de'Ath's parentage was even more distinguished.

"I'm never sure," Lassan answered carelessly. "It's an old title, officially abolished at the Revolution, but my grandfather used it and I'm his only direct male descendant. I suppose I lost any right to membership in the nobility when my mother and father made love on the wrong side of the blanket, but every now and then I resurrect the title to astonish the local peasantry."

"And you said you were a general?"

"Brevet only. Once the Austrian wars were over I reverted to being a plain and humble colonel."

"And your government sent you here to see how we fight?" Starbuck asked, astonished that such a man would have been ordered to America.

"Oh, no. They wanted me to command a recruiting depot, nothing but lumpish plowboys, spavined remounts, and drunken sergeants. They sent some bores from the academy and a couple of dull infantrymen to be their official observers here, but I wanted to look for myself so I took an indefinite leave of absence, and the government reluctantly accredited me once they realized I couldn't be stopped. I think of myself as being on holiday, Starbuck." Lassan tugged his horse onward. "Nearly there. I don't know what those silly bastards are fretting over. I could have waltzed a blindfolded division of galloping whores over this bridge."

Starbuck smiled at the outrageous claim, then twisted around as a stern voice hailed them from the river's northern bank. It was Colonel Ellis who called from beside the telegraph tent. "Stop!" Ellis shouted. "Right where you are! Stop!"

Starbuck waved as though he had misunderstood Ellis's order, then kept walking. He was almost off the bridge now and approaching the soggy, uncertain footing of the approach road. He began to hurry, dragging the horse behind him.

"Stop!" Ellis shouted again, and this time he reinforced the order by pulling out his revolver and firing a shot well

420

above Starbuck's head. The bullet ripped into the leaves of the trees that now lay some fifty yards ahead.

"Turn the horse toward him," Lassan said softly, "so he thinks you're obeying. Mount up at the same time, then keep the horse swinging around and ride like hell. Understand?"

"I understand," Starbuck said, and he waved again at the Engineer Colonel and he pulled the horse around to make it clear he was not trying to run away, and at the same time he put his muddy left boot into the stirrup. He gripped the saddle's pommel with his left hand and with a quick effort swung himself up into his brother's saddle. Lassan also mounted.

Colonel Ellis was hurrying toward the bridge, beckoning to the two fugitives. "Come back!"

"Goodbye, *mon Colonel*," Lassan said softly and turned his horse away. "Now ride with me!" the Frenchman shouted and Starbuck slashed back with his heels and his horse took off after the Frenchman's mount. The corduroy road was slippery and treacherous, but somehow the two horses kept their footing. "Ride!" Lassan encouraged Starbuck, and Colonel Ellis offered yet more encouragement by firing his revolver, only this time he was not aiming over the fugitives' heads, but at their horses. Yet the two men were already over a hundred yards away and revolvers were uncertain weapons at anything over forty or fifty yards. The Colonel fired his first two bullets much too fast and his aim was lamentably wide. Then he checked himself to take more careful aim, but Lassan was already in the shadow of the trees where he turned the black horse, drew his own revolver, and fired back past Starbuck. Lassan's shots splashed into the marsh or drove wet splinters up from the road. The Frenchman was not shooting to kill, but rather to throw off the engineer's aim, then

Starbuck spurred past him and turned a bend and so rode out of Ellis's sight.

Lassan caught up with Starbuck and the two men rode between woods as dank and overgrown as those on the river's northern bank. "They know where we are now," Lassan said. "Ellis will telegraph them." He was reloading his revolver, ramming the bullets down on the powder with the lever attached to the underside of the weapon's barrel. The sound of battle was louder now, filling the sultry land ahead with the menace of death. Lassan spotted a path in the woods and veered off the road, galloping along an open ride that widened into a field behind a sprawling house. Starbuck followed, tensing himself as the Frenchman jumped a rail fence. Starbuck gripped the reins, closed his eyes, and let the horse bump him up and over. Somehow he clung to the beast's back and when he opened his eyes again he saw they were trotting on a path that ran between a field and more woods. A drill barrow had been abandoned beside the path, a reminder of more peaceful times, while at the far side of the field there was an artillery park where the horses, limbers, and cannon of a northern battery waited for orders. "Best not to look in too much of a hurry," Lassan advised Starbuck. "There's nothing so suspicious on a battlefield as a man in a hurry. Have you noticed that? Soldiers do most things at half speed. The only people in a hurry are staff officers and fugitives."

He turned farther eastward, going into the open field and trotting casually behind the waiting guns. Starbuck rode beside him. A half mile to their left was another belt of timber, beyond which lay a range of low wooded hills that concealed the killing ground. A huge smear of smoke rose into the clouds beyond those hills, and Lassan was heading for the edge of that smoke. "No point in getting into the thick of things, Starbuck. We'll go for the flank."

"You're enjoying this, aren't you?" Starbuck said, content to let the more experienced Frenchman be his guide.

"It's better than sitting in McClellan's headquarters reading the New York *World* for the eighty-ninth time."

"But what about your belongings?" Starbuck asked, realizing suddenly that the Frenchman was proposing to move from the Federal to the Confederate lines with no apparent baggage.

"My belongings are in France. Here in America I have one cloak," Lassan patted the garment that was rolled at the cantle of his saddle. "Some money here." He patted a saddlebag. "Enough to make it worth your while to murder me, but I'd advise you not to try." He smiled happily. "A spare shirt, some tobacco, revolver cartridges, spare underclothes, a copy of Montaigne's essays, one toothbrush, three notebooks, two pencils, two razors, a steel, one compass, field glasses, one comb, one watch, one flute, letters of credit, and my official papers." He patted whatever pocket or saddlebag held these various possessions. "Once I'm safe with the rebels I'll buy a spare horse, and once again I will have possessions enough for all my needs. A soldier shouldn't carry more, and if I grew a beard I wouldn't even need the razors."

"What about the flute?"

"A man should possess some civilizing talent, *mon ami*, or else he's just a brute. God, I wouldn't like to fight in this country." He voiced this opinion as the two horsemen breasted a small rise to see a tangle of small fields and woods ahead. "This is no place for cavalry," Lassan said.

"Why not?"

"Because cavalry hates trees. Trees can hide guns and muskets and we cavalry like the long rolling plains. First you break the enemy infantry with artillery, then you loose the cavalry on them, and afterward you bury them. That's the old world's prescription for battle, but you can only do that in open country. And I tell you, my friend, that God gives no finer thrill than the experience of riding down a broken enemy. Hoofbeats, trumpets, the sun above, the enemy beneath, my God, but war is a wicked thrill." They trotted on, going past the first evidence of this day's battle. There was a casualty station in the field where ambulances were bringing the wounded and where nurses in a uniform of long skirts and men's shirts helped carry the bloody bodies out of the wagons and into the tents. Beside the casualty station was a small group of sullen men with powder-blackened faces, fugitives who had run from the rebels' first attacks and who had now been rounded up by northern provosts. Mules loaded with panniers of rifle ammunition were being led along a road toward the smoke plume.

Lassan and Starbuck trotted past the mules and into another belt of trees where northern infantry waited in the shadows. The men's faces were unstained with powder, evidence that they had not yet fought this day.

Beyond the trees the road dropped gently down to where the Richmond and York Railroad ran on its embankment through the damp meadows. The rebels had stripped the road of its rails and blown up the bridge across the Chickahominy, but the efficient northern engineers had restored both and a balloon train had stopped just to the right of the place where the road crossed the tracks. A locomotive puffed smoke into the air while the balloon's crew winched their ungainly vehicle up from a flatbed car. The wind had dropped in the wake of the storm, but even so the balloon's crew was having a hard struggle with the burgeoning envelope of gas.

"Trouble," Lassan grunted.

Starbuck had been gazing at the balloon, but now he

looked in the other direction and saw that a cavalry patrol was advancing along the railroad embankment.

"Maybe they're just hunting for skulkers," Lassan guessed. "We must risk it. Once we're in the far woods we'll be safe enough." He pointed to a thick belt of trees that lay on the far side of the railroad. "Just let the horse walk."

Lassan and Starbuck went slowly down the road. The Frenchman lit a cigar that he offered to Starbuck, then took one himself. The patrol was still a long way off and Starbuck felt his confidence rise as he drew nearer and nearer to the steel rails. The road climbed gently to the embankment's level between verges dotted with patches of burned grass where sparks from locomotives had started small fires. Two soldiers carried a reel mounted on a stick from which they unrolled a telegraph wire that would connect the balloon's basket with the wire that had been newly strung along the rail embankment. One of the men shimmied up a pole with a pair of pliers in his teeth. "I hate modern war," Lassan said as he and Starbuck reached the rail crossing. "War should be drumbeats and trumpets, not electric engineers and steam engines." Two ambulances were hurrying north along the road and Lassan drew his horse aside to let them pass. The wheels of the two white-painted wagons clattered over the boards that raised the roadbed to the level of the rails. The ambulances left a trail of fine blood drops on the road. Lassan grimaced at the sight of the ambulances' cargo of moaning, cursing, bleeding passengers, then took out his field glasses to examine the country south of the railroad. Off to the left were rows of tents and a line of earthworks where a battery of guns was emplaced, though the day's fighting all seemed to be a mile or so farther on beyond the trees. Two wig-wag men, their signal flags a blur of motion, stood on the redoubt's parapet to pass a message southward. Nearer at hand the cavalry patrol turned off the embankment and spurred onto the meadows.

"They've seen us," Starbuck warned the Frenchman, who looked leftward to see that the northern horsemen were angling across the fields in a maneuver that seemed designed to head off the two fugitives.

Lassan gazed for a second through his binoculars. "Your brother's there. And Pinkerton. I think we should become fugitives, yes?" He grinned at Starbuck, then trotted down the sloping road that led off the embankment's southern side. At the foot of the slope he looked again at the pursuers and evidently did not like what he saw for he took his heavy metal scabbard with its big, ugly sword and rammed it between his left thigh and the saddle so it would not bounce and bruise him. "Gallop!" he told Starbuck.

Both men rammed back their heels, and their horses threw up their heads and thumped their hooves into the road's red mud. A cavalry bugle sounded the charge and Starbuck twisted awkwardly in his saddle to see the blue-coated horsemen spreading across the field. The closest cavalry were still three hundred yards away and their horses were tired, but suddenly a pistol or carbine banged and Starbuck saw the puff of smoke snatched away behind the horsemen. He was not sure, but he thought he saw James, then another weapon cracked and Starbuck just ducked his head and rode hell-for-leather after Lassan. The Frenchman's horse pounded into the trees where Lassan swerved off the road into the tangled woodland. Starbuck followed, riding desperately around the denser patches of brush and ducking under the low branches until at last Lassan slowed to a trot and looked behind to make sure the pursuit had been avoided. Starbuck, his heart pounding, tried to calm his sweating horse. "I hate riding," he said.

Lassan held a finger to his lips, then pointed in the direction he wanted to go. He let the horses walk. Starbuck could smell the rank sweet stench of powder smoke while the sound of the guns was now so close that each gunshot gave a percussive thump to the ears, yet the trees still hid all sight of the battle. Lassan paused again. The Frenchman's face was alight with happiness. For him this was all a glorious adventure, a spree in the new world. "Onward," he said, "ever onward."

The two men emerged from the wood into a small, irregular meadow where a battalion of northern infantry waited. The officer leading the battalion's color party whirled his horse around eagerly as Lassan appeared. "Orders?" he asked.

"Not from us, good luck though," Lassan shouted in answer as he spurred past the color party. To Starbuck's left the country opened out and he could see wagons and gun limbers parked at a crossroads, and jets of smoke showing where the guns fired. There were a group of pine trees there and two gaunt houses that seemed to lie right beneath the plume of smoke. A Union flag lifted its scarlet and white stripes in the smoky breeze, then Starbuck lost sight of the crossroads as he followed Lassan into another belt of timber.

Lassan led him through a tangle of briers, over a fallen and fungi-ridden log, then they were in another clearing, and this time Starbuck could see the rail embankment to his right. There were no soldiers visible. "We've lost those cavalry," Starbuck said to the Frenchman.

"They're not so far away," Lassan cautioned. "We threw them off for a moment, but they'll be back. This way."

Their path led into trees again, then into another patch of open ground which proved to be so swampy that they had to dismount and lead their horses through the glutinous, sucking turf. Beyond the swamp was a patch of low scrub oak, then a stand of pines. The noise of the battle went on incessantly, but somehow, oddly, every evidence of soldiers had disappeared; indeed the woodland was so undisturbed that Lassan suddenly pointed to his right and Starbuck saw three wild turkeys in a small clearing. "Good eating?" Lassan asked.

"Very."

"Not today, though," Lassan said and turned to look ahead as an outbreak of rifle fire splintered the humid air. Then, over that fusillade, came the peculiar and chilling noise of the rebels' battle yell, and the sound of that defiant yelp gave Starbuck's heart a leap of excitement. "If I were you," Lassan said, "I'd take off that blue coat."

Starbuck was still wearing his brother's jacket. Now he hurriedly searched the pockets, taking out the Bible that James had left him in Richmond, then his handful of cheap cigars, the box of matches, the penknife, and the oilskin packet of papers. He pushed them all into a saddlebag, then peeled off his brother's coat and let it fall to the ground. Now he just wore his old gray rebel trousers, red suspenders, new shoes his brother had bought him from the sutler of a Pennsylvania regiment, and a broad-brimmed hat as ragged and stained as Lassan's eccentric headgear.

The Frenchman led him on through the trees. From time to time Starbuck would catch a glimpse of the rail embankment to their right, but he still could not see the troops who were giving the rebel yell. Every few seconds a stray rifle bullet tore through the leaves overhead, but it was hard to determine just where the fire was coming from. Lassan was picking his way carefully, as alert as a hunter edging toward a trapped prey. "We may have to cross the rails again," the Frenchman said, then there was no time for deliberation or thought, only for escape as a shout to their rear betrayed that the cavalry had found them again. Both men instinctively kicked their horses into a gallop.

A bullet slapped overhead, another cracked into a tree. Lassan whooped and ducked under a branch. Starbuck followed, gripping the pommel of his saddle as his horse thumped up a muddy path, across a small crest, and down to a road where a double file of Yankee infantry waited. "Make way! Make way!" Lassan shouted in his authoritative voice and the infantry moved magically aside to let the two horsemen pound past. They jumped a low hedge, crossed a field of arable, then once again the bullets came from behind and Starbuck feared that the whole infantry battalion would open fire, but suddenly he was in the woods again and could see soldiers to his left, only these soldiers were in full flight, running from some enemy ahead, and he let his hopes rise in anticipation. The fugitives were northerners, so surely there were rebels close by.

Lassan saw the running men and swerved away from them. Starbuck could hear hooves behind him now and he dared to snatch a glance over his shoulder to see a bearded horseman some twenty paces away. The man had a drawn saber, its blade wickedly bright in the day's cloudy gloom. There were infantry fusillades ahead, a rebel shout again, and more northerners running. Lassan looked over his shoulder and saw the cavalryman closing on Starbuck. The Frenchman pulled his horse left, slowed, and dragged his big sword from its scabbard. He let Starbuck overtake him, then he cut hard across the northerner's path and slammed the sword brutally down onto the skull of the man's horse. The blade drove into the horse's forehead and the beast screamed as it went down onto its knees. It was thrashing its head, spraying blood, then it collapsed and its rider went flying, cursing as he slid into a tangle of thorns beside the track. Lassan had already cut back to his left and was catching Starbuck again. "Always go for the horse, never the man," he shouted as he galloped to catch up with Starbuck.

The Frenchman sheathed his sword as he and Starbuck burst into a wide stretch of open country. To their right the rail embankment was topped by small groups of Yankees who were watching helplessly as a single rebel infantry brigade advanced boldly across the open heath. The brigade was composed of four battalions, three of which were flying the Confederacy's new battle flag while the fourth still carried the old three-striped flag. The brigade was advancing in two lines without either artillery or cavalry support, yet nothing seemed able to stop their progress. In front of them was a chaotic mass of fugitives and behind them a litter of dead and dying men. No other rebels were in sight. It was as if this one brigade had found a gap in the Yankee line and had decided to win the battle on its own.

Starbuck swerved toward the rebel brigade. "Virginia!" he shouted like a battle cry. "Virginia!" He waved to show he was unarmed. Lassan followed him, while sixty yards behind Lassan the northern cavalry burst out from beneath the trees.

The rebel brigade had been the first of General Longstreet's units to reach the battlefield, and its commander, Colonel Micah Jenkins, was just twenty-six years old. He had three battalions of South Carolinians and one of Georgians, and the four southern regiments had already torn through three Yankee positions. Jenkins had been ordered to attack, and no one had ordered him to stop, and so he was marching on deep into the Yankee rear. With a born soldier's luck his brigade had struck the Yankee defenses where there were few guns and only scattered units of infantry, and one by one the northern positions had been overwhelmed and put to panicked flight. Now his men were threatened by a handful of blue-coated cavalry who had appeared on their left flank. A South Carolina captain wheeled his company a half turn to the left. "Make sure you're loaded!" he called. "Aim for the horses!"

Some of the Yankees knew what was coming and sawed on their reins. One horse, turning too quickly, lost its footing in the wet soil and spilled over. Another reared up, whinnying, tipping its rider back over his saddle's cantle. But most of the Yankees whooped and galloped on, consumed with the fine frenzy of cavalrymen in full attack. Thirty horsemen had their sabers drawn, others carried revolvers. A bearded sergeant carried the guidon, a small triangular flag mounted on a lance shaft, and now he lowered the shaft's razor-sharp spear point until it pointed straight at the heart of the South Carolina Captain.

The Captain waited until the two strange fugitive horsemen were safely past his rifles, then he called the order to fire. Fifty rifles cracked.

Horses screamed and fell into the mud. The guidon plunged point-first into a tussock and stuck there quivering while the Sergeant flailed back off the horse, blood spilling suddenly from his open mouth. A dozen horses were down in the mud and another dozen rode into the chaos of hooves and scrambling men. Horses screamed in pain. The surviving beasts would not charge through the tangle of blood and beating hooves, but swerved aside instead. A few riders fired their revolvers into the bank of rifle smoke, then spurred away before the infantry could reload. Colonel Thorne was among the fallen, trapped in the mud beneath his wounded horse. The Colonel's left leg was broken and his fine dream of galloping across a smoky field to his country's rescue was reduced to the stench of blood and the scream of wounded beasts and the receding thump of hooves as the other cavalry wheeled hard away. The South Carolina Captain wheeled his company back into line and marched on.

Colonel Jenkins galloped across to the newcomers. "Who the devil are you?"

"Captain Starbuck, Faulconer Legion, Virginia," Starbuck panted.

"Lassan, Colonel of the French army, come to see some fighting," Lassan introduced himself.

"You've sure come to the right place, Colonel. What's up ahead?"

"My official position as an observer forbids me to tell you," Lassan said, "but my companion, if he had his breath back, would tell you there are two separate regiments of Yankee infantry, one in a clearing beyond the next stand of trees and the other a quarter mile beyond them. After that you hit their main defense works at the crossroads."

"Then we'd best keep going," Micah Jenkins said, "and whip the bastards some more." He looked at Starbuck. "You were a prisoner?"

"In a way, yes."

"Then welcome home, Captain, welcome home." He turned his horse and raised his voice. "On, boys, on! Roll the bastards back where they came from. On, boys, on!"

Starbuck turned to look back at the left flank. A squad of rebel skirmishers had gone to put the wounded horses out of their misery and their shots sounded flat and low in the day's gloom. The remnant of the Yankee cavalry had gathered by the far trees and now stood there impotent and watched while the infantrymen looted the saddlebags and pockets of the fallen riders. The southerners pulled Thorne's horse off the Colonel, took his sword and pistol, then left him cursing their parentage. Still more horsemen emerged from the woodland, and Starbuck could see James among them. Poor James, he thought, and the guilt whipped through him like a bullet's strike.

"What is it?" Lassan asked, seeing the stricken look on Starbuck's face.

"My brother."

"You're playing a game," Lassan said brusquely. "He lost, you won, you're both alive. There are thousands of men who will do worse than that today."

"I don't want him to suffer."

"How has he suffered?" Lassan asked. "The worst that will happen to your brother is that he will go back to his law practice, where he will spend the rest of his life telling his colleagues about his wastrel brother, and do you think he won't be secretly proud of you? You're doing all he would never dare, but would secretly like to do. Men like him need brothers like you, otherwise nothing would ever happen in their lives. My mother used to tell my sister and me one thing over and over again. Geese, she would say, go in gaggles, but eagles fly alone." Lassan grinned mischievously. "None of that may be true, *mon ami*, but if the notion helps your conscience then I would cling to it as though it were a warm woman in a deep bed on a cold night. Now stop feeling guilty and look for a weapon. There's a battle to fight."

Starbuck looked for a weapon. He was back under his chosen flag with a battle to fight, a noose to escape, and a friend to betray. He picked up a fallen man's rifle, found some cartridges, and looked for a target.

Northern reinforcements finally began crossing the rain-swollen river. The weight of a field gun broke the damaged bridge, though miraculously neither man nor weapon was lost. Instead the team horses were whipped bloody until they dragged the heavy gun out of the water and up to the corduroyed road on the southern bank.

McClellan stayed in bed, dosing himself with quinine,

honey, and brandy. He had taken so much medicine that he was dizzy and beset with headaches, but his doctor confirmed to the headquarters staff that the fevered General was aware that a battle was taking place, but claimed the patient was in no fit state to take command of the army. Tomorrow, perhaps, the Young Napoleon would be able to impose his granite will upon the battlefield, but till then he must rest and the army must manage without his guiding genius. The General's staff tiptoed away lest they disturb the great man's recovery.

General Johnston, waiting at his headquarters at the Old Tavern north of the railroad, had at last learned that the muffled noise of the guns was not an artillery duel, but rather a battle that had been raging without either his knowledge or his direction. General Longstreet had arrived at the Old Tavern to confirm that the first of his troops were now attacking south of the railroad. "I've lost Micah Jenkins," he told Johnston, "God only knows where his brigade is by now, and as for the rest, Johnston, they're exactly like virgins."

Johnston could have sworn Longstreet had said his men were like virgins. "They're like Virginians?"

"Like virgins, Johnston, virgins! Nervous of their flanks." Longstreet grinned. He was full of an excitable, quick energy. "We need an attack here" – he tapped a grimy fingernail on Johnston's map – "north of the rails."

Johnston rather believed he had given Longstreet specific orders to make just such an attack north of the rails, and that those orders had demanded the attack should have been made at dawn rather than now when the day was already dying. God only knew what had gone wrong with his careful three-pronged assault, but something had bent it dangerously askew and tomorrow, Johnston swore, he would find out exactly why it had gone awry and who was

434

responsible. But that inquiry must wait for victory and so he curbed his normally sharp tongue and instead sent an order for one of the reserve divisions to attack on the northern side of the railway embankment.

The new attackers marched past the Old Tavern, and Johnston, fretting to know exactly what was happening on the battlefield, joined the advancing troops. As he rode forward he wondered just why everything in this army seemed so needlessly complicated. It had been the same at Manassas, he reflected. At that battle the rebel headquarters had waited ignorant on the right while a battle flared on the left, while here he had waited on the left as a battle flared ungoverned on the right. Yet still he might pluck victory from chaos if only the Yankees had not sent too many reinforcements across the Chickahominy.

President Davis arrived at the Old Tavern to discover that General Johnston had gone eastward. Johnston's second-in-command, Gustavus Smith, who had been New York's street commissioner before the war, professed himself uncertain about the day's events, but delivered the broad verdict that everything seemed dandy as far as he understood, though he admitted his understanding did not stretch very far. General Lee, accompanying the President, was embarrassed by such a reply from a fellow soldier and shifted uncomfortably in his saddle. The tavern keeper brought the President a glass of sweetened lemonade that Davis drank on horseback. In the distance Davis could see the two yellow balloons of the Federal army's Aeronautical Corps wobbling precariously in the gusting wind. "Is there nothing we can do about those balloons?" Davis asked testily.

There was silence for a moment or two, then Lee quietly suggested that cannons did not have the necessary elevation and that the best answer might be high-powered sharpshooter rifles to make the lives of the gondola's occupants uncomfortable. "Even so, Mr. President, I doubt such rifles will have the necessary range."

"Something should be done," Davis said irritably.

"Eagles?" General Smith observed brightly. Both Lee and Davis looked at him quizzically and Smith hooked his fingers to demonstrate the action of a bird's claws. "Trained eagles, Mr. President, might well be persuaded to puncture the balloons' envelopes?"

"Quite so," Davis said, astonished. "Quite so." He glanced at his military adviser, but Lee was staring into a puddle as though, somehow, the answer to the Confederacy's problems might be found in its murky depths.

While out in the fields the guns banged on.

"On! On! On! On! On!" Micah Jenkins seemed to know only how to hurl his men forward. He ignored his own casualties, leaving them in the field behind while he chivvied and encouraged and inspired his men to keep advancing. They were deep inside Yankee territory now, without any other southern troops to support them, but the young South Carolinian did not care. "On! On!" he shouted. "No stopping now! Give the bastards hell. Come on, drummers! Let me hear you! Keep marching!" A bullet whistled within an inch of Jenkins's cheek, the wind of its passing like a small, warm slap. He saw a puff of smoke drifting away from the bushy top of a pine tree and he spurred forward to one of his marching companies. "See the smoke? The pine tree, there! To the left of the hawthorn. There's a sharpshooter up in the branches; I want the bastard's wife widowed this instant!"

A dozen men knelt, aimed, and fired. The tree seemed to shiver, then a body slumped into view, held in place by the rope that had tied the northern marksman to the tree. "Well done!" Jenkins shouted, "well done! Keep marching!"

Starbuck had collected a Palmetto rifle, a haversack of cartridges, and a gray uniform jacket from the corpse of a dead South Carolinian. The jacket had a small bullet hole in its left breast and a big, bloody rent in the back, but it still made a better uniform than his dirty shirt. Now he fought like a mounted infantryman, loading and firing from horseback. He rode just behind Jenkins's front line, caught up in the mad daring of this lunge that had carved its bloody hook deep into the Yankee rear. The main battle still thundered to the brigade's right, but that battle seemed like a quite separate action from this inspired South Carolinian charge.

The rebels marched in line across a road, throwing down the snake fence at its far side before moving into a belt of trees. The dead Yankee sharpshooter dripped blood from his tether at the top of the pine tree. His rifle, an expensive target model with a heavy barrel and a telescopic sight, had fallen to lodge in one of the lower branches from where it was retrieved by a jubilant Georgian who caught up with his comrades just as they emerged from the belt of trees to face yet another battalion of northern infantry. The northerners had just been ordered to their feet when the rebels burst from the trees. Micah Jenkins roared at his men to hold their fire and just charge. "Scream!" he shouted. "Scream!" And the ululating rebel yell began again.

The Yankee line disappeared behind its own bank of gunsmoke. Bullets whistled past Starbuck. Confederates were down, gasping and kicking on the grass, but still the gray line surged forward with Jenkins whipping it mercilessly on. "Leave the wounded! Leave them!" he shouted. "On! On! On!" The Yankees began reloading, their ramrods showing spiky above their two ranks, but then the banshee yell of the attackers and the glimmer of bayonet steel in the smoke convinced the northerners that this day was lost. The battalion broke and fled. "Follow them! Follow!" Jenkins shouted and the tired rebels swarmed into the woodland where they opened fire on the fugitives. Some Yankees tried to surrender, but Jenkins had no time for prisoners. The northerners had their rifles taken and were then told to make themselves scarce.

One more Yankee battalion waited at the wood's far edge and they, like all the other northern regiments that Jenkins's brigade had faced that afternoon, were unsupported by any other northern infantry. The first they knew of a rebel assault was when fleeing Yankees appeared among the trees, but before the Colonel could organize his defense, the rebels were in sight, whooping, yelling, and screaming for blood. The Yankees fled, pouring back across an open wheat field toward the crossroads where the bulk of their army had checked the strong central thrust of the rebels' main attack. And now, in sight of that larger battle, Micah Jenkins stopped his men.

The brigade had come deep into the Yankee rear, but to go farther was to invite annihilation. In front of them now there stretched an open plain crammed with tents, wagons, limbers, and caissons, while to their right was the crossroads by the two shell-riddled farmhouses and the seven bullet-shredded pine trees. It was there, by the rifle pits and the big redoubt, that the day's main battle raged. The main Confederate attack had stalled in front of the redoubt where the Yankees were putting up a solid defense. Cannon fire scorched the wheat and mowed down rebels. It was there that Johnston had planned to catch the stubborn Yankee defense in the pincers of his flank attacks, but the flank attacks had never happened and the central thrust was being bloodied and decimated by the northern gunners.

Except, by chance, Micah Jenkins's twelve hundred men were now in the Yankee rear. The brigade had started with nineteen hundred men, but seven hundred lay dead or wounded in the path of chaos that the South Carolinian had carved across the battlefield. Now he had a chance to make more chaos.

"Form line!" Jenkins shouted and waited while his second line of men caught up with the first. "Load!"

Twelve hundred rebels in two ragged ranks rammed minie balls on powder charges. Twelve hundred percussion caps were fumbled onto firing cones and twelve hundred hammers pulled back.

"Take aim!" Not that there was anything particular to aim at. No enemy were immediately confronting Jenkins's brigade; instead the rebel soldiers faced a wide field of Yankee encampments under a wind-fretted sky of smoky clouds. The rebel flags were hoisted high behind the line, the Palmetto flags of South Carolina and the three-pillared seal of Georgia, and above them all the crossed stars of the Confederacy's battle flag. Six enemy flags lay on the grass by Jenkins's horse, all captured in the charge and held now as trophies to be sent to his parents' plantation on Edisto Island.

Jenkins raised his saber high, paused for a heartbeat, then swept the curved blade down. "Fire!"

Twelve hundred bullets whipped across the damp evening fields. The volley did little physical damage, but its massive splintering crack announced to the northerners that there were rebels deep in their rear, and that realization was enough to start the retreat from the Seven Pines crossroads. One by one the Yankee guns were dragged out of the redoubt, then the infantry battalions began to back away from their parapets. Rebel yells whooped in the gloom and Starbuck saw a gray line of men swarm through the long shadows toward the earthen fort. A last northern gun fired, hurling a knot of attackers back in a mist of blood, then a flood of bayonets was carried up and over the sand-bagged parapets, and suddenly the wheat field in front of Micah Jenkins's brigade was dark with panicked men streaming eastward. The Yankees were abandoning their tents, their artillery, and their wounded. Horsemen galloped among the fugitives who ran toward the night, leaving the two houses and the shattered pines and the bloody redoubt to the rebels.

"My God." Jenkins spat a stream of tobacco juice that splattered onto one of the captured northern flags. "But Yankees sure make good runners."

There was enough light left to help the victorious rebels plunder the abandoned camps, but not enough to turn the day's victory into triumph. The northerners would not be driven into the swamps. Instead their officers halted the panicked flight a mile and a half east of the crossroads and there ordered the chastened battalions to dig new rifle pits and to fell trees to make new barricades. Guns came from the Yankee rear to stiffen the new defensive line, but in the day's dying light no rebels came to challenge the newly positioned batteries.

North of the railroad Johnston's flank attack waded through waist-deep swamps to attack emplaced guns protected by the infantry who had just marched across the river. The Yankee lines opened fire, their cannons cracking shell and canister and grape so that the gray lines reeled back, bloodied and shattered. The blue lines cheered in the twilight as they saw the shrieking enemy first silenced, then bloodied, then defeated. Wounded men drowned in the swamp, their blood oozing into the stinking mud.

General Johnston watched his men recoil from the

sudden and unexpected Yankee defense. He was sitting on his horse atop a small knoll that offered a fine view across the battlefield that was suddenly touched red by an evening sunlight that slanted underneath the clouds and battle smoke. Bullets whiplashed overhead, ripping through the leaves of a small sugarberry tree. One of his aides kept twitching in his saddle whenever a bullet came near, and the man's timidity annoyed the General. "You can't duck a bullet," he snapped at the aide. "By the time you hear them, they're past you." The General had been wounded five times in the service of the old U.S. Army and knew what it was to be under fire. He also knew that the careful battle that should have fetched him glory and fame had gone disastrously wrong. By God, he thought vengefully, but someone would suffer for this. "Does anyone know where Huger is?" he asked, but no one did. The General seemed to have vanished as completely as Longstreet had disappeared earlier, but at least Longstreet had finally reached the battlefield. Huger was still nowhere to be found. "Who gave Huger his orders?" Johnston demanded again.

"I told you, sir," Colonel Morton said respectfully. "It was young Faulconer."

Johnston turned on Adam. "He understood them?"

"I think so, sir."

"What do you mean? You think so? Did he have questions?"

"Yes, sir." Adam could feel himself coloring.

"What questions?" Johnston snapped.

Adam tried not to show his nervousness. "About the troops you put under General Longstreet's command, sir."

Johnston frowned. "He didn't have questions about the attack?"

"No, sir."

"Well tomorrow we'll get everyone into one room.

441

General Huger, General Longstreet, then we'll find out just what the devil happened today and I promise you that whoever made a hash of this day's work will wish they hadn't been born. Isn't that so, Morton?"

"Absolutely, sir."

"And I want every aide who carried a message to be there," Johnston insisted.

"Of course, sir," Morton said.

Adam stared doggedly into the gunsmoke. Somehow, in the raw glare of Johnston's anger, his febrile idea of the previous night did not seem so very bright after all. He had planned to plead forgetfulness, or just plain carelessness, but those excuses seemed extraordinarily weak right now.

"I'll have the responsible man shot!" Johnston spoke angrily, still obsessed with the failure of his careful plans, then he made a flamboyant gesture with his left arm that seemed curiously out of place, and Adam, who was terrified of what the morrow's investigation would bring, thought for a second that the General was trying to hit him, and then he saw that Johnston had been hit in the right shoulder and that he had merely flailed his left arm in a desperate attempt to keep his balance.

The General blinked rapidly, swallowed, then tentatively touched his left fingertips to his right shoulder. "Damn it, I've been hit," he said to Morton. "A bullet. Damn it." His breath was coming in big gasps.

"Sir!" Morton spurred forward to help Johnston.

"It's all right, Morton. Nothing vital touched. Just a bullet, that's all." Johnston clumsily fetched out a handkerchief and began folding it into a pad, but then a Yankee shell exploded at the foot of the knoll and a piece of the shrapnel case struck the General full in the chest and threw him back off his horse. He gave a cry, more in astonishment than in pain, then his aides gathered around to strip away his sword belt, pistols, and jacket. Blood was soaking the front of Johnston's uniform.

"You're going to be all right, sir," one aide said, but the General was quite unconscious now, and blood had started to spill from his mouth.

"Take him back!" Colonel Morton had taken charge. "A stretcher here, quick!" Another Yankee shell exploded nearby, its shrapnel hissing overhead to tear more leaves from the sugarberry.

Adam watched as men from the nearest infantry battalion brought a stretcher for the army's commander. Johnston's eyes were shut, his skin was pale, and his breath shallow. So much for the inquiry tomorrow, Adam thought, and his hopes soared. He would get away with it! He had engineered failure and no one would ever know!

Across the plain the guns fired on. The sun sank behind cloud again and the dead lay in the wet fields and the wounded cried and the living crouched to bite their cartridges and to fire their guns. The dusk made the gun flames stab ever brighter in the gloom. Then twilight brought the fireflies out and the guns slowly stopped until the cries of the dying were the loudest noise left between the city and the White Oak Swamp.

Flames flickered in the dark. There were no stars and no moonlight, just lanterns and small campfires. Men prayed.

In the morning, they knew, the battle would stir again like embers breathed to fire by a whispering breeze, but now, in the damp dark where the wounded cried for help, the two armies rested.

The battle died on the Sunday morning. The rebels, led now by General Smith, pushed on in the center, but the Yankees had sent reinforcements from north of the Chickahominy and would not be budged from their new defense line. Then the Yankees pushed back and the rebels gave ground until, at midday, the two armies gave up the struggle in mutual weariness. The rebels, finding no profit in holding on to the sliver of ground they had gained, pulled back to their original lines, thus letting the Yankees reoccupy the crossroads under the seven fire-blasted pine trees.

Work parties cut timbers and made pyres on which the dead horses were burned. The heat contracted the horses' tendons so that the dead beasts seemed to twitch in dreamy gallops as the flames hissed around them. The wounded were taken to field hospitals or, on the rebel side, loaded onto wagons and flatcars to be carried into Richmond. The northerners buried the dead in shallow graves because no one had the energy to dig deep ones, while the Confederates stacked their corpses in carts that were taken back to the cemeteries of Richmond. In the city, as the carts and wagons creaked through the streets with their uncovered cargoes of the dead and dying, women and children watched aghast.

The Yankees celebrated. One of the spoils of their battle was a double-decker horse bus that the Richmond Exchange Hotel had once used to carry hotel guests to the city's rail depots. The bus had been brought to the battlefield as an ambulance, but the vehicle had bogged down in the mud and been abandoned, so now the Union soldiers dragged it about their camp, offering two-cent rides down Broadway. All aboard for the Battery, they shouted. The northerners declared the battle a victory. Had they not repulsed the vaunted, outnumbering Confederates? And when the sick, shivering, weak McClellan appeared on horseback amid the wreckage of scorched limbers and shattered cannon and bloodied grass and broken rifles, he was welcomed with cheers as though he were a conquering hero. A New York band serenaded him with "Hail to the Chief." The General gallantly tried to give a speech, but his voice was pallid and only a few men heard him declare that they had witnessed the last despairing lunge of the rebel army, and that soon, very soon, he would lead them into the heart of secession and there defeat it utterly.

On both sides of the lines regiments formed squares for Sunday worship. Catholic regiments took Mass, Protestants listened to the Scriptures, and all thanked God for their deliverance. Strong men's voices sang hymns, the sound mournful across a battlefield that stank of death and smoke.

Starbuck and Lassan had spent the night with Micah Jenkins's brigade, but in the afternoon, after the battle died, they worked their way back through the shell holes and past the rows of dead men cut down by canister until they found the army headquarters in a small shingled farmhouse north of the railroad. Starbuck sought directions there and afterward, standing in the road, he parted from Lassan, but not before he insisted that the Frenchman take his brother's horse.

"You should sell the horse!" Lassan remonstrated.

Starbuck shook his head. "I'm in your debt."

"For what, *mon ami?*"

"My life," Starbuck said.

"Oh, nonsense! Such debts come and go on a battlefield like a child's wishes."

"But I am in your debt," Starbuck insisted.

Lassan laughed. "You are a puritan at heart. You let fear of sin ride you like a jockey. All right, I shall take the horse as a punishment for your imagined sins. We shall meet soon, yes?"

"I hope so," Starbuck said, but only if the gamble he was contemplating paid off. Otherwise, he thought, he would be hanging from a high beam in a cold dawn and he felt the temptation to throw away Pinkerton's paper. "I hope so," he said again, resisting the temptation.

"And remember what I taught you," Lassan said. "Aim low for men and high for women." He shook Starbuck's hand. "Good luck, my friend." The Frenchman went to make himself known to the Confederate headquarters while Starbuck walked slowly north with his handful of spoils from the battlefield. There was a fine northern-made razor with an ivory handle, a small pair of opera glasses, and a stone jug of cold coffee. He drank the coffee as he walked, tossing away the empty jug as he reached the fields where the Faulconer Brigade was camped.

It was time to do what Sally had told him to do so long before; it was time to fight.

He walked into the encampment just as the soldiers were being dismissed from the afternoon's church parade. He deliberately avoided the Legion's lines, going instead to the headquarters ridge-pole tents that were grouped about two pine trees that had been stripped of their branches to serve as flagpoles. The taller tree flew a Confederate battle flag, the slightly shorter carried the flag adapted from the Faulconer coat of arms with its motto "Forever Ardent." Nelson, General Washington Faulconer's servant, was the first man to see Starbuck in the encampment. "You must go away, Mr. Starbuck. If the master sees you, he'll have you arrested!"

"It's all right, Nelson. I'm told Master Adam's here?"

"That's right, sir. And sharing Captain Moxey's tent, sir, till they find him a new one. The master's so pleased he's back."

"Moxey's a captain now?" Starbuck asked, amused.

"He's an aide to the General, sir. And you shouldn't be here, sir, you shouldn't. The General can't abide you, sir."

"Show me to Moxey's tent, Nelson."

It was a big tent, serving not only as sleeping quarters but as a brigade office. There were two camp beds, two long tables, and two chairs, all set on a floor of wooden slats. Moxey's bed was piled with dirty clothes and discarded equipment while Adam's luggage was stacked at the foot of his neatly folded blankets. The tables held the stacks of paperwork that soldiering engendered, the piles all anchored by rocks that kept the forms safe from the small wind that stirred through the laced-back tent flaps.

Starbuck sat in one of the canvas folding chairs. The midday sunlight, watery at best, was turned into a leprous yellow by the canvas. He saw a Savage Navy revolver among the tangled belongings on Moxey's bed and Starbuck retrieved the gun just as the first officers began arriving back in the headquarters. Horses stamped their feet, servants and slaves ran to collect reins while the officers' cooks carried the evening meal across to the mess tables. Starbuck saw that the Savage was unloaded, but, typical of Moxey's carelessness, had an unfired percussion cap left on one of the cones. He turned the cylinder until the cap was in the next firing position, then looked up just as Captain Moxey ducked under the eaves. Starbuck smiled, but said nothing.

Moxey gaped at him. "You shouldn't be here, Starbuck."

"People keep telling me that. I'm beginning to feel distinctly unwanted, Moxey. But I'm here anyway, so you go and play somewhere else."

"This is my tent, Starbuck, so –" Moxey stopped abruptly as Starbuck leveled the heavy revolver. He raised his hands. "Now, Starbuck. Please! Be sensible!"

"Bang," Starbuck said, then pulled the gun's lower trigger that cocked the hammer and turned the cylinder. "Go away," he said.

"Now, Starbuck, please!" Moxey stammered, then

squealed as Starbuck pulled the upper trigger, making the percussion cap snap angrily. Moxey yelped and fled, while Starbuck levered the shattered and scorched scraps of copper off the cone. The tent was soured by a fine layer of astringent smoke.

Adam came in a few seconds later. He stopped when he saw Starbuck and his face suddenly seemed drained of color, though perhaps that was just the light-filtering effect of the canvas. "Nate," Adam said in a voice that was neither welcoming nor dismissive, but held a slightly guarded tone.

"Hello, Adam," Starbuck said happily.

"My father . . ."

". . . won't like it that I'm here," Starbuck continued the sentence for his friend. "Nor will Colonel Swynyard. Nor does Moxey approve of my presence, oddly enough, though why in the name of holy hell we should care what Moxey thinks, I don't know. I want to talk to you."

Adam looked at the gun in Starbuck's hand. "I've been wondering where you were."

"I've been with my brother James. Remember James? I've been with him, and with his chief who is a rugged little man called Pinkerton. Oh, and I've been with McClellan too. We mustn't forget Major General McClellan, the Young Napoleon." Starbuck peered into the Savage's barrel. "Moxey does keep a dirty gun. If he doesn't clean it he'll blow his hand off one day." Starbuck looked up at Adam again. "James sends his best wishes."

The tent gave a violent twitch as a man ducked through the entrance flaps. It was Washington Faulconer, his handsome face flushed with anger. Colonel Swynyard was behind the General, but Swynyard stayed out in the watery sunlight as Faulconer faced his enemy. "What the hell are you doing here, Starbuck?" General Faulconer demanded.

"Talking to Adam," Starbuck said mildly. He was sup-

448

pressing his nervousness. He might dislike Washington Faulconer, but the man was still a powerful enemy and a full general.

"You stand when you talk to me," Faulconer said. "And put that gun down," he added when Starbuck had obediently stood. Faulconer mistook the obedience for subservience. The General had come into the tent with his right hand on the hilt of his own revolver, but now he relaxed. "I ordered you out of my Legion, Starbuck," he said, "and when I gave that order I intended it to mean that you stayed well away from my men. All my men, and especially my family. You are not welcome here, not even as a visitor. You will leave now."

The General had spoken with dignity, keeping his voice low so that the curious bystanders would not hear the confrontation inside the tent.

"What if I don't go?" Starbuck asked just as quietly.

A muscle twitched on Faulconer's face, revealing that the General was a good deal more nervous than his demeanor betrayed. The last time these two men had faced each other had been on the evening of the battle at Manassas, and on that night it had been Faulconer who was humiliated and Starbuck who had triumphed. Faulconer was set on revenge. "You'll go, Starbuck," the General said confidently. "There's nothing for you here. We don't need you and we don't want you, so you can crawl back to your family or go back to that whore in Richmond, and you can do it on your own or you can do it under arrest. But you'll go. I command here and I'm ordering you away." Faulconer edged to one side and gestured toward the tent door. "Just go," he said.

Starbuck opened the top pocket of the threadbare uniform jacket that he had stripped from the dead South Carolinian and took out the Bible that James had given him. He looked at Adam and saw that his friend recognized the book.

"Father," Adam intervened softly.

"No, Adam!" the General said firmly. "I know your nature, I know you will appeal for your friend, but there is no appeal." Faulconer looked scornfully at Starbuck. "Put your Bible away and go. Else I'll call the provosts."

"Adam?" Starbuck prompted his friend.

Adam knew what Starbuck meant. The Bible was a symbol of James, and James was Adam's partner in espionage, and Adam's guilty conscience was more than strong enough to make the connection between the Bible and his own betrayal of his father's cause. "Father," Adam said again.

"No, Adam!" Faulconer insisted.

"Yes!" Adam snapped the word surprisingly loud, astonishing his father. "I have to talk with Nate," Adam insisted, "and afterward I'll talk with you." There was an utter misery in his voice.

Washington Faulconer felt his certainty crumble like a battle line shredding under cannon fire. He licked his lips. "What do you have to talk about?" he asked his son.

"Please, Father!"

"What's going on?" Faulconer demanded. Swynyard was crouching at the tent flap, trying to listen. "What's happening?" Faulconer appealed. "Tell me, Adam!"

Adam, his face still pale and sickly, just shook his head. "Please, Father."

But Washington Faulconer was not ready to surrender yet. He put his hand back to his pistol and glared at Starbuck. "I've had enough," he said. "I'm not standing here while you make our lives a misery again, so just get the hell away from us. Now!"

"General?" Starbuck said in a tone so mild and respectful

450

that it momentarily took Washington Faulconer aback.

"What is it?" Faulconer asked suspiciously.

Starbuck gave his enemy a glimmer of a smile. "All I'm asking of you, sir, is permission to rejoin the Legion. Nothing else, sir, that's all I want."

"I'm calling the provosts," General Faulconer said flatly and turned toward the tent's entrance.

"For whom?" Starbuck asked in a voice steely enough to check Washington Faulconer. "If I don't talk to Adam now," Starbuck went on remorselessly, "then I promise you that the name of Faulconer will go down in Virginia history alongside that of Benedict Arnold. I'll drag your family through mud so deep that even the hogs won't lie in your bedding. I'll break your name, General, and a whole nation will spit on its fragments."

"Nate!" Adam appealed.

"Faulconer and Arnold." Starbuck rubbed the threat home, and as he named the traitor, he felt the elation of a gambler, the same high feeling that had soared through him at the moment when he had turned the Yankee flank at Ball's Bluff. He had come here alone, armed only with a powerless shred of paper, and he was defeating a general surrounded by his own brigade. Starbuck could have laughed aloud for the arrogant success of this moment. He was a soldier, he was taking on a powerful enemy, and he was winning.

"Come and talk!" Adam said to Starbuck, and he twisted away toward the tent's entrance.

"Adam?" his father called after him.

"Soon, Father, soon. Nate and I have to talk first!" Adam said as he ducked out into the sunlight.

Starbuck smiled. "Nice to be back in the Legion, General."

For a second Starbuck thought Washington Faulconer

was going to unstrap the holster and pull out the revolver, but then the General turned and stalked out of the tent.

Starbuck followed. The General and Swynyard were striding away, scattering the knot of spectators who had gathered to listen to the conversation inside the tent. Adam seized Starbuck's arm. "Come," he said.

"You don't want to talk here?"

"We'll walk," Adam insisted, and he led Starbuck through the ring of bemused and silent officers. They crossed the field and climbed to the summit of a wooded knoll where redbuds and hornbeams grew. The redbuds were in blossom, cloudy pink and glorious. Adam stopped beside a fallen tree and turned to stare across the camp toward the distant city. "So how much do you know?" he asked Starbuck.

"Most everything, I guess," Starbuck said. He lit one of his cigars, then sat on the fallen trunk and watched the distant smoke trail of a locomotive. He guessed the train was hauling casualties to Richmond, more bodies for the sheds on Chimborazo Hill or the blossom-shaded graves at Hollywood.

"I want the war to end, you see." Adam broke the silence. "I've been wrong, Nate, all along. I should never have worn the uniform, ever. That was my mistake." He was flustered, uncertain, maybe unnerved by Starbuck's stillness. "I don't believe in the war," Adam went on defiantly. "I think it's a sin."

"But not a sin shared equally by both sides?"

"No," Adam said. "The North is morally right. We're wrong. You can see that, can't you? Surely you can see that?"

For answer Starbuck took the oilskin packet from his pocket and picked its stitches apart. As he plucked at the tightly sewn waxed cotton he told Adam how one of his letters had been intercepted when Webster was arrested, and how the authorities had suspected Starbuck of being its author, and how, once that ordeal had been endured, he had been sent across the lines to entrap the real traitor. "A very frightening man in Richmond sent me, Adam. He wanted to know who'd written that letter, but I knew it was you. Or I guessed it was you." Starbuck took the tightly folded piece of paper out of its oilskin package. "I'm supposed to take this paper back to Richmond. It's the proof they want. It names you as the spy." The piece of paper did nothing of the sort; it was merely the list of questions that Pinkerton and McClellan had concocted before the General went down with the Chickahominy fever, but there was a circular impression of an inked rubber stamp on the bottom of the letter which read "Sealed by Order of the Chief of the Army of the Potomac's Secret Service Bureau," and Starbuck let Adam see that seal before he folded the letter into a neat square.

Adam was too frightened to challenge Starbuck's bald assertion that the paper was proof of his guilt. He had seen the seal, and he had seen the elaborate precautions taken to protect the paper from damp, and what he had seen was proof enough. He had no idea that it was all a bluff, that the paper failed to incriminate him and that Starbuck's frightening man in Richmond was lying white-faced in a coffin. Starbuck, in truth, held a lousy hand of cards, but Adam felt too guilty to perceive that his friend was bluffing. "So what will you do?" Adam asked.

"What I won't do," Starbuck said, "is go to the very frightening man in Richmond and give him this letter." He placed the folded letter into his breast pocket beside the Bible. "What you can do," Starbuck suggested to Adam, "is shoot me right now. Then you can take the letter and no one will ever know you were a traitor."

"I'm not a traitor!" Adam bridled. "My God, Nate, this was all one country just a year ago! You and I took our hats off to the same flag, we cheered each July the Fourth together, and we had tears in our eyes when they played the 'Star Spangled Banner.' So how can I be a traitor if all that I'm doing is fighting for what I was brought up to love?"

"Because if you had succeeded," Starbuck said, "men who are your friends would have died."

"But fewer of them!" Adam shouted in protest. There were tears in his eyes as he looked away from Starbuck to gaze across the green land toward the spires and dark roofs of Richmond. "Don't you understand, Nate? The longer the war goes on, the more deaths there'll be?"

"So you were going to end it, single-handed?"

Adam heard the scorn. "I was going to do the right thing, Nate. Do you remember when you sought the right thing? When you prayed with me? When you read your Bible? When doing God's will was more important than anything on this earth? What happened to you, for God's sake?"

Starbuck looked up at his angry friend. "I found a cause," he said.

"A cause!" Adam scoffed at the word. "The South? Dixie? You don't even know the South! You haven't traveled south of Rockett's Landing in all your life! Have you seen the South Carolina rice fields? Have you seen the delta plantations?" Adam's anger was eloquent and fierce. "You want a view of hell on earth, Nate Starbuck, then you take a journey to see what it is you're defending. You go down the river, Nate, and hear the whips and see the blood and watch the children being raped! Then you come and tell me about your cause."

"So what's your moral cause?" Starbuck tried to retrieve the upper hand in the argument. "You think by winning this war the North will make the slaves happy? You think they'll be served better than the poor in northern factories? You've been to Massachusetts, Adam, you saw the factories in Lowell, is that your new Jerusalem?"

Adam shook his head wearily. "America's had these arguments a thousand times, Nate, and then we had an election and we settled the argument at the ballot box, and it was the South that wouldn't accept that decision." He spread his hands as if to show that he did not want to hear any more of the old, pointless discussion. "My cause is to do what's right, nothing else."

"And deceive your father?" Starbuck asked. "Do you remember last summer? In Faulconer County? You asked me how I could be scared of my father and not be scared of battle. So why don't you tell your father what you believe?"

"Because it would break his heart," Adam said simply. He fell silent, gazing north to where a bend in the Chickahominy showed as a flash of light in the green landscape. "I thought, you see, that I could ride both horses, that I could serve my country and my state, and that if the war was over quickly then my father would never know I had betrayed the one for the other." He paused. "And that might still happen. McClellan only has to push hard."

"McClellan can't push. McClellan is a turkey cock, all strut and no puff. Besides, McClellan thinks we outnumber him. I saw to that."

Adam flinched at Starbuck's tone, but said nothing for a long while. Then he sighed. "Did James betray me?"

"No one betrayed you. I worked it out for myself."

"Clever Nate," Adam said sadly. "Wrongheaded, clever Nate."

"What will your father do if he finds out you were betraying the South?" Starbuck asked.

Adam looked down at him. "Are you going to tell him?"

he asked. "You almost did already, so now you'll tell him the rest, is that it?"

Starbuck shook his head. "What I'm going to do, Adam, is walk down to those tents and I'm going to find Pecker Bird and I shall tell him that I've come back to be the Captain of K Company. That's all I'm going to do, unless someone comes to kick me out of the Legion again, in which case I'll go to Richmond and find a nasty, clever old man and let him deal with things instead of me."

Adam frowned at the implied threat. "Why?" he asked after a silence.

"Because that's what I'm good at. I've discovered I like being a soldier."

"In my father's brigade? He hates you! Why don't you go and join another regiment?"

Starbuck did not answer for a moment. The truth was that he had no leverage to join another regiment, not as a captain anyway, because his scrap of paper was only useful as a weapon against the Faulconer family. But there was also a deeper truth. Starbuck was beginning to understand that war could not be approached halfheartedly. A man did not dabble with killing any more than a Christian could flirt with sin. War had to be embraced, celebrated, drunk deep, and only a handful of men survived that process, but that handful blazed across history as heroes. Washington Faulconer was no such man. Faulconer enjoyed the trappings of high military office, but he had no taste for war, and Starbuck suddenly saw very clearly that if he survived the bullets and shells, then he would one day lead this half-hearted brigade into battle. There would be a Starbuck Brigade, and God help the enemy when that day came. "Because you don't run away from your enemies," he finally answered his friend's question.

Adam shook his head pityingly. "Nate Starbuck," he said

bitterly, "in love with war and soldiering. Is it because you failed at everything else?"

"This is where I belong." Starbuck ignored Adam's bitter question. "And you don't. So what you're going to do, Adam, is persuade your father to let me be the Captain of the Legion's K Company. How you do it is up to you. You don't have to tell him the truth."

"What else can I tell him?" Adam asked despairingly. "You've hinted enough."

"You and your father have a choice," Starbuck said, "to do this privately or to have it all dragged out into the open. I think I know which your father would prefer." He paused, then embellished his bluff with another lie. "And I'll write to the old man in Richmond and tell him the spy is dead. I'll say he was killed in battle yesterday. After all, you have finished your career as a spy, have you not?"

Adam heard the sarcasm and winced. Then he glanced sharply at Starbuck. "I do have another choice, remember."

"You do?"

Adam unbuttoned the flap that held the revolver in his holster and drew out the weapon. It was an expensive Whitney revolver with ivory sideplates on its handle and an engraved cylinder. He took out a small percussion cap and primed one of the loaded chambers.

"For God's sake don't kill yourself," Starbuck said in alarm.

Adam turned the cylinder so that the loaded chamber was ready to be turned under the hammer. "I've sometimes thought of suicide, Nate," he said in a mild voice. "In fact I've often thought how blessed it would be not to have to worry about doing the right thing, not to have to worry about Father, not to have to worry about whether Julia loves me, or whether I love her. Don't you find life complicated? Oh, God in His heaven, but I find it so tangled,

457

except in all the prayer, Nate, and in all the thinking of these last few weeks, I did find one certainty." He gestured with the loaded revolver, sweeping the weapon around the whole wide horizon. "This is God's country, Nate, and He put us here for His purpose, and that purpose was not to kill each other. I believe in the United States of America, not the Confederate States, and I believe God made the United States to be an example and a blessing to the world. So no, I'm not going to kill myself, because killing myself won't bring the American millennium one day nearer, just as none of the battle deaths have brought it one day nearer." He straightened his arm and lowered the gun's barrel until it was pointing straight at Starbuck's forehead. "But as you said, Nate, I could kill you and no one would be any the wiser."

Starbuck stared into the gun. He could see the pointed cones of the bullets in the lower chambers and he knew that one such bullet faced him down the dark muzzle. The weapon shook slightly in Adam's hand as Starbuck looked up beyond the gun into his friend's pale and earnest face.

Adam cocked the revolver. The sound of the hammer engaging sounded very loud. "Do you remember when we used to talk at Yale?" Adam asked. "How we took pride in the fact that God made being virtuous so difficult? It was easy to be a sinner, and so hard to be a Christian. But you gave up trying to be a Christian, didn't you, Nate?" The gun still shook, its muzzle catching and quivering the day's last sunlight. "I remember when I met you, Nate," Adam went on. "I used to worry so much about life's hardships, about the difficulties of knowing God's will, and then you came along and I thought nothing would ever be quite so hard again. I thought you and I would share the load. I thought we'd walk God's path together. I was wrong, wasn't I?"

Starbuck said nothing.

"What you're asking of me," Adam said, "is what you're not strong enough to do yourself. You're asking me to face my father and break his heart. I always thought you were the stronger of the two of us, but I was wrong, wasn't I?" Adam seemed very close to tears.

"If you had the courage," Starbuck said, "you wouldn't shoot me, but go fight for the Yankees."

"I don't need your advice anymore," Adam said. "I've had enough of your filthy advice to last me a lifetime, Nate." Then he pulled the trigger.

The gun crashed loud, but Adam had raised the barrel at the very last moment to fire into the tree above Starbuck's head. The bullet smashed through a bunch of redbud blossoms to scatter the petals across Starbuck's shoulders.

Starbuck stood. "I'm going to the Legion. You know where to find me."

"Do you know what they call that tree?" Adam asked as Starbuck walked away.

Starbuck turned and paused while he tried to find the trick in the question. He could find none. "A redbud, why?"

"They call it the Judas tree, Nate. The Judas tree."

Starbuck looked into his friend's face. "Goodbye, Adam," he said.

But there was no answer, and he walked down to the Legion alone.

"You've heard the news?" Thaddeus Bird said when Starbuck presented himself at his tent.

"I'm back."

"So you are," Bird said, as though Starbuck's sudden appearance were entirely ordinary. "Does my brother-in-law know you're under his command again?"

"He's finding out right now." Starbuck had watched Adam walk to his father's tent.

"And you think the General will approve?" Bird asked dubiously. He had been writing a letter and now rested his pen on the edge of the dry goods box that served as his table.

"I don't think he'll throw me out of the Legion."

"You are full of mystery, young Starbuck. Well, I'm sure Mr. Truslow will be pleased to see you. For some reason he seems to have regretted your absence." Bird picked up the pen and dipped its nib in ink. "I assume you've heard the news?"

"What news?"

"We have a new army commander."

"We do?" Starbuck asked.

"Robert E. Lee." Bird gave a shrug as if to suggest that the news were hardly worth mentioning.

"Ah."

"Exactly. Ah. It seems the President didn't trust Smith to replace Johnston, so Granny Lee, our King of Spades, has got the job. Still, even the King of Spades cannot be any worse than Johnston, can he? Or maybe he can. Perhaps the best we can hope for is that Lee is slightly better than his reputation."

"McClellan thinks Lee lacks moral strength," Starbuck said.

"You know that for a fact, do you, young Starbuck?"

"Yes, sir, I do. McClellan told me last week."

"Splendid, good, go away." Bird waved imperiously.

Starbuck paused. "It's nice to be back, sir."

"Get an early night, Starbuck, we're on picket duty from midnight. Major Hinton will have your orders."

"Yes, sir."

"And give Sergeant Truslow a dollar."

"A dollar, sir?"

"Give him a dollar! That's an order." Bird paused. "I'm glad you're back, Nate. Now go away."

"Yes, sir." Starbuck walked through the lines, listening to the distant sad sound of a violin. Yet the sadness did not touch him, not now, for now he was back where he belonged. The copperhead was home.

EPILOGUE

K COMPANY BEGAN ITS DYING three weeks later. Joseph May was the first. He was fetching water when a stray shell landed by the brook. His new spectacles were blown off his face, one lens was shattered, and the other so evenly coated in blood that it looked just like ruby-colored glass.

All that day the Legion waited while a battle hammered just to its north. The guns sounded from dawn to dusk, but the smoke plume never shifted, evidence that for all the rebel attacks the Yankees would not be moved back. Yet that night, after the fighting died, the northern army slipped away to new positions farther east and in the dawn they could be heard digging and the rebels knew there would be hard work ahead if the blue-bellies were to be pushed farther away from Richmond. James Bleasdale died that morning. He climbed a tree to get eggs from a nest and a Yankee sniper got him in the neck. He was dead before he hit the ground. Starbuck wrote to his mother, a widow, and tried to find words that might imply that her son had not died in vain. "He will be sorely missed," Starbuck wrote, but it was not really true. No one had particularly liked Bleasdale, or disliked him either for that matter. A flurry of shots announced that Sergeant Truslow's expedition had located the Yankee sharpshooter, but Truslow came back disconsolate. "Son of a bitch skedaddled," the Sergeant said, then turned to stare at Major Bird. "He's gone mad."

Major Bird was indeed behaving more oddly than usual.

He was progressing through the encampment with a curious, crablike motion, sometimes darting forward a few steps, then stopping with his feet together and one arm extended before suddenly turning completely around and beginning the strange sequence all over again. Every now and then he interrupted the strange capering to inform a group of men that they should be ready to march in half an hour's time. "He's gone mad," Truslow said again, after a further examination of the Major's strange gait.

"I am learning to dance," Bird announced to Starbuck and made a complete revolution with an imaginary partner in his ragged arms.

"Why?" Starbuck asked.

"Because dancing is a graceful accomplishment to high office. My brother-in-law has just made me a lieutenant colonel."

"Congratulations, Pecker." Starbuck was genuinely pleased.

"It seems he has small choice now that Adam has resigned from the fray." Pecker Bird, despite his avowed contempt for the formal military hierarchy, could not hide his pleasure.

"He had even less choice after everyone voted for you," Truslow growled.

"Voted! You think I owe my high military status to mere democracy? To mobocracy? I am a genius, Sergeant, rising like a comet through oceans of mediocrity. I mix metaphors too." Bird peered at the paper on Starbuck's lap. "Are you writing metaphors to Mother Bleasdale, Nate?"

"Just the usual lies, Pecker."

"Tell her some unusual ones, then. Say that her dull son is promoted to glory, that he has been loosed from his earthly bonds and now trills in the choir eternal. Say that he frolics in Abram's bosom. Sarah Bleasdale will like that, she was ever a fool. Half an hour, Starbuck, then we march." Bird danced away, whirling an invisible partner over the cow pats in the field where the Legion had slept under the stars.

General Lee was beside the road as the Legion marched out of its encampment. He sat straight-backed on a gray horse, surrounded by his staff and touching his hat to each company in turn. "We must drive them away," he said to each company in a conversational tone, and in between made awkward small talk with Washington Faulconer. "Drive them away, boys, drive them away," Lee said again, this time to the company marching immediately ahead of Starbuck's, and when the General turned to Faulconer once again he found that the brigadier had inexplicably moved away. "Push them hard, Faulconer!" Lee called after him, puzzled by Faulconer's sudden departure.

Faulconer's abrupt leaving was no mystery to the Legion, who had noticed how their general assiduously avoided K Company. He had dined with the officers from each of his brigade's other regiments, but he ignored the Legion in case he was forced to acknowledge Starbuck's presence. Faulconer told Swynyard he wanted to avoid the appearance of showing favoritism to the regiment that bore his name, and for that same reason he claimed to have decided not to appoint his son to command the Faulconer Legion, but no one believed the tale. Adam, it was said, was sick in his father's country house, though some, like Bird and Truslow, suspected the sickness was connected with Starbuck's return. Starbuck himself refused to speak of the matter.

"Drive them away, boys, drive them away," Lee said to K Company, touching a hand to his hat. Behind the general a stretch of woodland was splintered and charred from the previous day's fighting. A party of Negroes was collecting corpses, dragging them to a newly dug grave. Just around the corner another black man was hanging dead from a tree with a misspelled placard pinned to his chest. "This nigger was a gide to the yankees," the placard read. Lee, following K Company down the road, angrily ordered the corpse taken down.

Lee separated from the Legion at a crossroads where a tavern offered a night's lodging for five cents. A group of disconsolate northern prisoners was sitting on the tavern's steps under the guard of a pair of Georgia soldiers who looked scarcely a day over fourteen. A shell exploded in midair a half mile away, the smoke sudden and silent in the pearly sky. The sound followed an instant later, then a crackle of musketry ripped through the morning to scare a flock of birds up from the trees. A battery of Confederate cannon unlimbered in a field to the right of the road. Shirtsleeved men led the team horses back from the guns while other gunners filled sponge buckets with ditch water. They all had the efficient, unhurried look of workmen moving about their daily preparations.

"Colonel Bird! Colonel Bird!" Captain Moxey cantered down the Legion's line of march. "Where's Colonel Bird?"

"In the woods," Sergeant Hutton called back.

"What's he doing in the woods?"

"What do you think?"

Moxey turned his horse. "He's to report to General Faulconer. There's a mill down there." He pointed to a side road. "He's to go there. It's called Gaines' Mill."

"We'll tell him," Truslow said.

Moxey inadvertently caught Starbuck's eye and immediately slashed his spurs back to make his horse leap ahead. "We won't see him near the bullets today," Truslow commented drily.

The Legion waited beside the road while Bird learned

their fate. The Yankees were clearly not far away, for rebel shells were exploding over some nearby woods. Rifle fire sounded in sudden bursts, as though the skirmishers of either side were probing forward to make contact. The Legion waited as the sun rose higher and higher. Somewhere ahead of them a great veil of dust hung in the air, evidence that wheeled traffic was busy on a road, but whether it was the Yankees retreating or the rebels advancing, no one could tell. The morning passed and the Legion made a cold dinner from hardtack, rough rice, and water.

Bird returned just after midday and called his officers together. A half mile ahead of the Legion, he said, was a belt of woodland. The trees concealed a steep valley through which a stream ran through marshland toward the Chickahominy. The Yankees were dug in on the far bank of the stream and the Legion's job was to drive the sons of bitches away. "We're the front line," Bird told his company officers. "The Arkansas boys will be on our left, the rest of the brigade will be behind us."

"And the brigadier behind them," Captain Murphy said in his soft Irish accent.

Bird pretended not to have heard the jibe. "The river's not far beyond the Yankees," he said, "and Jackson's marching to cut them off, so maybe today we can break them forever." Stonewall Jackson had brought his army to the peninsula after driving the Yankees out of the Shenandoah Valley. The northern troops in the Shenandoah had outnumbered Jackson, but he had first marched rings around them, then whipped them bloody, and now his troops were under Lee's orders and facing McClellan's lumbering and hesitant army. That army, after the fight around the seven pines at the crossroads, had neither advanced nor retreated, but had instead busied itself with making a new supply base on the James River. Jeb Stuart had scornfully led twelve hundred rebel cavalrymen in a ride clean around the whole northern army, mocking McClellan's impotence and giving every southern patriot a new hero. Colonel Lassan had ridden with Stuart and brought news of the ride to Starbuck. "It was magnificent!" Lassan had enthused. "Worthy of the French cavalry!" He had brought three bottles of looted Yankee brandy that he shared with the Legion's officers while he filled an evening with tales of battles far away.

Yet McClellan would not be defeated by horsemen, however brilliant, but by infantrymen like those Bird now led toward the woods above the stream. The day was sweltering. Spring had turned into summer, the blossoms were gone, and the peninsula's muddy roads had dried to a cracked crust that scuffed into thick dust wherever men or horses passed.

Bird deployed eight companies of the Legion into a line of two ranks. The small Arkansas battalion formed on the left of the Legion beside Starbuck's men. They raised their colors. One was an old-fashioned three-striped Confederate flag while the other was a black banner with a crudely depicted white snake coiled at its center. "Ain't really our flag," the Arkansas Major confided to Starbuck, "but we kind of liked it and so we just took it. Bunch of boys from New Jersey had it first." He spat a viscous stream of tobacco juice, then told Starbuck how he and his men had arrived as volunteers in Richmond at the very beginning of the war. "Some of the boys wanted to go home to Arkansas after Manassas, and I could understand that, but I kept telling them there were more live Yankees here than there were back home and so I guess we just stayed on to do a bit of killing." His name was Haxall and his battalion numbered just over two hundred men, all of them as lean and ill-kempt as Haxall himself. "Luck to you, Captain," he said

470

to Starbuck, then slouched back to his small battalion just as Colonel Swynyard gave the order to advance. It was past midday so Swynyard was already hard put to stay in his saddle; by evening he would be incoherent and by midnight insensible. "Forward!" Swynyard shouted again, and the Legion trudged toward the shadowed woods.

"Does anyone know where we are?" Sergeant Hutton asked K Company.

No one did. It was just another piece of swampy woodland over which the shells began to burst. Starbuck could hear the missiles ripping through the trees, and every now and then a thrashing of leaves would show where a shell was passing through the upper branches. Some missiles exploded among the trees, others screamed over the Legion toward the Confederate battery in the field behind. The rebel guns answered, filling the sky with the thunderous wail of an artillery duel. "Skirmishers!" Major Hinton called. "Off you go, Nate!" he added more casually and Starbuck's company obediently broke ranks and trotted ahead to form a scattered line fifty paces ahead of the other companies. Starbuck's company formed teams of four men, though Starbuck, as an officer, was on his own and he suddenly felt very visible. He carried nothing that would denote to an enemy that he was an officer; no sword, no glint of braid, no metal bar on his collar, but his very solitariness suddenly seemed to make him a target. He watched the tree line, wondering whether northern skirmishers waited there or, worse, whether the green shadows hid a scatter of lethal sharpshooters with their telescopic sights and deadly rifles. He could feel his own heart beating and each step needed a deliberate effort. He instinctively kept his rifle's wooden stock over his crotch. A shell exploded just a few yards ahead and a scrap of shrapnel whipped past his shoulder. "Glad you came back!" Truslow called to him.

"This is how I always dreamed of spending my Friday afternoons, Sergeant," Starbuck said, astonished that his voice sounded so careless. He glanced around to make sure his men were not lagging behind and was astonished to see that the Legion was merely one small part of an immense line of gray-clad infantry that stretched away to his left for a half mile or more. He even forgot his fear for a few seconds as he gazed at the thousands of men in their wavering attack line who walked forward under their bright flags.

A shell exploded ahead of Starbuck, turning his attention back to the trees. He hurried past a scorched patch of turf where a fragment of shell smoked in the dirt. Another explosion sounded, this one from behind Starbuck and so huge that it seemed to punch a wave of hot air across the summer landscape. Starbuck turned to see that a Yankee shell had hit an artillery limber loaded with ammunition. Smoke boiled up from the shattered vehicle and a riderless horse limped away from the flames. A nearby gun fired, jetting a twenty-yard cloud of smoke behind its shell. The grass rippled outward in a shock wave from the gun's muzzle. The Faulconer Brigade's second line of men was deploying and somewhere a band was playing the popular Richmond song "God Will Defend the Right." Starbuck wished the musicians had chosen something more tuneful, then he forgot the music as he plunged into the trees where the day's harsh light was filtered green by the leaves. A squirrel ran ahead through the leaf mold. "When did we last eat squirrel?" he asked Truslow.

"We had plenty while you were away," the Sergeant said.

"I fancy some fried squirrel," Starbuck said. One year ago he would have gagged at the very idea of eating squirrels, whereas now he had a soldier's fastidious preference for young squirrels fried. The older animals were much tougher and were better stewed.

"Tonight we'll eat Yankee rations," Truslow said.

"That's true," Starbuck said. Where the hell were the enemy skirmishers? Where were their marksmen? A shell ripped through the treetops, provoking a clatter of pigeon wings. Where, for that matter, was the stream and the marshland? Then he saw the lip of a valley ahead, and beyond it the tall trees of the far slope, and under the trees there was a glimpse of freshly turned earth, and he understood that the Yankees were dug in on that far slope that would serve them like a giant earthwork. "Run!" he shouted. "Run!" He knew instinctively what was about to happen. "Charge!" he shouted,

And the world exploded.

The whole far side of the valley seemed to smother itself in a sudden, self-engendered fogbank. One moment the valley's far side was leaves and brush, then it was a layer of white smoke. The sound came a heartbeat later, and with the sound came a storm of bullets that ripped and shredded through the green woods. Men on the far slope were shouting and whooping; men on Starbuck's side of the valley were dying.

"Sergeant Carter's hit!" a man shouted.

"Keep running!" Starbuck bellowed. There was no point in lingering on the valley's lip to be the Yankees' victims. The gunsmoke was shredding and he could see a mass of blue-coated infantry among the far trees while, on the crest above, a line of cannon was emplaced behind newly dug ramparts. Rifle flames stabbed that blue line, then the cannon fired to roll a cloud of gray-white smoke among the trees. A man screamed as a canister ball disemboweled him, another crawled bleeding toward the bulk of the Legion that advanced into the wood behind the skirmishers. The trees above Starbuck sounded as if a sudden gale had snatched at their boughs. More cannon fired, and suddenly the whole wood was filled with the shriek and bellow of canister. Rifle bullets whistled and cracked. Fear was like vomit in Starbuck's craw, but survival lay in charging ahead and down into the green void of the valley. He leaped over the crest and half slid and half ran down the precipitous slope. The Arkansas men were giving the rebel yell. One of them was tumbling down the hill, blood smearing the dead leaves behind him. The Yankee gunfire was a constant splintering sound, a sustained, mind-numbing crackle as hundreds of rifles fired across the small valley. Amos Parks was hit in the belly, plucked backward with the force of a mule kick. More canister smashed overhead, bringing down a blizzard of leaf scraps and torn twigs. The Legion's only hope now was to keep running and so overwhelm the enemy with speed.

"Fix bayonets!" Haxall cried to Starbuck's left.

"Keep running!" Starbuck shouted to his men. He did not want his men slowing down to fix their clumsy bayonets. Better to keep moving into the morass at the valley's bottom where a stretch of black, stagnant water was broken by splintered trees, fallen logs, and marshy banks. The stream doubtless ran somewhere in the middle of the morass, but Starbuck could not see it. He reached the foot of the slope and leaped for a fallen log, then jumped again onto a bank of rich grass. A bullet churned water up ahead of him, another splintered a rotten length of wet timber from a log. He splashed through a stretch of water, then slipped as he tried to scramble up a short, slick bank of mud. He fell forward into grass, protected from the Yankees ahead and above by a huge, black, half-rotted tree trunk. He felt the temptation to stay behind the sheltering trunk, but knew his job was to keep his men moving. "Come on!" he shouted, and wondered why no one was using the rebel yell any longer, but just as he tried to stand up a hand

474

banged him in the small of the back and drove him down.

It was Sergeant Truslow who had pushed him. "Forget it!" Truslow said. The whole company had gone to ground. Not just the company, but the whole Legion. Indeed the whole rebel attack had taken cover because the entire valley was whipsawed with Yankee bullets, filled with the shriek and scream of canister and thick with powder smoke. Starbuck raised his head and saw the far rim of the valley wreathed in smoke above which the red and white stripes of the Yankee banners floated. A bullet smacked the log just inches from his face, driving a splinter into his cheek. "Keep your head down," Truslow growled. Starbuck twisted round. The only men in clear sight were the dead. Everyone else was crouching behind trees or sheltering in undergrowth. The bulk of the Legion was still at the top of the slope, gone to ground in the main stretch of woodland. Only the skirmishers had reached the valley's floor, and not all the skirmishers had made it safely. "Carter Hutton's dead," Truslow said, "so God knows how his wife will manage."

"Did he have children?" Starbuck asked and chided himself for needing to ask. An officer should know these things.

"Boy and a girl. Boy's a slobbering idiot. Doc Billy should have strangled him at birth like he usually does." Truslow raised his rifle above the log's parapet, sighted briefly, then fired and ducked straight down. "The girl's deaf as a stone. Carter never should have married the damn woman." He bit the top off a cartridge. "The women in that family all have weak litters. It's no good marrying for looks. Marry for strength."

"What did you marry for?" Starbuck asked.

"Looks, of course."

"I asked Sally to marry me," Starbuck confessed awkwardly.

"And?"

Starbuck knelt up, aimed the rifle at the top of the slope, pulled the trigger, and dropped down just an instant before a whole hornets' buzz of bullets slapped into the tree. "She turned me down," he confessed.

"So the girl's got some sense left then?" Truslow grinned. He was reloading his rifle, doing it lying down. The Yankees were cheering because the Confederate assault had been stopped so easily, but then a rebel yell announced the arrival of the Faulconer Brigade's second line and the Yankee fire seemed to double itself as they tore at these new attackers among the trees. Some men of the first line managed to throw themselves over the valley's lip and scrambled down the slope to find shelter. Cannon fired at point-blank range, hurling men back from the gray line. Starbuck was tempted to try and advance a few yards farther, but the second attack went to ground even faster than the first and the Yankee rifle fire switched back to the valley bottom where water and mud were churned by the bullet strikes. "Bastards have got their dander up this afternoon," Truslow grumbled.

"Reckon we're here till nightfall," Starbuck said, then bit a bullet off a cartridge. He shook the powder into the barrel, then spat the bullet into the muzzle. "Only darkness will get us out of this."

"Unless the bastards run," Truslow said, though not with any optimism. "I'll tell you one thing. We won't see Faulconer down here. He'll be keeping his pants dry." Truslow had found a niche in the fallen tree that offered him an oblique view up the enemy slope. Most of the enemy had gone to ground in rifle pits or trenches, but Truslow found one target on the crest and took careful aim. "Got you," he said, then pulled the trigger. "She really turn you down?"

"Gave me a tongue-lashing," Starbuck said, ramming the new bullet down his rifle barrel.

"She's a tough one," Truslow said with grudging admiration. A barrelful of canister slashed through the topmost branches, provoking a shower of broken twigs and torn leaves.

"She takes after you," Starbuck said. He knelt up, fired, and ducked back. He wondered, as the retaliatory bullets thudded into the log, just what Sally's new job entailed. There had been no opportunity to visit Richmond, nor would there be till the Yankees were driven away from the city, but when that happened both he and Truslow planned to visit Sally. Starbuck had other errands in the city. He wanted to make a social call on Lieutenant Gillespie. The anticipation of that revenge was a pleasure he relished, just as he relished seeing Julia Gordon again. If, indeed, she would receive him, for he suspected that her loyalty to Adam would most likely make her keep her front door shut.

The northerners began to jeer the stalled rebels. "Lost your spunk? What happened to your yelling, Johnny? Your slaves won't help you now!" The jeers stopped abruptly when the rebel artillery at last got the range of the far crest and began dropping shells onto the enemy. Truslow risked a quick look up the slope. "They're dug in deep," he said.

Too deep to be easily shifted, Starbuck reckoned, which meant the company was in for a long, hot wait. He took off his gray coat and dropped it beside the fallen tree, then sat with his back against the decaying wood to try and determine where his men had gone to earth. Only the dead were in plain sight. "Who's that?" he asked, pointing to a body that lay facedown and spreadeagled in a patch of water thirty yards away. There was an enormous hole in the gray jacket through which a mess of blood, flies, and the glint of a white rib could be seen. "Felix Waggoner," Truslow said after a cursory glance.

"How do you know it's not Peter?" Starbuck asked. Peter and Felix Waggoner were twins.

"It was Felix's turn to wear the good boots today," Truslow said. Somewhere a wounded man was moaning, but no one could move to help him. The valley was a death trap. The Yankee cannon could not depress far enough to rake the valley's bottom with canister, but the northern riflemen had a fine sight of anyone who tried to move across the swamp and so the wounded man would have to suffer.

"Starbuck!" Colonel Bird called from somewhere beyond the valley's rim. "Can you move?"

"Come on, Starbuck! Move!" a Yankee shouted, and suddenly a score of the enemy were chanting his name, mocking him, inviting him to try his luck against their rifles.

"No, Pecker!" Starbuck shouted. The wood fell silent again, or as silent as a battle could be. An artillery duel still thrashed the sky overhead, and every half hour or so a crescendo of rifle fire and cheering would mark yet another rebel attempt to push a brigade or a battalion across the swamp, but the Yankees had the whip hand here and were not going to let it go. They were a rearguard placed north of the Chickahominy to protect the bridges while the rest of the army crossed over to the southern part of the peninsula that McClellan had declared would be his new base of operations. Till now the steamers had unloaded their supplies at either Fort Monroe or West Point on the York River, but from now on they would sail to Harrison's Landing on the James. McClellan described the southward redeployment as a change of base, and had declared that it was a move "unparalleled in the annals of war," but to most of his soldiers the change of base felt more like a retreat, which is why they were taking such pleasure in whipping the rebels into quiescence in the bottom of this swamp-fever valley that ran a mile north of the Chickahominy River. And every hour that they kept the rebels at bay was an hour in which more men of the northern army could cross the river's precarious bridges to the temporary safety of the southern bank.

Starbuck took his brother's Bible out of his jacket pocket, turned to the blank pages at the back, and used a stub of pencil to write down the names of the men who had died thus far in the afternoon. He already knew about Sergeant Carter Hutton, Felix Waggoner, and Amos Parks, but now he learned another six names by calling to men nearby. "We've taken a licking," Starbuck said as he laid the Bible on top of his discarded coat.

"Aye." Truslow fired through his loophole in the log, and the puff of his rifle smoke was sufficient to draw an angry response from a score of northerners. The bullets chewed into the rotten wood, thumping splinters into the air. An Arkansas man fired, then another from K Company, but the sniping was desultory now. There were no reserves to feed into this part of the valley, and General Faulconer was making no effort to stir his men out of their muddy refuges. Farther up the valley, well out of Starbuck's sight, a more sustained attack was generating a storm of rifle and cannon fire that slowly died away as the rebel assault failed.

A black snake slithered across the heel of the mudbank where Starbuck and Truslow had found cover. It had a diamond pattern on the back of its skull. "Cottonmouth?" Starbuck asked.

"You're learning," Truslow said approvingly. The cottonmouth paused at the edge of the water, tasting the air with its tongue, then swam upstream to disappear into a tangle of fallen branches. A fire had started on the far side of the valley, burning and flickering in the dead leaves under a fallen tree. Starbuck scratched his belly and found a dozen ticks had buried themselves in the skin. He tried to pull the ticks away, but their heads broke off and stayed buried in the flesh. The afternoon heat was thick and humid, the marsh stagnant. The water in his canteen tasted salty and warm. He slapped and killed a mosquito. Somewhere upstream, out of sight around the valley's curve, another attack must have just started, for there was a sudden splintering of fire and the sound of screams. The attack lasted two minutes, then failed. "Poor bastards," Truslow said.

"Come on, rebs! Don't be shy! We've got enough bullets for you too!" a Yankee shouted, then laughed at the rebel silence.

The day seemed to grow even hotter. Starbuck had no watch and tried to judge the afternoon's passing by the motion of shadows, but it almost seemed as if the sun were standing still. "Maybe we won't be eating Yankee rations tonight," he said.

"I was looking forward to some coffee," Truslow said wistfully.

"It's thirty bucks a pound for real coffee in Richmond now," Starbuck said.

"Can't be."

"Sure is," Starbuck said, then he twisted around, raised his head, and aimed the rifle at the scar of a rifle pit on the opposite slope. He fired and dropped, expecting the usual retaliatory fusillade of bullets to shiver the rotting trunk, but instead the Yankees began shouting at each other to hold their fire. A couple of bullets slapped at the log, but immediately an authoritative voice demanded that the northerners cease their fire. Someone plaintively asked what was happening, then a score of voices shouted that it was safe. Truslow was staring in amazement at the rebel-held side of the valley. "Son of a bitch," he said in astonishment.

Starbuck turned. "Dear God," he said. The northerners had ceased fire and now Starbuck shouted to make sure that his own men did the same. "Hold your fire!" he called. Colonel Bird was shouting the same order from the top of the slope.

Because Adam had come to the battlefield.

He was making no effort to hide, but just strolling as though he were enjoying a late afternoon's walk. He was dressed in civilian clothes and was unarmed, though it was not that which had persuaded the Yankees to hold their fire, but rather the flag that he carried. Adam was holding a Stars and Stripes that he waved to and fro as he walked slowly downhill. Once the firing had stopped he draped the flag around his shoulders like a cape.

"He's gone soft in the brains," Truslow said.

"I don't think so." Starbuck cupped his hands. "Adam!"

Adam changed direction, angling downhill toward Starbuck. "I was looking for you, Nate!" he called cheerfully.

"Get your head down!"

"Why? No one's firing." Adam looked up at the Yankee slope and some of the northerners cheered him. Others asked him what he wanted, but in reply he just waved at them.

"What the hell are you doing?" Starbuck kept his head below the makeshift bullet-scarred parapet of the rotting log.

"What you told me to do, of course." Adam grimaced because he needed to wade through a patch of filthy swamp and he was wearing his best shoes. "Good afternoon, Truslow. How are you?"

481

"Been better, I reckon," Truslow said in a suspicious voice.

"I met your daughter in Richmond. I'm afraid I was unkind to her. Would you apologize to her for me?" Adam limped through the mud and water to reach the patch of dryer land where Truslow and Starbuck were sheltered. He stood upright and careless, as though no battle were taking place. Nor, for the moment, was there a battle in this part of the valley. Instead men on both sides had broken cover to stare at Adam and wonder just what kind of fool would walk so brazenly into a nest of rifle fire. A Yankee officer shouted to ask what he wanted, but Adam just waved again as if to suggest that all would be made clear in a short while. "You were right, Nate," he said to Starbuck.

"Adam, for God's sake, get down!"

Adam smiled. "For God's sake, Nate, I'm going up." He gestured toward the enemy-held slope. "I'm doing what you did, I'm changing sides. I'm going to fight for the North. I'm deserting, you could say. Would you like to come with me?"

"Just get down, Adam."

Instead of taking cover Adam looked all around the green, humid valley as though it were a place where no dead lay festering in the stagnant air. "I fear no evil, Nate. Not any longer." He put his hand into a coat pocket and brought out a bundle of letters tied in a green ribbon. "Will you make sure these reach Julia?"

"Adam!" Starbuck pleaded from the mud.

"Those are her letters. She should have them back. She wouldn't come with me, you see. I asked her and she said no, and then things got kind of bitter, and the long and short of it is that we won't be married." He tossed the bundled letters onto Starbuck's folded jacket and noticed the Bible there. He stooped, picked up the Scriptures, and leafed through the pages. "Still reading your Bible, Nate? It doesn't seem like your kind of book anymore. I'd have thought you'd be happier with a manual on hog butchery." He looked up from the Bible and gazed into Starbuck's eyes. "Why don't you stand up now, Nate, and come with me? Save your soul, my friend."

"Get down!"

Adam laughed at Starbuck's fear. "I'm doing God's work, Nate, so God will look after me. But you? You're a horse of a different color, aren't you?" He took a pencil from his pocket and made a note in Starbuck's Bible, which he then tossed down beside the letters. "A few moments ago I told Father what I was doing. I told him I was doing God's will, but Father thinks it's all your doing rather than God's, but Father would think that, wouldn't he?" Adam gave the rebel slope one last glance, then turned toward the Yankees. "Goodbye, Nate," he said, then he waved the bright flag in the warm air and clambered over the black log to wade knee-deep toward the far side of the valley. He lost his good shoes in the muddy bottom of the stream in the swamp's center, but just pushed on in his stockinged feet. The slight limp caused by the Yankee bullet he had taken at Manassas was more pronounced as he began to climb the hill on the far side of the quagmire.

"He's gone mad!" Truslow said.

"He's a holy goddamn fool," Starbuck said. "Adam!" he shouted, but Adam just waved the bright flag and kept going. Starbuck knelt upright. "Adam! Come back!" he shouted across the fallen tree. "For Christ's sake, Adam! Come back!" But Adam did not even look back; instead he just climbed up into the trees on the valley's far side and disappeared where the turned earth marked the Yankee entrenchments at the slope's crest. Adam's disappearance broke the spell that had held the two sides in suspense. Someone shouted an order to fire and Starbuck ducked

483

down behind the log just a second before the whole valley snapped and whistled with the sound of bullets. Smoke sifted among the leaves and across the black pools and broken tree stumps and dead soldiers.

Starbuck picked up the Bible. Adam had marked a page somewhere in the book's center and Starbuck now leafed through the pages to find his friend's message. Bullets whipcracked the valley as he flicked through the Psalms and the Proverbs and the Song of Solomon. Then he found it, a circle penciled around the twelfth verse of the sixty-fifth chapter of the book of Isaiah. Starbuck read the verse and, in the valley's mordant heat, suddenly felt cold. He closed the Bible fast.

"What does it say?" Truslow asked. He had seen Starbuck go pale.

"Nothing," Starbuck said curtly, then he put the Bible back into his jacket pocket and pulled on the frayed, threadbare garment. He pushed the letters into a pocket, then pulled the blanket roll over his head. "Nothing at all," he said and picked up his rifle and checked that a percussion cap was mounted on its cone. "Let's go and kill some goddamn Yankees," Starbuck said, then he flinched because the whole valley was suddenly crackling with the sound of killing. Artillery crashed and rifles splintered. The demonic rebel yell filled the trees as a new assault spilt gray over the valley's edge. Another infantry brigade had been sent to attack just to the left of Major Haxall's Arkansas men and the newcomers screamed their challenge as they leaped down the slope. The Yankees fired back, their rifle flames stabbing like fiery swords in the day's lengthening shadows. Shells burst on the far side of the valley, spreading patches of bitter smoke. Northern canister obliterated whole files of southern attackers, churning the leaf mold bloody where it struck, but still more men in gray and brown came surging from the upper woods and down the blood-slicked slope until the whole valley was filled with a scrabbling flood of yelling soldiers who charged through the mud and over the drowned dead.

Starbuck stood up. "K Company! Attack! Follow me! Come on!" He did not care now. He was accursed of God, a lost soul in the outer darkness. The slope ahead was dotted with smoke clouds, bright with flames. Starbuck began to scream, not the rebel yell, but a scream of a man who knows his soul is damned. He ran into the stream, forcing his steps through the clinging, sucking mud. He saw a Yankee take aim from a rifle pit ahead, then the man was snatched backward by a shot fired from the rebel side of the valley. Another northerner scrambled out of the hole and clambered upward and Starbuck looked past the fleeing man and thought this was how Ball's Bluff must have looked to the dying Yankees on the day when he and the other rebels had lined the crest and poured a dreadful fire down into their helpless ranks.

"Come on!" he yelled. "Kill the bastards, come on!" And he threw himself at the slope, pulling himself up on its roots and brambles. He passed two abandoned rifle pits, then there was a sudden movement to his right and he looked to see another pit half hidden by a screen of brushwood. A Yankee was taking aim at him, and Starbuck threw himself forward just as the man's rifle fired. Acrid smoke billowed around Starbuck's face. He was screaming defiance now, wanting the man's death. He rolled onto his back and pulled his rifle's trigger, firing from the hip. The gun crashed smoke and the bullet went wide. The Yankee scrambled out of his trench and began climbing to safety, but Starbuck was chasing him, screaming. The man turned, scared suddenly, trying to fend off Starbuck with an empty rifle, but Starbuck clumsily swatted the gun aside, then slammed his own rifle hard into the man's legs to tangle and trip him. The Yankee was keening in panic as he fell. He scrabbled for his sheathed bayonet, but Starbuck was above him with his rifle raised and its heavy brass-tipped butt pointing downward, and the man shouted something just as Starbuck struck. The blow jarred up through Starbuck's arms, blood spattered his boots, then he was aware that all around him the slope was moving with gray-clad bodies and the whole green valley was echoing with the murderous scream of a rebel attack. The star-crossed banners were moving forward and the Yankees' flags were going back. Starbuck left his victim bleeding and hurried upward, wanting to reach the valley's crest first, but all around him the rebels raced uphill, whipped on by the bugle calls that drove them up to a plateau skeined in smoke. A handful of Yankee gunners tried to save their cannon, but they were too late. A gray rush of men swarmed from the woods and the land between the swamp and the river suddenly became a chaos of panicked northerners.

A troop of northern horsemen tried to turn the rebels back. Two hundred and fifty horsemen had been waiting for the southern infantry to emerge from the trees and now, in three lines with their sabers drawn, the cavalry charged at the ragged rebel formations. The horses' hooves thumped the summer turf to make the whole hilltop shudder. The horses galloped, teeth bared and eyes white as a trumpeter sounded his challenge to the smoky sky and the guidon lance flags dipped into their killing slant. "Charge!" The cavalry commander drew the word out into one long, fine scream of defiance as he pointed his saber's blade at the rebel troops just forty yards ahead.

"Fire!" An Alabama officer called the command and the rebel infantry fired a volley that tore the guts and

486

glory from the northern cavalry. Horses screamed and fell, their hooves flailing in an evening air misted by blood. Riders were crushed, impaled on their own swords, killed by bullets. The second line of cavalry tried to swerve around the bloodied carnage of the leading rank.

"Fire!" A second volley crashed smoke and lead, this volley fired from the left flank, and the surviving cavalry were swatted sideways. Horses ran into other horses, men fell from saddles and were dragged along by stirrups. Others fell clear, only to be trampled by panicked horses.

"Fire!" A last volley pursued the fleeing handful of defeated horsemen who left behind a slaughteryard of dying horses and screaming men. The rebels swarmed over the horror, shooting the horses and looting the men.

Elsewhere on the plateau the rebels captured northern cannons still hot from the day's battle. Prisoners, some wearing straw summer hats, were herded into groups. A captured northern flag was paraded up and down the victorious ranks, while in the swamp the wounded cursed and bled and called for help.

Starbuck climbed onto the hot barrel of a northern twelve-pounder. The gun's venthole and muzzle were black with burned powder, black as the shadows that now stretched long across the wide hilltop. The fleeing northerners made a dark mass in the dying light. Starbuck looked for Adam, but knew he would never see one man among so many. A silver streak betrayed where the river curled between the darkening marshes beyond which the setting sun illuminated a northern balloon that wobbled slowly down toward its winch. Starbuck stared for a long while, then shouldered his rifle with its bloody, sticky butt and jumped to the ground.

That night the Legion ate Yankee victuals around a Yankee campfire. They drank Yankee coffee and listened to

Izard Cobb play a tune on a Yankee violin. The Legion had taken a whipping. Captain Carstairs and four other officers were dead, so was Sergeant Major Proctor. Eighty more men were dead or missing, and at least that number were wounded.

"We'll make eight companies instead of ten," Bird said. He had taken a bullet in his left arm, but had refused to take much note of the wound once it had been bandaged.

"Do we know what we're doing tomorrow?" Major Haxall of the Arkansas battalion had joined the Legion's officers around their fire.

"God knows," Bird said. He sipped at a captured flask of Yankee whiskey.

"Anyone seen Faulconer?" Haxall asked. "Swynyard, then?"

"Swynyard's drunk," Bird said, "and Faulconer is well on his way to being drunk, and even if he was sober he wouldn't want to talk to anyone."

"Because of Adam?" Captain Murphy asked.

"Yes," Bird said. "I guess."

"What the hell happened?" Murphy asked.

No one answered for a long time. A few of the men looked at Starbuck, expecting and wanting him to translate Adam's behavior, but Starbuck said nothing. He was just hoping that his erstwhile friend had the strength to be a stranger in a strange land.

"Adam thinks too much." Bird finally broke the silence. The firelight made the Colonel's thin face look more gaunt than ever. "Thinking isn't good for a man. It only confuses simple issues. We should make thinking illegal in our new and glorious country. We shall achieve the pursuit of happiness by abolishing education and outlawing all ideas that are deemed too difficult for the comprehension of snake-oil Baptists. In sublime stupidity will lie our nation's true

488